KU-068-638

Harlan COBEN

The Final Detail
Just One Look

The Final Detail
First published in Great Britain by Hodder & Stoughton in 1999

Just One Look
First published in Great Britain by Orion Books Ltd in 2004

This omnibus edition published in 2009
by Orion Books Ltd
Orion House, 5 Upper St. Martin's Lane,
London
WC2H 9EA

A CIP catalogue record for this book is available
at the British Library.

ISBN 9781407221175

Printed and bound in the UK by
CPI Mackays, Chatham ME5 8TD

The Orion Publishing Group's policy is to use papers that are
natural, renewable and recyclable products and made from wood
grown in sustainable forests. The logging and manufacturing
processes are expected to conform to the environmental
regulations of the country of origin.

www.orionbooks.co.uk

The Final Detail

For Aunt Evelyn in Revere,
with lots and lots of love

And in memory of Larry Gerson
1962–1998
Close your eyes and you can still see the smile

1

Myron lay sprawled next to a knee-knockingly gorgeous brunette clad only in a Class-B-felony bikini, a tropical drink sans umbrella in one hand, the aqua clear Caribbean water lapping at his feet, the sand a dazzling white powder, the sky a pure blue that could only be God's blank canvas, the sun as soothing and rich as a Swedish masseur with a snifter of cognac, and he was intensely miserable.

The two of them had been on this island paradise for, he guessed, three weeks. Myron had not bothered counting the days. Neither, he imagined, had Terese. The island seemed as remote as Gilligan's – no phone, some lights, no motorcar, plenty of luxury, not much like Robinson Crusoe, and well, not as primitive as can be either. Myron shook his head. You can take the boy out of the television, but you can't take the television out of the boy.

At the horizon's midway point, slicing toward them and ripping a seam of white in the aqua-blue fabric, came the yacht. Myron saw it, and his stomach clenched.

He did not know where they were exactly, though the island did indeed have a name: St Bacchanals. Yes, for real. It was a small patch of planet, owned by one of those mega-cruise lines that used one side of the island for passengers to swim and barbecue and enjoy a day on their 'own personal island paradise.' Personal. Just them and the other twenty-five hundred *turistas* squeezed onto a short stretch of beach. Yep, personal, bacchanallike.

This side of the island, however, was quite different.

There was only this one home, owned by the cruise line's CEO, a hybrid between a thatched hut and a plantation manor. The only person within a mile was a servant. Total island population: maybe thirty, all of whom worked as caretakers hired by the cruise line.

The yacht shut off its engine and drifted closer.

Terese Collins lowered her Bolle sunglasses and frowned. In three weeks no vessel except the mammoth cruise liners – they had subtle names like the *Sensation* or the *Ecstasy* or the *G Spot* – had ambled past their stretch of sand.

'Did you tell anybody where we were?' she asked.

'No.'

'Maybe it's John.'

John was the aforementioned CEO of said cruise line, a friend of Terese's.

'I don't think so,' Myron said.

Myron had first met Terese Collins, well, a little more than three weeks ago. Terese was 'on leave' from her high-profile job as prime-time anchorwoman for CNN. They both had been bullied into going to some charity function by well-meaning friends and had been immediately drawn to each other as though their mutual misery and pain were magnetic. It started as little more than a dare: Drop everything and flee. Just disappear with someone you found attractive and barely knew. Neither backed down, and twelve hours later they were in St Maarten. Twenty-four hours after that they were here.

For Myron, a man who had slept with a total of four women in his entire life, who had never really experienced one-night stands even in the days when they were fashionable or ostensibly disease-free, who had never had sex purely for the physical sensation and without the anchors of love or commitment, the decision to flee felt surprisingly right.

He had told no one where he was going or for how

long – mostly because he didn't have a clue himself. He'd called Mom and Dad and told them not to worry, a move tantamount to telling them to grow gills and breathe underwater. He'd sent Esperanza a fax and gave her power of attorney over MB SportsReps, the sports agency they now partnered. He had not even called Win.

Terese was watching him. 'You know who it is.'

Myron said nothing. His heartbeat sped up.

The yacht came closer. A cabin door in the front opened, and as Myron feared, Win stepped out on deck. Panic squeezed the air out of him. Win was not one for casual drop-bys. If he was here, it meant something was very wrong.

Myron stood. He was still too far to yell, so he settled for a wave. Win gave a small nod.

'Wait a second,' Terese said. 'Isn't that the guy whose family owns Lock-Horne Securities?'

'Yes.'

'I interviewed him once. When the market plunged. He has some long, pompous name.'

'Windsor Horne Lockwood the Third,' Myron said.

'Right. Weird guy.'

She should only know.

'Good-looking as all hell,' Terese continued, 'in that old-money, country-club, born-with-a-silver-golf-club-in-his-hands kinda way.'

As though on cue, Win put a hand through the blond locks and smiled.

'You two have something in common,' Myron said.

'What's that?'

'You both think he's good-looking as all hell.'

Terese studied Myron's face. 'You're going back.' There was a hint of apprehension in her voice.

Myron nodded. 'Win wouldn't have come otherwise.'

She took his hand. It was the first tender moment between them in the three weeks since the charity ball.

3

That might sound strange – lovers alone on an island, the sex constant, who had never shared a gentle kiss or a light stroke or soft words – but their relationship had been about forgetting and surviving: two desperate souls standing in the rubble with no interest in trying to rebuild a damn thing.

Terese had spent most days taking long walks by herself; he'd spent them sitting on the beach and exercising and sometimes reading. They met up for food, sleep, and sex. Other than that, they left each other alone to – if not heal – at least stave off the blood flow. He could see that she too had been shattered, that some recent tragedy had struck her deep and hard and to the bone. But he never asked her what had happened. And she never asked him either.

An unspoken rule of their little folly.

The yacht stopped and dropped anchor. Win stepped down onto a motorized dinghy. Myron waited. He shifted his feet, bracing himself. When the dinghy was close enough to the shore, Win snapped off the motor.

'My parents?' Myron called out.

Win shook his head. 'They're fine.'

'Esperanza?'

Slight hesitation. 'She needs your help.'

Win stepped gingerly into the water, almost as though he expected it to hold his weight. He was dressed in a white button-down oxford and Lilly Pulitzer shorts with colors loud enough to repel sharks. The Yacht Yuppie. His build was on the slight side, but his forearms looked like steel snakes coiling beneath the skin.

Terese stood as Win approached. Win admired the view without ogling. He was one of the few men Myron knew who could get away with that. Breeding. He took Terese's hand and smiled. They exchanged pleasantries. Fake smiles and pointless bandies followed. Myron stood frozen, not listening. Terese excused herself and headed to the house.

Win carefully watched her saunter away. Then he said, 'Quality derrière.'

'Would you be referring to me?' Myron asked.

Win kept his eyes keenly focused on the, er, target. 'On television she's always sitting behind that anchor desk,' he noted. 'One would never guess that she had such a high-quality derrière.' He shook his head. 'It's a shame really.'

'Right,' Myron said. 'Maybe she should stand a couple times during each broadcast. Twirl around a few times, bend over, something like that.'

'There you go.' Win risked a quick glance at Myron. 'Take any action snapshots, perhaps a videotape?'

'No, that would be you,' Myron said, 'or maybe an extra-perverse rock star.'

'Shame.'

'Yeah, shame, I got that.' Quality derrière? 'So what's wrong with Esperanza?'

Terese finally disappeared through the front door. Win sighed softly and turned toward Myron. 'The yacht will take half an hour to refuel. We'll leave then. Mind if I sit?'

'What happened, Win?'

He did not answer, choosing instead to sit on a chaise longue and ease back. He put his hands behind his head and crossed his ankles. 'I'll say this for you. When you decide to wig out, you do it in style.'

'I didn't wig out. I just needed a break.'

'Uh-hmm.' Win looked off, and a realization smacked Myron in the head: He had hurt Win's feelings. Strange but probably true. Win might be a blue-blooded, aristocratic sociopath, but hey, he was still human, sort of. The two men had been inseparable since college, yet Myron

5

had run off without even calling. In many ways Win had no one else.

'I meant to call you,' Myron said weakly.

Win kept still.

'But I knew if there was a problem, you'd be able to find me.' That was true. Win could find a Hoffa needle in a Judge Crater hay-stack.

Win waved a hand. 'Whatever.'

'So what's wrong with Esperanza?'

'Clu Haid.'

Myron's first client, a right-handed relief pitcher in the twilight of his career. 'What about him?'

'He's dead,' Win said.

Myron felt his legs buckle a bit. He let himself land on the chaise.

'Shot three times in his own abode.'

Myron lowered his head. 'I thought he'd straightened himself out.'

Win said nothing.

'So what does Esperanza have to do with this?'

Win looked at his watch. 'Right about now,' he said, 'she is in all likelihood being arrested for his murder.'

'What?'

Win said nothing again. He hated to repeat himself.

'They think Esperanza killed him?'

'Good to see your vacation hasn't dulled your sharp powers of deduction.' Win tilted his face toward the sun.

'What sort of evidence do they have?'

'The murder weapon, for one. Bloodstains. Fibers. Do you have any sunblock?'

'But how . . . ?' Myron studied his friend's face. As usual, it gave away nothing. 'Did she do it?'

'I have no idea.'

'Did you ask her?'

'Esperanza does not wish to speak with me.'

'What?'

'She does not wish to speak with you either.'

'I don't understand,' Myron said. 'Esperanza wouldn't kill anyone.'

'You're quite sure about that, are you?'

Myron swallowed. He had thought that his recent experience would help him understand Win better. Win had killed too. Often, in fact. Now that Myron had done likewise, he thought that there would be a fresh bond. But there wasn't. Just the opposite, in fact. Their shared experience was opening a whole new chasm.

Win checked his watch. 'Why don't you go get packed?'

'There's nothing I need to bring.'

Win motioned to the house. Terese stood there, watching them silently. 'Then say good-bye to La Derrière and let's be on our way.'

2

Terese had put on a robe. She leaned against the doorway and waited.

Myron was not sure what to say. He settled for 'Thank you.'

She nodded.

'Do you want to come along?' he asked.

'No.'

'You can't stay here forever.'

'Why not?'

Myron thought about it for a moment. 'You know anything about boxing?'

Terese sniffed the air. 'Do I detect the distinct odor of an upcoming sports metaphor?'

'I'm afraid so,' he said.

'Ugh. Go on.'

'This whole thing is sort of like a boxing match,' Myron began. 'We've been ducking and diving and weaving and trying to keep away from our opponent. But we can only do that for so long. Eventually we have to throw a punch.'

She made a face. 'Christ, that was lame.'

'Spur of the moment.'

'And inaccurate,' she added. 'Try this. We've tasted our opponent's power. It dropped us to the canvas. Somehow we managed to get back to our feet. But our legs are still rubbery, and our eyes are still hazed over. Another big blow and the fight will be over. Better to keep dancing. Better to avoid getting hit and hope to go the distance.'

Hard to argue.

They fell into silence.

Myron said, 'If you come up to New York, give me a call and—'

'Right.'

Silence.

'We know what would happen,' Terese said. 'We'd meet up for drinks, maybe hop back in the sack, but it won't be the same. We'll both be uncomfortable as all hell. We'll pretend that we'll get together again, and we won't even exchange Christmas cards. We're not lovers, Myron. We're not even friends. I don't know what the hell we are, but I'm grateful.'

A bird cawed. The small waves hummed their soft song. Win stood by the shore, his arms crossed, his body frighteningly patient.

'Have a good life, Myron.'

'You too,' he replied.

He and Win took the dinghy to the yacht. A crew member offered Myron his hand. Myron grabbed it and hoisted himself on board. The yacht took off. Myron stood on the deck and watched the shore grow smaller. He was leaning on a teakwood rail. Teakwood. Everything on this vessel was dark and rich and teak.

'Here,' Win said.

Myron turned. Win tossed him a Yoo-Hoo, Myron's favorite drink, kind of a cross between a soda pop and chocolate milk. Myron smiled. 'I haven't had one of these in three weeks.'

'The withdrawal pains,' Win said. 'They must have been agony.'

'No TV and no Yoo-Hoo. It's a wonder I survived.'

'Yes, you practically lived like a monk,' Win said. Then, looking back at the island, he added, 'Well, like a monk who gets laid a lot.'

They were both stalling.

'How long until we get back?' Myron asked.

'Eight hours on the boat,' Win said. 'A chartered jet is waiting at St Bart's. The flight should take about four hours.'

Myron nodded. He shook the can and popped it. He took a deep swig and turned back toward the water.

'I'm sorry,' he said.

Win ignored the statement. Or maybe it was enough for him. The yacht picked up speed. Myron closed his eyes and let the water and gentle spray caress his face. He thought a moment about Clu Haid. Clu hadn't trusted agents – 'a small step below pedophile' was how he put it – so he asked Myron to negotiate his contract, even though Myron was merely a first-year student at Harvard Law. Myron did it. He liked it. And MB SportsReps soon followed.

Clu was a lovable screwup. He unapologetically pursued wine, women, and song – not to mention any high he could get his hands/nose/veins on. Clu never met a party he didn't like. He was a red-headed big guy with a teddy bear gut, handsome in a boyish way, an almost old-fashioned cad, and immensely charming. Everyone loved Clu. Even Bonnie, his long-suffering wife. Their marriage was a boomerang. She'd throw him out, he'd spin in the air for a while, and then she'd catch him on the return.

Clu had seemed to be slowing down a bit. After all the times Myron had gotten him out of trouble – drug suspensions, drunk driving charges, whatever – Clu had gone puffy, reached the end of his charm reign. The Yankees had traded for him, putting him on strict probation, giving him one last chance at redemption. Clu had stayed in rehab for the first time. He'd been attending the AA meetings. His fastball was back up in the nineties.

Win interrupted his thoughts. 'Do you want to hear what happened?'

'I'm not sure,' Myron said.

'Oh?'

'I screwed up last time. You warned me, but I didn't listen. A lot of people died because of me.' Myron felt the tears come to his eyes. He pushed them back down. 'You have no idea how bad it ended.'

'Myron?'

He turned to his friend. Their eyes met.

'Get over yourself,' Win said.

Myron made a noise – one part sob, two parts chuckle. 'I hate when you coddle me.'

'Perhaps you would prefer it if I served up some useless platitudes,' Win said. He swirled his liquor and tasted a bit. 'Please select one of the following and then we'll move on: Life is hard; life is cruel; life is random; sometimes good people are forced to do bad things; sometimes innocent people die; yes, Myron, you screwed up, but you'll do better this time; no, Myron, you didn't screw up, it wasn't your fault; everyone has a breaking point and now you know yours. Can I stop now?'

'Please.'

'Then let us begin with Clu Haid.'

Myron nodded, took another swig of Yoo-Hoo, emptied the can.

'Everything seemed to be going swimmingly for our old college chum,' Win said. 'He was pitching well. Domestic bliss seemed to reign. He was passing his drug tests. He was making curfew with hours to spare. That all changed two weeks ago when a surprise drug test produced a positive result.'

'For what?'

'Heroin.'

Myron shook his head.

'Clu kept his mouth shut to the media,' Win said, 'but privately he claimed the test was fixed. That someone had tampered with his food or some such nonsense.'

'How do you know that?'

'Esperanza told me.'

'He went to Esperanza?'

'Yes, Myron. When Clu failed the test, he naturally looked to his agent for help.'

Silence.

'Oh,' Myron said.

'I don't want go into the fiasco that is MB SportsReps right now. Suffice to say that Esperanza and Big Cyndi did the best they could. But it's your agency. Clients hired you. Many have been more than unhappy at your sudden disappearance.'

Myron shrugged. He would probably care one day. 'So Clu failed the test.'

'And he was immediately suspended. The media moved in for the kill. He lost all his endorsement deals. Bonnie threw him out. The Yankees disowned him. With nowhere else to turn, Clu repeatedly visited your office. Esperanza told him that you were unavailable. His temper rose with each visit.'

Myron closed his eyes.

'Four days ago Clu confronted Esperanza outside the office. At the Kinney parking lot, to be more exact. They had words. Harsh and rather loud words. According to witnesses, Clu punched her in the mouth.'

'What?'

'I saw Esperanza the next day. Her jaw was swollen. She could barely talk, though she still managed to tell me to mind my own business. My understanding is more damage would have been inflicted had Mario and several other parking attendants not pulled them apart. Supposedly Esperanza made threats of the I'll-get-you-for-this-you-limp-dick-son-of-a-bitch variety as they were being held back.'

Myron shook his head. This made no sense.

'The next afternoon Clu was found dead in the

apartment he rented in Fort Lee,' Win continued. 'The police learned about the earlier altercation. They were then issued a slew of search warrants and found the murder weapon, a nine millimeter, in your office.'

'My office?'

'MB's office, yes.'

Myron shook his head again. 'It had to be a plant.'

'Yes, perhaps. There were also fibers that matched the carpeting in Clu's apartment.'

'The fibers are meaningless. Clu was in the office. He probably dragged them there.'

'Yes, perhaps,' Win said again. 'But the specks of blood in the trunk of the company car might be harder to explain.'

Myron almost fell over. 'Blood in the Taurus?'

'Yes.'

'And the police confirmed the blood as Clu's?'

'Same blood type. The DNA test will take several weeks.'

Myron could not believe what he was hearing. 'Had Esperanza been using the car?'

'That very day. According to the E-Z Pass records, the car crossed the Washington Bridge back into New York within an hour of the murder. And as I said, he was killed in Fort Lee. The apartment is maybe two miles from the bridge.'

'This is crazy.'

Win said nothing.

'What's her motive?' Myron asked.

'The police don't have a solid one yet. But several are being offered.'

'Such as?'

'Esperanza was a new partner at MB SportsReps. She'd been left in charge. The company's inaugural client was about to walk out the door.'

Myron frowned. 'Pretty flimsy motive.'

'He had also recently assaulted her. Perhaps Clu blamed her for all the bad things that were happening to him. Perhaps she wanted vengeance. Who knows?'

'You said something before about her not talking to you.'

'Yes.'

'So you asked Esperanza about the charges?'

'Yes.'

'And?'

'And she told me that she had the matter under control,' Win said. 'And she told me not to contact you. That she did not wish to speak with you.'

Myron looked puzzled. 'Why not?'

'I haven't a clue.'

He pictured Esperanza, the Hispanic beauty he had met in the days when she wrestled professionally under the moniker Little Pocahontas. A lifetime ago. She had been with MB SportsReps since its inception – first as a secretary and now that she'd graduated law school, as a full-fledged partner.

'But I'm her best friend,' Myron said.

'As I am well aware.'

'So why would she say something like that?'

Win guessed the question was rhetorical. He kept silent.

The island was out of sight now. In every direction there was nothing but the churning warm blue of the Atlantic.

'If I hadn't run away,' Myron began.

'Myron?'

'What?'

'You're whining again. I cannot handle whining.'

Myron nodded and leaned against the teakwood.

'Any thoughts?' Win asked.

'She'll talk to me,' Myron said. 'Count on it.'

'I just tried to call her.'

'And?'

'No answer.'

'Did you try Big Cyndi?'

'She now rooms with Esperanza.'

No surprise. 'What's today?' Myron asked.

'Tuesday.'

'Big Cyndi still bounces at Leather-N-Lust. She might be there.'

'During the day?'

Myron shrugged. 'Sexual deviancy has no off hours.'

'Thank God,' Win said.

They fell into silence, the ship gently rocking them.

Win squinted into the sun. 'Beautiful, no?'

Myron nodded.

'Must be sick of it after all this time.'

'Very,' Myron said.

'Come below deck. I think you'll be pleased.'

3

Win had stocked the yacht with videos. They watched episodes of the old *Batman* show (the one with Julie Newmar as Cat Woman and Lesley Gore as Pussycat – double meow!), the *Odd Couple* (Oscar and Felix on *Password*), a *Twilight Zone* ('To Serve Man'), and for something more current, *Seinfeld* (Jerry and Elaine visit Jerry's parents in Florida). Forget pot roast. This was comfort food. But on the off chance that it wasn't substantial enough, there were also Doritos and Cheez Doodles and more Yoo-Hoos and even rewarmed pizza from Calabria's Pizzeria on Livingston Avenue.

Win. He might be a sociopath, but what a guy.

The effect of all this was beyond therapeutic, the time spent at sea and later in the air an emotional pressure chamber of sorts, a chance for Myron's soul to adjust to the bends, to the sudden reemergence into the real world.

The two friends barely spoke, except to sigh over Julie Newmar as Cat Woman (whenever she came on the screen in her tight black cat suit, Win said, 'Puuuurrrr-fect'). They'd both been five or six years old when the show first aired, but something about Julie Newmar as Cat Woman completely blew away any Freudian notions of latency. Why, neither man could say. Her villainy perhaps. Or something more primal. Esperanza would no doubt have an interesting opinion. He tried not to think about her – useless and draining when he couldn't do anything about it – but the last time he had done something like this was in Philadelphia with both Win and Esperanza. He missed her. Watching the videos was not the same without her running commentary.

The boat docked and they headed for the private jet.

'We'll save her,' Win said. 'We are, after all, the good guys.'

'Questionable.'

'Have confidence, my friend.'

'No, I mean us being the good guys.'

'You should know better.'

'Not anymore I don't,' Myron said.

Win made his jutting jaw face, the one that had come over on the *Mayflower*. 'This moral crisis of yours,' he said. 'It's *très* unbecoming.'

A breathy blond bombshell like something out of an old burlesque skit greeted them in the cabin of the Lock-Horne company jet. She fetched them drinks between giggles and wiggles. Win smiled at her. She smiled back.

'Funny thing,' Myron said.

'What's that?'

'You always hire curvaceous stewardesses.'

Win frowned. 'Please,' he said. 'She prefers to be called a flight attendant.'

'Pardon my oafish insensitivity.'

'Try a little harder to be tolerant,' Win said. Then: 'Guess what her name is.'

'Tawny?'

'Close. Candi. With an *i*. And she doesn't dot it. She draws a heart over it.'

Win could be a bigger pig, but it was hard to imagine how.

Myron sat back. The pilot came over the loudspeaker. He addressed them by name, and then they took off. Private jet. Yacht. Sometimes it was nice having wealthy friends.

When they reached cruising altitude, Win opened what

looked like a cigar box and pulled out a telephone. 'Call your parents,' he said.

Myron stayed still for a moment. A fresh wave of guilt rolled over him, coloring his cheeks. He nodded, took the phone, dialed. He gripped the phone a bit too tightly. His mother answered.

Myron said, 'Mom—'

Mom started bawling. She managed to yell for Dad. Dad picked up the downstairs extension.

'Dad—'

And then he started bawling too. Stereo bawling. Myron held the phone away from his ear for a moment.

'I was in the Caribbean,' he said, 'not Beirut.'

An explosion of laughter from both. Then more crying. Myron looked at Win. Win sat impassively. Myron rolled his eyes, but of course he was also pleased. Complain all you want, but who didn't want to be loved like this?

His parents settled into a meaningless chatter – meaningless on purpose, Myron supposed. While they could undoubtedly be pests, Mom and Dad had a wonderful ability to know when to back off. He managed to explain where he'd been. They listened in silence. Then his mother asked, 'So where are you calling us from?'

'Win's airplane.'

Stereo gasps now. 'What?'

'Win's company has a private jet. I just told you he picked me—'

'And you're calling on his phone?'

'Yes.'

'Do you have any idea how much that costs?'

'Mom . . .'

But the meaningless chatter died down in a hurry then. When Myron hung up seconds later, he sat back. The guilt came again, bathing him in something ice cold. His parents were not young anymore. He hadn't thought about that before he ran. He hadn't thought about a lot of things.

'I shouldn't have done that to them,' Myron said. 'Or you.'

Win shifted in his seat – major body language for him. Candi wiggled back into view. She lowered a screen and hit a switch. A Woody Allen film came on. *Love and Death*. Ambrosia of the mind. They watched without speaking. When it was over, Candi asked Myron if he wanted to take a shower before they landed.

'Excuse me?' Myron said.

Candi giggled, called him a 'Big Silly,' and wiggled away.

'A shower?'

'There's one in the back,' Win said. 'I also took the liberty of bringing you a change of clothes.'

'You are a friend.'

'I am indeed, Big Silly.'

Myron showered and dressed, and then everyone buckled their seat belts for approach. The plane descended without delay, the landing so smooth it could have been choreographed by the Temptations. A stretch limousine was waiting for them on the dark tarmac. When they got off the plane, the air felt strange and unfamiliar, as though he'd been visiting another planet rather than another country. It was also raining hard. They ran down the steps and into the already-open limo doors.

They shook off the wet. 'I assume that you'll be staying with me,' Win said.

Myron had been living in a loft down on Spring Street with Jessica. But that was before. 'If it's okay.'

'It's okay.'

'I could move back in with my folks—'

'I said, it's okay.'

'I'll find my own place.'

'No rush,' Win said.

The limousine started up. Win steepled his fingers. He always did that. It looked good on him. Still holding the steeple, he bounced his forefingers against his lips. 'I'm not the best one to discuss these matters with,' he said, 'but if you want to talk about Jessica or Brenda or whatever . . .' He released the steeple, made a waving motion with his right hand. Win was trying. Matters of the heart were not his forte. His feelings on romantic entanglement could objectively be labeled 'appalling.'

'Don't worry about it,' Myron said.

'Fine then.'

'Thanks, though.'

Quick nod.

After more than a decade struggling with Jessica – years of being in love with the same woman, having one major breakup, finding each other again, taking tentative steps, growing, finally moving in together again – it was over.

'I miss Jessica,' Myron said.

'I thought we weren't going to talk about it.'

'Sorry.'

Win shifted in his seat again. 'No, go on.' Like he'd rather have an anal probe.

'It's just that . . . I guess part of me will always be enmeshed in Jessica.'

Win nodded. 'Like something in a machinery mishap.'

Myron smiled. 'Yeah. Like that.'

'Then slice off the limb and leave it behind.'

Myron looked at his friend.

Win shrugged. 'I've been watching *Sally Jessy* on the side.'

'It shows,' Myron said.

'The episode entitled "Mommy Took Away My Nipple Ring," ' Win said. 'I'm not afraid to say it made me cry.'

'Good to see you getting in touch with your sensitive side.' As if Win had one. 'So what next?'

Win checked his watch. 'I have a contact at the Bergen County house of detention. He should be in by now.' He hit the speakerphone and pressed in some numbers. They listened to the phone ring. After two rings a voice said, 'Schwartz.'

'Brian, this is Win Lockwood.'

The usual reverent hush when you first hear that name. Then: 'Hey, Win.'

'I need a favor.'

'Shoot.'

'Esperanza Diaz. Is she there?'

Brief pause. 'You didn't hear it from me,' Schwartz said.

'Hear what?'

'Good, okay, long as we understand each other,' he said. 'Yeah, she's here. They dragged her through here in cuffs a coupla hours ago. Very hush-hush.'

'Why hush-hush?'

'Don't know.'

'When is she being arraigned?'

'Tomorrow morning, I guess.'

Win looked at Myron. Myron nodded. Esperanza would be held overnight. This was not a good thing.

'Why did they arrest her so late?'

'Don't know.'

'And you saw them drag her in cuffs?'

'Yep.'

'Didn't they let her surrender on her own?'

'Nope.'

Again the two friends looked at each other. The late arrest. The handcuffs. The overnight. Someone in the DA's office was pissed off and trying to make a point. Very not a good thing.

'What else can you tell me?' Win asked.

'Not much. Like I said, they're being quiet on this one. The DA hasn't even released it to the media yet. But he will. Probably before the eleven o'clock news. Quick statement, no time for questions, that kind of thing. Hell, I wouldn't know about it if I wasn't a big fan.'

'A big fan?'

'Of professional wrestling. See, I recognized her from her old wrestling days. Did you know Esperanza Diaz used to be Little Pocahontas, the Indian Princess?'

Win glanced at Myron. 'Yes, Brian, I know.'

'Really?' Brian was big-time excited now. 'Little Pocahontas was my absolute fave, bar none. An awesome wrestler. Top drawer. I mean, she used to enter the ring in this skimpy suede bikini, right, and then she'd start grappling with other chicks, bigger chicks really, writhing around on the floor and stuff – swear to God, she was so hot my fingernails would melt.'

'Thank you for the visual,' Win said. 'Anything else, Brian?'

'No.'

'Do you know who her attorney of record is?'

'No.' Then: 'Oh, one other thing. She's got someone, well, sort of with her.'

'Sort of with her, Brian?'

'Outside. On the front steps of the courthouse.'

'I'm not sure I'm following you,' Win said.

'Out in the rain. Just sitting there. If I didn't know better, I'd swear it was Little Pocahontas's old tag team partner, Big Chief Mama. Did you know Big Chief Mama and Little Pocahontas were Intercontinental tag team champions three years running?'

Win sighed. 'You don't say.'

'Whatever Intercontinental means. I mean, what is that, Intercontinental? And I'm not talking about recently. Five, eight years ago, at least. But, man, they were awesome. Great wrestlers. Today, well, the league has no class anymore.'

'Grappling bikini-clad women,' Win said. 'They just don't make them like they used to.'

'Right, exactly. Too many fake, inflated breasts nowadays, at least that's how I see it. One of them is going to land on her stomach and bam, her boob is going to blow out like a worn tire. So I don't follow it much anymore. Oh, maybe if I'm flipping the channels and something catches my eye, I might watch a little—'

'You were talking about a woman out in the rain?'

'Right, Win, right, sorry. Anyway, she's out there, whoever she is. Just sitting there. The cops went by before and asked her what she was doing. She said she was going to wait for her friend.'

'So she's there right now?'

'Yep.'

'What does she look like, Brian?'

'Like the Incredible Hulk. Only scarier. And maybe greener.'

Win and Myron exchanged glances. No doubt. Big Chief Mama aka Big Cyndi.

'Anything else, Brian?'

'No, not really.' Then: 'So you know Esperanza Diaz?'

'Yes.'

'Personally?'

'Yes.'

Silent awe. 'Jesus, you lead some life, Win.'

'Oh, indeed.'

'Think you can get me her autograph?'

'I'll do my best, Brian.'

'A picture autograph maybe? Of Little Pocahontas in costume? I'm a really big fan.'

'So I gather, Brian. Good-bye.'

Win hung up and sat back. He looked over at Myron. Myron nodded. Win picked up the intercom and gave the driver directions to the courthouse.

4

By the time they arrived at the courthouse in Hackensack, it was nearly 10:00 p.m. Big Cyndi sat in the rain, shoulders hunched; at least Myron thought it was Big Cyndi. From a distance, it looked like someone had parked a Volkswagen Bug on the courthouse steps.

Myron stepped out of the car and approached. 'Big Cyndi?'

The dark heap let loose a low growl, a lioness warning off an inferior animal who'd wandered astray.

'It's Myron,' he said.

The growl deepened. The rain had plastered Big Cyndi's hair spikes to her scalp, as if she were sporting an uneven Caesar coif. Today's color was hard to decipher – Big Cyndi liked diversity in her follicular tint – but it didn't look like any hue found in the state of nature. Big Cyndi sometimes liked to combine dyes randomly and see what happened. She also insisted on being called Big Cyndi. Not Cyndi. Big Cyndi. She had even had her name legally changed. Official documents read: Cyndi, Big.

'You can't stay here all night,' Myron tried.

She finally spoke. 'Go home.'

'What happened?'

'You ran away.' Big Cyndi's voice was childlike, lost.

'Yes.'

'You left us alone.'

'I'm sorry about that. But I'm back now.'

He risked another step. If only he had something to placate her with. Like a half gallon of Häagen-Dazs. Or a sacrificial goat.

Big Cyndi started to cry. Myron approached slowly, semileading with his right hand in case she wanted to sniff it. But the growls were all gone now, replaced by sobs. Myron put his palm on a shoulder that felt like a bowling ball.

'What happened?' he asked again.

She sniffled. Loudly. The sound almost dented the limo's fender. 'I can't tell you.'

'Why can't you?'

'She said not to.'

'Esperanza?'

Big Cyndi nodded.

'She's going to need help,' Myron said.

'She doesn't want your help.'

The words stung. The rain continued to fall. Myron sat on the step next to her. 'Is she angry about my leaving?'

'I can't tell you, Mr Bolitar. I'm sorry.'

'Why not?'

'She told me not to.'

'Esperanza can't bear the brunt of this on her own,' Myron said. 'She's going to need a lawyer.'

'She has one.'

'Who?'

'Hester Crimstein.'

Big Cyndi gasped as though she realized she'd said too much, but Myron wondered if the slip had been intentional.

'How did she get Hester Crimstein?' Myron asked.

'I can't say any more, Mr Bolitar. Please don't be mad at me.'

'I'm not mad, Big Cyndi. I'm just concerned.'

Big Cyndi smiled at him then. The sight made Myron bite back a scream. 'It's nice to have you back,' she said.

'Thank you.'

She put her head on his shoulder. The weight made

26

him teeter, but he remained relatively upright. 'You know how I feel about Esperanza,' Myron said.

'Yes,' Big Cyndi said. 'You love her. And she loves you.'

'So let me help.'

Big Cyndi lifted her head off his shoulder. Blood circulated again. 'I think you should leave now.'

Myron stood. 'Come on. We'll give you a ride home.'

'No, I'm staying.'

'It's raining and it's late. Someone might try to attack you. It's not safe out here.'

'I can take care of myself,' Big Cyndi said.

He had meant that it wasn't safe for the attackers, but he let it pass. 'You can't stay out here all night.'

'I'm not leaving Esperanza alone.'

'But she won't even know you're here.'

Big Cyndi wiped the rain from her face with a hand the size of a truck tire. 'She knows.'

Myron looked back at the car. Win was leaning against the door now, arms crossed, umbrella resting on his shoulder. Very Gene Kelly. He nodded at Myron.

'You're sure?' Myron asked.

'Yes, Mr Bolitar. Oh, and I'll be late for work tomorrow. I hope you understand.'

Myron nodded. They stared at each other, the rain cascading down their faces. A howl of laughter made both of them turn to the right and look at the fortresslike structure that contained the holding cells. Esperanza, the person closest to them both, was incarcerated in there. Myron stepped toward the limousine. Then he turned back around.

'Esperanza wouldn't kill anyone,' he said.

He waited for Big Cyndi to agree or at least nod her head. But she didn't. She hunched the shoulders back up and disappeared within herself.

Myron slid back into the car. Win followed, handing Myron a towel. The driver started up.

'Hester Crimstein is her attorney,' Myron said.

'Ms Court TV?'

'The same.'

'Ah,' Win said. 'And what's the name of her show again?'

'*Crimstein on Crime*,' Myron said.

Win frowned. 'Cute.'

'She had a book with the same title.' Myron shook his head. 'This is weird. Hester Crimstein doesn't take many cases anymore. So how did Esperanza land her?'

Win tapped his chin with his forefinger. 'I'm not positive,' he said, 'but I believe Esperanza had a fling with her a couple of months back.'

'You're kidding.'

'Well, yes, I am such a mirthful fellow. And wasn't that just the funniest line?'

Wiseass. But it made sense. Esperanza was as perfect a bisexual as you could find – perfect because everyone, no matter what his or her sex or preference, found her immensely attractive. If you're going to go all ways, might as well have universal appeal, right?

Myron mulled this over a few moments. 'Do you know where Hester Crimstein lives?' he asked.

'Two buildings up from me on Central Park West.'

'So let's pay her a visit.'

Win frowned. 'Why?'

'Maybe she can fill us in.'

'She won't talk to us.'

'Maybe she will.'

'What makes you say that?'

'For one thing,' Myron said, 'I'm feeling particularly charming.'

'By God.' Win leaned forward. 'Driver, step on the gas.'

5

Win lived at the Dakota, one of Manhattan's swankiest buildings. Hester Crimstein lived two blocks north at the San Remo, an equally swanky building. Occupants included Diane Keaton and Dustin Hoffman, but the San Remo was perhaps best known as the building that had rejected Madonna's application for residence.

There were two entranceways, both with doormen dressed like Brezhnev strolling Red Square. Brezhnev One announced in a clipped tone that Ms Crimstein was 'not present.' He actually used the word *present* too; people don't often do that in real life. He smiled for Win and looked down his nose at Myron. This was no easy task – Myron was at least six inches taller – and required Brezhnev to tilt his head way back so that his nostrils looked like the westbound entrance to the Lincoln Tunnel. Why, Myron wondered, do servants of the rich and famous act snootier than their masters? Was it simple resentment? Was it because they were looked down upon all day and thus needed on occasion to be the one doing the looking down? Or – more simply – were people attracted to such jobs insecure asswipes?

Life's little mysteries.

'Are you expecting Ms Crimstein back tonight?' Win asked.

Brezhnev opened his mouth, stopped, cast a wary eye as if he feared Myron might defecate on the Persian rug. Win read his face and led him to the side, away from the lowly member of the unwashed.

'She should be back soon, Mr Lockwood.' Ah, so

Brezhnev had recognized Win. No wonder. 'Ms Crimstein's aerobics class concludes at eleven.'

Exercising at eleven o'clock at night. Welcome to the nineties, where leisure time is sucked away like something undergoing liposuction.

There were no waiting or sitting areas at the San Remo – most of your finer buildings did not encourage even approved guests to loiter – so they moved outside to the street. Central Park was across the roadway. Myron could see, well, trees and a stone wall, and that was about it. Lots of taxis sped north. Win's stretch limousine had been dismissed – they both figured they could walk the two blocks to Win's place – but there were four other stretch limousines sitting in a no parking zone. A fifth pulled up. A silver stretch Mercedes. Brezhnev rushed to the car door like he really had to pee and there was a bathroom inside.

An old man bald except for a white crown of hair stumbled out, his mouth twisted poststroke. A woman resembling a prune followed. Both were expensively dressed and maybe a hundred years old. Something about them troubled Myron. They looked wizened, yes. Old, certainly. But there was more to it, Myron sensed. People talk about sweet little old people, but these two were so blatantly the opposite, their eyes beady, their movements shifty and angry and fearful. Life had sapped them, sucked out all the goodness and hope of youth, leaving them with a vitality based on something ugly and hateful. Bitterness was the only thing left. Whether the bitterness was directed at God or at their fellowman, Myron could not say.

Win nudged him. He looked to his right and saw a figure he recognized from TV as Hester Crimstein coming toward them. She was on the husky side, at least by today's warped Kate Mossian standards, and her face was fleshy and cherubic. She wore Reebok white sneakers, white socks, green stretch pants that would probably make Kate snicker, a sweatshirt, a knit hat with frosted blond hair sticking out the back. The old man stopped when he saw the attorney, grabbed the prune lady's hand, hurried inside.

'Bitch!' the old man managed through the good side of his face.

'Up yours too, Lou,' Hester called out after him.

The old man stopped, looked like he wanted to say something more, limped off.

Myron and Win exchanged a glance and approached.

'Old adversary,' she said in way of explanation. 'You ever hear the old adage that only the good die young?'

'Uh, sure.'

Hester Crimstein gestured with both hands at the old couple like Carol Merrill showing off a brand-new car. 'There's your proof. Couple years back I helped his children sue the son of a bitch. You never saw anything like it.' She tilted her head. 'Ever notice how some people are like jackals?'

'Pardon?'

'They eat their young. That's Lou. And don't even get me started on that shriveled-up witch he lives with. Five-dollar whore who hit the jackpot. Hard to believe looking at her now.'

'I see,' Myron said, though he didn't. He tried to push ahead. 'Ms Crimstein, my name is—'

'Myron Bolitar,' she interrupted. 'By the way, that's a horrid name. Myron. What were your parents thinking?'

A very good question. 'If you know who I am, then you know why I'm here.'

'Yes and no,' Hester said.

'Yes and no?'

'Well, I know who you are because I'm a sports nut. I used to watch you play. That NCAA championship game against Indiana was a frigging classic. I know the Celtics drafted you in the first round, what, eleven, twelve years ago?'

'Something like that.'

'But frankly – and I mean no offense here – I'm not sure you had the speed to be a great pro, Myron. The shot, sure. You could always shoot. You could be physical. But what are you, six-five?'

'About that.'

'You would have had a tough time in the NBA. One woman's opinion. But of course the fates took care of that by blowing out your knee. Only an alternate universe knows the truth.' She smiled. 'Nice chatting with you.' She looked over at Win. 'You too, gabby boy. Good night.'

'Wait a second,' Myron said. 'I'm here about Esperanza Diaz.'

She faked a gasp of surprise. 'Really? And here I thought you just wanted to reminisce about your athletic career.'

He looked at Win. 'The charm,' Win whispered.

Myron turned back toward Hester. 'Esperanza is my friend,' he said.

'So?'

'So I want to help.'

'Great. I'll start sending you the bills. This case is going to cost a bundle. I'm very expensive, you know. You can't believe the upkeep of this building. And now the doormen want new uniforms. Something in mauve, I think.'

'That's not what I meant.'

'Oh?'

'I'd like to know what's going on with the case.'

She scrunched up her face. 'Where have you been the last few weeks?'

'Away.'

'Where away?'

'The Caribbean.'

She nodded. 'Nice tan.'

'Thanks.'

'But you could have gotten it at a tanning booth. You look like the kind of guy who hangs out at tanning booths.'

Myron looked at Win again. 'The charm, Luke,' Win whispered, doing his best Alec Guinness as Obi-Wan Kenobi. 'Remember the charm.'

'Ms Crimstein—'

'Anyone who can verify your whereabouts in the Caribbean, Myron?'

'Pardon me?'

'Hearing problems? I asked if anyone can verify your whereabouts at the time of the alleged murder.'

Alleged murder. The guy is shot three times in his home, but the murder is only 'alleged.' Lawyers. 'Why do you want to know that?'

Hester Crimstein shrugged. 'The alleged murder weapon was allegedly found at the offices of one MB SportsReps. That's your company, is it not?'

'It is.'

'And you use the company car where the alleged blood and alleged fibers were allegedly found.'

Win said, 'The key word here is *alleged*.'

Hester Crimstein looked at Win. 'It speaks.'

Win smiled.

Myron said, 'You think I'm a suspect?'

'Sure, why not? It's called reasonable doubt, sweet buns. I'm a defense attorney. We're big on reasonable doubt.'

'Much as I'd like to help, there was a witness to my whereabouts.'

'Who?'

'Don't worry about it.'

Another shrug. 'You're the one who said you wanted

33

to help. Good night.' She looked at Win. 'By the way, you're the perfect man – good-looking and nearly mute.'

'Careful,' Win said to her.

'Why?'

Win pointed at Myron with his thumb. 'Any minute now he's going to turn on the charm and reduce your willpower to rubble.'

She looked at Myron and burst out laughing.

Myron tried again. 'So what happened?' he asked.

'Excuse me?'

'I'm her friend.'

'Yeah, I think you already said that.'

'I'm her best friend. I care about her.'

'Fine. Tomorrow I'll pass her a note during study hall, find out if she likes you too. Then you can meet at Pop's and share a soda.'

'That's not what I—' Myron stopped, gave her the slow, slightly put-out-but-here-to-help smile. Smile 18: the Michael Landon model, except he couldn't crinkle the eyebrow. 'I'd just like to know what happened. You can appreciate that.'

Her face softened, and she nodded. 'You went to law school, right?'

'Yes.'

'At Harvard no less.'

'Yes.'

'So maybe you were absent the day they went over a little something we call attorney-client privilege. I can recommend some wonderful books on the subject, if you'd like. Or maybe you can watch any episode of *Law & Order*. They usually talk about it right before the old DA grouses to Sam Waterston that he's got no case and should cut a deal.'

So much for charm. 'You're just covering your ass,' Myron said.

She looked behind her and down. Then she frowned. 'No easy task, I assure you.'

'I thought you were supposed to be a hotshot attorney.'

She sighed, crossed her arms. 'Okay, Myron, let's hear it. Why am I covering my ass? Why am I not the hotshot attorney you thought I was?'

'Because they didn't let Esperanza surrender. Because they dragged her in in cuffs. Because they're holding her overnight instead of getting her through the system in the same day. Why?'

She dropped her hands to her sides. 'Good question, Myron. Why do you think?'

'Because someone there doesn't like her high-profile attorney. Someone in the DA's office probably has a hard-on for you and is taking it out on your client.'

She nodded. 'Good possibility. But I have another one.'

'What?'

'Maybe they don't like her employer.'

'Me?'

She started for the door. 'Do us all a favor, Myron. Stay out of this. Just keep away. And maybe get yourself a lawyer.'

Hester Crimstein spun around and disappeared inside then. Myron turned toward Win. Win was bent at the waist, squinting at Myron's crotch. 'What the hell are you doing?'

Still squinting. 'I wanted to see if she left you with even a sliver of a testicle.'

'Very funny. What do you think she meant about them not liking her employer?'

'Not a clue,' Win said. Then: 'You mustn't blame yourself.'

'What?'

'For your charm's seemingly lackluster performance. You forgot a crucial component in all this.'

35

'That being?'

'Ms Crimstein had an affair with Esperanza.'

Myron saw where he was going with this. 'Of course. She must be a lesbian.'

'Precisely. It's the only rational explanation for her ability to resist you.'

'That, or a really bizarre paranormal event.'

Win nodded. They started walking down Central Park West.

'This is also further proof of a very frightening adage,' Win said.

'What's that?'

'Most women you encounter are lesbians.'

Myron nodded. 'Almost every one.'

6

They walked the two blocks to Win's place, watched a little television, went to bed. Myron lay in the dark exhausted, but sleep remained elusive. He thought about Jessica. Then he tried to think about Brenda, but the automatic defense mechanism deflected that one. Still too raw. And he thought about Terese. She was alone on that island tonight for the first time. During the day the island's solitude was peaceful and quiet and welcome; at night the solitude felt more like dark isolation, the island's black walls closing in, silent and cloying as a buried coffin. He and Terese had always slept wrapped in each other's arms. Now he pictured her lying in that deep blackness alone. And he worried about her.

He woke up the next morning at seven. Win was already gone, but he'd scribbled a note that he'd meet up with Myron at the courthouse at nine. Myron grabbed a bowl of Cap'n Crunch, discerned with a digging left hand that Win had already extracted the free toy inside, showered, dressed, checked his watch. Eight o'clock. Plenty of time to reach the courthouse in time.

He took the elevator down and crossed the famed Dakota courtyard. He had just reached the corner of Seventy-second Street and Central Park West when he spotted the three familiar figures. Myron felt his pulse quicken. FJ, short for Frank Junior, was bookended by two huge guys. The two huge guys looked like lab experiments gone very wrong, as if someone had potently mixed genetic glandular excess with anabolic steroids.

They wore tank tops and those drawstring weightlifting pants that looked suspiciously like ugly pajama bottoms.

Young FJ silently smiled at Myron with thin lips. He sported a purple-blue suit so shiny it looked like someone had sprayed it with a sealant. FJ didn't move, didn't say anything, just smiled at Myron with unblinking eyes and those thin lips.

Today's word, boys and girls, is *reptilian*.

FJ finally took a step forward. 'Heard you were back in town, Myron.'

Myron bit back a rejoinder – it wasn't a very cutting one, something about the nice welcoming party – and kept his mouth shut.

'Remember our last conversation?' FJ continued.

'Vaguely.'

'I mentioned something about killing you, right?'

'It might have come up,' Myron said. 'I don't remember. So many tough guys, so many threats.'

The Bookends tried to scowl, but even their faces were overmuscled, and the movement took too much effort. They settled back into the steady frowns and lowered the eyebrows a bit.

'Actually, I was going to carry through with it,' FJ continued. 'About a month ago. I followed you out to some graveyard in New Jersey. I even sneaked up behind you with my gun out. Funny thing, no?'

Myron nodded. 'Like Henny Youngman wrote it.'

FJ tilted his head. 'Don't you want to know why I didn't kill you?'

'Because of Win.'

The sound of his name was like a cold glass of water in the faces of both Bookends. The two giants actually stepped back but recovered quickly with a few flexes. FJ remained unruffled. 'Win doesn't scare me,' he said.

'Even the dumbest animal,' Myron said, 'has an innate survival mechanism.'

FJ's eyes met Myron's. Myron tried to maintain contact, but it was hard. There was nothing behind FJ's eyes but rot and decay; it was like staring into the broken windows of an abandoned building. 'Sticks and stones, Myron. Sticks and stones. I didn't kill you because, well, you already looked so miserable. It was as though – how to put this? – as though killing you would have been an act of mercy. Like I said before, funny, right?'

'You should consider stand-up,' Myron agreed.

FJ chuckled and waved a well-manicured hand at nothing in particular. 'Anyway, bygones. My father and uncle like you, and yes, we see no reason to antagonize Win unnecessarily. They don't want you dead, so neither do I.'

His father and uncle were Frank and Herman Ache, two of New York's legendary leading leg breakers. The elder Aches had grown up on the streets, slaughtered more people than the next guy, moved up the ladder. Herman, the older brother and big cheese, was in his sixties now and liked to pretend he wasn't scum by surrounding himself with the finer things in life: restricted clubs that didn't want him, nouveau-riche art exhibits, well-coiffed charities, midtown French maître d's who treated anyone who tipped with less than a Jackson like something they couldn't scrape off the soles of their shoes. In other words, a higher-income scum. Herman's younger brother, Frank, the psycho who had produced the equally psycho offspring who now stood in front of Myron, remained what he had always been: an ugly hatchet man who considered Kmart velour sweatsuits haute couture. Frank had calmed down over the last few years, but it never quite worked for him. Life, it seemed, had little meaning for Frank Senior without someone to torture or maim.

'What do you want, FJ?'

'I have a business proposition for you.'

'Gee, I just know this is really going to interest me.'

'I want to buy you out.'

The Aches ran TruPro, a rather large sports representation firm. TruPro had always been devoid of any semblance of scruples, recruiting young athletes with as much moral restraint as a politician planning a fundraiser. But then their owner stacked up debts. Bad debts. The debts that attract the wrong kind of fungus. The appropriately named Ache brothers, the fungi in question, moved in and, like the parasitic entities they were, ate away all signs of life and were now gnawing on the carcass.

Still, being a sports agent was a legit way of making a living, sort of, and Frank Senior, wanting for his son what all fathers wanted, handed young FJ the reins straight out of business school. In theory FJ was supposed to run TruPro as legitimately as possible. His father had killed and maimed so that his son wouldn't have to – yep, the classic American dream with, granted, a rather deranged twist. But FJ seemed incapable of freeing himself from the old familial shackles. *Why* was a question that fascinated Myron. Was FJ's evil genetic, passed down from his father like a prominent nose, or was he, like so many other children, simply trying to gain his father's acceptance by proving the acorn could be as ferociously psychotic as the oak?

Nature or nurture. The argument rages on.

'MB SportsReps is not for sale,' Myron said.

'I think you're being foolish.'

Myron nodded. 'I'll file that under "One Day I Might Even Care." '

The Bookends sort of grumbled, took a step forward, and cracked their necks in unison. Myron pointed to one, then the other. 'Who does your choreography?'

They wanted to be insulted – you could just tell –

except neither one of them knew what the word *choreography* meant.

FJ asked, 'Do you know how many clients MB SportsReps lost in the last few weeks?'

'A lot?'

'I'd say a quarter of your list. A couple of them went with us.'

Myron whistled, feigned nonchalant, but he was not happy to hear this. 'I'll get them back.'

'You think so?' FJ again smiled the reptilian smile; Myron almost expected a forked tongue to dart out between his lips. 'Do you know how many more are going to leave when they hear about Esperanza's arrest?'

'A lot?'

'You'll be lucky to have one left.'

'Hey, then I'll be like Jerry Maguire. Did you see that movie? Show me the money? I love black people?' Myron gave FJ his best Tom Cruise earnest. 'You. Complete. Me.'

FJ remained cool. 'I'm willing to be generous, Myron.'

'I'm sure you are, FJ, but the answer is still no.'

'I don't care how clean your rep used to be. Nobody can survive the sort of money scandal you're about to go through.'

It wasn't a money scandal, but Myron was not in the mood to issue corrections. 'Are we finished, FJ?'

'Sure.' FJ gave him one last scaly smile. The smile seemed to jump off his face, crawl toward Myron, and then slither its way up his back. 'But why don't we get together and have lunch?'

'Any time,' Myron said. 'You have a cellular?'

'Of course.'

'Call my partner right away and set it up.'

'Isn't she in jail?'

Myron snapped his fingers. 'Drat.'

FJ found that amusing. 'I mentioned that some of your old clients are now using my services.'

'So you did.'

'If you contact any of them' – he paused, thought it over – 'I'd feel obliged to retaliate. Do I make myself clear?'

FJ was maybe twenty-five years old, less than a year out of Harvard Business School. He had gone undergrad to Princeton. Smart kid. Or powerful father. Either way, rumor had it that when a Princeton professor was about to accuse FJ of plagiarism, the professor disappeared and only his tongue was found – on the pillow of another professor who had considered leveling the same charges.

'Crystal, FJ.'

'Great, Myron. Then we'll talk again.'

If Myron still had his tongue.

The three men slid into their car and drove off without another word. Myron slowed his heart rate and checked his watch.

7

The courtroom in Hackensack looked very much like the ones you see on television. Shows like *The Practice* and *Law & Order* and even *Judge Judy* capture the physical appearance pretty well. They can't of course capture the essence emanating from the little things: the faint, underlying stench of fear-induced sweat, the overuse of disinfectant, the slightly sticky feel to all the benches and tables and handrails – what Myron liked to call the ooze factors.

Myron had his checkbook ready so bail could be posted immediately. He and Win had gone over it last night and figured the judge would come in around fifty to seventy-five grand. Esperanza had no record and a steady job. Those factors would play in her favor. If the money was higher, no problem. Myron's pockets might be only semideep, but Win's net worth was on par with the GNP of a small European country.

There were droves of reporters parked outside, tons of vans with wrapped cables and satellite dishes, and of course phallic antennas, stretching toward the heavens as though in search of the elusive god of higher ratings. Court TV was there. News 2 New York. ABC News. CNN. Eyewitness News. Every city in every region of the country had an Eyewitness News. Why? What was so appealing about that name? There were also the new sleazoid TV shows, like *Hard Copy, Access Hollywood, Current Affair*, though the distinction between them and the local news was becoming murky to the point of nonexistent. Hey, at least *Hard Copy* and the like were somewhat honest about the fact that they served no redeeming social value. And they didn't subject you to weathermen.

A couple of reporters recognized Myron and called out. Myron put on his game face – serious, unyielding, concerned, confident – and no-commented his way through them. When he entered the courtroom, he spotted Big Cyndi first – no surprise since she stuck out like Louis Farrakhan at B'nai B'rith. She was jammed into the aisle of a row empty except for Win. Not unusual. If you wanted to save seats, send Big Cyndi; people did not relish excusing themselves to squeeze past her. Most opted to stand. Or go home even.

Myron slid into Big Cyndi's row, actually high-stepping over two knees that looked like batting helmets, and sat between his friends.

Big Cyndi had not changed from last night or even washed up. The steady rain had rinsed out some of the hair dye; purple and yellow streaks had dried on the front and back of her neck. Her makeup, always applied in amounts thick enough to make a plaster bust, had also suffered under the rain's onslaught, her face now resembling multicolored menorah candles left too long in the sun.

In some major cities, murder arraignments were commonplace and handled in factory-line fashion. Not so here in Hackensack. This was big time – a murder case involving a celebrity. There would be no rush.

The bailiff started calling cases.

'I had a visitor this morning,' Myron whispered to Win.

'Oh?'

'FJ and two goons.'

'Ah,' Win said. 'Was the cover boy for *Modern Mobster* voicing his usual medley of colorful threats?'

'Yes.'

44

Win almost smiled. 'We should kill him.'

'No.'

'You're just putting off the inevitable.'

'He's Frank Ache's son, Win. You just don't kill Frank Ache's son.'

'I see. Then you'd rather kill somebody from a better family?'

Win logic. It made sense in the scariest way possible.

'Let's just see how it plays out, okay?'

'Don't put off until tomorrow what must be exterminated today.'

Myron nodded. 'You should write one of those life-instruction books.'

They fell into silence. Cases went by – a breaking and entering, a couple of assaults, too many car thefts. Every suspect looked young, guilty, and angry. Always scowling. Tough guys. Myron tried not to make a face, tried to remember innocent until proven guilty, tried to remember that Esperanza too was a suspect. But it didn't help much.

Finally Myron saw Hester Crimstein sweep into the courtroom, decked out in her best professional civvies: a sleek beige suit, cream blouse, and a tad overcoiffed, overfrosted hair. She took her spot at the defense table, and the room fell silent. Two guards led Esperanza through an open door. Myron saw her, and something akin to a mule kicked him in the chest.

Esperanza was dressed in a court-issued fluorescent orange jump-suit. Forget gray or stripes – if a prisoner wanted to escape, he was going to stick out like a neon light in a monastery. Her hands were cuffed in front of her. Myron knew that Esperanza was petite – maybe five-two, a hundred pounds – but he had never seen her look so small. She kept her head high, defiant. Classic Esperanza. If she was afraid, she wasn't showing it.

Hester Crimstein put a comforting hand on her client's

shoulder. Esperanza nodded at her. Myron tried desperately to catch her eye. It took a couple of moments, but eventually Esperanza turned his way, looking straight at him with a slight, resigned, I'm-okay smile. It made Myron feel better.

The bailiff called out, 'The People versus Esperanza Diaz.'

'What's the charge?' the judge asked.

The assistant district attorney, a fresh-faced kid who barely looked old enough to sport a pubic hair, stood by a pedestal. 'Murder in the second degree, Your Honor.'

'How do you plead?'

Esperanza's voice was strong. 'Not guilty.'

'Bail?'

The fresh-faced kid said, 'Your Honor, the People request that Ms Diaz be remanded without bail.'

Hester Crimstein shouted, 'What?' as if she had just heard the most irrational and dangerous words any human being had ever uttered under any circumstance.

Fresh Face was unfazed. 'Miss Diaz is accused of killing a man by shooting him three times. We have strong evidence—'

'They have nothing, Your Honor. Circumstantial nothings.'

'Miss Diaz has no family and no real roots in the community,' Fresh Face continued. 'We believe that she presents a substantial flight risk.'

'That's nonsense, Your Honor. Miss Diaz is a partner in a major sports representation firm in Manhattan. She is a law school graduate who is currently studying for the bar. She has many friends and roots in the community. And she has no record whatsoever.'

'But, Your Honor, she has no family—'

'So what?' Crimstein interrupted. 'Her mother and father are dead. Is that now a reason to punish a woman? Dead parents? This is outrageous, Your Honor.'

The judge, a woman in her early fifties, sat back. 'Your request to deny bail does seem extreme,' she said to Fresh Face.

'Your Honor, we believe that Miss Diaz has an unusual amount of resources at her disposal and very good reasons to flee the jurisdiction.'

Crimstein kept up with the apoplectic. 'What are you talking about?'

'The murder victim, Mr Haid, had recently withdrawn cash funds in excess of two hundred thousand dollars. That money is missing from his apartment. It's logical to assume that the money was taken during the commission of the murder—'

'What logic?' Crimstein shouted. 'Your Honor, this is nonsense.'

'Counsel for the defense mentioned that Miss Diaz has friends in the community,' Fresh Face continued. 'Some of them are here, including her employer, Myron Bolitar.' He pointed to Myron. All eyes turned. Myron stayed very still. 'Our investigation shows that Mr Bolitar has been missing for at least a week, perhaps in the Caribbean, even in the Cayman Islands.'

'So what?' Crimstein shouted. 'Arrest him if that's a crime.'

But Fresh Face was not done. 'And next to him is Miss Diaz's friend Windsor Lockwood of Lock-Horne Securities.' When all eyes turned to Win, he nodded and gave a small regal wave. 'Mr Lockwood was the victim's financial adviser and held the account where the two hundred thousand dollars was withdrawn.'

'So arrest him too,' Crimstein ranted. 'Your Honor, this has nothing to do with my client, except maybe to prove her innocence. Miss Diaz is a hardworking Hispanic woman who struggled her way through law school at night. She has no record and should be freed immediately. Short of that, she has a right to reasonable bail.'

'Your Honor, there's just too much cash floating around,' Fresh Face said. 'The missing two hundred thousand dollars. Miss Diaz's possible connection with both Mr Bolitar and, of course, Mr Lockwood, who comes from one of the wealthiest families in the region—'

'Wait a second, Your Honor. First, the district attorney suggests that Miss Diaz has stolen and hidden away this alleged missing money and will use it to run. Then he suggests that she'll ask Mr Lockwood, who is no more than a business associate, for the funds. Which is it? And while the district attorney's office is busy trying to manufacture some kind of money conspiracy, why would one of the already wealthiest men in the country deem it appropriate to conspire with a poor Hispanic woman to steal? The whole idea is ludicrous. The prosecution has no case, so they've come up with this money nonsense that sounds as plausible as an Elvis sighting—'

'Enough,' the judge said. She leaned back and strummed her fingers on the big desk. She stared at Win for a second, then back at the defense table. 'The missing money troubles me,' she said.

'Your Honor, I assure you that my client knows nothing about any money.'

'I'd be surprised if your position were different, Ms Crimstein. But the facts presented by the district attorney are sufficiently troublesome. Bail denied.'

Crimstein's eyes widened. 'Your Honor, this is an outrage—'

'No need to shout, Counselor. I hear you just fine.'

'I strenuously object—'

'Save it for the cameras, Ms Crimstein.' The judge hit the gavel. 'Next case?'

Suppressed mumbles broke forth. Big Cyndi started wailing like a widow in a war newsreel. Hester Crimstein put her mouth to Esperanza's ear and whispered something. Esperanza nodded, but it didn't look like she was listening. The guards led Esperanza toward a door. Myron tried to catch her eyes again, but she didn't – or maybe wouldn't – face him.

Hester Crimstein turned and shot Myron a glare so nasty it almost made him duck. She approached him and fought to keep her face neutral. 'Room seven,' she said to Myron, not looking at him, barely moving her lips. 'Down the hallway and to the left. Five minutes. Don't say anything to anyone.'

Myron did not bother with a nod.

Crimstein hurried out, already starting with the no comments before she hit the door. Win sighed, took a piece of paper and a pen from his jacket pocket, began to scribble something down.

'What are you doing?' Myron asked.

'You'll see.'

It did not take long. Two plainclothes cops accompanied by the stench of cheap cologne made their approach. Homicide division, no doubt. Before they could even introduce themselves, Win said, 'Are we under arrest?'

The cops looked confused. Then one said, 'No.'

Win smiled and handed him the piece of paper.

'What the hell is this?'

'Our attorney's phone number,' Win said. He rose and ushered Myron toward the door. 'Have a special day.'

They arrived in the defendant's conference room before the anointed five minutes. The room was empty.

'Clu withdrew cash?' Myron said.

'Yes,' Win said.

'You knew about it?'

'Of course.'

'How much?'

'The district attorney said two hundred thousand dollars. I have no reason to quibble with that estimate.'

'And you just let him?'

'Pardon?'

'You just let Clu withdraw two hundred grand?'

'It's his money.'

'But that much cash?'

'It was none of my business,' Win said.

'You know Clu, Win. It could have been for drugs or gambling or—'

'Probably was,' Win agreed. 'But I am his financial adviser. I instruct him on investment strategies. Period. I am not his conscience or his mommy or his baby-sitter – or even his agent.'

Ouch. But no time for that now. Once again Myron suppressed the guilt and mulled over the possibilities. 'Clu okayed us receiving his financial statements, right?'

Win nodded. MB SportsReps insisted that all clients use Win's services and meet with him in person at least quarterly to go over their accounts. This was for their sake more than Myron's. Too many athletes get taken advantage of because of ignorance. But most of Myron's clients had copies of their statements sent to Myron so that he too could help keep track of the ins and outs, set up some automatic bill paying, that kind of thing.

'So a withdrawal that big would have come up on our screen,' Myron said.

'Yes.'

'Esperanza would have known about it.'

'Yes again.'

Myron frowned. 'So that gives the DA another motive for the murder. She knew about the cash.'

'Indeed.'

Myron looked at Win. 'So what did Clu do with the money?'

Win shrugged.

'Maybe Bonnie knows?'

'Doubtful,' Win said. 'They've separated.'

'Big deal. They're always fighting, but she always takes him back.'

'Perhaps. But this time she made the separation legal.'

That surprised Myron. Bonnie had never gone that far before. Their turmoil cycle had always been consistent: Clu does something stupid, a big fight ensues, Bonnie throws him out for a couple of nights, maybe a week, Clu begs forgiveness, Bonnie takes him back, Clu behaves for a little while, Clu does something stupid, the cycle starts anew. 'She got a lawyer and filed papers?'

'According to Clu.'

'He told you that?'

'Yes, Myron. That's what 'According to Clu' means.'

'When did he tell you all this?'

'Last week. When he took out the cash. He said that she had already begun divorce proceedings.'

'How did he feel about it?'

'Badly. He craved yet another reconciliation.'

'Did he say anything else when he withdrew the cash?'

'Nothing.'

'And you have no idea—'

'None.'

The conference room door flew open. Hester Crimstein came in, red-faced and fuming. 'You dumb bastards. I told you to stay away.'

'Don't put this on us,' Myron said. 'This is your screwup.'

'What?'

'Getting her bail should have been a slam dunk.'

'If you weren't in the courtroom, it would have been. You played right into the DA's hands. He wants to show the judge that the defendant has the resources to run away, and boom, he points to a famous ex-jock and one

51

of the country's richest playboys sitting right in the front row.'

She started stomping about as though the industrial gray carpet contained small brushfires. 'This judge is a liberal schmuck,' she said. 'That's why I started with all that hardworking Hispanic crap. She hates rich people, probably because she is one. Having the *Preppy Handbook* here' – she gestured with her head at Win – 'sit in the front row was like waving a Confederate flag at a black judge.'

'You should drop the case,' Myron said.

Her head jerked toward him. 'Are you out of your mind?'

'Your fame is playing against you. The judge may not like rich people, but she doesn't much like celebrities either. You're the wrong attorney for this case.'

'Bullshit. I've had three cases before this judge. I'm three and oh.'

'Maybe she doesn't like that either.'

Crimstein seemed to lose a little steam. She moved back and collapsed into a chair. 'Bail denied,' she said more to herself than anyone else. 'I can't believe they even had the nerve to ask for no bail.' She sat a bit straighter. 'All right, here's how we play it. I'm going to press for answers. In the meantime you guys say nothing. No talking to the cops, the DA, the press. Nobody. Not until we figure out what exactly they think the three of you did.'

'The three of us?'

'Weren't you listening, Myron? They think it's a money scheme.'

'Involving the three of us?'

'Yes.'

'But how?'

'I don't know. They mentioned your going to the

Caribbean, maybe the Cayman Islands. We all know what that means.'

'Depositing cash in offshore accounts,' Myron said. 'But I left the country three weeks ago – before the money was even withdrawn. And I never went anywhere near the Caymans.'

'They're probably still grasping at straws,' Crimstein said. 'But they're going to go after you in a big way. I hope your books are in order because I guarantee you they'll have them subpoenaed within the hour.'

Money scandal, Myron thought. Hadn't FJ mentioned something about that?

Crimstein turned her attention to Win. 'Is that stuff about a big cash withdrawal true?'

'Yes.'

'Can they prove Esperanza knew about it?'

'Probably.'

'Damn.' She thought about this a moment.

Win moved into a corner. He took out his cell phone, dialed, started talking.

Myron said, 'Make me co-counsel.'

Crimstein looked up. 'Excuse me?'

'As you pointed out last night, I'm a bar-appointed attorney. Make me her attorney, and anything she tells me falls under attorney-client.'

She shook her head. 'One, that'll never fly. The judge will see it for what it is, a loophole to make sure you can't testify. Two, it's moronic. Not only will it reek of a desperate defensive move, but it'll look like we're shutting you up because we have something to hide. Three, you may still be charged in all this.'

'How? I already told you. I was in the Caribbean.'

'Right. Where nobody but Preppy Boy could find you. How convenient.'

'You think—'

'I don't think anything, Myron. I'm telling you what

the DA *might* be thinking. For now we're just guessing. Go back to your office. Call your accountant. Make sure your books are in order.'

'They're in order,' Myron said. 'I've never stolen a dime.'

She turned to Win. 'How about you?'

Win hung up the phone. 'What about me?'

'They'll subpoena your books too.'

Win arched the eyebrow. 'They'll try.'

'Are they clean?'

'You could eat off them,' Win said.

'Fine, whatever. I'll let your lawyers handle it. I got enough to worry about.'

Silence.

'So how do we get her out?' Myron asked.

'We don't get her out. I get her out. You stay away.'

'I don't take orders from you.'

'No? How about from Esperanza?'

'What about Esperanza?'

'This is her request as well as mine. Stay away from her.'

'I don't believe she'd say that.'

'Believe it.'

'If she wants me out,' Myron said, 'she'll have to tell me to my face.'

'Fine,' Crimstein said with a heavy sigh. 'Let's go take care of that now.'

'What?'

'You want her to tell you herself? Give me five minutes.'

8

Win said, 'I have to get back to the office.'

Myron was surprised. 'You don't want to hear what Esperanza has to say?'

'No time.'

His tone slammed the door on further discussion. Win reached for the knob.

'If you need my special talents,' he said, 'I'll have the cellular.'

He hurried out as Hester Crimstein entered. She watched him disappear down the corridor. 'Where's he going?'

'His office.'

'Why's he in such a rush all of a sudden?'

'I didn't ask.'

Hester Crimstein raised an eyebrow. 'Hmm.'

'Hmm what?'

'Win was the one in charge of the account with the missing money.'

'So?'

'So maybe he had a reason to silence Clu Haid.'

'That's ridiculous.'

'Are you saying he's incapable of murder?'

Myron did not reply.

'If even half the stories I've heard about Windsor Lockwood are true—'

'You know better than to listen to rumors.'

She looked at him. 'So if I subpoena you to testify and if I ask if you've ever witnessed Windsor Horne Lockwood the Third kill someone, what would you say?'

'No.'

'Uh-huh. Guess you also missed the class on perjury.'

Myron did not bother with a comeback. 'When can I see Esperanza?'

'Come on. She's waiting for you.'

Esperanza sat at a long table. She still wore the orange prison suit, her now-uncuffed hands folded in front of her, her expression serene as a church statue's. Hester signaled to the trooper, and they both left the room.

When the door closed, Esperanza smiled at him. 'Welcome back,' she said.

'Thanks,' Myron replied.

Her eyes took him in. 'If your tan was any darker, you could pass for my brother.'

'Thanks.'

'Still got the smooth tongue with the ladies, eh?'

'Thanks.'

She almost smiled. Even under these conditions, Esperanza still looked radiant. Her supple skin and ink black hair shimmered against the fluorescent orange backdrop. Her eyes still brought forth thoughts of Mediterranean moons and white peasant blouses.

'Are you feeling better now?' she asked him.

'Yes.'

'Where were you anyway?'

'A private island in the Caribbean.'

'For three weeks?'

'Yes.'

'By yourself?'

'No.'

When he didn't elaborate, Esperanza simply said, 'Details.'

'I ran off with a beautiful anchorwoman I barely knew.'

Esperanza smiled. 'Did she – how to put this delicately? – did she boff your brains out?'

'As it were.'

'Glad to hear it. If any guy needed to have his brain boffed out—'

'Right, I'm the guy. Voted Most Boff Needy by the senior class.'

She liked that one. She leaned back and crossed her legs cocktail-lounge casual. Odd in these surroundings, to put it mildly. 'You didn't tell anybody where you were?'

'That's right.'

'Yet Win still found you in a matter of hours,' she said.

It surprised neither of them. They sat in silence for a moment or two. Then Myron asked, 'You okay?'

'Fine.'

'Do you need anything?'

'No.'

Myron was not sure how to continue, what subject to broach or how to broach it. Once again Esperanza took the ball and started dribbling.

'So are you and Jessica through?' she asked.

'Yes.' It was the first time he had said it out loud. It felt weird.

That made her smile, big time. 'Ah, the silver lining,' she said triumphantly. 'So it's really over? Queen Bitch is gone for good?'

'Don't call her that.'

'Is she gone for good?'

'I think so.'

'Say yes, Myron. It'll make you feel better.'

But he couldn't. 'I'm not here to talk about me.'

Esperanza crossed her arms, said nothing.

'We'll get you out of this,' he said. 'I promise.'

She nodded, still playing casual; if she were a smoker, she'd be blowing rings. 'You better get back to the office. We've already lost too many clients.'

'I don't care about that.'

'I do.' Her voice had an edge now. 'I'm a partner now.'

'I know that.'

'So I own part of MB SportsReps. If you want to self-destruct, fine. But don't drag my lusted-after ass down with you, okay?'

'I didn't mean it like that. I just meant we've got bigger worries right now.'

'No.'

'What?'

'*We* don't have bigger worries. I want you to stay out of this.'

'I don't understand.'

'I have one of the top criminal defense attorneys in the country working on my case. Let her handle it.'

Myron tried to let her words settle in, but they were like unruly children after a sugar fix. He leaned forward a bit. 'What's going on here?'

'I can't talk about it.'

'What?'

'Hester told me I shouldn't talk about the case with anyone, even you. Our conversations are not protected.'

'You think I'd tell?'

'You can be forced to testify.'

'So I'd lie.'

'You won't have to.'

Myron opened his mouth, closed it, tried again. 'Win and I can help here. We're good at this.'

'No offense, Myron, but Win is psycho. I love him, but his kind of help I don't need. And you' – Esperanza stopped, looked up, unfolded her arms, lowered her gaze back to his – 'you're damaged goods. I don't blame you for running away. It was probably the right thing to do. But let's not pretend you're back to normal.'

'Not normal,' he agreed. 'But I'm ready for this.'

She shook her head. 'Concentrate on MB. It's going to take all your efforts to keep her afloat.'

'You're not going to tell me what happened?'

'No.'

'That doesn't make any sense.'

'I just spelled out the reasons—'

'You're really afraid I'd testify against you?'

'I didn't say that.'

'So what is it? If you think I'm not up for this, okay, maybe I buy it. But that wouldn't stop you from talking to me. In fact, you'd probably tell me just to keep me from poking around. So what's going on here?'

Her face slid closed. 'Go to the office, Myron. You want to help? Save our business.'

'Did you kill him?'

He regretted it the moment the words came out of his mouth. She looked at him as if he'd just reached across the table and slapped her face.

'I don't care if you did,' he pressed on. 'I'll stand by you no matter what. I want you to know that.'

Esperanza regained her composure. She slid her chair back and stood. For a few moments she stared at him, studying his face as though searching for something that was normally there. Then she turned away, called for the guard, and left the room.

9

Big Cyndi was already manning the reception desk when Myron reached the offices of MB SportsReps. They had a prime location, right smack on Park Avenue in midtown. The Lock-Horne high-rise had been owned by Win's family since Great-Great-Et-Cetera Grandpa Horne (or was it Lockwood?) had torn down a tepee and started building it. Myron rented space at a premium discount from Win. In return Win handled all the finances on Myron's clients. This deal was a bargain for Myron. Between the *primo* address and the ability to guarantee his clients the financial services of the near-legendary Windsor Horne Lockwood III, MB SportsReps had an air of legitimacy few small firms could boast.

MB SportsReps was on the twelfth floor. An elevator opened directly into their reception room. *Muy* classy. The phones were beeping. Big Cyndi put people on hold and looked up at him. She looked even more ridiculous than usual. No easy task. In the first place, the furniture was too small for her, the desk legs actually teetering on her knees like something a father might experience when visiting his child's elementary school. In the second place, she still had not washed up or changed from last night. Normally Myron, the image-conscious entrepreneur, would comment on this, but now did not seem an appropriate (or safe) time.

'The press is pulling out all the tricks to get up here, Mr Bolitar.' Big Cyndi always called him Mr Bolitar. She liked formalities. 'Two of them even pretended to be prospective clients coming out of Division One schools.'

Myron was hardly surprised. 'I told the guard downstairs to be extra wary.'

'A lot of clients are calling too. They're concerned.'

'Patch them through. Get rid of everybody else.'

'Yes, Mr Bolitar.' Like she wanted to salute. Big Cyndi handed him a pile of blue slips. 'These are this morning's calls from clients.'

He started thumbing through the stack.

'For your information,' Big Cyndi continued, 'we told everyone you were just gone for a day or two at first. Then a week or two. Then we started faking emergencies for you: family illnesses, helping a sick client, that sort of thing. But some clients got tired of the excuses.'

He nodded. 'You have a list of who left us?'

It was already in her hand. She handed it to him, and he started toward his office.

'Mr Bolitar?'

He turned. 'Yes?'

'Will Esperanza be okay?'

Again the tiny, distant voice belied her bulk, as though the looming form in front of him had swallowed a small child and the small child were now calling for help. 'Yes, Big Cyndi. She'll be fine.'

'You'll help her, won't you? Even though she doesn't want you to?'

Myron gave her a half nod. That didn't seem to satisfy her. So he said, 'Yes.'

'Good, Mr Bolitar. That's the right thing to do.'

He had nothing to add to that so he entered his inner office. Myron had not been to MB in six weeks. Strange. He had worked so hard and so long to build up MB SportsReps – M for Myron, B for Bolitar, snappy name, no? – and he had just abandoned her. Just like that. Abandoned his business. And his clients. And Esperanza.

The renovations had been completed – they'd sliced a bit of space out of the conference room and reception area so that Esperanza could have an office of her own – but the new room remained unfurnished. So Esperanza had been using his office. He sat at his desk and immediately the phone started ringing. He ignored it for a few seconds, his eyes latched on the client wall, the one with action photos of all the athletes MB represented. He zeroed in on Clu Haid's image. Clu was on the pitcher's mound, leaning forward, about to go into a stretch, his cheek bulging with tobacco chaw, his eyes squinting at a sign he would undoubtedly shake off.

'What did you do this time, Clu?' he said out loud.

The photo didn't reply, which was probably a good thing. But Myron continued to stare. He had pulled Clu out of so many jams over the years that he had to wonder: If he had not run off to the Caribbean, would he have been able to pull Clu out of this one too?

Useless introspection – one of Myron's many talents.

Big Cyndi buzzed him. 'Mr Bolitar?'

'Yes.'

'I know you told me to only patch through clients, but Sophie Mayor is on the line.'

Sophie Mayor was the new owner of the Yankees.

'Put her through.' He heard a click and said hello.

'Myron, my God. What the hell is going on here?' Sophie Mayor wasn't big on chitchat.

'I'm still trying to sort it out myself.'

'They think your secretary killed Clu.'

'Esperanza is my partner,' he corrected, though he was not sure why. 'And she didn't kill anyone.'

'I'm sitting here with Jared.' Jared was her son and the 'co-general manager' of the Yankees – *co* meaning *shares the title with someone who knows what he's doing because he got the job through nepotism. Jared* meaning *born after 1973.* 'We need to tell the press something.'

'I'm not sure how I can help, Ms Mayor.'

'You told me Clu was past all this, Myron.'

He said nothing.

'The drugs, the drinking, the partying, the trouble,' Sophie Mayor continued. 'You said it was in the past.'

He was about to defend himself but thought better of it. 'I think it's better if we talk about all this in person,' Myron said.

'Jared and I are on the road with the team. We're in Cleveland right now. We're flying home tonight.'

'How about tomorrow morning then?'

'We'll be at the stadium,' she said. 'Eleven o'clock.'

'I'll be there.'

He hung up the phone. Big Cyndi immediately put through a client call.

'Myron here.'

'Where the hell have you been?'

It was Marty Towey, a defensive tackle for the Vikings. Myron took a deep breath and let loose his semiprepared oration: he was back, things were great, don't worry, the financials are terrific, got the new contract right here, busy securing new endorsements, blah, blah, soothe, soothe.

Marty was a tough sell. 'Dammit, Myron, I chose MB because I didn't want underlings handling me. I wanted to deal with the big boss. You know what I'm saying?'

'Sure, Marty.'

'Esperanza's nice and all. But she ain't you. I hired you. Do you understand?'

'I'm back now, Marty. Everything is going to be fine, I promise. Look, you guys are in town in a couple of weeks, right?'

'We play the Jets in two weeks.'

'Great. So I'll meet you at the game and we'll go out to dinner afterward.'

When Myron hung up, it dawned on him that he'd been so uninvolved in his clients' affairs that he didn't even know if Marty was playing at an All-Pro level or nearly waived. Christ, he had a lot of catching up to do.

The calls went on in a similar vein for the next two hours. Most clients were assuaged. Some sat on the fence. No additional ones left him. He had not fixed anything, but he had managed to lessen the blood flow to a serious trickle.

Big Cyndi knocked and opened the office door. 'Trouble, Mr Bolitar.'

An awful, though not unfamiliar, stench started emanating from the doorway.

'What the hell . . . ?' Myron began.

'Out of the way, hot stuff.' The gruff voice came from behind Big Cyndi. Myron tried to see who it was, but Big Cyndi blocked his line of vision like a solar eclipse. Eventually she yielded, and the same two plainclothes officers from the courthouse hurried past her. The big one was fiftyish, bleary-eyed, world-weary and had the kind of face that looked unshaven even after a shave. He wore a trench coat with sleeves that barely reached his elbows and shoes that had more scuff marks than a Gaylord Perry baseball. The smaller guy was younger and really, well, ugly. His face reminded Myron of a magnified photo of head lice. He wore a light gray suit with vest – the Sears Casual Law Enforcer – and one of those *Looney Tunes* ties that screamed 1992.

The awful smell started permeating the walls.

'A warrant,' the big guy groused. He wasn't chewing on a cigar, but he should have been. 'And before you tell me we're out of our jurisdiction, we're still working with Michael Chapman, Manhattan North. Call him, you got a problem. Now get out of the chair, asshole, so we can search this place.'

Myron crinkled his nose. 'Jesus, which one of you is wearing the cologne?'

Head Lice gave a quick look toward his partner. The

look said, Hey, I'll take a bullet for this guy, but I'm not taking the fall for that smell. Understandable.

'Listen up, dip shit,' the big one said. 'My name is Detective Winters—'

'Really? Your mother named you Detective?'

Barely a sigh. '– and this is Detective Martinez. Move out here now, dim wad.'

The smell was getting to him. 'Yo, Winters, you got to stop borrowing cologne from male flight attendants.'

'Keep at it, funnyman.'

'Seriously, does the label include the words *glaze liberally*?'

'You're a real comedian, Bolitar. So many bad asses are funny it's a pity they don't televise Sing Sing.'

'I thought you already searched the place.'

'We did. Now we're back for the financials.'

Myron pointed to Head Lice. 'Can't he do it alone?'

'What?'

'I'll never get the smell out of here.'

Winters took out a pair of latex gloves, this so as not to mess up possible fingerprints. He snapped them on in dramatic fashion, including finger wiggling, and grinned.

Myron winked. 'You want me to bend down and grab my ankles?'

'No.'

'Dang, and me needing a date.' Want to needle a cop? Use gay humor. Myron had yet to meet one who wasn't a complete homophobe.

Winters said, 'We're going to trash this place, funnyman.'

'Doubtful,' Myron countered.

'Oh?'

Myron stood, reached into the file cabinet behind him. 'Hey, you can't touch anything in here.'

Myron ignored him, pulled out a small videocamera. 'Just keeping a record of your doings, officer. In today's climate of false police corruption charges, we wouldn't want any misunderstandings' – Myron snapped on the camera and aimed the lens at the big guy – 'would we?'

'No,' the big guy said, staring straight into the lens. 'We wouldn't want any misunderstandings.'

Myron kept his eye in the viewer. 'The camera captures the real you, Detective. I bet if we played it back, we'd still smell your cologne.'

Head Lice hid a smile.

'Please get out of our way, Mr Bolitar,' Winters said.

'Sure thing. Cooperation is my middle name.'

They began the search, which basically consisted of packing every document they could lay their hands on in crates and carrying them out. The gloved hands touched everything, and it felt to Myron like they were touching him. He tried to look innocent – whatever that looked like – but he couldn't help being nervous. Guilt was a funny thing. He knew that there was nothing amiss in any of the files, but he still felt oddly defensive.

Myron gave the video camera to Big Cyndi and started making calls to clients who had left MB. Most didn't pick up. The few who did tried to defect. Myron played it soft, figuring that any overaggression would backfire. He merely told them that he was back and would like very much to speak with them at their earliest convenience. A lot of hemming and hawing from those who actually spoke to him. Not unexpected. If he were to regain their confidence, it would take time.

The cops finished up and left without so much as a good-bye. Manners. Big Cyndi and Myron watched the elevators close.

'This is going to be very difficult,' Myron said.

'What?'

'Working without any files.'

Big Cyndi opened her purse and showed him computer disks. 'Everything is on these.'

'Everything?'

'Yes.'

'You backed up everything on these?'

'Yes.'

'Letters and correspondences, okay, but I need the contracts—'

'Everything,' she said. 'I bought a scanner and ran every paper in the office through it. There's a backup set in a safety-deposit box at Citibank. I update the disks every week. In case of fire or other emergency.'

When she smiled this time, Myron's cringe was barely perceptible.

'Big Cyndi, you are a surprising woman.'

It was hard to tell under the melted Masque de Crayola, but it almost looked like she was blushing.

The intercom buzzed. Big Cyndi picked up the phone. 'Yes?' Pause. Then her voice grew grave. 'Yes, send her up.' She replaced the receiver.

'Who is it?'

'Bonnie Haid is here to see you.'

Big Cyndi showed the Widow Haid into his office. Myron stood behind his desk, not sure what to do. He waited for her to make the first move, but she didn't. Bonnie Haid had let her hair grow out, and for a moment he was back at Duke. Clu and Bonnie were sitting on the couch in the basement of the frat house, another major kegger behind them, his arm draped over her shoulder, she wearing a gray sweatshirt, her legs tucked under her.

He swallowed and moved toward her. She took a step back and closed her eyes. She put a hand up to stop him as though she could not bear the pain of his intimacy. Myron stayed where he was.

'I'm sorry,' he said.

'Thank you.'

They both stood there, two dancers waiting for the music to begin.

'Can I sit down?' Bonnie asked.

'Of course.'

She sat. Myron hesitated and then chose to go back around his desk.

'When did you get back?' she asked.

'Last night,' he said. 'I didn't know about Clu before then. I'm sorry I wasn't here for you.'

Bonnie cocked her head. 'Why?'

'Pardon?'

'Why are you sorry you weren't here? What could you have done?'

Myron shrugged. 'Help maybe.'

'Help how?'

He shrugged again, spread his arms. 'I don't know what to say, Bonnie. I'm flailing here.'

She looked at him a moment, challenging, then dropped her eyes. 'I'm just lashing out at whoever's in front of me,' she said. 'Don't pay any attention.'

'I don't mind; lash away.'

Bonnie almost managed a smile. 'You're a good guy, Myron. You always were. Even at Duke there was something about you that was – I don't know – noble, I guess.'

'Noble?'

'Sounds silly, doesn't it?'

'Very,' he said. 'How are the boys?'

She shrugged. 'Timmy is only eighteen months old so he doesn't have a clue. Charlie is four so he's just pretty confused right now. My parents are taking care of them.'

'I don't want to keep sounding like a bad cliché,' Myron said, 'but if there's anything at all I can do . . .'

'One thing.'

'Name it.'

'Tell me about the arrest.'

Myron cleared his throat. 'What about it?'

'I've met Esperanza a few times over the years. I guess I find it hard to believe she'd kill Clu.'

'She didn't do it.'

Bonnie squinted a bit. 'What makes you so sure?'

'I know Esperanza.'

'That's it?'

He nodded. 'For now.'

'Have you spoken to her?'

'Yes.'

'And?'

'I can't talk about specifics' – mostly because he didn't know any; Myron was almost grateful that Esperanza had not told him anything – 'but she didn't do it.'

'What about all the evidence the police found?'

'I can't answer that yet, Bonnie. But Esperanza is innocent. We'll find the real killer.'

'You sound so sure.'

'I am.'

They fell into silence. Myron waited, mapping out an approach. There were questions that needed to be asked, but this woman had just lost her husband. One had to tread gently lest one trip an emotional land mine.

'I'm going to look into the murder,' Myron said.

She looked confused. 'What do you mean, look into?'

'Investigate.'

'But you're a sports agent.'

'I have some background in this.'

She studied his face. 'Win too?'

'Yes.'

She nodded as if something suddenly made sense. 'Win always scared the crap out of me.'

'That's only because you're sane.'

'And now you're going to try to figure out who killed Clu?'

'Yes.'

'I see,' she said. She shifted in her chair. 'Tell me something, Myron.'

'Anything.'

'What's your priority here: finding the murderer or getting Esperanza off?'

'One and the same.'

'And if they're not? If you learn Esperanza killed him?'

Time to lie. 'Then she'll be punished.'

Bonnie started smiling as though she could see the truth. 'Good luck,' she said.

Myron put an ankle up on a knee. *Gentle now*, he thought. 'Can I ask you something?'

She shrugged. 'Sure.'

Gently, gently. 'I don't mean any disrespect, Bonnie. I'm not asking this to be nosy—'

'Subtlety is not your strong suit, Myron. Just ask your question.'

'Were you and Clu having problems?'

A sad grin. 'Weren't we always?'

'I hear this was something more serious.'

Bonnie folded her arms below her chest. 'My, my. Back less than a day and already you've learned so much. You work fast, Myron.'

'Clu mentioned it to Win.'

'So what do you want to know?'

'Were you suing him for divorce?'

'Yes.' No hesitation.

'Can you tell me what happened?'

In the distance the fax machine started its primordial screech. The phone continued beeping. Myron had no fear that they'd be interrupted. Big Cyndi had worked for years as a bouncer at an S&M bar; when the situation called for it, she could be as nasty as a rabid rhino with a bad case of piles. Er, even when the situation didn't call for it.

'Why do you want to know?' Bonnie asked.

'Because Esperanza didn't kill him.'

'That's becoming something of a mantra for you, Myron. Say it often enough and you start to believe it, right?'

'I believe it.'

'So?'

'So if she didn't kill him, someone else did.'

Bonnie looked up. 'If she didn't kill him, someone else did,' she repeated. Pause. 'You weren't just bragging before. You really do have a background in this.'

'I'm just trying to find out who killed him.'

'By asking about our marriage?'

'By asking about anything turbulent in his life.'

'Turbulent?' She let out a stab of a laugh. 'This is Clu we're talking about here, Myron. Everything was turbulent. The hard thing to find would be patches of calm.'

'How long were you two together?' Myron asked.

'You know the answer to that.'

He did. Junior year at Duke. Bonnie had come bopping down to the frat house basement dressed in a monogram sweater and pearls and, yep, ponytail. Myron and Clu had been working the keg. Myron liked working the keg because it kept him so busy he didn't drink as much. Don't get the wrong idea here. Myron drank. It was pretty much a college requirement in those days. But he wasn't a very good drinker. He always seemed to miss that cusp of fun, that floaty buzz between sobriety and vomiting. It was almost nonexistent for him. Something in his ancestry, he assumed. It had actually helped him in recent months. Before running away with Terese, Myron had tried the old-fashioned approach of drowning one's sorrows. But, put bluntly, he usually threw up before reaching oblivion.

Nice way to prevent alcohol abuse.

Anyway, Clu and Bonnie's meeting was pretty simple. Bonnie walked in. Clu looked up from the keg and it was as if Captain Marvel had zapped him with a thunderbolt. 'Wow,' Clu muttered, the beer overflowing onto a floor so coated with beer that rodents often got stuck on it and died. Then Clu leaped over the bar, staggered toward Bonnie, dropped to one knee, and proposed. Three years later they tied the knot for real.

'So after all these years what happened?'

Bonnie looked down. 'It had nothing to do with his murder,' she said.

'That's probably true, but I need to get the full picture of his life, travel down any possible avenue—'

'Bullshit, Myron. I said it had nothing to do with the murder, okay? Leave it at that.'

He licked his lips, folded his hands, put them on the desktop. 'In the past you've thrown him out because of another woman.'

'Not woman. Women. Plural.'

'Is that what happened again this time?'

'He swore off women. He promised me that there'd be no more.'

'And he broke that promise?'

Bonnie didn't answer.

'What was her name?'

Her voice was soft. 'I never knew.'

'But there was someone else?'

Again she didn't answer. No need. Myron tried to put on his attorney skin for a moment. Clu's having an affair was a very good thing for Esperanza's defense. The more motives you can find, the more reasonable doubt you can create. Did the girlfriend kill him because he still wanted to be with his wife? Did Bonnie do it out of jealousy? And then there was the missing money. Wouldn't the girlfriend and/or Bonnie have known about it? Couldn't that be an added motive for murder? Yep, Hester Crimstein would like this. Throw enough possibilities into a trial, muddy the waters enough, and an acquittal is almost inevitable. It was a simple equation: Confusion equals reasonable doubt equals a not-guilty verdict.

'He's had affairs before, Bonnie. What was different this time?'

'Give it a rest, Myron, okay? Clu isn't even in the ground yet.'

He pulled back. 'I'm sorry.'

She looked away. Her chest rose and fell, her voice fighting to stay steady. 'I know you're just trying to help,' she said. 'But the divorce stuff . . . it hurts too much right now.'

'I understand.'

'If you have other questions . . .'

'I heard Clu failed a drug test.' So much for backing off.

'I only know what I read in the papers.'

'Clu told Win it was a fix.'

'What?'

'Clu claimed he was clean. What do you think?'

'I think Clu was a marvelous screwup. We both know that.'

'So he was taking again?'

'I don't know.' She swallowed and locked eyes with him. 'I hadn't seen him in weeks.'

'And before that?'

'He seemed clean, actually. But he was always good at hiding it. Remember that intervention we tried three years ago?'

Myron nodded.

'We all cried. We all begged him to stop. And finally Clu broke down too. He sobbed like a baby, said he was ready to turn his life around. Two days later he paid off a guard and sneaked out of rehab.'

'So you think he was just masking the symptoms?'

'He could have been. He was good at that.' She hesitated. 'But I don't think so.'

'Why not?'

'I don't know. Wishful thinking, I guess, but I really thought he was clean this time. In the past you could almost see he was going through the motions. He was playing a part for me or the kids. But this time he seemed more determined. Like he knew this trade was his last chance to start fresh. He worked at it like I've never seen him work at anything. I thought he was beating it too. But something must have pushed him back off . . .'

Bonnie's voice tailed off, and now her eyes filled. She was wondering, no doubt, if she had been that push, if Clu had indeed been clean and if she had thrown him out of their house and plunged him back into the world of his addictions. Myron almost told her not to blame herself, but good sense kept the grating cliché at bay.

'Clu always need someone or something,' she went on. 'He was the most dependent person I ever knew.'

Myron nodded, encouraging her.

'At first I found that attractive, that he needed me so much. But it got weary.' Bonnie looked at him. 'How many times did someone pull his ass out of the fire?'

'Too many,' Myron admitted.

'I wonder, Myron.' She sat up a bit, more clear-eyed now. 'I wonder if we all did him a disservice. Maybe if we weren't always there to save him, he would have had to change. Maybe if I had dumped him years ago, he would have straightened himself out and survived all this.'

Myron said nothing, not bothering to point out the inherent contradiction in her statement: She finally did dump him and he ended up dead.

'Did you know about the two hundred thousand dollars?' Myron asked.

'I heard about it from the police.'

'Do you have any idea where it might be?'

'No.'

'Or why he might have needed it?'

'No.' Her voice was far away now, her gaze drifting over his shoulder.

'Do you think it was for drugs?'

'The papers said he tested positive for heroin,' she said.

'That's my understanding.'

'That would be a new one for Clu. I know it's an expensive addiction, but two hundred thousand seems extreme.'

Myron agreed. 'Was he in any trouble?'

She looked at him.

'I mean, besides the usual. Loan sharks or gambling or something like that?'

'It's possible, I guess.'

'But you don't know.'

Bonnie shook her head, still looking off at nothing. 'You know what I was thinking about?'

'What?'

'Clu's first year as a pro. Class A with the New England Bisons. Right after he asked you to negotiate his contract. Do you remember that?'

Myron nodded.

'And again, I wonder.'

'Wonder what?'

'That was the first time we all banded together to save his ass.'

The late-night phone call. Myron swimming out of sleep and clutching the receiver. Clu crying, almost incoherent. He had been driving with Bonnie and his old Duke roommate, Billy Lee Palms, the Bisons' catcher. Drunk driving, to be more precise. He had smashed the car into a pole. Billy Lee's injuries were minor, but Bonnie had been rushed to the hospital. Clu, not a scratch on him, of course, had been arrested. Myron had hurried out to western Massachusetts, plenty of cash in hand.

'I remember,' Myron said.

'You'd just signed Clu to that big chocolate milk endorsement. Drunk driving was bad enough, but with an injury to boot, well, it would have destroyed him. But we took care of him. The right people were bought off. Billy Lee and I made a statement about some pickup truck cutting us off. We saved him. And now I wonder if we did the right thing. Maybe if Clu had paid a price right then and there, maybe if he'd gone to jail instead of skating by . . .'

'He wouldn't have gone to jail, Bonnie. A suspended license maybe. Some community service.'

'Whatever. Life is about ripples, Myron. There are some philosophers who think that everything we do changes the world forever. Even simple acts. Like if you left your house five minutes later, if you took a different route to work – it changes everything for the rest of your life. I don't necessarily buy that, but when it comes to the big things, yeah, sure, I think the ripples last. Or maybe it started before that. When he was a child. The first time he learned that because he could throw a white sphere with amazing velocity, people treated him special. Maybe we just continued the conditioning that day. Or brought it up to an adult level. Clu learned that someone would always save him. And we did. We got him off that night, and then there were the assault charges and the lewd behavior and the failed drug tests and whatever else.'

'And you think his murder was the inevitable result?'

'Don't you?'

'No,' Myron said. 'I think the person who shot him three times is responsible. Period.'

'Life is rarely that simple, Myron.'

'But murder usually is. In the end someone shot him. That's how he died. He didn't die because we helped him through some self-destructive excesses. Someone murdered him. And that person – not you or me or those who cared about him – is to blame.'

She thought about it. 'Maybe you're right.' But she didn't look convinced.

'Do you know why Clu would strike Esperanza?'

She shook her head. 'The police asked me that too. I don't know. Maybe he was high.'

'Did he get violent when he got high?'

'No. But it sounds like he was under a lot of pressure. Maybe he was just frustrated that she wouldn't tell him where you were.'

Another wave of guilt. He waited for it to recede.

'Who else would he have gone to, Bonnie?'

'What do you mean?'

'You said he was needy. I wasn't around. You weren't talking to him. So where would Clu go next?'

She thought about it. 'I'm not sure.'

'Any friends, teammates?'

'I don't think so.'

'How about Billy Lee Palms?'

She shrugged an I-don't-know.

Myron tossed out a few more questions, but nothing of consequence was batted back to him. After a while Bonnie feigned a check at the time. 'I have to get back to the kids,' she said.

He nodded, rose from his chair. This time she did not stop him. He hugged her and she hugged him back, gripping him fiercely.

'Do me one favor,' she said.

'Name it.'

'Clear your friend,' she said. 'I understand why you need to do that. And I wouldn't want her to go to jail for something she didn't do. But then let it be.'

Myron pulled back a bit. 'I don't understand.'

'Like I said before, you're a noble guy.'

He thought about the Slaughter family and how it all ended; something inside him was crushed anew. 'College was a long time ago,' he said softly.

'You haven't changed.'

'You'd be surprised.'

'You still need justice and neat endings and to do the right thing.'

He said nothing.

'Clu can't give you that,' Bonnie said. 'He wasn't a noble man.'

'He didn't deserve to be murdered.'

She put a hand on his arm. 'Save your friend, Myron. Then let Clu go.'

10

Myron took the elevator up two floors to the nerve center of Lock-Horne Securities and Investments. Exhausted white men – there were women and minorities too, more and more each year, but the overall numbers were still woefully inadequate – darted about, particles under blaring heat, gray phones tethered to their ears like life-sustaining umbilical cords. The noise level and the open space reminded Myron of a Vegas casino, though the toupees were better. People cried out in joy and agony. Money was won and lost. Dice were rolled and wheels were spun and cards were dealt. The men constantly glanced up at an electronic ticker, awe in their faces, ardently watching the stock prices like gamblers waiting for the wheel to settle on a number or ancient Israelites peering up at Moses and his new stone tablets.

These were the trenches of finance, armed soldiers crowded together, each trying to survive in a world where earning low six figures meant cowardice and probably death. Computer terminals twinkled through an onslaught of yellow Post-It notes. The warriors drank coffee and buried framed family photos under a volcanic outpouring of stock analyses and financial statements and corporate reviews. They wore white button-down shirts and Windsor-knotted ties, their suit jackets neatly arrayed on the backs of chairs as though the chairs were a tad chilly or preparing for lunch at Le Cirque.

Win did not sit out here, of course. The generals in this war – the rainmakers, big producers, heavy hitters, what have you – were tented on the perimeter, their offices running along the windows, cutting off from the foot soldiers any hint of blue sky or fresh air or any element endemic to human beings.

Myron headed up a carpeted incline and toward the left corner suite. Win was usually alone in his office. Not today. Myron stuck his head in the door, and a bunch of suitheads swiveled toward him. Lots of suits. Myron couldn't say how many. Might have been six, maybe eight. They were a lumpy blur of gray and blue with streaks of tie-and-hankie red, like the aftermath of a Civil War reenactment. The older ones, distinguished white-haired guys with manicures and cuff links, sat in the burgundy leather chairs closest to Win's desk and nodded a lot. The younger ones were squeezed onto the couches against the wall, heads down, scratching notes on legal pads as though Win were divulging the secret of eternal life. Every once in a while the younger men would peer up at the older men, glimpsing their glorious future, which would basically consist of a more comfortable chair and less note taking.

The legal pads gave it away. These were attorneys. The older men probably over four hundred bucks an hour, the younger ones two-fifty. Myron didn't bother with the math, mostly because it would take too much effort to count how many suits were in the room. Didn't matter. Lock-Horne Securities could afford it. Redistributing wealth – that is, the act of moving money around without creation or production or making anything new – was incredibly profitable.

Myron Bolitar, Marxist Sports Agent.

Win clapped his hands and the men were dismissed. They rose as slowly as possible – attorneys billed by the minute, sort of like 900 sex lines minus the guaranteed, er, payoff – and filed out the office door. The older men departed first, the younger men trailing not unlike Japanese brides.

Myron stepped inside. 'What's going on?'

Win signaled for Myron to sit. Then he leaned back and did the steeple thing with his hands. 'This situation,' he said, 'has me troubled.'

'You mean Clu's cash withdrawal?'

'In part, yes,' Win said. He bounced the fingertips before resting the indexes on his lower lip. 'I become very unhappy when I hear the words *subpoena* and *Lock-Horne* in the same sentence.'

'So? You have nothing to hide.'

Win smiled thinly. 'Your point being?'

'Let them look at your records. You're a lot of things, Win. Honest being chief among them.'

Win shook his head. 'You are so naive.'

'What?'

'My family runs a financial securities firm.'

'So?'

'So even the whiff of innuendo can destroy said firm.'

'I think you're overreacting,' Myron said.

Win arched an eyebrow, put a hand to his ear. 'Pardon *moi*?'

'Come on, Win. There's always some Wall Street scandal or other going on. People barely notice anymore.'

'Those are insider trading scandals mostly.'

'So?'

Win paused, looked at him. 'Are you being purposely obtuse?'

'No.'

'Insider trading is a completely different animal.'

'How so?'

'Do you really need me to explain this to you?'

'Guess so.'

'Fine then. Stripping it bare, insider trading is cheating or stealing. My clients do not care if I cheat or steal – as long it is done for their benefit. In fact, if a certain illegal act were to increase their portfolios, most clients would probably encourage it. But if their financial adviser is playing games with their personal accounts – or equally awful, if his banking institution is merely involved in something that will give the government the right to subpoena records – clients become understandably nervous.'

Myron nodded. 'I can see where there might be a problem.'

Win strummed the top of his desk with his fingers. For him, this was major agitation. Hard to believe, but for the first time Win actually appeared a touch unnerved. 'I have three law firms and two publicity firms working on the matter,' he continued.

'Working on it how?'

'The usual,' Win said. 'Calling in political favors, preparing a lawsuit against the Bergen County DA's office for libel and slander, planting positive spins in the media, seeing what judges will be running for reelection.'

'In other words,' Myron said, 'who can you pay off.'

Win shrugged. 'You say tomato, I say tomahto.'

'The files haven't been subpoenaed yet?'

'No. I plan on quashing the possibility before any judge even thinks of issuing them.'

'So maybe we should take the offensive.'

Win resteepled. His big mahogany desk was polished to the point where his reflection was near-mirror clear, like something out of an old dish detergent commercial where a housewife gets waaaaay too excited about seeing herself in a dinner plate. 'I'm listening.'

He recounted his conversation with Bonnie Haid. The red phone on Win's credenza – his Batphone, so enamored with the old Adam West vehicle that he actually kept it under what looked like a glass cake cover – interrupted him several times. Win had to take the calls. They were mostly from attorneys. Myron could hear the lawyerly panic travel through the earpiece and all the way across the desk. Understandable. Windsor Horne Lockwood III was not the kind of guy you wanted to disappoint.

Win remained calm. His end of the conversation could basically be broken down into two words: *How*. And *much*.

When Myron finished, Win said, 'Let's make a list.' He didn't reach for a pen. Neither did Myron. 'One, we need Clu's phone records.'

'He was staying at an apartment in Fort Lee,' Myron said.

'The murder scene.'

'Right. Clu and Bonnie rented the apartment when he first got traded in May.' To the Yankees. A huge deal that gave Clu, an aging veteran, one last chance to squander. 'They moved into the house in Tenafly in July, but the apartment's lease ran for another six months. So when Bonnie threw him out, that's where he ended up.'

'You have the address?' Win asked.

'Yep.'

'Fine then.'

'Send the records down to Big Cyndi. I'll have her check through it.'

Getting a phone record was frighteningly easy. Don't believe it? Open your local yellow pages. Choose a private investigator at random. Offer to pay him or her two grand for anyone's monthly phone bill. Some will simply say yes, but most will try to up you to three thousand, half the fee going to whatever phone company minion they bribe.

Myron said, 'We also need to check out Clu's credit cards, his checkbook, ATM, whatever, see what he's been up to lately.'

Win nodded. In Clu's case, this would be doubly easy. His entire financial portfolio was held by Lock-Horne Securities. Win had set up a separate management

83

account for Clu so that he could manage his finances easier. It included a Visa debit card, electronic payments of monthly bills, and a checkbook.

'We also need to find this mystery girlfriend,' Myron said.

'Shouldn't be too difficult,' Win said.

'No.'

'And as you suggested earlier, our old fraternity brother Billy Lee Palms might know something.'

'We can track him down,' Myron said.

Win raised a finger. 'One thing.'

'I'm listening.'

'You will have to do the majority of the legwork on your own.'

'Why's that?'

'I have a business to run.'

'So do I,' Myron said.

'You lose your business, you hurt two people.'

'Three,' Myron corrected. 'You forgot Big Cyndi.'

'No. I am speaking of Big Cyndi and Esperanza. I left you out for all the obvious reasons. Again if you require the prerequisite cliché, please choose one of the following: You made your bed, now lie in it—'

'I get the point,' Myron interrupted. 'But I still have a business to protect. For their sakes, if not my own.'

'No question.' Win motioned toward the trenches. 'But at the risk of sounding melodramatic, I am responsible for those people out there. For their jobs and financial security. They have families and mortgages and tuition payments.' He pierced Myron with the ice blues. 'That's not something I take lightly.'

'I know.'

Win leaned back. 'I'll stay involved, of course. And again if my particular talents are needed—'

'Let's hope they aren't,' Myron interrupted.

Win shrugged again. Then he said, 'Funny, isn't it?'

'What?'

'We haven't even mentioned Esperanza in all this. Why do you think that is?'

'I don't know.'

'Perhaps,' Win said, 'we have some doubt about her innocence.'

'No.'

Win arched the eyebrow but said nothing.

'I'm not just being emotional,' Myron said. 'I've been thinking about it.'

'And?'

'And it makes no sense. First off, why would Esperanza kill Clu? What's her motive?'

'The DA seems to think she killed him for the money.'

'Right. And I think it's fair to say we both know better.'

Win paused, nodded. 'Esperanza would not kill for money, no.'

'So we have no motive.'

Win frowned. 'I'd say that conclusion is at best premature.'

'Okay, but now let's look at the evidence. The gun, for example.'

'Go on,' Win said.

'Think this through for a second. Esperanza has a major altercation with Clu in front of witnesses, right?'

'Yes.'

Myron held up a finger. 'One, would Esperanza be dumb enough to kill Clu so soon after a public fight?'

'Fair point,' Win conceded. 'But perhaps the battle in the garage just raised the stakes. Perhaps after that Esperanza realized that Clu was out of control.'

'Fine, let's say that Esperanza was still dumb enough to kill him after the fight. She'd have to know she'd be a suspect, right? I mean, there were witnesses.'

Win nodded slowly. 'I'll go with that.'

'So why was the murder weapon in the office? Esperanza isn't that stupid. She's worked with us before. She knows the ins and out. Hell, anybody with a television set would have known you're supposed to dump the gun.'

Win hesitated. 'I see what you're saying.'

'So the gun had to be planted. And if the gun was planted, then it follows that the blood and the fibers were planted too.'

'Logical.' Win doing his best Mr Spock. The Batphone rang again. Win picked up the receiver and dispatched the matter in seconds. They went back to thinking.

'On the other hand,' Win said, 'I have never encountered a perfectly logical murder.'

'What do you mean?'

'Reality is messy and full of contradictions. Take the O.J. case.'

'The what?'

'The O.J. case,' Win repeated. 'If all that blood was spilled and the Juice was drenched in it, why was so little found?'

'He changed clothes.'

'So? Even if he did, you'd expect to find more than a few dashboard splatters, wouldn't you? If the Juice drove home and showered, why was no blood found on the tiles or in the pipes or what have you?'

'So you think O.J. was innocent?'

Win frowned again. 'You are missing my point.'

'Which is?'

'Murder investigations never make complete sense. There are always rips in the fabric of logic. Unexplainable flaws. Perhaps Esperanza made a mistake. Perhaps she did not believe the police would suspect her. Perhaps she thought the weapon would be safer in the office than, say, her house.'

'She didn't kill him, Win.'

Win spread his hands. 'Who amongst us is incapable – given the right circumstances – of murder?'

Heavy silence.

Myron swallowed hard. 'For the sake of argument, let's assume the weapon was planted.'

Win nodded slowly, keeping his eyes on Myron's.

'The question is, who set her up?'

'And why,' Win added.

'So we need to make a list of her enemies,' Myron said.

'And ours.'

'What?'

'This murder charge is seriously wounding both of us,' Win said. 'We thus have to look at several possibilities.'

'For example?'

'First,' Win said, 'we may be reading too much into the frame-up.'

'How so?'

'This may not be a personal vendetta at all. Perhaps the murderer heard about the garage altercation and concluded that Esperanza would make a convenient patsy.'

'So then this is all just a way of deflecting attention from the real killer? Nothing personal?'

'It's a possibility,' Win said. 'No more or less.'

'Okay,' Myron agreed, 'what else?'

'The murderer wants to do Esperanza great harm.'

'The obvious choice.'

'For whatever that's worth, yes,' Win said. 'And possibility number three: The murderer wants to do one of us great harm.'

'Or,' Myron said, 'our businesses.'

'Yes.'

Something like a giant cartoon anvil landed on Myron's head. 'Someone like FJ.'

Win merely smiled.

'And,' Myron went on, 'if Clu was doing something illicit, something that needed large amounts of cash—'

'Then FJ and his family would be a prime possible recipient,' Win finished for him. 'And of course, if we forget the money for a moment, FJ would relish any opportunity to crush you. What better way than decimating your business and incarcerating your best friend?'

'Two birds, one stone.'

'Precisely.'

Myron sat back, suddenly exhausted. 'I don't relish the idea of tangling with the Aches.'

'Neither do I,' Win said.

'You? Before, you wanted to kill FJ.'

'That's just my point. I can't anymore. If young FJ is behind this, we have to keep him alive in order to prove it. Trapping vermin is chancy. Simple extermination is the preferred course of action.'

'So we've now eliminated your favorite option.'

Win nodded. 'Sad, no?'

'Tragic.'

'But it gets worse, old friend.'

'How's that?'

'Innocent or guilty,' Win said, 'Esperanza is concealing something from us.'

Silence.

'We have no choice,' Win said. 'We need to investigate her too. Delve into her personal life a bit.'

'I don't relish the idea of tangling with the Aches,' Myron said, 'but I really don't relish the idea of invading Esperanza's privacy.'

'Be afraid,' Win agreed. 'Be very afraid.'

11

The first potential clue did two things to Myron: It scared the hell out of him, and it reminded him of *The Sound of Music*.

Myron liked the old Julie Andrews musical well enough – who didn't? – but he always found one song particularly dumb. One of the classics actually. 'My Favorite Things.' The song made no sense. Ask a zillion people to list their absolute favorite things, and how many of them are going to list doorbells, for crying out loud? You know what, Millie? I love doorbells! To hell with strolling on a quiet beach or reading a great book or making love or seeing a Broadway musical. Doorbells, Millie. Doorbells punch my ticket. Sometimes I just run up to people's houses and press their doorbells and well, I think I'm man enough to admit I shudder.

Another puzzling 'favorite' was brown paper packages tied up with string, mostly because it sounded like something sent by a mail-order pornographer (er, not that Myron would know that from personal experience). But that was what Myron found in the large stack of mail. Plain brown packaging. Typed address label with the word *Personal* across the bottom. No return address. Postmarked New York City.

Myron slit open the brown paper package, shook it, and watched a floppy disk drop to his desktop.

Hello.

Myron picked it up, turned it over, turned it back. No label on it. No writing. Just a plain black square with the metal across the top. Myron studied it for a moment, shrugged, popped it into his computer, hit some keys. He was about to hit Windows Explorer and see what kind of file it was when something started to happen. Myron sat back and frowned. He hoped that the diskette didn't contain a computer virus of some sort. He should, after all, know better than to just stick a strange diskette into his computer. He didn't know where it had been, what sleazy computer drive it had been inserted into before, if it wore a condom or had a blood test. Nothing. His poor computer. Just 'Wham, bam, thank you, RAM.'

Groan.

The screen went black.

Myron tugged his ear. His finger stretched forward to strike the escape button – the escape button being the last refuge of a desperate computerphobe – when an image appeared on the screen. Myron froze.

It was a girl.

She had long, semistringy hair with two flips in front and an awkward smile. He guessed her age at around sixteen, braces fresh off, the eyes looking to the side, the backdrop a fading swirl of school-portrait rainbow. Yep, the picture belonged in a frame on Mommy and Daddy's mantel or a suburban high school yearbook circa 1985, the kind of thing with a life-summing write-up underneath it, a life-defining quote from James Taylor or Bruce Springsteen followed by So-So enjoyed being secretary/treasurer of the Key Club, her fondest memories including hanging out with Jenny and Sharon T at the Big W, popcorn in Mrs Kennilworth's class, band practice behind the parking lot, that kind of apple-pie stuff. Typical. Kind of an obituary to adolescence.

Myron knew the girl.

Or at least he'd seen her before. He couldn't put his finger on where or when or if he'd seen her in person or in a photograph or what. But there was no doubt. He stared hard, hoping to conjure up a name or even a fleeting memory. Nothing. He kept staring. And that was when it happened.

The girl began to melt.

It was the only way to describe it. The girl's hair flips fell and blended into her flesh, her forehead sloped down, her nose dissolved, her eyes rolled back and then closed. Blood began to run down from the eye sockets, coating the face in crimson.

Myron bolted his chair back, nearly screaming.

The blood blanketed the image now, and for a moment Myron wondered if it would actually start coming out of the screen. A laughing noise came from the computer speakers. Not a psycho laugh or cruel laugh but the healthy, happy laugh of a teenage girl, a normal sound that raised the hairs on the back of Myron's neck as no howl ever could.

Without warning, the screen went mercifully black. The laughter stopped. And then the Windows 98 main menu reappeared.

Myron gulped down a few breaths. His hands gripped the edge of the desk to the point of white knuckles.

What the hell?

His heart beat against his rib cage as though it wanted to break free. He reached back and grabbed the brown paper wrappings. The postmark was almost three weeks old. Three weeks. This awful diskette had been sitting in his pile of mail since he'd run away. Why? Who had sent this to him? And who was the girl?

Myron's hand was still shaking when he picked up the phone. He dialed. Even though Myron had call block on his phone, a man answered by saying, 'What's up, Myron?'

'I need your help, PT.'

'Jesus, you sound like hell. This about Esperanza?'

'No.'

'So what have you got?'

'A computer diskette. Three-and-half-inch floppy. I need it analyzed.'

'Go to John Jay. Ask for Dr Czerski. But if you're looking for a trace, it's pretty unlikely. What's this about?'

'I got this diskette in the mail. It contains a graphic of a teenage girl. In an AVI file of some sort.'

'Who's the girl?'

'I don't know.'

'I'll call Czerski. You head over.'

Dr Kirstin Czerski sported a white lab coat and a frown as yielding as a former East German swimmer's. Myron tried Smile Patent 17 – moist Alan Alda, post-*M*A*S*H*.

'Hi,' Myron said. 'My name is—'

'The diskette.' She held out her hand. He handed it to her. She looked at it for a second and headed for a door. 'Wait here.'

The door opened. Myron got a brief view of a room that looked like the bridge on *Battlestar Galactica*. Lots of metal and wires and lights and monitors and reel-to-reel tapes. The door closed. Myron stood in a sparsely decorated waiting room. Linoleum floor, three molded plastic chairs, brochures on a wall.

Myron's cellular phone rang again. He stared at it for a second. Six weeks ago he had turned the phone off. Now that it was back on, the contraption seemed to be making up for lost time. He pressed a button and brought it to his ear.

'Hello?'

'Hi, Myron.'

Pow. The voice walloped him like a palm blast to the sternum. A rushing noise filled his ears, as though the phone were a seashell clamped against him. Myron slid into a yellow plastic chair.

'Hello, Jessica,' he managed.

'I saw you on the news,' she said, her voice a tad too controlled. 'So I figured you'd turn your phone back on.'

'Right.'

More silence.

'I'm in Los Angeles,' Jessica continued.

'Uh-huh.'

'But I needed to tell you a few things.'

'Oh?' Myron's Smooth-Lines Fountain – he just couldn't turn it off.

'First off, I'll be gone for at least another month. I didn't change the locks or anything so you can stay at the loft—'

'I'm, uh, bunking at Win's.'

'Yeah, I figured. But if you need anything or if you want to clear your stuff out—'

'Right.'

'Don't forget the TV too. That's yours.'

'You can keep it,' he said.

'Fine.'

More silence.

Jessica said, 'We're being so adult about this, aren't we?'

'Jess—'

'Don't. I called for a reason.'

Myron kept quiet.

'Clu called you several times. At the loft, I mean.'

Myron had guessed that.

'He sounded pretty desperate. I told him I didn't know where you were. He said that he had to find you. That he was worried about you.'

'About me?'

'Yes. He came by once, looking like absolute shit. He grilled me for twenty minutes.'

'About what?'

'About where you were. He said that he had to reach

you – for your sake more than his. When I insisted that I didn't know where you were, he started scaring me.'

'Scaring you how?'

'He asked how I knew you weren't dead.'

'Clu said those words? About my being dead?'

'Yes. I actually called Win when he left.'

'What did Win say?'

'That you were safe and that I shouldn't worry.'

'What else?'

'I'm talking about Win here, Myron. He said – and I quote – 'he's safe, don't worry.' Then he hung up. I let it drop. I figured that Clu was engaging in a little hyperbole to get my attention.'

'That was probably it,' Myron said.

'Yeah.'

More silence.

'How are you?' she asked.

'I'm good. And you?'

'I'm trying to get over you,' she said.

He could barely breathe. 'Jess, we should talk—'

'Don't,' she said again. 'I don't want to talk, okay? Let me put it simply: If you change your mind, call me. You know the number. If not, have a nice life.'

Click.

Myron put down the phone. He took several deep breaths. He looked at the phone. So simple. He did indeed know the number. How easy it would be to dial it.

'Worthless.'

He looked up at Dr Czerski. 'Pardon?'

She held up the diskette. 'You said there was graphic on it?'

Myron quickly explained what he had seen.

'It's not there now,' she said. 'It must have deleted itself.'

'How?'

'You say the program ran automatically?'

'Yes.'

'It probably self-extracted, self-ran, and then self-deleted. Simple.'

'Aren't there special programs so you can undelete a file?'

'Yes. But this file did more than that. It reformatted the whole diskette. Probably the final command in the chain.'

'Meaning?'

'Whatever you saw is gone forever.'

'Is there anything else on the diskette?'

'No.'

'Nothing we can trace? No unique characteristics or anything?'

She shook her head. 'Typical diskette. Sold in every software store in the country. Standard formatting.'

'How about fingerprints?'

'That's not my department.'

And, Myron knew, it would be a waste of time. If someone had gone to the trouble of destroying any computer evidence, chances were pretty good that all fingerprints had been wiped off too.

'I'm busy.' Dr Czerski handed him back the diskette and left without so much as a back glance. Myron stared at it and shook his head.

What the hell was going on here?

The cell phone rang again. Myron picked it up.

'Mr Bolitar?' It was Big Cyndi.

'Yes.'

'I am going through Mr Clu Haid's phone records, as you requested.'

'And?'

'Are you coming back to the office, Mr Bolitar?'

'I'm on the way there now.'

'There is something here you might find bizarre.'

12

When the elevator opened, Big Cyndi was waiting for him. She'd finally scrubbed her face clean. All the makeup was gone. Must have used a sand blaster. Or a jackhammer.

She greeted him by saying, 'Very bizarre, Mr Bolitar.'

'What's that?'

'Per your instructions, I was checking through Clu Haid's phone records,' she said. Then she shook her head. 'Very bizarre.'

'What's bizarre?'

She handed him a sheet of paper. 'I highlighted the number in yellow.'

Myron looked at it while walking into his office. Big Cyndi followed, closing the door behind her. The number was in the 212 area code. That meant Manhattan. Other than that, it was totally unfamiliar. 'What about it?'

'It's for a nightclub.'

'Which one?'

'Take A Guess?'

'Pardon?'

'That's the name of the place,' Big Cyndi said. 'Take A Guess. It's two blocks down from Leather-N-Lust.' Leather-N-Lust was the S&M bar that employed Big Cyndi as a bouncer. Motto: Hurt The Ones You Love.

'You know this place?' he asked.

'A little.'

'What kind of club is it?'

'Cross-dressers and transvestites, mostly. But they have a varied crowd.'

Myron rubbed his temples. 'When you say varied . . .'

'It's sort of an interesting concept really, Mr Bolitar.'

'I'm sure.'

'When you go to Take A Guess, you never know for sure what you're getting. You know what I mean?'

Myron didn't have a clue. 'Pardon my sexual naiveté, but could you explain?'

Big Cyndi scrunched her face in thought. It was not a pretty sight. 'In part, it's what you might expect: men dress like women, women dress like men. But then sometimes a woman is just a woman and a man is just a man. Follow?'

Myron nodded. 'Not even a little.'

'That's why it's called Take A Guess. You never know for sure. For instance, you might see a beautiful woman who is unusually tall with a platinum wig. So you figure it's a he-she. But – and this is what makes Take A Guess special – maybe it's not.'

'Not what?'

'A he-she. A transvestite or transsexual. Maybe it is indeed a beautiful woman who put on extra-high heels and a wig to confuse you.'

'And the reason for this is?'

'That's the fun of the place. The doubt. There's a sign inside. TAKE A GUESS: IT'S ABOUT AMBIGUITY, NOT ANDROGYNY.'

'Catchy.'

'But that's the idea. It's a place of mystery. You bring someone home. You think it's a beautiful woman or a handsome man. But until the pants are all the way down, you're never sure. People come dressed to fool. You just never know until – well, you saw *The Crying Game*.'

Myron made a face. 'And this is a desirable thing?'

'If you're into that, sure.'

'Into what?'

She smiled. 'Exactly.'

Myron rubbed the temples again. 'So the patrons don't have a problem with' – he searched for the right word, but there wasn't one – 'so a gay guy, for example, doesn't get pissed off when he finds out he brought home a woman?'

'It's why you go. The thrill. The uncertainty. The mystery.'

'Sort of the sexual equivalent of a grab bag.'

'Right.'

'Except in this case, you can really be surprised by what you grab.'

Big Cyndi considered that. 'If you really think about it, Mr Bolitar, there can be only one of two things.'

He was no longer so sure.

'But I like your grab bag analogy,' Big Cyndi continued. 'You know what you're bringing to the party, but you have no idea what you're going to take home. One time a guy left with what he thought was an overweight woman. It turned out that it was a guy with a midget hiding under the dress.'

'Please tell me you're joking.'

Big Cyndi just looked at him.

'So,' Myron continued, 'you, uh, frequent this place?'

'I've been a couple of times. But not recently.'

'Why not?'

'Two reasons. First, they compete with Leather-N-Lust. It's a different crowd, but we still draw from similar markets.'

Myron nodded. 'The pervert pool.'

'They're not hurting anybody.'

'At least nobody who doesn't want to be hurt.'

She pouted, not a great look on a three-hundred-pound wrestler, especially without her mortarlike makeup. 'Esperanza is right.'

'About?'

'You can be very closed-minded.'

'Yeah, I'm a regular Jerry Falwell. So what's the second reason?'

She hesitated. 'I'm obviously for sexual freedom. I don't care what you're doing as long as it's consensual. And I've done some wild things myself, Mr Bolitar.' She looked straight at him. '*Very* wild.'

Myron cringed, fearing she might share details.

'But Take A Guess started drawing the wrong kind of crowd,' she said.

'Gee, that's surprising,' Myron said. 'You'd think a place like that would be a natural for vacationing families.'

She shook her head. 'You are so repressed, Mr Bolitar.'

'Because I like to know my partner's gender before getting naked?'

'Because of your attitude. People like you cause sexual hang-ups. Society becomes sexually repressed – so repressed, in fact, that they cross the line between sex and violence, between playacting and real danger. They reach a stage where they get off by hurting people who do not want to be hurt.'

'And Take A Guess attracts that kind of crowd?'

'More than most.'

Myron sat back and rubbed his face with both hands. He started hearing brain clicks. 'This might explain a few things,' he said.

'Like what?'

'Why Bonnie finally threw Clu out for good. It's one thing to have a string of girlfriends. But if Clu was frequenting a place like this, if he started leaning toward' – again, what would be the word? – 'toward whatever. And if Bonnie found out, well, it would explain the legal separation.' He nodded to himself as he heard more internal clicks. 'And it would explain her odd behavior today.'

'How so?'

'She made a point of asking me not to dig too deeply. She just wanted me to clear Esperanza and then drop the investigation.'

Big Cyndi nodded. 'She was afraid this would get out.'

'Right. If something like this went public, what would it do to her kids?'

Another thought floating through Myron's brain got snagged on some jagged rock. He looked at Big Cyndi. 'I assume that Take A Guess appeals mostly to bisexuals. I mean, if you're not sure what you're getting, who better than someone who wouldn't care?'

'More like ambisexuals,' Big Cyndi said. 'Or people who want some mystery. Who want something new.'

'But bisexuals too.'

'Yes, of course.'

'How about Esperanza?'

Big Cyndi bristled. 'What about her?'

'Did she frequent this place?'

'I wouldn't know, Mr Bolitar. And I don't see the relevance.'

'I'm not asking because it gives me jollies. You want me to help her, right? That means digging where we don't want to dig.'

'I understand that, Mr Bolitar. But you know her better than I do.'

'Not this side of her,' Myron said.

'Esperanza is a private person. I really don't know. She usually has a steady, but I don't know if she's gone there or not.'

Myron nodded. Didn't matter much. If Clu had been hanging out in such a place, it would give Hester Crimstein more reasonable doubt. A rough trade place complete with a reputation for violence – it was a natural recipe for disaster. Clu could have brought home the wrong package. Or been the wrong package. And there was the cash to consider. Blackmail money? Did a customer recognize him? Threaten him? Videotape him?

Yep, lots of murky reasonable doubt.

And a good place to search for the elusive girlfriend. Or boyfriend. Or in-between friend. He shook his head. It was not a question of the ethics or moral dilemma for Myron; deviancy simply confused him. Repugnancy aside, he didn't get it. Lack of imagination, he supposed.

'I'll have to pay the Take A Guess a visit,' he said.

'Not alone,' Big Cyndi said. 'I'll go with you.'

Subtle surveillance was out. 'Fine.'

'And not now. Take A Guess doesn't open until eleven.'

'Okay. We'll go tonight then.'

'I have just the outfit,' she said. 'What are you going to go as?'

'A repressed heterosexual man,' he said. 'All I'll have to do is slip on my Rockports.' He looked at the phone record again. 'You have another number highlighted in blue.'

She nodded. 'You mentioned an old friend named Billy Lee Palms.'

'This his number?'

'No. Mr Palms doesn't exist anywhere. No phone listing. And he hasn't paid taxes in four years.'

'So whose number is this?'

'Mr Palms's parents. Mr Haid called them twice in the past month.'

Myron checked the address. Westchester. He vaguely remembered meeting Billy Lee's parents during a Family Day at Duke. He looked at his watch. It would take an hour to get there. He grabbed his coat and headed for the elevator.

13

Myron's car, the business's Ford Taurus, had been confiscated by the police, so he rented a maroon Mercury Cougar. He hoped the women would be able to resist. When he started the car, the radio was tuned to Lite FM 106.7. Patti LaBelle and Michael McDonald were crooning a sad lite staple entitled 'On My Own.' This once blissfully happy couple were breaking up. Tragic. So tragic that, as Michael McDonald put it, 'Now we're up to talking divorce . . . and we weren't even married.'

Myron shook his head. For this Michael McDonald left the Doobie Brothers?

In college Billy Lee Palms had been the quintessential party boy. He had sneaky good looks, jet black hair, and a magnetic, albeit oily, combination of charisma and machismo, the kind of thing that played well with young coeds away from home for the first time. At Duke the frat brothers had dubbed him Otter, the pseudosuave character in the movie *Animal House*. It fitted. Billy Lee was also a great baseball player, a catcher who managed to reach the major leagues for a half season, riding the bench for the Baltimore Orioles the year they won the World Series.

But that was years ago.

Myron knocked on the door. Seconds later the door swung open fast and wide. No warning, nothing. Strange. In this day and age people looked through peepholes or cracks in chain-held doors or at the very least asked who it was.

A woman he vaguely recognized as Mrs Palms said,

'Yes?' She was small with a squirrel mouth and eyes that bulged like something behind them was pushing to get out. Her hair was tied back, but several strands escaped and drooped in front of her face. She pushed them back with splayed fingers.

'Are you Mrs Palms?' he asked.

'Yes.'

'My name is Myron Bolitar. I went to Duke with Billy Lee.'

Her voice dropped an octave or two. 'Do you know where he is?'

'No, ma'am. Is he missing?'

She frowned and stepped back. 'Come in, please.'

Myron moved into the foyer. Mrs Palms was already heading down a corridor. She pointed to her right without turning around or breaking stride. 'Just go into Sarah's wedding room. I'll be there in a second.'

'Yes, ma'am.'

Sarah's wedding room?

He followed where she had pointed. When he turned the corner, he heard himself give a little gasp. Sarah's wedding room. The decor was run-of-the-mill living room, something out of a furniture store circular. An off-white couch and matching love seat formed a broken L, probably the monthly special, $695 for both, the couch might fold out into a Serta sleeper, something like that. The coffee table was a semi oak square, a short stack of attractive, unread magazines on one end, silk flowers in the middle, a couple of coffee books on the other end. The wall-to-wall carpeting was light beige, and there were two torchère lamps à la the Pottery Barn.

But the walls were anything but ordinary.

Myron had seen plenty of houses with photographs on the walls. They were hardly uncommon. He had even been in a house or two where the photographs dominated rather than complemented the surroundings. That too would hardly give him reason to pause. But this was beyond surreal. Sarah's Wedding Room – heck, it should be capitalized – was a re-creation of that event. Literally. Color wedding photographs had been blown up to life size and pasted on as a wallpaper substitute. The bride and groom smiled at him invitingly from the right. On the left, Billy Lee in a tux, probably the best man or maybe just an usher, smiled at him. Mrs Palms, dressed in a summer gown, danced with her husband. In front of him were the wedding tables, lots of them. Guests looked up and smiled at him – all life size. It was as though a panoramic wedding photo had been blown up to the size of Rembrandt's *Night Watch*. People slow-danced. A band played. There was a minister of sorts and floral arrangements and a wedding cake and fine china and white linen – again, all life size.

'Please sit down.'

Myron turned to Mrs Palms. Was it the real Mrs Palms or one of the reproductions? No, she was casually dressed. The real McCoy. He almost reached out and touched her to make sure. 'Thank you,' he said.

'This is our daughter Sarah's wedding. She was married four years ago.'

'I see.'

'It was a very special day for us.'

'I'm sure.'

'We had it at the Manor in West Orange. You know it?'

'I was bar mitzvahed there,' Myron said.

'Really? Your parents must have very fond memories of the day.'

'Yes.' But now he wondered. I mean, Mom and Dad kept most of the photos in an album.

Mrs Palms smiled at him. 'It's odd, I know, but . . . oh, I've explained this a thousand times. What's one more?'

She sighed, signaled to a couch. Myron sat. She did likewise.

Mrs Palms folded her hands and looked at him with the blank stare of a woman who sat too close to life's big screen. 'People take pictures of their most special times,' she began too earnestly. 'They want to capture the important moments. They want to enjoy them and savor them and relive them. But that's not what they do. They take the picture, they look at it once, and then they stick it in a box and forget about it. Not me. I remember the good times. I wallow in them – re-create them, if I can. After all, we live for those moments, don't we, Myron?'

He nodded.

'So when I sit in this room, it warms me. I'm surrounded by one of the happiest moments in my life. I've created the most positive aura imaginable.'

He nodded again.

'I'm not a big art fan,' she continued. 'I don't relish the idea of hanging impersonal lithographs on the walls. What's the point of looking at images of people and places I don't know? I don't care that much about interior design. And I don't like antiques or phony-baloney Martha Stewart stuff. But do you know what I do find beautiful?' She stopped and looked at him expectantly.

Myron picked up his cue. 'What?'

'My family,' she replied. 'My family is beautiful to me. My family is art. Does that make sense to you, Myron?'

'Yes.' Oddly enough, it did.

'So I call this Sarah's Wedding Room. I know that's silly. Naming rooms. Blowing up old photographs and using them as wallpaper. But all the rooms are like this. Billy Lee's bedroom upstairs I call the Catcher's Mitt. It's where he still stays when he's here. I think it comforts him.' She raised her eyebrows. 'Would you like to see it?'

'Sure.'

She practically leaped off the couch. The stairwell was plastered with giant, seemingly old black and whites. A stern-faced couple in wedding gear. A soldier in full uniform. 'This is the Generational Wall. That's my great-grandparents over there. And Hank's. My husband. He died three years ago.'

'I'm sorry.'

She shrugged. 'This stairwell goes back three generations. I think it's a nice way of remembering our ancestors.'

Myron didn't argue. He looked at the photograph of the young couple, just starting out their life together, probably a little scared. Now they were dead.

Deep Thoughts by Myron Bolitar.

'I know what you're thinking,' she said. 'But is it any stranger than hanging oils of dead relatives? Just more lifelike.'

Hard to argue.

The walls in the upstairs corridor featured some sort of costume party from the seventies. Lots of leisure suits and bell-bottoms. Myron didn't ask, and Mrs Palms didn't explain. Just as well. She turned left and Myron trailed her into the Catcher's Mitt. It lived up to its billing. Billy Lee's baseball life was laid out like a Hall of Fame display room. It started with Billy Lee in Little League, squatting in his catcher's stance, his smile huge and strangely confident for so young a child. The years flashed by. Little League to Babe Ruth League to high school to Duke, ending with his one glorious year with the Orioles, Billy Lee proudly showing off his World Series ring. Myron studied the Duke photographs. One had been taken out in front of Psi U, their frat house. A uniformed Billy Lee had his arm around Clu, plenty of frat brothers in the background, including, he saw now, him and Win. Myron remembered when the picture had been taken. The baseball team had just beaten Florida

State to win the national championship. The party had lasted three days.

'Mrs Palms, where is Billy Lee?'

'I don't know.'

'When you say you don't know—'

'He ran off,' she interrupted. 'Again.'

'He's done this before?'

She stared at the wall. Her eyes were glassy now. 'Maybe Billy Lee doesn't find this room comforting,' she said softly. 'Maybe it reminds him of what could have been.' She turned to him. 'When was the last time you saw Billy Lee?'

Myron tried to remember. 'It's been a long time.'

'How come?'

'We were never that close.'

She pointed to the wall. 'That's you? In the background?'

'That's right.'

'Billy Lee spoke about you.'

'Really?'

'He said you were a sports agent. Clu's agent, if I'm not mistaken.'

'Yes.'

'You stayed friendly with Clu then?'

'Yes.'

She nodded as though this explained everything. 'Why are you looking for my son, Myron?'

He was not sure how to explain. 'You've heard about Clu's death?'

'Yes, of course. That poor boy. A lost soul. Like Billy Lee in many ways. I think that's why they were drawn to each other.'

'Have you seen Clu lately?'

'Why do you want to know?'

In for a penny and all that. 'I'm trying to find out who killed him.'

Her body stiffened as though his words held a small electric shock. 'And you think Billy Lee had something to do with it?'

'No, of course not.' But even as he said it, he began to wonder. Clu is murdered; maybe his killer runs away. More reasonable doubt. 'It's just that I know how close they were. I thought maybe Billy Lee could help me out.'

Mrs Palms was staring at the image of the two ballplayers in front of Psi U. She reached out as though to stroke her son's face. But she pulled back. 'Billy Lee was handsome, wasn't he?'

'Yes.'

'The girls,' she said. 'They all loved my Billy Lee.'

'I'd never seen anybody better with them,' he said.

That made her smile. She kept staring at the image of her son. It was kinda creepy. Myron remembered the old episode of *The Twilight Zone* where the aging movie queen escapes reality by stepping into one of her old movies. It looked like Mrs Palms craved doing likewise.

She finally tore her eyes away. 'Clu came by a few weeks ago.'

'Can you be more specific?'

'Funny.'

'What?'

'That's just what the police asked.'

'The police were here?'

'Sure.'

They must have gone through the phone records too, Myron thought. Or found another link.

'I'll tell you the same thing I told them. I can't be more specific.'

'Do you know what Clu wanted?'

'He came to see Billy Lee.'

'Billy Lee was here?'

'Yes.'

'He lives here then?'

'On and off. The past few years have not been very good to my son.'

Silence.

'I don't mean to pry,' Myron began, 'but—'

'What happened to Billy Lee?' she finished. 'Life caught up with him, Myron. The drinking, the drugs, the womanizing. He had stints in rehab. Are you familiar with Rockwell?'

'No, ma'am.'

'It's a private clinic. He finished his fourth trip to Rockwell not two months ago. But he couldn't stay clean. When you're in college or even in your twenties, you can survive it. When you're a big star and people are looking out for you, you can get away with it. But Billy Lee wasn't good enough to reach that level. So he had no one to fall back upon. Except me. And I'm not that strong.'

Myron swallowed. 'Do you know why Clu came to see Billy Lee?'

'For old times' sake, I guess. They went out. Maybe they had a few beers and chased women. I really don't know.'

'Did Clu visit Billy Lee a lot?'

'Well, Clu's been out of town,' she said, a little too defensively. 'He was only traded back to this area a few months ago. But of course, you know that.'

'So this was just a casual visit?'

'I thought so at the time.'

'And now?'

'Now my son is missing and Clu is dead.'

Myron thought about it. 'Where does he usually go when he runs off like this?'

'Wherever. Billy Lee is a bit of a nomad. He goes off, he does whatever horrible thing he does to himself, and when he hits rock bottom, he comes back here.'

'So you don't know where he is?'

'That's right.'

'Any idea at all?'

'No.'

'No favorite haunts?'

'No.'

'A girlfriend maybe?'

'No one I know about anyway.'

'Any close friends he might stay with?'

'No,' she said slowly. 'He has no friends like that.'

Myron took out his card and handed it to her. 'If you hear from him, Mrs Palms, could you please let me know?'

She studied the card as they moved out of the room and back down the stairs.

Before she opened the door, Mrs Palms said, 'You were the basketball player.'

'Yes.'

'The one who hurt his knee.'

First preseason game as a pro. Myron had been the Boston Celtics' first-round draft pick. A terrible collision and his career was over. Just like that. Finished before it started. 'Yes.'

'You managed to put it behind you,' she said. 'You managed to get on with your life and be happy and productive.' She cocked her head. 'Why couldn't Billy Lee?'

Myron had no answer – in part because he was not sure her supposition was entirely accurate. He said his good-byes and left her alone with her ghosts.

14

Myron checked his watch. Dinnertime. Mom and Dad were expecting him. He'd hit the Garden State Parkway when the cell phone rang again.

'Are you in the car?' Win asked. Always with the pleasantries.

'Yes.'

'Flip on 1010 WINS. I'll call back.'

One of New York's all-news radio stations. Myron did as he was told. The guy in the helicopter was finishing up the traffic report. He handed it back to the woman at the news desk. She provided the teaser: 'The latest bombshell in the murder of baseball superstar Clu Haid. In sixty seconds.'

It was a long sixty seconds. Myron had to put up with a truly annoying Dunkin' Donuts commercial, and then some excited bozo had a way of turning five thousand dollars into twenty thousand dollars, though a softer, fast-speaking voice added that it didn't work all the time and in fact you could lose money too and probably would and you'd have to be a major moron to take investment advice from a radio ad. Finally the woman at the news desk came back on. She told the audience her name – like anyone cared – the name of her male counterpart, and the time. Then:

'ABC is reporting from an anonymous source in the Bergen Country district attorney's office that hairs and quote other bodily materials unquote matching the murder suspect Esperanza Diaz have been found at the murder scene. According to the source, DNA tests are pending, but preliminary tests show a clear match with Ms Diaz. The source also says that the hairs, some small, were found in various locations throughout the house.'

Myron felt a flutter beneath his heart. Small hairs, he thought. Euphemism for pubic.

'No further details are available, but the district attorney's office clearly believes that Mr Clu Haid and Ms Esperanza Diaz were having a sexual relationship. Stay tuned to 1010 WINS for all the details.'

The cell phone rang. Myron picked it up. 'Jesus Christ.'

'Not even close,' Win said.

'I'll call you right back.' Myron hung up. He called Hester Crimstein's office. The secretary said that Ms Crimstein was unavailable. Myron stressed that this was urgent. Ms Crimstein was still unavailable. But, Myron asked, doesn't Ms Crimstein have a cell phone? The secretary disconnected the call. Myron hit the memory button. Win picked up.

'What's your take on this?' Myron asked.

'Esperanza was sleeping with him,' Win said.

'Maybe not.'

'Yes, of course,' Win said. 'Perhaps someone planted Esperanza's pubic hairs at the murder scene.'

'It could be a false leak.'

'Could be.'

'Or maybe she visited his apartment. To talk business.'

'And left stray pubic hairs behind?'

'Maybe she used the bathroom. Maybe she—'

'Myron?'

'What?'

'Please don't go into further detail, thank you. There is something else to consider.'

'What?'

'The E-Z Pass records.'

'Right,' Myron said. 'She crossed the Washington

Bridge an hour after the murder. We know that. But maybe that fits now. Esperanza and Clu have a big argument at the parking garage. Esperanza wants to clear the air. So she drives out to his apartment.'

'And when she gets there?'

'I don't know. Maybe she saw the body and panicked.'

'Yes, of course,' Win said. 'So she ripped out a few pubic hairs and ran.'

'I didn't say it was her first visit out there.'

'Indeed not.'

'What do you mean?'

'The E-Z Pass records for the Ford Taurus. According to the bill that arrived last week, the car crossed the bridge eighteen times in the past month.'

Myron frowned. 'You're kidding.'

'Yes, I am a mirthful fellow. I also took the liberty of checking the month before. Sixteen crosses of the Washington Bridge.'

'Maybe she had another reason for going out to North Jersey.'

'Yes, of course. The malls in Paramus are quite an attraction.'

'Okay,' Myron said. 'Let's assume they were having an affair.'

'That would seem most prudent, especially since it offers a reasonable explanation for much that has happened.'

'How's that?'

'It would explain Esperanza's silence.'

'How?'

'Lovers always make wonderful suspects,' Win said. 'If, for example, Esperanza and Clu were dancing the sheet mambo, then we can assume that the altercation in the parking garage was something of a lovers' tiff. All in all, this development looks bad for her. She would want to hide it.'

'But from us?' Myron countered.

'Yes.'

'Why? She trusts us.'

'Several reasons come to mind. Her attorney probably ordered her not to say anything.'

'That wouldn't stop her.'

'It might. But more important, Esperanza was probably embarrassed. You have recently promoted her to partner. She was in charge of the entire operation. I know that you believe Esperanza is too tough to care about such things, but I do not think she would relish your disapproval.'

Myron mulled that one over. It made some sense, but he wasn't sure he bought it entirely. 'I still think we're missing something.'

'That's because we're ignoring the strongest motive for her keeping silent.'

'That being?'

'She killed him.'

Win hung up on that cheery note. Myron took Northfield Avenue toward Livingston. The familiar landmarks of his hometown popped into view. He thought about the news report and what Win had said. Could Esperanza be the mystery woman, the reason for Clu and Bonnie's breakup? If so, why wouldn't Bonnie say that? Maybe she didn't know. Or maybe—

Hold the phone.

Maybe Clu and Esperanza met up at Take A Guess. Did they go there together or just bump into each other? Is that how the affair started? Did they go there and participate in – in whatever? Maybe it was an accident. Maybe they both arrived there in disguise and didn't realize who they were until, well, it was too late to stop? Did that make sense?

He made the right at Nero's Restaurant and onto Hobart Gap Road. Not far now. He was in the land of his childhood – check that, his entire life. He had lived here with his parents until a year or so ago, when he finally severed the apron strings and moved in with Jessica. Psychologists and psychiatrists and the like, he knew, would have a field day with the fact that he had lived with his parents into his thirties, theorizing all kinds of unnatural preoccupations that kept him so close to Mom and Dad. Maybe they'd be right. But for Myron, the answer had been far simpler. He liked them. Yes, they could be pests – what parents weren't? – and they liked to pry. But most of the pestering and prying were over the incidentals. They had given him privacy yet made him feel cared for and wanted. Was that unhealthy? Maybe. But it seemed a damn sight better than his friends who thrived on blaming their parents for any unhappiness in their lives.

He turned onto his street. The old neighborhood was wholly unspectacular. There were thousands like it in New Jersey, hundreds of thousands throughout the US of A. This was suburbia, the backbone of this country, the battleground of the fabled American Dream. Corny to say, but Myron loved it here. Sure, there was unhappiness and dissatisfaction and fights and all that, but he still thought that this was the 'realest' place he had ever been. He loved the basketball court in the driveway and the training wheels on the new two-wheelers and the routine and the walking to school and the caring too much about the color of the grass. This was living. This was what it was all about.

In the end Myron guessed that he and Jessica had broken up for all the classic reasons, albeit with a gender twist. He wanted to settle down, buy a house in the 'burbs, raise a family; Jessica, fearing commitment, did not. He pulled into the driveway now, shaking his head. Too simple an explanation. Too pat. The commitment stuff had been an ongoing source of tension, no question, but there was more to it. There was the recent tragedy, for one thing.

There was Brenda.

Mom rushed out the door, sprinting toward him with her arms spread wide. She always greeted him like he was a recently released POW, but today was something extra special. She threw her arms around him, nearly knocking him over. Dad trailed behind, equally excited but playing it cool. Dad had always been about balance, the total love without the smothering, the caring without pushing. An amazing man, his father. When Dad reached him, there was no handshake. The two men hugged fiercely and without any hint of embarrassment. Myron kissed his father's cheek. The familiar feel of Dad's rough skin made him understand a bit what Mrs Palms was trying to accomplish with the wallpapered images.

'Are you hungry?' Mom asked. Always her opening gambit.

'A little.'

'You want me to fix something?'

Everyone froze. Dad made a face. 'You're going to cook?'

'What's the big deal?'

'Let me make sure I have the number of poison control.'

'Oh, Al, that's so funny. Ha-ha, I can't stop laughing. What a funny man your father is, Myron.'

'Actually, Ellen, go ahead and cook something. I need to drop a few pounds.'

'Wow, what a knee slapper, Al. You're killing me here.'

'Better than a fat farm.'

'Ho-ho.'

'Just the thought is better than an appetite suppressor.'

'It's like being married to Shecky Greene.' But she was smiling.

They were in the house now. Dad took Mom's hand. 'Let me show you something, Ellen,' Dad said. 'See that big metal box over there? That's called an oven. O-v-e-n. Oven. See that knob, the one with all the numbers on it? That's how you turn it on.'

'You're funnier than a sober Foster Brooks, Al.'

But they were all smiling now. Dad was speaking the truth. Mom didn't cook. Almost never did. Her culinary skills could cause a prison riot. When he was a kid, Myron's favorite home-cooked dinner was Dad's scrambled eggs. Mom was an early career woman. The kitchen was a place to read magazines.

'What do you want to eat, Myron?' Mom asked. 'Chinese maybe. From Fong's?'

'Sure.'

'Al, call Fong's. Order something.'

'Okay.'

'Make sure you get shrimp with lobster sauce.'

'I know.'

'Myron loves Fong's shrimp with lobster sauce.'

'I know, Ellen. I raised him too, remember?'

'You might forget.'

'We've been ordering from Fong's for twenty-three years. We always order shrimp with lobster sauce.'

'You might forget, Al. You're getting old. Didn't you forget to pick up my blouse at the laundry two days ago.'

'It was closed.'

'So you never picked up my blouse, am I right?'

'Of course not.'

'I rest my case.' She looked at her son. 'Myron, sit. We need to talk. Al, call Fong's.'

The men obeyed her orders. As always. Myron and Mom sat at the kitchen table.

'Listen to me closely,' Mom said. 'I know Esperanza is your friend. But Hester Crimstein is a fine lawyer. If she told Esperanza not to talk to you, it's the right thing.'

'How do you know—'

'I've known Hester for years.' Mom was a defense attorney, one of the best in the state. 'We've worked cases together before. She called me. She said you're interfering.'

'I'm not interfering.'

'Actually she said you're bothering her and to butt out.'

'She talked to you about this?'

'Of course. She wants you to leave her client alone.'

'I can't.'

'Why can't you?'

Myron squirmed a bit. 'I have some information that might be important.'

'Such as?'

'According to Clu's wife, he was having an affair.'

'And you think Hester doesn't know that? The DA thinks he was having an affair with Esperanza.'

'Wait a second.' It was Dad. 'I thought Esperanza was a lesbian.'

'She's a bisexual, Al.'

'A what?'

'Bisexual. It means she likes both boys and girls.'

Dad thought about that. 'I guess that's a good thing to be.'

'What?'

'I mean, it gives you double the options of everyone else.'

'Great, Al, thanks for the insight.' She rolled her eyes and turned back to Myron. 'So Hester already knows that. What else?'

'Clu was desperate to find me before he was killed,' Myron said.

'Most logically, *bubbe*, to say something incriminating about Esperanza.'

'Not necessarily. Clu came to the loft. He told Jessica that I was in danger.'

'And you think he meant it?'

'No, he was probably exaggerating. But shouldn't Hester Crimstein judge the significance?'

'She already has.'

'What?'

'Clu came here too, darling.' Her voice was suddenly soft. 'He told your father and me the same thing he told Jessica.'

Myron didn't push it. If Clu had told his parents the same thing he told Jessica, if he had used all that death talk when Mom and Dad didn't know where Myron was . . .

As though reading his mind, Dad said, 'I called Win. He said you were safe.'

'Did he tell you where I was?'

Mom took that one. 'We didn't ask.'

Silence.

She reached over and put a hand on his arm. 'You've been through a lot, Myron. Your father and I know that.'

They both looked at him with the deep-caring eyes. They knew part of what happened. About his breakup with Jessica. About Brenda. But they would never know it all.

'Hester Crimstein knows what's she doing,' Mom went on. 'You have to let her do her job.'

More silence.

'Al?'

'What?'

'Hang up the phone,' she said. 'Maybe we should go out to eat.'

Myron checked his watch. 'It'll have to be quick. I have to get back to the city.'

'Oh?' Mom raised an eyebrow. 'You have a date already?'

He thought about Big Cyndi's description of Take A Guess.

'Not likely,' he said. 'But you never know.'

15

From the outside Take A Guess looked pretty much like your standard Manhattan cantina-as-pickup-joint. The building was brick, the windows darkened to highlight the neon beer signs. Above the door, faded lettering spelled out *Take A Guess*. That was it. No 'Bring Your Perversions.' No 'The Kinkier the Better.' No 'You Better Like Surprises.' Nothing. A suit trudging home might happen by here, stop in, lay down his briefcase, spot something attractive, buy it a drink, make a few quasi-smooth moves warmed over from college mixers, take it home. Surprise, surprise.

Big Cyndi met him at the front door dressed like Earth, Wind, and Fire – not so much any one member as the entire group. 'Ready?'

Myron hesitated, nodded.

When Big Cyndi pushed open the door, Myron held his breath and ducked in behind her. The interior too was not what he'd visualized. He had expected something . . . blatantly wacko, he guessed. Like the bar scene in *Star Wars* maybe. Instead Take A Guess just had the same neodesperate feel and stench of a zillion other singles' joints on a Friday night. A few patrons were colorfully dressed, but most wore khakis and business suits. There were also a handful of outrageously clad cross-dressers and leather devotees and one babe-a-rama packed into a vinyl catsuit, but nowadays you'd be hard pressed to find a Manhattan nightspot that didn't have any of that. Sure, some folks were in disguise, but when it came right down to it, who didn't wear a facade at a singles' bar?

Whoa, that was deep.

Heads and eyes swerved in their direction. For a moment Myron wondered why. But only for a moment. He was, after all, standing next to Big Cyndi, a six-six three-hundred-pound multihued mass blanketed with more sparkles than a Siegfried and Roy costume party. She drew the eye.

Big Cyndi seemed flattered by the attention. She lowered her eyes, playing demure, which was like Ed Asner playing coquettish. 'I know the head bartender,' she said. 'His name is Pat.'

'Male or female?'

She smiled, punched him on the arm. 'Now you're getting the hang of it.'

A jukebox played the Police's 'Every Little Thing She Does Is Magic.' Myron tried to count how many times Sting repeated the words *every little*. He lost count at a million.

They found two stools at the bar. Big Cyndi looked for Pat. Myron cased the joint, very detectivelike. He turned his back to the bar, eased his elbows against it, bobbed his head slightly to the music. Señor Slick. The babe-a-rama in the black catsuit caught his eye. She slithered to the seat next to him and curled into it. Myron flashed back to Julie Newmar as Cat Woman circa 1967, something he did far too often. This woman was dirty blond but otherwise frighteningly comparable.

Catsuit gave him a look that made him believe in telekinesis. 'Hi,' she said.

'Hi back.' The Lady Slayer awakens.

She slowly reached for her neck and started toying with the catsuit's zipper. Myron managed to keep his tongue in the general vicinity of his mouth. He took a quick peek at Big Cyndi.

'Don't be too sure,' Big Cyndi warned.

Myron frowned. There was cleavage here, for crying

out loud. He stole another look – for the sake of science. Yep, cleavage. And plenty of it. He looked back at Big Cyndi and whispered, 'Bosoms. Two of them.'

Big Cyndi shrugged.

'My name is Thrill,' Catsuit said.

'I'm Myron.'

'Myron,' she repeated, her tongue circling as though testing the word for taste. 'I like that name. It's very manly.'

'Er, thanks, I guess.'

'You don't like your name?'

'Actually, I've always sort of hated it,' he said. Then he gave her the big-guy look, cocking the eyebrow like Fabio going for deep thought. 'But if you like it, maybe I'll reconsider.'

Big Cyndi made a noise like a moose coughing up a turtle shell.

Thrill gave him another smoldering glance and picked up her drink. She did something that could roughly be called 'taking a sip,' but Myron doubted the Motion Picture Association would give it less than an R rating. 'Tell me about yourself, Myron.'

They started chatting. Pat, the bartender, was on break, so Myron and Thrill kept at it for a good fifteen minutes. He didn't want to admit it, but he was sort of having fun. Thrill turned toward him, full body. She slid a little closer. Myron again looked for telltale gender signs. He checked for the two Five O'clocks: Shadow and Charlie. Nothing. He checked the cleavage again. Still there. Damn if he wasn't a trained detective.

Thrill put her hand on his thigh. It felt hot through his jeans. Myron stared at the hand for a moment. Was the size odd? He tried to figure out if it was big for a woman or maybe small for a man. His head started spinning.

'I don't mean to be rude,' Myron finally said, 'but you're a woman, right?'

Thrill threw her head back and laughed. Myron looked for an Adam's apple. She had a black ribbon tied around the neck. Made it hard to tell. The laugh was a touch hoarse, but oh, come on now. This couldn't be a guy. Not with that cleavage. Not when the catsuit was so tight about the, er, nether region, if you catch the drift.

'What's the difference?' Thrill asked.

'Pardon?'

'You find me attractive, don't you?'

'What I see.'

'So?'

Myron raised his hands. 'So – and let me just state this plainly – if, during a moment of passion, there is a second penis in the room . . . well, it definitely kills the mood for me.'

She laughed. 'No other penises, eh?'

'That's right. Just mine. I'm funny that way.'

'Are you familiar with Woody Allen?' she asked.

'Of course.'

'Then let me quote him.' Myron stayed still. Thrill was about to quote the Woodman. If she was a she, Myron was close to proposing. ' "Sex is a beautiful thing between two people. Between five it's fantastic." '

'Nice quote,' Myron said.

'Do you know what it's from?'

'His old nightclub act. When Woody did stand-up comedy in the sixties.'

Thrill nodded, pleased that the pupil had passed the test.

'But we're not talking group sex here,' Myron said.

'Have you ever had group sex?' she asked.

'Well, uh, no.'

'But if you did – if there were, say, five people – would it be a problem if one of them had a penis?'

'We're talking hypothetically here, right?'

'Unless you want me to call some friends.'

'No, that's okay, really, thanks.' Myron took a deep breath. 'Yeah, okay, hypothetically, I guess it wouldn't be a huge problem, as long as the man kept his distance.'

Thrill nodded. 'But if I had a penis—'

'A major mood killer.'

'I see.' Thrill made small circles on Myron's thigh. 'Admit you're curious.'

'I am.'

'So?'

'So I'm also curious about what goes through a person's mind when he jumps out of a skyscraper. Before he goes splat on the sidewalk.'

She arched an eyebrow. 'It's probably a hell of a rush.'

'Yeah, but then there's that splat at the end.'

'And in this case . . . '

'The splat would be a penis, yes.'

'Interesting,' Thrill said. 'Suppose I'm a transsexual.'

'Pardon?'

'Suppose I *had* a penis, but now it's gone. You'd be safe, right?'

'Wrong.'

'Why?'

'Phantom penis,' Myron said.

'Pardon?'

'Like in a war when a guy loses his limb and still thinks it's there. Phantom penis.'

'But it's not your penis that would be missing.'

'Still. Phantom penis.'

'But that doesn't make any sense.'

'Exactly.'

Thrill showed him nice, even white teeth. Myron looked at them. Can't tell much about gender from teeth. Better to check the cleavage again. 'You realize that you're massively insecure about your sexuality,' she said.

'Because I like to know if a potential partner has a penis?'

'A real man wouldn't worry about being thought of as a fag.'

'It's not what people think that bothers me.'

'It's just the penis issue,' she finished for him.

'Bingo.'

'I still say you're sexually insecure.'

Myron shrugged, palms raised. 'Who isn't?'

'True.' She shifted her rear. Vinyl on vinyl. Grrrr sound. 'So why don't you ask me out on a date?'

'I think we just went over this.'

'You find me attractive, right? What you see, I mean.'

'Yes.'

'And we're having a nice talk?'

'Yes.'

'You find me interesting? Fun to be with?'

'Yes and yes.'

'And you're single and unattached?'

He swallowed. 'Two more yesses.'

'So?'

'So – and again, don't take this personally—'

'But it's that penis thing again.'

'Bingo.'

Thrill leaned back, fiddled with the neckline zipper, pulled it up a bit. 'Hey, it's a first date. We don't have to end up naked.'

Myron thought about that. 'Oh.'

'You sound surprised.'

'No . . . I mean—'

'Maybe I'm not that easy.'

'My mistake for presuming . . . I mean, you're hanging out in this bar.'

'So?'

'So I didn't think most of the patrons in here played hard to get. To quote Woody Allen, "How did I misread those signs?" '

Thrill didn't hesitate. '*Play It Again, Sam.*'

'If you are a woman,' Myron said, 'I may be falling in love.'

'Thank you. And if we're reading signs from being in this bar, what are you doing here? You with your penis issue.'

'Good point.'

'So?'

'So what?'

'So why don't you ask me out?' Again with the smolder. 'We could hold hands. Maybe kiss. You might even sneak a hand under my shirt, go for a little second base. The way you've been ogling, it's almost like you're there anyway.'

'I'm not ogling,' Myron said.

'No?'

'If I've been looking – and note I said *if* – it would be purely for the sake of gender clarification, I assure you.'

'Thanks for straightening that out. But my point is, we can just go and have dinner. Or go to a movie. We don't have to have any genital contact.'

Myron shook his head. 'I'd still be wondering.'

'Ah, but don't you like a little mystery?'

'I like mystery in lots of arenas. But when it comes to trouser content, well, I'm a pretty traditional guy.'

Thrill shrugged. 'I still don't understand why you're here.'

'I'm looking for someone.' He took out a photograph of Clu Haid and showed it to her. 'Do you know him?'

Thrill looked at the photograph and frowned. 'I thought you said you're a sports agent.'

'I am. He was a client.'

'Was?'

'He was murdered.'

'He's the baseball player?'

Myron nodded. 'Have you seen him here?'

Thrill grabbed a piece of paper and wrote something

down. 'Here's my phone number, Myron. Call me sometime.'

'What about the guy in the photograph?'

Thrill handed him the scrap of paper, jumped off the stool, and undulated away. Myron watched her movements closely, looking for, umm, a concealed weapon. Big Cyndi elbowed him. He almost fell off the stool.

'This is Pat,' Big Cyndi said.

Pat the bartender looked like someone Archie Bunker might have hired to work his place. He was mid-fifties, short, gray-haired, slouch-shouldered, world-weary. Even his mustache – one of those gray-turning-to-yellow models – drooped as though it'd seen it all. Pat's sleeves were rolled up, revealing Popeye-size forearms covered with hair. Myron hoped like hell Pat was a guy. This place was giving him a headache.

Behind Pat was a giant mirror. Next to that, a wall with the words *Customer Hall of Fame* painted in pink. The wall was covered with framed head shots of big-time right-wingers. Pat Buchanan. Jerry Falwell. Pat Robertson. Newt Gingrich. Jesse Helms.

Pat saw him looking at the photographs. 'Ever notice that.'

'Notice what?'

'How all the big antifags have sexually ambiguous first names? Pat, Chris, Jesse, Jerry. Could be a guy, could be a girl. See what I'm saying?'

Myron said, 'Uh-huh.'

'And what kind of name is Newt?' Pat added. 'I mean, how the hell do you grow up with a healthy sexual attitude with a name like Newt?'

'I don't know.'

'My theory?' Pat shrugged, wiped the bar with a dishrag. 'These narrow assholes were all teased a lot as children. Makes them hostile on the whole gender issue.'

'Interesting theory,' Myron said. 'But isn't your name Pat?'

'Yeah, well, I hate fags too,' Pat said. 'But they tip well.'

Pat winked at Big Cyndi. Big Cyndi winked back. The jukebox changed songs. Lou Rawls crooned 'Love Is in the Air.' Timing.

The right-wing head shots were all 'autographed.' Jesse Helms's read: 'I'm sore all over, Love and kisses, Jesse.' Blunt. Several Xs and Os followed. There was also a big lipstick kiss impression as though Jesse himself had puckered up and laid down a wet one. Eeeuw.

Pat started cleaning out a beer mug with the dishrag. Casually. Myron half expected him to spit in it like in an old western. 'So what can I get you?'

'Are you a sports fan?' Myron asked.

'You taking a poll?'

That line. It was always such a riot. Myron tried again. 'Does the name Clu Haid mean anything to you?'

Myron watched for a reaction but didn't get one. Meant nothing. The guy looked like a lifetime bartender. They show about as much range as a *Baywatch* regular. Hmm. Now why was that show on his mind?

'I asked you—'

'Name means nothing to me.'

Big Cyndi said, 'Please, Pat.'

He shot her a look. 'You heard me, Big C. I don't know him.'

Myron pressed it. 'Never heard of Clu Haid?'

'That's right.'

'How about the New York Yankees?'

'I haven't followed them since the Mick retired.'

Myron put the photograph of Clu Haid on the bar. 'Ever seen him in here?'

Someone called out for a draft. Pat drew it. When he came back, he spoke to Big Cyndi. 'This guy a cop?'

'No,' Big Cyndi said.

'Then the answer is no.'

'And if I was a cop?' Myron asked.

'Then the answer would be no . . . sir.' Myron noticed that Pat had never so much as glanced at the photograph. 'I might also add a little song and dance about how I'm too busy to notice faces in here. And how most people, especially celebrities, don't show their real faces in here anyway.'

'I see,' Myron said. He reached into his wallet, took out a fifty. 'And if I showed you a photograph of Ulysses S. Grant?'

The jukebox changed songs. The Flying Machine started crooning for Rosemarie to 'smile a little smile for me, Rosemarie.' The Flying Machine. Myron had remembered the group's name. What did that say about a man?

'Keep your money,' Pat said. 'Keep your picture. Keep your questions. I don't like trouble.'

'And this guy means trouble?'

'I haven't even looked at the picture, pal. And I don't plan to. Take a hike.'

Big Cyndi stepped in. 'Pat,' she said, 'please can't you help' – she batted her eyelashes; picture two crabs on their backs in the blazing sun – 'for me?'

'Hey, Big C, I love you, you know that. But suppose I came into Leather-N-Lust with pictures? You gonna be anxious to help?'

Big Cyndi thought about that. 'I guess not.'

'There you go. I got customers.'

'Fine,' Myron said. He picked up the photograph. 'Then maybe I'll stick around. Pass the picture around the room. Ask some questions. Maybe I'll stake this place out. Indiscreetly. Take photos of people entering and leaving this fine establishment.'

Pat shook his head, smiled a bit. 'You're one dumb son of a bitch, you know that.'

'I'll do it,' Myron said. 'I don't want to, but I'll camp out on your doorstep with a camera.'

Pat gave Myron a long look. Hard to read. Part hostile maybe. Mostly bored. 'Big C, head out of here for a few minutes.'

'No.'

'Then I don't talk.'

Myron turned to her, nodded. Big Cyndi shook her head. Myron pulled her aside. 'What's the problem?'

'You shouldn't make threats in here, Mr Bolitar.'

'I know what I'm doing.'

'I warned you about this place. I can't leave you alone.'

'You'll be right outside. I can take care of myself.'

When Big Cyndi frowned, her face resembled a freshly painted totem pole. 'I don't like it.'

'We have no choice.'

She sighed. Picture Mount Vesuvius bubbling up a bit of lava. 'Be careful.'

'I will.'

She lumbered toward the exit. The place was packed and Big Cyndi took up a wide berth. Still, people parted with a speed that would have made Moses jot notes. When she was all the way out the door, Myron turned back to Pat. 'Well?'

'Well, you're a dumb asshole.'

It happened without warning. Two hands snaked under Myron's arms, the fingers locking behind his neck. A classic full nelson. The hold was tightened, pushing back his arms like chicken wings. Myron felt something hot rip across his shoulder blades.

A voice near his ear whispered, 'Care to dance, dreamboat?'

When it came to hand-to-hand combat, Myron was no Win, but he was no slouch either. He thus knew that if the perpetrator was good, there was no way to break a full nelson. That was why they were illegal in real wrestling matches. If you were standing, you could try to stomp on the person's instep. But only a moron fell for that, and a moron would not have had the speed or the strength to get this far. And Myron was not standing.

Myron's elbows were high up in the air, marionette fashion, his face helplessly exposed. The powerful arms locking him were covered in cardigan. Soft yellow cardigan, as a matter of fact. As in a soft yellow cardigan sweater. Jesus. Myron struggled. Nothing doing. The cardigan-clad arms pulled Myron's head back and then snapped it toward the bar, face first. Myron could do nothing but close his eyes. He tucked his chin just enough to keep his nose from taking the brunt of the blow. But his head bounced off the varnished teak in a way it was never intended to, jarring his skull. Something on his forehead split open. His head swam. He saw stars.

Another set of hands scooped up Myron's feet. He was in the air now and moving and very dizzy. Hands emptied his pockets. A door opened. Myron was carried through it into a dark room. The grip was released, and Myron fell like a potato sack onto his tailbone. The whole process, from the onset of the full nelson to the moment he was dumped on the floor, took all of eight seconds.

A light was snapped on. Myron touched his forehead and felt something sticky. Blood. He looked up at his attackers.

Two women.

No, cross-dressers. Both with blond wigs. One had gone with early-eighties Mall Girl hair – lots of height and teased more than a bed-wetter. The other one – the one with the soft yellow cardigan sweater (mono-grammed, for those who cared) – had hair like Veronica Lake on a particularly nasty bender.

Myron started to get to his feet. Veronica Lake let out a squeal and threw a side kick. The kick was fast and landed hard on his chest. Myron heard himself make a noise like 'pluuu' and landed back on his rear. His hand automatically reached for his cellular. He'd hit the memory button and call Win. Then stall.

The phone was gone.

He looked up. Mall Girl had it. Damn. He took in his surroundings. There was a great view of the bar and Pat the bartender's back. He remembered the mirror. Of course. One-way glass. The patrons saw a mirror. The people back here saw, well, everything. Hard to steal from the till when you never knew who was watching.

The walls were corked and thus soundproof. The floor was cheap linoleum. Easier to clean, he guessed. Despite that, there were specks of blood on it. Not his. These specks were old and dried. But they were there. No mistaking them for something else. And Myron knew why. In a word: intimidation.

This was a classic pounding room. Lots of places have them. Especially sports arenas. Not so much now as in the old days. There was a time when an unruly fan was more than just escorted out of the stadium. The security guards took him into a back room and pounded on him a bit. It was fairly safe. What could the unruly fan claim after the fact? He was drunk off his rocker, had probably gotten into a fight in the stands, whatever. So the security boys added a few extra bruises for good measure. Who's to say where the bruises came from? And if the unruly fan threatened to press charges or make noise, stadium officials could whack him back with charges of public drunkenness and assault and whatever else they could dream up. They could also produce a dozen security guards to back their story and none to back the unruly fan's.

So the fan let it drop. And the pounding rooms remained. Probably still do in some places.

Veronica Lake giggled. It was not a pretty sound. 'Care to dance, dreamboat?' he-she asked again.

'Let's wait for a slow song,' Myron said.

A third cross-dresser stepped into the room. A redhead. He-she looked a lot like Bonnie Franklin, the plucky mother on the old sitcom *One Day at a Time*. The resemblance was, in fact, rather uncanny – the perfect mix of determination and cutes. Spunky. Scrappy.

'Where's Schneider?' Myron asked.

No reply.

Veronica Lake said, 'Stand up, dreamboat.'

'The blood on the floor,' Myron said.

'What?'

'It's a nice touch, but it's overkill, don't you think?'

Veronica Lake lifted her right foot and pulled on her heel. It came off. Sort of. The heel was a covering actually. A sheath. For a steel blade. Veronica showed it to Myron with an impressive display of martial art high kicks, the blade gleaming in the light.

Bonnie Franklin and Mall Girl started giggling.

Myron kept the fear at bay and looked steadily at Veronica Lake. 'Are you new at cross-dressing?' he asked.

Veronica stopped kicking. 'What?'

'I mean, aren't you taking the whole *stiletto* heel thing too far?'

Not his best joke, but anything to stall. Veronica looked at Mall Girl. Mall Girl looked at Bonnie Franklin. Then Veronica suddenly threw a sweep kick, leading with the blade heel. Myron saw the glint of steel shoot toward him. He rolled back, but the blade still sliced through his shirt and into his skin. He let out a little cry and looked down wide-eyed. The cut wasn't deep, but he was bleeding.

The three spread out, making fists. Bonnie Franklin had something in her hand. A black club maybe. Myron did not like this. He tried to spring to his feet, but again Veronica threw a kick. He leaped high, but the blade still hit his lower leg. he actually felt the blade get caught on the shin bone before scraping itself off.

Myron's heart was pounding now. More blood. Jesus Christ. Something about seeing your own blood. His breathing was too fast. *Keep cool*, he reminded himself. *Think*.

He faked left to the spot where Bonnie Franklin stood with the baton. Then he coiled right, his fist at the ready. Without hesitating, he threw a punch at the advancing Mall Girl. His knuckles landed flush below the eye and Mall Girl went down.

That was when Myron felt his heart stop.

There was a zapping sound and the back of his knee exploded. Myron spun in pure agony. His body jolted. Searing pain burst out of the nerve bundle behind the knee and traveled everywhere in an electric surge. He looked behind him. Bonnie Franklin had merely touched him with the baton. His legs seized up, lost power. He collapsed back to the floor and writhed fish-on-boat-deck fashion. His stomach clenched. Nausea consumed him.

'That was the lowest setting,' Bonnie Franklin said, voice high-pitched little girl. 'Just gets the cow's attention.'

Myron looked up, trying to stop his body from quaking. Veronica lifted her leg and placed the heel blade near his face. One quick stomp and he was done. Bonnie showed him the cattle prod again. Myron felt a fresh shiver go through him. He looked through the one-way glass. No sign of Big Cyndi or any cavalry.

Now what?

Bonnie Franklin did the talking. 'Why are you here?'

He focused on the cattle prod and how to avoid experiencing its wrath again. 'I was asking about someone,' he said.

Mall Girl had recovered. She-he stood up over him holding her-his face. 'He hit me!' Her tone was a little deeper now, the shock and hurt dropping the feminine facade a bit.

Myron stayed still.

'You bitch!'

Mall Girl grimaced and threw a kick as though Myron's rib cage were a football. Myron saw the kick coming, saw the heel blade, saw the cattle prod, closed his eyes, and let it land.

He fell back.

Bonnie Franklin continued with the questions. 'Who were you asking about?'

No secret. 'Clu Haid.'

'Why?'

'Because I wanted to know if he'd been here.'

'Why?'

Telling them he was looking for his killer might not be the wisest course of action, especially if said killer was in the room. 'He was a client of mine.'

'So?'

'Bitch!' It was Mall Girl again. Another kick. It again landed on the bottom tip of the rib cage and hurt like hell. Myron swallowed away some bile that had worked its way up. He looked through the one-way glass again. Still no Big Cyndi. Blood flowed from the knife wounds to his chest and leg. His insides still trembled from the electric shock. He looked into the eyes of Veronica Lake. The calm eyes. Win had them too. The great ones always do.

'Who do you work for?' Bonnie asked.

'No one.'

'Then why would you care if he came here?'

'I'm just trying to put some things together,' he said.

'What things?'

'Just general stuff.'

Bonnie Franklin looked at Veronica Lake. Both nodded. Then Bonnie Franklin made a show of turning up the cattle prod. ' "General stuff" is an unacceptable response.'

Panic squeezed Myron's gut. 'Wait—'

'No, I think not.' Bonnie reached toward him with the cattle prod.

Myron's eyes widened. No choice really. He had to try it now. If the prod hit him again, he'd have nothing left. He just had to hope Veronica would not kill him.

He had been planning the move for the past ten seconds. Now he rolled all the way back over his neck and head. He landed on his feet and without warning shot himself forward as though from a cannon. The three cross-dressers backed off, prepared for the attack. But an attack would be suicide. Myron knew that. There were three of them, two armed, at least one very good. Myron could never beat them. He needed to surprise them. So he did. By *not* going for them.

He went instead for the one-way glass.

His legs had pushed off full throttle, propelling him rocket-ship fashion toward the glass. By the time his three captors realized what he was doing, it was too late. Myron squeezed his eyes shut, made two fists, and hit the glass with his full weight, Superman style. He held nothing back. If the glass did not give, he was a dead man.

The glass shattered on impact.

The sound was enormous, all-consuming. Myron flew through it, glass clattering to the floor around him. When he landed, he tucked himself into a tight ball. He hit the floor and rolled. Tiny shards of mirror bit into his skin. He ignored the pain, kept rolling, crashing hard into the bar. Bottles fell.

Big Cyndi had talked about the place's reputation.

Myron was counting on that. And the Take A Guess clientele did not disappoint.

A pure New York melee ensued.

Tables were thrown. People screamed. Someone flew over the bar and landed on top of Myron. More glass shattered. Myron tried to get to his feet, but it wasn't happening. From his right, he saw a door open. Mall Girl emerged.

'Bitch!'

Mall Girl started toward him, carrying Bonnie's cattle prod. Myron tried to scramble away, but he couldn't get his bearings. Mall Girl kept coming, drawing closer.

And then Mall Girl disappeared.

It was like a scene from a cartoon, where the big dog punches Sylvester the Cat, and Sylvester flies across the room and the oversize fist stays there for a few seconds.

In this case the oversize fist belonged to Big Cyndi.

Bodies flew. Glasses flew. Chairs flew. Big Cyndi ignored it all. She scooped Myron up and threw him over her shoulder like a firefighter. They rushed outside as police sirens clawed through the milky night air.

16

Back at the Dakota, Win tsk-tsked and said, 'You let a couple of girls beat you up?'

'They weren't girls.'

Win took a sip of cognac. Myron gulped some Yoo-Hoo. 'Tomorrow night,' Win said, 'we'll go back to this bar. Together.'

It was not something Myron wanted to think about right now. Win called a doctor. It was after two in the morning, but the doctor, a gray-haired man straight from central casting, arrived in fifteen minutes. Nothing broken, he declared with a professional chuckle. Most of the medical treatment consisted of cleaning out the cuts from the heel blade and window bits. The two heel slices – the one on his stomach was shaped like a Z – required stitches. All in all, painful but relatively harmless.

The doctor tossed Myron some Tylenol with codeine, closed up his medical bag, tipped his hat, departed. Myron finished his Yoo-Hoo and stood slowly. He wanted to take a shower, but the doctor had told him to wait until the morning. He swallowed a couple of tablets and hit the sheets. When he fell asleep, he dreamed about Brenda.

In the morning he called Hester Crimstein at her apartment. The machine picked up. Myron said it was urgent. Midway through his message Hester took the call.

'I need to see Esperanza,' he told the attorney. 'Now.'

Surprisingly, the attorney hesitated for only a moment before saying, 'Okay.'

'I killed someone,' Myron said.

Esperanza sat across from him.

'I don't mean I actually fired a gun. But I might as well have. In many ways what I did was worse.'

Esperanza kept her eyes on him. 'This happened right before you ran away?'

'Within a couple of weeks, yes.'

'But that's not why you left.'

His mouth felt dry. 'I guess not.'

'You ran away because of Brenda.'

Myron did not answer.

Esperanza crossed her arms. 'So why are you sharing this little tidbit with me?'

'I'm not sure.'

'I am,' she said.

'Oh?'

'It's something of a ploy. You hoped that your big confession would help me open up.'

'No,' Myron said.

'Then?'

'You're the one I talk to about things like this.'

She almost smiled. 'Even now?'

'I don't understand why you're shutting me out,' he said. 'And okay, maybe I do hold out some hope that talking about this will help us return to – I don't know – some kind of sense of normalcy. Or maybe I just need to talk about this. Win wouldn't understand. The person I killed was evil incarnate. It would have presented him with a moral dilemma no more complex than choosing a tie.'

'And this moral dilemma haunts you?'

'The problem is,' Myron said, 'it doesn't.'

Esperanza nodded. 'Ah.'

'The person deserved it,' he went on. 'The courts had no evidence.'

'So you played vigilante.'

'In a sense.'

'And that bothers you? No, wait, it doesn't bother you.'

'Right.'

'So you're losing sleep over the fact that you're not losing sleep.'

He smiled, spread his hands. 'See why I come to you?'

Esperanza crossed her legs and looked up in the air. 'When I first met you and Win, I wondered about your friendship. About what first attracted you to each other. I thought maybe Win was a latent homosexual.'

'Why does everyone say that? Can't two men just—'

'I was wrong,' she interrupted. 'And don't get all defensive, it'll make people wonder. You guys aren't gay. I realized that early on. Like I said, it was just a thought. Then I wondered if it was simply the old adage "Opposites attract." Maybe that's part of it.' She stopped.

'And?' Myron prompted.

'And maybe you two are more alike than either one of you wants to believe. I don't want to get too deep here, but Win sees you as his humanity. If you like him, he reasons, how bad can he be? You, on the other hand, see him as a cold dose of reality. Win's logic is scary, but it's oddly appealing. There is a little part in all of us that likes what he does, the same side of us that thinks the Iranians might be on to something when they cut off a thief's hand. You grew up with all that suburban liberal crap about the disadvantaged. But now real-life experience is teaching you that some people are just plain evil. It shifts you a little closer to Win.'

'So you're saying I'm becoming like Win? Gee, that's comforting.'

'I'm saying your reaction is human. I don't like it. I don't think it's right. You may indeed be sinking into a quagmire. Bending the rules is getting easier and easier for you. Maybe the person you killed deserved it, but if you want to hear that, if you want absolution, go to Win.'

Silence.

Esperanza's fingers fluttered near her mouth, debating between biting the nails and plucking her lower lip. 'You've always been the finest person I know,' she said. 'Don't let anybody change that, okay?'

He swallowed, nodded.

'You're not bending the rules anymore,' she continued. 'You're decimating them. Just yesterday you told me you'd lie under oath to protect me.'

'That's different.'

Esperanza looked straight at him. 'Are you sure about that?'

'Yes. I'll do whatever I have to to protect you.'

'Including breaking laws? That's my point, Myron.'

He shifted in his chair.

'And one other thing,' she said. 'You're using this whole moral dilemma thing to distract yourself from two truths you don't want to face.'

'What truths?'

'One, Brenda.'

'And two?'

Esperanza smiled. 'Skipped over one pretty fast.'

'And two?' he repeated.

Her smile was gentle, understanding. 'Two, it gets your mind off why you're really here.'

'And why's that?'

'You're starting to do more than wonder if I killed Clu. And you're trying to find a way to rationalize it away if I did. You killed once, ergo it may be justifiable if I killed too. You just want to hear a reason.'

'He hit you,' Myron said. 'In the parking garage.'

She said nothing.

'The radio said they found pubic hairs in his apart-ment—'

'Don't go there,' she said.

'I have to.'

'Just stay out.'

'I can't.'

'I don't need your help.'

'There's more to it than that. I'm involved in this.'

'Only because you want to be.'

'Did Clu tell you I was in danger?'

She said nothing.

'He told my parents that. And Jessica. I thought at first it was hyperbole. But maybe it's not. I got this weird diskette in the mail. There was an image of a young girl.'

'You're ranting,' she said. 'You think you're ready for this, but you're not. Learn something from your past mistakes. Keep away from this.'

'But it won't keep away from me,' Myron said. 'Why did Clu say I was in danger? Why did he hit you? What happened at the Take A Guess bar?'

She shook her head. 'Guard.'

The guard opened the door. Esperanza kept her eyes down. She turned and left the room without looking back at Myron. Myron sat alone for a few seconds, gathered his thoughts. He checked his watch. Nine forty-five. Plenty of time to get to Yankee Stadium for his eleven o'clock meeting with Sophie and Jared Mayor. He had barely left the room when a man approached him.

'Mr Bolitar?'

'Yes.'

'This is for you.'

The man handed him an envelope and disappeared. Myron opened it. A subpoena from the Bergen County district attorney's office. Case heading: 'People of Bergen County v. Esperanza Diaz.' Well, well. Esperanza and Hester had been right not to tell him anything.

He stuffed it into his pocket. At least now he wouldn't have to lie.

17

Myron did what every good boy should do when he gets into legal trouble: He called his mommy.

'Your aunt Clara will handle the subpoena,' Mom said.

Aunt Clara wasn't really his aunt, just an old friend from the neighborhood. On the High Holy Days she still pinched Myron's cheek and cried out, 'What a *punim*!' Myron sort of hoped she wouldn't do that in front of the judge: 'Your Honor, I ask you to look at this face: Is that a *punim* or is that a *punim*?'

'Okay,' Myron said.

'I'll call her, she'll call the DA. In the meantime you say nothing, understand?'

'Yes.'

'See now, Mr Smarty Pants? See what I was telling you now? About Hester Crimstein being right?'

'Yeah, Mom, whatever.'

'Don't whatever me. They've subpoenaed you. But because Esperanza wouldn't tell you anything, you can't hurt her case.'

'I see that, Mom.'

'Good. Now let me go call Aunt Clara.'

She hung up. And Mr Smarty Pants did likewise.

Bluntly put, Yankee Stadium was located in a cesspool section of the ever-eroding Bronx. It didn't much matter. Whenever you first caught sight of the famed sports edifice, you still fell into an immediate church hush. Couldn't help it. Memories swarmed in and burrowed down. Images flashed in and out. His youth. A small child crammed standing on the 4 train, holding Dad's seemingly giant hand, looking up into his gentle face, the pregame anticipation tingling through every part of him. Dad had caught a fly ball when Myron was five years old. He could still see it sometimes – the arc of white rawhide, the crowd standing, his dad's arm stretching to an impossible height, the ball landing on the palm with a happy smack, the warm beam coming off Dad's face when he handed the prized possession to his son. Myron still had that ball, browning in the basement of his parents' house.

Basketball was Myron's sport of choice, and football was probably his favorite to watch on TV. Tennis was the game of princes, golf the game of kings. But baseball was magic. Early childhood memories are faint, but almost every boy can recall his first major-league baseball game. He can remember the score, who hit a home run, who pitched. But mostly he remembers his father. The smell of his after-shave is wrapped up in the smells of baseball – the freshly cut grass, the summer air, the hot dogs, the stale popcorn, the spilled beer, the overoiled glove complete with baseball breaking in the pocket. He remembers the visiting team, the way Yaz tossed grounders to warm up Petrocelli at short, the way the hecklers made gentle fun of Frank Howard's TV commercials for Nestlé's Quik, the way the game's greats rounded second and slid headfirst into third. You remember your sibling keeping stats, studying the lineups the way rabbinical scholars study the Talmud, baseball cards gripped in your hand, the ease and pace of a slow summer afternoon, Mom spending more time sunning herself than watching the action. You remember Dad buying you a pennant of the visiting team and later hanging it on your wall in a ceremony equal to the Celtics raising a banner in the old Boston Garden. You remember the way the players in the bullpen looked so relaxed, big wads of chew distorting their cheeks. You remember your healthy, respectful hate for the visiting team's superstars, the pure joy of going on Bat Day and treasuring that piece of wood as though it'd come straight from Honus Wagner's locker.

Show me a boy who didn't dream of being a big leaguer before age seven, before Training League or whatever slowly began to thin the herd in one of life's earliest lessons that the world can and will disappoint you. Show me a boy who doesn't remember wearing his Little League cap to school when the teachers would allow it, keeping it pitched high with a favorite baseball card tucked inside, wearing it to the dinner table, sleeping with it on the night table next to his bed. Show me a boy who doesn't remember playing catch with his father on the weekends or, better, on those precious summer nights when Dad would rush home from his job, shake off his work clothes, put on a T-shirt that was always a little too small, grab a mitt, and head into the backyard before the final rays faded away. Show me a boy who didn't stare in awe at how far his father could hit or throw a baseball – no matter how bad an athlete his father was, no matter how spastic or what have you – and for that shining moment Dad was transformed into a man of unimaginable ability and strength.

Only baseball had that magic.

The new majority owner of the New York Yankees was Sophie Mayor. She and her husband, Gary, had shocked the baseball world by buying the team from the longtime unpopular owner Vincent Riverton less than a year ago. Most fans had applauded. Vincent Riverton, a publishing mogul, had a love-hate relationship with the public (mostly hate) and the Mayors, a techno-nouveau-riche pair who had found their fortune through computer software, promised a more hands-off approach. Gary Mayor had grown up in the Bronx and promised a return to the days of the Mick and DiMaggio. The fans were thrilled.

But tragedy struck pretty fast. Two weeks before the

deal to buy was finalized, Gary Mayor died of a sudden heart attack. Sophie Mayor, who had always been an equal, if not dominating, partner in the software business, insisted on going ahead with the transaction. She had public support and sympathy, but Gary and his roots had been the rope tethering her to the public. Sophie was a midwesterner, and with her love of hunting mixed with her background as a math genius, she hit the prenatally suspicious New Yorkers as being something of a kook.

Soon after taking over the helm, Sophie made her son Jared, a man with virtually no baseball experience, co-general manager. The public frowned. She made a quick trade, gutting the Yankee farm system on the chance that Clu Haid still had a good year or two left. The public cried. She had stood firm. She wanted a World Series in the Bronx immediately. Trading for Clu Haid was the way to get it. The public was skeptical.

But Clu pitched amazingly well during his first month with the team. His fastball was back over ninety, and his curves were breaking as if they were accepting signals from a remote control. He got better with each outing, and the Yankees grabbed first place. The public was appeased. For a little while anyway, Myron guessed. He had stopped paying attention, but he could imagine the backlash against the Mayor family when Clu tested positive for drugs.

Myron was led immediately into Sophie Mayor's office. She and Jared both stood to greet him. Sophie Mayor was probably mid-fifties, what was commonly called a handsome woman, her hair gray and neat, her back straight, her handshake firm, her arms tawny, her eyes twinkling with hints of mischief and cunning. Jared was twenty-fiveish. He wore his hair parted on the right with no hint of style, wire-rimmed glasses, a blue blazer, and a polka dot bow tie. Youths for George Will.

The office was sparsely decorated, or maybe it just

appeared that way because the scene was dominated by a moose head hanging on a wall. A dead moose actually. A live moose is so hard to hang. Quite the decorating touch. Myron tried not to make a face. He almost said, 'You must have hated this moose,' à la Dudley Moore in *Arthur* but refrained. With age comes maturity.

Myron shook Jared's hand, then turned toward Sophie Mayor.

Sophie pounced. 'Where the hell have you been, Myron?'

'Excuse me?'

She pointed to a chair. 'Sit.'

Like he was a dog. But he obeyed. Jared too. Sophie stayed on her feet and glowered down at him.

'In court yesterday they said something about your being in the Caribbean,' she continued.

Myron made a noncommittal 'uh-huh' sound.

'Where were you?'

'I was away.'

'Away?'

'Yes.'

She looked over at her son, then back at Myron. 'For how long?'

'Three weeks.'

'But Miss Diaz told me you were in town.'

Myron said nothing.

Sophie Mayor made two fists and leaned toward him. 'Why would she tell me that, Myron?'

'Because she didn't know where I was.'

'In other words, she lied to me.'

Myron did not bother replying.

'So where were you?' she pressed.

'Out of the country.'

'The Caribbean?'

'Yes.'

'And you never told anyone?'

147

Myron shifted in his chair, trying to find an opening or gain some sort of footing here. 'I don't mean to sound rude,' he said, 'but I don't see how my whereabouts are any of your business.'

'You don't?' A sharp chortle passed her lips. She looked at her son as if to say, *Do you believe this guy?*, then redirected her laser grays back toward Myron. 'I relied on you,' she said.

Myron said nothing.

'I bought this team and I decided to be hands-off. I know software. I know computers. I know business. I really don't know much about baseball. But I made one decision. I wanted Clu Haid. I had a feeling about him. I thought he still had something left. So I traded for him. People thought I was nuts – three good prospects for one has-been. I understood that concern. So I went to you, Myron, remember?'

'Yes.'

'And you assured me he was going to stay clean.'

'Wrong,' Myron said. 'I said he *wanted* to stay clean.'

'Wanted, was going to ... What is this, a lesson in semantics?'

'He was my client,' Myron said. 'It's my job to worry about his interests.'

'And damn mine?'

'That's not what I said.'

'Damn integrity and ethics too? Is that the way you work, Myron?'

'That's not it at all. Sure, we wanted this trade to happen—'

'You wanted it badly,' she corrected him.

'Fine, we wanted it badly. But I never promised you he'd stay clean because it's not something I or anyone else can guarantee. I assured you we would try our hardest. I made it part of the deal. I gave you the right to randomly test him at any time.'

'You *gave* me the right? I demanded it! And you fought me on it every step of the way.'

'We shared the risk,' Myron said. 'I made his salary contingent on his staying clean. I let you put in a strict morals clause.'

She smiled, crossed her arms. 'You know who you sound like? Those hypocritical car commercials where General Motors or Ford tout all the pollution-saving devices they've put on their cars. As though they did it on their own. As though they woke up one day more concerned with the environment than the bottom line. They leave out the fact that the government forced them to put on those devices, that they fought the government tooth and nail the whole way.'

'He was my client,' Myron said again.

'And you think that's an all-purpose excuse?'

'It's my job to get him the best deal.'

'Keep telling yourself that, Myron.'

'I can't stop a man from returning to an addiction. You knew that.'

'But you said you'd watch him. You said you'd work on keeping him straight.'

Myron swallowed and shifted in his chair again. 'Yes.'

'But you didn't watch him, Myron, did you?'

Silence.

'You took a vacation and didn't tell anyone. You left Clu alone. You acted irresponsibly, and so I blame you in part for his falling off the wagon.'

Myron opened his mouth, closed it. She was right, of course, but he didn't have the luxury of wallowing in that right now. Later. He'd think about his role in this later. The pain from last night's beating was angrily stirring from its snooze. He reached into his pocket and shook out a couple of extra-strength Tylenols.

Satisfied – or maybe satiated – Sophie Mayor sat

down. Seeing the pills, she asked, 'Would you like some water?'

'Please.'

She nodded at Jared. Jared poured Myron a glass of water and handed it to him. Myron thanked him and swallowed the tablets. The placebo effect jumped in, and he immediately felt better.

Before Sophie Mayor could strike again, Myron tried to shift gears. 'Tell me about Clu's failed drug test,' he said.

Sophie Mayor looked puzzled. 'What's to tell?'

'Clu claimed he was clean.'

'And you believe that?'

'I want to look into it.'

'Why?'

'Because when Clu was caught in the past, he begged forgiveness and promised to get help. He never pretended a test result was wrong.'

She crossed her arms. 'And that's evidence of what exactly?'

'Nothing. I'd just like to ask a few questions.'

'Ask away then.'

'How often did you test him?'

Sophie looked over at her son. His cue. Jared spoke for the first time since greeting Myron at the door. 'At least once a week,' he said.

'Urine tests?' Myron asked.

'Yes,' Jared said.

'And he passed them all? I mean, except for the last one.'

'Yes.'

Myron shook his head. 'Every week? And no other positives? Just that one?'

'That's right.'

He looked back at Sophie. 'Didn't you find that odd?'

'Why?' she countered. 'He'd been trying to stay clean,

and he fell off the wagon. It happens every day, doesn't it?'

It did, Myron guessed, and still something about it didn't sit right with him. 'But Clu knew you were testing him?'

'I assume so, yes. We'd been testing him at least once a week.'

'And how were the tests conducted?'

Sophie again looked over at Jared. Jared asked, 'What do you mean?'

'Step by step,' Myron said. 'What did he do?'

Sophie took that one. 'He peed in the cup, Myron. It's pretty simple.'

It was never pretty simple. 'Did someone watch him urinate?'

'What?'

'Did someone actually witness Clu peeing or did he step into a stall?' Myron said. 'Was he naked when he did it or did he have on shorts—'

'What difference does any of that make?'

'Plenty. Clu had spent his lifetime beating these tests. If he knew they were coming, he'd be prepared.'

'Prepared how?' Sophie asked.

'Lots of ways, depending on the sophistication of the test,' Myron said. 'If the testing was more primitive, you can put motor oil on your fingers and let the urine hit them while urinating. The phosphates throw the results out of whack. Some testers know this, so they check for phosphates. If the tester lets the guy urinate in a stall, he can strap clean urine onto his inner thigh and use that. Or the testee keeps the clean urine hidden in a condom or small balloon. He stores it in the lining of his boxer shorts maybe. Or between his toes. Under his armpit. In his mouth even.'

'Are you serious?'

'It gets worse. If the testee gets tipped off a strict test is coming up – one where the administrators are watching every move he makes – he'll drain his bladder and use a catheter to pump in clean urine.'

Sophie Mayor looked horror-stricken. 'He pumps someone else's urine into his bladder?'

'Yes,' Myron said.

'Jesus.' Then she pinned him down with her eyes. 'You seem to know quite a bit about this, Myron.'

'So did Clu.'

'What are you saying?'

'It raises some questions, that's all.'

'He probably got caught by surprise.'

'Maybe,' Myron said. 'But if you were testing him every week, how surprised could he have been?'

'He might have just messed up,' Sophie went on. 'Drug addicts have a way of doing that.'

'Could be. But I'd like to speak with the person who administered the test.'

'Dr Stilwell,' Jared said. 'He's the team doctor. He handled it. Sawyer Wells assisted him.'

'Sawyer Wells, as in the self-help guru?'

'He's a psychologist specializing in human behavior and an excellent motivational therapist,' Jared corrected.

Motivational therapist. Uh-huh. 'Are either of them around now?'

'No, I don't think so. But they'll be here later. We have a home game tonight.'

'Who on the team was especially friendly with Clu? A coach, a player?'

'I really wouldn't know,' Jared said.

'Who did he room with on the road?'

Sophie almost smiled. 'You really were out of touch, weren't you?'

'Cabral,' Jared said. 'Enos Cabral. He's a Cuban pitcher.'

Myron knew him. He nodded, glancing about, and

that was when he saw it. His heart lurched, and it took all his willpower not to scream.

He had just been sweeping the room with his eyes, taking the room in but not really seeing anything, just the normal thing everyone does, when an object snagged his gaze as though on a rusted hook. Myron froze. On the credenza. On the right side of the credenza, mixed in with the other framed photos and the trophies and those latex cubes that encased civic awards and the first issue of Mayor Software stock and the like. Right there. A framed photograph.

A framed photograph of the girl on the computer diskette.

Myron tried to maintain a calm facade. Deep breath in, deep breath out. But he could feel his pulse quicken. His mind fought through the haze, searching for a temporary clearing. He scanned his internal memory banks. *Okay, slow down. Breathe. Keep breathing.*

No wonder the girl had looked familiar to him.

But what was her deal? More memory bank scanning. She was Sophie Mayor's daughter, of course. Jared Mayor's sister. What was her name again? His recollections were vague. What had happened to her? A runaway, right? Ten, fifteen years ago. There had been an estrangement or something. Foul play was not suspected. Or was it? He didn't remember.

'Myron?'

He needed to think. Calmly. He needed space, time. He couldn't just blurt out, 'Oh, I got this weird diskette with an image of your daughter melting in blood on it.' He had to get out of here. Do some research. Think it through. He stood, clumsily looking at his watch.

'I have to go,' he said.

'What?'

'I'd like to speak with Dr Stilwell as soon as possible,' he said.

Sophie's eyes stayed on him. 'I don't see the relevance.'

'I just explained—'

'What difference would it make? Clu is dead now. The drug test isn't relevant.'

'There might be a connection.'

'Between his death and a drug test?'

'Yes.'

'I'm not sure I agree.'

'I'd still like to check it out. I have that right.'

'What right?'

'If the drug test was inconclusive, it changes things.'

'Changes what—' Then Sophie stopped, smiled a bit, and nodded to herself. 'I think I see now.'

Myron said nothing.

'You mean in terms of his contract, don't you?'

'I have to go,' he repeated.

She leaned back and recrossed her arms. 'Well, Myron, I have to hand it to you. You are definitely an agent. Trying to squeeze one more commission out of a corpse, eh?'

Myron let the insult roll off. 'If Clu was clean, his contract would still be valid. You'd owe the family at least three million dollars.'

'So this is a shakedown? You're here for money?'

He glanced at the picture of the young girl again. He remembered the diskette, the laugh, the blood. 'Right now,' he said, 'I'd just like to talk with the team doctor.'

Sophie Mayor looked at him like he was a turd on the carpet. 'Get out of my office, Myron.'

'Will you let me speak to the doctor?'

'You don't have any legal standing here.'

'I think I do.'

'You don't, believe me. The blood money has run dry here. Get out, Myron. Now.'

He took one more look at the photograph. Now was not the time to argue the point. He hurried out the door.

18

Myron was starting to hurt. The Tylenol alone wasn't doing the trick. He had Tylenol with codeine in his back pocket, but he did not dare. He needed to stay sharp, and that stuff put him to sleep faster than, er, sex. He quickly cataloged the sore spots. His sliced-up shin hurt most, followed closely by his bruised ribs. The rest of the aches were an almost welcome distraction. But the pain made him conscious of every movement.

When he got back to his office, Big Cyndi handed him a huge pile of message slips.

'How many reporters have called?' he asked.

'I stopped counting, Mr Bolitar.'

'Any messages from Bruce Taylor?'

'Yes.'

Bruce covered the Mets, not the Yankees. But every reporter wanted in on this story. Bruce was also something of a friend. He would know about Sophie Mayor's daughter. The question was, of course, how to raise the subject without getting him overly curious.

Myron closed his office door, sat down, dialed a number. A voice answered on the first ring.

'Taylor.'

'Hey, Brucie.'

'Myron? Jesus Christ. Hey, I appreciate you calling me back.'

'Sure, Bruce. I love to cooperate with my favorite reporter.'

Pause. Then: 'Uh-oh.'

'What?' Myron said.

'This is too easy.'

'Pardon.'

'Okay, Myron, let's skip the part where you break down my defenses with your supernatural charisma. Cut to it.'

'I want to make a deal.'

'I'm listening.'

'I'm not willing to make a statement yet. But when I do, you get first crack. An exclusive.'

'An exclusive? Sheesh, Myron, you really do know your media lingo, don't you?'

'I could have said scoop. It's one of my favorite words.'

'Okay, Myron, great. So in return for your *not* telling me anything, you get what?'

'Just some information. But you don't read anything into what I ask and you don't report on it. You're just my source.'

'More like your bitch,' Bruce said.

'If that's what you're into.'

'Not today, dear, I have a headache. So let me get this straight. You tell me nothing. I report nothing. In return I get to tell you everything. Sorry, big guy, no deal.'

'Bye-bye, Brucie.'

'Whoa, whoa, Myron, hold up. Christ, I'm not a general manager. Don't pull that negotiating crap on me. Look, let's stop tugging each other's chains here. This is what we do: You give me something. A statement, anything. It can be as innocuous as you want to make it. But I want to be the first with a statement from Myron Bolitar. Then I tell you what you want, I keep quiet, you give me the exclusive scoop or whatever before everyone else. Deal?'

'Deal,' Myron said. 'Here's your statement: Esperanza Diaz did not kill Clu Haid. I stand behind her one hundred percent.'

'Was she having an affair with Clu?'

'That's my statement, Bruce. Period.'

'Okay, fine, but what's this about your being out of the country at the time of the murder?'

'A statement, Bruce. As in, "no further comment." As in, "I'll be answering no questions today." '

'Hey, it's already public knowledge. I just want a confirmation. You were in the Caribbean, right?'

'Right.'

'Where in the Caribbean?'

'No comment.'

'Why not? Were you really in the Cayman Islands?'

'No, I was not in the Caymans.'

'Then where?'

See how reporters work? 'No comment.'

'I called you immediately following Clu's positive drug test. Esperanza said you were in town but would not comment.'

'And I still won't,' Myron said. 'Now it's your turn, Bruce.'

'Come on, Myron, you're giving me nothing here.'

'We had a deal.'

'Yeah, all right, sure, I want to be fair,' he said in a tone that made it clear he would start up again later. 'Ask away.'

Casual, casual. He couldn't just ask about Sophie Mayor's daughter. Subtlety. That was the key. Myron's office door opened, and Win swept into the room. Myron signaled with one finger. Win nodded and opened a closet door. There was a full-length mirror on the inside back. Win stared at his reflection and smiled. A nice way of passing the time.

'What were the rumors about Clu?' Myron asked.

'You mean before the positive test results?'

'Yes.'

'Time bomb,' Bruce said.

'Explain.'

'He was pitching great, no question. And he looked good. Thinned down, seemed focused. But then a week or so before the drug test, he started looking like hell. Christ, you must have seen it, right? Or were you out of the country then too?'

'Just go on, Bruce.'

'What else can I tell you? With Clu you've seen it a hundred times before. The guy breaks your heart. His arm was touched by God. The rest of him was, well, just touched, if you follow my meaning.'

'So there were signs before the positive test?'

'Yeah, I guess. In hindsight, sure there were lots of signs. I hear his wife threw him out. He was unshaven, red-eyed, that kind of thing.'

'It didn't have to be drugs,' Myron said.

'True. It could have been booze.'

'Or maybe it was just the strain of marital discord.'

'Look, Myron, maybe some guys like Orel Hershiser get the benefit of the doubt. But when it comes to Clu Haid or Steve Howe or some other perennial screwup, you figure it's substance abuse, and eleven times out of ten you're right.'

Myron looked over at Win. Win had finished patting the blond locks and was now using the mirror to practice his different smiles. Right now he was working on roguish.

Subtle, Myron reminded himself, subtle . . . 'Bruce?'

'Yeah?'

'What can you tell me about Sophie Mayor?'

'What about her?'

'Nothing specific.'

'Just curious, huh?'

'Right, curious.'

'Sure you are,' Bruce said.

'How much damage did Clu's drug test do to her?'

'Tremendous damage. But you know this. Sophie

Mayor stuck her neck out, and for a while she was a genius. Then Clu fails the drug test, and presto, she's an idiotic bimbo who should let the men run things.'

'So tell me about her background.'

'Background?'

'Yes. I want to get a feel for her.'

'Why?' Bruce asked. Then: 'Ah, what the hell. She's from Kansas, I think, or Iowa or Indiana or Montana. Someplace like that. An aged Ivory Girl type. Loves fishing, hunting, all that nature stuff. She was also something of a math prodigy. Came East to go to MIT. That's where she met Gary Mayor. They got married and lived most of their lives as science professors. He taught at Brandeis; she taught at Tufts. They developed a software program for personal finance in the early eighties and suddenly went from middle-class professors to millionaires. They took the company public in '94 and changed the *m* to a *b*.'

'The *m* to a *b*?'

'Millionaire to billionaire.'

'Oh.'

'So the Mayors did what lots of superwealthy people do: They bought a sports franchise. In this case, the Yankees. Gary Mayor grew up loving them. It was going to be a nice toy for him, but of course he never got to enjoy it.'

Myron cleared his throat. 'And they, uh, have children?' Señor Subtle-o.

'They had two. You know Jared. He's actually a pretty good kid, smart, went to your alma mater Duke. But everyone hates him because he got the job through nepotism. His main responsibility is to keep an eye on Mommy's investment. My understanding is that he's actually pretty good at that and that he leaves the baseball to the baseball guys.'

'Uh-huh.'

'They also have a daughter. Or had a daughter.'

With great effort, Win sighed, closed the closet door. So difficult to pull himself away from a mirror. He sat across from Myron looking, as always, completely at ease. Myron cleared his throat and said into the phone, 'What do you mean, *had* a daughter?'

'The daughter's very estranged. Don't you remember the story?'

'Vaguely. She ran away, right?'

'Right. Her name was Lucy. She took off with a boyfriend, some grunge musician, a few weeks before her eighteenth birthday. This was, I don't know, ten, fifteen years ago. Before the Mayors had any money.'

'So where does she live now?'

'Well, that's the thing. No one knows.'

'I don't understand.'

'She ran away, that much is known for sure. She left them a note, I think. She was going to hit the road with her boyfriend and seek her fortune, the usual teenage stuff. Sophie and Gary Mayor were typical East Coast college professors who read too much Dr Spock, so they gave their daughter "space," figuring of course that she'd come back.'

'But she didn't.'

'Duh.'

'And they never heard from her?'

'Duh again.'

'But I remember reading about this a few years ago. Didn't they start a search for her or something?'

'Yeah. First off, the boyfriend came back after a few months. They'd broken up and gone their separate ways. Big shock, right? Anyway, he didn't know where she went. So the Mayors called the police, but they treated it like no big deal. Lucy was eighteen by this time, and she had clearly run away on her own. There was no evidence of foul play or anything and remember that this was before the Mayors had beaucoup bucks.'

'And after they became rich?'

'Sophie and Gary tried to find her again. They made it like a search for the missing heiress. The tabloids loved it for a while. There were some wild reports but nothing concrete. Some say Lucy moved overseas. Some say she's living on a commune somewhere. Some say she's dead. Whatever. They never found her, and there was still no sign of foul play, so the story eventually petered out.'

Silence. Win looked at Myron and arched an eyebrow. Myron shook his head.

'So why the interest?' Bruce asked.

'I just want to get a feel for the Mayors.'

'Uh-huh.'

'No big deal.'

'Okay, I buy that. Not.'

'It's the truth,' Myron lied. 'And how about using a more up-to-date reference? No one says *not* anymore.'

'They don't?' Pause. 'Guess I gotta watch more MTV. But Vanilla Ice is still hip, right?'

'Ice, ice, baby.'

'Fine, okay, we'll play it your way for now, Myron. But I don't know anything else about Lucy Mayor. You can try a search on Lexis. The papers might have more detail.'

'Good idea, thanks. Listen, Bruce, I got another call coming in.'

'What? You're just going to cut me loose?'

'That was our deal.'

'So why all the questions about the Mayors?'

'Like I said, I want to get a feel for them.'

'Does the phrase *what a crock* mean anything to you?'

'Good-bye, Bruce.'

'Wait.' Pause. Then Bruce said, 'Something serious is going down here, right?'

'Clu Haid has been murdered. Esperanza's been arrested for the crime. I'd say that's pretty serious.'

'There's more to it. Tell me that much. I won't print it, I promise.'

'Truth, Bruce? I don't know yet.'

'And when you do?'

'You'll be the first to know.'

'You really think Esperanza's innocent? Even with all that evidence?'

'Yes.'

'Call me, Myron. If you need anything else. I like Esperanza. I want to help if I can.'

Myron hung up. He looked over at Win. Win seemed in deep thought. He was tapping his chin with his index finger. They sat in silence for several seconds.

Win stopped tapping and asked, 'Whatever happened to the King Family?'

'You mean the ones with the Christmas specials?'

Win nodded. 'Every year you were supposed to watch the King Family Christmas Special. There must have been a hundred of the buggers – big Kings with beards, little Kings in knickers, Mommy Kings, Daddy Kings, Uncle and Aunt and Cousin Kings. Then one year – poof – they're gone. All of them. What happened?'

'I don't know.'

'Strange, isn't it?'

'I guess.'

'And what did the King clan do the rest of the year?'

'Prepared for the next Christmas special?'

'What a life, no?' Win said. 'Christmas passes, and you start thinking about next Christmas. You live in a snow globe of Christmas.'

'I guess.'

'I wonder where they are now, all those suddenly unemployed Kings. Do they sell cars? Insurance? Are they drug dealers? Do they get sad every Christmas?'

'Yeah, poignant point, Win. By the way, did you come down here for a reason?'

'Discussing the King Family isn't reason enough? Weren't you the one who came up to my office because you didn't understand the meaning of a Sheena Easton song?'

'You're comparing the King Family to Sheena Easton?'

'Yes, well, in truth, I came up here to inform you that I quashed the subpoenas against Lock-Horne.'

Myron shouldn't have been surprised. 'The power of payoffs,' he said with a shake of his head. 'It never fails to amaze me.'

'*Payoff* is such an offensive term,' Win said. 'I prefer the more politically correct *assisting the contribution-challenged*.' He sat back, crossed his legs in that way of his, folded his hands on his lap. He gestured at the phone and said, 'Explain.'

So Myron did. He filled him in on everything, especially on the Lucy Mayor incident. When Myron was finished, Win said, 'Puzzling.'

'Agreed.'

'But I am not sure I see a connection.'

'Someone mails me a diskette with Lucy Mayor's image on it and a little while later Clu is murdered. You think that's just a coincidence?'

Win mulled that over. 'Too early to tell,' he concluded. 'Let's do a little recap, shall we?'

'Go ahead.'

'Let's start with a straight time line: Clu gets traded to New York, he pitches well, he gets thrown out by Bonnie, he starts collapsing, he fails a drug test, he desperately searches for you, he comes to me and withdraws two hundred thousand dollars, he strikes Esperanza, he gets murdered.' Win stopped. 'That sound fair?'

'Yes.'

'Now let's explore some possible tangents from this line.'

'Let's.'

'One, our old fraternity chum Billy Lee Palms appears to be missing. Clu purportedly contacted him shortly before the murder. Aside from that, is there any reason to tie Billy Lee into all this?'

'Not really. And according to his mother, Billy Lee isn't the most dependable tool in the shed.'

'So maybe his disappearance has nothing to do with this.'

'Maybe.

'But that would be yet another bizarre coincidence,' Win said.

'It would at that.'

'Fine, let's move on for the moment. Tangent two, this Take A Guess nightspot.'

'All we know is that Clu called them.'

Win shook his head. 'We know a great deal more.'

'For example?'

'They overreacted to your visit. Tossing you out would have been one thing. Roughing you up a bit would have been one thing. But this sort of interrogation complete with knife slashes and electrocution – that's overkill.'

'Meaning?'

'Meaning that you struck a nerve, poked the hive, stirred the nest, choose your favorite cliché.'

'So they're connected into all this.'

'Logical,' Win said, again doing his best Spock.

'How?'

'Heavens, I haven't a clue.'

Myron chewed it over a bit. 'I had thought maybe Clu and Esperanza hooked up there.'

'And now?'

'Let's say they did hook up there. What would be the big deal about that? Why the overkill?'

'So it's something else.'

Myron nodded. 'Any more tangents?'

'The big one,' Win said. 'The disappearance of Lucy Mayor.'

'Which happened more than ten years ago.'

'And we must confess that her connection is tenuous at best.'

'So confessed,' Myron said.

Win steepled his fingers and raised the pointers. 'But the diskette was addressed to you.'

'Yes.'

'Ergo we cannot be sure that Lucy Mayor is connected to Clu Haid at all—'

'Right.'

'—but we can be sure that Lucy Mayor is somehow connected to you.'

'Me?' Myron made a face. 'I can't imagine how.'

'Think hard. Perhaps you met her once.'

Myron shook his head. 'Never.'

'You might not have known. The woman has been living in some sort of clandestine state for a very long time. Perhaps she was someone you met in a bar, a one-night stand.'

'I don't one-night stand.'

'That's right,' Win said. Then with flat eyes: 'God, I wish I were you.'

Myron waved him off. 'But suppose you're right. Suppose I did meet her but didn't know it. So what? She decides to repay me by sending me a diskette of her face melting into a puddle of blood?'

Win nodded. 'Puzzling.'

'So where does that leave us?'

'Puzzled.'

The speaker buzzed. Myron said, 'Yes?'

Big Cyndi said, 'Your father is on line one, Mr Bolitar.'

'Thank you.' Myron picked up the receiver. 'Hi, Dad.'

'Hey, Myron. How are you?'

'Good.'

'You readjusting to being home?'

'Yeah, I am.'

'Happy to be back?'

Dad was stalling. 'Yeah, Dad, I'm great.'

'All this stuff with Esperanza. It must be keeping you hopping, huh?'

'I guess so, yeah.'

'Soooo,' Dad said, stretching out the word, 'think you have time for lunch with your old man?'

There was a strain in the voice.

'Sure, Dad.'

'How about tomorrow? At the club?'

Myron bit back a groan. Not the club. 'Sure. Noon, okay?'

'Good, son, that'll be fine.'

Dad didn't call him son very often. More like never. Myron switched hands. 'Anything wrong, Dad?'

'No, no,' he said too quickly. 'Everything's fine. I just want to talk to you about something.'

'About what?'

'It'll keep, no biggie. See you tomorrow.'

Click.

Myron looked at Win. 'That was my father.'

'Yes, I picked up on that when Big Cyndi said your father was on the line. It was further reemphasized when you said "Dad" four times during the conversation. I'm gifted that way.'

'He wants to have lunch tomorrow.'

Win nodded. 'And I care because—?'

'Just telling you.'

'I'll write about it in my diary tonight,' Win said. 'In the meantime, I had another thought, vis-à-vis Lucy Mayor.'

'I'm listening.'

'If you recall, we were trying to figure out who was being injured in all this.'

'I recall.'

'Clu obviously. Esperanza. You. I.'

'Yes.'

'Well, we must add a new person: Sophie Mayor.'

Myron thought about it. Then he started nodding. 'That could very well be the connection. If you wanted to destroy Sophie Mayor, what would you do? First, you'd do something to undermine any support she had with the Yankee fans and management.'

'Clu Haid,' Win said.

'Right. Then you might hit her in what has to be a vulnerable spot – her missing daughter. I mean, if someone sent her a similar diskette, can you imagine the horror?'

'Which raises an interesting question,' Win said.

'What?'

'Are you going to tell her?'

'About the diskette?'

'No, about recent troop movements in Bosnia. Yes, the diskette.'

Myron thought about it but not for very long. 'I don't see where I have any choice. I have to tell her.'

'Perhaps that too is part of the theoretical plan to wear her down,' Win said. 'Perhaps someone sent you the diskette knowing it would get back to her.'

'Maybe. But she still has the right to know. It's not my place to decide what Sophie Mayor is strong enough to handle.'

'Too true.' Win rose. 'I have some contacts trying to locate the official reports on Clu's murder – autopsy, crime scene, witness statements, labs, what have you. But everyone is tight-lipped.'

'I got a possible source,' Myron said.

'Oh?'

'The Bergen County medical examiner is Sally Li. I know her.'

'Through Jessica's father?'

'Yes.'

'Go for it,' Win said.

Myron watched him head for the door. 'Win?'

'Yes?'

'You have any thoughts on how I should break the news to Sophie Mayor?'

'None whatsoever.'

Win left then. Myron stared at the phone. He picked it up and dialed Sophie Mayor's phone number. It took some time, but a secretary finally patched him through to her. Sophie sounded less than thrilled to hear his voice.

She opened sharply. 'What?'

'We need to talk,' Myron said. There was distortion on the line. A cell or car phone probably.

'We already talked.'

'This is different.'

Silence. Then: 'I'm in the car right now, about a mile from my house out on the Island. How important is this?'

Myron picked up a pen. 'Give me your address,' he said. 'I'll be right over.'

19

On the street the man was still reading a newspaper.

Myron's elevator trip down to the lobby featured mucho stops. Not atypical. No one spoke, of course, everyone busying themselves by staring up at the descending flashing numbers as though awaiting a UFO landing. In the lobby he joined the stream of suits and flowed out onto Park Avenue, salmons fighting upstream against the tide until, well, they died. Many of the suits walked with heads high, their expressions kick-ass-runway-model; others walked with backs bent, flesh versions of the statue on Fifth Avenue of Atlas carrying the world on his shoulders, but for them the world was simply too heavy.

Whoa, again with the deep.

Perfectly situated on the corner of Forty-sixth and Park, standing reading a newspaper but positioned in such a way as to watch all entering or leaving the Lock-Horne building, was the same man Myron had noticed standing there when he entered.

Hmm.

Myron took out his cell phone and hit the programmed button.

'Articulate,' Win said.

'I think I got a tail.'

'Hold please.' Maybe ten seconds passed. Then: 'The newspaper on the corner.'

Win keeps a variety of telescopes and binoculars in his office. Don't ask.

'Yep.'

'Good Lord,' Win said. 'Could he be any more obvious?'

'Doubt it.'

'Where's the pride in his work? Where's the professionalism?'

'Sad.'

'That, my friend, is the whole problem with this country.'

'Bad tails?'

'It's an example. Look at him. Does anybody really stand on a street corner and read a newspaper like that? He might as well cut out two eyeholes.'

'Uh-huh,' Myron said. 'You got some free time?'

'But of course. How would you like to play it?'

'Back me up,' Myron said.

'Give me five.'

Myron waited five minutes. He stood there and studiously avoided looking at the tail. He checked his watch and huffed a bit as though he expected someone and was getting impatient. When the five minutes passed, Myron walked straight over to the tail.

The tail spotted his approach and ducked into the newspaper.

Myron kept walking until he stood directly next to the tail. The tail kept his face in the newspaper. Myron gave him Smile 8. Big and toothy. A televangelist being handed a hefty check. Early Wink Martindale. The tail kept his eyes on the newspaper. Myron kept smiling, his eyes wide as a clown's. The tail ignored him. Myron inched closer, leaned his *über*-wattage smile within inches of the tail's face, wriggled his eyebrows.

The tail snapped closed the newspaper and sighed. 'Fine, hotshot, you made me. Congratulations.'

Still with the Wink Martindale smile: 'And thank you for playing our game! But don't worry, we won't let you go home empty-handed! You get the home version of

Incompetent Tail and a year's subscription to *Modern Doofus.*'

'Yeah, right, see you around.'

'Wait! Final *Jeopardy!* round. Answer: He or she hired you to follow me.'

'Bite me.'

'Ooo, sorry, you needed to put that in the form of a question.'

The tail started walking away. When he looked back, Myron gave him the smile and a big wave. 'This has been a Mark Goodson-Bill Todman production. Good-bye, everybody!' More waving.

The tail shook his head and continued down the street, joining another stream of people. Lots of people in this stream; Win happened to be one of them. The tail would probably find a clearing and then call his boss. Win would listen in and learn all. What a plan.

Myron headed to his rented car. He circled the block once. No more tails. At least none as obvious as the last. No matter. He was driving out to the Mayor estate on Long Island. It didn't much matter if anyone knew.

He spent his time in the car working on the cell phone. He had two arena football players – indoor football on a smaller field, for those who don't know – both of whom were hoping to scratch a bench spot on an NFL roster before the waiver wire closed down. Myron called teams, but nobody was interested. Lots of people asked him about the murder. He brushed them off. He knew his efforts were fairly futile, but he stuck to it. Big of him. He tried concentrating on his work, tried to lose himself in the numb bliss of what he did for a living. But the world kept creeping in. He thought about Esperanza in jail. He thought about Jessica in California. He thought about Bonnie Haid and her fatherless boys at home. He thought about Clu in formaldehyde. He thought about his father's phone call. And strangely, he kept thinking about Terese alone on that island.

He blocked out the rest.

When he reached Muttontown, a section of Long Island that had somehow escaped him in the past, he turned right onto a heavily wooded road. He drove about two miles, passing maybe three driveways. He finally reached a simple iron gate with a small sign that read THE MAYORS. There were several security cameras and an intercom. He pressed the button. A woman's voice came on and said, 'May I help you?'

'Myron Bolitar to see Sophie Mayor.'

'Please drive up. Park in front of the house.'

The gate opened. Myron drove up a rather steep hill. Tall hedges lined both sides of the driveway, giving the aura of being a rat in a maze. He spotted a few more security cameras. No sign of the house yet. When he reached the top of the hill, he hit upon a clearing. There was a slightly overgrown grass tennis court and croquet field. Very Norma Desmond. He made another turn. The house was dead straight ahead. It was a mansion, of course, though not as huge as some Myron had seen. Vines clung to pale yellow stucco. The windows looked leaded. The whole scene screamed Roaring Twenties. Myron half expected Scott and Zelda to pull up behind him in a slick roadster.

This part of the driveway was made up of small loose pebbles rather than pavement. His tires crunched them as he drew closer. There was a fountain in the middle of the circular drive, about fifteen feet in front of the door. Neptune stood naked with a triton in his hand. The fountain, Myron realized, was a smaller version of the one in the Piazza della Signoria in Florence. Water spouted up but not very high or with much enthusiasm, as if someone had set the water pressure on 'light urination.'

Myron parked the car. There was a perfectly square swimming pool on his right, complete with lily pads floating on the top. A poor man's Giverny. There were statues in the gardens, again something from old Italy or Greece or the like. Venus de Milo-like except with all the limbs.

He got out of the car and stopped. He thought about what he was about to unearth, and for a brief moment he considered turning back. *How*, he wondered again, *do I tell this woman about her missing daughter melting on a computer diskette?*

No answer came to him.

The door opened. A woman in casual clothes led him through a corridor and into a large room with high tin ceilings and lots of windows and a semidisappointing view of more white statues and woods. The interior was art deco, but it didn't try too hard. Nice. Except, of course, for the hunting trophies. Taxidermy birds of some sort sat on the shelves. The birds looked upset. Probably were. Who could blame them?

Myron turned and stared at a mounted deer. He waited for Sophie Mayor. The deer waited too. The deer seemed very patient.

'Go ahead,' a voice said.

Myron turned around. It was Sophie Mayor. She was wearing dirt-smeared jeans and a plaid shirt, the very essence of the weekend botanist.

Never short of a witty opening gambit, Myron countered, 'Go ahead and what?'

'Make the snide remark about hunting.'

'I didn't say anything.'

'Come, come, Myron. Don't you think hunting is barbaric?'

Myron shrugged. 'I never really thought about it.' Not true, but what the hey.

'But you don't approve, do you?'

'Not my place to approve.'

'How tolerant.' She smiled. 'But you of course would never do it, am I right?'

'Hunt? No, it's not for me.'

'You think it's inhumane.' She gestured with her chin to the mounted deer. 'Killing Bambi's mother and all.'

'It's just not for me.'

'I see. Are you a vegetarian?'

'I don't eat much red meat,' Myron said.

'I'm not talking about your health. Do you ever eat any dead animals?'

'Yes.'

'So do you think it's more humane to kill, say, a chicken or a cow than it is to kill a deer?'

'No.'

'Do you know what kind of awful torture that cow goes through before it's slaughtered?'

'For food,' Myron said.

'Pardon?'

'Slaughtered for food.'

'I eat what I kill, Myron. Your friend up there' – she nodded to the patient deer – 'she was gutted and eaten. Feel better?'

Myron thought about that. 'Uh, we're not having lunch, are we?'

That got a small chuckle. 'I won't go into the whole food chain argument,' Sophie Mayor said. 'But God created a world where the only way to survive is to kill. Period. We all kill. Even the strict vegetarians have to plow fields. You don't think plowing kills small animals and insects?'

'I never really thought about it.'

'Hunting is just more hands-on, more honest. When you sit down and eat an animal, you have no appreciation for the process, for the sacrifice made so that you could survive. You let someone else do the killing. You're above even thinking about it. When I eat an animal, I have a fuller understanding. I don't do it casually. I don't depersonalize it.'

'Okay,' Myron said, 'while we're on the subject, what about those hunters who don't kill for food?'

'Most do eat what they kill.'

'But what about those who kill for sport? I mean, isn't that part of it?'

'Yes.'

'So what about that? What about killing merely for sport?'

'As opposed to what, Myron? Killing for a pair of shoes? Or a nice coat? Is spending a full day outdoors, coming to understand how nature works and appreciating her bountiful glory, is that worth any less than a leather pocketbook? If it's worth killing an animal because you prefer your belt made of animal skin instead of something man-made, is it not worth killing one because you simply enjoy the thrill of it?'

He said nothing.

'I'm sorry to ride you about this. But the hypocrisy of it all drives me somewhat batty. Everyone wants to save the whale, but what about the thousands of fish and shrimp a whale eats each day? Are their lives worthless because they aren't as cute? Ever notice how no one ever wants to save ugly animals? And the same people who think hunting is barbaric put up special fences so the deer can't eat their precious gardens. So the deer overpopulate and die of starvation. Is that better? And don't even get me started on those so-called ecofeminists. Men hunt, they say, but women are too genteel. Of all the sexist nonsense. They want to be environmentalists? They want to stay as close to a state of nature as possible? Then understand the one universal truth about nature: You either kill or you die.'

They both turned and stared at the deer for a moment. Proof positive.

'You didn't come here for a lecture,' she said.

Myron had welcomed this delay. But the time had come. 'No, ma'am.'

'Ma'am?' Sophie Mayor chuckled without a hint of humor. 'That sounds grim, Myron.'

Myron turned and looked at her. She met his gaze and held it.

'Call me Sophie,' she said.

He nodded. 'Can I ask you a very personal, maybe hurtful question, Sophie?'

'You can try.'

'Have you heard anything from your daughter since she ran away?'

'No.'

The answer came fast. Her gaze remained steady, her voice strong. But her face was losing color.

'Then you have no idea where she is?'

'No idea.'

'Or even if she's . . .'

'Alive or dead,' she finished for him. 'None.'

Her voice was so monotone it seemed on the verge of a scream. There was a quaking near her mouth now, a fault line starting to give way. Sophie Mayor stood and waited for his explanation, afraid perhaps to say any more.

'I got a diskette in the mail,' he began.

She frowned. 'What?'

'A computer diskette. It came in the mail. I put it in my A drive, and it just started up. I didn't have to hit any keys.'

'Self-starting program,' she said, suddenly the computer expert. 'That's not complicated technology.'

Myron cleared his throat. 'A graphic came on. It started out as a photograph of your daughter.'

Sophie Mayor took a step back.

'It was the same photograph that's in your office. On the right side of the credenza.'

'That was Lucy's junior year of high school,' she said. 'The school portrait.'

Myron nodded, though he didn't know why. 'After a few seconds her image started melting on the screen.'

'Melting?'

'Yes. It sort of dissolved into a puddle of, uh, blood. Then a sound came on. A teenage girl laughing, I think.'

Sophie Mayor's eyes were glistening now. 'I don't understand.'

'Neither do I.'

'This came in the mail?'

'Yes.'

'On a floppy disk?'

'Yes,' Myron said. Then he added for no reason: 'A three-and-a-half-inch floppy.'

'When?'

'It arrived in my office about two weeks ago.'

'Why did you wait so long to tell me?' She put a hand up. 'Oh, wait. You were out of the country.'

'Yes.'

'So when did you first see it?'

'Yesterday.'

'But you saw me this morning. Why didn't you tell me then?'

'I didn't know who the girl was. Not at first anyway. Then when I was in your office, I saw the photograph on the credenza. I got confused. I wasn't sure what to say.'

She nodded slowly. 'So that explains your abrupt departure.'

'Yes. I'm sorry.'

'Do you have the diskette? My people will analyze it.'

He reached into his pocket and withdrew it. 'I don't think it'll be any help.'

'Why not?'

'I took it to a police lab. They said it automatically reformatted itself.'

'So the diskette is blank?'

'Yes.'

It was as though her muscles had suddenly decided to flee the district. Sophie Mayor's legs gave way. She dropped to a chair. Her head lolled into her hands. Myron waited. There were no sounds. She just sat there, head in hands. When she looked up again, the gray eyes were tinged with red.

'You said something about a police lab.'

He nodded.

'You used to work in law enforcement.'

'Not really.'

'I remember Clip Arnstein saying something about it.'

Myron said nothing. Clip Arnstein was the man who had drafted Myron in the first round for the Boston Celtics. He also had a big mouth.

'You helped Clip when Greg Downing vanished,' she continued.

'Yes.'

'I've been hiring private investigators to search for Lucy for years. Supposedly the best in the world. Sometimes we seem to get close but ... ' Her voice drifted off, her eyes far away. She looked at the diskette in her hand as if it had suddenly materialized there. 'Why would someone send this to you?'

'I don't know.'

'Did you know my daughter?'

'No.'

Sophie took a couple of careful breaths. 'I want to show you something. Wait here a minute.' It took maybe half that time. Myron had just begun to stare into the eyes of some dead bird, noting with some dismay how closely they resembled the eyes of some human beings he

178

knew, and Sophie was back. She handed him a sheet of paper.

Myron looked at it. It was an artist's rendering of a woman nearing thirty years of age.

'It's from MIT,' she explained. 'My alma mater. A scientist there has developed a software package that helps with age progression. For missing people. So you can see what they might look like today. He made this up for me a few months ago.'

Myron looked at the image of what the teenage Lucy might look like as a woman heading toward thirty. The effect was nothing short of startling. Oh, it looked like her, he guessed, but talk about ghosts, talk about life being a series of what-ifs, talk about the years slipping away and then smacking you in the face. Myron stared at the image, at the more conservative haircut, the small frown lines. How painful must it be for Sophie Mayor to look at this?

'Does she look familiar at all?' Sophie asked.

Myron shook his head. 'No, I'm sorry.'

'You're sure?'

'As sure as you can be in these situations.'

'Will you help me find her?'

He wasn't sure how to answer. 'I can't see how I can help.'

'Clip said you're good at these things.'

'I'm not. But even if I were, I can't see what I can do. You've hired experts already. You have the cops—'

'The police have been useless. They view Lucy as a runaway, period.'

Myron said nothing.

'Do you think it's hopeless?' she asked.

'I don't know enough about it.'

'She was a good girl, you know.' Sophie Mayor smiled at him, her eyes misty with time travel. 'Headstrong, sure. Too adventurous for her own good. But then again I raised Lucy to be independent. The police. They think she was simply a troubled kid. She wasn't. Just confused. Who isn't at that age? And it wasn't as if she ran off in the middle of the night without telling anyone.'

Against his better judgment Myron asked, 'Then what happened?'

'Lucy was a teenager, Myron. She was sullen and unhappy, and she didn't fit in. Her parents were college math professors and computer geeks. Her younger brother was considered a genius. She hated school. She wanted to see the world and live on the road. She had the whole rock 'n' roll fantasy. One day she told us she was going off with Owen.'

'Owen was her boyfriend?'

She nodded. 'An average musician who fronted a garage band, certain that his immense talent was being held back by them.' She made a lemon-sucking face. 'They wanted to run off and get a record deal and become famous. So Gary and I said okay. Lucy was like a wild bird trapped in a small cage. She wouldn't stop flapping her wings no matter what we did. Gary and I felt we had no choice in the matter. We even thought it might be good for her. Lots of her classmates were backpacking through Europe. What was the difference?'

She stopped and looked up at him. Myron waited. When she didn't say anything, he said, 'And?'

'And we never heard from her again.'

Silence.

She turned back to the mounted deer. The deer looked back at her with something akin, it seemed, to pity.

Myron said, 'But Owen came back, right?'

'Yes.' She was still staring at the deer. 'He's a car salesman in New Jersey. He plays in a wedding band on weekends. Can you imagine? He dresses up in a cheap tuxedo and belts out "Tie a Yellow Ribbon" and "Celebration" and introduces the bridal party.' She shook her head at the irony. 'When Owen came back, the police questioned him, but he didn't know anything. Their story was so typical: They went out to Los Angeles, failed miserably, started fighting, and broke up after six months. Owen stayed out there another three months, certain this time it had been Lucy who was holding back his immense talent. When he failed again, he came back home with his tail between his legs. He said he hadn't seen Lucy since their breakup.'

'The police checked it out?'

'So they said. But it was a dead end.'

'Do you suspect Owen?'

'No,' she said bitterly. 'He's too big a nothing.'

'Have there been any solid leads at all?'

'Solid?' She thought about it. 'Not really. Several of the investigators we've hired think she joined a cult.'

Myron made a face. 'A cult?'

'Her personality fit the profile, they said. Despite my attempts to make her independent, they claim she was just the opposite – someone needing guidance, alone, suggestible, alienated from friends and family.'

'I don't agree,' Myron said.

She looked at him. 'You said you never met Lucy.'

'The psychological profile may be right, but I doubt she's with a cult.'

'What makes you say that?'

'Cults like money. Lucy Mayor is the daughter of an extraordinarily wealthy family. Maybe you didn't have money when she first would have joined, but believe me, they'd know about you by now. And they would have been in touch, if for no other reason than to extort vast sums.'

She started blinking again. Her eyes closed, and she turned her back to him. Myron took a step forward and then stopped, not sure what to do. He chose discretion, kept his distance, waited.

'The not knowing,' Sophie Mayor said after some time had passed. 'It gnaws at you. All day, all night, for twelve years. It never stops. It never goes away. When my husband's heart gave out, everyone was so shocked. Such a healthy man, they said. So young. Even now I don't know how I'll get through the day without him. But we rarely spoke about Lucy after she disappeared. We just lay in bed at night and pretended that the other one was asleep and stared at the ceiling and imagined all the horrors only parents with missing children can conjure up.'

More silence.

Myron had no idea what to say. But the silence was growing so thick he could barely breathe. 'I'm sorry,' he said.

She didn't look up.

'I'll go to the police,' he said. 'Tell them about the diskette.'

'What good will that do?'

'They'll investigate.'

'They already have. I told you. They think she's a runaway.'

'But now we have this new evidence. They'll take the case more seriously. I can even go to the media. It'll jump-start their coverage.'

She shook her head. Myron waited. She stood and wiped her palms on the thighs of her jeans. 'The diskette,' she said, 'was sent to you.'

'Yes.'

'Addressed to you.'

'Yes.'

'So,' she said, 'someone is reaching out to you.'

Win had said something similar. 'You don't know that,' Myron said. 'I don't want to douse your hopes, but it could be nothing more than a prank.'

'It's not a prank.'

'You can't be sure.'

'If it was a prank, it would have been sent to me. Or Jared. Or someone who knew her. It wasn't. It was sent to you. Someone is reaching out to you specifically. It might even be Lucy.'

He took a deep breath. 'Again I don't want to douse your—'

'Don't patronize me, Myron. Just say what you want to say.'

'Okay ... if it were Lucy, why would she send an image of herself melting into a puddle of blood?'

Sophie Mayor did not wince, but she came close. 'I don't know. Maybe you're right. Maybe it's not her. Maybe it's her killer. Either way, they're seeking *you* out. It's the first solid lead in years. And if we make it loud and public, I fear that whoever sent this will go back into hiding. I can't risk that.'

'I don't know what I can do,' Myron said.

'I'll pay you whatever you want. Name a price. A hundred thousand? A million?'

'It's not the money. I just don't see where I can help.'

'You can investigate.'

He shook his head. 'My best friend and business partner is in jail for murder. My client was shot in his own home. I have other clients who rely on me for their job security.'

'I see,' she said. 'So you don't have time, is that it?'

'It's not a question of time. I really have nothing to go on. No clue, no connection, no source. There's nothing to start with here.'

Her eyes pinned him down. 'You can start with you. You're my clue, my connection, my source.' She reached out and took his hand. Her flesh was cold and hard. 'All I'm asking is that you look closer.'

'At what?'

'Maybe,' she said, 'at yourself.'

Silence. They stood there, she holding his hand.

'That sounds good, Sophie, but I'm not sure what it means.'

'You don't have children, do you?'

'No,' Myron said. 'But that doesn't mean I don't sympathize.'

'So let me ask you, Myron: What would you do if you were me? What would you do if the first real clue in ten years just walked in your door?'

'The same thing you're doing.'

So under the mounted deer, he told her he would keep his eyes open. He told her he would think about it. He told her he would try to figure out the connection.

20

Back at the office Myron strapped on the Ultra Slim phone headset and started making phone calls. Very Jerry Maguire. Not just in appearance but in the fact that clients were abandoning him left and right. And he hadn't even written a mission statement.

Win called. 'Newspaper Tail's name is Wayne Tunis. He lives in Staten Island and works in construction. He placed one call to a John McClain, telling him that he had been spotted. That's it. They're pretty careful.'

'So we don't yet know who hired him?'

'That would be correct.'

'When in doubt,' Myron said, 'we should go with the obvious choice.'

'Young FJ?'

'Who else? He's been following me for months.'

'Course of action?'

'I'd like to get him off my back.'

'May I recommend a well-placed bullet through the back of the skull?'

'We've got enough problems without adding one more.'

'Fine. Course of action?'

'We confront him.'

'He usually hangs out at a Starbucks on Forty-ninth Street,' Win said.

'Starbucks?'

'The old mob espresso bars have gone the way of leisure suits and disco music.'

'Both of them are coming back.'

'No,' Win said, 'bizarre mutations of them are coming back.'

'Like coffee bars in place of espresso bars?'

'Then you understand.'

'So let's pay FJ a visit.'

'Give me twenty minutes,' Win said before hanging up.

As soon as Myron hit the disconnect, Big Cyndi buzzed his line.

'Mr Bolitar?'

'Yes?'

'A Miss or Mr Thrill is on the phone,' Big Cyndi said.

Myron closed his eyes. 'You mean from last night?'

'Unless you know someone else named Thrill, Mr Bolitar.'

'Take a message.'

'Both her words and tone suggest urgency, Mr Bolitar.'

Suggest urgency? 'Fine. Patch her – or him – through.'

'Yes, Mr Bolitar.'

There was a click.

'Myron?'

'Uh, yeah, hi, Thrill.'

'That was some exit you made last night, big fella,' Thrill said. 'You really know how to impress a girl.'

'Yeah, I usually don't jump through a plate glass window until the second date.'

'So how come you haven't called me?'

'I've been really busy.'

'I'm downstairs,' Thrill said. 'Tell the guard to let me up.'

'It's not a good time. Like I said before—'

'Men rarely say no to Thrill. I must be losing my touch.'

'It's not that,' he said. 'It's just that the timing is all wrong.'

'Myron, my name isn't really Thrill.'

186

'I hate to burst your bubble, but I kinda suspected it read something else on your birth certificate.'

'No, that's not what I mean. Look, let me up. We need to talk about last night. About something that happened after you left.'

So he shrugged and called down to the guard at the front desk and told him to let up anyone identifying themselves as Thrill. The guard was puzzled but said okay. The headset was still strapped on so Myron speed-dialed a sports apparel company. Before dashing to the Caribbean, Myron had been on the verge of landing a sneaker deal for a track and field client with said company. But now he was being put on hold. An assistant to an assistant finally came on the line. Myron asked him about the deal. It had fallen through, he was told. Why? he asked.

'Ask your client,' the assistant said. 'Oh, and ask his new agent too.'

Click.

Myron closed his eyes and pulled off his headset. Damn.

There was a knock on his office door. The alien sound caused a ripple of pain. Esperanza had never knocked. Never. She prided herself on interrupting him. She would sooner give up a limb than knock.

'Come in.'

The door opened. Someone stepped inside and said, 'Surprise.'

Myron tried not to stare. He took off the headset. 'You're . . . ?'

'Thrill, yup.'

Nothing was the same. Gone was the Cat Woman costume, the blond wig, the high heels, the, uh, prodigious bosom. Thrill was still female, thank heavens. Still quite attractive in her conservative navy suit with matching blouse, her hair done in a pixie style, her eyes

187

less luminous behind round tortoiseshell glasses, her makeup now applied with a far lighter hand. Her figure was thinner, more toned, less, uh, shapely. Nothing to complain about, mind you. Just different.

'To answer your first question,' she said, 'when I dress like Thrill, I wear the aptly named Raquel Wonder Breast Enhancements.'

Myron nodded. 'That the stuff that looks like flattened Silly Putty?'

'The very. You jam them in your bra. Guess you've seen the infomercial on TV.'

'Seen it? I bought the video.'

Thrill laughed. Last night her laugh – not to mention her walk, her movements, her tone of voice, her choice of words – had been a double entendre. In the light of day the sound was melodic and almost childlike.

'I also strap on the aptly named Miracle Bra,' she continued. 'To lift it all up high.'

'Any higher,' Myron said, 'and they could have doubled as earrings.'

'Too true,' she said. 'The legs and ass, however, are mine. And for the record, I do not have a penis.'

'So noted.'

'Can I sit down?'

Myron looked at his watch. 'I hate to be a pest—'

'You'll want to hear this, believe me.' She sat in the chair in front of his desk. Myron folded his arms and leaned his butt on the desk's lip. 'My real name is Nancy Sinclair. I don't dress like Thrill for kicks. I'm a journalist, and I'm doing a story on Take A Guess. An insider's look at what goes on, what kind of people go there, what makes them tick. In order to get people to open up, I go undercover as Thrill.'

'So you do all this for a story?'

'I do all what?'

'Dress up and, uh . . .' His gestures were unintelligible.

'Not that I see where it's even vaguely any of your concern, but the answer is no. I dress a part. I strike up conversations. I flirt. Period. I like to watch people's reaction to me.'

'Oh.' Then Myron cleared his throat and said, 'Just, uh, out of curiosity, I'm not going to be in your story, am I? I mean, I've really never been there before and I was—'

'Relax. I recognized you as soon as you came in the door.'

'You did?'

'I follow basketball. I got season tickets to the Dragons.'

'I see.' The Dragons were New Jersey's pro basketball team. Myron had tried a comeback with them not long ago.

'That's why I approached you.'

'To see if I was into, uh, gender ambiguity?'

'Everyone else there is. Why not you?'

'But I explained to you that I was there to ask about someone.'

'Clu Haid, right. Still, your reaction to me was interesting.'

'I found you to be a witty conversationalist,' Myron said.

'Uh-huh.'

'And I also have a Julie-Newmar-as-Cat-Woman fetish.'

'You'd be surprised how many people have that same fetish.'

'No, I don't think I would be,' Myron said. 'So why are you here, Nancy?'

'Pat saw us talking last night.'

'The bartender?'

'He's also one of the owners. He has shares in a couple of places in the city.'

'And?'

'And after the smoke cleared from your exit, Pat pulled me aside.'

'Because he saw us talking?'

'Because he saw me giving you my phone number.'

'So?'

'So I'd never done that before.'

'I'm flattered.'

'Don't be. I'm just making a point. I come on to a ton of girls and guys and whatever in there. But I never give out a phone number.'

'So why did you give it to me?'

'Because I was curious to see if you'd call. You rebuffed Thrill, so you clearly weren't there for sex. I wondered what you were up to.'

Myron frowned. 'That was the only reason?'

'Yes.'

'Nothing about my rugged good looks and brawny body?'

'Oh, yeah. I almost forgot.'

'So what did Pat want?'

'He wants me to bring you to another club tonight.'

'Tonight?'

'Yes.'

'How did he know I'd call?'

Again the smile. 'Nancy Sinclair might not guarantee an immediate phone call . . .'

'But Thrill does?'

'Bosoms are empowerment. And if you didn't, he told me I could look up your business number in the phone book.'

'Which is what you did.'

'Yes. He also promised me you wouldn't be hurt.'

'How comforting. And your interest in all this?'

'Isn't it obvious? A story. The Clu Haid murder is huge news. Now you're tying this week's murder-of-the-century to a kinky New York nightclub.'

'I don't think I can help you.'

'Cow dooky.'

'Cow dooky?'

She shrugged.

'What else did Pat say to you?' Myron asked.

'Nothing much. He just said that he wanted to talk.'

'If he wanted to talk, he could have looked up my phone number too.'

'Thrill, not the brightest bulb on the tree, didn't pick up on that.'

'But Nancy Sinclair did.'

She smiled again. It was a damn nice smile. 'Pat was also huddled up with Zorra.'

'Who?'

'That's their psycho bouncer. A cross-dresser with a blond wig.'

'Like Veronica Lake?'

She nodded. 'He's absolutely nuts. Lift up your shirt.'

'Pardon?'

'He can do anything with that razor heel. His favorite is a Z slash on the right side. You were in the back room with him.'

Made sense. Myron hadn't made him miss. Zorra – *Zorra?* – just wanted to brand him. 'I have one.'

'He's seriously whacked out. Did some sort of stuff in the Persian Gulf War. Undercover. Worked for the Israelis too. There are all kinds of rumors about him, but if five percent of the stories I've heard are true, he's killed dozens.'

Just what he needed – Cross-Dressing Mossad. 'Did they talk about Clu at all?'

'No. But Pat said something about your trying to kill somebody.'

'Me?'

'Yes.'

'They think I killed Clu?'

'I don't think so. It sounded more like they thought you were at the club to find someone and kill him.'

'Who?'

'No idea. They just said you were out to kill him.'

'They didn't say who?'

'If they did, I didn't hear them.' She smiled. 'So do we have a date?'

'Guess so.'

'You're not scared?'

'I'll have backup.'

'Someone good?'

Myron nodded. 'Oh, yeah.'

'Then I better go home and strap up my breasts.'

'Need any help?'

'My hero. But no, Myron, I think I can handle it myself.'

'And if you can't?'

'I have your phone number,' she said. 'See you tonight.'

21

Win frowned. 'Nonsurgical breast enhancements?'

'Yes. They're an accessory of some sort.'

'An accessory? Like a matching pocketbook?'

'In a way.' Then thinking about it, Myron added, 'But they're probably more noticeable.'

Win showed him the flat eyes. Myron shrugged.

'False advertising,' Win said.

'Pardon?'

'Breast enhancements. It's false advertising. There should be a law.'

'Right, Win. But the politicians in Washington – where are they when it comes to the real issues?'

'Then you understand.'

'I understand that you're a snorting pig.'

'A thousand pardons, Oh, Enlightened One.' Win put a hand to his ear and tilted his head to the side. 'Tell me again, Myron: What first attracted you to this Thrill?'

'The catsuit,' Myron said.

'I see. So if, say, Big Cyndi came into the office in the catsuit—'

'Hey, c'mon, I just ate a muffin.'

'Exactly.'

'Fine, I'm a pig too. Happy?'

'Yes, ecstatic. And perhaps you misread me. Perhaps I wish to outlaw such accessories because of what they do to a woman's self-esteem. Perhaps I tire of a society that forces unobtainable beauty on a woman – size four dresses with D cups.'

'The key word here being *perhaps*.'

Win smiled. 'Love me for all my faults.'

'What else is there?'

Win adjusted his tie. 'FJ and the two oversized hormonal glands that guard him are at Starbucks. Shall we?'

'Let's. Then I want to head over to Yankee Stadium. I need to question a couple of folks.'

'Sounds almost like a plan,' Win said.

They strolled up Park Avenue. The light changed, and they waited at the corner. Myron stood next to a man in a business suit talking on a cell phone. Nothing unusual about that, except the man was having phone sex. He was actually rubbing his, uh, nether parts and saying into the phone, 'Yeah, baby, like that,' and other stuff not worth repeating. The light changed. The man crossed, still rubbing and talking. Talk about I Love New York.

'About tonight,' Win said.

'Yes.'

'You trust this Thrill?'

'She checks out.'

'There is of course a chance that they'll just shoot you when you show up.'

'I doubt it. This Pat is part owner. He wouldn't want the trouble in his own place.'

'So you think they're extending this invitation to buy you a drink?'

'Could be,' Myron said. 'With my preference-crossing animal magnetism, I'm considered something of a tasty morsel to the swinger set.'

Win chose not to argue.

They headed east on Forty-ninth Street. The Starbucks was four blocks up on the right. When they arrived, Win signaled for Myron to wait. He leaned in and took a quick peek through the glass before backing away. 'Young FJ is at a table with someone,' Win reported.

'Hans and Franz are two tables over. Only one other table is occupied.'

Myron nodded. 'Shall we?'

'You first,' Win said. 'Let me trail.'

Myron had stopped questioning Win's methods a long time ago. He immediately stepped inside and headed toward FJ's table. Hans and Franz, the Mr Universe Bookends, were still wearing the tank tops and the semipajama pants smeared with a pattern that resembled melted paisley. They bolted upright when Myron entered, fingers tightened into fists, necks in midcrack.

FJ was decked out in a light herringbone sports coat, collared shirt buttoned all the way to the top, cuffed pants, and Cole-Haan tasseled loafers. Too natty for words. He spotted Myron and raised his hand in the bruisers' direction. Hans and Franz froze.

'Hi, FJ,' Myron said.

FJ was sipping something foamy; it kinda looked like shaving cream. 'Ah, Myron,' he said with what he must have been sure was *savoir faire*. He gestured at his table companion. His companion got up without a word and scooted toward the exit like a scared gerbil. 'Please, Myron, join me. This is such a strange coincidence.'

'Oh?'

'You saved me a trip. I was just going to pay you a visit.' FJ tossed Myron the snake smile. Myron let it land on the floor and watched it slither away. 'I guess it's kismet, huh, Myron? Your coming here. Pure kismet.'

FJ cracked up at that. Hans and Franz laughed too.

'Kismet,' Myron repeated. 'Good one.'

FJ waved a modest hand as if to say, *I got a million like that.* 'Please sit, Myron.'

Myron pulled out a chair.

'Care for a drink?'

'An iced latte would be fine. Grande, skim, with a dash of vanilla.'

FJ motioned to the guy working behind the coffee bar. 'He's new,' FJ confided.

'Who?'

'The guy working the espresso machine. The last guy who worked here made a wonderful latte. But he quit for moral reasons.'

'Moral reasons?'

'They started selling Kenny G CDs,' FJ said. 'Suddenly he couldn't sleep at night. It was tearing him apart. Suppose an impressionable kid bought one? How could he live with himself? Pushing caffeine was okay. But Kenny G . . . the man had scruples.'

Myron said, 'Commendable.'

Win chose that moment to enter. FJ spotted him and looked over at Hans and Franz. Win did not hesitate. He beelined straight toward FJ's table. Hans and Franz went to work. They stepped in Win's path and expanded their chests to dimensions large enough to apply for a parking permit. Win kept walking. Both men wore turtlenecks so high and loose they looked like something awaiting circumcision.

Hans managed a smirk. 'You Win?'

'Yes,' Win said, 'me Win.'

'You don't look so tough.' Hans looked at Franz. 'He look tough to you, Keith?'

Keith said, 'Not so tough.'

Win did not break stride. Almost casually and without the slightest warning, he struck Hans with the knife-edge of his hand behind the ear. Hans's whole body stiffened and then collapsed as though someone had ripped the skeleton out of him. Franz gaped at the sight. But not for long. In the same motion Win pirouetted and struck Franz in the oft vulnerable throat. An awful gurgling noise shot out of Franz's lips, as though he were choking on a slew of small bones. Win reached for the carotid artery, found it, and squeezed with his pointer and thumb. Franz's eyes closed, and he too slid into Nighty-Night Land.

The couple at the other table exited quickly. Win smiled down at the unconscious bruisers. Then he glanced at Myron. Myron shook his head. Win shrugged and turned to the guy manning the coffee bar.

'Barista,' Win said. 'One caffe mocha.'

'What size?'

'Grande, please.'

'Skim or whole milk?'

'Skim. I'm watching my figure.'

'Right away.'

Win joined Myron and FJ. He sat and crossed his legs. 'Nice sports coat, FJ.'

'Glad you like it, Win.'

'It really brings out the demonic red in your eyes.'

'Thank you.'

'So where were we?'

Myron played along. 'I was just about to tell FJ that I'm getting a little tired of the tail.'

'And I was just about to tell Myron that I'm getting tired of him meddling into my affairs,' FJ said.

Myron looked at Win. 'Meddling? Does anybody really use that word anymore?'

Win thought about it. 'The old man at the end of every *Scooby Doo*.'

'Right. You meddling kids, stuff like that.'

'You will never guess who does the voice for Shaggy,' Win said.

'Who?'

'Casey Kasem.'

'Get out,' Myron said. 'The top-forty radio guy?'

'The very same.'

'Live and learn.'

On the floor Hans and Franz started to stir. Win showed FJ the gun he had semihidden in his one hand.

'For the safety of all concerned,' Win said, 'please ask your employees to refrain from moving.'

FJ told them. He was not scared. His father was Frank Ache. That was protection enough. The muscles here were for show.

'You've been following me for weeks now,' Myron said. 'I want it to end.'

'Then I suggest that you stop interfering with my company.'

Myron sighed. 'Fine, FJ, I'll bite. How am I interfering with your company?'

'Did you or did you not visit Sophie and Jared Mayor this morning?' FJ asked.

'You know I did.'

'For what purpose?'

'It had nothing to do with you, FJ.'

'Wrong answer.'

'Wrong answer?'

'You visited the owner of the New York Yankees even though you currently represent no one who plays for the team.'

'So?'

'So why were you there?'

Myron looked at Win. Win shrugged. 'Not that I need to explain myself to you, FJ, but just to assuage your paranoid delusions, I was there about Clu Haid.'

'What about him?'

'I was asking about his drug tests.'

FJ's eyes narrowed. 'That's interesting.'

'Glad you think so, FJ.'

'You see, I'm just a new guy trying to learn this confusing business.'

'Uh-huh.'

'I'm young and inexperienced.'

Win said, 'Ah, how often I've heard that line.'

Myron just shook his head.

FJ leaned forward, his scaly features coming closer. Myron feared his tongue would dart out and sniff him. 'I want to learn, Myron. So please tell me: What possible significance could Clu's drug test results have now?'

Myron quickly debated answering and decided, What's the harm? 'If I can show the drug test was faulty, his contract would still be active.'

FJ nodded, seeing the thought trail now. 'You'd be able to get his contract paid out.'

'Right.'

'Do you have reason to believe that the test was faulty?'

'I'm afraid that's confidential, FJ. Agent-client privilege or whatever you want to call it. I'm sure you understand.'

'I do,' FJ said.

'Good.'

'But you, Myron, are not his agent.'

'I am still responsible for his estate's financial well-being. Clu's death doesn't alter my obligation.'

'Wrong answer.'

Myron looked at Win. 'Again with the wrong answer?'

'You are not responsible.' FJ reached to the floor and pulled a briefcase into view. He snapped it open with as much flair as possible. His finger danced through a stack of papers before withdrawing the one he sought. He handed it to Myron and smiled. Myron looked into FJ's eyes, and again he was reminded of the eyes of that mounted deer.

Myron skimmed it over. He read the first line, felt a thump, checked the signature. 'What the hell is this?'

FJ's smile was like a dripping candle now. 'Exactly what it looks like. Clu Haid changed representation. He fired MB SportsReps and hired TruPro.'

He remembered what Sophie Mayor had said in her office, about his having no legal standing. 'He never told us.'

'Never told *us*, Myron, or never told *you*?'

'What the hell does that mean?'

'You weren't around. Perhaps he tried to tell you. Perhaps he told your associate.'

'So he just happened by you, FJ?'

'How I recruit is none of your business. If you kept your clients happy, the best recruitment efforts wouldn't work.'

Myron checked the date. 'This is quite a coincidence, FJ.'

'What's that?'

'He dies two days after he signs with you.'

'Yes, Myron, I agree. I don't think it was a coincidence. Fortunately for me, it means that I had no motive to kill him. Unfortunately for the sizzling Esperanza, the opposite is true.'

Myron glanced over at Win. Win was staring down at Hans and Franz. They were both awake now, face to the floor, hands behind their heads. Customers occasionally came into the coffee bar. Some saw the two men on the floor and exited right away. Others were unfazed, walking past as though Hans and Franz were just two more Manhattan panhandlers.

'Very convenient,' Myron said.

'What's that?'

'Clu signing with you so close to his death. On the surface it eliminates you as a serious suspect.'

'On the surface?'

'It draws attention away from you, makes it look like his death hurts your interests.'

'It does hurt my interests.'

Myron shook his head. 'He had failed a drug test. His contract was null and void. He's thirty-five years old with several suspensions. As a monetary commodity Clu was fairly worthless.'

'Clu had overcome adversity before,' FJ said.

'Not like this. He was through.'

'If he stayed with MB, yes, that's probably true. But TruPro has influence. We would have found a way to relaunch his career.'

Doubtful. But all this raised some interesting questions. The signature looked real, the contract legit. So maybe Clu had left him. Why? Well, lots of reasons. His life was being flushed down the toilet while Myron lollygagged in the sands of the Caribbean. Okay, but why TruPro? Clu knew their reputation. He knew what the Aches were all about. Why would he choose them?

Unless he had to.

Unless Clu was in debt to them. Myron remembered the missing two hundred thousand dollars. Could Clu have been in debt to FJ? Had he gotten in too deep – so deep he had to sign with TruPro? But if that was the case, why not take out more money? He still had more in the account.

No, maybe this was far simpler. Maybe Clu got himself in big trouble. He looked to Myron for help. Myron wasn't there. Clu felt abandoned. He had no one. In desperation he turned to his old friend Billy Lee Palms. But Billy Lee was too messed up to help anyone. He looked again for Myron. But Myron was still gone, possibly avoiding him. Clu was weak and alone, and FJ was there with promises and power.

So maybe Clu didn't have an affair with Esperanza after all. Maybe Clu told her he was leaving the agency and she got upset and then he got upset. Maybe Clu gave her a good-bye smack in that garage.

Hmm.

But there were problems with that scenario too. If there was no affair, how do you explain Esperanza's hairs at the crime scene? How do you explain the blood in the car, the gun in the office, and Esperanza's continued silence?

FJ was still smiling.

'Let's cut to it,' Myron said. 'How do I get you off my back?'

'Stay away from my clients.'

'The same way you stayed away from mine?'

'Tell you what, Myron.' FJ sipped more shaving cream. 'If I desert my clients for six weeks, I give you carte blanche to pursue them with as much gusto as you can muster.'

Myron looked at Win. No solace. Scary as it might sound, FJ had a point.

'Esperanza has been indicted for Clu's murder,' Myron said. 'I'm involved until she's cleared. Outside of that, I'll stay out of your business. And you stay out of mine.'

'Suppose she's not cleared,' FJ said.

'What?'

'Have you considered the possibility that Esperanza did indeed kill him?'

'You know something I don't, FJ?'

FJ put his hand to his chest. 'Me?' The most innocent lamb ever to lie next to a lion. 'What would I know?' He finished his coffee whatever and stood. He looked down at his goons, then at Win. Win nodded. FJ told Hans and Franz to get up. They did. FJ ordered them out the door. They went out, heads high, chests out, eyes up, but still looking like a pair of whipped dogs.

'If you find anything that might help me get Clu's contract reinstated, you'll let me know?'

'Yeah,' Myron said. 'I'll let you know.'

'Great. Then let's stay in touch, Myron.'

'Oh,' Myron said. 'Let's.'

22

They took the subway to Yankee Stadium. The 4 train was fairly empty this time of the day. After they found seats, Myron asked, 'Why did you beat up those two muscleheads?'

'You know why,' Win said.

'Because they challenged you?'

'I hardly call what they mustered a challenge.'

'So why did you beat them up?'

'Because it was simple.'

'What?'

Win hated repeating himself.

'You overreacted,' Myron said. 'As usual.'

'No, Myron, I reacted perfectly.'

'Meaning?'

'I have a reputation, do I not?'

'As a violent psycho, yes.'

'Exactly – a reputation that I've culled and created through what you call overreacting. You trade off that reputation sometimes, do you not?'

'I guess I do.'

'It helps us?'

'I guess so.'

'Guess nothing,' Win said. 'Friends and foes believe I snap too easily – overreact, as you put it. That I'm unstable, out of control. But that's nonsense, of course. I'm never out of control. Just the opposite. Every attack has been well thought out. The pros and cons have been weighed.'

'And in this case, the pros won?'

'Yes.'

'So you knew you were going to beat up those two before we entered?'

'I considered it. Once I realized that they were unarmed and that taking them out would be easy, I made the final decision.'

'Just to enhance your reputation?'

'In a word, yes. My reputation keeps us safe. Why do you think FJ was ordered by his father not to kill you?'

'Because I'm a ray of sunshine? Because I make the world a better place for all?'

Win smiled. 'Then you understand.'

'Does it bother you at all, Win?'

'Does what?'

'Attacking someone like that.'

'They're goons, Myron, not nuns.'

'Still. You just walloped them without provocation.'

'Oh, I see. You don't like the fact that I sucker-punched them. You would have preferred a fairer fight?'

'I guess not. But suppose you miscalculated?'

'Highly unlikely.'

'Suppose one of them was better than you thought and didn't go down so easily. Suppose you had to maim or kill one.'

'They're goons, Myron, not nuns.'

'So you would have done it?'

'You know the answer to that.'

'I guess I do.'

'Who would have mourned their passing?' Win asked. 'Two scums in the night who freely chose a profession that bullies and maims.'

Myron did not answer. The train stopped. Passengers exited. Myron and Win stayed in their seats.

'But you enjoy it,' Myron said.

Win said nothing.

'You have other reasons, sure, but you enjoy violence.'

'And you don't, Myron?'

'Not like you.'

'No, not like me. But you feel the rush.'

'And I usually feel sick after it's all over.'

'Well, Myron, that's probably because you're such a fine humanitarian.'

They exited the subway at 161st Street and walked in silence to Yankee Stadium. Four hours to game time, but there were already several hundred fans lining up to watch the warm-ups. A giant Louisville Slugger bat cast a long shadow. Cops aplenty stood near clusters of unfazed ticket scalpers. Classic détente. There were hot dog carts, some with – gasp! – Yoo-Hoo umbrellas. Yum. At the press entrance Myron flashed his business card, the guard made a call, they were let in.

They traveled down the stairs on the right, reached the stadium tunnel, and emerged into bright sunshine and green grass. Myron and Win had just been discussing the nature of violence, and now Myron thought again about his dad's phone call. Myron had seen his father, the most gentle man he had ever known, grow violent only once. And it was here at Yankee Stadium.

When Myron was ten years old, his father had taken him and his younger brother, Brad, to a game. Brad was five at the time. Dad had secured four seats in the upper tier, but at the last minute a business associate had given him two more seats three rows behind the Red Sox bench. Brad was a huge fan of the Red Sox. So Dad suggested that Brad and Myron sit by the dugout for a few innings. Dad would stay in the upper tier. Myron held Brad's hand, and they walked down to the box seats. The seats were, in a word, awesome.

Brad started cheering his five-year-old lungs out. Cheering like mad. He spotted Carl Yastrzemski in the batter's box and started calling out, 'Yaz! Yaz!' The guy sitting in front of them turned around. He was maybe twenty-five and bearded and looked a bit like a church image of Jesus. 'That's enough,' the bearded guy snapped at Brad. 'Quiet down.'

Brad looked hurt.

'Don't listen to him,' Myron said. 'You're allowed to yell.'

The bearded man's hands moved fast. He grabbed the ten-year-old Myron by his shirt, bunching the Yankee emblem in his seemingly giant fist, and pulled Myron closer to him. There was beer on his breath. 'He's giving my girlfriend a headache. He shuts up now.'

Fear engulfed Myron. Tears filled his eyes, but he wouldn't let them escape. He remembered being shocked, scared, and mostly, for some unknown reason, ashamed. The bearded man glared at Myron another few seconds and then pushed him back. Myron grabbed Brad's hand and rushed back to the upper tier. He tried to pretend everything was all right, but ten-year-olds are not great actors, and Dad could read his son as if he lived inside his skull.

'What's wrong?' Dad asked.

Myron hesitated. Dad asked again. Myron finally told him what happened. And something happened to Myron's father, something Myron had never seen before or since. There was an explosion in his eyes. His face turned red; his eyes went black.

'I'll be right back,' he said.

Myron watched the rest through binoculars. Dad moved down to the seat behind the Red Sox dugout. His father's face was still red. Myron saw Dad cup his hands around his mouth, lean forward, and start screaming for all he was worth. The red in his face turned to crimson. Dad kept screaming. The bearded man tried to ignore him. Dad leaned into his ear à la Mike Tyson and screamed some more. When the bearded man finally turned around, Dad did something that shocked Myron to the core. He pushed the man. He pushed the man twice and then gestured toward the exit, the international sign inviting another man to step outside. The guy with the beard refused. Dad pushed him again.

Two security guards raced down the steps and broke it up. No one was tossed. Dad came back to the upper tier. 'Go back down,' Dad said. 'He won't bother you again.'

But Myron and Brad shook their heads. They liked the seats up here better.

Win said, 'Time travelling again, are we?'

Myron nodded.

'You realize, of course, that you are far too young for so many reflective spells.'

'Yeah, I know.'

A group of Yankee players were sitting on the outfield grass, legs sprawled, hands back, still kids under the collars waiting for their Little League game to start. A man in a too-nicely-fitted suit was talking to them. The man gestured wildly, smiling and enthusiastic and as enraptured with life as the new born-again on the block. Myron recognized him. Sawyer Wells, the motivational speaker né con man of the moment. Two years ago Wells was an unknown charlatan, spouting the standard reworded dogma about finding yourself, unlocking your potential, doing something for yourself – as though people weren't self-centered enough. His big break came when the Mayors hired him to do talks for their work force. The speeches were, if not original, successful, and Sawyer Wells caught on. He got a book deal – cleverly monikered *The Wells Guide to Wellness* – along with an infomercial, audiotapes, video, a planner, the full self-help schematic. Fortune 500 companies started hiring him. When the Mayors took over the Yankees, they brought him on board as a consultant motivational psychologist or some such drivel.

When Sawyer Wells spotted Win, he almost started panting.

'He smells a new client,' Myron said.

'Or perhaps he's never seen anyone quite this handsome before.'

'Oh, yeah,' Myron said. 'That's probably it.'

Wells turned back to the players, shouted out a bit more enthusiasm, spasmed with gestures, clapped once, and then bade them goodbye. He looked back over at Win. He waved. He waved hard. Then he started bounding over like a puppy chasing a new squeaky toy or a politician chasing a potential contributor.

Win frowned. 'In a word, decaf.'

Myron nodded.

'You want me to befriend him?' Win asked.

'He was supposedly present for the drug tests. And he's also the team psychologist. He probably hears a lot of rumors.'

'Fine,' Win said. 'You take the roommate. I'll take Sawyer.'

Enos Cabral was a good-looking wiry Cuban with a flame-throwing fastball and breaking pitches that still needed work. He was twenty-four, but he had the kind of looks that probably got him carded at any liquor store. He stood watching batting practice, his body slack except for his mouth. Like most relief pitchers, he chewed gum or tobacco with the ferocity of a lion gnawing on a recently downed gazelle.

Myron introduced himself.

Enos shook his hand and said, 'I know who you are.'

'Oh?'

'Clu talked about you a lot. He thought I should sign with you.'

A pang. 'Clu said that?'

'I wanted a change,' Enos continued. 'My agent. He treats me well, no? And he made me a rich man.'

'I don't mean to knock the importance of good representation, Enos, but you made you a rich man. An agent facilitates. He doesn't create.'

Enos nodded. 'You know my story?'

The thumbnail sketch. The boat trip had been rough. Very rough. For a week everyone had assumed they had been lost at sea. When they finally did pop up, only two of the eight Cubans were still alive. One of the dead was Enos's brother Hector, considered the best player to come out of Cuba in the past decade. Enos, considered the lesser talent, was nearly dead of dehydration.

'Just what I've read in the papers,' Myron said.

'My agent. He was there when I arrived. I had family in Miami. When he heard about the Cabral brothers, he lent them money. He paid for my hospital stay. He gave me money and jewelry and a car. He promised me more money. And I have it.'

'So what's the problem?'

'He has no soul.'

'You want an agent with a soul?'

Enos shrugged. 'I'm Catholic,' he said. 'We believe in miracles.'

They both laughed.

Enos seemed to be studying Myron. 'Clu was always suspicious of people. Even me. He had something of a hard shell.'

'I know,' Myron said.

'But he believed in you. He said you were a good man. He said that he had trusted you with his life and would gladly do so again.'

Another pang. 'Clu was also a lousy judge of character.'

'I don't think so.'

'Enos, I wanted to talk to you about Clu's last few weeks.'

He raised an eyebrow. 'I thought you came here to recruit me.'

'No,' Myron said. Then: 'But have you heard the expression *killing two birds with one stone*?'

Enos laughed. 'What do you want to know?'

'Were you surprised when Clu failed the drug test?'

He picked up a bat. He gripped and regripped it in his hands. Finding the right groove. Funny. He was an American League pitcher. He would probably never have the opportunity to bat. 'I have trouble understanding addictions,' he said. 'Where I come from, yes, a man may try to drink away his world, if he can afford it. You live in such stink, why not leave, no? But here, when you have as much as Clu had . . .'

He didn't finish the thought. No point in stating the obvious.

'One time Clu tried to explain it to me,' Enos continued. ' "Sometimes," he said, "you don't want to escape the world; sometimes you want to escape yourself." ' He cocked his head. 'Do you believe that?'

'Not really,' Myron said. 'Like a lot of cute phrases, it sounds good. But it also sounds like a load of self-rationalization.'

Enos smiled. 'You're mad at him.'

'I guess I am.'

'Don't be. He was a very unhappy man, Myron. A man who needs so much excess . . . there is something broken inside him, no?'

Myron said nothing.

'Clu tried. He fought hard, you have no idea. He wouldn't go out at night. If our room had a minibar, he'd make them take it out. He didn't hang out with old friends because he was afraid of what he might do. He was scared all the time. He fought long and hard.'

'And he lost,' Myron added.

'I never saw him take drugs. I never saw him drink.'

'But you noticed changes.'

Enos nodded. 'His life began to fall apart. So many bad things happened.'

'What bad things?'

The organ music revved immediately into high gear, the legendary Eddie Layton opening up with his rendition of that ballpark classic 'The Girl from Ipanema.' Enos lifted the bat to his shoulder, then lowered it again. 'I feel uncomfortable talking about this.'

'I'm not prying for the fun of it. I'm trying to find out who killed him.'

'The papers said your secretary did it.'

'They're wrong.'

Enos stared at the bat as though there were a message hidden beneath the word *Louisville*. Myron tried to prompt him.

'Clu withdrew two hundred thousand dollars not long before he died,' Myron said. 'Was he having financial problems?'

'If he did, I didn't see it.'

'Did he gamble?'

'I didn't see him him gamble, no.'

'Do you know that he changed agents?'

Enos looked surprised. 'He fired you?'

'Apparently he was going to.'

'I didn't know,' he said. 'I know he was looking for you. But no, I didn't know that.'

'So what was it then, Enos? What made him cave?'

He lifted his eyes and blinked into the sun. The perfect weather for a night game. Soon fans would arrive, and memories would be made. Happened every night in stadiums around the world. It was always some kid's first game.

'His marriage,' Enos said. 'That was the big thing, I think. You know Bonnie?'

'Yes.'

'Clu loved her very much.'

'He had an odd way of showing it.'

Enos smiled. 'Sleeping with all those women. I think he did it more to hurt himself than anyone else.'

'That sounds like another one of those big, fat rationalizations, Enos. Clu may have made self-destruction an art form. But that's not an excuse for what he put her through.'

'I think he'd agree with that. But Clu hurt himself most of all.'

'Don't kid yourself. He hurt Bonnie too.'

'Yes, you're right, of course. But he still loved her. When she threw him out, it hurt him so much. You have no idea.'

'What can you tell me about their breakup?'

Another hesitation. 'Not much to tell. Clu felt betrayed, angry.'

'You know that Clu had fooled around before.'

'Yes.'

'So what made it different this time? Bonnie was used to his straying. What made her finally snap? Who was his girlfriend?'

Enos looked puzzled. 'You think Bonnie threw him out over a girl?'

'She didn't?'

Enos shook his head.

'You're sure.'

'It was never about girls with Clu. They were just part of the drugs and alcohol. They were easy for him to give up.'

Myron was confused. 'So he wasn't having an affair?'

'No,' Enos said. '*She* was.'

That was when it clicked. Myron felt a cold wave roll through him, squeezing the pit of his stomach. He barely said good-bye before he hurried away.

23

He knew Bonnie would be home.

The car had barely come to a full stop when he shot out the driver's door. There were perhaps a dozen other vehicles parked on the street. Mourners. The front door was opened. Myron headed inside without knocking. He wanted to find Bonnie and confront her and end this. But she wasn't in the living room. Just mourners. Some approached him, slowing him down. He offered his condolences to Clu's mother, her face ravaged with grief. He shook other hands, trying to swim through the thick sea of grief-stricken and glad-handers and find Bonnie. He finally spotted her outside in the backyard. She sat alone on the deck, her knees tucked under her chin, watching her children play. He steeled himself and pushed open the sliding glass doors.

The porch was cedarwood and overlooked a large swing set. Clu's boys were on it, both dressed in red ties and untucked short-sleeve shirts. They ran and laughed. Miniature versions of their dead father, their smiles so like his, their features eternal echoes of Clu's. Bonnie watched them. Her back was to Myron, a cigarette in her hand. She did not turn around as he approached.

'Clu didn't have the affair,' Myron said. 'You did.'

Bonnie inhaled deeply and let it out. 'Great timing, Myron.'

'That can't be helped.'

'Can't we talk about this later?'

Myron waited a beat. Then: 'I know who you were sleeping with.'

She stiffened. Myron looked down at her. She finally turned and met his gaze.

'Let's take a walk,' Bonnie said.

She reached out a hand, and Myron helped her to her feet.

They walked down the backyard to a wooded area. The din of traffic filtered through a sound barrier up the hill. The house was spanking new, large and innately nouveau-riche. Airy, lots of windows, cathedral ceilings, small living room, huge kitchen flowing into huge California room, huge master bedroom, closets large enough to double as Gap outlets. Probably went for about eight hundred thou. Beautiful and sterile and soulless. Needing to be lived in a bit. Properly aged like a fine Merlot.

'I didn't know you smoked,' he said.

'You don't know a lot of things about me, Myron.'

Touché. He looked at her profile, and again he saw that young coed heading into the fraternity basement. He flashed back to that very moment, to the sound of Clu's sharp intake of air when he first laid eyes on her. Suppose she'd come down a little later, after Clu had passed out or hooked up with another woman. Suppose she had gone to another frat party that night. Dumb thoughts – life's arbitrary forks in the road, the series of what ifs – but there you go.

'So what makes you think I was the one having an affair?' she said.

'Clu told Enos.'

'Clu lied.'

'No,' Myron said.

They kept walking. Bonnie took a last drag and tossed the cigarette on the ground. 'My property,' she said. 'I'm allowed.'

Myron said nothing.

'Did Clu tell Enos who he thought I was sleeping with?'

'No.'

'But you think you know who this mystery lover is.'

'Yes,' Myron said. 'It's Esperanza.'

Silence.

'Would you believe me if I insisted you were wrong?' she said.

'You'd have a lot of explaining to do.'

'How's that?'

'Let's start with you coming to my office after Esperanza was arrested.'

'Okay.'

'You wanted to know what they had on her – that was the real reason. I wondered why you warned me away from finding the truth. You told me to clear my friend but not dig too hard.'

She nodded. 'And you think I said that because I didn't want you to know about this affair?'

'Yes. But there's more. Like Esperanza's silence, for one thing. Win and I theorized that she didn't want us to know about her affair with Clu. It would look bad on several levels to be having an affair with a client. But to be having an affair with a client's wife? What could be dumber than that?'

'That's hardly evidence, Myron.'

'I'm not finished. You see, all the evidence that points to an affair between Esperanza and Clu actually points to an affair between you two. The physical evidence, for example. The pubic hairs and DNA found at the Fort Lee apartment. I started thinking about that. You and Clu lived there for a short time. Then you moved into this house. But you still had the lease on the apartment. So before you threw him out, it was empty, right?'

'Right.'

'What better place to meet for a tryst? It wasn't Clu and Esperanza meeting there. It was you two.'

Bonnie said nothing.

'The E-Z Pass records – most of the bridge crossings were on days when the Yankees were out of town. So Esperanza wasn't coming out to see Clu. She was coming out to see you. I checked the office phone records. She never called the apartment after you threw Clu out – only this house. Why? Clu wasn't living here. You were.'

She took out another cigarette and struck a match.

'And lastly, the fight in the garage when Clu struck Esperanza. That bothered the hell of me. Why would he hit her? Because she broke off an affair? That didn't make sense. Because he wanted to find me or was crazed from taking drugs? Again, no. I couldn't figure it out. But now the answer is obvious. Esperanza was having an affair with his wife. He blamed her for breaking up the marriage. Enos said the breakup shook him to the core. What could be worse for a psyche as fragile as Clu's than his wife having an affair with a woman?'

Her voice was sharp. 'Are you blaming me for his death?'

'Depends. Did you kill him?'

'Would it help if I said no?'

'It would be a start.'

She smiled, but there was no joy in it. Like.the house, it was beautiful and sterile and almost soulless. 'Do you want to hear something funny?' she said. 'Clu's beating the drugs and the drinking didn't help our marriage – it ended it. For so long Clu was . . . I don't know . . . a work in progress. I blamed his shortcomings on the drugs and drinking and all that. But once he finally exorcised his demons, what was left was just' – she lifted her palms and shrugged – 'just him. I saw Clu clearly for the first time, Myron, and you know what I realized? I didn't love him.'

Myron said nothing.

'And don't blame Esperanza. It wasn't her fault. I held on purely for the sake of my kids, and when Esperanza came along—' Bonnie stopped, and this time her smile seemed more genuine. 'You want to hear something else funny? I'm not a lesbian. I'm not even a bisexual. It's just . . . she treated me tenderly. We had sex, sure, but it was never about sex. I know that sounds weird, but her gender was irrelevant. Esperanza is just a beautiful person, and I fell in love with that. Does that make sense?'

'You know how this looks,' Myron said.

'Of course I know how it looks. Two dykes got together and offed the husband. Why do you think we're trying so hard to keep it secret? The weakness in their case right now is motive. But if they find out we were lovers—'

'Did you kill him?'

'What do you expect me to say to that, Myron?'

'I'd like to hear it.'

'No, we didn't kill him. I was leaving him. Why would I throw him out and start filing papers if I planned on killing him?'

'To prevent a scandal that would surely hurt your kids.'

She made a face. 'Come on, Myron.'

'So how do you explain the gun in the office and the blood in the car?'

'I can't.'

Myron thought about it. His head hurt – from the physical altercation or this latest revelation, he couldn't say. He tried to concentrate through the haze. 'Who else knows about the affair?'

'Just Esperanza's lawyer, Hester Crimstein.'

'No one else?'

'No one. We were very discreet.'

'You're sure?'

'Yes. Why?'

'Because,' Myron said, 'if I were going to murder Clu and I wanted to frame someone for it, his wife's lover would be my first choice.'

Bonnie saw where he was heading. 'So you think the killer knew about us?'

'It might explain a lot.'

'I didn't tell anyone. And Esperanza said she didn't either.'

Pow. Right between the eyes. 'You couldn't have been too careful,' Myron said.

'What makes you say that?'

'Clu found out, didn't he?'

She thought about it, nodded.

'Did you tell him?' he asked.

'No.'

'What did you say when you threw him out?'

She shrugged. 'That there was no one else. That was true in a sense. It wasn't about Esperanza.'

'So how did he find out?'

'I don't know. I assumed he became obsessed. That he followed me.'

'And he found out the truth?'

'Yes.'

'And then he went after Esperanza and attacked her?'

'Yes.'

'And before he has a chance to tell anyone else about this, before it has a chance of getting out and hurting either of you, he ends up dead. And the murder weapon ends up with Esperanza. And Clu's blood ends up in the car she's been driving. And the E-Z Pass records show Esperanza came back to New York an hour after the murder.'

'Again, yes.'

Myron shook his head. 'It doesn't look good, Bonnie.'

'That's what I've been trying to tell you,' she said. 'If even you won't believe us, how do you think a jury is going to react?'

There was no need to answer. They headed back to the house then. The two young boys were still at play, oblivious of what was going on around them. Myron watched for a moment. *Fatherless*, he thought, shuddering at the word. With one last look he turned and walked away.

24

Thrill, not Nancy Sinclair, met him outside a bar called the Biker Wannabee. Honesty in advertising. Nice to see.

'Howdy,' Myron said. Tex Bolitar.

Her smile was full of pornographic promise. Totally into Thrill mode now. 'Howdy yourself, pardner,' she cooed. With some women, every syllable is cooed. 'How do I look?'

'Mighty tasty, ma'am. But I think I prefer you as Nancy.'

'Liar.'

Myron shrugged, not sure if he was telling the truth or not. This whole thing reminded him of when Barbara Eden would play her evil sister on *I Dream of Jeannie*. He was often torn back then too, not sure if Larry Hagman should stay with Jeannie or run off with the enticingly evil sister. But hey, talk about your great dilemmas.

'I thought you were bringing backup,' Thrill said.

'I am.'

'Where is he?'

'If things go well, you won't see him.'

'How mysterious.'

'Isn't it?'

They headed inside and grabbed a corner booth in the back. Yep, biker wanna-be. Lots of guys aiming for that hairy, Vietnam-vet-cum-hit-the-road look. The jukebox played 'God Only Knows (What I'd Be Without You)' – the Beach Boys, but unlike anything else the Beach Boys did. The song was a plaintive wail, and despite its pop misgivings, it always struck Myron to the bone, the trepidation of what the future might hold so naked in Brian's voice, the words so hauntingly simple. Especially now.

Thrill was studying his face. 'You okay?' she asked.

'Fine. So what happens next?'

'We order a drink, I guess.'

Five minutes passed. 'Lonely Boy' came on the juke-box. Andrew Gold. Serious seventies AM bubble gum. Chorus: 'Oh, oh, oh . . . oh what a lonely boy . . . oh what a lonely boy . . . oh what a lonely boy.' By the time the chorus was repeated for the eighth time, Myron had it down pat so he sang along. Megamemory. Maybe he should do an infomercial.

Men at nearby tables checked out Thrill, some surreptitiously, most not. Thrill's smile was practically a leer now, sinking deeper into the role.

'You get into this,' Myron said.

'It's a part, Myron. We're all actors on a stage and all that.'

'But you enjoy the attention.'

'So?'

'So I was just saying.'

She shrugged. 'I find it fascinating.'

'What's that?'

'What a large bosom does to a man. They get so obsessed.'

'You just reached the conclusion that men are mammary-obsessed? I hate to break this to you, Nancy, but the research has been done.'

'But it's weird when you think about it.'

'I try not to.'

'Bosoms do weird things to men, no doubt,' she said, 'but I don't like what they do to women either.'

'How's that?'

Thrill put her palms on the table. 'Okay, everyone

knows that we women put too much of our self-worth into our bodies. Old news, right?'

'Right.'

'I know it, you know it, everyone knows it. And unlike my more feminist sisters, I don't blame men for this.'

'You don't?'

'*Mademoiselle, Vogue, Bazaar, Glamour* – those are run by women and have a totally female clientele. They want to change the image, start there. Why ask the men to change a perception that women themselves won't change?'

'Refreshing viewpoint,' Myron noted.

'But bosoms do funny things to people. Men, okay, that's obvious. They become brain-dead. It's as if the nipples shoot out like two grapefruit spoons, dig into their frontal lobe, and scrape away all cognitive thought.'

Myron looked up, the imagery giving him pause.

'But for women, well, it starts when you're young. A girl develops early. Adolescent boys start lusting after her. How do her girlfriends react? They take it out on her. They're jealous of the attention or feeling inadequate or whatever. But they take it out on the young girl who can't help what her body is going through. With me?'

'Yes.'

'Even now. Look at the glances the women in here give me. Pure hatred. You get a group of women together and a chesty counterpart walks by and they all sigh, "Oh, please." Professional women, for example, feel the urge to dress down – not just because of leering men but because of women. Because of how women treat them. A businesswoman sees a big-chested businesswoman with a better title – well, she got the job because of her tits. Plain and simple. Might be true, might not be. Is this animosity spawned again from dormant jealousy or a misplaced feeling of inadequacy or because they unfairly equate bosoms with stupidity? Any way you look at it, it's an ugly thing.'

'I never really thought about it,' Myron said.

'And finally I don't like what it does to me.'

'Your reaction to seeing a big chest or having one?'

'The latter.'

'Why?'

'Because the big-breasted woman gets used to it. She takes it for granted. She uses them to her advantage.'

'So?'

'What do you mean, so?'

'All attractive people do that,' Myron said. 'It's not just bosoms. If a woman is beautiful, she knows it and uses it. Nothing wrong with that. Men use it too, if they can. Sometimes – I'm ashamed to admit this – even I shake my little tush to get my way.'

'Shocking.'

'Well, not really. Because it never works.'

'I think you're being modest. But either way, don't you see anything wrong with that?'

'With what?'

'With using a physical attribute to get your way.'

'I didn't say there was nothing wrong with it. I'm simply noting that what you're talking about is not merely a mammarial phenomenon.'

She made a face. 'Mammarial phenomenon?'

Myron shrugged, and mercifully the waitress came over. Myron made a point of not looking anywhere near her chest, which was tantamount to telling yourself not to scratch that irksome itch. The waitress had a pen behind her ear. Her overtreated hair aimed for on-the-farm strawberry blond but landed far closer to fell-at-the-4H-fair cotton candy.

'Get you?' she said. Skipping the preliminaries like 'Hello' and 'What can I . . . ?'

'Rob Roy,' Thrill said.

The pen came out of the ear holster, jotted it down, back in the holster. Wyatt Earp. 'You?' she said to Myron.

Myron doubted that they had any Yoo-Hoo. 'A diet soda, please.'

She looked at him as if he'd ordered a bedpan.

'Maybe a beer,' Myron said.

She clacked her gum. 'Bud, Michelob, or some pansy brew?'

'Pansy would be fine, thank you,' Myron said. 'And do you have any of those little cocktail umbrellas?'

The waitress rolled her eyes and walked away.

They chatted for a while. Myron had just started relaxing and yes, even enjoying himself when Thrill said, 'Behind you. By the door.'

He was not much in the mood for clandestine games. They wanted him here for a reason. No sense beating around the bush. He turned without an iota of subtlety and spotted Pat the bartender and Veronica Lake aka Zorra dressed again in a cashmere sweater – peach-toned, for those keeping score – long skirt, and a strand of pearls. Zorra, the Steroid Debutante. Myron shook his head. Bonnie Franklin and Mall Girl were nowhere to be seen.

Myron gave a big wave. 'Over here, fellas!'

Pat scowled, feigning surprise. He looked toward Zorra, She-Man of the Saber Heel. Zorra showed nothing. The great ones never do. Myron always wondered if their blaséness was an act or if, in truth, nothing really surprised them. Probably a bit of both.

Pat strode toward their table, acting as though he were shocked – shocked! – that Myron was in his bar. Zorra followed, more gliding than walking, the eyes soaking in everything. Like Win, Zorra moved economically – albeit in stylish red pumps – no motion wasted. Pat was still scowling when he reached the table.

'What the hell are you doing here, Bolitar?' Pat asked.

Myron nodded. 'Not bad, but it could use work. Do me a favor. Try it again. But add a little gasp first. Gasp, what the hell are you doing here, Bolitar? Like that. Better yet, why not give a wry shake of your head and say something like "All the gin joints in all the world, you have to walk into mine – two nights in a row." '

Zorra was smiling now.

'You're crazy,' Pat said.

'Pat.' It was Zorra. He looked at Pat and shook his head just once. The shake said, Stop with the games.

Pat turned to Thrill. 'Do me a favor, hon.'

Thrill offered up breathless. 'Sure, Pat.'

'Go powder your nose or something, okay?'

Myron made a face. 'Go powder your nose?' He looked pleadingly at Zorra. Zorra's small shrug was semiapologetic. 'What next, Pat? You going to threaten to make me sleep with the fishes? Make me an offer I can't refuse. I mean, go powder your nose?'

Pat was fuming. He looked over at Thrill. 'Please, hon.'

'No problem, Pat.' She slid out of the booth. Pat and Zorra immediately took her place. Myron frowned at the change in scenery.

'We need some information,' Pat said.

'Yeah, I picked up on that last night,' Myron said.

'That got out of control. I'm sorry.'

'I bet.'

'Hey, we let you go, right?'

'As soon as I was electrocuted with a cattle prod, slashed twice with a heel blade, kicked in the ribs, and then jumped through a glass mirror. Yeah, you let me go.'

Pat smiled. 'If Zorra here didn't want you to escape, you wouldn't have escaped. Get my meaning?'

Myron looked at Zorra. Zorra looked at Myron. Myron said, 'A peach sweater with red pumps?'

Zorra smiled, shrugged.

'Zorra here could have killed you easy as pie,' Pat continued.

'Right, fine, Zorra is a tough guy, you're supergenerous to me. Get to it.'

'Why were you asking about Clu Haid?'

'Sorry to disappoint you, but I was telling you the truth last night. I'm trying to find his killer.'

'So what does my club have to do with that?'

'Before I got dragged into the back room, I would have said, "Nothing." But now, well, that's what I'd like to know.'

Pat looked at Zorra. Zorra did not move. Pat said, 'We want to take you for a ride.'

'Damn.'

'What?'

'You'd gone nearly three minutes without a mob cliché. Then you come up with the take a ride bit. It's sad really. Can I powder my nose first?'

'You want to crack wise or you want to come with us?'

'I can do both,' Myron said. 'I'm rather multitalented.'

Pat shook his head. 'Let's go.' Myron started to slide out the booth.

'No,' Zorra said.

Everyone stopped. 'What's wrong?' Pat said.

Zorra looked at Myron. 'We are not interested in hurting you,' Zorra said.

More reassurances.

'But we can't let you know where you're going, dreamboat. You'll have to be blindfolded.'

'You're kidding, right?'

'No.'

'Fine, blindfold me. Let's go.'

'No,' Zorra said again.

'What now?'

'Your friend Win. Zorra assumes he's close by.'

'Who?'

Zorra smiled. He-she wasn't pretty. Lots of transvestites are. Lots of times you can't even tell. But Zorra had a five o'clock shadow (a look Myron found to be less than alluring in a woman), big hands with hairy knuckles (ditto), a skewered wig (call him picky), a rather masculine, whispery voice (*comme ci, comme ça*) and despite the outer trappings, Zorra looked like, well, a guy wearing a dress. 'Don't insult Zorra's intelligence, dreamboat.'

'You see him?'

'If Zorra could,' Zorra said, 'then someone has grossly overexaggerated his reputation.'

'So what makes you so sure Win's here?'

'You're doing it again,' Zorra said.

'Doing what?'

'Insulting Zorra's intelligence.'

Nothing like a psycho who refers to himself in the third person.

'Please ask him to come forward,' Zorra said. 'We have no interest in hurting anyone. But Zorra knows that your colleague will follow wherever you go. Then Zorra will have to follow him. It will lead to conflict. None of us wants that.'

Win's voice came from Myron's cell phone. Must have taken off the mute. 'What guarantee do we have that Myron will return?'

Myron lifted the cell phone into view.

'You and Zorra will sit and enjoy a drink, dreamboat,' Zorra said into the phone. 'Myron will travel with Pat.'

'Travel where?' Myron asked.

'We can't tell you.'

Myron frowned. 'Is this cloak-and-dagger stuff really necessary?'

Pat leaned back now, letting Zorra handle it. 'You have questions, we have questions,' Zorra said. 'This meeting is the only way to satisfy both.'

'So why can't we talk here?'

'Impossible.'

'Why?'

'You have to go with Pat.'

'Where?'

'Zorra cannot tell you.'

'Who are you taking me to see?'

'Zorra cannot tell you that either.'

Myron said, 'Does the fate of the free world rest in Zorra's maintaining silence?'

Zorra adjusted his lips, forming what he probably read someplace was known as a smile. 'You mock Zorra. But Zorra has kept silent before. Zorra has seen horrors you cannot imagine. Zorra has been tortured. For weeks on end. Zorra has felt pain that makes what you felt with that cattle prod seem like a lover's kiss.'

Myron nodded solemnly. 'Wow,' he said.

Zorra spread his hands. Hairy knuckles and pink nail polish. Hold me back. 'We can always choose to part ways, dreamboat.'

From the cell phone Win said, 'Good idea.'

Myron lifted the receiver. 'What?'

'If we agree to their terms,' Win said, 'I cannot guarantee they won't kill you.'

'Zorra guarantees it,' Zorra said. 'With her life.'

Myron said, 'Excuse me?'

'Zorra stays here with Win,' Zorra went on, the glint in the overmascaraed eye sparkling anew. Something was there, and it was not lucidity. 'Zorra will be unarmed. If you don't return in perfect health, Win kills Zorra.'

'Heck of a guarantee,' Myron said. 'Ever thought about becoming a car mechanic?'

Win entered the bar now. He walked straight toward

the table, sat down, hands under it. 'If you'd be so kind,' Win said to Zorra and Pat, 'please put all hands on the table.'

They did.

'And, Ms Zorra, if you wouldn't mind kicking off your heels?'

'Sure, dreamboat.' Win kept his eyes on Zorra. Zorra kept his on Win. There would be no blinking here. Win said, 'I still cannot guarantee his safety. Yes, I have the option of killing you if he does not return. But for all I know, Pat the Bunny here doesn't give a rodent's buttocks about you.'

'Hey,' Pat said, 'you have my word.'

Win just looked at him for a moment. Then he turned back to Zorra. 'Myron goes armed. Pat drives. Myron keeps the gun on him.'

Zorra shook his head. 'Impossible.'

'Then we have no deal.'

Zorra shrugged. 'Then Zorra and Pat must bid you adieu.'

They rose to leave. Myron knew that Win wouldn't call them back. He whispered to Win, 'I need to know what's going on here.'

Win shrugged. 'It's a mistake,' he said, 'but it's your call.'

Myron looked up. 'We agree,' he said.

Zorra sat back down. Under the table Win kept the gun on him.

'Myron keeps his cell phone on,' Win said. 'I listen to every word.'

Zorra nodded. 'Fair enough.'

Pat and Myron started to leave.

'Oh, Pat?' Win said.

Pat stopped.

Win's voice was how's-the-weather casual. 'If Myron isn't returned, I may or may not kill Zorra. I will decide at the appropriate time. Either way, I will use all my considerable influence and money and time and effort to find you. I will offer rewards. I will search. I will not sleep. I will find you. And when I do, I *won't* kill you. Do you understand?'

Pat swallowed, nodded.

'Go,' Win said.

25

When they reached the car, Pat frisked him. Nothing. Then he handed Myron a black hood. 'Put this on.'

Myron made a face. 'Tell me you're joking.'

'Put it on. Then lie down in the backseat. Don't look up.'

Myron rolled his eyes, but he did as he was asked. His six-four frame wasn't all that comfortable, but he made do. Big of him. Pat got in the front seat and started the car.

'Quick suggestion,' Myron said.

'What did you say?'

'Next time you do this, try vacuuming out the car first. It's disgusting back here.'

Pat drove. Myron tried to concentrate, listening for sounds that would give him a clue where they were going. That always worked on TV. The guy would hear, say, a boat horn and know he'd gone to Pier 12 or something, and they'd all rush in and find him. But all Myron heard were, not surprisingly, traffic noises: the occasional horn, cars passing or being passed, loud radios, that kind of thing. He tried to keep track of turns and distances but quickly realized the futility. What did he think he was, a human compass?

The drive lasted maybe ten minutes. Not enough time to leave the city. Clue: He was still in Manhattan. Gee, that was helpful. Pat turned off the engine.

'You can sit up,' he said. 'But keep the hood on.'

'You sure the hood goes with this ensemble? I want to look my best for Mr Big.'

'Someone once tell you were funny, Bolitar?'

'You're right. Black goes with everything.'

Pat sighed. When nervous, some people run. Some hide. Some grow silent. Some get chatty. And some make dumb jokes.

Pat helped Myron out of the car and led him by the elbow. Myron again tried to pick up sounds. The cooing of a seagull maybe. That too always seemed to happen on TV. But in New York seagulls didn't coo as much as phlegm cough. And if you heard a seagull in New York, it was more likely you were near a trash canister than a pier. Myron tried to think of the last time he had seen a seagull in New York. There was a picture of one on a sign for his favorite bagel store. Caption: 'If a bird flying over the sea is a seagull, what do you call a bird flying over the bay?' Clever when you think about it.

The two men walked – where to, Myron had no idea. He stumbled on uneven pavement, but Pat kept him upright. Another clue. Find the spot in Manhattan with uneven pavement. Christ, he practically had the guy cornered.

They walked up what felt like a stoop and entered a room with heat and humidity slightly more stifling than a Burmese forest fire. Myron was still blindfolded, but light from what might be a bare bulb filtered through the cloth. The room reeked of mildew and steam and dried sweat – like the most popular sauna at Jack La Lanne's gone to seed. It was hard to breathe through the hood. Pat put a hand on Myron's shoulder.

'Sit,' Pat said before pushing down slightly.

Myron sat. He heard Pat's footsteps, then low voices. Whispers actually. Mostly from Pat. An argument of some sort. Footsteps again. Coming closer to Myron. A body suddenly cut off the bare lightbulb, bathing Myron in total darkness. One more step. Someone stopped directly over him.

'Hello, Myron,' the voice said.

There was a tremor there, an almost manic twang in the tone. But there was no doubt. Myron was not great with names and faces, but voices were imprints. Memories flooded in. After all these years his recall was instantaneous.

'Hello, Billy Lee.'

The missing Billy Lee Palms, to be exact. Former frat brother and Duke baseball star. Former best bud of Clu Haid. Son of Mrs My-Life-Is-but-a-Wallpaper-Tapestry.

'Mind if I take the hood off now?' Myron asked.

'Not at all.'

Myron reached up and grabbed the top of the hood. He pulled it off. Billy Lee was standing over him. Or at least he assumed it was Billy Lee. It was as if the former pretty boy had been kidnapped and replaced with this fleshier counterpart. Billy Lee's formerly prominent cheekbones looked malleable, tallow skin in mid-shed clung to sagging features, his eyes sunken deeper than any pirate treasure, his complexion the gray of a city street after a rainfall. His hair was greasy and jutting all over the place, as unwashed as any MTV video jockey's.

Billy Lee was also holding what looked like a sawed-off shotgun about six inches from Myron's face.

'He's holding what looks like a sawed-off shotgun about six inches from my face,' Myron said for the benefit of the cell phone.

Billy Lee giggled. That sound too was familiar.

'Bonnie Franklin,' Myron said.

'What?'

'Last night. You were the one who hit me with the cattle prod.'

Billy Lee spread his hands impossibly wide. 'Bingo, baby!'

Myron shook his head. 'You definitely look better with the makeup, Billy Lee.'

Billy Lee giggled again and retrained the shotgun on Myron. Then he held out his free hand. 'Give me the phone.'

Myron hesitated but not for long. The sunken eyes, once Myron could see them, were wet and unfocused and tinged with a dull red. Billy Lee's body was one tremor. Myron checked out the short sleeves and saw the needle tracks. Billy Lee looked like the wildest and most unpredictable of animals: a cornered junkie. Myron handed him the phone. Billy Lee put it to his ear.

'Win?'

Win's voice was clear. 'Yes, Billy Lee.'

'Go to hell.'

Billy Lee giggled again. Then he clicked off the phone, untethering them from the outside world, and Myron felt the dread rise in his chest.

Billy Lee stuck the phone in Myron's pocket and looked over at Pat. 'Tie him to the chair.'

Pat said, 'What?'

'Tie him to the chair. There's rope right behind it.'

'Tie him how? I look like a goddamn Boy Scout?'

'Just wrap it around him and tie a knot. I want to slow him down in case he gets dumb before I kill him.'

Pat moved toward Myron. Billy Lee kept an eye on Myron.

Myron said, 'It's not really a good idea to upset Win.'

'Win doesn't scare me.'

Myron shook his head.

'What?'

'I knew you were strung out,' Myron said. 'But I didn't realize how badly.'

Pat started winding the rope around Myron's chest. 'Maybe you should call him back,' Pat said. If the San Andreas quaked like his voice, they'd be calling for an evacuation. 'We don't need him searching for us too, you know what I'm saying?'

'Don't worry about it,' Billy Lee said.

'And Zorra's still there—'

'*Don't worry about it!*' Screaming this time. A shrill, awful scream. The shotgun bounced closer to Myron's face. Myron tensed his body, preparing to make a move before the rope was knotted. But Billy Lee jumped back suddenly, as if realizing for the first time that Myron was in the room.

Nobody spoke. Pat tightened the rope and tied it in a knot. Not well done, but it'd serve its stated purpose – i.e., slow him down so that Billy Lee would have plenty of time to blow Myron's head off.

'You trying to kill me, Myron?'

Strange question. 'No,' Myron said.

Billy Lee's fist slammed into the lower part of Myron's belly. Myron doubled over, the air gone, his lungs spasming in the pure, naked need for oxygen. He felt tears push into his eyes.

'Don't lie to me, asshole.'

Myron fought for breath.

Billy Lee sniffed, wiped his face with his sleeve. 'Why are you trying to kill me?'

Myron tried to respond, but it took too long. Billy Lee hit him hard with the butt of the shotgun, exactly on the Z spot Zorra had sliced into him the night before. The stitches split apart, and blood mushroomed onto Myron's shirt. His head began to swim. Billy Lee giggled some more. Then he raised the butt of the shotgun over his head and started it in an arc toward Myron's head.

'Billy Lee!' Pat shouted.

Myron saw it coming, but there was no escape. He managed to tilt the chair with his toes and roll back. The blow glanced the top of his head, scraping his scalp. The chair teetered over, and Myron's head banged against the wooden floor. His skull tingled.

Oh Christ . . .

He looked up. Billy Lee was raising the butt of the shotgun again. A straight blow would crush his skull. Myron tried to roll, but he was hopelessly tangled up. Billy Lee smiled down at him. He held the shotgun high above his head, letting the moment drag out, watching Myron struggle the way some people watch an injured ant before stomping it with their foot.

Billy Lee suddenly frowned. He lowered the weapon, studying it for a moment. 'Hmm,' he said. 'Might break my gun that way.'

Myron felt Billy Lee grab his shoulders and lift him and the chair back up. The shotgun was at eye level now.

'Fuck it,' Billy Lee said. 'Might as well just shoot your sorry ass, am I right?'

Myron barely heard the giggling now. When a gun is pointed so directly in your face, it has a tendency to block out everything else. The double barrel's opening grows, moves closer, surrounds you until everything you are and see and hear is consumed in its black mouth.

Pat tried again. 'Billy Lee . . .'

Myron felt the sweat under his arms begin to gush. Calm. Keep the tone calm. Don't excite him. 'Tell me what's going on, Billy Lee. I want to help.'

Billy Lee snickered, the shotgun still shaking in his hand. 'You want to help me?'

'Yes.'

That made him laugh. 'Bullshit, Myron. Total bullshit.'

Myron kept still.

'We were never even friends, were we, Myron? I mean, we were frat brothers, and we hung out and stuff. But we were never really friends.'

Myron tried to keep his eyes on Billy Lee's. 'This is a heck of a time to go tiptoeing through the past, Billy Lee.'

'I'm trying to make a point here, asshole. You're peddling this crap about wanting to help me. Like we're friends. But that's a load of bullshit. We're not friends. You never really liked me.'

Never really liked me. Like they were third graders during recess. 'I still helped pull your ass out of a few fires, Billy Lee.'

The smile. 'Not my ass, Myron. Clu's. It was always about Clu, wasn't it? The drunk driving thing when we were living in Massachusetts. You didn't drive up to save my ass. You drove up because of Clu. And that brawl at that bar in the city. That was also because of Clu.'

Billy Lee suddenly tilted his head like a dog hearing a new sound. 'Why weren't we friends, Myron?'

'Because you didn't invite me to your birthday party at the roller rink?'

'Don't fuck with me, asshole.'

'I liked you just fine, Billy Lee. You were a fun guy.'

'But it got tired after a while, didn't it? My whole act, I mean. While I was a college star, it was pretty cool, right? But when I failed in the pros, I wasn't so cute and funny anymore. I was suddenly pathetic. That sound about right, Myron?'

'You say so.'

'So what about Clu?'

'What about him?'

'You were friends with him.'

'Yes.'

'Why? Clu partied the same way. Maybe even harder. He was always getting his ass in trouble. Why were you his friend?'

'This is stupid, Billy Lee.'

'Is it?'

'Put the gun down already.'

Billy Lee's smile was wide and knowing and somewhere just south of sane. 'I'll tell you why you stayed friendly with Clu. Because he was a better baseball player than me. He was going to the bigs. And you knew that.

That's the only difference between Clu Haid and Billy Lee Palms. He got drunk and took drugs and screwed tons of women, but it was all so funny because he was a pro.'

'So what are you trying to say, Billy Lee?' Myron countered. 'That pro athletes are treated differently from the rest of us? Hell of a revelation.'

But the revelation sat uneasily on Myron. Probably because Billy Lee's words, while wholly irrelevant, were at least in part true. Clu was charming and quirky simply because he was a pro athlete. But if the velocity of his fastball had dropped a few miles per hour, if the rotation of his arm had been just a little askew or if his finger position had not allowed for good ball movement on his pitches, Clu would have ended up like Billy Lee. Alternate worlds – totally different lives and fates – are right there, separated by a curtain no thicker than membrane. But with athletes, you can see your alternate life a little too clearly. You have the ability to throw the ball just a little faster than the next guy, you end up a god rather than the most pitiful of mortals. You get the girls, the fame, the big house, the money instead of the rats, the dull anonymity, the crummy apartment, the menial job. You get to go on TV and offer life insights. People want to be near you and hear you speak and touch the hem of your cloak. Just because you can hurl the rawhide with great velocity or put an orange ball in a metallic circle or swing a stick with a slightly more pure arc. You are special.

Nuts when you think about it.

'Did you kill him, Billy Lee?' Myron said.

Billy Lee looked like he'd been slapped. 'What?'

'You were jealous of Clu. He had everything. He left you behind.'

'He was my best friend!'

'A long time ago, Billy Lee.'

Myron again debated making a move. He could try to

slip the ropes – they were not on very tightly – but it would take time and he was still too far away. He wondered how Win was reacting to being cut off from all this and shuddered. Not worth dwelling upon.

A funny, tranquil flat line crossed Billy Lee's face. He stopped shaking, looked straight at Myron without jerking or twitching. His voice was suddenly soft.

'Enough,' he said.

Silence.

'I have to kill you, Myron. It's self-defense.'

'What are you talking about?'

'You killed Clu. And now you want to kill me.'

'That's crazy.'

'Maybe you had your secretary do it. And she got caught. Or maybe Win did it. That guy's always been your lapdog. Or maybe you did it yourself, Myron. The gun was found in your office, right? The blood in your car?'

'Why would I kill Clu?'

'You use people, Myron. You used him to start up your business. But after he failed his last drug test, Clu was finished. So you figured, why not cut your losses?'

'That makes no sense,' Myron said. 'And even if it did, why would I want to kill you?'

'Because I can talk too.'

'Talk about what?'

'About how helpful you are.'

Tears started rolling down Billy Lee's face. His voice tailed off. And Myron knew he was in huge trouble.

The moment of calm was over. The barrel of the gun was shaking. Myron tested the ropes. Nope. Despite the heat, something icy flooded his veins. He was trapped. No chance of making a move.

Billy Lee tried to giggle again, but something inside him was too weary now. 'Bye.'

Panic squeezed Myron's insides. Billy Lee was only seconds away from killing him. Period. There was no chance of talking him out of it. The combo of drugs and paranoia had scooped out all his ability to reason. Myron assessed his options and liked none of them.

'Win,' Myron said.

'I already told you. I ain't afraid of him.'

'I'm not talking to you.' Myron glanced over at Pat. The bartender was breathing hard, and his shoulders were drooping as though someone had packed them with wet sand. 'Once he pulls that trigger,' Myron said to him, 'I'm better off than you are.'

Pat started toward Billy Lee. 'Let's just calm down a second, Billy Lee. Think this through, okay?'

'I'm going to kill him.'

'Billy Lee, this Win guy. I've heard stories—'

'You don't understand, Pat. You just don't get it.'

'Then tell me, man. I'm here to help.'

'After I kill him.'

Billy Lee stepped toward Myron. He put the barrel of the gun against Myron's temple. Myron went rigid.

'Don't!'

Pat was close enough now. Or at least that was what he thought. He made his move, diving for Billy Lee's legs. But beneath the diminished drug addict lurked some of the athlete's old reflexes. Enough of them anyway. Billy Lee spun and fired. The bullet hit Pat's chest. For the briefest moment Pat looked surprised. Then he went down.

Billy Lee screamed, 'Pat!' He dropped onto his knees and crawled toward the still body.

Myron's heart was flapping like a caged condor. He did not wait. He struggled with the ropes. No go. He slid down in a frenzied slither. The rope was tighter than he thought, but he made some headway.

'Pat!' Billy Lee screamed again.

Myron's knees were on the floor now, his body contorted, his spine bow-bending in a way it was never supposed to. Billy Lee was wailing over a too-silent Pat.

The rope got caught under Myron's chin, pushing his head back and temporarily strangling him. How long did he have? How long before Billy Lee regained his senses? Impossible to say. Myron tilted his chin even higher, and the rope began to pass over him. He was almost out.

Billy Lee startled and turned around.

Myron was still caught in the rope. The two men locked eyes. It was over. Billy Lee lifted the shotgun. Maybe eight feet separated them. Myron saw the barrel, saw Billy Lee's eyes, saw the distance.

No chance. Too late.

The gun fired.

The first bullet hit Billy Lee's hand. He screamed in pain and dropped the shotgun. The second bullet hit Billy Lee's knee. Another scream. Blood spurted. The third bullet came so fast Billy Lee didn't have time to hit the floor. His head flew back from the impact, his legs splaying in midair. Billy Lee dropped out of sight like something at a shooting gallery.

The room was still.

Myron pulled the rope the rest of the way off and rolled into a corner.

'Win?' he shouted.

No answer.

'Win?'

Nothing.

Pat and Billy Lee did not so much as twitch. Myron stood, the only sound his own breath. Blood. Everywhere blood. They had to be dead. Myron pressed back into the corner. Someone was watching him. He knew that now. He crossed the room and looked out a window. He looked left. Nothing. He looked right.

Someone stood in the shadows. A silhouette. Fear engulfed Myron. The silhouette seemed to hover and then vanished into the darkness. Myron spun around and found the doorknob. He threw the door open and began to run.

26

He vomited three blocks away. He pulled up, leaned against a building, and puked his guts out. Several homeless men stopped and applauded. Myron gave a wave, acknowledging his fans. Welcome to New York.

Myron tried his cell phone, but it'd been crushed in the melee. He found a street sign and saw that he was only ten blocks south of the Biker Wannabee bar, in the meat-packing district near the West Side Highway. He jogged, holding his side, trying to stop the blood flow. He located a working pay phone, a feat that in this section of Manhattan normally involved a burning bush, and dialed Win's cellular.

Win picked up on the first ring. 'Articulate.'

'They're dead,' Myron said. 'Both of them.'

'Explain.'

Myron did.

When he finished, Win said, 'I'll be there in three minutes.'

'I have to call the cops.'

'Unwise.'

'Why?'

'They will not believe your tale of woe,' Win said, 'especially the part about a mystery savior.'

'Meaning they'll think you killed them?'

'Precisely.'

Win had a point.

'But we'd be able to clear it up,' Myron said.

'Yes perhaps, eventually. But it would take serious time.'

'Time we don't have.'

'Then you understand.'

Myron thought about it. 'But witnesses saw me leave the bar with Pat.'

'So?'

'So the police will question people. They'll learn about that. They'll be able to place me at the scene.'

'No more.'

'What?'

'On the phone. No more discussion. I'll be there in three minutes.'

'What about Zorra? What did you do to him?'

But Win was already off the line. Myron hung up the phone. A new set of homeless guys eyed him like he was a dropped sandwich. Myron met their gaze and did not look away until they did. He was not in the mood to be afraid anymore tonight.

A car pulled up in the promised three minutes. A Chevy Nova. Win had a collection of them – all old, all very used, all untraceable. Disposable cars, he called them. Win liked to use them for certain night activities. Don't ask.

The front passenger door opened. Myron glanced inside and saw Win behind the wheel. Myron slid in next to him.

'The die is cast,' Win said.

'What?'

'The police are already at the scene. It was on the scanner.'

Bad news. 'I can still come forward.'

'Yes, of course. And why, Mr Bolitar, did you not call the police? Why, in fact, did you call your friend before the proper authorities? Are you or are you not suspected of aiding Ms Esperanza Diaz in the murder of Billy Lee Palms's oldest friend? What exactly were you doing in that bar in the first place? Why would Mr Palms want to kill you?'

'It can all be explained.'

Win shrugged. 'Your call.'

'Just as it was my call to go alone with Pat.'

'Yes.'

'Which I called wrong.'

'Yes. You were too vulnerable going in like that. There were other ways.'

'What other ways?'

'We could have grabbed Pat at another time and made him tell us.'

'Made him?'

'Yes.'

'You mean, rough him up? Or torture him?'

'Yes.'

'I don't do that.'

'Grow up,' Win said. 'It is a simple cost-benefit analysis: By causing temporary discomfort to a malfeasant, you greatly lower the risk of being killed. It's a no-brainer.' Win glanced at him. 'By the way, you look like hell.'

'You should see the other guy,' he said. Then: 'Did you kill Zorra?'

Win smiled. 'You know me better than that.'

'No, Win, I don't. Did you kill him?'

Win pulled up to the Biker Wannabee bar. He put the car in park. 'Take a look inside.'

'Why are we back here?'

'Two reasons. One, you never left.'

'I didn't?'

'That's what I'll swear to. You were here all night. You just walked Pat out for a moment. Thrill will back me on it.' He smiled. 'So will Zorra.'

'You didn't kill him?'

'Her. Zorra prefers to be called a her.'

'Her. You didn't kill her?'

'Of course not.'

They got out of the car.

'I'm surprised,' Myron said.

'Why?'

'Usually when you threaten—'

'I never threatened Zorra. I threatened Pat. I said I *may* kill Zorra. But what would have been the point? Should Zorra suffer because a drugged-out psychotic like Billy Lee Palms hangs up a phone? Methinks not.'

Myron shook his head. 'You're a constant surprise.'

Win stopped. 'And lately you're a constant screwup. You got lucky. Zorra said she'd be willing to use her life to guarantee your safety. I recognized that she couldn't do it. It's why I told you not to go.'

'I didn't think I had a choice.'

'Now you know better.'

'Maybe.'

Win put a stilling hand on Myron's arm. 'You're not over her yet. Esperanza has a point when she tells you that.'

Myron nodded. Win dropped his arm.

'Take this,' Win said, handing him a small bottle. 'Please.'

Trial-size mouthwash. Count on Win. They made their way inside the Biker Wannabee. Myron stopped in the bathroom, rinsed out his mouth, splashed water on his face, checked the wound. It hurt. He looked in the mirror. His face was still tan from his three weeks with Terese, but Win was right: He looked like hell.

He met up with Win outside the bathroom door. 'You said two reasons before, that there were two reasons you wanted me to come back here.'

'Reason two,' Win said. 'Nancy – or Thrill, if you prefer. She was worried about you. I thought it best if you saw her.'

When they reached the corner booth, Zorra and Thrill were busy chatting like, well, two single women at a bar.

Zorra smiled at Myron. 'Zorra is sorry, dreamboat.'

'Not your fault,' Myron said.

'Zorra means that they're dead,' Zorra said. 'Zorra would have liked a few hours alone with them first.'

'Yeah,' Myron said. 'Pity.'

'Zorra already told Win all Zorra knows, which is very little. Zorra is just a beautiful hired gun. She likes to know as little as possible.'

'But you worked for Pat?'

She-he nodded, but the wig did not. 'Zorra was a bouncer and bodyguard. Do you believe that? Zorra Avrahaim having to settle for work as a common bouncer?'

'Yeah, times are tough. So what was Pat into?'

'A little of everything. Mostly drugs.'

'And how were Billy Lee and Pat connected?'

'Billy Lee claimed to be his uncle.' Zorra shrugged. 'But that could have been a lie.'

'Did you ever meet Clu Haid?'

'No.'

'Do you know why Billy Lee was hiding?'

'He was terrified. He thought someone was trying to kill him.'

'That someone being me?'

'So it seemed.'

Myron couldn't figure that one out. He asked a few more questions, but there was nothing else to learn. Win offered his hand. Zorra took it and stepped out of the booth. She handled the high heels well. Not everyone does.

Zorra kissed Win on the cheek. 'Thanks for not killing Zorra, dreamboat.'

Win bowed slightly. 'A pleasure, madame.' Win the charmer. 'I'll walk you out.'

246

Myron slid into the booth next to Thrill. Without saying a word, she grabbed his face with both hands and kissed him hard. He kissed her back. Win and his mouthwash. What a guy.

When they came up for air, Thrill said, 'You do know how to show a girl a good time.'

'Ditto.'

'You also scared the hell out of me.'

'I didn't mean to.'

She searched his face. 'Are you okay?'

'I will be.'

'Part of me wants to invite you back to my place.'

He said nothing, lowering his eyes. She kept her eyes on his face.

'This is it, isn't it?' she said. 'You won't call, will you?'

Myron said, 'You're beautiful, intelligent, fun—'

'And about to get the big kiss-off.'

'It's not you.'

'Oh, that's original. Don't tell me. It's you, right?'

He tried a smile. 'You know me so well.'

'I'd like to.'

'I'm damaged goods, Nancy.'

'Who isn't?'

'I'm just over a long-term relationship—'

'Who said anything about a relationship? We could just go out, right?'

'No.'

'What?'

'I don't work that way,' he said. 'I can't help it. I go out with someone, I start picturing kids and a backyard barbecue and a rusted hoop in the driveway. I try to size up all that stuff right away.'

She looked at him. 'Christ, you're strange.'

Hard to argue.

She started fiddling with a mixing straw. 'And you can't imagine me in any of those domestic settings?'

'Just the opposite,' Myron said. 'That's the problem.'

'I see. At least I think I see.' She shifted in her seat. 'I better go.'

'I'll take you home.'

'No, I'll get a taxi.'

'That's not necessary.'

'I think it is. Good night, Myron.'

She walked away. Myron stood. Win moved up next to him. They watched her disappear out the door.

'You'll make sure she gets home safely?' Myron asked.

Win nodded. 'I already called a car service for her.'

'Thanks.'

Silence. Then Win put his hand on Myron's shoulder.

'May I make one observation at this juncture?' Win asked.

'Shoot.'

'You're a total moron.'

They stopped at the doctor's apartment on the Upper West Side. He restitched the wound, making a tsk-tsk noise as he sewed. When they reached Win's apartment at the Dakota building, the two friends settled into the Louis the Someteenth decor with their favorite beverages. Myron chugged on a Yoo-Hoo; Win sipped an amber liquor.

Win flipped channels with a remote control. He stopped on CNN. Myron looked at the screen and thought of Terese on that island by herself. He checked the time. This was normally Terese's anchor slot. A bad dye job filled in. Myron wondered when or if Terese would be back on the air. And he wondered why he kept thinking about her.

Win turned the TV off. 'Need a refill?'

Myron shook his head. 'So what did Sawyer Wells tell you?'

'Not very much, I'm afraid. Clu was a drug addict. He

tried to help him. Blah, blah, blah. Sawyer is leaving the Yankees, you know.'

'I didn't.'

'He credits them with raising him out of obscurity. But alas, now it's time for dear Sawyer to take hold of his reins and motivate more minions. He's going to start touring soon.'

'Like a rock star?'

Win nodded. 'Complete with overpriced T-shirts.'

'Are they black?'

'I don't know. But at the end of each performance he encores after frenzied fans flick their Bics and shout, "Freebird!" '

'That's so 1977.'

'Isn't it? But I did a little checking. Guess who's sponsoring the tour.'

'Budweiser, the undisputed King of Beer?'

'Close,' Win said. 'His new publisher. Riverton Press.'

'As in Vincent Riverton, former owner of the New York Yankees?'

'The very.'

Myron whistled, processed it, came up with nothing. 'With all the buyouts in publishing, Riverton owns half the books in town. Probably means nothing.'

'Probably,' Win agreed. 'If you have more questions, Sawyer is giving a seminar tomorrow at the Cagemore Auditorium at Reston University. He invited me to attend. I'm allowed to bring a date.'

'I don't put out on the first date.'

'And you're proud of that?'

Myron took a deep chug. Maybe he was getting older, but Yoo-Hoo didn't have the same kick anymore. He craved a venti-size skim iced latte with a splash of vanilla, though he hated ordering it in front of other men. 'I'm going to try to find out about Clu's autopsy tomorrow.'

'Through this Sally Li?'

Myron nodded. 'She's been in court, but she's supposed to be back at the morgue tomorrow morning.'

'Think she'll tell you anything?'

'I don't know.'

'You may have to turn on the charm again,' Win said. 'Is this Sally Li of the heterosexual persuasion?'

'She is now,' Myron said. 'But once I turn on the charm—'

'All bets are off, yes.'

'Charm so potent,' Myron said, 'he can turn a woman against men.'

'You should print that on your business card.' Win did that snifter circle, palm up and under the glass. 'Before our old chum Billy Lee perished, did he reveal anything of import?'

'Not really,' Myron said. 'Just that he thought I was the one who killed Clu and now wanted to kill him.'

'Hmm.'

'Hmm what?'

'Once again, your name rears its ugly head.'

'He was a strung-out addict.'

'I see,' Win said. 'So he was just ranting?'

Silence.

'Somehow,' Myron said, 'I keep ending up in the middle of this.'

'So it seems.'

'But I can't imagine why.'

'Life's little mysteries.'

'I also can't figure out how Billy Lee fits into any of this: into Clu's murder, into Esperanza's affair with Bonnie, into Clu getting thrown off the team, into Clu signing with FJ, into any of it.'

Win put down his snifter and stood. 'I suggest we sleep on it.'

Good advice. Myron crawled under the covers and plunged immediately into slumber land. It was several hours later – after the REM and alpha sleep cycles, when he started rising to consciousness and his brain activity started going haywire – that it came to him. He thought again about FJ and about his having tailed Myron. He thought about what FJ had said, about how he had even seen Myron at the cemetery before Myron disappeared with Terese in the Caribbean.

And a big click sounded in his head.

27

He called FJ at nine in the morning. FJ's secretary said that Mr Ache could not be disturbed. Myron told her it was urgent. Sorry, Mr Ache was out of the office. But, Myron reminded her, you just said he could not be disturbed. He cannot be disturbed, the secretary countered, because he is not in the office. Ah.

'Tell him I want to meet with him,' Myron said. 'And it has to be today.'

'I can't promise you—'

'Just tell him.'

He looked at his watch. He was meeting Dad at 'the Club' at noon. It gave him time to try to rendezvous with Sally Li, chief medical examiner for Bergen County. He called her office and told her he wanted to talk.

'Not here,' Sally said. 'You know the Fashion Center?'

'It's one of the malls on Route Seventeen, right?'

'On the Ridgewood Avenue intersection, yeah. There's a sub shop outside the Bed, Bath and Beyond. Meet me there in an hour.'

'Bed, Bath and Beyond is part of the Fashion Center?'

'Must have something to do with the Beyond part.'

She hung up. He got in the rental car and started out to Paramus, New Jersey. Motto: There's No Such Thing as Too Much Commerce. The town of Paramus was like a muggy, jam-packed elevator with some jerk holding the door-open button and shouting, 'Come on, we can squeeze in one more strip mall.'

Nothing about the Fashion Center was particularly fashionable; the mall was in fact so unhip that teenagers didn't even hang out there. Sally Li sat on a bench, an unlit cigarette dangling from her lips. She wore green hospital scrubs and rubber sports sandals with no socks – footwear sported by many a coroner because it made cleaning off blood and guts and other human debris easy with a simple garden hose.

Okay, a little background here: For the past decade or so, Myron had been involved in an on-again, off-again romance with Jessica Culver. More recently they'd been in love. They'd moved in together. And now it was over. Or so he thought. He was not sure what exactly had happened. Objective observers might point to Brenda. She came along and changed a lot of things. But Myron was not sure.

So what's that have to do with Sally Li?

Jessica's father, Adam Culver, had been the Bergen County chief medical examiner until he was murdered several years ago. Sally Li, his assistant and close friend, had taken his place. That was how Myron knew her.

He approached. 'Another no-smoking mall?'

'No one uses the word *no* anymore,' Sally said. 'They say *free* instead. This isn't a no-smoking mall; it's a smoke-free zone. Next they'll call underwater an air-free zone. Or the Senate a brain-free zone.'

'So why did you want to meet here?'

Sally sighed, sat up. 'Because you want to know about Clu Haid's autopsy, right?'

Myron hesitated, nodded.

'Well, my superiors – and I use that term knowing I don't even have equals – would frown upon seeing us together. In fact, they'd probably try to fire my ass.'

'So why take the risk?' he asked.

'First off, I'm going to change jobs. I'm going back West, probably UCLA. Second, I'm cute, female, and what they now call Asian-American. It makes it harder to fire me. I might make a stink and the politically ambitious hate to look like they're beating up a minority. Third, you're a good guy. You figured out the truth when Adam was killed. I figure I owe you.' She took the cigarette out of her mouth, put it back in the package, took out another one, put it in her mouth. 'So what do you want to know?'

'Just like that?'

'Just like that.'

Myron said, 'I thought I'd have to turn on my charm.'

'Only if you want to get me naked.' She waved a hand. 'Ah, who am I kidding? Go ahead, Myron, fire away.'

'Injuries?' Myron asked.

'Four bullet wounds.'

'I thought there were three.'

'So did we at first. Two to the head, both at close range, either one of which would have been fatal. The cops thought there was only one. There was another in the right calf, and another in the back between the shoulder blades.'

'Longer range?'

'Yeah, I'd say at least five feet. Looked liked thirty-eights, but I don't do ballistics.'

'You were at the scene, right?'

'Yup.'

'Could you tell if there was forced entry?'

'The cops said no.'

Myron sat back and nodded to himself. 'Let me see if I got the DA's theory right. Correct me if I'm wrong.'

'I look forward to it.'

'They figure Clu knew the killer. He let him or her in voluntarily, they talked or whatever, and something went wrong. The killer draws a gun, Clu runs, the killer fires two shots. One hits his calf, the other his back. Could you tell which came first?'

'Which what?'

'The calf shot or the back shot.'

'No,' Sally said.

'Okay, so Clu goes down. He's hurt but not dead. The killer puts the gun to Clu's head. Bang, bang.'

Sally arched an eyebrow. 'I'm impressed.'

'Thanks.'

'As far as it goes.'

'Pardon?'

She sighed and shifted on the bench. 'There are problems.'

'Such as?'

'The body was moved.'

Myron felt his pulse pick up. 'Clu was killed someplace else?'

'No. But his body was moved. After he was killed.'

'I don't understand.'

'The lividity wasn't affected, so the blood didn't have time to settle. But he was dragged around on the floor, probably immediately after death, though it could be up to an hour later. And the room was tossed.'

'The killer was searching for something,' Myron said. 'Probably the two hundred thousand dollars.'

'Don't know about that. But there were blood smears all over the place.'

'What do you mean, smears?'

'Look, I'm an ME. I don't interpret crime scenes. But the place was a mess. Overturned furniture and bookshelves, drawers emptied out, and blood everywhere. On the walls. And on the floor. Like he'd been dragged like a rag doll.'

'Maybe he was dragging himself around. After he was shot in the leg and back.'

'Could be, I guess. Of course it's hard to drag yourself across walls unless you're Spider-Man.'

Myron's blood chilled a few degrees. He tried to sort and sift and process. How did all this fit? The killer was on a rampage to find the cash. Okay, that makes sense.

But why drag around the body? Why smear the walls with blood?

'We're not finished,' Sally said.

Myron blinked as though coming out of a trance.

'I also ran a full tox screen on the deceased. Know what I found?'

'Heroin?'

She shook her head. 'El Zippo.'

'What?'

'*Nada*, nothing, the big zero.'

'Clu was clean?'

'Not even a Tums.'

Myron made a face. 'But that could have been temporary, right? I mean, the drugs might have just been out of his system.'

'Nope.'

'What do you mean, nope?'

'Let's keep the science simple here, shall we? If a guy abuses drugs or alcohol, it shows up somewhere. Enlarged heart, liver damage, lung modules, whatever. And it did. There was no question that Clu Haid had liked some pretty potent chemicals. *Had*, Myron. Had. There are other tests – hair tests, for example – that give you a more recent snapshot. And those were clean. Which means he'd been off the stuff for a while.'

'But he failed a drug test two weeks ago.'

She shrugged.

'Are you telling me that test was fixed?'

Sally held up both hands. 'Not me. I'm telling you that my data disputes that data. I never said anything about a fix. It could have been an innocent error. There are such things as false positives.'

Myron's head swam. Clu had been clean. His body had been dragged around after being shot four times. Why? None of this made any sense.

They chatted a few more minutes, mostly about the

past, and headed for the exit ten minutes later. Myron started back to his car. Time to see Dad. He tried the new cellular – count on Win to have 'extras' lying about his apartment – and called Win.

'Articulate,' Win answered.

'Clu was right. The drug test was fixed.'

Win said, 'My, my.'

'Sawyer Wells witnessed the drug test.'

'More my, my.'

'What time is he doing the motivational talk at Reston?'

'Two o'clock,' Win said.

'In the mood to get motivated?'

'You have no idea.'

28

The Club.

Brooklake Country Club, to be more exact, though there was no brook, no lake, and they were not in the country. It was, however, most definitely a club. As Myron's car made its way up the steep drive, the clubhouse's white Greco-Roman pillars rising through the clouds, childhood memories popped up in fluorescent flashes. It was how he always saw the place. In flashes. Not always pleasant ones.

The Club was the epitome of nouveau-riche, Myron's wealthy brethren proving that they could be just as tacky and exclusive as their goyish counterparts. Older women with perpetual tans on large, freckled chests sat by the pool, their hair shellacked into place by fake French hairdressers to the point where the strands resembled frozen fiber optics, never allowing it, God forbid, to touch the water, sleeping, he imagined, without putting their heads down lest they shatter the dos like so much Venetian glass; there were nose jobs and liposuction and face-lifts so extreme that the ears almost touched in the back, the overall effect bizarrely sexy in the same way you might find Yvonne De Carlo on *The Munsters* sexy; women fighting off old age and on the surface winning, but Myron wondered if they doth protest too much, their fear just a little too bare in the scar-revealing, harsh overhead lights of the dining room.

Men and women were separated at the Club, the women animatedly playing mah-jongg, the men silently chewing on cigars over a hand of cards; women still had special tee times so as not to interfere with the bread-winners' – i.e., their husbands' – precious leisure moments; there was tennis too, but that was more for fashion than exercise, giving everyone an excuse to wear sweatsuits that rarely encountered sweat, couples some-times sporting matching ones; a men's grill, a women's lounge, the oak boards memorializing golf champions in gold leaf, the same man winning seven years in a row, now dead, the large locker rooms with masseur's tables, the bathrooms with combs sitting in blue alcohol, the pickle-and-coleslaw bar, cleat marks on the rug, the Founders Board with his grandparents' names still on it, immigrant dining room help, all referred to by their first names, always smiling too hard and at the ready.

What shocked Myron now was that people *his* age were members. The same young girls who had sneered at their mothers' idleness now abandoned their own found-ering careers to 'raise' the kids – read: hire nannies – came here to lunch and bore each other silly with a continuous game of one-upmanship. The men Myron's age had manicures and long hair and were well fed and too well dressed, kicking back with their cellular phones and casually swearing to a colleague. Their kids were there too, dark-eyed youngsters walking through the clubhouse with hand-held video games and Walkmans and too regal a bearing.

All conversations were inane and depressed the hell out of Myron. The grandpas in Myron's day had the good sense not to talk much to one another, just discarding and picking up what was dealt, occasionally grumbling about a local sports team; the grandmothers interrogated one another, measuring their own children and grand-children against the competition, seeking an opponent's weakness and any conversational opening to jab forward with tales of offspring heroics, no one really listening, just preparing for the next frontal assault, familial pride getting confused with self-worth and desperation.

The main clubhouse dining room was as expected: waaaay too overstated. The green carpeting, the curtains that resembled corduroy leisure suits, the gold tablecloths on huge round mahogany, the floral centerpieces piled too high and with no sense of proportion, not unlike the plates traipsing down the buffet line. Myron remembered attending a sports-themed bar mitzvah here as a child: jukeboxes, posters, pennants, a Wiffle ball batting cage, a basket for foul shots, an artist wanna-be stuck sketching sports-related caricatures of thirteen-year-old boys – thirteen-year-old boys being God's most obnoxious creation short of television lawyers – and a wedding band complete with an overweight lead singer who handed the kids silver dollars shrouded in leather pouches that were emblazoned with the band's phone number.

But this view – these flashes – was too quick and thus simplistic. Myron knew that. His remembrances were all screwed up about this place – the derision blending with the nostalgia – but he also remembered coming here as a child for family dinners, his clip-on tie slightly askew, sent by Mom into the inner sanctum of the men's card room to find his grandfather, the undisputed family patriarch, the room reeking of cigar smoke, his pop-pop greeting him with a ferocious embrace, his gruff compatriots who wore golf shirts that were too loud and too tight barely acknowledging the interloper because their own grandkids would do the same soon, the card game trickling down, participant by participant.

These same people he so easily picked apart were the first generation fully out of Russia or Poland or Ukraine or some other shtetl-laced combat zone. They'd hit the New World running – running away from the past, the poverty, the fear – and they just ran a bit too far. But under the hair and the jewelry and the gold lamé, no mother bear would ever be so quick to kill for her cubs, the women's hard eyes still seeking out the pogrom in the distance, suspicious, always expecting the worst, bracing themselves to take the blow for their children.

Myron's dad sat in a yellow, pseudo-leather swivel chair in the brunch room, fitting in with this crowd about as well as a camel-riding mufti. Dad did not belong here. Never had. He didn't play golf or tennis or cards. He didn't swim and he didn't brag and he didn't brunch and he didn't talk stock tips. He wore his work clothes of all things: charcoal gray slacks, loafers, and a white dress shirt over a sleeveless white undershirt. His eyes were dark, his skin pale olive, his nose jutting forward like a hand waiting to be shook.

Interestingly enough, Dad was not a member of Brooklake. Dad's parents, on the other hand, had been founding members, or in the case of Pop-pop, a ninety-two-year-old quasi vegetable whose rich life had been dissolved into useless fragments by Alzheimer's, still was. Dad hated the place, but he kept up the membership for the sake of his father. That meant showing up every once in a while. Dad looked at it as a small price to pay.

When Dad spotted Myron, he rose, more slowly than usual, and suddenly the obvious hit Myron: The cycle was beginning anew. Dad was the age Pop-pop had been back then, the age of the people they'd made fun of, his ink-black hair wispy, static gray now. The thought was far from comforting.

'Over here!' Dad called, though Myron had seen him. Myron threaded his way through the brunchers, mostly overkept women who constantly pendulumed between chewing and chatting, bits of coleslaw caught in the corners of their glossy mouths, water glasses stained with pink lipstick. They eyed Myron as he walked by for three reasons: under forty, male, no marriage band. Measuring his son-in-law potential. Always on the lookout, though not necessarily for their own daughters, the yenta from the shtetl never too far away.

Myron hugged his father and as always kissed his cheek. The cheek still felt wonderfully rough, but the skin was loosening. The scent of Old Spice wafted gently in the air, as comforting as any hot chocolate on the coldest of days. Dad hugged him back, released, then hugged him again. No one noticed the display of affection. Such acts were not uncommon here.

The two men sat. The paper place mats had an overhead diagram of the golf course's eighteen holes and an ornate letter *B* in the middle. The club's logo. Dad picked up a stubby green pencil, a golf pencil, to scribble down their order. That was how it worked. The menu had not changed in thirty years. As a kid Myron always ordered either the Monte Cristo or Reuben sandwich. Today he asked for a bagel with lox and cream cheese. Dad wrote it down.

'So,' Dad began. 'Getting acclimated to being back?'

'Yeah, I think so.'

'Hell of a thing with Esperanza.'

'She didn't do it.'

Dad nodded. 'Your mother tells me that you've been subpoenaed.'

'Yep. But I don't know anything.'

'You listen to your aunt Clara. She's a smart lady. Always has been. Even in school, Clara was the smartest girl in the class.'

'I will.'

The waitress came by. Dad handed her the order. He turned back to Myron and shrugged. 'It's getting near the end of the month,' Dad said. 'I have to use your pop-pop's minimum before the thirtieth. I didn't want the money to go to waste.'

'This place is fine.'

Dad made a face signaling disagreement. He grabbed

some bread, buttered it, then pushed it away. He shifted in his chair. Myron watched him. Dad was working up to something.

'So you and Jessica broke up?'

In all the years Myron had been dating Jessica, Dad had never inquired about their relationship past the polite questions. It just wasn't his way. He'd ask how Jessica was, what she was up to, when her next book was coming out. He was polite and friendly and greeted her warmly, but he'd never given a true indication of how he really felt about her. Mom had made her own feelings on the subject crystal clear: Jessica was not good enough for her son, but then again, who was? Dad was like a great newscaster, the kind of guy who asks questions without giving the viewer any hint of how he was really leaning on the issue.

'I think it's over,' Myron said.

'Because' – Dad stopped, looked away, looked back – 'of Brenda?'

'I'm not sure.'

'I'm not big on giving advice. You know that. Maybe I should have been. I read those life instruction books fathers write for their children. You ever see those?'

'Yes.'

'All kinds of wisdom in there. Like: Watch a sunrise once a year. Why? Suppose you want to sleep in? Another one: Overtip a breakfast waitress. But suppose she's grumpy? Suppose she's really bad? Maybe that's why I never dealt with it. I always see the other side.'

Myron smiled.

'So I was never big on advice. But I have learned one thing for sure. One thing. So listen to me because this is important.'

'Okay.'

'The most important decision you'll ever make is who you marry,' Dad said. 'You can take every other decision you'll ever make, add them together, and it still won't be as important as that one. Suppose you choose the wrong job, for example. With the right wife, that's not a problem. She'll encourage you to make a change, cheer you on no matter what. You understand?'

'Yes.'

'Remember that, okay?'

'Okay.'

'You have to love her more than anything in the world. But she has to love you just as much. Your priority should be her happiness, and her priority should be yours. That's a funny thing – caring about someone more than yourself. It's not easy. So don't look at her as just a sexual object or as just a friend to talk to. Picture every day with the person. Picture paying bills with that person, raising children with that person, being stuck in a hot room with no air-conditioning and a screaming baby with that person. Am I making sense?'

'Yes.' Myron smiled and folded his hands on the table. 'Is that how it is with you and Mom? Is she all those things to you?'

'All those things,' Dad agreed, 'plus a pain in the *tuchus.*'

Myron laughed.

'If you promise not to tell your mother, I'll let you in on a little secret.'

'What?'

He leaned in and whispered conspiratorially. 'When your mother walks in the room – even now, even after all these years, if she were to, say, stroll by us right now – my heart still does a little two-step. You understand what I'm saying?'

'I think so, yeah. That used to happen with Jess.'

Dad spread his hands. 'Enough then.'

'Are you saying Jessica is that person?'

'Not my place to say one way or the other.'

'Do you think I'm making a mistake?'

Dad shrugged. 'You'll figure that out, Myron. I have tremendous confidence in you. Maybe that's why I never gave you much advice. Maybe I always thought you were smart enough without me.'

'Bull.'

'Or maybe it was easier parenting, I don't know.'

'Or maybe you led by example,' Myron said. 'Maybe you led gently. Maybe you showed rather than told.'

'Yeah, well, whatever.'

They fell into silence. The women around them chatted up their white noise.

Dad said, 'I turn sixty-eight this year.'

'I know.'

'Not a young man anymore.'

Myron shook his head. 'Not old either.'

'True enough.'

More silence.

'I'm selling the business,' Dad said.

Myron froze. He saw the warehouse in Newark, the place Dad had worked for as long as Myron could remember. The *schmata* business – in Dad's case, undergarments. He could picture Dad with his ink-black hair in his glass-walled warehouse office, barking out orders, sleeves rolled up, Eloise, his long-time secretary, fetching him whatever he needed before he knew he needed it.

'I'm too old for it now,' Dad went on. 'So I'm getting out. I spoke to Artie Bernstein. You remember Artie?'

Myron managed a nod.

'The man's a rat bastard, but he's been dying to buy me out for years. Right now his offer is garbage, but I still might take it.'

Myron blinked. 'You're selling?'

'Yes. And your mother is going to cut back at the law firm.'

'I don't understand.'

Dad put a hand on Myron's arm. 'We're tired, Myron.'
Myron felt two giant hands press down on his chest.
'We're also buying a place in Florida.'
'Florida?'
'Yes.'
'You're moving to Florida?' Myron's Theory on East
Coast Jewish Life: You grow up, you get married, you
have kids, you go to Florida, you die.
'No, maybe part of the year, I don't know. Your
mother and I are going to start traveling a little more.'
Dad paused. 'So we'll probably sell the house.'
They'd owned that house Myron's entire life. Myron
looked down at the table. He grabbed a wrapped Saltine
cracker from the bread basket and tore open the
cellophane.
'Are you okay?' Dad asked.
'I'm fine,' he said. But he wasn't fine. And he couldn't
articulate why, even to himself.
The waitress served them. Dad was having a salad with
cottage cheese. Dad hated cottage cheese. They ate in
silence. Myron kept feeling tears sting his eyes. Silly.
'There's one other thing,' Dad said.
Myron looked up. 'What?'
'It's not a big deal really. I didn't even want to tell you,
but your mother thought I should. And you know how it
is with your mother. When she has something in her
mind, God himself—'
'What is it, Dad?'
Dad fixed his eyes on Myron's. 'I want you to know
this has nothing to do with you or your going to the
Caribbean.'
'Dad, what?'
'While you were gone' – Dad shrugged and started
blinking; he put down his fork, and there was the faintest
quiver in his lower lip— 'I had some chest pains.'
Myron felt his own heart sputter. He saw Dad with the

ink-black hair at Yankee Stadium. He saw Dad's face turning red when he told him about the bearded man. He saw Dad rise and storm off to avenge his sons.

When Myron spoke, his voice sounded tinny and far away. 'Chest pains?'

'Don't make a thing of it.'

'You had a heart attack?'

'Let's not blow it out of proportion. The doctors weren't sure what it was. It was just some chest pains, that's all. I was out of the hospital in two days.'

'The hospital?' More images: Dad waking up with the pains, Mom starting to cry, calling an ambulance, rushing to the hospital, the oxygen mask on his face, Mom holding his hand, both their faces devoid of any color . . .

And then something broke open. Myron couldn't stop himself. He got up and half sprinted to the bathroom. Someone said hello to him, called out his name, but he kept moving. He pushed open the bathroom door, opened a stall, locked himself in, and nearly collapsed.

Myron started to cry.

Deep, bone-crushing cries, full-body sobs. Just when he thought he couldn't cry anymore. Something inside him had finally given way, and now he sobbed without pause or letup.

Myron heard the bathroom door open. Someone leaned against the stall door. Dad's voice, when he finally spoke, was barely a whisper. 'I'm fine, Myron.'

But Myron again saw Dad at Yankee Stadium. The ink-black hair was gone, replaced with the gray, fly-away wisps. Myron saw Dad challenge the bearded man. He saw the bearded man rise, and then he saw Dad clutch his chest and fall to the ground.

29

Myron tried to shake it off. No choice really. But he couldn't stop thinking about it. And he couldn't stop worrying. Worrying had never been his style in the past, even when a crisis loomed. All of a sudden he had the worry-queasies in his stomach. It was true what they said: The older you become, the more you are like your parents. Soon he'd be telling a kid not to stick his elbow out the car window or he'd lose it.

Win met him in front of the auditorium. He was in classic Win pose, eyes level, arms crossed, totally relaxed. He wore designer sunglasses and looked ultrasleek. *GQ* casual.

'Problem?' Win said.

'No.'

Win shrugged.

'I thought we were going to meet inside,' Myron said.

'That would mean I'd have to listen to more of Sawyer Wells.'

'That bad?'

'Imagine, if you will, a Mariah Carey-Michael Bolton duet,' Win said.

'Eeuw.'

Win checked his watch. 'He should be finishing up now. We must be brave.'

They headed inside. The Cagemore Center was a sprawling facility that featured oodles of concert and lecture halls that could be cut to any size by sliding walls back and forth. There was a summer camp for young children in one room. Win and Myron stopped and listened to the children sing 'Farmer in the Dell.' The sound made Myron smile.

'. . . the farmer in the dell, the farmer in the dell, hi-ho-the-dairy-o, the farmer in the dell . . .'

Win turned to Myron. 'What's a dell?' Win asked.

'No idea.'

Win shrugged and moved on to the main auditorium. There was a table out front selling Sawyer Wells paraphernalia. Cassettes, videos, books, magazines, posters, pennants (though what one does with a Sawyer Wells pennant went beyond Myron's capacity to imagine) and yep, T-shirts. Groovy titles too: *The Wells Guide to Wellness, The Wells Rules for Wellness, Key to Wellness: It's All About You.* Myron shook his head.

The auditorium was packed, the crowd so silent they'd put the Vatican to shame. Up on the stage, jittering to and fro like Robin Williams in his stand-up comic days, was the self-help guru himself. Sawyer Wells was resplendent in a business suit with the jacket off, shirt cuffs turned once, fancy suspenders cutting into his shoulders. A good look for a self-help guru: The expensive suit makes you reek of success while the jacket off and rolled-up sleeves give you the air of a regular guy. A perfectly balanced ensemble.

'It's all about you,' Sawyer Wells told the enraptured audience. 'If you remember nothing else today, remember that. It's all about you. Make everything about you. Every decision is about you. Everything you see, everything you touch is a reflection of you. No . . . more than that – it *is* you. You are everything. And everything is you.'

Win leaned toward Myron. 'Isn't that a song?'

'The Stylistics, I think. Circa early seventies.'

'I want you to remember that,' Sawyer continued. 'Visualize. Visualize everything as you. Your family is you. Your job is you. When you're walking down the street, that beautiful tree is you. That blooming rose is you.'

Win said, 'That dirty commode at the bus terminal.'

Myron nodded. 'You.'

'You see the boss, the leader, the breadwinner, the successful, fulfilled person. That person is you. No one can lead you because the leader is you. You stand in front of your opponent, and you know you can win because you are your opponent. And you know how to beat you. Remember you are your opponent. Your opponent is you.'

Win frowned. 'But don't you know how to beat you too?'

'It's a paradox,' Myron agreed.

'You fear the unknown,' Sawyer Wells ranted. 'You fear success. You fear taking chances. But now you know that the unknown is you. Success is you. Taking chances is you. You don't fear you, do you?'

Win frowned.

'Listen to Mozart. Take long walks. Ask yourself what you did today. Do that every night. Before you go to sleep, ask yourself if the world is better because of you. After all, it's your world. You are the world.'

Win said, 'If he breaks into a rendition of "We Are the World," I'm using my gun.'

'But you are your gun,' Myron countered.

'And he is my gun too.'

'Right.'

Win considered that. 'So if he is my gun and my gun kills him, it's a suicide.'

'Take responsibility for your actions,' Wells said. 'That's one of the Wells Rules for Wellness. Take responsibility. Cher once said, "Excuses won't lift your butt, 'kay?" Listen to that. Believe that with all your heart.'

The man was quoting Cher. The crowd was nodding. There is no God.

'Confess something about yourself to a friend – something awful, something you'd never want anyone to know. You'll feel better. You'll still see that you're worthy of love. And since your friend is you, you are really just telling yourself. Have an interest in everything. Thirst for knowledge. That's another rule. Remember that it's all about you. When you learn about other things, you are actually learning about yourself. Get to know you better.'

Win looked at Myron, his face pained.

'Let's wait outside,' Myron said.

But luck was with them. Two sentences later Sawyer Wells was done. The crowd went ballistic. They stood, they applauded, they hooted like an old Arsenio Hall audience.

Win shook his head. 'Four hundred dollars a pop.'

'That what this thing costs?'

'He is your money.'

People approached the stage, stretching their hands toward the heavens in the vain hope that Sawyer Wells might reach out and touch them. Myron and Win watched. The table with the Wells paraphernalia was swarmed now like rotting fruit with buzzing flies.

'The citified version of a tent revival,' Win noted.

Myron nodded.

Eventually Sawyer Wells waved and ran offstage. The crowd continued to cheer and purchase. Myron half expected a voice-over to announce that Elvis had left the building. Win and Myron swam through the crowd.

'Come,' Win said. 'I have backstage passes.'

'Please tell me you're joking.'

He wasn't. They actually said 'Backstage Pass' on them. A plainclothes security guard scowled at them and scrutinized the passes as if they were the Zapruder film.

Satisfied, he let them past the velvet rope. Yep, velvet rope. Sawyer Wells spotted Win and bounced toward them.

'So glad you could come, Win!' He turned to Myron and stuck out his hand. 'Hi, I'm Sawyer Wells.'

Myron shook it. 'Myron Bolitar.'

Sawyer's smile flickered but stayed on. 'Nice to meet you, Myron.'

Myron decided to try a frontal assault. 'Why did you fix Clu Haid's drug test so it would appear he was taking heroin?'

The smile was still there, but it wasn't sitting right. 'Pardon?'

'Clu Haid. The name ring a bell?'

'Of course. As I told Win yesterday, I worked very hard with him.'

'Worked how?'

'To keep him off drugs. I have an extensive background as a drug counselor. That's how I was trained. To help addicts.'

'Not so different from what you're doing now,' Myron said.

'Pardon?'

'People with addictive personalities need an addiction. If it's not booze or drugs, maybe it's religion or self-help mumbo jumbo. They're simply swapping addictions; we hope to one less damaging.'

Sawyer Wells overnodded. 'That's a really interesting viewpoint, Myron.'

'Gee, thanks, Sawyer.'

'I learned much about human frailty, about our lack of self-esteem, from addicts like Clu Haid. As I said, I worked very hard with him. His failure hurt me greatly.'

Win said, 'Because it was your failure.'

'Pardon?'

'You are everything, and everything is you,' Win said. 'You are Clu Haid. He failed, ergo you failed.'

Sawyer Wells maintained the smile. But it was different when he looked at Win. His gestures were tighter too, more controlled. He was one of those guys who tried to imitate the person with whom he was conversing. Myron hated that. 'I see you came in at the end of my seminar, Win.'

'Did I misunderstand your message?'

'No, it's not that. But a man creates his own world. That's my point. You are what you create, what you perceive. Take responsibility. That's the most important component of the Wells Guide to Wellness. You take responsibility for your own actions. And you admit fault. You know what the two most beautiful sentences in the world are?'

Win opened his mouth, stopped, looked at Myron, shook his head. 'Too easy,' he said.

' "I am responsible," ' Sawyer continued. ' "It's my fault." ' He turned toward Myron. 'Say it, Myron.'

'What?'

'Come on. It's exhilarating. Say, "I am responsible. It's my fault." Stop passing the buck in your life. Say it. Come on, I'll say it with you. Win, you too.'

Myron and Sawyer said, 'I am responsible. It's my fault.' Win remained silent.

'Feel better?' Sawyer said.

'It was almost like sex,' Myron said.

'It can be powerful, yes.'

'Yeah, uh-huh. Look, Sawyer, I'm not here to critique your seminar. I want to know about Clu's drug test. It was fixed. We have evidence that proves that fact. You helped administer that test. I want to know why you made it look like Clu was on drugs.'

'I don't know what you're talking about.'

'The autopsy shows conclusively that Clu hadn't taken

273

drugs for at least two months before his death. Yet you tested him positive two weeks ago.'

'Maybe the test was faulty,' Sawyer said.

Win tsk-tsked. 'Say, "I am responsible. It's my fault." '

'Stop passing the buck in your life,' Myron added.

'Come on, Sawyer. It's exhilarating.'

'That's not funny,' Sawyer said.

'Wait,' Win said. 'You are everything, thus you are the drug test.'

'And you are a positive guy,' Myron added.

'Ergo the test result was positive.'

Sawyer said, 'I think I've had just about enough.'

'You're finished, Wells,' Myron said. 'I'll blab to the papers.'

'I don't know what you're talking about. I don't know anything about a fixed test.'

'Want to hear my theory?' Myron said.

'No.'

'You're leaving the Yankees and going to work for Vincent Riverton, right?'

'I'm not working exclusively for anyone. His conglomerate publishes my book.'

'He's also Sophie Mayor's archenemy.'

'You don't know that,' Sawyer said.

'He lived for owning the team. When she took over, he was pissed. She ends up being everything New York wants in an owner because she minds her own business. She makes only one move, acquiring Clu Haid, and it's a beauty. Clu pitches better than anyone dared hope. The Yankees start heading for greatness. Then you step in. Clu fails a drug test. Sophie Mayor looks incompetent. The Yankees tumble.'

Sawyer seemed to recoup a bit. Something in what Myron had just said had given him a new lease. Odd. 'That makes no sense whatsoever.'

'What part?'

'All of it,' Sawyer said, chest back out. 'Sophie Mayor has been good to me. I was working as a drug counselor at the Sloan State and Rockwell rehab centers when she gave me my chance to move up. Why would I want to hurt her?'

'You tell me.'

'I have no idea. I firmly believed that Clu was on drugs. If he wasn't, then the test was faulty.'

'You know the results are double-tested. There was no mistake. Someone had to fix it.'

'It wasn't me. Maybe you should speak to Dr Stilwell.'

'But you were there? You admit that?'

'Yes, I was there. And I will no longer dignify your questions with answers.' With that Sawyer Wells abruptly spun and stormed off.

'I don't think he liked us,' Myron said.

'But if it's all about you, then we are he.'

'So he doesn't like himself?'

'Sad, isn't it?'

'Not to mention confusing,' Myron said.

They headed for the exit.

'So where to, Oh, Motivated One?' Win asked.

'Starbucks.'

'Latte time?'

Myron shook his head. 'Confront FJ time.'

30

FJ was not there. Myron called his office again. The same secretary told him that FJ was still unavailable. Myron repeated that it was imperative that he speak to Francis Ache Junior as soon as humanly possible. The secretary remained unimpressed.

Myron returned to his office.

Big Cyndi wore a bright green spandex bodysuit with a slogan across the chest – this on a woman who could barely squeeze into a caftan. The fabric screamed in pain, the letters in the slogan so elongated that Myron couldn't read them, kinda like what happens to Silly Putty after you press it against a newspaper headline and stretch it out.

'Lots of clients have been calling, Mr Bolitar,' Big Cyndi said. 'They are not pleased by your absence.'

'I'll take care of it,' he said.

She gave him the messages. 'Oh, and Jared Mayor called,' she said. 'He seemed very anxious to talk to you.'

'Okay, thanks.'

He called Jared Mayor first. He was in his mother's office at Yankee Stadium. Sophie switched on the speakerphone.

'You called?' Myron said.

'I was hoping you could give us an update,' Jared said.

'I think someone is setting up your mother.'

Sophie said, 'Setting me up how?'

'Clu's drug test was a fix. He was clean.'

'I know you want to believe that—'

'I have proof,' Myron said.

Silence.

'What kind of proof?' Jared asked.

'There's no time for that now. But trust me on this. Clu was clean.'

'Who would have fixed the test?' Sophie asked.

'That's what I want to know. The logical suspects are Dr Stilwell and Sawyer Wells.'

'But why would they want to hurt Clu?'

'Not Clu, Sophie. You. It fits in with everything else we have. Raising the specter of your missing daughter, taking your big baseball trade and turning it against you – I think someone's out to hurt you.'

'You're jumping to conclusions,' Sophie said.

'Could be.'

'Who would want to hurt me?'

'I'm sure you've made your share of enemies. How about Vincent Riverton, for one?'

'Riverton? No. Our whole takeover was far more amicable than the press portrayed it.'

'Still, I wouldn't rule him out.'

'Listen, Myron, I don't really care about any of this. I just want you to find my daughter.'

'They're probably connected.'

'How?'

Myron changed ears. 'You want me to be blunt, right?'

'Absolutely.'

'Then I have to remind you what the odds are that your daughter is still alive.'

'Slim,' she said.

'Very slim.'

'No, I'll stay with slim. In fact, I think it's better than slim.'

'Do you really believe Lucy is alive someplace?'

'Yes.'

'She's out there somewhere, waiting to be found?'

'Yes.'

'Then the big question,' Myron said, 'is why.'

'What do you mean?'

'Why isn't she home?' he asked. 'Do you think someone's been holding her hostage all these years?'

'I don't know.'

'Well, what other choices are there? If Lucy is still alive, why hasn't she come home? Or phoned home? What is she hiding from?'

Silence.

Sophie broke it. 'You think someone has resurrected my daughter's memory as part of some vendetta against me?'

Myron was not sure how to answer. 'I think it's a possibility we have to consider.'

'I appreciate your bluntness, Myron. I want you to remain honest with me. Don't hold back. But I'll also keep my hope. When your child disappears into thin air, it creates a huge void. I need something to fill that void, Myron. So until I find out otherwise, I'll fill it with hope.'

Myron said, 'I understand.'

'Then you'll keep looking.'

There was a knock on the door. Myron put his hand over the phone and said to come in. Big Cyndi opened the door. Myron gestured to a chair. She took it. In the bright green she looked a bit like a planet.

'I'm not sure what I can do, Sophie.'

'Jared will investigate Clu's drug test,' she said. 'If there was anything amiss, he'll find out about it. You keep your eyes open for my daughter. You may be right about Lucy's fate. Then again you may be wrong. Don't give up.'

Before he could reply, the line was disconnected. Myron put the phone back in the cradle.

'Well?' Big Cyndi asked.

'She still has hope.'

Big Cyndi scrunched up her face. 'There's a fine line between hope and delusion, Mr Bolitar,' she said. 'I think Ms Mayor may have crossed it.'

Myron nodded. He shifted in his chair. 'Something I can do for you?' he asked.

She shook her head. Her head was a nearly perfect cube and reminded Myron of the old game of Rock'Em Sock'Em Robots. Not sure what else to do, Myron folded his hands and put them on his desk. He wondered how many times he had been alone with Big Cyndi like this. Less than a handful for sure. Wrong to say, but she made him uncomfortable.

After some time had passed, Big Cyndi said, 'My mother was a big, ugly woman.'

Myron had no comeback for that one.

'And like most big, ugly women, she was a shrinking violet. That's how it is with big, ugly women, Mr Bolitar. They get used to standing alone in the corner. They hide. They become angry and defensive. They keep their heads down, and they let themselves be treated with disdain and disgust and—'

She stopped suddenly, waved a meaty paw. Myron sat still.

'I hated my mother,' she said. 'I swore that I would never be like that.'

Myron risked a small nod.

'That's why you have to save Esperanza.'

'I'm not sure I see the connection.'

'She's the only one who sees past this.'

'Past what?'

She thought about that one for a moment. 'What's the first thing you think when you see me, Mr Bolitar?'

'I don't know.'

'People like to stare,' she said.

'Hard to blame them, don't you think?' Myron said. 'I mean, the way you dress and stuff.'

She smiled. 'I'd rather see shock on their faces than pity,' she said. 'And I'd rather they see brazen or outrageous than shrinking or scared or sad. Do you understand?'

'I think so.'

'I'm not standing alone in the corner anymore. I've done enough of that.'

Myron, unsure what to say, settled for a nod.

'When I was nineteen, I started wrestling professionally. And of course I was cast as a villain. I sneered. I made faces. I cheated. I hit opponents when they weren't looking. It was all an act, of course. But that was my job.'

Myron sat back and listened.

'One night I was scheduled to fight Esperanza – Little Pocahontas, I should say. It was the first time we'd met. She was already the most beloved wrestler on the circuit. Cute and pretty and small and all the things . . . all the things that I'm not. Anyway, we were performing in some high school gym outside Scranton. The script was the usual. A back-and-forth match. Esperanza winning with her skill. Me cheating. Twice I was supposed to nearly have her pinned when the crowd would go wild and she'd start stamping her foot, like the cheers were giving her strength, and then everyone would start clapping in unison with her stomps. You know how it works, right?'

Myron nodded.

'She was supposed to pin me with a backflip at the fifteen-minute mark. We executed it perfectly. Then as she was raising her hands in victory, I was supposed to sneak up on her and whack her in the back with a metal chair. Again it went perfectly. She collapsed to the canvas. The crowd gasped. I, the Human Volcano – that's what I was called then – raised my hands in victory. They started booing and throwing things. I sneered. The announcers acted all concerned for poor Little Pocahontas. They brought out the stretcher. Again you've seen the same act a million times on cable.'

He nodded again.

'So there was another match or two, and then the crowd was ushered out. I decided not to change until I got back to the motel. I left for the bus a few minutes before the other girls. It was dark, of course. Nearly midnight. But some of the spectators were still out there. They confronted me. There must have been twenty of them. They started shouting at me. I decided to play back. I did my ring sneer and flexed' – her voice caught – 'and that was when a rock hit me square in the mouth.'

Myron kept perfectly still.

'I started bleeding. Then another rock hit me in the shoulder. I couldn't believe what was happening. I tried to head back inside, but they circled around me. I didn't know what to do. They started moving in closer. I ducked down. Someone hit me over the head with a beer bottle. My knees hit the pavement. Then someone kicked me in the stomach and someone else pulled my hair.'

She stopped. Her eyes blinked a few times and she looked up and away. Myron thought about reaching out to her, but he didn't. Later he'd wonder why.

'And that's when Esperanza stepped in,' Big Cyndi said after a few moments had passed. 'She jumped over someone in the crowd and landed right on me. The morons thought she was there to help beat me up. But she just wanted to put herself between me and the blows. She told them to stop. But they wouldn't listen. One of them pulled her away so they could keep beating me. I felt another kick. Someone yanked my hair so hard my neck snapped back. I really thought they were going to kill me.'

Big Cyndi stopped again and took a deep breath. Myron stayed where he was and waited.

'You know what Esperanza did then?' she asked.

He shook his head.

'She announced that we were going to be tag team partners. Just like that. She shouted that after she'd been taken off on the stretcher, I'd visited her and we realized that we were actually long-lost sisters. The Human Volcano was now going to be called Big Chief Mama and we were going to be partners and friends. Some of the spectators backed off then. Others looked wary. "It's a trap!" they warned her. "The Human Volcano is setting you up!" But Esperanza insisted. She helped me to my feet and by then the police showed up and the moment was over. The crowd dispersed pretty easily.'

Big Cyndi threw up her thick arms and smiled. 'The end.'

Myron smiled back. 'So that's how you two became tag team partners?'

'That's how. When the president of FLOW heard about the incident, he decided to capitalize on it. The rest, as they say, is history.'

They both sat back in silence, still smiling. After some time had passed, Myron said, 'I had my heart broken six years ago.'

Big Cyndi nodded. 'By Jessica, right?'

'Right. I walked in on her with another man. A guy named Doug.' He paused. He could not believe he was telling her this. And it still hurt. After all this time it still hurt. 'Jessica left me then. Isn't that weird? I didn't throw her out. She just left. We didn't speak for four years – until she came back and we started up again. But you know about that.'

Big Cyndi made a face. 'Esperanza hates Jessica.'

'Yeah, I know. She doesn't exactly go to pains to hide that fact.'

'She calls her Queen Bitch.'

'When she's in a good mood,' Myron said. 'But that's why. Up until we broke up that first time, she was more or less indifferent. But after that—'

'Esperanza doesn't forgive easily,' Big Cyndi said. 'Not when it comes to her friends.'

'Right. Anyway, I was devastated. Win was no help. When it comes to matters of the heart, well, it's like explaining Mozart to a deaf man. So about a week after Jess left me, I moped into the office. Esperanza had two airplane tickets in her hand. "We're going away," she said. "Where?" I asked. "Don't worry about it," she said. "I already called your folks. I told them we'd be gone for a week." ' Myron smiled. 'My parents love Esperanza.'

'That should tell you something,' Big Cyndi said.

'I told her I didn't have any clothes. She pointed to two suitcases on the floor. "I bought you all you'll need." I protested, but I didn't have much left, and you know Esperanza.'

'Stubborn,' Big Cyndi said.

'To put it mildly. You know where she took me?'

Big Cyndi smiled. 'On a cruise. Esperanza told me about it.'

'Right. One of those big new ships with four hundred meals a day. And she made me go to every dumb activity. I even made a wallet. We drank. We danced. We played friggin' bingo. We slept in the same bed and she held me and we never so much as kissed.'

They sat for another long moment, both smiling again.

'We never asked her for help,' Big Cyndi said. 'Esperanza just knows and does the right thing.'

'And now it's our turn,' Myron said.

'Yes.'

'She's still hiding something from me.'

Big Cyndi nodded. 'I know.'

'Do you know what it is?'

'No,' she said.

Myron leaned back. 'We'll save her anyway,' he said.

At eight o'clock Win called down to Myron's office. 'Meet me at the apartment in an hour. I have a surprise for you.'

'I'm not much in the mood for surprises, Win.'

Click.

Great. He tried FJ's office again. No answer. He didn't much like waiting. FJ was a key in all this, he was sure of it now. But what choice did he have? It was getting late anyway. Better to go home and be surprised by whatever Win had in store and then get some rest.

The subway was still crowded at eight-thirty; the so-called Manhattan rush hour had grown to more like five or six. People worked too hard, Myron decided. He got off and walked to the Dakota. The same doorman was there. He had been given instructions to let Myron in at any time, that indeed Myron was now officially a resident of the Dakota, but the doorman still made a face like there was a bad odor whenever he passed.

Myron took the elevator up, fumbled for his key, and opened the door.

'Win?'

'He's not here.'

Myron turned. Terese Collins gave him a small smile. 'Surprise,' she said.

He gaped. 'You left the island?'

Terese glanced in a nearby mirror, then back at him. 'Apparently.'

'But—'

'Not now.'

She stepped toward him and they embraced. He kissed her. They fumbled with buttons and zippers and snaps. Neither one spoke. They made it into the bedroom, and then they made love.

When it was over, they clung to each other, the sheets tangled and binding them close together. Myron rested his cheek against her soft breast, hearing her heartbeat. Her chest was hitching a bit, and he knew that she was quietly crying.

'Tell me,' he said.

'No.' Terese's hand stroked his hair. 'Why did you leave?'

'A friend is in trouble.'

'That sounds so noble.'

Again with that word. 'I thought we agreed we wouldn't do this,' he said.

'You complaining?'

'Hardly,' he said. 'Just curious why you changed your mind.'

'Does it matter?'

'I don't think so.'

She stroked his hair some more. He closed his eyes, not moving, wanting only to enjoy the wonderful suppleness of her skin against his cheek and ride the rise and fall of her chest.

'Your friend in trouble,' she said. 'It's Esperanza Diaz.'

'Win told you?'

'I read it in the papers.'

He kept his eyes closed.

'Tell me about it,' she said.

'We were never great at talking on the island.'

'Yeah, but that was then, this is now.'

'Meaning?'

'Meaning you look a little worse for wear,' she said. 'I think you'll need the recovery time.'

Myron smiled. 'Oysters. The island had oysters.'

'So tell me.'

So he did. Everything. She stroked his hair. She interrupted a lot with follow-up questions, relaxing in the more familiar role of interviewer. It took him almost an hour.

'Some story,' she said.

'Yes.'

'Does it hurt? I mean, where you got beaten up?'

'Yes. But I'm a tough guy.'

She kissed the top of his head. 'No,' she said. 'You're not.'

They sat in comfortable silence.

'I remember the Lucy Mayor disappearance,' Terese said. 'At least the second round.'

'The second round?'

'When the Mayors had the money to run the big campaign to find her. Before that there really wasn't much of a story. An eighteen-year-old runaway. No big deal.'

'You remember anything that might help me?'

'No. I hate covering stories like that. And not just for the obvious reason that lives are being shattered.'

'Then what?'

'There's just too much denial,' she said.

'Denial?'

'Yes.'

'You mean with the family?'

'No, with the public. People block when it comes to their children. They deny because it's too painful to accept. They tell themselves it can't happen to them. God is not that fickle. There has to be a reason. Do you remember the Louise Woodward case a couple of years ago?'

'The nanny who killed the baby in Massachusetts?'

'Reduced to manslaughter by the judge, but yes. The public kept denying, even those who thought she was guilty. The mother shouldn't have been working, they said. Never mind the fact that the mother worked only part-time and came home at lunch every day to breast-feed the baby. It was her fault. And the father. He should have checked out the nanny's background better. The parents should have been more careful.'

'I remember,' Myron said.

'In the Mayors' case it was the same kind of thing. If Lucy Mayor had been raised right, she would have never run away in the first place. That's what I mean by denial. It's too painful to think about, so you block and convince yourself it can't happen to you.'

'Do you think there's any merit to that argument in this case?'

'What do you mean?'

'Were Lucy Mayor's parents part of the problem?'

Terese's voice was soft. 'It's not important.'

'What makes you say that?'

She was silent, her breathing a little more hitched again.

'Terese?'

'Sometimes,' she said, 'a parent is to blame. But that doesn't change anything. Because either way – your fault or not – your child is gone and that's all that matters.'

More silence.

Myron broke it. 'You okay?' he asked.

'Fine.'

'Sophie Mayor told me that the worst part was the not knowing.'

'She's wrong,' Terese said.

Myron wanted to ask her more, but she got out of bed then. When she came back, they made love again – languid and bittersweet, as the song says – both feeling loss, both searching for something in the moment or at least settling for the numb.

They were still snarled in the sheets when the phone woke Myron early in the morning. He reached over her head and picked up the receiver.

'Hello?'

'What's so important?'

It was FJ. Myron quickly sat up.

'We need to chat,' Myron said.

'Again?'

'Yes.'

'When?'

'Now.'

'Starbucks,' FJ said. 'And Myron?'

'What?'

'Tell Win to stay outside.'

31

FJ sat alone at the same table. He had his legs crossed at the knee and sipped as if maybe there were something in the bottom of the cup he wanted no part of. A bit of foam clung to his upper lip. His face was clean and wax-treatment smooth. Myron checked for Hans and Franz or some new goons, but nobody was there. FJ smiled and as always, something cold scrambled down Myron's back.

'Where's Win?' FJ asked.

'Outside,' Myron said.

'Good. Have a seat.'

'I know why Clu signed with you, FJ.'

'Care for an iced latte? You take it skim, correct?'

'It was bugging the hell out of me,' Myron said. 'Why would Clu sign with you? Don't get me wrong. He had every reason to leave MB. But he knew about TruPro's reputation. Why would he go there?'

'Because we offer a valuable service.'

'At first I figured it was a gambling or drug debt. It's how your dad always worked. He gets his hooks into someone, and then he gnaws on the carcass. But Clu was clean. And he had plenty of cash. So that wasn't it.'

FJ put his elbow on the table and leaned his chin against his palm. 'This is so fascinating, Myron.'

'It gets better. When I ran off to the Caribbean, you were keeping tabs on me. Because of the whole Brenda Slaughter situation. You even admitted it when I first got back, remember? You knew I'd been visiting the cemetery.'

'A very poignant moment for us all,' FJ agreed.

'When I vanished, you still wanted to keep tabs on me. If anything, my disappearance probably piqued your curiosity. You also saw an opening for TruPro, but that's not here or there. You wanted to know where I was. But I wasn't around. So you did the next best thing: You followed Esperanza, my partner and closest friend.'

FJ made a clucking noise. 'And here I thought Win was your closest friend.'

'They both are. But that's not the point. Following Win would be too difficult. He'd spot the tail before you even had him in place. So you followed Esperanza instead.'

'I still don't see what any of this has to do with Clu's decision to improve his representation.'

'I was missing. You knew that. You took advantage. You called my clients, telling them that I'd abandoned them.'

'Was I wrong?'

'I don't care about that now. You saw a weakness and you exploited it. You couldn't help yourself. It's how you were raised.'

'Ouch.'

'But the important thing here is that you were following Esperanza, hoping she'd lead you to me or at least give you a clue to how long I'd be gone. You followed her out to New Jersey. And you stumbled upon something you were never supposed to learn.'

His smile was positively wet. 'And what would that be?'

'Wipe that smile off your face, FJ. You're no better than a peeping Tom. Even your father wouldn't stoop that low.'

'Oh, you'd be surprised how low my father would stoop.'

'You're a pervert, and worse, you used what you learned as leverage against a client. Clu went nuts when Bonnie threw him out. He had no idea why. But now you knew. So you made a deal with him. He signs with TruPro, he learns the truth about his wife.'

FJ leaned back, recrossed the legs, folded his hands, and placed them on his lap. 'Quite a spin, Myron.'

'It's true, isn't it?'

FJ tilted his head in a maybe-yes, maybe-no fashion. 'Let me tell you how I see it,' he began. 'Clu Haid's old agency, MB SportsReps, was clearly screwing him. In every way. His agent – that would be you, Myron – abandoned him when he needed him most. Your partner – that would be the lovely and rather lithe Esperanza – was engaging in a lick fest with his wife. True?'

Myron said nothing.

FJ unfolded the hands, took a sip of foam, refolded the hands. 'What I did,' he continued, 'was take Clu Haid out of this awful situation. I brought him to an agency that would not abuse his trust. An agency that would look out for his interests. One of the ways we do that is through information. Valuable information. So the client understands what is happening to him. That's part of an agent's job, Myron. One of our agencies engaged in questionable ethics here. And it wasn't TruPro.'

It was a reverse spin, but it was also true. One day, when Myron had the time to dwell upon them, the words would undoubtedly wound. But not now.

'So you admit it?'

FJ shrugged.

'But if you were following Esperanza, you know she didn't do it.'

Again the head tilt. 'Do I?'

'Stop playing games with me, FJ.'

'Please hold a moment.' FJ took out his cell phone and dialed a number. He stood, walked toward the corner, chatted. He put the phone between his shoulder and ear, took out a pen and paper, jotted something down. He hung up and returned to the table.

'You were saying?'

'Did Esperanza do it?'

He smiled. 'You want the truth?'

'Yes.'

'I don't know. Honest. Yes, I followed her. But as I am sure you know, even lesbian scenes get repetitive. So after a while we'd stop watching her once she crossed the Washington Bridge. There was no point.'

'So you really don't know who killed Clu?'

'Afraid not.'

'Are you still following me, FJ?'

'No.'

'Last night. You didn't have a man on me?'

'No. And truth be told, I didn't have a man on you when you came in here yesterday.'

'The guy I spotted outside my office wasn't yours?'

'Sorry, no.'

Myron was missing something here.

FJ leaned forward again. His smile was so creepy that his teeth seemed to wiggle. 'How far are you willing to go to save Esperanza?' he whispered.

'You know how far.'

'The ends of the earth?'

'What are you getting at, FJ?'

'You're right, of course. I did learn about Esperanza and Bonnie. And I saw an opening. So I called Clu at the apartment in Fort Lee. But he wasn't there. I left a rather intriguing message on his machine. Something to the effect of "I know who your wife is sleeping with." He called me back on my private line within the hour.'

'When was this?'

'What . . . three days before his death?'

'What did he say?'

'His reaction was the obvious. But the *what* is not nearly as important as the *where*.'

'The where?'

'I have caller ID on my private line.' FJ sat back. 'Clu was out of town when he returned my call.'

'Where?'

FJ took his time. He picked up the coffee, took a long sip, made an aaah noise as if he were filming a 7-Up commercial, put the cup back down. He looked at Myron. Then he shook his head. 'Not so fast.'

Myron waited.

'My specialty, as you've now seen, is gathering information. Information is power. It's currency. It's cash. I just don't give away cash.'

'How much, FJ?'

'Not money, Myron. I don't want your money. I could buy you ten times over; we both know that.'

'So what do you want?'

He took another long sip. Myron wanted so very much to reach across the table and throttle him. 'Sure you don't want anything to drink?'

'Cut the crap, FJ.'

'Temper, temper.'

Myron made two fists and hid them under the table. He willed himself to stay calm. 'What do you want, FJ?'

'You are familiar, are you not, with Dean Pashaian and Larry Vitale.'

'They're two of my clients.'

'Correction. They are seriously considering leaving MB SportsReps and joining TruPro. They are on the fence as we speak. So here is my deal. You stop pursuing them. You don't call them and hand them crap about TruPro being run by gangsters. You promise to do that' – he showed Myron the piece of paper he'd been writing on in the corner – 'I give you the number Clu called from.'

'Your agency will destroy their careers. It always does.'

FJ smiled again. 'I can guarantee you, Myron, that no one on my staff will have a lesbian affair with their wives.'

'No deal.'

'Good-bye then.' FJ stood.

'Wait.'

'Your promise or I walk.'

'Let's talk about this,' Myron said. 'We can come up with something.'

'Good-bye.'

FJ started for the door.

'Okay,' Myron said.

FJ put a hand to his ear. 'I missed that.'

Selling out two clients. What would he stoop to next, running political campaigns? 'You have a deal. I won't talk to them.'

FJ spread his hands. 'You really are a master negotiator, Myron. I'm in awe of your skills.'

'Where did he call from, FJ?'

'Here's the phone number.' He handed Myron the piece of paper. Myron read it and sprinted back to the car.

32

Myron was on the cell phone before he reached Win. He pressed in the number and heard three rings.

'Hamlet Motel,' a man said.

'Where are you located?'

'In Wilston. On Route Nine off Ninety-one.'

Myron thanked the man and hung up. Win looked at him. Myron dialed Bonnie's number. Bonnie's mother answered. Myron identified himself and asked to speak with Bonnie.

'She was very upset after you left yesterday,' Bonnie's mother said.

'I'm sorry about that.'

'Why do you want to talk to her?'

'Please. It's very important.'

'She's in mourning. You realize that. Their marriage may have been in trouble—'

'I understand that, Mrs Cohen. Please let me speak to her.'

A deep sigh, but two minutes later Bonnie came on. 'What is it, Myron?'

'What does the Hamlet Motel in Wilston, Massachusetts, mean to you?'

Myron thought he heard a short intake of air. 'Nothing.'

'You and Clu lived there, didn't you?'

'Not at the motel.'

'I mean, in Wilston. When Clu was playing for the Bisons in the minor leagues.'

'You know we did.'

'And Billy Lee Palms. He lived there too. At the same time.'

'Not Wilston. I think he was in Deerfield. It's the neighboring town.'

'So what was Clu doing staying at the Hamlet Motel three days before he died?'

Silence.

'Bonnie?'

'I don't have the slightest idea.'

'Think. Why would Clu need to go up there?'

'I don't know. Maybe he was visiting an old friend.'

'What old friend?'

'Myron, you're not listening. I don't know. I haven't been up there in almost ten years. But we lived there for eight months. Maybe he made a friend. Maybe he went up there to fish or take a vacation or get away from it all. I don't know.'

Myron gripped the phone. 'You're lying to me, Bonnie.'

Silence.

'Please,' he said. 'I'm just trying to help Esperanza.'

'Let me ask you something, Myron.'

'What?'

'You keep digging and digging, right? I asked you not to. Esperanza asked you not to. Hester Crimstein asked you not to. But you keep digging.'

'Is there a question in there?'

'It's coming now: Has all your digging helped? Has all your digging made Esperanza look more guilty or less?'

Myron hesitated. But it didn't matter. Bonnie hung up before he had the chance to answer. Myron put the phone back in his lap. He looked at Win.

'I'll take Awful Songs for two hundred, Alex,' Win said.

'What?'

'Answer: Barry Manilow and Eastern Standard.'

Myron almost smiled. 'What is "Time in New England," Alex?'

'Correct answer.' Win shook his head. 'Sometimes when our minds are that in tune—'

'Yeah,' Myron said. 'It's scary.'

'Shall we?'

Myron thought about it. 'I don't think we have a choice.'

'Call Terese first.'

Myron nodded, started dialing. 'You know how to get there?'

'Yes.'

'It'll probably take three hours.'

Win hit the accelerator. No easy trick in midtown Manhattan. 'Try two.'

33

Wilston is in western Massachusetts, about an hour shy of the New Hampshire and Vermont borders. You could still see remnants of the old days, the oft artistically rendered New England town with V-shaped brick walks, colonial clapboard homes, the historical society bronze signs welded onto the front of every other building, the white-steepled chapel in the center of the town – the whole scene screaming for the lush leaves of autumn or a major snowstorm. But like everywhere else in the US of A, the superstore boom was playing havoc with the historical. The roads between these postcard villages had widened over the years, as though guilty of gluttony, feeding off the warehouse-size stores that now lined them. The stores sucked out the character and the quaintness and left in their wake a universal blandness that plagued the byroads and highways of America. Maine to Minnesota, North Carolina to Nevada – there was little texture and individuality left. It was about Home Depot and Office Max and the price clubs.

On the other hand, whining about the changes progress imposes upon us and longing for the good ol' days make for easy pickings. Harder to answer the question of why, if these changes are so bad, does every place and everybody so quickly and warmly welcome them.

Wilston had the classic New England Christmas card-conservative facade, but it was a college town, the college in question being Wilston College, and was thus liberal – liberal in the way only a college town can be, liberal in the way only the young can be, liberal in the way only the isolated and protected and rose-tinted can be. But that was okay. In fact, that was how it should be.

But even Wilston was changing. Yes, the old signs of liberalism were there: the tofu sweet shop, the migrant-friendly coffeehouse, the lesbian bookstore, the shop with the black lightbulbs and the pot paraphernalia, the clothing store that sold only ponchos. But the franchises were sneaking in quietly, slowly eating away at the gray stone corners: Dunkin' Donuts, Angelo's Sub Shop, Baskin-Robbins, Seattle Coffee.

Myron started softly singing 'Time in New England.'

Win looked at him. 'You realize, of course, that I'm well armed.'

'Hey, you're the one who got the song stuck in my head.'

They sped through town – with Win driving, you only sped – and arrived at the Hamlet Motel, a quasi-dump on Route 9 hovering on the town's edge. A sign advertised FREE HBO! and the ice machine was so large you could see it from your average space station. Myron checked his watch. Less than two hours to get here. Win parked the Jag.

'I don't get it,' Myron said. 'Why would Clu stay here?'

'Free HBO?'

'More likely because he could pay in cash. That's why we didn't see anything about this on his credit cards. But why wouldn't he want anyone to know he was here?'

'Such good questions,' Win said. 'Perhaps you should go inside and see if you can find some of the answers.'

They both stepped out of the car. Win noticed a restaurant next door. 'I'll try there,' he said. 'You take the desk clerk.'

Myron nodded. The desk clerk, definitely a college kid on break, sat behind the counter and stared straight ahead at nothing. He could have looked more bored, but only if a qualified physician induced a coma. Myron took a glance around and spotted the computer terminal. This was a good thing.

'Hello?'

The kid's eyes slid toward Myron. 'Yeah?'

'This computer. It keeps track of outgoing calls, right? Even local ones.'

The kid's eyes narrowed. 'Who wants to know?'

'I need to see records for all outgoing guest calls from the tenth and eleventh of this month.'

That got the kid to his feet. 'You a cop? Let me see your badge.'

'I'm not a cop.'

'Then—'

'I'll pay you five hundred dollars for the information.' No sense in playing around here, Myron thought. 'No one will ever know.'

The kid hesitated but not for long. 'Hell, even if I get canned, that's more money than I clear in a month. What dates did you need?'

Myron told him. The kid punched a few buttons. The printer started cranking. It all fitted on one sheet. Myron handed the kid the money. The kid handed him the sheet. Myron quickly scanned the list.

Instant bingo.

He spotted the long-distance call to FJ's office. It had come from room 117. Myron looked for other calls made from the same room. Clu had called his answering machine at home twice. Okay, good, fine. Now how about something more local? No reason to come up here just to make long-distance calls.

Bingo again.

Room 117. The first call on the list. A local number. Myron's heart started pumping, his breath growing shallow. He was close now. So close. He walked outside. The driveway was gravel. He kicked it around a bit. He took out his phone and was about to dial the number. No. That might be a mistake. He should learn all he could first. If he called, he might tip someone off. Of course, he didn't know whom he'd tip off or how they'd be tipped off or what they'd be tipped off about. But he didn't want to screw up now. He had the phone number. Big Cyndi at the office would have a reverse directory. These were easy to come by now. Any software store sold CD-ROMs that had the entire country's phone books on them or you could visit www.infospace.com on the Web. You plug in a number, it tells you who the number belongs to and where they live. More progress.

He called Big Cyndi.

'I was just about to call you, Mr Bolitar.'

'Oh?'

'I have Hester Crimstein on the line. She says that she urgently needs to talk to you.'

'Okay, put her through in a sec. Big Cyndi?'

'Yes.'

'About what you said yesterday. About people staring. I'm sorry if—'

'No pity, Mr Bolitar. Remember?'

'Yes.'

'Please don't change a thing, okay?'

'Okay.'

'I mean it.'

'Put Hester Crimstein through,' he said. 'And while I'm on the line, do you know where Esperanza keeps the reverse phone directory CDs?'

'Yes.'

'I want you to look up a number for me.' He read it off to her. She repeated it. Then she put Hester Crimstein through.

'Where are you?' the attorney barked at him.

'Why do you care?'

Hester was not pleased. 'God damn it, Myron, stop acting like a child. Where are you?'

'None of your business.'

'You're not helping.'

'What do you want, Hester?'

'You're on a cell phone, right?'

'Right.'

'Then we don't know if the line is safe,' she said. 'We have to meet right away. I'll be in my office.'

'No can do.'

'Look, do you want to help Esperanza or not?'

'You know the answer to that.'

'Then get your ass in here, pronto,' Hester said. 'We got a problem, and I think you can help.'

'What kind of problem?'

'Not on the phone. I'll be waiting for you.'

'It'll take me some time,' Myron said.

Silence.

'Why will it take some time, Myron?'

'It just will.'

'It's almost noon,' she said. 'When can I expect you?'

'Not until at least six.'

'That's too late.'

'Sorry.'

She sighed. 'Myron, get here now. Esperanza wants to see you.'

Myron's heart did a little flip. 'I thought she was in jail.'

'I just got her released. It's hush-hush. Get your ass over here, Myron. Get over here now.'

Myron and Win stood in the Hamlet Motel parking lot.

'What do you make of it?' Win asked.

'I don't like it,' Myron said.

'How so?'

'Why is Hester Crimstein so desperate to see me all of

a sudden? She's been trying to get rid of me from the moment I returned. Now I'm the answer to a problem?'

'It is bizarre,' Win agreed.

'And not only that, I don't like this whole hush-hush release for Esperanza.'

'It happens.'

'Sure, it happens. But if it did, why hasn't Esperanza called me? Why is Hester making the call for her?'

'Why indeed?'

Myron thought about it. 'Do you think she's involved in all this?'

'I cannot imagine how,' Win said. Then: 'Except that she may have spoken to Bonnie Haid.'

'So?'

'So then she may have deduced that we are in Wilston.'

'And now she urgently wants us to return,' Myron said.

'Yes.'

'So she's trying to get us out of Wilston.'

'It is a possibility,' Win said.

'So what is she afraid we'll find?'

Win shrugged. 'She's Esperanza's advocate.'

'So something detrimental to Esperanza.'

'Logical,' Win said.

A couple in their eighties stumbled out of one of the motel rooms. The old man had his arm around the woman's shoulder. They both looked postsex. At noon. Nice to see. Myron and Win watched them in silence.

'I pushed too hard last time,' Myron said.

Win did not reply.

'You warned me. You told me I didn't keep my eye on the prize. But I didn't listen.'

Win still said nothing.

'Am I doing the same now?'

'You are not good at letting things go,' Win said.

'That's not an answer.'

Win frowned. 'I'm not some holy wise man on the mount,' he said. 'I don't have all the answers.'

'I want to know what you think.'

Win squinted, though the sun was pretty much gone by now. 'Last time, you lost sight of your goal,' he said. 'Do you know what your goal is this time?'

Myron thought about it. 'Freeing Esperanza,' he said. 'And finding the truth.'

Win smiled. 'And if those two are mutually contradictory?'

'Then I bury the truth.'

Win nodded. 'You seem to have a good handle on the goal.'

'Should I let it go anyway?' Myron asked.

Win looked at him. 'There's one other complication.'

'What's that?'

'Lucy Mayor.'

'I'm not actively looking for her. I'd love to find her, but I don't expect to.'

'Still,' Win said, 'she is your personal connection into all this.'

Myron shook his head.

'The diskette came to you, Myron. You can't run away from that. You're not built that way. Somehow you and this missing girl are linked.'

Silence.

Myron checked the address and name Big Cyndi had given him. The phone was listed to a Barbara Cromwell at 12 Claremont Road. The name meant nothing to him. 'There's a rental car place down the street,' Myron said. 'You go back. Talk to Hester Crimstein. See what you can learn.'

'And you?'

'I'm going to check out Barbara Cromwell of Twelve Claremont Road.'

'Sounds like a plan,' Win said.
'A good one?'
'I didn't say that.'

34

Massachusetts, like Myron's home state of New Jersey, can quickly turn from big city to full-fledged town to hickville. That was the case here. Twelve Claremont Road – why the numbers reached twelve when the whole road had only three buildings on it Myron could not say – was an old farmhouse. At least it looked old. The color, probably once a deep red, had faded to a barely visible, watery pastel. The top of the structure curled forward as though suffering from osteoporosis. The front roof overhang had split down the middle, the right lip dipping forward like the mouth of a stroke victim. There were loose boards and major cracks and the grass was tall enough to go on the adult rides at a Six Flags.

He stopped in front of Barbara Cromwell's house and debated his approach. He hit the redial button and Big Cyndi answered.

'Got anything yet?'

'Not very much, Mr Bolitar. Barbara Cromwell is thirty-one years old. She was divorced four years ago from a Lawrence Cromwell.'

'Children?'

'That's all I have right now, Mr Bolitar. I'm terribly sorry.'

He thanked her and said to keep trying. He looked back at the house. There was a dull, steady thudding in his chest. Thirty-one years old. He reached into his pocket and took out the computer rendering of the aged Lucy Mayor. He stared at it. How old would Lucy be if she were still alive? Twenty-nine, maybe thirty. Close in age, but who cares? He shook the thought away, but it didn't go easy.

Now what?

He turned off the engine. A curtain jumped in an upstairs window. Spotted. No choice now. He opened the door and walked up the drive. It had been paved at one time, but the grass now laid claim to all but a few patches of tar. The side yard had one of those plastic Fisher-Price tree houses with a slide and rope ladder; the loud yellow, blue, and red of the play set shone through the brown grass like gems against black velvet. He reached the door. No bell, so he knocked and waited.

He could hear house sounds, someone running, someone whispering. A child called out, 'Mom!' Someone hushed him.

Myron heard footsteps, and then a woman said, 'Yes?'

'Ms Cromwell?'

'What do you want?'

'Ms Cromwell, my name is Myron Bolitar. I'd like to talk to you a moment.'

'I don't want to buy anything.'

'No, ma'am, I'm not selling—'

'And I don't accept door-to-door solicitations. You want a donation, you ask by mail.'

'I'm not here for any of that.'

Brief silence.

'Then what do you want?' she said.

'Ms Cromwell' – he'd clipped on his most reassuring voice now – 'would you mind opening your door?'

'I'm calling the police.'

'No, no, please, just wait a second.'

'What do you want?'

'I want to ask you about Clu Haid.'

There was a long pause. The little boy started talking again. The woman hushed him. 'I don't know anybody by that name.'

'Please open the door, Ms Cromwell. We need to talk.'

'Look, mister, I'm friendly with all the cops around here. I say the word, they'll lock you up for trespassing.'

'I understand your concerns,' Myron said. 'How about if we talk by phone?'

'Just go away.'

The little boy started crying.

'Go away,' she repeated. 'Or I'll call the police.'

More crying.

'Okay,' Myron said. 'I'm leaving.' Then, figuring what the hey, he shouted, 'Does the name Lucy Mayor mean anything to you?'

The child's crying was the only reply.

Myron let loose a sigh and started back to the car. Now what? He hadn't even been able to see her. Maybe he could poke around the house, try to peek in a window. Oh, that was a great idea. Get arrested for peeping. Or worse, scare a little kid. And she'd call the cops for sure—

Hold the phone.

Barbara Cromwell said that she was friendly with the police in town. But so was Myron. In a way. Wilston was the town where Clu had been nabbed on that first drunk driving charge when he was in the minors. Myron had gotten him off with the help of two cops. He scanned the memory banks for names. It didn't take him long. The arresting officer was named Kobler. Myron didn't remember his first name. The sheriff was a guy named Ron Lemmon. Lemmon was in his fifties then. He might have retired. But odds were pretty good one of them would still be on the force. They might know something about the mysterious Barbara Cromwell.

Worth a shot anyway.

35

One might expect the Wilston police station to be in a dinky little building. Not so. It was in the basement of a tall, fortresslike structure of dark, old brick. The steps down had one of those old bomb shelter signs, the black and yellow triangles still bright in the ominous circle. The image brought back memories of Burnet Hill Elementary School and the old bombing drills, a somewhat intense activity in which children were taught that crouching in a corridor was a suitable defense against a Soviet nuclear blitzkrieg.

Myron had never been to the station house before. After Clu's accident he'd met with the two cops in the back booth of a diner on Route 9. The whole episode took less than ten minutes. No one wanted to hurt the up-and-coming superstar. No one wanted to ruin Clu's promising young career. Dollars changed hands – some for the arresting officer, some for the sheriff in charge. Donations, they'd called it with a chuckle. Everyone smiled.

The desk sergeant looked up at Myron when he came in. He was around thirty and, like so many cops nowadays, built as if he spent more time in the weight room than the doughnut shop. His nametag read 'Hobert.' 'May I help you?'

'Does Sheriff Lemmon still work here?'

'No, sorry to say. Ron died, oh, gotta be a year now. Retired about two years before that.'

'I'm sorry to hear that.'

'Yeah, cancer. Ate through him like a hungry rat.' Hobert shrugged as if to say, What can you do?

'How about a guy named Kobler? I think he was a deputy about ten years ago.'

Hobert's voice was suddenly tight. 'Eddie's not on the force anymore.'

'Does he still live in the area?'

'No. I think he lives in Wyoming. May I ask your name, sir?'

'Myron Bolitar.'

'Your name sounds familiar.'

'I used to play basketball.'

'Nah, that's not it. I hate basketball.' He thought a moment, then shook his head. 'So why are you asking about two former cops?'

'They're sort of old friends.'

Hobert looked doubtful.

'I wanted to ask them about someone a client of mine has become involved with.'

'A client?'

Myron put on his helpless-puppy-dog smile. He usually used it on old ladies, but hey, waste not, want not. 'I'm a sports agent. My job is to look after athletes and, well, make sure they're not being taken advantage of. So this client of mine has an interest in a lady who lives in town. I just wanted to make sure she's not a gold digger or anything.'

Two words: *truly lame*.

Hobert said, 'What's her name?'

'Barbara Cromwell.'

The officer blinked. 'This a joke?'

'No.'

'One of your athletes is interested in dating Barbara Cromwell?'

Myron tried a little backpedal. 'I might have gotten the name wrong,' he said.

'I think maybe you have.'

'Why's that?'

'You mentioned Ron Lemmon before. The old sheriff.'

'Right.'

'Barbara Cromwell is his daughter.'

For a moment Myron just stood there. A fan whirred. A phone rang. Hobert said, 'Excuse me a second,' and picked it up. Myron heard none of it. Someone had frozen the moment. Someone had suspended him above a dark hole, giving Myron plenty of time to stare down at the nothingness, until suddenly the same someone let go. Myron plunged down into the black, his hands wheeling, his body turning, waiting, almost hoping, to smash against the bottom.

36

Myron stumbled back outside. He walked the town square. He grabbed something to eat at a Mexican place, wolfing it down without even tasting the food. Win called.

'We were correct,' Win said. 'Hester Crimstein was trying to divert our attention.'

'She admitted it?'

'No. She offers no explanation. She claims that she will speak with you and only you and only in person. She then pushed me for details on your whereabouts.'

No surprise.

'Would you like me to' – Win paused – 'interrogate her?'

'Please no,' Myron said. 'Ethics aside, I don't think there's much need anymore.'

'Oh?'

'Sawyer Wells said he was a drug counselor at Rockwell.'

'I remember.'

'Billy Lee Palms was treated at Rockwell. His mother mentioned it when I visited her house.'

'Hmm,' Win said. 'Wonderful coincidence.'

'Not a coincidence,' Myron said. 'It explains everything.'

When he finished talking to Win, he strolled the main street of Wilston seven or eight times over. The shopkeepers, light on business, smiled at him. He smiled back. He nodded hello to the large assortment of people passing by. The town was so stuck in the sixties, the kind of place where people still wore unkempt beards and black caps and looked like Seals and Crofts at an outdoor concert. He liked it here. He liked it a lot.

He thought about his mother and his father. He thought about them getting old and wondered why he could not accept it. He thought about how his father's 'chest pains' were partially his fault, how the strain of his running away had at least tangentially contributed to what happened. He thought about what it would have been like for his parents if they had suffered the same fate as Sophie and Gary Mayor, if he had disappeared at seventeen without a trace and were never found. He thought about Jessica and how she claimed she would fight for him. He thought about Brenda and what he had done. He thought about Terese and last night and what, if anything, it meant. He thought about Win and Esperanza and the sacrifices that friends make.

For a long time he did not think about Clu's murder or Billy Lee's death. He did not think about Lucy Mayor and her disappearance and his connection to it. But that lasted only so long. Eventually he made a few phone calls, did some digging, confirmed what he already suspected.

The answers never come with cries of 'Eureka!' You stumble toward them, often in total darkness. You stagger through an unlit room at night, tripping over the unseen, lumbering forward, bruising your shins, toppling over and righting yourself, feeling your way across the walls and hoping your hand happens upon the light switch. And then – to keep within this piss-poor but sadly accurate analogy – when you find the switch, when you flick it on and bathe the room in light, sometimes the room is just as you pictured it. And then sometimes, like now, you wonder if you'd have been better off staying forever stumbling in the dark.

Win of course would say that Myron was limiting the

analogy. He would point out that there were other options. You could simply leave the room. You could let your eyes get accustomed to the dark, and while you would never see everything clearly, that was okay. You could even flick the switch back off once you turned it on. In the case of Horace and Brenda Slaughter, Win would be right. In the case of Clu Haid, Myron was not so sure.

He had found the light switch. He had flicked it on. But the analogy did not hold – and not just because it was a dumb one from the start. Everything in the room was still murky, as though he were looking through a shower curtain. He could see lights and shadows. He could make out shapes. But to know exactly what had happened, he would have to push aside the curtain.

He could still back off, let the curtain rest or even flick the light back off. But that was the problem with darkness and Win's options. In the dark you cannot see the rot fester. The rot is free to continue to eat away, undisturbed, until it consumes everything, even the man huddled in the corner, trying like hell to stay away from that damned light switch.

So Myron got in his car. He drove back out to the farmhouse on Claremont Road. He knocked on the door, and again Barbara Cromwell told him to go away. 'I know why Clu Haid came here,' he told her. He kept talking. And eventually she let him in.

When he left, Myron called Win again. They talked a long time. First about Clu Haid's murder. Then about Myron's dad. It helped. But not a lot. He called Terese and told her what he knew. She said that she'd tried to check some of the facts with her sources.

'So Win was right,' Terese said. 'You are personally connected.'

'Yes.'

'I blame myself every day,' Terese said. 'You get used to it.'

Again he wanted to ask more. Again he knew that it wasn't time.

Myron made two more calls on the cell phone. The first was to the law office of Hester Crimstein.

'Where are you?' Hester snapped.

'I assume you're in contact with Bonnie Haid,' he said.

Pause. Then: 'Oh Christ, Myron, what did you do?'

'They aren't telling you everything, Hester. In fact, I bet Esperanza barely told you anything.'

'Where are you, dammit?'

'I'll be in your office in three hours. Have Bonnie there.'

His final call was to Sophie Mayor. When she answered, he said three words: 'I found Lucy.'

37

Myron tried to drive like Win, but that was beyond his capabilities. He sped, but he still hit construction on Route 95. You always hit construction on Route 95. It was a Connecticut state law. He listened to the radio. He made phone calls. He felt frightened.

Hester Crimstein was a senior partner in a high-rise, higher-bill, mega New York law firm. The attractive receptionist had clearly been expecting him. She led him down a hallway lined with what looked like mahogany wallpaper and into a conference room. There was a rectangular table big enough to seat twenty, pens and legal pads in front of each chair, billable no doubt to some unsuspecting client at wildly inflated prices. Hester Crimstein sat next to Bonnie Haid, their backs to the window. They started to rise when he entered.

'Don't bother,' he said.

Both women stopped.

'What's this all about?' Hester asked.

Myron ignored her and looked at Bonnie. 'You almost told me, didn't you, Bonnie? When I first came back. You said you wondered if we did Clu a disservice by helping him. You wondered if our sheltering him and protecting him had eventually led to his death. I said you were wrong. The only person to blame is the person who shot him. But I didn't know everything, did I?'

'What the hell are you talking about?' Hester said.

'I want to tell you a story,' he said.

'What?'

'Just listen, Hester. You might find out what you've gotten yourself involved in.'

Hester closed her mouth. Bonnie kept silent.

'Twelve years ago,' Myron said, 'Clu Haid and Billy Lee Palms were minor-league players for a team called the New England Bisons. They were both young and reckless in the way athletes tend to be. The world was their oyster, they thought they were the cat's pajamas, you know the fairy tale. I won't insult you by going into details.'

Both women slid back into their seats. Myron sat across from them and continued.

'One day Clu Haid drove drunk – well, he probably drove drunk more than once, but on this occasion he wrapped his car around a tree. Bonnie' – he gestured to her with his chin – 'was injured in the accident. She suffered a bad concussion and spent several days in the hospital. Clu was unhurt. Billy Lee broke a finger. When it happened, Clu panicked. A drunk driving charge could ruin a young athlete, even as little as twelve years ago. I had just signed him to several profitable endorsement deals. He was going to move up to the majors in a matter of months. So he did what a lot of athletes did. He found someone who'd get him out of trouble. His agent. Me. I drove up to the scene like a madman. I met with the arresting officer, a guy named Eddie Kobler, and the town sheriff, Ron Lemmon.'

Hester Crimstein said, 'I don't understand any of this.'

'Give me time, you will,' Myron said. 'The officers and I came to an understanding. It happens all the time with big-time athletes. Matters like this are swept under the rug. Clu was a good kid, we all agreed. No reason to destroy his life over this little incident. It was a somewhat victimless crime – the only person hurt was Clu's own wife. So money changed hands, and an agreement was reached. Clu wasn't drunk. He swerved to avoid another car. That's what caused the accident. Billy Lee Palms and Bonnie would swear to it. Incident over and forgotten.'

Hester wore her annoyed-but-curious scowl. Bonnie's face was losing color fast.

'It's twelve years later now,' Myron said. 'And the incident is almost like one of those mummy curses. The drunk driver, Clu, is murdered. His best friend and passenger, Billy Lee Palms, is shot to death – I won't call that murder because the shooter saved my life. The sheriff I bought off – he died of prostate cancer. Nothing too strange about that or perhaps God got to him before the mummy. And as for Eddie Kobler, the other officer, he was caught last year taking bribes in a big drug sting. He was arrested and plea-bargained down. His wife left him. His kids won't talk to him. He lives alone in a bottle in Wyoming.'

'How do you know about this Kobler guy?' Hester Crimstein asked.

'A local cop named Hobert told me what happened. A reporter friend confirmed it.'

'I still don't see the relevance,' Hester said.

'That's because Esperanza kept you in the dark,' Myron said. 'I was wondering how much she told you. Apparently not much. Probably just insisted that I be kept totally out of this, right?'

Hester gave him the courtroom eyes. 'Are you saying Esperanza has something to do with all this?'

'No.'

'You're the one who committed a crime here, Myron. You bribed two police officers.'

'And there's the rub,' Myron said.

'What are you talking about?'

'Even that night something struck me as odd about the whole incident. The three of them in the car together. Why? Bonnie didn't much care for Billy Lee Palms. Sure, she'd go out with Clu and Clu would go out with Billy

317

Lee and maybe they'd even double-date or something. But why were the three of them in that car so late at night?'

Hester Crimstein stayed the lawyer. 'Are you saying one of them wasn't in the car?'

'No. I'm saying that there were four people in the car, not three.'

'What?'

They both looked at Bonnie. Bonnie lowered her head.

'Who were the four?' Hester asked.

'Bonnie and Clu were one couple.' Myron tried to meet Bonnie's eyes, but she wouldn't look up. 'Billy Lee Palms and Lucy Mayor were the other.'

Hester Crimstein looked as if she'd been hit with a two-by-four. 'Lucy Mayor?' she repeated. 'As in the missing Mayor girl?'

'Yes.'

'Jesus Christ.'

Myron kept his eyes on Bonnie. Eventually she raised her head. 'It's true, isn't it?'

Hester Crimstein said, 'She's not talking.'

'Yes,' Bonnie said. 'It's true.'

'But you never knew what happened to her, did you?'

Bonnie hesitated. 'Not then, no.'

'What did Clu tell you?'

'That you bought her off too,' Bonnie said. 'Like with the police. He said you paid her to keep silent.'

Myron nodded. It made sense. 'There's one thing I don't get. There was a ton of publicity about Lucy Mayor a few years back. You must have seen her picture in the paper.'

'I did.'

'Didn't it ring a bell?'

'No. You have to remember. I only saw her that one time. You know Billy Lee. A different girl every night.

And Clu and I sat in the front. Her hair was a different color too. She was a blonde then. So I didn't know.'

'And neither did Clu.'

'That's right.'

'But eventually you learned the truth.'

'Eventually,' she said.

'Whoa,' Hester Crimstein said. 'I'm not following any of this. What does an old traffic accident have to do with Clu's murder?'

'Everything,' Myron said.

'You better explain, Myron. And while you're at it, why did Esperanza get framed for it?'

'That was a mistake.'

'What?'

'Esperanza wasn't the one they intended to frame,' Myron said. 'I was.'

38

Yankee Stadium hunched over in the night, crouching shoulders low as though trying to escape the glow from its own lights. Myron parked in Lot 14, where the executives and players parked. There were only three other cars there. The night guard at the press entrance said he was expected, that the Mayors would meet him on the field. Myron moved down the lower tier and hopped the wall near the batter's box. The stadium lights were on, but nobody was there. He stood alone on the field and took a deep breath. Even in the Bronx nothing smelled like a baseball diamond. He turned toward the visitors' dugout, scanning the lower boxes and finding the exact seats he and his brother had sat in all those years ago. Funny what you remember. He walked toward the pitcher's mound, the grass making a gentle whooshing sound, and sat down on the rubber and waited. Clu's home. The one place he'd always felt at peace.

Should have buried him here, Myron thought. *Under a pitcher's mound.*

He stared up into the thousands of seats, empty like the shattered eyes of the dead, the vacant stadium merely a body now without a soul. The whites of the foul lines were muddied, nearly dirt-toned now. They'd be put down anew tomorrow before game time.

People say that baseball is a metaphor for life. Myron did not know about that, but staring down the foul line, he wondered. The line between good and evil is not so different from the foul line on a baseball field. It's often made of stuff as flimsy as lime. It tends to fade over time.

It needs to be constantly redrawn. And if enough players trample on it, the line becomes smeared and blurred to the point where fair is foul and foul is fair, where good and evil become indistinguishable from each other.

Jared Mayor's voice broke the stillness. 'You said you found my sister.'

Myron squinted toward the dugout. 'I lied,' he said.

Jared stepped up the cement stairs. Sophie followed. Myron rose to his feet. Jared started to say something more, but his mother put her hand on his arm. They kept walking as though they were coaches coming out to talk to the relief pitcher.

'Your sister is dead,' Myron said. 'But you both know that.'

They kept walking.

'She was killed in a drunk driving accident,' he went on. 'She died on impact.'

'Maybe,' Sophie said.

Myron looked confused. 'Maybe?'

'Maybe she died on impact, maybe she didn't,' Sophie continued. 'Clu Haid and Billy Lee Palms weren't doctors. They were dumb, drunk jocks. Lucy might have just been injured. She may have been alive. A doctor might have been able to save her.'

Myron nodded. 'I guess that's possible.'

'Go on,' Sophie said. 'I want to hear what you have to say.'

'Whatever your daughter's condition actually was, Clu and Billy Lee believed that she was dead. Clu was terrified. Drunk driving charges would be serious enough, but this was vehicular homicide. You don't walk away from that, no matter how far your curveball breaks. He and Billy Lee panicked. I don't know the details here. Sawyer Wells can tell us. My guess is that they hid the body. It was a quiet road, but there still wouldn't be

321

enough time to bury Lucy before the police and ambulance arrived. So they probably stashed her in the brush. And when it all calmed down, they came back and buried her. Like I said, I don't know the details. I don't think they're particularly relevant. What is relevant is that Clu and Billy Lee got rid of the body.'

Jared stepped into Myron's face. 'You can't prove any of this.'

Myron ignored him, keeping his eyes on Jared's mother. 'The years pass. Lucy is gone. But not in the minds of Clu Haid and Billy Lee Palms. Maybe I'm overanalyzing. Maybe I'm being too easy on them. But I think what they did that night defined the rest of their lives. Their self-destructive tendencies. The drugs—'

'You're being too easy,' Sophie said.

Myron waited.

'Don't give them credit for having consciences,' she continued. 'They were worthless scum.'

'Maybe you're right. I shouldn't analyze. And I guess it doesn't matter. Clu and Billy Lee may have created their own hell, but it wasn't close to the agony your family experienced. You told me about the awful torment of not knowing the truth, how it lives with you every day. With Lucy dead and buried like that, the torment just went on.'

Sophie's head was still high. There was no flinch in her. 'Do you know how we finally learned our daughter's fate?'

'From Sawyer Wells,' Myron said. 'The Wells Rules of Wellness, Rule Eight: 'Confess something about yourself to a friend – something awful, something you'd never want anyone to know. You'll feel better. You'll still see that you're worthy of love.' Sawyer was a drug counselor at Rockwell. Billy Lee was a patient there. My guess is that he caught him during a withdrawal episode. When he was delirious probably. He did what his therapist asked. Rule eight. He confessed the worst thing he could imagine, the one moment in his life that shaped all others. Sawyer suddenly saw his ticket out of Rockwell and into the spotlight. Through the wealthy Mayor family, owners of Mayor Software. So he went to you and your husband. And he told you what he'd heard.'

Again Jared said, 'You have no proof of any of this!'

And again Sophie silenced him with her hand. 'Go on, Myron,' she said. 'What happened then?'

'With this new information, you found your daughter's body. I don't know if your private investigators did it or if you just used your money and influence to keep the authorities quiet. It wouldn't have been difficult for someone in your position.'

'I see,' Sophie said. 'But if all that's true, why would I want to keep it quiet? Why not prosecute Clu and Billy Lee – and even you?'

'Because you couldn't,' Myron said.

'Why not?'

'The corpse had been buried for twelve years. There was no evidence there. The car was long gone – no evidence there either. The police report listed a Breathalyzer test that showed Clu was not drunk. So what did you have: the ranting of a drug addict going through withdrawal? Billy Lee's confession to Sawyer Wells would probably be suppressed, and even if it wasn't, so what? His testimony about the police payoffs was complete hearsay since he wasn't even there when it happened. You realized all that, didn't you?'

She said nothing.

'And that meant justice was up to you, Sophie. You and Gary would have to avenge your daughter.' He stopped, looked at Jared, then back at Sophie. 'You told me about a void. You said that you preferred to fill that void with hope.'

Sophie nodded. 'I did.'

'And when the hope was gone – when the discovery of

your daughter's body sucked it all away – you and your husband still needed to fill that void.'

'Yes.'

'So you filled it with revenge.'

She fixed her gaze on his. 'Do you blame us, Myron?'

He said nothing.

'The crooked sheriff was dying of cancer,' Sophie said. 'There was nothing to be done about him. The other officer, well, as your friend Win could tell you, money is influence. The Federal Bureau of Investigation set him up at our behest. He took the bait. And yes, I shattered his life. Gladly.'

'But Clu was the one you wanted to hurt most,' Myron said.

'Hurt nothing. I wanted to crush him.'

'But he too was fairly broken down,' Myron said. 'In order to really crush him, you had to give him hope. Just like you and Gary had all these years. Give him hope, then snatch it away. Hope hurts like nothing else. You knew that. So you and your husband bought the Yankees. You overpaid, but so what? You had the money. You didn't care. Gary died soon after the transaction.'

'From heartache,' Sophie interrupted. She raised her head, and for the first time he saw a tear. 'From years of heartache.'

'But you carried on without him.'

'Yes.'

'You concentrated on one thing and one thing only: getting Clu in your grasp. It was a silly trade – everyone thought so – and it was strange coming from an owner who kept out of every other baseball decision. But it was all about getting Clu on the team. That's the only reason you bought the Yankees. To give Clu a last chance. And even better, Clu cooperated. He started straightening out his life. He was clean and sober. He was pitching well.

He was as happy as Clu Haid was ever going to get. You had him in the palm of your hand.

'And then you closed your fist.'

Jared put his arm around her shoulders and pressed her close.

'I don't know the order,' Myron went on. 'You sent Clu a computer diskette like you sent me. Bonnie told me that. She also told me that you blackmailed him. Anonymously. That explains the missing two hundred thousand dollars. You made him live in terror. And Bonnie even inadvertently helped you by filing for divorce. Now Clu was in the perfect position for your coup de grace: the drug test. You fixed it so he would fail. Sawyer helped. Who better, since he already knew what was going on? It worked beautifully. Not only did it destroy Clu, but it also diverted any attention from you. Who would ever suspect you, especially since the test seemingly hurt you too? But you didn't care about any of that. The Yankees meant nothing to you except as a vehicle to destroy Clu Haid.'

'So true,' Sophie said.

'Don't,' Jared said.

She shook her head and patted her son's arm. 'It's okay.'

'Clu had no idea the girl he buried in the woods was your daughter. But after you bombarded him with the calls and the diskette and especially after he failed the drug test, he put it together. But what could he do about it? He certainly couldn't say the drug test was fixed because he'd killed Lucy Mayor. He was trapped. He tried to figure out how you'd learned the truth. He thought maybe it was Barbara Cromwell.'

'Who?'

'Barbara Cromwell. She's Sheriff Lemmon's daughter.'

'How did she know?'

'Because as quiet as you tried to keep the investigation,

Wilston is a small town. The sheriff was tipped off about the discovery. He was dying. He had no money. His family was poor. So he told his daughter about what had really happened that night. She could never get in trouble for it – it was his crime, not hers. And they could use the information to blackmail Clu Haid. Which they did. On several occasions. Clu figured Barbara had been the one who opened her mouth. When he called her to find out if she'd told anyone, Barbara played coy. She demanded more money. So Clu drove up to Wilston a few days later. He refused to pay her. He said it was over.'

Sophie nodded. 'So that's how you put it together.'

'It was the final piece, yes,' Myron said. 'When I realized that Clu had visited Lemmon's daughter, it all fell into place. But I'm still surprised, Sophie.'

'Surprised about what?'

'That you killed him. That you let Clu out of his misery.'

Jared's arm dropped off his mother. 'What are you talking about?' he said.

'Let him speak,' Sophie said. 'Go on, Myron.'

'What more is there?'

'For starters,' she said, 'how about your part in all this?'

A lead block formed in his chest. He said nothing.

'You're not going to claim that you were blameless in all this, are you, Myron?'

His voice was soft. 'No.'

In the distance, out beyond center field, a janitor started cleaning off the memorials to the Yankees' greats. He sprayed and wiped, working, Myron knew from past stadium visits, on Lou Gehrig's stone. The Iron Horse. Such bravery in the face of so awful a death.

'You've done this too, haven't you?' Sophie said.

Myron kept his eyes on the janitor. 'Done what?' But he knew.

'I've looked into your past,' she said. 'You and your business associate often take the law into your own hands, am I right? You play judge and jury.'

Myron said nothing.

'That's all I did. For the sake of my daughter's memory.'

The blurry line between fair and foul again. 'So you decided to frame me for Clu's murder.'

'Yes.'

'The perfect way to wreak vengeance on me for bribing the officers.'

'I thought so at the time.'

'But you messed up, Sophie. You ended up framing the wrong person.'

'That was an accident.'

Myron shook his head. 'I should have seen it,' he said. 'Even Billy Lee Palms said it, but I didn't pay attention. And Hester Crimstein said it to me the first time I met her.'

'Said what?'

'They both pointed out that the blood was found in *my* car, the gun in *my* office. Maybe I killed Clu, they said. A logical deduction except for one thing. I was out of the country. You didn't know that, Sophie. You didn't know that Esperanza and Big Cyndi were playing a shell game with everybody, pretending I was still around. That's why you were so upset with me when you found out I'd been away. I messed up your plan. You also didn't know that Clu had an altercation with Esperanza. So all the evidence that was supposed to point to me—'

'Pointed instead to your associate, Miss Diaz,' Sophie said.

'Exactly,' Myron said. 'But there's one other thing I want to clear up.'

'More than one thing,' Sophie corrected.

'What?'

327

'There's more than one thing you'll want to clear up,' Sophie said. 'But please go ahead. What would you like to know?'

'You were the one who had me followed,' he said. 'The guy I spotted outside the Lock-Horne building. He was yours.'

'Yes. I knew Clu had tried to hook up with you. I hoped the same might happen with Billy Lee Palms.'

'Which it did. Billy Lee thought that maybe I killed Clu to keep my part in the crime buried. He thought I wanted to kill him too.'

'It makes sense,' she agreed. 'You had a lot to lose.'

'So you were following me then? At the bar?'

'Yes.'

'Personally?'

She smiled. 'I grew up a hunter and a tracker, Myron. The city or the woods, it makes little difference.'

'You saved my life,' he said.

She did not reply.

'Why?'

'You know why. I didn't come there to kill Billy Lee Palms. But there are degrees of guilt. Simply put, he was more guilty than you. When it came down to a question of you or him, I chose to kill him. You deserve to be punished, Myron. But you didn't deserve to be killed by scum like Billy Lee Palms.'

'Judge and jury again?'

'Luckily for you, Myron, yes.'

He sat down hard on the pitcher's mound, his whole body suddenly drained. 'I can't just let you get away with this,' he said. 'I may sympathize. But you killed Clu Haid in cold blood.'

'No.'

'What?'

'I didn't kill Clu Haid.'

'I don't expect you to confess.'

'Expect or don't expect. I didn't kill him.'

Myron frowned. 'You had to. It all adds up.'

Her eyes remained placid pools. Myron's head started spinning. He turned and looked up at Jared.

'He didn't kill him either,' Sophie said.

'One of you did,' Myron said.

'No.'

Myron looked at Jared. Jared said nothing. Myron opened his mouth, closed it, tried to come up with something.

'Think, Myron.' Sophie crossed her arms and smiled at him. 'I told you my philosophy when you were last here. I'm a hunter. I don't hate what I kill. Just the opposite. I respect what I kill. I honor my kill. I consider the animal brave and noble. Killing, in fact, can be merciful. That's why I kill with one shot. Not Billy Lee Palms, of course. I wanted him to have at least a few moments of agony and fear. And of course, I would never show Clu Haid mercy.'

Myron tried to sort through it. 'But—'

And then he heard yet another click. His conversation with Sally Li started uncoiling in his head.

The crime scene . . .

Christ, the crime scene. It was in such a state of disarray. Blood on the walls. Blood on the floor. Because blood splatters would show the truth. So splatter some more. Destroy the evidence. Fire more shots into the corpse. To the calf, to the back, even to the head. Take the gun with you. Mess things up. Cover up what really happened.

'Oh God . . .'

Sophie nodded at him.

Myron's mouth felt dry as a sandstorm. 'Clu committed suicide?'

Sophie tried a smile, but she just couldn't quite make it.

Myron started to stand, his bad knee audibly creaking as he rose. 'The end of his marriage, the failed drug test, but mostly the past coming back at him – it was all too much. He shot himself in the head. The other shots were just to throw the police off. The crime scene was messed up so no one would be able to analyze the blood splatters and see it was a suicide. It was all a diversion.'

'A coward to the end,' Sophie said.

'But how did you know he killed himself? Did you have his place bugged or under surveillance?'

'Nothing so technical, Myron. He wanted us to find him – me specifically.'

Myron just stared at her.

'We were supposed to have our big confrontation that night. Yes, Clu had hit rock bottom, Myron. But I was not through with him. Not by a long shot. An animal deserved a quick kill. Not Clu Haid. But when Jared and I arrived, he'd already taken the gutless way out.'

'And the money?'

'It was there. As you noted, the anonymous stranger who sent him the diskette and made all those phone calls was blackmailing him. But he knew it was us. I took the money that night and donated it to the Child Welfare Institute.'

'You caused him to kill himself.'

She shook her head, her posture still ramrod. 'Nobody causes someone to kill himself. Clu Haid chose his fate. It was not what I intended but—'

'Intended? He's dead, Sophie.'

'Yes, but it was not what I *intended*. Just as you, Myron, did not *intend* to cover up my daughter's murder.'

Silence.

'You took advantage of his death,' Myron said. 'You planted the blood and gun in my car and office. Or you hired someone to do it.'

330

'Yes.'

He shook his head. 'The truth has to come out,' he said.

'No.'

'I'm not letting Esperanza rot in jail—'

'It's done,' Sophie Mayor said.

'What?'

'My attorney is meeting with the DA as we speak. Anonymously, of course. They won't know whom he represents.'

'I don't understand.'

'I kept evidence that night,' she said. 'I took pictures of the body. They'll test Clu's hand for powder residue. I even have a suicide note, if need be. The charges against Esperanza will be dropped. She'll be released in the morning. It's over.'

'The DA isn't going to settle for that. He's going to want to know the whole story.'

'Life is full of wants, Myron. But the DA won't get it in this case. He'll just have to live with that reality. And in the end it's just a suicide anyway. High profile or not, it won't be a priority.' She reached into her pocket and took out a piece of paper. 'Here,' she said. 'It's Clu's suicide note.'

Myron hesitated. He took the note, immediately recognizing Clu's handwriting. He started reading:

Dear Mrs Mayor,

The torment has gone on long enough. I know you won't accept my apology and I can't say that I blame you. But I also don't have the strength to face you. I've been running away from that night all my life. I hurt my family and my friends, but I hurt nobody so much as I hurt you. I hope my death gives you some measure of comfort.

I am the one to blame for what happened. Billy

*Lee Palms just did what I told him to. The same
goes for Myron Bolitar. I paid off the police. Myron
just delivered the money. He never knew the truth.
My wife was knocked out in the accident. She also
never knew the truth and she still doesn't.*

*The money is all here. Do with it what you will.
Tell Bonnie that I'm sorry and that I understand
everything. And let my children know that their
father always loved them. They were the only thing
pure and good in my life. You, of all people, should
understand that.*

Clu Haid

Myron read the note again. He pictured Clu writing it,
then putting it aside, then picking up the gun and
pressing it against his head. Did he close his eyes then?
Did he think of his children, the two boys with his smile,
before he pulled the trigger? Did he hesitate at all?

His eyes stayed on the note. 'You didn't believe him,'
he said.

'About the culpability of the others? No. I knew he was
lying. You, for example. You were more than a delivery
boy. You bribed those officers.'

'Clu lied to protect us,' Myron said. 'In the end he
sacrificed himself for those he loved.'

Sophie frowned. 'Don't make him out to be a martyr.'

'I'm not. But you just can't walk away from what you
did.'

'I did nothing.'

'You made a man – the father of two boys – kill
himself.'

'He made a choice, that's all.'

'He didn't deserve that.'

'And my daughter didn't deserve to be murdered and
buried in an anonymous pit,' she said.

Myron looked up into the stadium lights, letting them blind him a bit.

'Clu was off drugs,' he said. 'You'll pay the rest of his salary.'

'No.'

'You'll also let the world know – and his children – that in the end Clu wasn't on drugs.'

'No,' Sophie said again. 'The world won't know that. And they also won't know Clu was a murderer. I'd say that's a pretty good bargain, wouldn't you?'

He read the note again, tears stinging his eyes.

'One heroic moment in the end doesn't redeem him,' Sophie said.

'But it says something.'

'Go home, Myron. And be glad it's over. If the truth were ever to come out, there is only one guilty party left to take the fall.'

Myron nodded. 'Me.'

'Yes.'

They stared at each other.

'I didn't know about your daughter,' he said.

'I know that now.'

'You thought I helped Clu cover it up.'

'No, I *know* you helped Clu cover it up. What I wasn't sure about is if you knew what you were doing. It was why I asked you to look for Lucy – so I could see how deep your involvement was.'

'The void,' Myron said.

'What about it?'

'Did this help fill it?'

Sophie thought about it. 'Strangely enough, the answer is yes, I think. It doesn't bring Lucy back. But I feel as though she's been properly buried now. I think we can begin to heal.'

'So we all just go on?'

Sophie smiled. 'What else can we do?'

She nodded to Jared. Jared took his mother's hand, and they started back for the dugout.

'I am very sorry,' Myron said.

Sophie stopped. She dropped her son's hand and studied Myron for a moment, her eyes moving over his face. 'You committed a felony by bribing those police officers. You put my family and me through years of agony. You probably contributed to my husband's premature death. You had a hand in the deaths of Clu Haid and Billy Lee Palms. And in the end you made me commit horrible acts I always thought I was incapable of committing.' She stepped back toward her son, her gaze more tired now than accusatory. 'I won't hurt you any further. But if you don't mind, I'll let you keep your apology.'

She gave Myron a moment for rebuttal. He didn't use it. They strode down the steps and disappeared, leaving Myron alone with the grass and the dirt and the bright stadium lights.

39

In the lot Win frowned and holstered his .44. 'No one even pulled a gun.'

Myron said nothing. He got into his car. Win got into his. Myron's cellular phone rang before he had driven five minutes. It was Hester Crimstein.

'They're dropping the charges,' she said to him. 'Esperanza will be out tomorrow morning. They're offering up a full exoneration and apology if we promise not to sue.'

'Will you accept that?'

'It's up to Esperanza. But I think she'll agree.'

Myron drove to Bonnie's house. Her mother opened the door and looked angry. Myron pushed past her and found Bonnie alone. He showed her the note. She cried. He held her. He looked in on the two sleeping boys and stayed in the doorway until Bonnie's mother tapped him on the shoulder and asked him to leave. He did.

He headed back to Win's apartment. When he opened the door, Terese's suitcase was by the entrance. She stepped into the foyer.

'You're packed,' Myron said.

She smiled. 'I love a man who misses nothing.'

He waited.

'I'm leaving in an hour for Atlanta,' she said.

'Oh.'

'I spoke to my boss at CNN. Ratings have been down. He wants me back on the air tomorrow.'

'Oh,' Myron said again.

Terese pulled at a ring on her finger. 'You ever try a long-distance relationship?' she asked.

'No.'

'Might be worth a try.'

'Might be,' he said.

'I hear the sex is great.'

'That's never been our trouble, Terese.'

'No,' she said. 'It hasn't.'

He checked his watch. 'Only an hour, you said?'

She smiled. 'Actually, an hour and ten minutes.'

'Whew,' he said, moving closer.

At midnight Myron and Win were in the living room watching television.

'You'll miss her,' Win said.

'I'm flying down to Atlanta this weekend.'

Win nodded. 'Best-case scenario.'

'Meaning?'

'Meaning you are the pitiful, needy type who feels incomplete without a steady girlfriend. Who better than a career woman who lives a thousand miles away?'

More silence. They watched a repeat of *Frasier* on Channel 11. The show was starting to grow on them both.

'An agent represents his clients,' Win said during a commercial. 'You're his advocate. You can't worry about the repercussions.'

'You really believe that?'

'Sure, why not?'

Myron shrugged. 'Yeah, why not?' He watched another commercial. 'Esperanza said I'm starting to get too comfortable with breaking the rules.'

Win said nothing.

'Truth is,' Myron said, 'I've been doing it for a while. I paid off police officers to cover up a crime.'

'You didn't know the severity.'

'Does that matter?'

'Of course it does.'

Myron shook his head. 'We trample on that damned foul line until we can't see it anymore,' he said softly.

'What are you talking about?'

'I'm talking about us. Sophie Mayor said that you and I do the same thing she did. We take the law into our own hands. We break the rules.'

'So?'

'So it's not right.'

Win frowned. 'Oh, please.'

'The innocent get hurt.'

'The police hurt the innocent too.'

'Not like this. Esperanza suffered when she had nothing to do with any of this. Clu deserved to be punished, but what happened to Lucy Mayor was still an accident.'

Win drummed his chin with two fingers. 'If we put aside an argument on the relative severity of drunk driving,' he said, 'in the end it was not merely an accident. Clu chose to bury the body. The fact that he couldn't live with it doesn't excuse it.'

'We can't keep doing this, Win.'

'Keep doing what?'

'Breaking the rules.'

'Let me pose a question to you, Myron.' Win continued his chin drumming. 'Suppose you were Sophie Mayor and Lucy Mayor were your daughter. What would you have done?'

'Maybe the same thing,' Myron said. 'Does that make it right?'

'Depends,' Win said.

'On?'

'On the Clu Haid factor: Can you live with yourself?'

'That's it?'

'That's it. Can you live with yourself? I know that I could.'

'And you're comfortable with that?'

'With what?'

'With a world where people take the law into their own hands,' Myron said.

'Good lord, no. I'm not prescribing this remedy for others.'

'Just you.'

Win shrugged. 'I trust my judgment. I'd trust yours too. But now you want to go back in time and take an alternate route. Life is not like that. You made a decision. It was a good one based on what you knew. A tough call, but aren't they all? It could have worked out the other way. Clu might have smartened up from the experience, become a better person. My point is, you can't concern yourself with distant, impossible-to-see consequences.'

'Just worry about the here and now.'

'Precisely.'

'And what you can live with.'

'Yes.

'So maybe next time,' Myron said, 'I should opt for doing the right thing.'

Win shook his head. 'You're confusing the right thing with the legal or seemingly moral thing. But that's not the real world. Sometimes the good guys break the rules because they know better.'

Myron smiled. 'They cross the foul line. Just for a second. Just to do good. Then they scramble back into fair territory. But when you do that too often, you start smearing the line.'

'Perhaps the line is supposed to be smeared,' Win said.

'Perhaps.'

'On balance, you and I do good.'

'That balance might be better if we didn't stray across

338

the line so much – even if that meant letting a few more injustices remain injustices.'

Win shrugged. 'Your call.'

Myron sat back. 'You know what's bothering me the most about this conversation?'

'What's that?'

'That I don't think it'll change anything. That I think you're probably right.'

'But you're not sure,' Win said.

'No, I'm not sure.'

'And you still don't like it.'

'I definitely don't like it,' Myron said.

Win nodded. 'That's all I wanted to hear.'

40

Big Cyndi was totally in orange. An orange sweatshirt. Orange parachute pants like something stolen from MC Hammer's 1989 closet. Dyed orange hair. Orange fingernail polish. Orange – don't ask how – skin. She looked like a mutant teenage carrot.

'Orange is Esperanza's favorite color,' she told Myron.

'No, it's not.'

'It's not?'

Myron shook his head. 'Blue is.' For a moment, he pictured a giant Smurf.

Big Cyndi mulled that one over. 'Orange is her second favorite color?'

'Sure, I guess.'

Satisfied, Big Cyndi smiled and strung up a sign across the reception area that read WELCOME BACK, ESPERANZA!

Myron moved into his inner office. He made some calls, managed to do a little work, kept listening for the elevator.

Finally, the elevator dinged at 10:00 A.M. The doors slid open. Myron stayed put. He heard Big Cyndi's squeal of delight; the floors below them almost evacuated at the sound. He felt the vibrations of Big Cyndi leaping to her feet. Myron stood now and still waited. He heard cries and sighs and reassurances.

Two minutes later Esperanza entered Myron's office. She didn't knock. As always.

Their hug was a little awkward. Myron backed off, shoved his hands in his pockets. 'Welcome back.'

Esperanza tried a smile. 'Thanks.'

Silence.

'You knew about my personal involvement the whole time, didn't you?'

Esperanza said nothing.

'That's the part I could never resolve,' Myron said.

'Myron, don't—'

'You're my best friend,' he continued. 'You know I'd do anything for you. So I couldn't for the life of me figure out why you wouldn't talk to me. It made no sense. At first I thought you were angry at me for disappearing. But that isn't like you. Then I thought you had an affair with Clu and you didn't want me to know. But that was wrong. Then I thought it was because you had an affair with Bonnie—'

'Showing very poor judgment,' Esperanza added.

'Yes. But I'm hardly in a position to lecture you. And you wouldn't be afraid to tell me about it. Especially with the stakes so high. So I kept wondering, What could be so bad that you wouldn't talk to me? Win thought that the only explanation was that you did indeed kill Clu.'

'That Win,' Esperanza said. 'Always the sunny side.'

'But even that wouldn't do it. I'd still stick by you. You knew that. There is only one reason you wouldn't tell me the truth—'

Esperanza sighed. 'I need a shower.'

'You were protecting me.'

She looked at him. 'Don't get all mushy on me, okay? I hate when you do that.'

'Bonnie told you about the car accident. About my bribing the cops.'

'Pillow talk,' Esperanza said with a shrug.

'And once you were arrested, you made her swear to keep her mouth shut. Not for your sake or hers. But for mine. You knew that if the bribes ever became public, I'd be ruined. I'd committed a serious felony. I'd be disbarred or worse. And you knew that if I ever found out, you wouldn't be able to stop me from telling the DA because it would've been enough to get you off.'

Esperanza put her hands on her hips. 'Is there a point to this, Myron?'

'Thank you,' he said.

'Nothing to thank me for. You were too weak coming off Brenda. I was afraid you'd do something stupid. You have that habit.'

He hugged her again. She hugged him back. Nothing felt awkward this time. When they broke the embrace, he stepped back. 'Thank you.'

'Stop saying that.'

'You are my best friend.'

'And I did it for my sake too, Myron. For the business. My business.'

'I know.'

'So do we still have any clients left?' she asked.

'A few.'

'Maybe we better get on the horn then.'

'Maybe,' he said. 'I love you, Esperanza.'

'Shut up before I puke my guts out.'

'And you love me.'

'If you start singing "Barney," I'll kill you. I've already done prison time. I'm not afraid to do more.'

Big Cyndi stuck her head in. She was smiling. With the orange skin, she looked like the most frightening jack-o'-lantern imaginable. 'Marty Towey on line two.'

'I'll take it,' Esperanza said.

'And I have Enos Cabral on line three.'

'Mine,' said Myron.

At the end of a wonderfully long workday Win came into the office. 'I spoke to Esperanza,' he said. 'We're all doing pizza and old CBS Sunday at my place.'

'I can't.'

Win arched an eyebrow. '*All in the Family, M*A*S*H, Mary Tyler Moore, Bob Newhart, Carol Burnett*?'

'Sorry.'

'The Sammy Davis episode of *All in the Family*?'

'Not tonight, Win.'

Win looked concerned. 'I know you want to punish yourself,' he said, 'but this is taking self-flagellation too far.'

Myron smiled. 'It's not that.'

'Don't tell me you want to be alone. You never want to be alone.'

'Sorry, I got other plans,' Myron said.

Win arched the eyebrow, turned, left without another word.

Myron picked up the phone. He dialed the familiar number. 'I'm on my way,' he said.

'Good,' Mom said. 'I already called Fong's. I got two orders of shrimp with lobster sauce.'

'Mom?'

'What?'

'I really don't like their shrimp in lobster sauce anymore.'

'What? You've always loved it. It's your favorite.'

'Not since I was fourteen.'

'So how come you never told me?'

'I have. Several times.'

'And what, you expect me to remember every little thing? So what are you trying to tell me, Myron, your taste buds are too mature for Fong's shrimp with lobster sauce now? Who do you think you are, the Galloping Gourmet or something?'

Myron heard his father yell in the background. 'Stop bothering the boy.'

'Who's bothering him? Myron, am I bothering you?'

'And tell him to hurry,' Dad shouted. 'The game's almost on.'

'Big deal, Al. He doesn't care.'

Myron said, 'Tell Dad I'm on my way.'

'Drive slowly, Myron. There's no rush. The game will wait.'

'Okay, Mom.'

'Wear a seat belt.'

'Sure thing.'

'And your father has a surprise for you.'

'Ellen!' It was Dad again.

'What's the big deal, Al?'

'I wanted to tell him—'

'Oh stop being silly, Al. Myron?'

'Yeah, Mom?'

'Your father bought tickets to a Mets game. For Sunday. Just the two of you.'

Myron swallowed, said nothing.

'They're playing the Tunas,' Mom said.

'The Marlins!' Dad shouted.

'Tunas, marlins – what's the difference? You going to be a marine biologist now, Al? Is that what you're going to do with your leisure time, study fish?'

Myron smiled.

'Myron, you there?'

'I'm on my way, Mom.'

He hung up. He slapped his thighs and stood. He said good night to Esperanza and Big Cyndi. He stepped into the elevator and managed a smile. Friends and lovers were great, he thought, but sometimes a boy just wanted his mom and dad.

Just One Look

Acknowledgments

The author wishes to thank the following for their technical expertise: Mitchell F. Reiter, MD, Chief, Division of Spine Surgery, UMDNJ (aka 'Cuz'); David A. Gold, MD; Christopher J. Christie, United States attorney for the state of New Jersey; Captain Keith Killion of the Ridgewood Police Department; Steven Miller, MD, Director of Pediatric Emergency Medicine, Children's Hospital of New York Presbyterian; John Elias; Anthony Dellapelle (the non-fictional one); Jennifer van Dam; Linda Fairstein; and Craig Coben (aka 'Bro'). As always, if there are errors, technical or otherwise, the fault is with these people. I'm tired of being the fall guy.

A nod of gratitude to Carole Baron, Mitch Hoffman, Lisa Johnson, and all at Dutton and Penguin Group USA; Jon Wood, Malcolm Edwards, Susan Lamb, Juliet Ewers, Nicky Jeanes, Emma Noble and the gang at Orion; Aaron Priest, Lisa Erbach Vance, Bryant and Hil (for helping me over that first hump), Mike and Taylor (for helping me over the second one), and Maggie Griffin.

Characters in this book may share a name with people I know, but they are still completely fictional. In fact, this entire novel is a work of fiction. That means I make stuff up.

A special thanks to Charlotte Coben for Emma's poems. All rights reserved, as they say.

Scott Duncan sat across from the killer.

The windowless room of thundercloud gray was awkward and still, stuck in that lull when the music first starts and neither stranger is sure how to begin the dance. Scott tried a noncommittal nod. The killer, decked out in prison-issue orange, simply stared. Scott folded his hands and put them on the metal table. The killer – his file said he was Monte Scanlon, but there was no way that was his real name – might have done likewise had his hands not been cuffed.

Why, Scott wondered yet again, am I here?

His specialty was prosecuting corrupt politicians – something of a vigorous cottage industry in his home state of New Jersey – but three hours ago, Monte Scanlon, a mass executioner by any standards, had finally broken his silence to make a demand.

That demand?

A private meeting with Assistant U.S. Attorney Scott Duncan.

This was strange for a large variety of reasons, but here were two: one, a killer should not be in a position to make demands; two, Scott had never met or even heard of Monte Scanlon.

Scott broke the silence. 'You asked to see me?'

'Yes.'

Scott nodded, waited for him to say more. He didn't. 'So what can I do for you?'

Monte Scanlon maintained the stare. 'Do you know why I'm here?'

Scott glanced around the room. Besides Scanlon and

himself, four people were present. Linda Morgan, the United States attorney, leaned against the back wall trying to give off the ease of Sinatra against a lamppost. Standing behind the prisoner were two beefy, nearly identical prison guards with tree-stump arms and chests like antique armoires. Scott had met the two cocky agents before, had seen them go about their task with the sereneness of yoga instructors. But today, with this well-shackled prisoner, even these guys were on edge. Scanlon's lawyer, a ferret reeking of checkout-counter cologne, rounded out the group. All eyes were on Scott.

'You killed people,' Scott answered. 'Lots of them.'

'I was what is commonly called a hit man. I was' – Scanlon paused – 'an assassin for hire.'

'On cases that don't involve me.'

'True.'

Scott's morning had started off normal enough. He'd been drafting a subpoena on a waste-disposal executive who was paying off a small-town mayor. Routine matter. Everyday graft in the Garden State of New Jersey. That had been, what, an hour, an hour and a half ago? Now he sat across the bolted-down table from a man who had murdered – according to Linda Morgan's rough estimate – one hundred people.

'So why did you ask for me?'

Scanlon looked like an aging playboy who might have squired a Gabor sister in the fifties. He was small, wizened even. His graying hair was slicked back, his teeth cigarette-yellow, his skin leathery from midday sun and too many long nights in too many dark clubs. No one in the room knew his real name. When captured, his passport read Monte Scanlon, an Argentinean national, age fifty-one. The age seemed about right, but that would be about it. His fingerprints had not popped up in the NCIC computer banks. Facial recognition software had come up with a big goose egg.

'We need to speak alone.'

'This is not my case,' Scott said again. 'There's a U.S. attorney assigned to you.'

'This has nothing to do with her.'

'And it does with me?'

Scanlon leaned forward. 'What I'm about to tell you,' he said, 'will change your entire life.'

Part of Scott wanted to wiggle his fingers in Scanlon's face and say, 'Ooooo.' He was used to the captured criminal mindset – their serpentine maneuverings, their quest for an edge, their search for a way out, their overblown sense of importance. Linda Morgan, perhaps sensing his thoughts, shot a warning glare across his bow. Monte Scanlon, she'd told him, had worked for various connected families for the better part of thirty years. RICO hungered for his cooperation in a starving-man-near-a-buffet way. Since his capture, Scanlon had refused to talk. Until this morning.

So here Scott was.

'Your boss,' Scanlon said, gesturing with his chin at Linda Morgan, 'she hopes for my cooperation.'

'You're going to get the needle,' Morgan responded, still trying to give off the scent of nonchalance. 'Nothing you say or do will change that.'

Scanlon smiled. 'Please. You fear losing what I have to say much greater than I fear death.'

'Right. Another tough guy who doesn't fear death.' She peeled herself off the wall. 'Know what, Monte? The tough guys are always the ones who soil their pants when we strap them to the gurney.'

Again Scott fought off the desire to wiggle his fingers, this time at his boss. Scanlon kept smiling. His eyes never left Scott's. Scott didn't like what he saw. They were, as one would expect, black and shiny and cruel. But – and Scott might have been imagining things – maybe he saw something else there. Something beyond the standard

3

vacancy. There seemed to be a pleading in the eyes; Scott couldn't turn away from them. There was regret there maybe.

Remorse even.

Scott looked up at Linda and nodded. She frowned, but Scanlon had called her bluff. She touched one of the beefy guards on the shoulder and gestured for them to leave. Rising from his seat, Scanlon's lawyer spoke for the first time. 'Anything he says is off the record.'

'Stay with them,' Scanlon ordered. 'I want you to make sure that they don't listen in.'

The lawyer picked up his briefcase and followed Linda Morgan to the door. Soon Scott and Scanlon were alone. In the movies, killers are omnipotent. In real life, they are not. They don't escape from handcuffs in the middle of a high-security federal penitentiary. The Beef Brothers, Scott knew, would be behind the one-way glass. The intercom, per Scanlon's instructions, would be off. But they'd all be watching.

Scott shrugged a *well?* at him.

'I am not your typical assassin for hire.'

'Uh huh.'

'I have rules.'

Scott waited.

'For example, I only kill men.'

'Wow,' Scott said. 'You're a prince.'

Scanlon ignored the sarcasm. 'That is my first rule. I kill only men. No women.'

'Right. Tell me, does rule two have anything to do with not putting out until the third date?'

'You think I'm a monster?'

Scott shrugged as if the answer was obvious.

'You don't respect my rules?'

'What rules? You kill people. You make up these so-called rules because you need the illusion of being human.'

Scanlon seemed to consider that. 'Perhaps,' he allowed,

4

'but the men I've killed were scum. I was hired by scum to kill scum. I am no more than a weapon.'

'A weapon?' Scott repeated.

'Yes.'

'A weapon doesn't care who it kills, Monte. Men, women, grannies, little kids. A weapon doesn't differentiate.'

Scanlon smiled. 'Touché.'

Scott rubbed his palms on his pant legs. 'You didn't call me here for an ethics class. What do you want?'

'You're divorced, aren't you, Scott?'

He said nothing.

'No children, amicable split, still friendly with the ex.'

'What do you want?'

'To explain.'

'To explain what?'

He lowered his eyes but only for a moment. 'What I did to you.'

'I don't even know you.'

'But I know you. I've known you for a long time.'

Scott let the silence in. He glanced at the mirror. Linda Morgan would be behind the glass, wondering what they were talking about. She wanted information. He wondered if they had the room bugged. Probably. Either way, it would pay to keep Scanlon talking.

'You are Scott Duncan. Thirty-nine years old. You graduated from Columbia Law School. You could be making a great deal more money in private practice, but that bores you. You've been with the U.S. attorney's office six months. Your mother and father moved to Miami last year. You had a sister, but she died in college.'

Scott shifted in his seat. Scanlon studied him.

'You finished?'

'Do you know how my business operates?'

Change of subject. Scott waited a beat. Scanlon was playing a head game, trying to keep him off balance or

5

some such nonsense. Scott was not about to fall for it. Nothing he had 'revealed' about Scott's family was surprising. A person could pick up most of that info with a few well-placed keystrokes and phone calls.

'Why don't you tell me,' Scott said.

'Let's pretend,' Scanlon began, 'that you wanted someone dead.'

'Okay.'

'You would contact a friend, who knows a friend, who knows a friend, who can reach me.'

'And only that last friend would know you?'

'Something like that. I had only one go-between man, but I was careful even with him. We never met face to face. We used code names. The payments always went to offshore accounts. I would open a new account for every, shall we say, transaction, and I closed it as soon as the transaction was completed. You still with me?'

'It's not that complicated,' Scott said.

'No, I guess not. But you see, nowadays we communicate by e-mail. I'll set up a temporary e-mail account with Hotmail or Yahoo! or whatever, with fake names. Nothing that can be traced back. But even if it could, even if you could find out who sent it, where would it lead you? All e-mails were sent and read at libraries or public places. We were totally covered.'

Scott was about to mention that this total coverage had eventually landed Scanlon's ass in jail, but he decided to save it. 'What does this have to do with me?'

'I'm getting to that.' Scott could see that Scanlon was warming up to his own tale. 'In the old days – when I say old days, I mean, eight, ten years ago – we did it mostly with pay phones. I'd never see the name written. The guy would just tell me over the phone.'

Scanlon stopped and made sure that he had Scott's full attention. His tone softened a bit, became less matter-of-fact. 'That's the key, Scott. It was by phone. I'd only hear

6

the name on the phone, not see it.'

He looked at Scott expectantly. Scott had no idea what he was trying to say, so he went, 'Uh huh.'

'Do you understand why I'm stressing that it was done by phone?'

'No.'

'Because a person like me, a person with rules, could make a mistake with the phone.'

Scott thought about that. 'I still don't get it.'

'I never kill women. That was rule number one.'

'So you said.'

'So if you wanted to put a hit on someone named Billy Smith, I'd figure Billy was a man. You know, with a y. I'd never think Billy would be a woman. With an ie at the end. You understand?'

Scott went very still. Scanlon saw it. He dropped the smile. His voice was very soft.

'We talked before about your sister, didn't we, Scott?'

Scott did not respond.

'Her name was Geri, am I right?'

Silence.

'You see the problem, Scott? Geri is one of those names. If you heard it on the phone, you'd assume it would be with a J in the front and a y at the end. So fifteen years ago, I got a phone call. From that go-between man I told you about. . . .'

Scott shook his head.

'I was given an address. I was told exactly what time "Jerry"' – Scanlon made quote marks with his fingers – 'would be home.'

Scott's own voice seemed to come from very far away. 'It was ruled an accident.'

'Most arsons are, if you know what you're doing.'

'I don't believe you.'

But Scott looked at the eyes again and felt his world teeter. The images flooded in: Geri's contagious smile, the unruly hair, the braces, the way she stuck her tongue out at him during family gatherings. He remembered her first real boyfriend (a dork named Brad), her not getting a date to the junior prom, the gung-ho speech she made when she ran for student council treasurer, her first rock band (they were awful), her college acceptance letter.

Scott felt his eyes well up. 'She was only twenty-one.'

No response.

'Why?'

'I don't get into the whys, Scott. I'm just a hired hand – '

'No, not that.' Scott looked up. 'Why are you telling me this now?'

Scanlon studied his reflection in the mirror. His voice was very quiet. 'Maybe you were right.'

'Right about what?'

'What you said before.' He turned back toward Scott. 'Maybe after all is said and done, I need the illusion of being human.'

three months later

1

There are sudden rips. There are tears in your life, deep knife wounds that slash through your flesh. Your life is one thing, then it is shredded into another. It comes apart as though gutted in a belly slit. And then there are those moments when your life simply unravels. A loose thread pulled. A seam gives way. The change is slow at first, nearly imperceptible.

For Grace Lawson, the unraveling began at the Photomat.

She was about to enter the photo developing shop when she heard a somewhat familiar voice. 'Why don't you get a digital camera, Grace?'

Grace turned toward the woman. 'I'm not good with that techno stuff.'

'Oh, come now. Digital technology is a snap.' The woman raised her hand and actually snapped, just in case Grace didn't know what the word meant. 'And digital cameras are sooo much more convenient than conventional cameras. You just erase the photos you don't want. Like computer files. For our Christmas card? Barry, well, he must have taken a zillion pictures of the kids, you know, snapping away because Blake blinked or Kyle was looking the wrong way, whatever, but when you shoot that many, well, like Barry says, you're going to get one that's pretty decent, am I right?'

Grace nodded. She was trying to unearth the woman's name, but it wouldn't surface. The woman's daughter – Blake, was it? – was in Grace's son's class in first grade. Or maybe it was last year in kindergarten. Hard to keep track. Grace kept the smile frozen to her face. The woman was nice enough, but she blended in with the others. Grace wondered, not for the first time, if she was blending in too, if her once great individuality had joined the unpleasant swirl of suburban uniformity.

The thought was not a comforting one.

The woman kept describing the wonders of the digital age. Grace's frozen smile began to ache. She glanced at her watch, hoping Tech Mom would pick up the hint. Two-forty-five. Almost time to pick up Max at school. Emma had swim team practice, but another mom was driving the carpool today. A car*pool* to the *pool*, as the too-jolly mother had reminded Grace with a little tee-hee. Yeah, funny stuff.

'We have to get together,' the woman said, winding down. 'With Jack and Barry. I think they'd get along.'

'Definitely.'

Grace took advantage of the pause to wave good-bye, pull open the door, and disappear inside the Photomat. The glass door closed with a snap, ringing a little bell. The chemical smell, not unlike model glue, hit her first. She wondered about the long-term effects of working in such an environment and decided the short-term ones were annoying enough.

The kid working – Grace's use of the term *working* being overly generous here – behind the counter had a white fuzz pellet under his chin, hair dyed a color that'd intimidate Crayola, and enough piercings to double as a wind instrument. One of those wrap-around-low head-phones snaked around the back of his neck. The music was so loud that Grace could feel it in her chest. He had tattoos, lots of them. One read STONE. Another read KILLJOY. Grace thought that a third should read SLACKER.

'Excuse me?'

He did not look up.

'Excuse me?' she said a little louder.

Still nothing.

'Yah, like, dude?'

That got his attention. He snarled up, narrowed his eyes, offended by the interruption. He removed the headphones but grudgingly. 'Stub.'

'Pardon me?'

'Stub.'

Ah. Grace handed him the receipt. Fuzz Pellet then asked her for her name. This reminded Grace of those damn customer service phones that ask you to dial in your home phone, and then as soon as you get a real live person, they ask you for the same phone number. Like the first request was just for practice.

Fuzz Pellet – Grace was warming up to this nickname – flipped through a file of photo packets before extracting one. He ripped off the tag and told her an exorbitant price. She handed him a Val-Pak coupon, one dug out of her purse in an excavation that rivaled the search for the Dead Sea Scrolls, and watched the price drop to something closer to reasonable.

He handed her the packet of photographs. Grace thanked him, but he already had the music plugged back into his cerebrum. She waved in his direction. 'I come not for the pictures,' Grace said, 'but for the sparkling repartee.'

Fuzz Pellet yawned and picked up his magazine. The latest issue of *Modern Slacker*.

Grace hit the sidewalk. The weather was brisk. Autumn had shoved summer aside with a patented gust. The leaves hadn't really started turning yet, but the air had that apple-cider quality to it. The shop windows had started up with the Halloween decorations. Emma, her third grader, had convinced Jack to buy an eight-foot blowup Homer-Simpson-as-Frankenstein balloon. It looked, she had to admit, terrific. Her children liked *The Simpsons*, which meant that maybe, despite their best efforts, she and Jack were raising them right.

Grace wanted to slit open the envelope now. There was always an excitement with a newly developed roll of film, an opening-a-gift expectation, a hurry-to-the-mailbox-even-though-it's-always-bills rush that digital photography, for all its conveniences, could never duplicate. But there wasn't time before school let out.

As her Saab climbed up Heights Road, she took a small detour so that she could pass the town's lookout. From here, the skyline of Manhattan, especially at night, lay spread out like diamonds on black velvet. The longing tugged at her. She loved New York City. Until four years ago, that wonderful island had been their home. They'd had a loft on Charles Street down in the Village. Jack worked on the medical research for a large pharmaceutical company. She painted in her home studio while scoffing at her suburban counterparts and their SUVs and corduroy pants and toddler-referenced dialogues. Now she was one of them.

Grace parked behind the school with the other mothers. She turned the engine off, picked up the Photomat envelope, and ripped it open. The roll was from last week's annual trip to Chester for apple picking. Jack had snapped away. He liked being the family photographer. He considered it paternal manly work, taking the photos, as if this was a sacrifice a father was supposed to make for his family.

The first image was of Emma, their eight-year-old daughter, and Max, their six-year-old son, on the hayride, shoulders hunched, their cheeks reddened by wind. Grace stopped and stared for a moment. Feelings of, yes, maternal warmth, both primitive and evolutionary, rocked her back. That was the thing with kids. It was the little things that got to you. She'd remembered that it had been cold that day. The orchard, she knew, would be too crowded. She had not wanted to go. Now, looking at this photograph, she wondered about the idiocy of her priorities.

The other mothers were gathering by the school fence, making small talk and planning play-dates. It was, of course, the modern era, post-feminist America, and yet, of the roughly eighty parents waiting for their charges, only two were male. One, she knew, was a father who'd been laid off for more than a year. You could see it in his eyes, his slow shuffle, the missed spots when he shaved. The other guy was a stay-at-home journalist who always seemed a little too anxious to chat up the moms. Lonely maybe. Or something else.

Someone knocked on the car window. Grace looked up. Cora Lindley, her best friend in town, signaled for her to unlock the door. Grace did. Cora slid into the passenger seat next to her.

'So how did the date go last night?' Grace asked.

'Poorly.'

'Sorry.'

'Fifth-date syndrome.'

Cora was a divorcee, a little too sexy for the nervous, ever-protective 'ladies who lunch.' Clad in a low-cut, leopard-print blouse with spandex pants and pink pumps, Cora most assuredly did not fit in with the stream of khakis and loose sweaters. The other mothers eyed her with suspicion. Adult suburbia can be a lot like high school.

'What's fifth-date syndrome?' Grace asked.

'You're not dating much, are you?'

'Well, no,' Grace said. 'The husband and two kids have really cramped my style.'

'Pity. See – and don't ask me why – but on the fifth date, the guys always raise the subject . . . how should I word this delicately? . . . of a ménage à trois.'

'Please tell me you're joking.'

'I joke with you not. Fifth date. At the latest. The guy asks me, on a purely theoretical basis, what my opinion is on ménage à trois. Like it's peace in the Middle East.'

'What do you say?'

'That I usually enjoy them, especially when the two men start French-kissing.'

Grace laughed and they both got out of the car. Grace's bad leg ached. After more than a decade, she shouldn't be self-conscious about it anymore, but Grace still hated for people to see the limp. She stayed by the car and watched Cora walk away. When the bell rang, the kids burst out as if they'd been fired from a cannon. Like every other parent, Grace only had eyes for her own. The rest of the pack, uncharitable as this might sound, was scenery.

Max emerged in the second exodus. When Grace saw her son – one sneaker lace untied, his Yu-Gi-Oh! backpack looking four sizes too big, his New York Rangers knit hat tilted to the side like a tourist's beret – the warmth rushed over anew. Max made his way down the stairs, adjusting the backpack up his shoulders. She smiled. Max spotted her and smiled back.

He hopped in the back of the Saab. Grace strapped him into the booster seat and asked him how his day was. Max answered that he didn't know. She asked him what he did in school that day. Max answered that he didn't know. Did he learn math, English, science, arts and crafts? Answer: Shrug and dunno. Grace nodded. A classic case of the epidemic known as Elementary-School Alzheimer's. Were the kids drugged to forget or sworn to secrecy? One of life's mysteries.

It was not until after she got home and gave Max his Go-GURT snack – think yogurt in a toothpaste-like squeeze tube – that Grace had the chance to take a look at the rest of the photographs.

The message light on the answering machine was blinking. One message. She checked the Caller ID and saw that the number was blocked. She pressed play and was surprised. The voice belonged to an old . . . friend, she guessed. Acquaintance was too casual. Father-figure was probably more accurate, but only in the most bizarre sense.

'Hi, Grace. It's Carl Vespa.'

He did not have to say his name. It had been years, but she'd always know the voice.

'Could you give me a call when you have the chance? I need to talk to you about something.'

The message beeped again. Grace did not move, but she felt an old fluttering in her belly. Vespa. Carl Vespa had called. This could not be good. Carl Vespa, for all his kindnesses to her, was not one for idle chitchat. She debated calling him back and decided for the time being against it.

Grace moved into the spare bedroom that had become her makeshift studio. When she was painting well – when she was, like any artist or athlete, 'in the zone' – she saw the world as if preparing to put it on canvas. She would look at the streets, the trees, the people and imagine the type of brush she would use, the stroke, the mix of colors, the differing lights and casts of shadows. Her work should reflect what she wanted, not reality. That was how she looked at art. We all see the world through our own prism, of course. The best art tweaked reality to show the artist's world, what she saw or, more precisely, what she wanted others to see. It was not always a more beautiful reality. It was often more provocative, uglier maybe, more gripping and magnetic. Grace wanted a reaction. You might enjoy a beautiful setting sun – but Grace wanted you immersed in her sunset, afraid to turn away from it, afraid not to.

Grace had spent the extra dollar and ordered a second set of prints. Her fingers dipped into the envelope and plucked out the photographs. The first two were the ones of Emma and Max on the hayride. Next came Max with his arm stretched up to pick a Gala apple. There was the compulsory blurry shot of flesh, the one where Jack's hand had slipped too close to the lens. She smiled and shook her head. Her big doofus. There were several more shots of

Grace and the children with a variety of apples, trees, baskets. Her eyes grew moist, the way they always did when she looked at photographs of her children.

Grace's own parents had died young. Her mother was killed when a semi crossed the divide on Route 46 in Totowa. Grace, an only child, was eleven at the time. The police did not come to the door like in the movies. Her father had learned what happened from a phone call. Grace still remembered the way her father, wearing blue slacks and a gray sweater-vest, had answered the phone with his customary musical hello, how his face had drained of color, how he suddenly collapsed to the floor, his sobs first strangled and then silent, as if he could not gather enough air to express his anguish.

Grace's father raised her until his heart, weakened from a childhood bout with rheumatic fever, gave out during Grace's freshman year of college. An uncle out in Los Angeles volunteered to take her in, but Grace was of age by now. She decided to stay east and make her own way.

The deaths of her parents had been devastating, of course, but they had also given Grace's life a strange sense of urgency. There is a left-behind poignancy for the living. Those deaths added amplification to the mundane. She wanted to jam in the memories, get her fill of the life moments and – morbid as it sounds – make sure her kids had plenty to remember her by when she too was no more.

It was at that moment – thinking about her own parents, thinking about how much older Emma and Max looked now than in last year's apple-picking photo shoot – when she stumbled across the bizarre photograph.

Grace frowned.

The picture was near the middle of the pack. Closer to the back maybe. It was the same size, fitting neatly in with the others, though the backing sheet was somewhat flimsier. Cheaper stock, she thought. Like a high-end office-supply photocopy maybe.

Grace checked the next picture. No duplicate this time. That was strange. Only one copy of this photograph. She thought about that. The picture must have fallen in somehow, mixed up with another roll.

Because this photograph did not belong to her.

It was a mistake. That was the obvious explanation. Think for a moment about the quality workmanship of, say, Fuzz Pellet. He was more than capable of screwing up, right? Of putting the wrong photograph in the middle of her pack?

That was probably what was going on here.

Someone else's photograph had gotten mixed in with hers.

Or maybe . . .

The photograph had an old look about it – not that it was black-and-white or antique sepia. Nothing like that. The print was in color, but the hues seemed . . . off somehow – saturated, sun-faded, lacking the vibrancy one would expect in this day and age. The people in it too. Their clothes, their hair, their makeup – all dated. From fifteen, maybe twenty years ago.

Grace put it down on the table to take a closer look.

The images in the photograph were all slightly blurred. There were four people – no, wait, one more in the corner – five people in the photograph. There were two men and three women, all in their late teens, early twenties maybe – at least, the ones she could see clearly enough appeared to be around that age.

College students, Grace thought.

They had the jeans, the sweatshirts, the unkempt hair, that attitude, the casual stance of budding independence. The picture looked as if it'd been snapped when the subjects were not quite ready, in mid-gather. Some of the heads were turned so you only saw a profile. One dark-haired girl, on the very right edge of the photo, you could only see the back of her head, really, and a denim jacket.

Next to her there was another girl, this one with flaming-red hair and eyes spaced wide apart.

Near the middle, one girl, a blonde, had – God, what the hell was that about? – her face had a giant X across it. Like someone had crossed her out.

How had this picture . . . ?

As Grace kept staring, she felt a small ping in the center of her chest. The three women – she didn't recognize them. The two men looked somewhat alike, same size, same hair, same attitude. The guy on the far left too was not someone she knew.

She was sure, however, that she recognized the other man. Or boy. He wasn't really old enough to call a man. Old enough to join the army? Sure. Old enough to be called a man? He was standing in the middle, next to the blonde with the X through her face . . .

But it couldn't be. His head was in mid-turn for one thing. That adolescent-thin beard covered too much of his face . . .

Was it her husband?

Grace bent closer. It was, at best, a profile shot. She hadn't known Jack when he was this young. They had met thirteen years ago on a beach in the Côte d'Azur on southern France. After more than a year of surgery and physical therapy, Grace was still not all the way back. The headaches and memory loss remained. She had the limp – still had it now – but with all the publicity and attention from that tragic night still suffocating her, Grace had just wanted to get away for a while. She matriculated at the University of Paris, studying art in earnest. It was while on break, lying in the sun on the Côte d'Azur, that she met Jack for the first time.

Was she sure it was Jack?

He looked different here, no doubt about it. His hair was a lot longer. He had this beard, though he was still too young and baby-faced for it to come in full. He wore glasses. But there was something in the way he stood, the tilt of his head, the expression.

This was her husband.

She quickly sifted through the rest of the roll. There were more hayrides, more apples, more arms raised in mid-pick. She saw one that she'd taken of Jack, the one time he'd let her have the camera, control freak that he was. He was reaching so high, his shirt had moved up enough to show his belly. Emma had told him that it was eeuw, gross. That, of course, made Jack pull up the shirt more. Grace had laughed. 'Work it, baby!' she'd said, snapping the next photo. Jack, much to Emma's ultimate mortification, obliged and undulated.

'Mom?'

She turned. 'What's up, Max?'

'Can I have a granola bar?'

'Let's grab one for the car,' she said, rising. 'We need to take a ride.'

Fuzz Pellet was not at the Photomat.

Max checked out the various themed picture frames – 'Happy Birthday,' 'We Love You, Mom,' that kind of thing. The man behind the counter, resplendent in a polyester tie, pocket protector, and short-sleeve dress shirt flimsy enough to see the V-neck tee beneath it, wore a name tag that informed one and all that he, Bruce, was an assistant manager.

'May I help you?'

'I'm looking for the young man who was here a couple of hours ago,' Grace said.

'Josh is gone for the day. Something I can do for you?'

'I picked up a roll of film a little before three o'clock . . .'

'Yes?'

Grace had no idea how to put this. 'There was a photo in there that shouldn't have been.'

'I'm not sure I understand.'

'One of the pictures. I didn't take it.'

He gestured toward Max. 'I see you have young children.'

'Excuse me?'

Assistant Manager Bruce pushed his glasses up off the end of his nose. 'I was just pointing out that you have young children. Or at least, one young child.'

'What does that have to do with anything?'

'Sometimes a child picks up the camera. When the parent isn't looking. They snap a picture or two. Then they put the camera back.'

'No, it's not that. This picture had nothing to do with us.'

'I see. Well, I'm sorry for the inconvenience. Did you get all the photos you took?'

'I think so.'

'None were missing?'

'I really didn't check that closely, but I think we got them all.'

He opened a drawer. 'Here. This is a coupon. Your next roll will be developed for free. Three by fives. If you want the four by sixes, there is a small surcharge.'

Grace ignored his outstretched hand. 'The sign on the door says you develop all the pictures on site.'

'That's right.' He petted the large machine behind him. 'Old Betsy here does the job for us.'

'So my roll would have been developed here?'

'Of course.'

Grace handed him the Photomat envelope. 'Could you tell me who developed this roll?'

'I'm sure it was just an honest error.'

'I'm not saying it wasn't. I just want to know who developed my roll.'

He took a look at the envelope. 'May I ask why you want to know?'

'Was it Josh?'

'Yes, but –'

22

'Why did he leave?'

'Pardon me?'

'I picked up the photos a little before three o'clock. You close at six. It's nearly five now.'

'So?'

'It seems strange that a shift would end between three and six for a store that closes at six.'

Assistant Manager Bruce straightened up a bit. 'Josh had a family emergency.'

'What kind of emergency?'

'Look, Miss . . .' – he checked the envelope – 'Lawson, I'm sorry for the error and inconvenience. I'm sure a photograph from another set fell into your packet. I can't recall it happening before, but none of us are perfect. Oh, wait.'

'What?'

'May I see the photograph in question please?'

Grace was afraid he'd want to keep it. 'I didn't bring it,' she lied.

'What was it a picture of?'

'A group of people.'

He nodded. 'I see. And were these people naked?'

'What? No. Why would you ask that?'

'You seem upset. I assumed that the photograph was in some way offensive.'

'No, nothing like that. I just need to speak to Josh. Could you tell me his last name or give me a home phone number?'

'Out of the question. But he'll be in tomorrow first thing. You can talk to him then.'

Grace chose not to protest. She thanked the man and left. Might be better anyway, she thought. By driving here she had merely reacted. Check that. She had probably overreacted.

Jack would be home in a few hours. She would ask him about it then.

Grace had homebound carpool duties for the swim practice. Four girls, ages eight and nine, all delightfully energetic, piled two into the backseat and two into the 'way, way' back of the minivan. There was a swirl of giggles, of 'Hello, Ms. Lawson,' wet hair, the gentle perfume of both YMCA chlorine and bubble gum, the sound of backpacks being shucked off, of seat belts fastening. No child sat in the front – new safety rules – but despite the chauffeur feel, or maybe because of it, Grace liked doing carpool. It was time spent seeing her child interact with her friends. Children spoke freely during carpool; the driving adult might as well have been in another time zone. A parent could learn much. You could find out who was cool, who was not, who was in, who was out, what teacher was totally rad, what teacher was most assuredly not. You could, if you listened closely enough, decipher where on the pecking order your child was currently perched.

It was also entertaining as all get-out.

Jack was working late again, so when they got home, Grace quickly made Max and Emma dinner – veggie chicken nuggets (purportedly healthier and, once dipped in ketchup, the kids can never tell the difference), Tater Tots, and Jolly Green Giant frozen corn. Grace peeled two oranges for dessert. Emma did her homework – too big a load for an eight-year-old, Grace thought. When she had a free second, Grace headed down the hallway and flipped on the computer.

Grace might not be into digital photography, but she understood the necessity and even advantages of computer graphics and the World Wide Web. There was a site that featured her work, how to buy it, how to commission a portrait. At first, this had hit her as too much like shilling, but as Farley, her agent, reminded her, Michelangelo painted for money and on commission. So did Da Vinci and Raphael and pretty much every great artist the world has ever known. Who was she to be above it?

Grace scanned in her three favorite apple-picking photos for safekeeping and then, more on a whim than anything else, she decided to scan in the strange photograph too. That done, she started bathing the children. Emma went first. She was just getting out of the tub when Grace heard his keys jangle in the back door.

'Hey,' Jack called up in a whisper. 'Any hot love monkeys up there waiting for their stud muffin?'

'Children,' she said. 'Children are still awake.'

'Oh.'

'Care to join us?'

Jack bounded up the stairs, taking them two at a time. The house shook from the onslaught. He was a big man, six-two, two-ten. She loved the substance of him sleeping beside her, the rise and fall of his chest, the manly smell of him, the soft hairs on his body, the way his arm snaked around her during the night, the feeling of not only intimacy but safety. He made her feel small and protected, and maybe it was un-PC, but she liked that.

Emma said, 'Hi, Daddy.'

'Hey, Kitten, how was school?'

'Good.'

'Still have a crush on that Tony boy?'

'Eeuw!'

Satisfied with the reaction, Jack kissed Grace on the cheek. Max came out of his room, stark naked.

'Ready for your bath, mah man?' Jack asked.

'Ready,' Max said.

They high-fived. Jack scooped Max up in a sea of giggles. Grace helped Emma get in her pajamas. Laughter spilled from the bath. Jack was singing a rhyming song with Max where some girl named Jenny Jenkins couldn't decide what color to wear. Jack would start off with the color and Max filled in the rhyme line. Right now they were singing that Jenny Jenkins couldn't wear 'yellow' because she'd look like a 'fellow.' Then they both cracked up anew. They did pretty much the same rhymes every night. And they laughed their asses off over them every night.

Jack toweled Max off, got him into his pajamas, and put him to bed. He read two chapters of *Charlie and the Chocolate Factory*. Max listened to every word, totally riveted. Emma was old enough to read by herself. She lay in her bed, devouring the latest tale of the Baudelaire orphans from Lemony Snicket. Grace sat with her and sketched for half an hour. This was her favorite time of the day – working in silence in the same room as her eldest child.

When Jack finished, Max begged for just one more page. Jack stayed firm. It was getting late, he said. Max grudgingly acquiesced. They talked for another moment or two about Charlie's impending visit to Willy Wonka's factory. Grace listened in.

Roald Dahl, both her men agreed, totally rocked.

Jack turned down the lights – they had a dimmer switch because Max didn't like complete darkness – and then he entered into Emma's room. He bent down to give Emma a kiss good night. Emma, a total Daddy's Girl, reached up, grabbed his neck, and wouldn't let him go. Jack melted at Emma's nightly technique for both showing affection and stalling going to sleep.

'Anything new for the journal?' Jack asked.

Emma nodded. Her backpack was next to her bed. She dug through it and produced her school journal. She turned the pages and handed it to her father.

'We're doing poetry,' Emma said. 'I started one today.'

'Cool. Want to read it?'

Emma's face was aglow. So was Jack's. She cleared her throat and began:

'Basketball, basketball,
Why are you so round?
So perfectly bumpy,
So amazingly brown.
Tennis ball, tennis ball,
Why are you so fizzy,
When you're hit with a racket,
Do you feel kind of dizzy?'

Grace watched the scene from the doorway. Jack's hours had gotten bad lately. Most of the time Grace didn't mind. Quiet moments were becoming scarce. She needed the solace. Loneliness, the precursor to boredom, is conducive to the creative process. That was what artistic meditation was all about – boring yourself to the point where inspiration must emerge if only to preserve your sanity. A writer friend once explained that the best cure for writer's block was to read a phone book. Bore yourself enough and the Muse will be obligated to push through the most slog-filled of arteries.

When Emma was done, Jack fell back and said, 'Whoa.'

Emma made the face she made when she was proud of herself but didn't want to show it. She tucked her lips over and back under her teeth.

'That was the most brilliant poem I've ever heard ever ever,' Jack said.

Emma gave a head-down shrug. 'It's only the first two verses.'

'That was the most brilliant first two verses I've ever heard ever ever.'

'I'm going to write a hockey one tomorrow.'

'Speaking of which . . .'

Emma sat up. 'What?'

Jack smiled. 'I got tickets for the Rangers at the Garden on Saturday.'

Emma, part of the 'jock' group as opposed to the group who worshipped the latest boy band, gave a yippee and reached up for another hug. Jack rolled his eyes and accepted it. They discussed the team's recent performance and set odds on their chances of beating the Minnesota Wild. A few minutes later, Jack disentangled himself. He told his daughter that he loved her. She told him that she loved him too. Jack started for the door.

'Gotta grab something to eat,' he whispered to Grace.

'There's leftover chicken in the fridge.'

'Why don't you slip into something more comfortable?'

'Hope springs eternal.'

Jack arched an eyebrow. 'Still afraid you're not enough woman for me?'

'Oh, that reminds me.'

'What?'

'Something about Cora's date last night.'

'Hot?'

'I'll be down in a second.'

He arched the other eyebrow and hustled downstairs with a whistle. Grace waited until she heard Emma's breathing deepen before following. She turned off the light and watched for a moment. This was Jack's bit. He paced the corridors at night, unable to sleep, guarding them in their beds. There were nights she'd wake up and find the spot next to her empty. Jack would be standing in one of their doorways, his eyes glassy. She'd approach and he'd say, 'You love them so much . . .' He didn't need to say more. He didn't even have need to say that.

Jack didn't hear her approach, and for some reason, a reason Grace wouldn't want to articulate, she tried to stay quiet. Jack stood stiffly, his back to her, his head down. This was unusual. Jack was usually hyper, constant motion. Like Max, Jack could not stay still. He fidgeted. His leg shook whenever he sat. He was high energy.

But right now he was staring down at the kitchen

counter – more specifically, at the strange photograph – still as a stone.

'Jack?'

He startled upright. 'What the hell is this?'

His hair, she noticed, was a shade longer than it should be. 'Why don't you tell me?'

He didn't say anything.

'That's you, right? With the beard?'

'What? No.'

She looked at him. He blinked and looked away.

'I picked up this roll of film today,' she said. 'At the Photomat.'

He said nothing. She stepped closer.

'That photograph was in the middle of the pack.'

'Wait.' He looked up sharply. 'It was in with our roll of film?'

'Yes.'

'Which roll?'

'The one we took at the apple orchard.'

'That doesn't make any sense.'

She shrugged. 'Who are the other people in the photo?'

'How should I know?'

'The blonde standing next to you,' Grace said. 'With the X through her. Who is she?'

Jack's cell phone rang. He snapped it up like a gunfighter on a draw. He mumbled a hello, listened, put his hand over the mouthpiece, and said, 'It's Dan.' His research partner at Pentocol Pharmaceuticals. He lowered his head and headed into the den.

Grace headed upstairs. She started getting ready for bed. What had started as a gentle nagging was growing stronger, more persistent. She flashed back to their years living in France. He would never talk about his past. He had a wealthy family and a trust fund, she knew – and he wanted nothing to do with either. There was a sister, a lawyer out in Los Angeles or San Diego. His father was still alive but very old. Grace had wanted to know more, but Jack refused to elaborate, and sensing something foreboding, she had not pushed him.

They fell in love. She painted. He worked in a vineyard in Saint-Emilion in Bordeaux. They lived in Saint-Emilion until Grace had gotten pregnant with Emma. Something called her home then – a yearning, corny as it might sound, to raise her children in the land of the free and the home of the brave. Jack wanted to stay, but Grace had insisted. Now Grace wondered why.

Half an hour passed. Grace slipped under the covers and waited. Ten minutes later, she heard a car engine start up. Grace looked out the window.

Jack's minivan was pulling out.

He liked to shop at night, she knew – hit the grocery store when it wasn't crowded. So going out like this was not unusual for him. Except, of course, he hadn't called up to tell her he was going or to ask if they needed anything in particular.

Grace tried his cell phone but the voice mail picked up. She sat back and waited. Nothing. She tried to read. The words swam by in a meaningless haze. Two hours later, Grace tried Jack's cell phone again. Still voice mail. She checked on the children. They slept soundly, appropriately oblivious.

When she could stand it no longer Grace headed downstairs. She looked through the packet of film.

The strange photograph was gone.

2

Most people check out the online personals to find a date. Eric Wu found victims.

He had seven different accounts using seven different made-up personas – some male and some female. He tried to stay in e-mail contact with an average of six 'potential dates' per account. Three of the accounts were on standard any-age straight personals. Two were for singles over the age of fifty. One was for gay men. The final site hooked up lesbians looking for serious commitment.

At any one time Wu would be conducting online flirtations with as many as forty or even fifty of the forlorn. He would slowly get to know them. Most were cautious, but that was okay. Eric Wu was a patient man. Eventually they would give him enough tidbits to find out if he should pursue the relationship or cut them loose.

He only dealt with women at first. The theory was that they would be the easiest victims. But Eric Wu, who received no sexual gratification from his work, realized that he was leaving untapped an entire market that would be less likely to worry about online safety. A man does not, for example, fear rape. He does not fear stalkers. A man is less cautious, and that makes him more vulnerable.

Wu was seeking singles with few ties. If they had children, they were no good to him. If they had family living close by, they were no good to him. If they had roommates, important jobs, too many close friends, well, ditto. Wu wanted them lonely, yes, but also secluded and shut off from the many ties and bonds that connect the rest of us to something greater than the individual. Right now, he also required one with geographical proximity to the Lawson household.

He found such a victim in Freddy Sykes.

Freddy Sykes worked for a storefront tax-filing company in Waldwick, New Jersey. He was forty-eight years old. His parents were both deceased. He had no siblings. According to his online flirtations at BiMen.com, Freddy had taken care of his mother and never had the time for a relationship. When she passed away two years ago, Freddy inherited the house in Ho-Ho-Kus, a scant three miles from the Lawson residence. His online photograph, a headshot, hinted that Freddy was probably on the plump side. His hair was shoe-polish black, thin, styled in a classic comb-over. His smile seemed forced, unnatural, as if he were wincing before a blow.

Freddy had spent the past three weeks flirting online with one Al Singer, a fifty-six-year-old retired Exxon executive who'd been married twenty-two years before admitting that he was interested in 'experimenting.' The Al Singer persona still loved his wife, but she didn't understand his need to be with both men and women. Al was interested in European travel, fine dining, and watching sports on TV. For his Singer persona, Wu used a photograph he'd grabbed off a YMCA online catalogue. His Al Singer looked athletic but not too handsome. Someone too attractive might raise Freddy's suspicion. Wu wanted him to buy the fantasy. That was the key thing.

Freddy Sykes's neighbors were mostly young families who paid him no attention. His house looked like every other on the block. Wu watched now as Sykes's garage door opened electronically. The garage was attached. You could enter and exit your car without being seen. That was excellent.

Wu waited ten minutes and then rang his doorbell.

'Who is it?'

'Delivery for Mr. Sykes.'

'From whom?'

Freddy Sykes had not opened the door. That was strange. Men usually did. Again that was part of their vulnerability, part of the reason that they were easier prey than their female counterparts. Overconfidence. Wu spotted the peephole. Sykes would no doubt be peering at the twenty-six-year-old Korean man with baggy pants and a squat, compact build. He might notice Wu's earring and bemoan how today's youth mutilated their bodies. Or maybe the build and earring would turn Sykes on. Who knew?

'From Topfit Chocolate,' Wu said.

'No, I mean, who sent them?'

Wu pretended to read the note again. 'A Mr. Singer.'

That did it. The deadbolt slid open. Wu glanced about him. No one. Freddy Sykes opened the door with a smile. Wu did not hesitate. His fingers formed a spear and then darted for Sykes's throat like a bird going for food. Freddy went down. Wu moved with a speed that defied his bulk. He slid inside and closed the door behind him.

Freddy Sykes lay on his back, his hands wrapped around his own neck. He was trying to scream, but all he could make were small squawking noises. Wu bent down and flipped him onto his stomach. Freddy struggled. Wu pulled up his victim's shirt. Freddy kicked at him. Wu's expert fingers traced up his spine until he found the right spot between the fourth and fifth vertebrae. Freddy kicked some more. Using his index finger and thumb like bayonets, Wu dug into the bone, nearly breaking skin.

Freddy stiffened.

Wu applied a bit more pressure, forcing the facet joints to sublux. Still burrowing deeper between the two vertebrae, he took hold and plucked. Something in Freddy's spine snapped like a guitar string.

The kicking stopped.

All movement stopped.

33

But Freddy Sykes was alive. That was good. That was what Wu wanted. He used to kill them right away, but now he knew better. Alive, Freddy could call his boss and tell him that he was taking time off. Alive, he could offer up his PIN if Wu wanted money from the ATM. Alive, he could answer messages in case someone did indeed call.

And alive, Wu would not have to worry about the smell.

Wu jammed a gag in Freddy's mouth and left him naked in the bathtub. The pressure on the spine had made the facet joints jump out of position. This dislocation of the vertebrae would contuse rather than completely sever the spinal column. Wu tested the results of his handiwork. Freddy could not move his legs at all. His deltoids might work, but the hands and lower arms would not function. Most important, he could still breathe on his own.

For all practical purposes, Freddy Sykes was paralyzed.

Keeping Sykes in the tub would make it easier to rinse off any mess. Freddy's eyes were open a little too widely. Wu had seen this look before: somewhere past terror but not yet death, a hollowness that fell in that awful cusp between the two.

There was obviously no need to tie Freddy up.

Wu sat in the dark and waited for night to fall. He closed his eyes and let his mind drift back. There were prisons in Rangoon where they studied spinal fractures during hangings. They learned where to place the knot, where to apply force, what effects different placement would have. In North Korea, in the political prison Wu had called home from the age of thirteen to eighteen, they had taken the experiments one step further. Enemies of the state were killed creatively. Wu had done many with his bare hands. He had hardened his hands by punching boulders. He had studied the anatomy of the human body in a way most medical students would envy. He had practiced

34

on human beings, perfecting his techniques.

The exact spot between the fourth and fifth vertebrae. That was key. Any higher and you could paralyze them completely. That would lead to death fairly quickly. Forget their arms and legs – their internal organs would stop working. Any lower and you would only get the legs. The arms would still work. If the pressure applied was too great, you'd snap the entire spinal column. It was all about precision. Having the right touch. Practice.

Wu turned on Freddy's computer. He wanted to keep up with the other singles on his list because he never knew when he would need a new place to live. When he was finished, Wu allowed himself to sleep. Three hours later he awoke and looked in on Freddy. His eyes were glassier now, staring straight up, blinking without focus.

When his contact called Wu's cell phone, it was nearly 10 P.M.

'Are you settled in?' the contact asked.

'Yes.'

'We have a situation.'

Wu waited.

'We need to move things up a bit. Is that a problem?'

'No.'

'He needs to be taken now.'

'You have a place?'

Wu listened, memorizing the location.

'Any questions?'

'No,' Wu said.

'Eric?'

Wu waited.

'Thanks, man.'

Wu hung up. He found the car keys and took off in Freddy's Honda.

3

Grace couldn't call the police yet. She couldn't sleep either.

The computer was still on. Their screen saver was a family photo taken last year at Disney World. The four of them posed with Goofy at Epcot Center. Jack was wearing mouse ears. His grin was ear to ear. Hers was more reserved. She'd felt silly, which just encouraged Jack. She touched the mouse – the other mouse, the computer mouse – and her family disappeared.

Grace clicked the new icon and the strange photograph of the five college-aged kids appeared. The image came up with Adobe Photoshop. For several minutes Grace just stared at the young faces, searching for – she didn't know – a clue maybe. Nothing came to her. She cropped each face, blowing them up into something approaching four inches by four inches. Any bigger and the already-blurred image became undecipherable. The good paper was in the color inkjet, so she hit the print button. She grabbed a pair of scissors and went to work.

Soon she had five separate headshots, one for each person in the picture. She studied them again, this time taking extra care with the young blonde next to Jack. She was pretty with that girl-next-door complexion and long flaxen hair. The young woman's eyes were on Jack, and the look was more than casual. Grace felt a pang of, what, jealousy? How bizarre. Who was this woman? Obviously an old girlfriend – one Jack had never mentioned. But so what? Grace had a past. So did Jack. Why would the look in that photograph bother her?

So what now?

She would have to wait for Jack. When he came home, she would demand answers.

But answers about what?

Back up here a second. What was really going on? An old photograph, probably of Jack, had popped up in her packet of pictures. It was weird, sure. It was even a little creepy, what with the blonde crossed out like that. And Jack had stayed out late before without calling. So really, what was the big deal here? Something in the photo had probably upset him. He turned off his phone and was probably in a bar. Or at Dan's house. This whole thing was probably just a bizarre joke.

Yeah, Grace, sure. A joke. Like the one about the carpool to the pool.

Sitting alone, the room dark except for the glow from the computer monitor, Grace tried a few more ways to rationalize away what was going on. She stopped when she realized that this was only scaring her more.

Grace clicked onto the face of the young woman, the one who stared at her husband with longing, zooming in for a better view. She stared at the face, really stared, and a tingle of dread began to travel across her scalp. Grace did not move. She just kept looking at the woman's face. She didn't know the wheres or whens or hows, but she now realized something with thudding certainty.

Grace had seen this young woman before.

4

Rocky Conwell took up post by the Lawson residence.

He tried to get comfortable in his 1989 Toyota Celica, but that was impossible. Rocky was too big for this piece-of-crap car. He pulled harder on that damned seat lever, nearly ripping it out, but the seat would go back no farther. It would have to do. He settled in and let his eyes start to close.

Man, was Rocky tired. He was working two jobs. The first, his steady gig to impress his parole officer, was a ten-hour shift on the Budweiser assembly line in Newark. The second, sitting in this damn car and staring at a house, was strictly off the books.

Rocky jerked up when he heard a noise. He picked up his binoculars. Damn, someone had started up the mini-van. He focused in. Jack Lawson was on the move. He lowered the binoculars, shifted into drive, and prepared to follow.

Rocky needed two jobs because he needed cash in a big, bad way. Lorraine, his ex, was making overtures about a possible reconciliation. But she was still skittish about it. Cash, Rocky knew, could tip the balance in his favor. He loved Lorraine. He wanted her back in a big, bad way. He owed her some good times, didn't he? And if that meant he had to work his butt off, well, he'd been the one to screw up. It was a price he was willing to pay.

It hadn't always been like this for Rocky Conwell. He'd been an All-State defensive end at Westfield High. Penn State – Joe Paterno himself – had recruited him and transformed him into a hard-hitting inside linebacker. Six-four, two-sixty, and blessed with a naturally aggressive nature, Rocky had been a standout for four years. He'd been All Big-Ten for two years. The St. Louis Rams drafted him in the seventh round.

For a while, it was like God Himself had perfectly planned out his life from the get-go. His real name was Rocky, his parents naming him that when his mother went into labor as they watched the movie *Rocky* in the summer of 1976. You gonna have a name like Rocky, you better be big and strong. You better be ready to rumble. Here he was, a pro football draft pick itching to get to camp. He and Lorraine – a knockout who could not only stop traffic but make it go backward – hooked up during his junior year. They fell for each other pretty hard. Life was good.

Until, well, it wasn't.

Rocky was a great college player, but there is a big difference between Division IA and the pros. At the Rams rookie camp, they loved his hustle. They loved his work ethic. They loved the way he would sacrifice his body to make a play. But they didn't love his speed – and in today's game, what with the emphasis on passing and coverage, Rocky was simply not good enough. Or so they said. Rocky would not surrender. He started taking more steroids. He got bigger but still not big enough for the front line. He managed to hang around one season playing special teams for the Rams. The next year he was cut.

The dream wouldn't die. Rocky wouldn't let it. He pumped iron nonstop. He began 'roiding big time. He had always taken some kind of anabolic supplement. Every athlete does. But desperation had made him less cautious. He didn't worry about cycling or overdoing it. He just wanted mass. His mood darkened from either the drugs or the disappointment – or more likely, the potent blend of the two.

To make ends meet, Rocky took up work with the Ultimate Fighting Federation. You may remember their octagon grudge matches. For a while, they were all the rage on pay-per-view – real, bloody, no-holds-barred brawls. Rocky was good at it. He was big and strong and a natural fighter. He had great endurance and knew how to wear down an opponent.

Eventually the violence in the ring got to be too much for people's sensibilities. States began to outlaw ultimate fighting. Some of the guys started battling in Japan where it was still legal – Rocky guessed that they had different sensibilities over there – but he didn't go. Rocky still believed that the NFL was within his grasp. He just had to work harder. Get a little bigger, a little stronger, a little faster.

Jack Lawson's minivan pulled onto Route 17. Rocky's instructions were clear. Follow Lawson. Write down where he went, who he talked to, every detail of his trip, but do not – repeat not – engage him. He was to observe. Nothing more.

Right, easy cash.

Two years ago, Rocky got into a bar fight. It was typical stuff. Some guy stared at Lorraine too long. Rocky had asked him what he was looking at, and the guy responded, 'Not much.' You know the drill. Except Rocky was juiced up from the 'roids. He pulverized the guy – put him in traction – and got nailed on an assault beef. He spent three months in jail and was now on probation. That had been the final straw for Lorraine. She called him a loser and moved out.

So now he was trying to make it up to her.

Rocky had quit the junk. Dreams die hard, but he now realized that the NFL was not going to be. But Rocky had talents. He could be a good coach. He knew how to motivate. A friend of his had an in at his old alma mater, Westfield High. If Rocky could get his record cleared, he'd be made varsity defensive coordinator. Lorraine could get a job there as a guidance counselor. They'd be on their way.

They just needed a little set-up cash.

Rocky kept the Celica a decent distance back of the minivan. He was not too worried about being spotted. Jack Lawson was an amateur. He wouldn't be looking for a tail. That was what his boss had told him.

Lawson crossed the New York border and took the thruway north. The time was ten P.M. Rocky wondered if he should call it in, but no, not yet. There was nothing here to report. The man was taking a ride. Rocky was following him. That was his job.

Rocky felt his calf start cramping. Man, he wished this piece of junk had more legroom.

Half an hour later Lawson pulled off by the Woodbury Commons, one of those massive outdoor malls where all the stores were purportedly 'outlets' for their more expensive counterparts. The Commons was closed. The minivan pulled down a quiet stretch of road on the side. Rocky hung back. If he followed now, he'd be spotted for sure.

Rocky found a position on the right, shifted into park, turned off his headlights, and picked up his binoculars.

Jack Lawson stopped the minivan, and Rocky watched him step out. There was another car not too far away. Must be Lawson's girlfriend. Strange place for a romantic rendezvous, but there you go. Jack looked both ways and then headed toward the wooded area. Damn. Rocky would have to follow on foot.

He put down the binoculars and slid out. He was still seventy, eighty yards away from Lawson. Rocky didn't want to get any closer. He squatted down and peered through the binoculars again. Lawson stopped walking. He turned around and . . .

What's this?

Rocky swung the binoculars to the right. A man was standing to Lawson's left. Rocky took a closer look. The man wore fatigues. He was short and squat, built like a perfect square. Looked like he worked out, Rocky thought. The guy – he looked Chinese or something – stood perfectly still, stonelike.

At least for a few seconds.

Gently, almost like a lover's touch, the Chinese guy reached up and put his hand on Lawson's shoulder. For a fleeting moment Rocky thought that maybe he had stumbled across a gay tryst. But that wasn't it. That wasn't it at all.

Jack Lawson dropped to the ground like a puppet with his strings cut.

Rocky stifled a gasp. The Chinese guy looked down at the crumpled form. He bent down and picked Lawson up by . . . hell, it looked like the neck. Like you'd pick up a puppy or something. By the scruff of his neck.

Oh damn, Rocky thought. I better call this in.

Without breaking a sweat, the Chinese guy started carrying Lawson toward his car. With one hand. Like the guy was a briefcase or something. Rocky reached for his cell phone.

Crap, he'd left it in the car.

Okay, think, Rocky. The car the Chinese guy was driving. It was a Honda Accord. New Jersey plates. Rocky tried to memorize the number. He watched while the Chinese guy opened the trunk. He dumped Lawson in as if he were a load of laundry.

Oh man, now what?

Rocky's orders were firm. Do not engage. How many times had he heard that? Whatever you do, just observe. Do not engage.

He didn't know what to do.

Should he just follow?

Uh-uh, no way. Jack Lawson was in the trunk. Look, Rocky did not know the man. He didn't know why he was supposed to follow him. He'd figured that they'd been hired to follow Lawson for the usual reason – his wife sus-

42

pected him of having an affair. That was one thing. Follow and prove infidelity. But this . . . ?

Lawson had been assaulted. For crying out loud, he'd been locked in the trunk by this muscle-headed Jackie Chan. Could Rocky just sit back and let that happen?

No.

Whatever Rocky had done, whatever he had become, he was not about to let that stand. Suppose he lost the Chinese guy? Suppose there wasn't enough air in the trunk? Suppose Lawson had been seriously injured already and was dying?

Rocky had to do something.

Should he call the police?

The Chinese guy slammed the trunk closed. He started for the front seat.

Too late to call anyone. He had to make his move now.

Rocky remained six-four, two-sixty, and rock solid. He was a professional fighter. Not a show boxer. Not a phony, staged wrestler. A real fighter. He didn't have a gun, but he knew how to take care of himself.

Rocky started running toward the car.

'Hey!' he shouted. 'Hey, you! Stop right there!'

The Chinese guy – as he got closer, Rocky could see he was more like a kid – looked up. His expression did not change. He just stared as Rocky ran toward him. He did not move. He did not try to get in the car and drive away. He waited patiently.

'Hey!'

The Chinese kid stayed still.

Rocky stopped a yard in front of him. Their eyes met. Rocky did not like what he saw. He had played football against some true headcases. He'd fought pain-happy crazies in the Ultimate Fighting ring. He had stared into the eyes of pure psychos – guys who got off on hurting people. This was not like this. This was like staring into the eyes of . . . something not alive. A rock maybe. An

43

inanimate object of some kind. There was no fear, no mercy, no reason.

'May I help you?' the Chinese kid said.

'I saw . . . Let that man out of the trunk.'

The kid nodded. 'Of course.'

The kid glanced toward the trunk. So did Rocky. And that was when Eric Wu struck.

Rocky never saw the blow. Wu ducked down, twisted his hips for power, and smashed his fist into Rocky's kidney. Rocky had taken shots before. He had been punched in the kidney by men twice this size. But nothing had ever hit him like this. The blow landed like a sledgehammer.

Rocky gasped but stayed on his feet. Wu moved in and jabbed something hard into Rocky's liver. It felt like a barbecue skewer. The pain exploded through him.

Rocky's mouth opened, but the scream wouldn't come out. He fell to the ground. Wu dropped down next to him. The last thing Rocky saw – the last thing he would ever see – was Eric Wu's face, calm and serene, as he placed his hands under Rocky's rib cage.

Lorraine, Rocky thought. And then nothing more.

5

Grace caught herself mid-scream. She jerked upright. The light was still on in the hallway. A silhouette stood in her doorway. But it wasn't Jack.

She awoke, still gasping. A dream. She knew that. On some elusive level, she had known that midway through. She'd had this dream before, plenty of times, though not in a long time. Must be the upcoming anniversary, she thought.

She tried to settle back. It wouldn't happen. The dream always started and ended the same. The variations occurred in the middle.

In the dream Grace was back at the old Boston Garden. The stage was directly in front of her. There was a steel blockade, short, maybe waist-high, like something you might use to lock your bike. She leaned against it.

The loudspeaker played 'Pale Ink,' but that was impossible because the concert hadn't even started yet. 'Pale Ink' was the big hit from the Jimmy X Band, the best-selling single of the year. You still hear it on the radio all the time. It would be played live, not on some waiting-time recording. But if this dream was like some movie, 'Pale Ink' was, if you will, the soundtrack.

Was Todd Woodcroft, her boyfriend at the time, standing next to her? She sometimes imagined holding his hand – though they were never the hand-holding kind of couple – and then, when it went wrong, the stomach-dropping feel of his hand slipping away from hers. In reality, Todd was probably right next to her. In the dream, only sometimes. This time, no, he was not there. Todd had escaped that night unscathed. She never blamed him for what happened to her. There was nothing he could have done. Todd had never even visited her in the hospital. She didn't blame him for that either. Theirs was a college romance already on the skids, not a soul-mate situation. Who needed a scene at this stage of the game? Who'd want to break up with a girl in the hospital? Better for both, she thought, to let it just sort of drift away.

In the dream, Grace knows that tragedy is about to strike, but she does nothing about it. Her dream self does not call out a warning or try to make for the exit. She often wondered why, but wasn't that how dreams worked? You are powerless even with foreknowledge, a slave to some advanced hardwiring in your subconscious. Or perhaps the answer is simpler: There was no time. In the dream, the tragedy begins in seconds. In reality, according to witnesses, Grace and the others had stood in front of that stage for more than four hours.

The crowd's mood had slid from excited to antsy to restless before stopping at hostile. Jimmy X, real name James Xavier Farmington, the gorgeous rocker with the glorious hair, was supposed to take the stage at 8:30 P.M., though no one really expected him before nine. Now it was closing in on midnight. At first the crowd had been chanting Jimmy's name. Now a chorus of boos had started up. Sixteen thousand people, including those, like Grace, who had been lucky enough to get standing seats in the pit, rose as one, demanding their performance. Ten minutes passed before the loudspeaker finally offered up some feedback. The crowd, having reverted to their earlier state of fevered excitement, went wild.

But the voice that came over the loudspeaker did not introduce the band. In a straight monotone, it announced that tonight's performance had been delayed again for at least an hour. No explanation. For a moment nobody moved. Silence filled the arena.

This was where the dream began, during that lull before the devastation. Grace was there again. How old was she? She had been twenty-one, but in the dream she seemed to be older. It was a different, parallel Grace, one who was married to Jack and mother to Emma and Max and yet was still at that concert during her senior year of college. Again that was how it worked in dreams, a dual reality, your parallel self overlapping with your actual one.

Was all this, these dream moments, coming from her subconscious or from what she had read about the tragedy after the fact? Grace did not know. It was, she'd long surmised, probably a combination of both. Dreams open up memories, don't they? When she was awake, she couldn't recall that night at all – or for that matter, the few days before. The last thing she remembered was studying for a political science final she'd taken five days earlier. That was normal, the doctors assured, with her type of head trauma. But the subconscious was a strange terrain. Perhaps the dreams were actual memories. Perhaps imagination. Most likely, as with most dreams or even memories, both.

Either way, be it from memory or press reports, it was at this very moment when someone fired a shot. Then another. And another.

This was before the days of metal detector sweeps when you entered an arena. Anyone could carry in a gun. For a while, there had been much debate over the origins of those shots. Conspiracy nuts still argued over the point, as if the arena had a grassy knoll in the upper tier. Either way, the young crowd, already in a frenzy, snapped. They screamed. They broke. They rushed for exits.

They rushed toward the stage.

Grace was in the wrong spot. Her waist was crushed against the top of the steel girder. It dug into her belly. She could not pry herself free. The crowd cried out and surged as one. The boy next to her – she would later learn that he was nineteen years old and named Ryan Vespa – didn't get his hands up in time. He smacked the girder at a bad angle.

Grace saw – again was it just in the dream or in reality too? – the blood shoot from Ryan Vespa's mouth. The girder finally gave way. It tilted over. She fell to the floor. Grace tried to get her footing, tried to stand, but the current of screaming humans drove her back down.

This part, she knew, was real. This part, being buried under a mass of people, haunted more than just her dreams.

The stampede continued. People stomped on her. Trampled her arms and legs. Tripped and fell, slamming down on her like stone tablets. The weight grew. Crushing her. Dozens of desperate, struggling, slithering bodies rushed over her.

Screams filled the air. Grace was underneath it now. Buried. There was no light anymore. Too many bodies on top of her. It was impossible to move. Impossible to breathe. She was suffocating. Like someone had buried her in concrete. Like she was being dragged underwater.

There was too much weight on her. It felt as if a giant hand was pressing down on her head, squashing her skull like it was a Styrofoam cup.

There was no escape.

And that, mercifully, was when the dream ended. Grace woke up, still gulping for air.

In reality, Grace had woken up four days later and remembered almost nothing. At first she thought it was the morning of her political science final. The doctors took their time explaining the situation. She had been seriously injured. She had, for one, a skull fracture. That, the doctors surmised, explained the headaches and memory loss. This was not a case of amnesia or repressed memory or even anything psychological. The brain was damaged, which is not infrequent with this kind of severe head trauma and loss of consciousness. Losing hours, even days, was not unusual. Grace also shattered her femur, her tibia, and three ribs. Her knee had split in two. Her hip had been ripped out of its joint.

Through a haze of painkillers, she eventually learned that she had been 'lucky.' Eighteen people, ranging in age from fourteen to twenty-six, had been killed in the stampede that the media dubbed the Boston Massacre.

The silhouette in the doorway said, 'Mom?'

It was Emma. 'Hi, sweetheart.'

'You were screaming.'

'I'm okay. Even moms have bad dreams sometimes.'

Emma stayed in the shadows. 'Where's Daddy?'

Grace checked the bedside clock. It was nearly 4:45 A.M. How long had she been asleep? No more than ten, fifteen minutes. 'He'll be home soon.'

Emma did not move.

'You okay?' Grace asked.

'Can I sleep with you?'

Plenty of bad dreams tonight, Grace thought. She pulled back the blanket. 'Sure, honey.'

Emma crawled onto Jack's side of the bed. Grace threw the blanket back over her and held tight. She kept her eyes on the bedside clock. At exactly 7 A.M. – she watched the digital clock switch from 6:59 A.M. – she let panic in.

Jack had never done anything like this before. If it had been a normal night, if he had come up and told her that he was going grocery shopping, if he had made some clumsy double entendre before leaving, something about melons or bananas, something funny and stupid like that, she'd have been on the phone with the police already.

But last night had not been normal. There had been that photograph. There had been his reaction. And there had been no kiss good-bye.

Emma stirred beside her. Max entered in mid–eye rub a few minutes later. Jack was usually the one who made breakfast. He was more the early riser. Grace managed to whip up the morning meal – Cap'n Crunch with sliced banana – and deflected their questions about their father's absence. While they were busy wolfing down breakfast, she slid into the den and tried Jack's office, but nobody picked up the line. Still too early.

She threw on a pair of Jack's Adidas sweats and walked them to the bus stop. Emma used to hug her before she boarded, but she was too old for that. She hurried aboard, before Grace could mumble something idiotically parental about Emma being too old for hugs but not too old to visit Mom when she was scared at night. Max still gave her a hug but it was quick and with a serious lack of enthusiasm. They both stepped inside, the bus door swooshing to a close as though swallowing them whole.

Grace blocked the sun with her hand and, as always, watched the bus until it turned down Bryden Road. Even now, even after all this time, she still longed to hop in her car and follow just to be sure that that seemingly fragile box of yellow tin made it safely to school.

What had happened to Jack?

She started back toward the house, but then, thinking better of it, she sprinted toward her car and took off. Grace caught up to the bus on Heights Road and followed it the rest of the way to Willard School. She shifted into park and watched the children disembark. When Emma and Max appeared, weighed down by their backpacks, she felt the familiar flutter. She sat and waited until they both headed up the path, up the stairs, and disappeared through the school doors.

And then, for the first time in a long time, Grace cried.

Grace expected cops in plainclothes. And she expected two of them. That was how it always worked on television. One would be the gruff veteran. The other would be young and handsome. So much for TV. The town police had sent one officer in the regulation stop-you-for-speeding uniform and matching car.

He had introduced himself as Officer Daley. He was indeed young, very young, with a smattering of acne on his shiny baby face. He was gym muscular. His short sleeves worked like tourniquets on his bloated biceps. Officer Daley spoke with annoying patience, a suburban-cop monotone, as if addressing a class of first graders on bike safety.

He had arrived ten minutes after her call on the non-emergency police line. Normally, the dispatcher told her, they would ask her to come in and fill out a report on her own. But it just so happened that Officer Daley was in the area, so he'd be able to swing by. Lucky her.

Daley took a letter-size sheet of paper and placed it out on the coffee table. He clicked his pen and started asking questions.

'The missing person's name?'

'John Lawson. But he goes by Jack.'

He started down the list.

'Address and phone number?'

She gave them.

'Place of birth?'

'Los Angeles, California.'

He asked his height, weight, eye and hair color, sex (yes, he actually asked). He asked if Jack had any scars, marks, or tattoos. He asked for a possible destination.

'I don't know,' Grace said. 'That's why I called you.'

Officer Daley nodded. 'I assume that your husband is over the age of emancipation?'

'Pardon?'

'He is over eighteen years old.'

'Yes.'

'That makes this harder.'

'Why?'

'We got new regulations on filling out a missing person report. It was just updated a couple weeks back.'

'I'm not sure I understand.'

51

He gave a theatrical sigh. 'See, in order to put someone in the computer, he needs to meet the criteria.' Daley pulled out another sheet of paper. 'Is your husband disabled?'

'No.'

'Endangered?'

'What do you mean?'

Daley read from the sheet. ' 'A person of age who is missing and in the company of another person under circumstances indicating that his/her physical safety is in danger.' '

'I don't know. I told you. He left here last night . . .'

'Then that would be a no,' Daley said. He scanned down the sheet. 'Number three. Involuntary. Like a kidnapping or abduction.'

'I don't know.'

'Right. Number four. Catastrophe victim. Like in a fire or airplane crash.'

'No.'

'And the last category. Is he a juvenile? Well, we covered that already.' He put the sheet down. 'That's it. You can't put the person into the system unless he fits in one of those categories.'

'So if someone goes missing like this, you do nothing?'

'I wouldn't put it that way, ma'am.'

'How would you put it?'

'We have no evidence that there was any foul play. If we receive any, we will immediately upgrade the investigation.'

'So for now you do nothing?'

Daley put down the pen. He leaned forward, his forearms on his thighs. His breathing was heavy. 'May I speak frankly, Mrs. Lawson?'

'Please.'

'Most of these cases – no, more than that, I'd say ninety-nine out of a hundred – the husband is just running around. There are marital problems. There is a mistress. The husband doesn't want to be found.'

'That's not the case here.'

He nodded. 'And in ninety-nine out of a hundred cases, that's what we hear from the wife.'

The patronizing tone was starting to piss her off. Grace hadn't felt comfortable confiding in this youth. She'd held back, as if she feared telling the entire truth would be a betrayal. Plus, when you really thought about it, how would it sound?

Well, see, I found this weird photo from the Photomat in the middle of my pack from Apple Orchard, in Chester, right, and my husband said it wasn't him and really, it's hard to tell because the picture is old and then Jack left the house . . .

'Mrs. Lawson?'

'Yes.'

'Do you understand what I'm telling you?'

'I think so. That I'm hysterical. My husband ran off. I'm trying to use the police to drag him back. That sound about right?'

He remained unruffled. 'You have to understand. We can't fully investigate until we have some evidence that a crime has been committed. Those are the rules set up by the NCIC.' He pointed to the sheet of paper again and said in his gravest tone: 'That's the National Crime Information Center.'

She almost rolled her eyes.

'Even if we find your husband, we wouldn't tell you where he was. This is a free country. He is of age. We can't force him to come back.'

'I'm aware of that.'

'We could make a few calls, maybe make a few discreet inquiries.'

'Great.'

'I'll need the vehicle make and license plate number.'

'It's a Ford Windstar.'

'Color?'

'Dark blue.'

'Year?'

She didn't remember.

'License plate?'

'It begins with an M.'

Officer Daley looked up. Grace felt like a moron.

'I have a copy of the registration upstairs,' she said. 'I can check.'

'Do you use E-ZPass at tollbooths?'

'Yes.'

Officer Daley nodded and wrote that down. Grace headed upstairs and found the file. She made a copy with her scanner and gave it to Officer Daley. He wrote something down. He asked a few questions. She stuck with the facts: Jack had come home from work, helped put the children to bed, gone out, probably for groceries . . . and that was it.

After about five minutes, Daley seemed satisfied. He smiled and told her not to worry. She stared at him.

'We'll check back with you in a few hours. If we hear nothing by then, let's talk some more.'

He left. Grace tried Jack's office again. Still no answer. She checked the clock. It was nearly 10 A.M. The Photomat would be opening now. Good.

She had some questions for Josh the Fuzz Pellet.

6

Charlaine Swain slipped on her new online lingerie purchase – a Regal Lace babydoll with matching G-string – and pulled up her bedroom shade.

Something was wrong.

The day was Tuesday. The time was 10:30 A.M. Charlaine's children were at school. Her husband Mike would be at his desk in the city, the phone wedged between shoulder and ear, his fingers busy rolling and unrolling his shirtsleeves, his collar tighter by the day but his ego too proud to admit the need for a bigger size.

Her neighbor, the scuzzy creepazoid named Freddy Sykes, should be home by now.

Charlaine glanced toward the mirror. She didn't do that often. There was no need to remind herself that she was over forty. The image that stared back was still shapely, she guessed, helped no doubt by the babydoll's underwired support – but what had once been considered buxom and curvaceous had weakened and loosened. Oh, Charlaine worked out. There was yoga class – yoga being this year's Tae Bo or Step – three mornings a week. She stayed fit, battling against the obvious and unbeatable, holding tight even as it slipped away.

What had happened to her?

Forget the physical for a second. The young Charlaine Swain had been a bundle of energy. She had zest for life. She was ambitious and a go-getter. Everyone said it. There was always a spark with Charlaine, a crackle in the air, and somewhere, somehow, life – just plain living – had extinguished it.

Were the children to blame? Was it Mike? There was a time when he couldn't get enough of her, when an outfit like this would make his eyes widen and his mouth water. Now when she strutted by, he would barely look up.

When had that started?

She couldn't put her finger on it. She knew the process had been gradual, the change so slow as to be almost indiscernible, until, alas, it was a *fait accompli*. It hadn't all been his fault. She knew that. Her drive had waned, especially during the years of pregnancies, postnatal nursing, the ensuing exhaustion of infants. That was natural, she supposed. Everyone went through that. Still she wished that she had made more of an effort before the temporary changes hardened into something apathetic and enduring.

The memories, however, were still there. Mike used to romance her. He used to surprise her. He used to lust after her. He used to – and yes, this might sound crude – jump her bones. Now what he wanted was efficiency, something mechanical and precise – the dark, a grunt, a release, sleep.

When they talked, it was about the kids – the class schedules, the pickups, the homework, the dentist appointments, the Little League games, the Biddy Basketball program, the play-dates. But that wasn't just Mike's fault either. When Charlaine had coffee with the women in the neighborhood – the Mommy and Me meetings at Starbucks – the conversations were so cloying, so boring, so stuffed with all things children, that she wanted to scream.

Charlaine Swain was being smothered.

Her mother – the idle queen of the country-club lunch – told her that this was life, that Charlaine had everything a woman could want, that her expectations were simply unrealistic. The saddest part was, Charlaine feared that her mother was right.

She checked her makeup. She applied more lipstick and rouge and then sat back and appraised herself. Yep, she looked like a whore. She grabbed a Percodan, the mommy equivalent of the lunchtime cocktail, and swallowed it. Then she took a closer look in the mirror, squinting even.

Was the old Charlaine still there somewhere?

There was this woman who lived two blocks down, a nice mother of two like Charlaine. Two months ago, this nice mother of two walked up to the Glen Rock train tracks and committed suicide by stepping in front of the 11:10 A.M. Bergen line heading south. Horrible story. Everyone talked about it for weeks. How could this woman, this nice mother of two, just abandon her children like that? How could she be so selfish? And yet, as Charlaine tsk-tsked with her fellow suburbanites, she felt a small pang of jealousy. For this nice mother, it was over. There had to be relief in that.

Where was Freddy?

Charlaine actually looked forward to this, her Tuesdays at ten, and perhaps that was the saddest thing of all. Her initial reaction to Freddy's peeping had been revulsion and rage. When and how had that slid into acceptance and even, God forgive her, arousal? No, she thought. It wasn't arousal. It was . . . something. That was all. It was a spark. It was something to feel.

She waited for his shade to come up.

It didn't.

Strange. Come to think of it, Freddy Sykes never pulled down his shades. Their properties backed up to each other's, so that only they could see in each other's window. Freddy never pulled down the shade in the back. Why would he?

Her eyes roamed toward the other windows. All the shades were pulled down. Curious. The curtains in what she assumed was the den – she had never, of course, stepped foot in his house – were drawn closed.

Was Freddy traveling? Had he perhaps gone away?

Charlaine Swain caught her reflection in the window and felt a fresh wave of shame. She grabbed a robe – her husband's ratty terrycloth – and slipped into it. She wondered if Mike was having an affair, if another woman had drained that once insatiable sex drive, or was he just not interested in her? She wondered which was worse.

Where was Freddy?

And how degrading, how truly scraping-the-bottom pitiful it was, that this meant so much to her. She stared at the house.

There was movement.

It was slight. A shadow had crossed the side of a shade. But movement nonetheless. Maybe, just maybe, Freddy was truly peeping again, upping, if you will, his excitement level. That could be it, right? Most peepers got off on the stealth, *I Spy* aspects of the act. Maybe he simply didn't want her to see him. Maybe he was watching her right now, surreptitiously.

Could that be it?

She loosened the robe and let it slide down her shoulders. The terrycloth reeked of man sweat and the aging remnants of cologne she'd bought Mike, what, eight, nine years ago. Charlaine felt the tears sting her eyes. But she didn't turn away.

Something else suddenly appeared between the window shades. Something . . . blue?

She squinted. What was it?

The binoculars. Where were they? Mike kept a box of crap like that in his closet. She found it, dug through the many power cords and adapters, and unearthed the Leicas. She remembered when they bought them. They were on a cruise in the Caribbean. The stop was one of the Virgin Islands – she didn't remember which one – and the purchase had been spontaneous. That was why she remembered it, the buying of the binoculars, because of the spontaneity of such a mundane act.

Charlaine put the binoculars up to her eyes. They were auto-focus, so there was nothing to adjust. It took her a moment or two to find the space between the window and the shade. But the blue spot was there. She saw the flicker and her eyes closed. She should have known.

The television. Freddy had turned on the television.

He was home.

Charlaine stood without moving. She didn't know how she felt anymore. The numb was back. Her son Clay liked to play a song from the *Shrek* movie about a guy forming an L with his fingers on his forehead. Loser. That was Freddy Sykes. And now Freddy, this scuzzy creepazoid, this Loser with a finger-capital L, would rather watch television than her lingerie-clad body.

Something was still strange.

All those shades pulled down. Why? She had lived next to the Sykes house for eight years. Even when Freddy's mother was alive, the shades were never pulled down, the curtains never closed. Charlaine took another look through her binoculars.

The television flicked off.

She stopped, waiting for something to happen. Freddy had lost track of the time, she thought. The shade would open now. They would begin their perverted ritual.

But that's not what happened.

Charlaine heard the slight whir and knew immediately what it was. Freddy's electric garage door had been activated.

She moved closer to the window. There was the sound of a car starting up, and then Freddy's hunk-of-junk Honda pulled out. Sunlight reflected off the windshield. The glare made her squint. She blocked it by cupping her hand above her eyes.

The car moved and the glare cleared. She could now see who was driving.

It wasn't Freddy.

Something, something base and primitive, commanded Charlaine to duck out of sight. She did. She dropped down and crawled for the robe. She pressed the terrycloth

59

against herself. The smell – that combination of Mike and stale cologne – now seemed oddly comforting.

Charlaine moved toward the side of the window. She pressed her back against the wall and peaked out.

The Honda Accord had stopped. The driver – the Asian man behind the wheel – was staring at her window.

Charlaine quickly flattened herself back against the wall. She stayed still, holding her breath. She stayed that way until she heard the car start moving again. And then, just to be on the safe side, she stayed down another ten minutes.

When she looked again, the car was gone.

The house next door was still.

7

At exactly 10:15 A.M., Grace arrived at the Photomat.

Josh the Fuzz Pellet was not there. As a matter of fact, nobody was there. The sign in the store window, probably left from the night before, read CLOSED.

She checked the printed hours. Opens at 10 A.M. She waited. At ten-twenty, the first customer, a harried woman in her mid-thirties, spotted the CLOSED sign, read the hours, tried the door. She sighed in high drama. Grace gave her a commiserating shrug. The woman huffed off. Grace waited.

When the store had still not opened at 10:30 A.M., Grace knew that it was bad. She decided to try Jack's office again. His line kept going into voice mail – eerie hearing Jack's too-formal recorded voice – so she tried Dan's line this time. The two men had, after all, spoken last night. Maybe Dan could offer a clue.

She dialed his work number.

'Hello?'

'Hi, Dan, it's Grace.'

'Hey!' he said with a tad too much enthusiasm. 'I was just about to call you.'

'Oh?'

'Where's Jack?'

'I don't know.'

He hesitated. 'When you say you don't know –'

'You called him last night, right?'

'Yes.'

'What did you two talk about?'

'We're supposed to be making a presentation this afternoon. On the Phenomytol studies.'

'Anything else?'

'What do you mean, anything else? Like what?'

'Like what else did you talk about?'

'Nothing. I wanted to ask him about a PowerPoint slide. Why? What's going on, Grace?'

'He went out after that.'

'Right, so?'

'I haven't seen him since.'

'Wait, when you say you haven't seen him . . . ?'

'I mean, he hasn't come home, he hasn't called, I have no idea where he is.'

'Jesus, did you call the police?'

'Yes.'

'And?'

'And nothing.'

'My God. Look, let me get out of here. I'll be right over.'

'No,' she said. 'I'm fine.'

'You sure?'

'Positive. I have some things to do,' she said lamely. She moved the phone to the other ear, unsure how to put this. 'Has Jack been okay?'

'You mean, at work?'

'I mean anywhere.'

'Yeah, sure, he's Jack. You know.'

'You haven't noticed any change?'

'We've both been stressed about these drug trials, if that's what you mean. But nothing unusual. Grace, are you sure I shouldn't come up?'

There was a beep on her phone. Call Waiting. 'I need to go, Dan. That's the other line.'

'Probably Jack. Call me if you need anything.'

She clicked him off and checked the Caller ID. Not Jack. At least, not his cell. The number was blocked.

'Hello?'

'Ms. Lawson, this is Officer Daley. Has there been any word from your husband?'

'No.'

'We tried you at home.'

'Right, I'm out.'

There was a pause. 'Where are you?'

'In town.'

'Where in town?'

'I'm at the Photomat store.'

A longer pause. 'I don't mean to sound judgmental, but isn't that a strange place to be when you're concerned about your husband?'

'Officer Daley?'

'Yes?'

'There's this new invention. It's called the cell phone. In fact, you're calling me on it right now.'

'I didn't mean to –'

'Have you learned anything about my husband?'

'That's why I'm calling, actually. My captain is in now. He'd like to do a follow-up interview.'

'A follow-up?'

'Yes.'

'Is that standard?'

'Sure.' He sounded like it was anything but.

'Have you found something?'

'No, I mean, nothing to be alarmed about.'

'What does that mean?'

'Captain Perlmutter and I just need more information, Mrs. Lawson.'

Another Photomat customer, a recently streaked quasi-blonde about Grace's own age, approached the empty store. She cupped her hands around her eyes and peered inside. She too frowned and scoffed away.

'You're both at the station now?' Grace asked.

'Yes.'

'I'll be there in three minutes.'

*

63

Captain Perlmutter asked, 'How long have you and your husband lived in town?'

They were jammed into an office more fitting for the school custodian than the police captain of a town. The Kasselton cops had moved their station house to the former town library, a building with history and tradition but very little comfort. Captain Stu Perlmutter sat behind his desk. He leaned back at the first question, hands resting on a tidy paunch. Officer Daley leaned against the door frame, trying to look comfortable.

Grace said, 'Four years.'

'Like it here?'

'Well enough.'

'Great.' Perlmutter smiled at her, a teacher approving of the answer. 'And you have kids, right?'

'Yes.'

'How old?'

'Eight and six.'

'Eight and six,' he repeated with a wistful smile. 'Man, those are great ages. Not babies, and not teens yet.'

Grace decided to wait him out.

'Mrs. Lawson, has your husband ever disappeared before?'

'No.'

'Are there any problems with the marriage?'

'None.'

Perlmutter gave her a skeptical look. He didn't wink, but he came close. 'Everything is perfect, eh?'

Grace said nothing.

'How did you and your husband meet?'

'Pardon?'

'I asked –'

'What does that have to do with anything?'

'I'm just trying to get a feel here.'

'A feel for what? Have you found something or not?'

'Please.' Perlmutter tried on what he must have believed

was a disarming smile. 'I just need to get some stuff down. For background, okay? Where did you and Jack Lawson meet?'

'In France.'

He wrote it down. 'You're an artist, aren't you, Mrs. Lawson?'

'Yes.'

'So you were overseas studying your art?'

'Captain Perlmutter?'

'Yes.'

'No offense, but this line of questioning is bizarre.'

Perlmutter glanced at Daley. He shrugged to signal that he meant no harm. 'Maybe you're right.'

'Have you learned something or not?'

'I believe Officer Daley explained to you that your husband is of age, that we really aren't obligated to tell you anything?'

'He did.'

'Right, well, we don't think he's met up with foul play, if that's your concern.'

'What makes you say that?'

'No evidence of such.'

'Meaning,' she said, 'that you haven't found bloodstains or anything like that?'

'That's correct. But more than that' – Perlmutter looked over at Daley again – 'we did find something that, well, we probably shouldn't share with you.'

Grace adjusted herself in the seat. She tried very hard to meet his eye, but he wouldn't face her. 'I'd very much appreciate knowing what you found.'

'It's not much,' Perlmutter said.

She waited.

'Officer Daley called your husband's office. He's not there, of course. I'm sure you know that already. He also didn't call in sick. So we decided to investigate a little more. Unofficially, you understand.'

'Right.'

'You were helpful enough to give us your car's E-ZPass number. We ran it through the computer. What time did you say your husband went out last night?'

'Around ten o'clock.'

'And you thought that maybe he went to the grocery store?'

'I didn't know. He didn't tell me.'

'He just upped and left?'

'Right.'

'And you never asked him where he was going?'

'I was upstairs. I heard the car start up.'

'Okay, here's what I need to know.' Perlmutter let go of the paunch. His chair creaked as he leaned forward. 'You called him on the cell phone. Pretty much right away. Is that correct?'

'Yes.'

'Well, see, that's the problem. Why didn't he answer you? I mean, if he wanted to talk to you?'

Grace saw where he was going with this.

'Do you think your husband – what? – got in an accident right away? Or maybe someone grabbed him within minutes of leaving your house?'

Grace hadn't really thought about that. 'I don't know.'

'Do you ever drive up the New York Thruway?'

The change of subject threw her. 'Not often, but sure, I've taken it.'

'Ever go to Woodbury Commons?'

'The outlet mall?'

'Yes.'

'I've been, yes.'

'How long do you figure it takes to get there?'

'Half an hour. Is that where he went?'

'I doubt it, not at that hour. The stores are all closed. But he used his E-ZPass at the tollbooth on that exit at precisely 10:26 P.M. It leads to Route 17, and heck, that's how I go to the Poconos. Give or take ten minutes either way, that would fit a scenario where your husband left your house and drove straight in that direction. From there, well, who knows where he went? It's fifteen miles to Interstate 84. From there you can go straight to California if you'd like.'

She sat there.

'So add it up, Mrs. Lawson. Your husband leaves the house. You call him immediately. He doesn't answer. Within a half hour or so, we know he's driving in New York. If someone had attacked him or if he got in an accident, well, there's no way he could have been snatched and then his E-ZPass used up there in that short a time frame. Do you understand what I'm telling you?'

Grace met his eye. 'That I'm a hysterical bimbo whose husband ran out on her.'

'That's not what I'm saying at all. It's just . . . Well, we really can't investigate any further at this point. Unless . . .' He leaned a little closer. 'Mrs. Lawson, is there anything else you can think of that could help us here?'

Grace tried not to squirm. She glanced behind her. Officer Daley had not moved. She had a copy of the strange photograph in her purse. She thought about Fuzz Pellet Josh and the store not opening. It was time to tell them. In hindsight she should have told Daley about it when she first showed up.

'I'm not sure it's relevant,' she began, reaching into her purse. She pulled out a copy of the photograph and passed it to Perlmutter. Perlmutter took out a pair of reading glasses, cleaned them with his shirttail, and pushed them into place. Daley walked around and bent down over the captain's shoulder. She told them about finding the photograph mixed in with her others. The two officers stared at her as if she'd taken out a razor and started shaving her head.

When Grace was done, Captain Perlmutter pointed to

the picture and said, 'And you're sure that's your husband?'

'I think so.'

'But you're not sure?'

'I'm pretty sure.'

He nodded in that way people do when they think you're a lunatic. 'And the other people in the photo? The young lady somebody crossed out?'

'I don't know them.'

'But your husband. He said it wasn't him, right?'

'Right.'

'So if it isn't him, well, this is irrelevant. And if it is him' – Perlmutter took off the glasses – 'he lied to you. Isn't that correct, Mrs. Lawson?'

Her cell phone rang. Grace grabbed it fast and checked the number.

It was Jack.

For a moment she went very still. Grace wanted to excuse herself, but Perlmutter and Daley were both looking at her. Asking for privacy was not really an option here. She hit the answer button and brought the phone to her ear.

'Jack?'

'Hey.'

The sound of his voice should have filled her with relief. It didn't.

Jack said, 'I tried you at home. Where are you?'

'Where am *I*?'

'Listen, I can't talk long. I'm sorry about running out on you like that.'

His tone was aiming for casual, but it wasn't hitting the mark.

'I need a few days,' he said.

'What are you talking about?'

'Where are you, Grace?'

'I'm at the police station.'

'You called the police?'

68

Her eyes met Perlmutter's. He wiggled his fingers, as if to say, *Give me the phone, little lady. I'll handle it.*

'Look, Grace, just give me a few days. I . . .' Jack stopped. And then he said something that made the dread grow tenfold. 'I need some space.'

'Space,' she repeated.

'Yes. A little space. That's all. Please tell the police that I apologize. I have to go now. Okay? I'll be back soon.'

'Jack?'

He didn't reply.

'I love you,' Grace said.

But the phone was dead.

8

Space. Jack said he needed space. And that was all wrong.

Never mind that 'needing space' was one of those lame, cloying, namby-pamby, New Age we-are-the-world terms that was worse than meaningless – 'needing space' – a terrible euphemism for 'I'm soooo outta here.' That would have been a clue perhaps, but this went much deeper.

Grace was home now. She had mumbled an apology to Perlmutter and Daley. Both men looked at her with pity and told her that it was all part of the job. They said that they were sorry. Grace offered up a solemn nod and headed for the door.

She had learned something crucial from the phone call.

Jack was in trouble.

She had not been overreacting. His disappearance had nothing to do with running away from her or fear of commitment. It was no accident. It had not been expected or planned. She had picked up the photograph from the store. Jack had seen it and run out.

And now he was in serious danger.

She could never explain this to the police. First off, they wouldn't believe her. They would claim that she was either delusional or naïve to the point of a learning disability. Maybe not to her face. Maybe they would humor her, which would be both a tremendous irritant and waste of time. They'd been convinced that Jack was on the run before the call. Her explanation would not change their minds.

And maybe that was best.

Grace was trying to read between the lines here. Jack

had been concerned about police involvement. That was obvious. When she said that she was at the police station, the regret in his voice was real. That was no act.

Space.

That was the main clue. If he had just told her that he was leaving for a few days, blowing off steam, running off with a stripper he'd met at the Satin Dolls, okay, she might not believe him, but it would be in the realm of possibility. But Jack hadn't done that. He had been specific about his reasons for disappearing. He even repeated himself.

Jack needed space.

Marital codes. All couples have them. Most were pretty stupid. For example, there was a scene in the Billy Crystal movie *Mr. Saturday Night* when the comic Crystal played – Grace couldn't remember the name, barely remembered the movie – pointed at an old man with a terrible toupee and said, 'Is that a toupee? I, for one, was fooled.' So now, whenever she and Jack saw a man with a possible toupee, one would turn to the other and say, 'I for one?' and the spouse would either agree or disagree. Grace and Jack started using 'I for one' for other vanity enhancements too – nose jobs, breast implants, whatever.

The origin of 'Need space' was a bit more risqué.

Despite her current predicament, Grace's cheeks couldn't help but flush from the memory. Sex had always been very good with Jack, but in any long-term relationship, there are ebbs and flows. This was two years ago, during a time of, uh, great flow. A stage of more corporeal creativity, if you will. Public creativity, to be more specific.

There had been the quick nooky in the changing room at one of those upscale hair salons. There had been under-the-coat manipulation in a private balcony at a lush Broadway musical. But it was midway through a particularly daring encounter in a British-style red phone booth located, in of all places, a quiet street in Allendale, New Jersey, when Jack suddenly panted, 'I need space.'

Grace had looked up at him. 'Excuse me?'

'I mean, literally. Back up! The phone receiver is pressing into my neck!'

They'd both laughed. Grace closed her eyes now, a faint smile on her lips. 'Need space' had thus joined the ranks of their private marital language. Jack would not use that phrase haphazardly. He was sending her a message, warning her, letting her know that he was saying something he didn't mean.

Okay, so what did he mean then?

Jack couldn't speak freely for one thing. Someone was listening. Who? Was someone with him – or was he afraid because she was with the cops? She hoped the latter, that he was alone and simply didn't want police involvement.

But when she considered all the facts, that possibility seemed unlikely.

If Jack had been free to talk, why hadn't he called her back? He'd have to realize that she'd be out of the police station by now. If he were okay, if he was alone, Jack would have called again, just to let her know what was going on. He hadn't done that.

Conclusion: Jack was with somebody and in serious trouble.

Did he want her to react or sit tight? In the same way she knew Jack – in the same way she knew that he'd been sending her a signal – Jack would know that Grace's reaction would not be to go quietly into that good night. That was not her personality. Jack understood that. She would try to find him.

He had probably counted on that.

Of course, this was all no more than conjecture. She knew her husband well – or maybe she didn't? – so her conjectures were more than mere fancy. But how much more? Maybe she was just justifying her decision to take action.

Didn't matter. Either way, she was involved.

Grace thought about what she'd already learned. Jack had taken the Windstar up the New York Thruway. Who did they know up there? Why would he have gone that way so late at night?

She had no idea.

Hold up.

Roll it back to the start: Jack comes home. Jack sees the photograph. That was what set it off. The photograph. He sees it on the kitchen counter. She starts asking him about it. He gets a call from Dan. And then he goes into his study . . .

Stop. His study.

Grace hurried down the hall. *Study* was a rather ornate word for this converted screened-in porch. The plaster was cracking in spots. There was always a draft in the winter and a stifling lack of anything approaching air in the summer. There were photographs of the kids in cheap frames and two of her paintings in expensive ones. The study felt strangely impersonal to her. Nothing in here told you about the past of the room's main occupant – no mementos, no softball signed by friends, no photo of a golf foursome taking to the links. Other than some pharmaceutical freebies – pens, pads, a paperclip holder – there were no clues as to who Jack really was other than a husband, father, and researcher.

But maybe that was all there was.

Grace felt weird, snooping. There had been strength, she thought, in respecting one another's privacy. They each had a room closed off to the other. Grace had always been okay with that. She'd even convinced herself it was healthy. Now she wondered about looking away. She wondered if it'd derived from a desire to give Jack privacy – needing space?! – or because she feared poking a beehive.

His computer was up and online. Jack's default page was the 'official' Grace Lawson Web site. Grace stared at the chair for a moment, the ergonomic gray from the local Staples store, imagining Jack there, turning on the computer every morning, having her face greet him. The site's home page had a glam shot of Grace along with several examples of her work. Farley, her agent, had recently insisted that she include the photograph in all sales material because, as he put it, 'You a babe.' She reluctantly acquiesced. Looks had always been used by the arts to promote the work. On stage and in movies, well, the importance of looks was obvious. Even writers, with their glossy touched-up portraits, the smoldering dark eyes of the next literati wunderkind, marketed appearances. But Grace's world – painting – had been fairly immune to this pressure, ignoring the creator's physical beauty, perhaps because the form itself was all about the physical.

But not anymore.

An artist appreciates the importance of the aesthetical, of course. Aesthetics do more than alter perception. They altered reality. Prime example: If Grace had been fat or homely, the TV crews would not have been monitoring her vital signs after she'd been pulled from the Boston Massacre. If she'd been physically unappealing, she would have never been adopted as the 'people's survivor,' the innocent, the 'Crushed Angel,' as one tabloid headline dubbed her. The media always broadcasted her image while giving medical updates. The press – nay, the country – demanded constant updates on her condition. The families of victims visited her room, spent time with her, searched her face for ghostly wisps of their own lost children.

Would they have done the same had she been unattractive?

Grace didn't want to speculate. But as one too-honest art critic had told her: 'We have little interest in a painting that has little aesthetic appeal – why should it be different with a human being?'

Even before the Boston Massacre Grace had wanted to

be an artist. But something – something elusive and impossible to explain – had been missing. The whole experience had helped take her artistic sensibilities to the next level. Yes, she knew how pretentious that sounded. She had disdained that art-school clatter: You have to suffer for your art; you need tragedy to give your work texture. It had always rung hollow before, but now she understood that there was indeed something to it.

Without her conscious viewpoint changing, her work developed that vague intangible. There was more emotion, more life, more . . . swirl. Her work was darker, angrier, more vivid. People often wondered if she'd ever painted any scenes from that horrible day. The simple answer was only one portrait – a young face so full of hope that you knew it would soon be crushed – but the truer answer was that the Boston Massacre shaded and colored everything she touched.

Grace sat down at Jack's desk. The phone was to her right. She reached for it, deciding to try the simplest thing first: Hit redial on Jack's phone.

The phone – a new Panasonic model she'd picked up at Radio Shack – had an LCD screen so she could see the redialed number come up. The 212 area code. New York City. She waited. On the third ring a woman answered and said, 'Burton and Crimstein, law office.'

Grace wasn't sure how to proceed.

'Hello?'

'This is Grace Lawson calling.'

'How may I transfer your call?'

Good question. 'How many attorneys work at the firm?'

'I really couldn't say. Would you like me to connect you with one?'

'Yes, please.'

There was a pause. The voice had a shade of that trying-to-be-helpful impatience now. 'Is there one in particular?'

Grace checked the Caller ID. There were too many numbers. She saw that now. Usually long distance calls had eleven numbers. But here there were fifteen, including an asterisk. She mulled that over. If Jack had made the call, it would have been late last night. The receptionists would not have been on duty. Jack probably hit the asterisk button and plugged in an extension.

'Ma'am?'

'Extension four-six-three,' she said, reading off the screen.

'I'll connect you.'

The phone rang three times.

'Sandra Koval's line.'

'Ms. Koval please.'

'May I ask who is calling?'

'My name is Grace Lawson.'

'And what is this in reference to?'

'My husband, Jack.'

'Please hold.'

Grace gripped the phone. Thirty seconds later, the voice came back on.

'I'm sorry. Ms. Koval is in a meeting.'

'It's urgent.'

'I'm sorry –'

'I just need a second of her time. Tell her it's very important.'

The sigh was intentionally audible. 'Please hold.'

The hold music was a Muzak version of Nirvana's 'Smells Like Teen Spirit.' It was strangely calming.

'Can I help you?' The voice was all clipped professionalism.

'Ms. Koval?'

'Yes?'

'My name is Grace Lawson.'

'What do you want?'

'My husband Jack Lawson called your office yesterday.'

She did not reply.

'He's missing.'

'Pardon?'

'My husband is missing.'

'I'm sorry to hear that, but I don't see –'

'Do you know where he is, Ms. Koval?'

'Why on earth would I know?'

'He made a phone call last night. Before he disappeared.'

'So?'

'I hit the redial button. This number came up.'

'Ms. Lawson, this firm employs more than two hundred attorneys. He could have been calling any of them.'

'No. Your extension is here, on the redial display. He called you.'

No reply.

'Ms. Koval?'

'I'm here.'

'Why did my husband call you?'

'I have nothing more to say to you.'

'Do you know where he is?'

'Ms. Lawson, are you familiar with attorney-client privilege?'

'Of course.'

More silence.

'Are you saying my husband called you for legal advice?'

'I cannot discuss the situation with you. Good-bye.'

9

It didn't take Grace long to put it together.

The Internet could be a wonderful tool when used properly. Grace had Googled the words 'Sandra Koval,' for Web hits, for newsgroups, for images. She checked the Burton and Crimstein Web site. There were bios of all their lawyers. Sandra Koval had graduated from Northwestern. She had gotten her law degree at UCLA. Based on the years of graduation, Sandra Koval would be forty-two or so. She was married, according to the site, to one Harold Koval. They had three children.

They lived in Los Angeles.

That had been the giveaway.

Grace had done a little more research, some the old-fashioned way: with a telephone. The pieces started to come together. The problem was, the picture made no sense.

The drive into Manhattan had taken less than an hour. Burton and Crimstein's reception desk was on the fifth floor. The receptionist/security guard gave her a closed-mouth smile. 'Yes?'

'Grace Lawson to see Sandra Koval.'

The receptionist made a call, speaking in a voice below a whisper. A moment later, she said, 'Ms. Koval will be right out.'

That was something of surprise. Grace had been prepared to launch threats or accept a long wait. She knew what Koval looked like – there had been a photograph of her on the Burton and Crimstein Web site – so she'd even accepted the fact that she might have to confront her as she left.

In the end Grace had decided to take the chance and

drive into Manhattan without calling first. Not only did she feel she'd need the element of surprise, but she very much wanted to confront Sandra Koval face to face. Call it necessity. Call it curiosity. Grace had to see this woman for herself.

It was still early enough. Emma had a play-date after school. Max attended an 'enrichment program' today. She wouldn't need to pick either of them up for several hours yet.

The reception area of Burton and Crimstein was part old-world attorney – rich mahogany, lush carpeting, tapestry-clad seating, the décor that foreshadows the billing – and part Sardi's celebrity wall. Photographs, mostly of Hester Crimstein, the famed TV attorney, adorned the walls. Crimstein had a show on Court TV cleverly dubbed *Crimstein on Crime*. The photos included Ms. Crimstein with a bevy of actors, politicos, clients, and, well, combinations of all three.

Grace was studying a photograph of Hester Crimstein standing alongside an attractive olive-skinned woman when a voice behind her said, 'That's Esperanza Diaz. A professional wrestler falsely accused of murder.'

Grace turned. 'Little Pocahontas,' she said.

'Excuse me?'

Grace pointed at the photograph. 'Her wrestling name. It was Little Pocahontas.'

'How do you know that?'

Grace shrugged. 'I'm a swarm of useless facts.'

For a moment Grace openly stared at Sandra Koval. Koval cleared her throat and made a big production of looking at her watch. 'I don't have much time. Please come this way.'

Neither woman spoke as they headed down the corridor and into a conference room. There was a long table, maybe twenty chairs, one of those gray speakerphones in the middle that looks suspiciously like a dropped octopus.

There was a variety of soft drinks and bottled water on a counter in the corner.

Sandra Koval kept her distance. She crossed her arms and made a gesture that said, *Well?*

'I did some research on you,' Grace said.

'Care to sit?'

'No.'

'Mind if I do?'

'Suit yourself.'

'How about a drink?'

'No.'

Sandra Koval poured herself a Diet Coke. She was what you'd call a handsome woman rather than pretty or beautiful. Her hair was going a gray that worked for her. Her figure was slim, her lips full. She had one of those lick-the-world postures that let your adversaries know that you were comfortable with yourself and more than ready to do battle.

'Why aren't we in your office?' Grace asked.

'You don't care for this room?'

'It's a tad large.'

Sandra Koval shrugged.

'You don't have an office here, do you?'

'You tell me.'

'When I called, the woman answered 'Sandra Koval's line.' '

'Uh huh.'

'Line, she said. Line. Not office.'

'And that's supposed to mean something?'

'On its own, no,' Grace said. 'But I looked up the law firm on the Web. You live in Los Angeles. Near the Burton and Crimstein West Coast office.'

'True enough.'

'That's your home base. You're visiting here. Why?'

'A criminal case,' she said. 'An innocent man wrongly accused.'

'Aren't they all?'

'No,' Sandra Koval said slowly. 'Not all.'

Grace moved closer to her. 'You're not Jack's lawyer,' she said. 'You're his sister.'

Sandra Koval stared at her drink.

'I called your law school. They confirmed what I suspected. Sandra Koval was the married name. The woman who graduated was named Sandra Lawson. I double-checked it through LawMar Securities. Your grandfather's firm. Sandra Koval is listed as a member of the board.'

She smiled without humor. 'My, aren't we the little Sherlock.'

'So where is he?' Grace asked.

'How long have you two been married?'

'Ten years.'

'And in all that time, how many times has Jack talked about me?'

'Pretty much never.'

Sandra Koval spread her hands. 'Precisely. So why would I know where he is?'

'Because he called you.'

'So you say.'

'I hit the redial button.'

'Right, you told me that on the phone.'

'Are you saying he didn't call you?'

'When did this call purportedly take place?'

'Purportedly?'

Sandra Koval shrugged. 'Always the lawyer.'

'Last night. Around ten o'clock.'

'Well, there's your answer then. I wasn't here.'

'Where were you?'

'At my hotel.'

'But Jack called your line.'

'If he did, nobody would have answered. Not at that hour. It would have gone into voice mail.'

'You checked the messages today?'

'Of course. And no, none from Jack.'

Grace tried to digest that. 'When was the last time you spoke to Jack?'

'A long time ago.'

'How long?'

Her gaze flicked away. 'We haven't spoken since he went overseas.'

'That was fifteen years ago.'

Sandra Koval took another sip.

'How would he still know your phone number?' Grace asked.

She didn't reply.

'Sandra?'

'You live at 221 North End Ave in Kasselton. You have two phone lines, one the phone, one the fax.' Sandra repeated the two numbers from memory.

The two women looked at each other. 'But you've never called?'

Her voice was soft. 'Never.'

The speakerphone squawked. 'Sandra?'

'Yes.'

'Hester wants to see you in her office.'

'On my way.' Sandra Koval broke the eye contact. 'I have to go now.'

'Why would Jack try to call you?'

'I don't know.'

'He's in trouble.'

'So you say.'

'He's disappeared.'

'Not for the first time, Grace.'

The room felt smaller now. 'What happened between you and Jack?'

'It's not my place to say.'

'The hell it isn't.'

Sandra shifted in her seat. 'You said he disappeared?'

'Yes.'

82

'And Jack hasn't called?'

'Actually, he has.'

That puzzled her. 'And when he called, what did he say?'

'That he needed space. But he didn't mean it. It was code.'

Sandra made a face. Grace took out the photograph and placed it on the table. The air rushed out of the room. Sandra Koval looked down and Grace could see her body jolt.

'What the hell is this?'

'Funny,' Grace said.

'What?'

'Those are the exact words Jack used when he saw it.'

Sandra was still staring at the picture.

'That's him, right? In the middle with the beard?' Grace asked.

'I don't know.'

'Sure you do. Who's the blonde next to him?'

Grace dropped the blowup of the young woman onto the table. Sandra Koval looked up. 'Where did you get these?'

'The Photomat.' Grace quickly explained. Sandra Koval's face clouded over. She wasn't buying it. 'Is it Jack, yes or no?'

'I really can't say. I've never seen him with a beard.'

'Why would he call you immediately after seeing this picture?'

'I don't know, Grace.'

'You're lying.'

Sandra Koval pushed herself to a stand. 'I have a meeting.'

'What happened to Jack?'

'What makes you so sure he didn't just run away?'

'We're married. We have two kids. You, Sandra, have a niece and nephew.'

83

'And I had a brother,' she countered. 'Maybe neither one of us knows him that well.'

'Do you love him?'

Sandra stood there, shoulders slumped. 'Leave it alone, Grace.'

'I can't.'

Shaking her head, Sandra turned toward the door.

'I'm going to find him,' Grace said.

'Don't count on it.'

And then she was gone.

10

Okay, Charlaine thought, mind your own business.

She drew the curtains and changed back into her jeans and sweater. She put the babydoll back in the bottom of her drawer, taking her time, folding it very carefully for some reason. As if Freddy would notice if it was wrinkled. Right.

She took a bottle of seltzer water and mixed in a little of her son's fruit punch Twister. Charlaine sat on a stool at the marble kitchen block. She stared at the glass. Her finger traced loops in the condensation. She glanced at the Sub-Zero refrigerator, the new 690 model with the stainless steel front. There was nothing on it – no kid pictures, no family photographs, no finger smears, not even magnets. When they had the old yellow Westinghouse, the front had been blanketed with that stuff. There had been vitality and color. The remodeled kitchen, the one she had wanted so much, was sterile, lifeless.

Who was the Asian man driving Freddy's car?

Not that she kept tabs on him, but Freddy had very few visitors. She could, in fact, recall none. That didn't mean he didn't have any, of course. She did not spend her entire day watching his house. Still a neighborhood has a routine of its own. A vibe, if you will. A neighborhood is an entity, a body, and you can feel when something is out of place.

The ice in her drink was melting. Charlaine had not yet taken a sip. There was food shopping to be done. Mike's shirts would be ready at the cleaner. She was having lunch with her friend Myrna at Baumgart's on Franklin Avenue.

Clay had karate with Master Kim after school.

She mentally ran through the rest of her to-do list and tried to come up with an order. Mindless stuff. Would there be time before lunch to do the food shopping and get back to the house? Probably not. The frozen goods would melt in the car. That errand would have to wait.

She stopped. To hell with this.

Freddy should be at work now.

That was how it'd always worked. Their perverted little dance lasted from around ten to ten-thirty. By ten-forty-five, Charlaine always heard that garage door open. She'd watch his Honda Accord pull out. Freddy worked, she knew, for H&R Block. It was in the same strip mall as the Blockbuster where she rented the DVDs. His desk was near the window. She avoided walking past it, but some days, when she parked, she would look over and see Freddy staring out the window, pencil resting against his lips, lost.

Charlaine found the yellow pages and looked up the number. A man identifying himself as a supervisor said that Mr. Sykes was not in but was expected at any moment. She pretended to be put out. 'He told me he'd be in by now. Doesn't he normally get in at eleven?'

The supervisor admitted that he did.

'So where is he? I really need those figures.'

The supervisor apologized and assured her that Mr. Sykes would call the moment he arrived at his desk. She hung up.

Now what?

Something still felt very wrong here.

But so what? Who was Freddy Sykes to her anyway? Nothing. In a way, less than nothing. He was a reminder of her failures. He was a symptom of how pathetic she had become. She owed him nothing. More than that, imagine, just imagine, if poking around got her caught. Imagine if somehow the truth came out.

Charlaine looked over at Freddy's place. The truth coming out.

Somehow that no longer bothered her all that much.

She grabbed her coat and headed toward Freddy's house.

11

Eric Wu had seen the lingerie-clad woman in the window.

The previous night had been a long one for Wu. He had not anticipated any interference, and while the large man – his wallet said his name was Rocky Conwell – had presented no threat, Wu now had to get rid of a body and another car. That meant an extra trip back up to Central Valley, New York.

First things first. He packed Rocky Conwell into the trunk of his Toyota Celica. He moved Jack Lawson, whom he had originally jammed into the Honda Accord's trunk, to the back of the Ford Windstar. Once the bodies were out of sight, Wu changed license plates, got rid of the E-ZPass, and drove the Ford Windstar back to Ho-Ho-Kus. He parked the minivan in Freddy Sykes's garage. There was still enough time to catch a bus back up to Central Valley. Wu searched Conwell's car. Satisfied that it was cleared out, he took it to the Park-n-Ride on Route 17. He found a remote spot near the fence. A car being left there for days, even weeks, was not unusual. The smell would eventually bring attention, but that would not be anytime soon.

The Park-n-Ride was only three miles from Sykes's house in Ho-Ho-Kus. Wu walked. Early the next morning, he rose and caught the bus back to Central Valley. He picked up Sykes's Honda Accord. On the way back, he took a brief detour past the Lawson residence.

A patrol car was in the driveway.

Wu considered that. It did not cause him great concern, but perhaps he should nip any police involvement in the bud. He knew just how.

Wu drove back to Freddy's residence and turned on the television. Wu liked daytime TV. He enjoyed watching shows like *Springer* and *Ricki Lake*. Most people poo-pooed them. Wu did not. Only a truly great society, a free one, could allow such nonsense to air. But more than that, stupidity made Wu happy. People were sheep. The weaker they are, the stronger you are. What could be more comforting or entertaining?

During a commercial – the theme of the show, according to a graphic on the bottom: 'Mommy Won't Let Me Get a Nipple Ring!' – Wu rose. It was time to take care of the potential police problem.

Wu didn't need to touch Jack Lawson. All he had to say was one sentence: 'I know that you have two children.'

Lawson cooperated. He made the call to his wife's cell phone and told her he needed space.

At ten-forty-five – with Wu watching a mother and daughter wrestle across a stage while a crowd chanted 'Jerry!' – a call came in from a prison acquaintance.

'All okay?'

Wu said yes.

He pulled the Honda Accord out of the garage. As he did, he noticed the woman who lived next door standing in the window. She was wearing lingerie. Wu might not have thought much about the scene – a woman still in her unmentionables after ten in the morning – but something about the way she suddenly ducked away...

That might have been a natural reaction. You parade around in lingerie, forgetting to pull down your shade, and then you spot a stranger. Many people, perhaps most people, would move away or cover up. So it could be nothing.

But the woman had moved very fast, as if in a panic. More than that, she had not moved when the car first pulled out – only when she'd spotted Wu. If she had been afraid of being seen, wouldn't she have pulled the shade or ducked down when she first heard or saw the car?

Wu pondered that. He had, in fact, been pondering it all day.

He picked up his cell phone and hit the button to dial the last incoming number.

A voice said, 'Problem?'

'I don't think so.' Wu turned the car around and started back toward the Sykes house. 'But I may be late.'

12

Grace didn't want to make the phone call.

She was still in New York City. There was a law against using a cell phone while driving unless it was hands-free, though that had nothing to do with her hesitation. With one hand on the steering wheel, she felt around on the floor of the car. She located the ear attachment, managed to untangle the cord, and jammed the earpiece deep into the canal.

This was supposed to be safer than using a handheld?

She turned on the cell phone. Though Grace hadn't called the number in years, she still had it programmed into the cell. For emergencies, she supposed. Like this one.

The phone was answered on the first ring.

'Yes?'

No name. No hello. No company greeting.

'This is Grace Lawson.'

'Hold.'

The wait was not long. First Grace heard the static and then, 'Grace?'

'Hello, Mr. Vespa.'

'Please call me Carl.'

'Carl, right.'

'You got my message?' he asked.

'Yes.' She did not tell Carl Vespa that it had nothing to do with why she was calling now. There was feedback on the line. 'Where are you?' she asked.

'My jet. We're about an hour outside of Stewart.'

Stewart was an air force base and airport about an hour and a half from her house.

Silence.

'Is something wrong, Grace?'

'You said to call if I ever needed anything.'

'And now, fifteen years later, you do?'

'I think so.'

'Good. And your timing couldn't be better. There's something I want to show you.'

'What's that?'

'Listen, are you home?'

'I'll be there soon.'

'I'll pick you up in two, two and a half, hours. We can talk then, okay? Do you have someone to watch the kids?'

'I should be able to find someone.'

'If you can't, I'll leave my assistant at your house. See you then.'

Carl Vespa hung up. Grace kept driving. She wondered what he wanted from her now. She wondered about the wisdom of calling him in the first place. She hit the first number on her speed-dial again – Jack's cell phone – but there was still no answer.

Grace had another idea. She called her friend of the no-ménage, Cora.

'Didn't you used to date a guy who worked in e-mail spam?' Grace asked.

'Yep,' Cora said. 'Obsessive creep named – get this – Gus. Hard to get rid of. I had to use my own version of a bunker buster on him.'

'What did you do?'

'I told Gus he had a small wee-wee.'

'Ouch.'

'Like I said, the bunker buster. Works every time, but there's often, uh, collateral damage.'

'I might need his help.'

'How?'

Grace was not sure how to put this. She decided to concentrate on the blonde with the X across her face, the one she was sure she'd seen before. 'I found this photograph . . . ,' she began.

'Right.'

'And there's this woman in it. She's probably late teens, early twenties.'

'Uh-huh.'

'It's an old picture. I'd say fifteen, twenty years old. Anyway, I need to find out who the girl is. I was thinking maybe I could send it out via spam mail. It could ask if anyone can identify the girl for a research project, something like that. I know most people erase those e-mails, but if a few looked, I don't know, maybe I could get a response.'

'Long shot.'

'Yeah, I know.'

'And wow, talk about creeps coming out of the wood-work. Imagine the replies.'

'Got a better idea?'

'Not really, no. It could work, I guess. By the way, you notice I'm not asking you why you need to find the identity of a woman in a picture from fifteen, twenty years ago?'

'I do.'

'I just wanted it noted for the record.'

'So noted. It's a long story.'

'You need someone to tell?'

'I might. I might also need someone to watch the kids for a few hours.'

'I'm available and alone.' Pause. 'Sheesh, I have to stop saying that.'

'Where's Vickie?' Vickie was Cora's daughter.

'She's spending the night at the McMansion with my ex and his horse-faced wife. Or as I prefer to put it, she's spending the night in the bunker with Adolf and Eva.'

Grace managed a smile.

'My car is in the shop,' Cora said. 'Can you pick me up on the way?'

'I'll be there right after I grab Max.'

Grace swung by the Montessori Enrichment program and grabbed her son. Max had that near-tears thing going on, having lost several of his Yu-Gi-Oh! cards to a classmate in some dumb game. Grace tried to humor him, but he wasn't in the mood. She gave up. She helped him get his jacket on. His hat was missing. So was one of his gloves. Another mother smiled and whistled while bundling up her little bundle in color-coordinated knit (hand-knit, no doubt) hat, scarf, and yes, matching gloves. She looked over at Grace and faked a sympathetic smile. Grace did not know this woman, but she disliked her intensely.

Being a mother, Grace thought, was a lot like being an artist – you are always insecure, you always feel like a phony, you know that everybody else is better at it than you. The mothers who doted obsessively on their off-spring, the ones who performed their numbing tasks with that Stepford-ready smile and supernatural patience – you know, those mothers who always, *always,* have the right supplies for the ideal after-school craft . . . Grace suspected that these women were profoundly disturbed.

Cora was waiting in the driveway of her bubble-gum-pink house. Everybody on the block hated the color. For a while, one neighbor, a prissy thing properly named Missy, had started up a petition demanding that Cora repaint it. Grace had seen Prissy Missy passing around the petition at a first-grade soccer game. Grace had asked to see it, ripped it up, and walked away.

The color was hardly to Grace's taste, but memo to the Missys of the world: Get over yourselves.

Cora teetered toward them in her stiletto heels. She was dressed slightly more demurely – a sweatshirt over the leotard – but it really didn't matter. Some women oozed sex, even if dressed in a burlap sack. Cora was one of them. When she moved, new curves were formed even as old ones disappeared. Every line from her husky voice, no matter how innocuous, came out as a double entendre. Every tilt of the head was a come-on.

Cora slid in and looked back at Max. 'Hey, handsome.'

Max grunted and didn't look up.

'Just like my ex.' Cora spun back around. 'You got that photo?'

'I do.'

'I called Gus. He'll do it.'

'Did you promise anything in return?'

'Remember what I said about fifth-date syndrome? Well, are you free Saturday night?'

Grace looked at her.

'Kidding.'

'I knew that.'

'Good. Anyway, Gus said to scan the photo and e-mail it to him. He can set up an anonymous e-mail address for you to receive replies. No one will know who you are. We'll keep the text to a minimum, just say that a journalist is doing a story and needs to know the origin of the photograph. That sound okay?'

'Yeah, thanks.'

They arrived at the house. Max stomped upstairs and then shouted down, 'Can I watch *SpongeBob*?'

Grace acquiesced. Like every parent, Grace had strict rules about no TV during the day. Like every parent, she knew that rules were made to be broken. Cora headed straight for the cupboard and made coffee. Grace thought about which photograph to send and decided to use a blowup of the right side, the blonde with the X on her face and the redhead on her left. She left Jack's image – again, assuming that *was* Jack – out. She didn't yet want him involved. She decided that having two people increased chances of getting an identity hit and made the solicitation look less like the work of a crazed stalker.

Cora looked at the original photograph. 'May I make an observation?'

'Yes.'

'This is pretty weird.'

'The guy over here' – Grace pointed – 'the one with the beard. Who does that look like to you?'

Cora squinted. 'I guess it could be Jack.'

'Could be or is?'

'You tell me.'

'Jack's missing.'

'Come again?'

She told Cora the story. Cora listened, tapping a too-long fingernail painted up in Chanel's Rouge Noir, a color not unlike blood, on the tabletop. When Grace finished, Cora said, 'You know, of course, that I have a low opinion of men.'

'I know.'

'I believe that, for the most part, they are two floors below dog turd.'

'I know that too.'

'So the obvious answer is that, yes, this is a picture of Jack. That, yes, this little blondie, the one gazing up at him like he's the messiah, is an old flame. That yes, Jack and Mary Magdalene here are having an affair. That someone, maybe her current husband, wanted you to find out about it, so he sent you that picture. That everything came to a head when Jack realized that you were onto him.'

'And that's why he ran away?'

'Correct.'

'That doesn't add up, Cora.'

'You have a better theory?'

'I'm working on it.'

'Good,' Cora said, 'because I don't buy it either. I'm just talking. The rule is thus: Men are scum. Jack, however, has always hit me as the exception that proves the rule.'

'I love you, you know.'

Cora nodded. 'Everybody does.'

Grace heard a sound and glanced out the window. A

stretch limousine of glistening black slid up the driveway with the smoothness of a Motown background singer. The chauffeur, a rat-faced man with the build of a whippet, hurried to open the car's back door.

Carl Vespa had arrived.

Despite his rumored vocation, Carl Vespa did not dress in Sopranos-style velour or shiny, sealant-coated suits. He preferred khakis, Joseph Abboud sports coats, and loafers *sans* socks. He was mid-sixties but looked a solid decade younger. His hair was tickling-the-shoulders long, the color a distinguished shade of blond-gone-to-gray. His face was tanned and had the sort of waxy smoothness that suggests Botox. His teeth were aggressively capped, as if the front cuspids had taken growth hormones.

He nodded an order at the whippetlike driver and approached the house on his own. Grace opened the door to greet him. Carl Vespa gave her the toothy dazzler. She smiled back, glad to see him. He greeted her with a kiss on the cheek. No words were exchanged. They didn't need them. He held both her hands and looked at her. She could see his eyes start to well up.

Max moved to his mother's right. Vespa let go and took a step back.

'Max,' Grace began, 'this is Mr. Vespa.'

'Hello, Max.'

'That your car?' Max asked.

'Yes.'

Max looked at the car, then at Vespa. 'Got a TV inside?'

'It does.'

'Whoa.'

Cora cleared her throat.

'Oh, and this is my friend, Cora.'

'Charmed,' Vespa said.

Cora looked at the car, then at Vespa. 'You single?'

'I am.'

'Whoa.'

Grace repeated the baby-sitting instructions for the sixth time. Cora pretended to listen. Grace gave her twenty dollars to order pizza and that cheesy bread Max had become enamored with of late. A classmate's mom would bring Emma home in an hour.

Grace and Vespa headed toward the limousine. The rat-faced driver had the door opened and at the ready. Vespa said, 'This is Cram,' gesturing to the driver. When Cram shook her hand, Grace had to bite back a scream.

'A pleasure,' Cram said. His smile brought on visions of a Discovery Channel documentary on sea predators. She slid in first and Carl Vespa followed.

There were Waterford glasses and a matching decanter half-filled with a liquid that appeared both caramel and luxurious. There was, as noted, a television set. Above her seat was a DVD player, multiple CD player, climate controls, and enough buttons to confuse an airline pilot. The whole thing – the crystal, the decanter, the electronics – was overstated, but maybe that was what you wanted in a stretch limousine.

'Where are we going?' Grace asked.

'It's a little hard to explain.' They were sitting next to each other, both facing forward. 'I'd rather just show it to you, if that's okay.'

Carl Vespa had been the first lost parent to loom over her hospital bed. When Grace first came out of the coma, his was the first face she saw. She had no idea who he was, where she was, what day it was. More than a week was gone from her memory banks. Carl Vespa ended up sitting in her hospital room for days on end, sleeping in the chair next to her. He made sure that plenty of flowers surrounded her. He made sure that she had a good view, soothing music, enough pain medication, private nursing. He made sure that once Grace was able to eat, the hospital staff didn't give her the standard slop.

He never asked her for details of that night because, in

truth, she really could not provide any. Over the next few months they talked for countless hours. He told her stories, mostly about his failures as a father. He had used his connections to get into her hospital room that first night. He had paid off security – interestingly enough, the security firm at the hospital was actually controlled by organized crime – and then he had simply sat with her.

Eventually other parents followed his lead. It was weird. They wanted to be around her. That was all. They found comfort in it. Their child had died in Grace's presence and it was as if maybe a small part of their souls, their forever-lost son or daughter, somehow still lived inside of her. It made no sense and yet Grace thought that maybe she understood.

These heartbroken parents came to talk about their dead children, and Grace listened. She figured that she owed them at least that much. She knew that these relationships were probably unhealthy, but there was no way she could turn them away. The truth was, Grace had no family of her own. She'd thrived, for a little while at least, on the attention. They needed a child; she needed a parent. It wasn't that simple – this malaise of cross-projection – but Grace wasn't sure she could explain it any better.

The limo headed south on the Garden State Parkway now. Cram flipped on the radio. Classical music, a violin concerto from the sound of it, came through the speakers.

Vespa said, 'You know, of course, that the anniversary is coming up.'

'I do,' she said, though she had done her best to ignore it all. Fifteen years. Fifteen years since that awful night at the Boston Garden. The papers had run all the expected 'Where Are They Now?' commemorative pieces. The parents and survivors all handled it differently. Most participated because they felt it was one way to keep the memory of what happened alive. There had been heart-wrenching articles on the Garrisons and the Reeds and the Weiders.

The security guard, Gordon MacKenzie, who was credited with saving many by forcing open locked emergency exits, now worked as a police captain in Brookline, a Boston suburb. Even Carl Vespa had allowed a picture of him and his wife, Sharon, sitting in their yard, both still looking as if someone had just hollowed out their insides.

Grace had gone the other way. With her art career in full swing, she did not want even the appearance of capitalizing on the tragedy. She had been injured, that was all, and to make more of it than that reminded her of those washed-up actors who come out of the woodwork to shed crocodile tears when a hated costar suddenly dies. She wanted no part of it. The attention should be given to the dead and those they left behind.

'He's up for parole again,' Vespa said. 'Wade Larue, I mean.'

She knew, of course.

The stampede that night had been blamed on Wade Larue, currently a resident of Walden Prison outside Albany, New York. He was the one who fired the shots creating the panic. The defense's claim was interesting. They argued that Wade Larue didn't do it – forget the gun residue found on his hands, the gun belonging to him, the bullet match to the gun, the witnesses who saw him fire – but if he *did* do it, he was too stoned to remember. Oh, and if neither of those rationales floated your boat, Wade Larue couldn't have known that firing a gun would cause the death of eighteen people and the injury of dozens more.

The case proved to be controversial. The prosecutors went for eighteen counts of murder, but the jury didn't see it that way. Larue's lawyer ended up cutting a deal for eighteen counts of manslaughter. Nobody really worried too much about sentencing. Carl Vespa's only son had died that night. Remember what happened when Gotti's son was killed in a car accident? The man driving the car, a family man, has never been heard from again. A similar fate, most agreed, would befall Wade Larue, except this time, the general public would probably applaud the outcome.

For a while, Larue was kept isolated in Walden Prison. Grace didn't follow the story closely, but the parents – parents like Carl Vespa – still called and wrote all the time. They needed to see her every once in a while. As a survivor, she had become a vessel of some sort, carrying the dead. Putting aside the physical recuperation, this emotional pressure – this awesome, impossible responsibility – was a big part of the reason for Grace's going overseas.

Eventually Larue had been put in general population. Rumor had it he was beaten and abused by his fellow inmates, but for whatever reason, he lived. Carl Vespa had decided to forgo the hit. Maybe it was a sign of mercy. Or maybe it was just the opposite. Grace didn't know.

Vespa said, 'He finally stopped claiming total innocence. Did you hear that? He admits he fired his gun, but that he just freaked out when the lights went out.'

Which made sense. For her part, Grace had seen Wade Larue only once. She had been called to testify, though her testimony had nothing to do with guilt and innocence – she had almost no memory of the stampede, never mind who fired the gun – and everything to do with inflaming the passion of the jury. But Grace didn't need revenge. To her Wade Larue was stoned out of his mind, a souped-up punk more worthy of pity than hate.

'Do you think he'll get out?' she asked.

'He has a new lawyer. She's damn good.'

'And if she gets him released?'

Vespa smiled. 'Don't believe everything you read about me.' Then he added, 'Besides, Wade Larue isn't the only one to blame for that night.'

'What do you mean?'

He opened his mouth and then fell silent. Then: 'It's like I said. I'd rather show you.'

Something about his tone told her to change subjects. 'You said you were single,' Grace said.

'Pardon?'

'You told my friend you were single.'

He waved his finger. No ring. 'Sharon and I divorced two years ago.'

'I'm sorry to hear that.'

'It hasn't been right for a long time.' He shrugged, looking off. 'How is your family?'

'Okay.'

'I sense some hesitation.'

She may have shrugged.

'On the phone, you said you needed my help.'

'I think so.'

'So what's wrong?'

'My husband . . .' She stopped. 'I think my husband is in trouble.'

She told him the story. His eyes stayed straight ahead, avoiding her gaze. He nodded every once in a while, but the nods seemed strangely out of context. His expression didn't change, which was strange. Carl Vespa was usually more animated. After she stopped talking, he didn't say anything for a long time.

'This photograph,' Vespa said. 'Do you have it with you?'

'Yes.' She handed it to him. His hand, she noticed, had a small quake. Vespa stared at the picture for a very long time.

'Can I keep this?' he asked.

'I have copies.'

Vespa's eyes were still on the images. 'Do you mind if I ask you a few personal questions?' he asked.

'I guess not.'

'Do you love your husband?'

'Very much.'

'Does he love you?'

'Yes.'

Carl Vespa had only met Jack once. He had sent a wedding gift when they got married. He sent gifts on Emma's and Max's birthdays too. Grace wrote him thank-you notes and gave the gifts to charity. She didn't mind being connected to him, she guessed, but she didn't want her children . . . what was the phrase? . . . tainted by the association.

'You two met in Paris, right?'

'Southern France, actually. Why?'

'And how did you meet again?'

'What's the difference?'

He hesitated a second too long. 'I guess I'm trying to learn how well you know your husband.'

'We've been married ten years.'

'I understand that.' He shifted in his seat. 'You were there on vacation when you met?'

'I don't know if I'd call it a vacation exactly.'

'You were studying. You were painting.'

'Yes.'

'And, well, mostly you were running away.'

She said nothing.

'And Jack?' Vespa continued. 'Why was he there?'

'Same reason, I guess.'

'He was running away?'

'Yes.'

'From what?'

'I don't know.'

'May I state the obvious then?'

She waited.

'Whatever he was running from' – Vespa gestured toward the photograph – 'it caught up to him.'

The thought had occurred to Grace too. 'That was a long time ago.'

'So was the Boston Massacre. Your running away. Did it make it go away?'

In the rearview mirror she saw Cram glance at her, waiting for an answer. She kept still.

'Nothing stays in the past, Grace. You know that.'

'I love my husband.'

He nodded.

'Will you help me?'

'You know I will.'

The car veered off the Garden State Parkway. Up ahead, Grace saw an enormous bland structure with a cross on it. It looked like an airplane hangar. A neon sign stated that tickets were still available for the 'Concerts with the Lord.' A band called Rapture would be playing. Cram pulled the limo into a parking lot big enough to declare statehood.

'What are we doing here?'

'Finding God,' Carl Vespa said. 'Or maybe His opposite. Let's go inside, I want to show you something.'

13

This was nuts, Charlaine thought.

Her feet moved steadily toward Freddy Sykes's yard without thought or emotion. It had crossed her mind that she could be raising the danger stakes out of desperation, hungry as she was for any kind of drama in her life. But okay, again, so what? Really, when she thought about it, what was the worst that could happen? Suppose Mike did find out. Would he leave her? Would that be so bad?

Did she want to get caught?

Oh, enough with the amateur self-analysis. It wouldn't hurt to knock on Freddy's door, pretend to be neighborly. Two years ago, Mike had put up a four-foot-high stockade fence in the backyard. He had wanted one higher, but the town ordinance wouldn't allow it unless you owned a swimming pool.

Charlaine opened the gate separating her backyard from Freddy's. Odd. This was a first. She had never opened the gate before.

As she got closer to Freddy's back door, she realized how weathered his house was. The paint was peeling. The garden was overgrown. Weeds sprouted up through the cracks in the walk. There were patches of dead grass everywhere. She turned and glanced at her own house. She had never seen it from this angle. It too looked tired.

She was at Freddy's back door.

Okay, now what?

Knock on it, stupid.

She did. She started with a soft rap. No answer. She pounded louder. Nothing. She pressed her ear against the door. Like that would do any good. Like she'd hear a muffled cry or something.

There was no sound.

The shades were still down, but there were wedges that the shades couldn't quite cover. She put an eye up to an opening and peered in. The living room had a lime-green couch so worn it looked like it was melting. There was a vinyl recliner of maroon in the corner. The television looked new. The wall had old paintings of clowns. The piano was loaded with old black-and-white photographs. There was one of a wedding. Freddy's parents, Charlaine figured. There was another of the groom looking painfully handsome in an army uniform. There was one more photograph of the same man holding a baby, a smile spread across his face. Then the man – the soldier, the groom – was gone. The rest of the photographs were of either Freddy alone or with his mother.

The room was immaculate – no, preserved. Stuck in a time warp, unused, untouched. There was a collection of small figurines on a side table. More photographs too. A life, Charlaine thought. Freddy Sykes had a life. It was a strange thought, but there you have it.

Charlaine circled toward the garage. There was one window in the back. A flimsy curtain of pretend lace hung across it. She stood on her tiptoes. Her fingers gripped the window ledge. The wood was so old it almost broke away. Peeling paint flaked off like dandruff.

She looked into the garage.

There was another car.

Not a car actually. A minivan. A Ford Windstar. When you live in a town like this, you know all the models.

Freddy Sykes did not own a Ford Windstar.

Maybe his young Asian guest did. That would make sense, right?

She was not convinced.

So what next?

Charlaine stared down at the ground and wondered. She had been wondering since she first decided to approach the house. She had known before leaving the safety of her own kitchen that there would be no answer to her knocks. She also knew that peeking in the windows – peeping on the peeper? – would do no good.

The rock.

It was there, in what had once been a vegetable garden. She had seen Freddy use it once. It wasn't a real rock. It was one of those hide-a-keys. They were so common now that criminals probably looked for them before checking under the mat.

Charlaine bent down, picked up the rock, and turned it over. All she had to do was slide the little panel back and take the key out. She did so. The key rested in her palm, glistening in the sunlight.

Here was the line. The no-going-back line.

She moved toward the back door.

14

Still wearing the sea-predator smile, Cram opened the door and Grace stepped out of the limousine. Carl Vespa slid out on his own. The huge neon sign listed a church affiliation that Grace had never heard of. The motto, according to several signs around the edifice, seemed to indicate that this was 'God's House.' If that were true, God could use a more creative architect. The structure held all the splendor and warmth of a highway mega-store.

The interior was even worse – tacky enough to make Graceland look understated. The wall-to-wall carpeting was a shiny shade of red usually reserved for a mall girl's lipstick. The wallpaper was darker, more blood-colored, a velvet affair adorned with hundreds of stars and crosses. The effect made Grace dizzy. The main chapel or house of worship – or, most suitably, arena – held pews rather than seats. They looked uncomfortable, but then again wasn't standing encouraged? The cynical side of Grace suspected that the reason all religious services had you sporadically stand had nothing to do with devotion and everything to do with keeping congregants from falling asleep.

As soon as she entered the arena, Grace felt a flutter in her heart.

The altar, done up in the green and gold of a cheer-leader's uniform, was being wheeled offstage. Grace looked for preachers with bad toupees, but none were to be found. The band – Grace assumed this was Rapture – was setting up. Carl Vespa stopped in front of her, his eyes on the stage.

'Is this your church?' she asked him.

A small smile came to his lips. 'No.'

'Is it safe to assume that you're not a fan of, uh, Rapture?'

Vespa didn't answer the question. 'Let's move down closer to the stage.'

Cram took the lead. There were security guards, but they swept aside as if Cram were toxic.

'What's going on here?' Grace asked.

Vespa kept moving down the steps. When they reached what a theater would call the orchestra – what do you call the good seats in a church? – she looked up and got a whole new feel for the size of the place. It was a huge theater-in-the-round. The stage was in the center, surrounded on all sides. Grace felt the constriction in her throat.

Dress it up in a religious cloak, but there was no mistake.

This felt like a rock concert.

Vespa took her hand. 'It'll be okay.'

But it wouldn't be. She knew that. She had not been to a concert or sporting event in any 'arena venue' in fifteen years. She used to love going to concerts. She remembered seeing Bruce Springsteen and the E Street Band at Asbury Park Convention Center during her high school days. What was strange to her, what she had realized even back then, was that the line between rock concert and intense religious service was not all that thick. There was a moment when Bruce played 'Meeting Across the River' followed by 'Jungleland' – two of Grace's favorites – when she was on her feet, her eyes closed, sheen of sweat on her face, when she was simply gone, lost, shaking with bliss, the same bliss she'd witness on TV when a televangelist got the crowd on its feet, hands raised and shaking.

She loved that feeling. And she knew that she never wanted to experience it again.

Grace pulled her hand away from Carl Vespa's. He nodded as if he understood. 'Come on,' he said gently.

Grace limped behind him. The limp, it seemed to her, was getting more pronounced. Her leg throbbed. Psychological. She knew that. Tight spaces did not terrify her; huge auditoriums, especially jammed with people, did. The place was fairly empty now, thank He Who Lives Here, but her imagination entered the fray and provided the absent commotion.

Shrill feedback from the amplifier made her pull up. Someone was doing a sound test.

'What's this all about?' she asked Vespa.

His face was set. He veered to the left. Grace followed. There was a scoreboard-type sign above the stage announcing that Rapture was in the middle of a three-week gig and that they, Rapture, were: 'What God Has on His MP3.'

The band came onstage now for sound check. They gathered at center stage, had a brief discussion, and then started playing. Grace was surprised. They sounded pretty good. The lyrics were syrupy, full of stuff about skies and spread wings and ascensions and being lifted up. Eminem told a potential girlfriend to 'sit your drunk ass on that f***ing runway, ho.' These lyrics, in their own way, were equally jarring.

The lead singer was female. She had platinum blond hair, cut with bangs, and sang with her eyes cast toward the heavens. She looked about fourteen years old. A guitarist stood to her right. He was more heavy-metal rock, what with the medusa-black locks and a tattoo of a giant cross on his right bicep. He played hard, slashing at the strings as if they had pissed him off.

When there was a lull, Carl Vespa said, 'The song was written by Doug Bondy and Madison Seelinger.'

She shrugged.

'Doug Bondy wrote the music. Madison Seelinger – that's the singer up there – wrote the lyrics.'

'And I care because?'

'Doug Bondy is playing the drums.'

They moved to the side of the stage for a better look. The music started again. They stood by a speaker. Grace's ears took the pounding, but under normal conditions, she would actually have been enjoying the sound. Doug Bondy, the drummer, was pretty much hidden by the array of cymbals and snares surrounding him. She moved a little more to the side. She could see him better now. He was banging the skins, as they say, his eyes closed, his face at peace. He looked older than the other members of the band. He had a crewcut. His face was clean-shaven. He wore those black Elvis Costello glasses.

Grace felt that flutter in her chest expand. 'I want to go home,' she said.

'It's him, isn't it?'

'I want to go home.'

The drummer was still smacking the skins, lost in the music, when he turned and saw her. Their eyes met. And she knew. So did he.

It was Jimmy X.

She didn't wait. She started limping toward the exit. The music chased her down.

'Grace?'

It was Vespa. She ignored him. She pushed through the emergency exit door. The air felt cool in her lungs. She sucked it down, tried to let the dizziness fade. Cram was outside now, as if he knew that she'd take this exit. He smiled at her.

Carl Vespa came up behind her. 'It's him, right?'

'And what if it is?'

'What if . . .' Vespa repeated, surprised. 'He's not innocent here. He's as much to blame –'

'I want to go home.'

Vespa stopped short as if she'd slapped him.

Calling him had been a mistake. She knew that now. She had lived. She had recovered. Sure, there was the limp.

There was some pain. There was the occasional nightmare. But she was okay. She had gotten over it. They, the parents, never would. She saw it that first day – the shatter in their eyes – and while progress had been made, lives had been lived, pieces had been picked up, the shatter had never left. She looked now at Carl Vespa – at the eyes – and saw it all over again.

'Please,' she said to him. 'I just want to go home.'

15

Wu spotted the empty hide-a-key.

The rock was on the path by the back door, turned over like a dying crab. The cover had been slid open. Wu could see the key was gone. He remembered the first time he had approached a house that had been violated. He was six years old. The hut – it was one room, no plumbing – had been his own. The Kim government had not bothered with the niceties of keys. They had knocked the door down and dragged his mother away. Wu found her two days later. They had hung her from a tree. No one was allowed to cut her down, under penalty of death. A day later the birds found her.

His mother had been wrongly accused of being a traitor to the Great Leader, but guilt or innocence was irrelevant. An example was made of her anyway. This is what happens to those who defy us. Check that: This is what happens to anyone we *think may be* defying us.

No one took in the six-year-old Eric. No orphanage picked him up. He did not become a ward of the state. Eric Wu ran away. He slept in the woods. He ate out of garbage cans. He survived. At thirteen, he was arrested for stealing and thrown in jail. The chief guard, a man more crooked than anyone he housed, saw Wu's potential. And so it began.

Wu stared down at the empty hide-a-key.

Someone was in the house.

He glanced at the house next door. His best guess would be that it was the woman who lived there. She liked to watch out the window. She would know where Freddy Sykes hid a key.

He considered his options. There were two.

One, he could simply leave.

Jack Lawson was in the trunk. Wu had a vehicle. He could take off, steal another car, begin his journey, set up residence elsewhere.

Problem: Wu's fingerprints were inside the house, along with the severely wounded, perhaps dead, Freddy Sykes. The lingerie-clad woman, if it was the woman, would be able to identify him too. Wu was fresh out of prison and on parole. The DA had suspected him of terrible crimes, but they could not prove them. So they cut a deal in exchange for his testimony. Wu had spent time in a maximum security penitentiary in Walden, New York. Next to what he had experienced in his homeland, the prison might as well have been a Four Seasons.

But that didn't mean he wanted to go back.

No, option one was no good. So that left option two.

Wu silently opened the door and slid inside.

Back in the limousine, Grace and Carl Vespa fell into silence.

Grace kept flashing back to the last time she'd seen Jimmy X's face – fifteen years ago in her hospital. He'd been forced to visit, a photo op arranged by his promoter, but he couldn't even look at her, never mind speak. He just stood by her bed, flowers clutched in his hand, his head down like a little boy's waiting for the teacher to scold him. She never said a word. Eventually he handed her the flowers and walked out.

Jimmy X quit the business and ran off. Rumor had it he moved to a private island near Fiji. Now, fifteen years later, here he was in New Jersey, playing drums for a Christian rock band.

When they pulled onto her street, Vespa said, 'It hasn't gotten any better, you know.'

Grace looked out the window. 'Jimmy X didn't fire the gun.'

'I know that.'

'So what do you want from him?'

'He's never said he's sorry.'

'And that would be enough?'

He thought about that, and then said, 'There was a boy who survived. David Reed. You remember him?'

'Yes.'

'He was standing next to Ryan. They were body to body. But when the crush began, this Reed kid somehow got lifted up on someone's shoulder. He got on the stage.'

'I know.'

'You remember what his parents said?'

She did but she said nothing.

'Jesus lifted up their son. It was God's will.' Vespa's voice had not changed, but Grace could feel the hidden rage like a blast furnace. 'You see, Mr. and Mrs. Reed prayed and God responded. It was a miracle, they said. God looked out for their son, that's what they kept repeating. As if God didn't have the desire or inclination to save mine.'

They fell into silence. Grace wanted to tell him that many good people died that day, many people with good parents who prayed, that God does not discriminate. But Vespa knew all that. It would not comfort.

By the time they pulled into the driveway, night was falling. Grace could see the silhouettes of Cora and the kids in the kitchen window. Vespa said, 'I want to help you find your husband.'

'I'm not even sure what you can do.'

'You'd be surprised,' he said. 'You have my number. No matter what you need, call me. No matter what time it is, I don't care. I'll be there.'

Cram opened the door. Vespa walked her to the door.

'I'll be in touch,' he said.

'Thank you.'

'I'm also going to assign Cram here to watch your house.'

She looked at Cram. Cram sort of smiled back.

'That won't be necessary.'

'Humor me,' he said.

'No, really, I don't want that. Please.'

Vespa thought about it. 'If you change your mind . . . ?'

'I'll let you know.'

He turned to leave then. She watched him walk back to the car and wondered about the wisdom of making deals with the devil. Cram opened the door. The limo seemed to swallow Vespa whole. Cram nodded at her. Grace did not move. She considered herself pretty good at reading people, but Carl Vespa had changed her view. She never saw or even sensed a hint of evil in him. Yet she knew it was there.

Evil – real evil – was like that.

Cora put on boiling water for the Ronzoni penne. She threw a jar of Prego into a saucepan and then leaned close to Grace's ear.

'I'm going to check the e-mail to see if we got any replies,' Cora whispered.

Grace nodded. She was helping Emma do her homework and trying like hell to care. Her daughter was dressed in a Jason Kidd Nets basketball jersey. She called herself Bob. She wanted to be a jock. Grace didn't know how she felt about it, but she guessed it was better than buying *Teen Beat* magazine and lusting after nonthreatening boy bands.

Mrs. Lamb, Emma's young-but-quickly-aging teacher, had the kids working on the multiplication tables. They were doing the sixes. Grace tested Emma. At six times seven, Emma paused for a long time.

'You should know it by heart,' Grace said.

'Why? I can figure it out.'

'That's not the point. You learn it by heart so you can build off that when you start multiplying numbers with multiple digits.'

'Mrs. Lamb didn't say to memorize them.'

'You should.'

'But Mrs. Lamb –'

'Six times seven.'

And so it went.

Max had to find an item to put in the 'Secret Box.' You put something in the box – in this case, a hockey puck – and you made up three clues so that your fellow kindergartners could guess what it was. Clue one: The item is black. Clue two: It's used in a sport. Clue three: Ice. Fair enough.

Cora came back from the computer shaking her head. Nothing yet. She grabbed a bottle of Lindemans, a decent-yet-cheap Chardonnay from Australia, and popped the cork. Grace put the kids to bed.

'Where's Daddy?' Max asked.

Emma echoed the sentiment. 'I wrote the hockey verse for my poem.'

Grace said something vague about Jack having to work. The kids looked wary.

'I'd love to hear the poem,' Grace said.

Grudgingly Emma produced her journal.

'Hockey stick, hockey stick,
Do you love to score?
When you are used to shoot,
Do you feel like you want more?'

Emma looked up. Grace said, 'Wow' and clapped, but she was simply not as good at the enthusiasm game as Jack. She kissed them both good night and headed back downstairs. The wine bottle was open. She and Cora began to drink. She missed Jack. He'd been gone less than twenty-four hours – he'd been gone longer on business trips plenty of times – and yet the house seemed to sag somehow. Something felt lost, irretrievably so. The missing of him had already become a physical ache.

Grace and Cora drank some more. Grace thought about her children. She thought about a life, a whole life, without Jack. We do anything to shield our children from pain. Losing Jack would, no doubt, crush Grace. But that was okay. She could take it. Her pain, however, would be nothing next to what it would do to the two children upstairs who, she knew, lay awake, sensing something was amiss.

Grace looked at the photographs lining the walls.

Cora moved next to her. 'He's a good man.'

'Yeah.'

'You okay?'

'Too much wine,' Grace said.

'Not enough, you ask me. Where did Mr. Mobster take you?'

'To see a Christian rock band.'

'Quite the first date.'

'It's a long story.'

'I'm all ears.'

But Grace shook her head. She didn't want to think about Jimmy X. An idea came to her. She mulled it over, let it settle.

'What?' Cora said.

'Maybe Jack made more than one call.'

'You mean, besides the call to his sister?'

'Yes.'

Cora nodded. 'Have you set up an online account?'

'We have AOL.'

'No, I mean for your phone bill.'

'Not yet.'

'No time like the present then.' Cora stood up. There was a teeter to her step now. The wine was making them both warm. 'Who do you use for long distance?'

'Cascade.'

They were back by Jack's computer. Cora sat at the

desk, cracked her knuckles, and went to work. She brought up Cascade's Web site. Grace gave her the necessary information – address, social security number, credit card. They came up with a password. Cascade sent an e-mail to Jack's account verifying that he'd just signed up for online billing.

'We're in,' Cora said.

'I don't get it.'

'An online billing account. I just set it up. You can now view and pay your phone bill over the Internet.'

Grace looked over Cora's shoulder. 'That's last month's bill.'

'Yep.'

'But it won't have the calls from last night.'

'Hmm. Let me e-mail a request. We can also call Cascade and ask.'

'They're not open twenty-four-seven. Part of the discount service.' Grace leaned closer to the monitor. 'Let me see if he called his sister before last night.'

Her eyes skimmed down the list. Nothing. No unfamiliar numbers either. She no longer felt weird doing this, spying on the husband she loved and trusted, which of course felt weird in and of itself.

'Who pays the bills?' Cora asked.

'Jack does most of them.'

'The phone bill comes to the house?'

'Yes.'

'You look at it?'

'Sure.'

Cora nodded. 'Jack has a cell phone, right?'

'Right.'

'What about that bill?'

'What about it?'

'Do you look at it?'

'No, it's his.'

Cora smiled.

'What?'

'When my ex was cheating on me, he used the cell because I never looked at those bills.'

'Jack isn't cheating.'

'But he may be keeping secrets, right?'

'Could be,' Grace allowed. 'Okay, yeah, probably.'

'So where would he keep the phone bills for his mobile?'

Grace checked the file cabinet. He saved the bills from Cascade. She checked under the Vs for Verizon Wireless. Nothing. 'They're not here.'

Cora rubbed her hands together. 'Ooo, suspicious.' She was into it now. 'So let's do that voodoo that they do that we do.'

'And what exactly do we do?'

'Let's say Jack is keeping something from you. He would probably destroy the bills the minute he gets them, right?'

Grace shook her head. 'This is so bizarre.'

'But am I right?'

'Yeah, okay, if Jack is keeping secrets from me –'

'Everyone has secrets, Grace. C'mon, you know that. Are you telling me that this all comes as a total surprise?'

This truth would normally have made Grace pause, but there was no time for such indulgences. 'Okay, so let's say Jack did destroy the cell phone bills – how are we going to get them?'

'Same way I just did. We set up another online account, this time under Verizon Wireless.' Cora started typing.

'Cora?'

'Yep.'

'Can I ask you something?'

'Shoot.'

'How do you know how to do all this?'

'Practical experience.' She stopped typing and looked back at Grace. 'How do you think I found out about Adolf and Eva?'

'You spied on them?'

'Yup. I bought a book called *Spying for Dodos* or something like that. It's all in there. I wanted to make sure I had all the facts before I confronted his sorry ass.'

'What did he say when you showed it to him?'

'That he was sorry. That he'd never do it again. That he'd give up Ivana of the Implant and never see her again.'

Grace watched her friend type. 'You really love him, don't you?'

'More than life itself.' Still typing, Cora added, 'How about opening another bottle of wine?'

'Only if we're not driving tonight.'

'You want me to sleep here?'

'We shouldn't drive, Cora.'

'Okay, deal.'

Grace stood and felt her head reel from the drink. She headed back into the kitchen. Cora often drank too much, but tonight Grace was happy to join her. She opened another bottle of the Lindemans. The wine was warm so she put an ice cube in both. Gauche, but they liked it cold.

When Grace got back into the office, the printer was whirring. She handed Cora a glass and sat. Grace stared at the wine. She started shaking her head.

'What?' Cora said.

'I finally met Jack's sister.'

'So?'

'I mean, think about it. Sandra Koval. I didn't even know her name before now.'

'You never asked Jack about her?'

'Not really.'

'Why not?'

Grace took a sip. 'I can't really explain it.'

'Try.'

She looked up and wondered how to put it. 'I thought it was healthy. You know, keeping parts of yourself private.

I was running away from something. He never pushed me on it.'

'So you never pushed him either?'

'It was more than that.'

'What?'

Grace thought about it. 'I never bought into that 'we have no secrets' stuff. Jack had a wealthy family and he wanted no part of it. There had been a falling out. I knew that much.'

'Wealthy from what?'

'What do you mean?'

'What business are they in?'

'Some kind of securities firm. Jack's grandfather started it. They have trust funds and options and voting shares, stuff like that. Nothing Onassis-like, but enough, I guess. Jack won't have anything to do with it. He won't vote. He won't touch the money. He set it up so the trust skips a generation.'

'So Emma and Max will get it?'

'Yep.'

'How do you feel about that?'

Grace shrugged. 'You know what I'm realizing?'

'I'm all ears.'

'The reason I never pushed Jack? It had nothing to do with respecting privacy.'

'Then what?'

'I loved him. I loved him more than any man I'd ever met . . .'

'I feel a "but" coming here.'

Grace felt the tears press against her eyes. 'But it all felt so fragile. Does that make sense? When I was with him – this is going to sound so stupid – but when I was with Jack, it was the first time I was happy since, I don't know, since my father died.'

'You've had a lot of pain in your life,' Cora said.

Grace did not reply.

'You were scared it would go away. You didn't want to open yourself up to more.'

'So I chose ignorance?'

'Hey, ignorance is supposed to be bliss, right?'

'You buy that?'

Cora shrugged. 'If I never checked up on Adolf, he probably would have had his fling and gotten over it. Maybe I'd be living with the man I love.'

'You could still take him back.'

'Nope.'

'Why not?'

Cora thought about it. 'I need the ignorance, I guess.' She picked up her glass and took a long sip.

The printer finished whirring. Grace picked up the sheets and started examining them. Most of the phone numbers she knew. Point of fact, she knew almost all of them.

But one immediately jumped out at her.

'Where's six-oh-three area code?' Grace asked.

'Beats me. Which call?'

Grace showed her on the monitor. Cora moved the cursor over it.

'What are you doing?' Grace asked.

'You click the number, they tell you who called.'

'For real?'

'Man, what century do you live in? They have talkies now.'

'So all you have to do is click the link?'

'And it'll tell all. Unless the number is unlisted.'

Cora clicked the left mouse button. A box appeared saying:

NO RECORD OF THAT NUMBER.

'There you go. Unlisted.'

Grace checked her watch. 'It's only nine-thirty,' she said. 'Not too late to call.'

'Under the missing-husband rule, no, not too late at all.'

Grace picked up the phone and inputted the number. A piercing feedback, not unlike the one at the Rapture concert, slapped her eardrum. Then: 'The number you have called' – the robotic voice stated the number – 'has been disconnected. No further information is available.'

Grace frowned.

'What?'

'When was the last time Jack called it?'

Cora checked. 'Three weeks ago. He talked for eighteen minutes.'

'It's disconnected.'

'Hmm, six-oh-three area code,' Cora said, moving to another Web site. She typed in '603 area code' and hit the enter button. The answer came right up. 'It's in New Hampshire. Hold on, let's Google it.'

'Google what? New Hampshire?'

'The phone number.'

'What will that do?'

'Your number is unlisted, right?'

'Right.'

'Hold on, let me show you something. This doesn't work every time, but watch.' Cora typed Grace's phone number into the search engine. 'What it will do is search the entire Web for those numbers in a row. Not just phone directories. That won't do it because, like you said, your number is unlisted. But . . .'

Cora hit return. There was one search hit. The site was for an art prize offered at Brandeis University, her alma mater. Cora clicked the link. Grace's name and number came up. 'You were judging some painting award?'

Grace nodded. 'They were giving out an art scholarship.'

'Yep, there you are. Your name, address, and phone number with other judges. You must have given it to them.'

Grace shook her head.

'Throw away your eight-tracks and welcome to the Information Age,' Cora said. 'And now that I know your name, I can do a million different searches. Your gallery Web page will come up. Where you went to college. Whatever. Now let's try with this six-oh-three number. . . .'

Cora's fingers flew again. She hit return. 'Hold on. We got something.' She squinted at the screen. 'Bob Dodd.'

'Bob?'

'Yes. Not Robert. Bob.' Cora looked back at Grace. 'Is the name familiar?'

'No.'

'The address is a PO box in Fitzwilliam, New Hampshire. You ever been?'

'No.'

'How about Jack?'

'I don't think so. I mean, he went to college in Vermont, so he might have visited New Hampshire, but we've never been there together.'

There was a sound from upstairs. Max cried out in his sleep.

'Go,' Cora said. 'I'll see what I can dig up on our friend Mr. Dodd.'

As Grace headed up toward her son's bedroom, another pang struck deep in her chest: Jack was the house's night sentinel. He handled nightmares and nocturnal requests for water. He was the one who held the kid's foreheads at 3 A.M. when they woke up to, er, throw up. During the day, Grace took care of the sniffles, the taking of the temperatures, the heating of chicken soup, the forcing down of Robitussin. The night shift was Jack's.

Max was sobbing when she reached his room. His cries were soft now, more a whimper, and somehow that was more pitiful than the loudest of screams. Grace wrapped her arms around him. His little body was shaking. She rocked back and forth and gently shushed him. She whispered that

Mommy was here, that everything was okay, that he was safe.

It took Max a while to settle. Grace brought him to the bathroom. Even though Max was barely six, he peed like a man – that is to say, he missed the bowl entirely. He swayed, falling back asleep as he stood. When he finished, she helped him pull up his *Finding Nemo* pajamas. She tucked him back in and asked if he wanted to tell her about his dream. He shook his head and fell back asleep.

Grace watched his little chest rise and fall. He looked very much like his father.

After a while she headed back downstairs. There was no sound. Cora was no longer clacking the keyboard. Grace entered the office. The chair was empty. Cora stood in the corner. She gripped the wineglass.

'Cora?'

'I know why Bob Dodd's phone was disconnected.'

There was a tightness in Cora's voice, one Grace had never heard. She waited for her friend to continue, but she seemed to be shrinking into the corner.

'What happened?' Grace asked.

Cora downed a quick sip. 'According to an article in the *New Hampshire Post*, Bob Dodd is dead. He was murdered two weeks ago.'

16

Eric Wu stepped inside the Sykes house.

The house was dark. Wu had left all the lights out. The intruder – whoever had taken the key out of the rock – had not turned them on. Wu wondered about that.

He had assumed the intruder was the nosey woman in the lingerie. Would she be smart enough to know not to turn the lights on?

He stopped. More than that: If you have the forethought not to turn on the lights, wouldn't you have the forethought not to leave the hide-a-key in plain sight?

Something did not add up.

Wu lowered himself and moved behind the recliner. He stopped and listened. Nothing. If someone was in the house, he would hear them move. He waited some more.

Still nothing.

Wu mulled it over. Could the intruder have come and gone?

He doubted it. A person who would take the risk of entering with a hidden key would look around. They would probably find Freddy Sykes in the upstairs bathroom. They would call for help. Or if they left, if they found nothing amiss, they would have put the key back in the rock. None of that had happened.

What then was the most logical conclusion?

The intruder was still in the house. Not moving. Hiding.

Wu trod gently. There were three exits. He made sure all the doors were locked. Two doors had bolt locks. He carefully slid them into place. He took the dining room chairs and placed them in front of all three exits. He wanted something, anything, to block or at least slow down an easy escape.

Trap his adversary.

The stairway was carpeted. That made it easier to pad up in silence. Wu wanted to check the bathroom, to see if Freddy Sykes was still in the tub. He thought again about the hide-a-key in plain sight. Nothing about this setup made sense. The more he thought about it, the slower his step.

Wu tried to think it through. Start from the beginning: A person who knows where Sykes keeps a hide-a-key opens the door. He or she comes inside. Now what? If he finds Sykes, panic would ensue. He would call the police. If he doesn't find Sykes, well, he leaves. He puts the key back in the rock and puts the rock away.

But neither one of those things had happened.

So again, what could Wu conclude?

The only other possibility that came to mind – unless he was missing something – was that the intruder had indeed found Sykes, just as Wu entered the house. There had been no time to call for help. There had only been time to hide.

But that scenario had problems too. Wouldn't the intruder have turned on a light? Perhaps she had. Perhaps she had turned on the light, but then she saw Wu approach. She might have turned off the lights and hidden where she was.

In the bathroom with Sykes.

Wu was in the master bedroom now. He could see the crack under the bathroom door. The light was still off. Do not underestimate your foe, he reminded himself. He had made mistakes recently. Too many of them. First, Rocky Conwell. Wu had been sloppy enough to allow him to follow. That had been mistake one. Second, Wu had been spotted by the woman next door. Sloppy.

And now this.

It was tough to look at yourself critically, but Wu tried to step away and do just that. He was not infallible. Only fools believe that. Perhaps his time in prison had rusted him somehow. Didn't matter. Wu needed to focus now. He needed to concentrate.

There were more photographs in Sykes's bedroom. This had been Freddy's mother's room for fifty years. Wu knew that from his online encounters. Sykes's father had died during the Korean War. Sykes had been an infant. The mother had never gotten over it. People react differently to the death of a loved one. Mrs. Sykes had decided to dwell with her ghost instead of the living. She spent the rest of her life in this same bedroom – in the same bed even – that she'd shared with her soldier husband. She slept on her side, Freddy said. She never let anyone, not even when young Freddy had a nightmare, touch the side of the bed where her beloved had once lain.

Wu's hand was on the doorknob now.

The bathroom, he knew, was small. He tried to picture an angle someone might use to attack. There really was none. Wu had a gun in his duffel bag. He wondered if he should take it out. If the intruder was armed, then it could be a problem.

Overconfident? Maybe. But Wu didn't think he'd need a weapon.

He turned the knob and pushed hard.

Freddy Sykes was still in the tub. The gag was in his mouth. His eyes were closed. Wu wondered if Freddy was dead. Probably. No one else was here. There was no place to hide. Nobody had come to Freddy's rescue.

Wu moved toward the window. He looked out at the house now, at the house next door.

The woman – the one who'd been in the lingerie – was there.

In her house. Standing by the window.

She stared back at him.

That was when Wu heard the car door slam. There was no siren, but now, as he turned toward the driveway, he could see the red cruiser lights.

The police were here.

Charlaine Swain was not crazy.

She watched movies. She read books. Lots of them. Escapism, she had thought. Entertainment. A way to numb the boredom every day. But maybe these movies and books were oddly educational. How many times had she shouted at the plucky heroine – the oh-so-guileless, witch-skinny, raven-haired beauty – not to go into that damned house?

Too many. So now, when it had been her turn . . . uh-uh, no way. Charlaine Swain was not about to make that mistake.

She had stood in front of Freddy's back door staring at that hide-a-key. She couldn't go inside per her movie and book training, but she couldn't just leave it alone either. Something was wrong. A man was in trouble. You can't just walk away from that.

So she came up with an idea.

It was simple really. She took the key out of the rock. It was in her pocket now. She left the hide-a-key in plain view, not because she wanted the Asian guy to see it, but because that would be her excuse for calling the police.

The moment the Asian guy entered Freddy's house, she dialed 911. 'Someone is in the neighbor's house,' she told them. The clincher: The hide-a-key was strewn on the walkway.

Now the police were here.

One cruiser had made the turn onto her block. The siren was silent. The car was not speeding bat-out-of-hell style, just moving at a clip solidly above the speed limit. Charlaine risked a look back at Freddy's house.

The Asian man was watching her.

17

Grace stared at the headline. 'He was murdered?'

Cora nodded.

'How?'

'Bob Dodd was shot in the head in front of his wife. Gangland style, they called it, whatever that means.'

'They catch who did it?'

'Nope.'

'When?'

'When was he murdered?'

'Yeah, when?'

'Four days after Jack called him.'

Cora moved back toward the computer. Grace considered the date.

'It couldn't have been Jack.'

'Uh huh.'

'It would be impossible. Jack hasn't traveled out of the state in more than a month.'

'You say so.'

'What's that supposed to mean?'

'Nothing, Grace. I'm on your side, okay? I don't think Jack killed anybody either, but c'mon, let's get a grip here.'

'Meaning?'

'Meaning stop with the "hasn't traveled out of state" nonsense. New Hampshire is hardly California. You can drive up in four hours. You can fly up in one.'

Grace rubbed her eyes.

'Something else,' Cora went on. 'I know why he's listed as Bob, not Robert.'

'Why?'

'He's a reporter. That's his byline. Bob Dodd. Google listed one hundred and twenty-six hits on his name over the past three years for the *New Hampshire Post*. The obituary called him – where's the line? – "a hard-nosed investigative reporter, famous for his controversial exposés"– like the New Hampshire mob rubbed him out to keep him quiet.'

'And you don't think that's the case?'

'Who knows? But skimming through his articles, I'd say Bob Dodd was more like an "On Your Side" reporter, you know – he finds dishwasher repairmen scamming old ladies, wedding photographers who bail out with the deposit, that sorta thing.'

'He could have pissed someone off.'

Cora's tone was flat. 'Yup, could have. And, what, you think it's a coincidence – Jack calling the guy before he died?'

'No, there's no coincidence here.' Grace tried to process what she was hearing. 'Hold up.'

'What?'

'That photograph. There were five people in it. Two women, three men. This is a long shot . . .'

Cora was already typing. 'But maybe Bob Dodd is one of them?'

'There are image search engines, right?'

'Already there.'

Her fingers flew, her cursor pointed, her mouse slid. There were two pages, a total of twelve picture hits for Bob Dodd. The first page featured a hunter with the same name living out in Wisconsin. On the second page – the eleventh hit – they found a table photograph taken at a charity function in Bristol, New Hampshire.

Bob Dodd, a reporter for the *New Hampshire Post*, was the first face on the left.

They didn't need to study it closely. Bob Dodd was African-American. Everyone in the mystery photograph was white.

Grace frowned. 'There still has to be a connection.'

'Let me see if I can dig up a bio on him. Maybe they went to college together or something.'

There was a gentle rapping at the front door. Grace and Cora looked at each other. 'Late,' Cora said.

The knocking came again, still soft. There was a doorbell. Whoever was there had chosen not to use it. Must know she had kids. Grace rose and Cora followed. At the door she flicked on the outside light and peered out the window on the side of the door. She should have been more surprised, but Grace guessed that maybe she was beyond that.

'Who's that?' Cora asked.

'The man who changed my life,' Grace said softly.

She opened the door. Jimmy X stood on the stoop looking down.

Wu had to smile.

That woman. As soon as he saw those siren lights, he put it together. Her ingenuity was both admirable and grating.

No time for that.

What to do . . . ?

Jack Lawson was tied up in the trunk. Wu realized now that he should have fled the moment he saw that hide-a-key. Another mistake. How many more could he afford?

Minimize the damage. That was the key here. There was no way to prevent it all – the damage, that is. He would be hurt here. It would cost him. His fingerprints were in the house. The woman next door had probably already given the police a description. Sykes, alive or dead, would be found. There was nothing he could do about that either.

Conclusion: If he was caught, he would go to jail for a very long time.

The police cruiser pulled into the driveway.

Wu snapped into survival mode. He hurried downstairs. Through the window he saw the cruiser glide to a stop. It was dark out now, but the street was well lit. A tall black man in full uniform came out. He put on his police cap. His gun remained in his holster.

That was good.

The black police officer was barely on the walk when Wu opened the front door and smiled widely. 'Something I can do for you, Officer?'

He did not draw his weapon. Wu had counted on that. This was a family neighborhood in the great American expanse known as the suburbs. A Ho-Ho-Kus police officer probably responds to several hundred possible burglaries during his career. Most, if not all, were false alarms.

'We got a call about a possible break-in,' the officer said.

Wu frowned, feigning confusion. He took a step outside but kept his distance. Not yet, he thought. Be nonthreatening. Wu's moves were intentionally laconic, setting a slow pace. 'Wait, I know. I forgot my key. Someone probably saw me going in through the back.'

'You live here, Mr . . . ?'

'Chang,' Wu said. 'Yes, I do. Oh, but it's not my house, if that's what you mean. It belongs to my partner, Frederick Sykes.'

Now Wu risked another step.

'I see,' the officer said. 'And Mr. Sykes is . . . ?'

'Upstairs.'

'May I see him please?'

'Sure, come on in.' Wu turned his back to the officer and yelled up the stairs. 'Freddy? Freddy, throw something on. The police are here.'

Wu did not have to turn around. He knew the tall black man was moving up behind him. He was only five yards away now. Wu stepped back into the house. He held the door open and gave the officer what he thought was an effeminate smile. The officer – his name tag read Richardson – moved toward the door.

When he was only a yard away, Wu uncoiled.

Office Richardson had hesitated, perhaps sensing something, but it was too late. The blow, aimed for the center of his gut, was a palm strike. Richardson folded in half like a deck chair. Wu moved closer. He wanted to disable. He did not want to kill.

An injured policeman produces heat. A dead policeman raises the temperature tenfold.

The cop was doubled over. Wu hit him behind the legs. Richardson dropped to his knees. Wu used a pressure point technique. He dug the knuckles of his index fingers into both sides of Richardson's head, up and into the ear cavity under the cartilage, an area known as Triple Warmer 17. You need to get the right angle. Go full strength and you could kill someone. You needed precision here.

Richardson's eyes went white. Wu released the hold. Richardson dropped like a marionette with its strings cut.

The knockout would not last long. Wu took the handcuffs from the man's belt and cuffed his wrist to the stairwell. He ripped the radio from his shoulder.

Wu considered the woman next door. She'd be watching.

She would surely call the police again. He wondered about that, but there was no time. If he tried to attack, she would see him and lock the door. It would take too long. His best bet was to use time and surprise here. He hurried to the garage and got into Jack Lawson's minivan. He checked the cargo area in the back.

Jack Lawson was there.

Wu moved to the driver's seat now. He had a plan.

Charlaine had a bad feeling the moment she saw the policeman step out of the car.

For one thing, he was alone. She had assumed that there would be two of them, partners, again from TV – *Starsky and Hutch*, *Adam-12*, Briscoe and Green. She realized now that she had made a mistake. Her call had been too casual. She should have claimed to see something menacing, something frightening, so that they would have arrived more wary and prepared. Instead she had simply come across as a nosey neighbor, a dotty woman who had nothing better to do but call the cops for any little thing.

The policeman's body language too was all wrong. He sauntered toward the door, slack and casual, not a care in the world. Charlaine couldn't see the front door from where she was, only the driveway. When the officer disappeared from view, Charlaine felt her stomach drop.

She considered shouting out a warning. The problem was – and this might sound strange – the new Pella windows they had installed last year. They opened vertically, with a hand crank. By the time she slid open both locks and cranked the handle, well, the officer would already be out of sight. And really, what could she yell? What kind of warning? What in the end did she really know?

So she waited.

Mike was in the house. He was downstairs in the den, watching the Yankees on the YES Network. The divided night. They never watched TV together anymore. The way he flipped the remote was maddening. They liked different shows. But really, she didn't think that was it. She could watch anything. Still Mike took the den; she had the bedroom. They both watched alone, in the dark. Again she didn't know when that had started. The children weren't home tonight – Mike's brother had taken them to the movies – but when they were, they stayed in their own rooms. Charlaine tried to limit the Web surf time, but it was impossible. In her youth, friends talked on the phone for hours. Now they instant-messaged and lord-knew-what over the Internet.

This was what her family became – four separate entities in the dark, interacting with one another only when necessary.

She saw the light go on in the Sykes garage. Through the window, the one covered with flimsy lace, Charlaine could see a shadow. Movement. In the garage. Why? There would be no need for the police officer to be in there. She reached for the phone and dialed 911, even as she began to head for the stairs.

'I called you a little while ago,' she told the 911 operator.

'Yes?'

'About a break-in at my neighbor's house.'

'An officer is responding.'

'Yeah, I know that. I saw him pull up.'

Silence. She felt like a dope.

'I think something might have happened.'

'What did you see?'

'I think he may have been attacked. Your officer. Please send someone quickly.'

She hung up. The more she'd explain, the stupider it would sound.

The familiar churning noise started up. Charlaine knew what it was. Freddy's electric garage door. The man had done something to the cop. He was going to escape.

And that was when Charlaine decided to do something truly stupid.

She thought back to those wicked-witch-thin heroines, the ones with the mind-scooped stupidity, and wondered if any of them, even the most brain dead, had ever done something so colossally stupid. She doubted it. She knew that when she looked back on the choice she was about to make – assuming she survived it – she would laugh and maybe, just maybe, have a little more respect for the protagonists who enter dark homes in just their bra and panties.

Here was the thing: The Asian guy was about to escape. He had hurt Freddy. He had hurt a cop; she was sure of it. By the time the cops responded, he would be gone. They wouldn't find him. It would be too late.

And if he got away, then what?

He had seen her. She knew that. At the window. He had probably already figured out that she was the one who called the police. Freddy could be dead. So too the cop. Who was the only witness left?

Charlaine.

He would come back for her, wouldn't he? And even if he didn't, even he decided to let her be, well, at best, she would live in fear. She'd be jumpy in the night. She'd look for him in crowds during the days. Maybe he would simply want revenge. Maybe he would go after Mike or the kids . . .

She could not let that happen. She had to stop him now. How?

Wanting to prevent his escape was all fine and good, but let's stay real here. What could she do? They didn't own a gun. She couldn't just run outside and jump on his back and try to claw his eyes. No, she had to be cleverer than that.

She had to follow him.

On the surface it sounded ridiculous, but add it up. If he got away, the result would be fear. Pure, unadulterated, probably unending terror until he was captured, which might be never. Charlaine had seen the man's face. She had seen his eyes. She couldn't live with that.

Following him – running a tail, as they say on TV – made sense, when you considered the alternatives. She would follow him in her car. She would keep her distance. She would have the cell phone. She would be able to tell the police where he was. The plan did not involve following him long, just until the police could take over. Right now, if she didn't act, she knew what would happen: The police would arrive; the Asian man would be gone.

There was no alternative.

The more she thought about it, the less nutsy it sounded. She'd be in a moving car. She'd stay comfortably behind him. She'd be on her cell phone with a 911 operator.

Wasn't that safer than letting him go?

She ran downstairs.

'Charlaine?'

It was Mike. He stood there, in the kitchen, standing over the sink eating peanut-butter crackers. She stopped for a second. His eyes probed her face in a way only he could, in a way only he ever had. She was taken back to her days at Vanderbilt, when they first fell in love. The way he looked at her then, the way he looked at her now. He was skinnier back then and so handsome. But the look, the eyes, they were the same.

'What's wrong?' he asked.

'I need' – she stopped, caught her breath – 'I need to go somewhere.'

His eyes. Probing. She remembered the first time she ever saw him, that sunny day at Centennial Park in Nashville. How far had they come? Mike still saw. He still saw her in a way that no one else ever had. For a moment Charlaine could not move. She thought that she might cry. Mike dropped the crackers into the sink and started toward her.

'I'll drive,' Mike said.

18

Grace and the famous rocker known as Jimmy X were alone in the den-cum-playroom. Max's Game Boy was lying on its back. The battery case had broken, so now the two double As were held in place by Scotch tape. The game cartridge, lying next to it as if it'd been spit out, was called Super Mario Five, which, according to Grace's less than sophisticated eye, appeared to be exactly the same as Super Mario One through Four.

Cora had left them alone and returned to her role as cybersleuth. Jimmy had still not spoken. He sat with his forearms against his thighs, his head hanging, reminding Grace of the first time she'd seen him, in her hospital room not long after she regained consciousness.

He wanted her to talk first. She could see that. But she had nothing to say to him.

'I'm sorry to stop by so late,' he said.

'I thought you had a gig tonight.'

'Already over.'

'Early,' she said.

'The concerts usually end by nine. It's how the promoters like it.'

'How did you know where I lived?'

Jimmy shrugged. 'I guess I've always known.'

'What's that supposed to mean?'

He didn't answer and she didn't push it. For several seconds the room was dead silent.

'I'm not sure how to begin,' Jimmy said. Then, after a brief pause, he added, 'You still limp.'

'Good opening,' she said.

He tried to smile.

'Yes, I limp.'

'From . . . ?'

'Yes.'

'I'm sorry.'

'I got off easy.'

The shadow crossed his face. His head, the one he'd finally worked up the nerve to lift, dropped back down as if it had learned its lesson.

Jimmy still had the cheekbones. The famed blond locks were gone, from either genetics or a razor's edge, she couldn't tell which. He was older, of course. His youth was over and she wondered if that was true for her too.

'I lost everything that night,' he began. Then he stopped and shook his head. 'That didn't come out right. I'm not here for pity.'

She said nothing.

'Do you remember when I came to see you at the hospital?'

She nodded.

'I'd read every newspaper story. Every magazine story. I watched all the news reports. I can tell you about every kid that died that night. Every one of them. I know their faces. I close my eyes, I still see them.'

'Jimmy?'

He looked up again.

'You shouldn't be telling me this. Those kids had families.'

'I know that.'

'I'm not the one to give you absolution.'

'You think that's what I came here for?'

Grace did not reply.

'It's just . . .' He shook his head. 'I don't know why I came, okay? I saw you tonight. At the church. And I could see you knew who I was.' He tilted his head. 'How did you find me anyway?'

'I didn't.'

'The man you were with?'

'Carl Vespa.'

'Oh Christ.' He closed his eyes. 'Father of Ryan.'

'Yes.'

'He brought you?'

'Yes.'

'What does he want?'

Grace thought about that. 'I don't think he knows.'

Now it was Jimmy's turn to stay silent.

'He thinks he wants an apology.'

'Thinks?'

'What he really wants is his son back.'

The air felt heavy. She shifted in her chair. Jimmy's face had no color.

'I tried, you know. To apologize, I mean. He's right about that. I owe them that. At the very least. And I'm not talking about that stupid photo op with you at the hospital. My manager wanted that. I was so stoned I just went along. I could barely stand.' He stared at her. He had those same intense eyes that had made him an instant MTV darling. 'Do you remember Tommy Garrison?'

She did. He had died in the stampede. His parents were Ed and Selma.

'His picture touched me. I mean, they all did, you know. These lives, they were all just starting out . . .' He stopped again, took a deep breath, tried again. 'But Tommy, he looked like my kid brother. I couldn't get him out of my head. So I went to his house. I wanted to apologize to his parents . . .' He stopped.

'What happened?'

'I got there. We sat at their kitchen table. I remember I put my elbows on it and the whole thing teetered. They had this linoleum floor, half coming up. The wallpaper, this awful yellow flowered stuff, was peeling off the walls. Tommy was their only child. I looked at their lives, at their empty faces . . . I couldn't bear it.'

She said nothing.

'That was when I ran.'

'Jimmy?'

He looked at her.

'Where have you been?'

'Lot of places.'

'Why?'

'Why what?'

'Why did you just give it all up?'

He shrugged. 'There wasn't all that much, really. The music business, well, I won't go into it, but let's just say I hadn't received much money yet. I was new. It takes a while to get serious money. I didn't care. I just wanted out.'

'So where do you go?'

'I started in Alaska. Worked gutting fish, if you can believe that. Did that for about a year. Then I started traveling, played with a couple of small bar bands. In Seattle I found a group of old hippies. They used to do IDs for members of the Weather Underground, that kinda thing. They got me new papers. The closest I came back here, I played with a cover band in an Atlantic City casino for a while. At the Tropicana. I dyed my hair. I stuck to the drums. Nobody recognized me, or if they did, they didn't much care.'

'Were you happy?'

'You want the truth? No. I wanted to come back. I wanted to make amends and move on. But the longer I was gone, the harder it was, the more I longed for it. The whole thing was a vicious circle. And then I met Madison.'

'The lead singer of Rapture?'

'Yeah. Madison. Can you believe that name? It's huge now. You remember that movie *Splash*, the one with Tom Hanks and what's-her-name?'

'Daryl Hannah,' Grace said automatically.

'Right, the blond mermaid. Remember that scene where Tom Hanks is trying to come up with a name for her and he says all kinds of stuff like Jennifer or Stephanie and they're walking past Madison Avenue and he just mentions the street name and she wants it to be her name and that's a big laugh in the movie, right, a woman named Madison. Now it's a top-ten name.'

Grace let it go.

'Anyway, she's from a farm town in Minnesota. She ran away to the Big Apple when she was fifteen, ended up strung out and homeless in Atlantic City. She landed at a homeless shelter for runaway teens. She found Jesus, you know the deal, trading one addiction for another, and started singing. She has a voice like a Janis Joplin angel.'

'Does she know who you are?'

'No. You know how Shania has Mutt Lange in the background? That's what I wanted. I like working with her. I like the music, but I wanted to stay out of the spotlight. At least that's what I tell myself. Madison is painfully shy. She won't perform unless I'm onstage with her. She'll get over that, but for now I figured drums are a pretty good disguise.'

He shrugged, tried a smile. There was still a hint of the old knock-'em-back charisma. 'Guess I was wrong about that.'

They were silent for a moment.

'I still don't understand,' Grace said.

He looked at her.

'I said before I'm not the one to give you absolution. I meant that. But the truth is, you didn't fire a gun that night.'

Jimmy stayed still.

'The Who. When they had that stampede in Cincinnati, they got over it. And the Stones, when that Hell's Angel killed a guy at their concert. They're still playing. I can see wanting out for a little while, a year or two . . .'

Jimmy looked to the right. 'I should leave.'

He stood.

'Going to disappear again?' she asked.

He hesitated and then reached into his pocket. He pulled out a card and handed it to her. There were ten digits on it and nothing more. 'I don't have a home address or anything, just this mobile phone.'

He turned and started for the door. Grace did not follow. Under normal circumstances, she might have pushed him, but in the end, his visit was an aside, a not very important one in the scheme of things. Her past had a curious pull, that was all. Especially now.

'Take care of yourself, Grace.'

'You too, Jimmy.'

She sat in the den, feeling the exhaustion begin to weigh on her shoulders, and wondered where Jack was right now.

Mike did indeed drive. The Asian man had nearly a minute head start, but what was good about their twisty development of cul-de-sacs, tract houses, nicely wooded lots – this wondrous serpentine sprawl of suburbia – was that there was only one true entrance and exit road.

In this stretch of Ho-Ho-Kus, all roads led to Hollywood Avenue.

Charlaine filled Mike in as quickly as possible. She told him most of it, about how she'd looked out the window and spotted the man and grown suspicious. Mike listened without interrupting. There were holes the size of a heartache in her story. She left out why she had been looking out the window in the first place, for example. Mike must have seen the holes, but right now he was letting it go.

Charlaine studied his profile and traveled back to the first time they met. She had been a freshman at Vanderbilt University. There was a park in Nashville, not far from campus, with a replica of the Parthenon, the one in

Athens. Originally built in 1897 for the Centennial Expo, the structure was thought to be the most realistic replica of the famed site atop the Acropolis anywhere in the world. If you wanted to know what the actual Parthenon looked like in its heyday, well, people would travel to Nashville, Tennessee.

She was sitting there on a warm fall day, just eighteen years old, staring at the edifice, imagining what it must have been like in Ancient Greece, when a voice said, 'It doesn't work, does it?'

She turned. Mike had his hands in his pocket. He looked so damned handsome. 'Excuse me?'

He took a step closer, a half smile on his lips, moving with a confidence that drew her. Mike gestured with his head toward the enormous structure. 'It's an exact replica, right? You look at it, and this is what they saw, great philosophers like Plato and Socrates, and all I can think is' – he stopped, shrugged – 'is that all there is?'

She smiled at him. She saw his eyes widen and knew that the smile had landed hard. 'It leaves nothing to the imagination,' she said.

Mike tilted his head. 'What do you mean?'

'You see the ruins of the real Parthenon and you try to imagine what it would have looked like. But the reality, which this is, can never live up to what your mind conjures up.'

Mike nodded slowly, considering.

'You don't agree?' she asked.

'I had another theory,' Mike said.

'I'd like to hear it.'

He moved closer and bent down on his haunches. 'There are no ghosts.'

Now she did the head tilt.

'You need the history. You need the people in their sandals walking through it. You need the years, the blood, the deaths, the sweat from, what, four hundred years B.C.

146

Socrates never prayed in there. Plato didn't argue by its door. Replicas never have the ghosts. They're bodies without souls.'

The young Charlaine smiled again. 'You use this line on all the girls?'

'It's new, actually. I'm trying it out. Any good?'

She lifted her hand, palm down, and turned it back and forth. 'Eh.'

Charlaine had been with no other man since that day. For years they returned to the fake Parthenon on their anniversary. This had been the first year they hadn't gone back.

'There he is,' Mike said.

The Ford Windstar was traveling west on Hollywood Avenue toward Route 17. Charlaine was back on the phone with a 911 operator. The operator was finally taking her seriously.

'We lost radio contact with our officer at the scene,' she said.

'He's heading onto Route 17 south at the Hollywood Avenue entrance,' Charlaine said. 'He's driving a Ford Windstar.'

'License plate?'

'I can't see it.'

'We have officers responding to both scenes. You can drop your pursuit now.'

She lowered the phone. 'Mike?'

'It's okay,' he said.

She sat back and thought about her own house, about ghosts, about bodies without souls.

Eric Wu was not easily surprised.

Seeing the woman from the house and this man he assumed was her husband following him – that definitely registered as something he would not have predicted. He wondered how to handle it.

The woman.

She had set him up. She was following him. She had called the police. They had sent an officer. He knew then that she would call again.

What Wu had counted on, however, was putting enough distance between himself and the Sykes household before the police responded to her call. When it comes to tracking down vehicles the police are far from omnipotent. Think about the Washington sniper a few years back. They had hundreds of officers. They had roadblocks. For an embarrassingly long time they couldn't locate two amateurs.

If Wu could get enough miles ahead, he would be safe.

But now there was a problem.

That woman again.

That woman and her husband were following him. They would be able to tell the police where he was going, what road he was on, what direction he was heading. He would not be able to put the distance between him and the authorities.

Conclusion: Wu had to stop them.

He spotted the sign for the Paramus Park Mall and took the jug-handle back over the highway. The woman and her husband followed. It was late at night. The stores were closed. The lot was empty. Wu pulled into it. The woman and her husband kept their distance.

That was okay.

Because it was time to call their bluff.

Wu had a gun, a Walther PPK. He didn't like using it. Not that he was squeamish. Wu simply preferred his hands. He was decent with a gun; he was expert with his hands. He had perfect control with them. They were a part of him. With a gun you are forced to trust the mechanics, an outside source. Wu did not like that.

But he understood the need.

He stopped the car. He made sure the gun was loaded.

His car door was unlocked. He pulled the handle, stepped out of the vehicle, and aimed his weapon.

Mike said, 'What the hell is he doing?'

Charlaine watched the Ford Windstar enter the mall lot. There were no other cars. The lot was well lit, bathed in a shopping-center fluorescent glow. She could see Sears up ahead, the Office Depot, Sports Authority.

The Ford Windstar drifted to a stop.

'Keep back,' she said.

'We're in a locked car,' Mike said. 'What can he do?'

The Asian man moved with fluidity and grace, and yet there was also deliberation, as if each movement had been carefully planned in advanced. It was a strange combination, the way he moved, almost inhuman. But right now the man stood next to his car, his entire body still. His arm swept forward, only the arm, the rest of him so undisturbed by the motion that you might think it was an optical illusion.

And then their windshield exploded.

The noise was sudden and deafening. Charlaine screamed. Something splashed on her face, something wet and syrupy. There was a coppery smell in the air now. Instinctively Charlaine ducked. The glass from the windshield rained down on her head. Something slumped against her, pushing her down.

It was Mike.

She screamed again. The scream mixed with the sound of another bullet being fired. She had to move, had to get out, had to get them out of here. Mike was not moving. She shoved him off her and risked raising her head.

Another shot whistled past her.

She had no idea where it landed. Her head was back down. There was a screaming in her ears. A few seconds passed. Charlaine finally risked a glance.

The man was walking toward her.

What now?

Escape. Flee. That was the only thought that came through.

How?

She shifted the car into reverse. Mike's foot was still on the brake. She dropped low. Her hand stretched out and took hold of his slack ankle. She slid his foot off the brake. Still wedged into the foot area Charlaine managed to jam her palm on the accelerator. She pushed down with everything she had. The car jerked back. She could not move. She had no idea where she was going.

But they were moving.

She kept her palm pressed down to the floor. The car jolted over something, a curb maybe. The bounce banged her head against the steering column. Using her shoulder blades, she tried to keep the wheel steady. Her left hand still pressed down on the accelerator. They hit another bump. She held on. The road was smoother now. But just for a moment. Charlaine heard the honking of horns, the screech of tires and brakes, and the awful whir of cars spinning out of control.

There was an impact, a terrible jarring, and then, a few seconds later, darkness.

19

The color in Officer Daley's face had ebbed away.

Perlmutter sat up. 'What is it?'

Daley stared at the sheet of paper in his hand as if he feared it might flee. 'Something doesn't make sense here, Cap.'

When Captain Perlmutter had started working as a cop, he hated the night shift. The quiet and solitude got to him. He had grown up in a big family, one of seven kids, and he liked that life. He and his wife Marion planned on having a big family. He had the whole thing figured out – the barbecues, the weekends coaching one kid or the other, the school conferences, the family movies on Friday night, the summer nights on the front porch – the life he'd experienced growing up in Brooklyn, but with a suburban, bigger-house twist.

His grandmother used to spew Yiddish quotes all the time. Stu Perlmutter's personal favorite had been this: 'Man plans and God laughs.' Marion, the only woman he had ever loved, died of a sudden embolism when she was thirty-one. She'd been in the kitchen, making Sammy – that was their son, their only child – a sandwich when the embolism hit. She was dead before she landed on the linoleum.

Perlmutter's life pretty much ended that day. He did what he could to raise Sammy, but the truth was, his heart was never really in it. He loved the boy and enjoyed his job, but he had lived for Marion. This precinct, his work, had become his solace. Home, being with Sammy, reminded him of Marion and all they'd never have. Here, alone, he could almost forget.

All of that was a long time ago. Sammy was in college now. He had turned into a good man, despite his father's inattentiveness. There was something to be said for that, but Perlmutter did not know what.

Perlmutter signaled for Daley to sit down. 'So what's up?'

'That woman. Grace Lawson.'

'Ah,' Perlmutter said.

'Ah?'

'I was just thinking about her too.'

'Something about her case bothering you, Captain?'

'Yep.'

'I thought it was just me.'

Perlmutter tipped his chair back. 'Do you know who she is?'

'Ms. Lawson?'

'Yup.'

'She's an artist.'

'More than that. You notice the limp?'

'Yes.'

'Her married name is Grace Lawson. But once upon a time, her name – her maiden name, I guess – was Grace Sharpe.'

Daley looked at him blankly.

'You ever hear of the Boston Massacre?'

'Wait, you mean that rock concert riot?'

'More a stampede, but yeah. Lot of people died.'

'She was there?'

Perlmutter nodded. 'Badly injured too. In a coma for a while. Press gave her the full fifteen minutes and then some.'

'How long ago was that?'

'What, fifteen, sixteen years ago maybe.'

'But you remember?'

'It was big news. And I was a big fan of the Jimmy X Band.'

Daley looked surprised. 'You?'

'Hey, I wasn't always an old fart.'

'Heard their CD. It was pretty damn good. Radio still plays 'Pale Ink' all the time.'

'One of the best songs ever.'

Marion had liked the Jimmy X Band. Perlmutter remembered her constantly blasting 'Pale Ink' on an old Walkman, her eyes closed, her lips moving as she silently sang along. He blinked the image away.

'So what happened to them?'

'The massacre destroyed the band. They broke up. Jimmy X – I don't remember his real name anymore – was the front man and wrote all the songs. He just up and quit.' Perlmutter pointed to the piece of paper in Daley's hand. 'So what's that?'

'That's what I wanted to talk to you about.'

'Something to do with the Lawson case?'

'I don't know.' Then: 'Yeah, maybe.'

Perlmutter put his hands behind his head. 'Start talking.'

'DiBartola got a call early tonight,' Daley said. 'Another missing husband case.'

'Similarities to Lawson?'

'No. I mean, not at first. This guy wasn't even her husband anymore. An ex. And he isn't exactly squeaky clean.'

'He's got a record?'

'Did time for assault.'

'Name?'

'Rocky Conwell.'

'Rocky? For real?'

'Yep, that's what it says on his birth certificate.'

'Parents.' Perlmutter made a face. 'Wait, why does that name ring a bell?'

'He played a little pro ball.'

Perlmutter searched the memory banks, shrugged. 'So what's the deal?'

'Okay, like I said, this case looks even more cut-and-dry than Lawson. Ex-husband who was supposed to take his wife out shopping this morning. I mean, it's nothing. It's less than nothing. But DiBartola sees the wife – her name is Lorraine – well, she's a royal babe. So you know DiBartola.'

'A pig,' Permutter said with a nod. 'Ranked in the top ten by both the AP and UPI.'

'Right, so he figures, what the hell, humor her, right? She's separated, so you never know. Maybe something would swing his way.'

'Very professional.' Perlmutter frowned. 'Go on.'

'This is where it gets weird.' Daley licked his lips. 'DiBartola, he does the simple thing. He runs the E-ZPass.'

'Like you.'

'*Exactly* like me.'

'What do you mean?'

'He gets a hit.' Daley took another step into the room. 'Rocky Conwell crossed the tollbooth off Exit 16 on the New York Thruway. At exactly ten-twenty-six last night.'

Perlmutter looked at him.

'Yeah, I know. Exact same time and place as Jack Lawson.'

Perlmutter scanned the report. 'You're sure about this? DiBartola didn't accidentally run the same number we did or something?'

'Checked it twice. There's no mistake. Conwell and Lawson crossed the toll at the exact same time. They had to be together.'

Perlmutter mulled it over and shook his head. 'No.'

Daley looked confused. 'You think it's a coincidence?'

'Two separate cars, crossing the toll at the same time? Not likely.'

'So how do you figure it?'

'I'm not sure,' Perlmutter said. 'Let's say they, I don't know, ran away together. Or Conwell kidnapped Lawson.

154

Or hell, Lawson kidnapped Conwell. Whatever. They'd be in the same car. There would be only one E-ZPass hit, not two.'

'Right, okay.'

'But they were in two separate cars. That's what's throwing me. Both men in separate cars cross the toll at the same time. And now both men are missing.'

'Except Lawson called his wife,' Daley added. 'He needed space, remember?'

They both thought about it.

Daley said, 'You want me to call Ms. Lawson? See if she knows this Conwell guy?'

Perlmutter plucked on his bottom lip and thought about it. 'Not yet. Besides it's late. She's got kids.'

'So what should we do?'

'A little more investigating. Let's talk to Rocky Conwell's ex-wife first. See if we dig up a connection between Conwell and Lawson. Put his car out there, see if we get a hit.'

The phone rang. Daley was working the switchboard as well. He picked it up, listened, and then turned to Perlmutter.

'Who was that?'

'Phil over at the Ho-Ho-Kus station.'

'Something wrong?'

'They think an officer might be down. They want our help.'

20

Beatrice Smith was a fifty-three-year-old widow.

Eric Wu was back in the Ford Windstar. He took Ridgewood Avenue to the Garden State Parkway north. He headed east on Interstate 287 toward the Tappan Zee Bridge. He exited at Armonk in New York. He was on side roads now. He knew exactly where he was going. He had made mistakes, yes, but the basics were still with him.

One of those basics: Have a backup residence lined up.

Beatrice Smith's husband had been a popular cardiologist, even serving a term as town mayor. They'd had lots of friends, but they were all 'couple' friends. When Maury – that was her husband's name – died of a sudden heart attack, the friends stayed around for a month or two and then faded away. Her only child, a son, and a doctor like his father, lived in San Diego with his wife and three children. She kept the house, the same house she had shared with Maury, but it was big and lonely. She was thinking about selling it and moving into Manhattan, but the prices were just too steep right now. And she was afraid. Armonk was all she knew. Would it be jumping from the frying pan into the fire?

She had confided all of this online to the fictional Kurt McFaddon, a widower from Philadelphia who was considering relocating to New York City. Wu pulled onto her street and slowed. The surroundings were quiet and woodsy and very private. It was late. A fake delivery would not work at this hour. There would be no time or even need for subtlety. Wu would not be able to keep this host alive.

There could be nothing to connect Beatrice Smith to Freddy Sykes.

In short, Beatrice Smith could not be found. Not ever.

Wu parked the car, put on his gloves – no fingerprints this time – and approached the house.

21

At 5 A.M., Grace threw on a bathrobe – Jack's robe – and headed downstairs. She always wore Jack's clothes. He'd kindly request lingerie, but she preferred his pajama tops. 'Well?' she'd ask, modeling the top. 'Not bad,' he'd reply, 'but why not try wearing just the bottoms instead. Now *that* would be a look.' She shook her head at the memory and reached the computer room.

The first thing Grace did was check the e-mail address they were using to receive replies from their spam of the photograph. What she saw surprised her.

They were no replies.

Not one.

How could that be? It was conceivable, she guessed, that nobody recognized the women in the photograph. She'd been prepared for that possibility. But by now they had sent out hundreds of thousands of e-mails to people. Even with spam blocks and all that, *someone* should have responded with at the very least an expletive, some crack-pot with time on his hands, someone fed up with the over-flow of spam who'd need to vent.

Someone.

But she had not received even one reply.

What should she make of that?

The house was quiet. Emma and Max were still asleep. So too was Cora. Cora was snoring, stretched out on her back, her mouth open.

Switch gears, Grace thought.

She knew that Bob Dodd, the murdered reporter, was now her best, perhaps only, lead, and let's face it, it was a pretty flimsy one. She had no phone contact for him, no next of kin, not even a street address. Still, Dodd had been a reporter for a fairly major newspaper, the *New Hampshire Post*. She decided that was the best place to start.

Newspapers don't really close – at least, that was what Grace figured. Someone has to be manning the *Post* desk in case a big story broke. It also figured that the reporter stuck working at 5 A.M. might be bored and more apt to talk to her. So she picked up the phone.

Grace was not sure how to approach this. She considered various angles, pretending, for example, to be a reporter doing a story, asking for collegial assistance, but she wasn't sure she'd be able to talk the talk.

In the end she decided to try to keep as close to the truth as possible.

She pressed *67 to block the Caller ID. The newspaper had a toll-free line. Grace didn't use it. You can't block Caller ID from toll-free numbers. She had learned that somewhere and stockpiled it in the back brain closet, the same closet where she stored information about Daryl Hannah being in *Splash* and Esperanza Diaz being the wrestler dubbed Little Pocahontas, the same closet that helped make Grace, in Jack's words, 'Mistress of the Useless Factoid.'

The first two calls to the *New Hampshire Post* went nowhere. The guy at the news desk simply could not be bothered. He hadn't really known Bob Dodd and barely listened to her pitch. Grace waited twenty minutes and tried again. This time she got routed to Metro, where a woman who sounded very young informed Grace that she had just started at the paper, that this was her first job ever, that she didn't know Bob Dodd, but gee, wasn't it awful what happened to him?

Grace checked the e-mails again. Still nothing.

'Mommy!'

It was Max.

'Mommy, come quick!'

Grace hurried up the stairs.

'What is it, honey?'

Max sat in his bed and pointed to his foot. 'My toe is growing too fast.'

'Your toe?'

'Look.'

She moved next to him and sat down.

'See?'

'See what, honey?'

'My second toe,' he began. 'It's bigger than my big toe. It's growing too fast.'

Grace smiled. 'That's normal, honey.'

'Huh?'

'Lots of people have a second toe that's longer than their big one. Your daddy has that.'

'No way.'

'Yup, way. His second toe is longer than the big one on the end.'

That seemed to appease him. Grace felt another pang. 'You want to watch *The Wiggles*?' she asked him.

'That's a baby show.'

'Let's see what's on *Playhouse Disney*, okay?'

Rolie Polie Olie was on, and Max settled into the couch to watch. He liked to use the cushions as blankets, making a total mess of the place. Grace was beyond caring. She tried the *New Hampshire Post* again. This time she asked for features.

The man who answered had a voice like old tires on a gravel road. 'What's up?'

'Good morning,' Grace said, too cheerfully, smiling into the phone like a dimwit.

The man made a noise which, loosely translated, said: *Get on with it.*

'I'm trying to get some information on Bob Dodd.'

'Who is this?'

'I'd rather not say.'

'You're kidding, right? Look, sweetheart, I'm going to hang up now –'

'Wait a second. I can't go into details, but if it turns into a major scoop –'

'Major scoop? Did you just say major scoop?'

'Yes.'

The man started cackling. 'And what, you think I'm like Pavlov's dog or something. Say major scoop and I'll salivate.'

'I just need to know about Bob Dodd.'

'Why?'

'Because my husband is missing and I think it might have something to do with his murder.'

That made him pause. 'You're kidding me, right?'

'No,' Grace said. 'Look, I just need to find someone who knew Bob Dodd.'

The voice was softer now. 'I knew him.'

'Did you know him well?'

'Well enough. What do you want?'

'Do you know what he was working on?'

'Look, lady, do you have information on Bob's murder? Because if you do, forget the major scoop crap and tell the police.'

'Nothing like that.'

'Then what?'

'I was going through some old phone bills. My husband talked to Bob Dodd not long before he was murdered.'

'And your husband is?'

'I'm not going to tell you that. It's probably just a co-incidence.'

'But you said your husband is missing?'

'Yes.'

'And you're concerned enough to be following up on this old phone call?'

'I've got nothing else,' Grace said.

There was a pause. 'You're going to have to do better than that,' the man said.

'I don't think I can.'

Silence.

'Ah, what's the harm? I don't know anything. Bob didn't confide in me.'

'Who would he confide in?'

'You can try his wife.'

Grace almost slapped herself in the head. How could she not have thought of something so obvious? Man, she was in over her head here. 'Do you know how I can locate her?'

'Not sure. I only met her, what, once, maybe twice.'

'What's her name?'

'Jillian. That's with a J, I think.'

'Jillian Dodd?'

'I guess.'

She wrote it down.

'There's another person you might try. Bob's father, Robert Senior. He must be in his eighties, but I think they were pretty close.'

'Do you have an address for him?'

'Yeah, he's in some nursing home in Connecticut. We shipped Bob's stuff there.'

'Stuff?'

'Cleaned out his desk myself. Put the stuff in a cardboard box for him.'

Grace frowned. 'And you sent it to his father's nursing home?'

'Yup.'

'Why not to Jillian, the wife?'

There was a brief pause. 'Don't know actually. I think she freaked after the murder. She was there, you know. Hold on a second, let me find the number of the nursing home. You can ask yourself.'

*

Charlaine wanted to sit next to the hospital bed.

You always see that in movies and on TV – doting wives sitting bedside, holding the hand of their beloved – but in this room there was no chair made for that. The one chair in the room was too low to the ground, the sort of thing that opened up into a sleeper, and yes, that might come in handy later, but now, right now, Charlaine just wanted to sit and hold her husband's hand.

She stood instead. Every once in a while she sat on the bed's edge, but she feared that might disturb Mike. So she'd stand again. And maybe that was good. Maybe that felt a little like penance.

The door behind her opened. Her back was to it. She did not bother turning around. A man's voice, one she hadn't heard before, said, 'How are you feeling?'

'I'm fine.'

'You were lucky.'

She nodded. 'I feel like I won the lottery.'

Charlaine reached up and touched the bandage on her forehead. A few stitches and possible slight concussion. That was all she had suffered during the accident. Scrapes, bruises, a few stitches.

'How is your husband?'

She did not bother replying. The bullet had hit Mike in the neck. He still had not regained consciousness, though the doctors had informed her that they believed 'the worst was over,' whatever that meant.

'Mr. Sykes is going to live,' the man behind her said. 'Because of you. He owes you his life. A few more hours in that tub . . .'

The man – she assumed that he was yet another police officer – let his voice drift off. She finally turned and faced him. Yep, a cop. In uniform nonetheless. The patch on his arm said he was from the Kasselton Police Department.

'I already talked to the Ho-Ho-Kus detectives,' she said.

'I know that.'

'I really don't know any more, Officer . . . ?'

'Perlmutter,' he said. 'Captain Stuart Perlmutter.'

She turned back toward the bed. Mike had his shirt off. His belly rose and fell as if it were being inflated at a gas station. He was overweight, Mike, and the act of breathing, just breathing, seemed to put undue stress on him. He should have taken better care of his health. She should have insisted on it.

'Who's with your kids?' Perlmutter asked.

'Mike's brother and sister-in-law.'

'Anything I can get you?'

'No.'

Charlaine changed her grip on Mike's hand.

'I was going over your statement.'

She did not reply.

'Do you mind if I ask you a few follow-up questions?'

'I'm not sure I understand,' Charlaine said.

'Pardon?'

'I live in Ho-Ho-Kus. What does Kasselton have to do with it?'

'I'm just helping out.'

She nodded, though she had no idea why. 'I see.'

'According to your statement, you were looking out your bedroom window when you saw the hide-a-key on Mr. Sykes's back path. Is that correct?'

'Yes.'

'And that's why you called the police?'

'Yes.'

'Do you know Mr. Sykes?'

She shrugged, keeping her eyes on that rising and falling stomach. 'To say hello.'

'You mean like a neighbor?'

'Yes.'

'When was the last time you talked to him?'

'I didn't. I mean, I never really talked to him.'

'Just the neighborly hellos.'

She nodded.

'And the last time you did that?'

'Waved hello?'

'Yes.'

'I don't know. A week ago maybe.'

'I'm a little confused, Mrs. Swain, so maybe you can help me out here. You saw a hide-a-key on the path and just decided to call the police –'

'I also saw movement.'

'Pardon?'

'Movement. I saw something move in the house.'

'Like someone was inside?'

'Yes.'

'How did you know it wasn't Mr. Sykes?'

She turned around. 'I didn't. But I also saw the hide-a-key.'

'Lying there. In plain sight.'

'Yes.'

'I see. And you put two and two together?'

'Right.'

Perlmutter nodded as if suddenly understanding. 'And if Mr. Sykes had been the one to use the hide-a-key, he wouldn't have just tossed it onto the path. Was that your thinking?'

Charlaine said nothing.

'Because, see, that's what's weird to me, Mrs. Swain. This guy who broke into the house and assaulted Mr. Sykes. Why would he have left the hide-a-key out in plain sight like that? Wouldn't he have hidden it or taken it in-side with him?'

Silence.

'And there's something else. Mr. Sykes sustained his in-juries at least twenty-four hours before we found him. Do you think the hide-a-key was out on that path the whole time?'

'I wouldn't know.'

'No, I guess you wouldn't. It's not like you stare at his backyard or anything.'

She just looked at him.

'Why did you and your husband follow him, the guy who broke into the Sykes place, I mean?'

'I told the other officer –'

'You were trying to help out, so we wouldn't lose him.'

'I was also afraid.'

'Of what?'

'That he'd know I called the police.'

'Why would you worry about that?'

'I was watching from the window. When the police arrived. He turned and looked out and saw me.'

'And you thought, what, he'd go after you?'

'I don't know. I was scared, that's all.'

Perlmutter did that over-nod bit again. 'I guess that fits. I mean some of the pieces, well, you have to force them down, but that's normal. Most cases don't make perfect sense.'

She turned away from him again.

'You say he was driving a Ford Windstar.'

'That's right.'

'He pulled out of the garage in that vehicle, right?'

'Yes.'

'Did you see the license plate?'

'No.'

'Hmm. Why do you think he did that?'

'Did what?'

'Parked in the garage.'

'I have no idea. Maybe so no one would see his car.'

'Yeah, okay, that adds up.'

Charlaine took her husband's hand again. She remembered the last time they'd held hands. Two months ago, when they went to see a romantic comedy with Meg Ryan. Strangely enough Mike was a sucker for 'chick flicks.' His eyes welled up during bad romance movies. In real life, she could only remember seeing him cry once, when his father died. But at movies Mike sat in the dark and you would see a little quake in the face and then, yes, the tears would start. That night he reached out and took her hand, and what Charlaine remembered most – what tormented her now – was being unmoved. Mike had tried to interlace their fingers, but she shifted hers just enough to block him. That was how little it meant to Charlaine, nothing really, this overweight man with the comb-over reaching out to her.

'Could you please leave now?' she asked Perlmutter.

'You know I can't.'

She closed her eyes.

'I know about your tax problem.'

She stayed still.

'In fact, you called H&R Block this morning about it, isn't that right? That's where Mr. Sykes worked.'

She didn't want to let go of the hand, but it felt as though Mike was pulling away.

'Mrs. Swain?'

'Not here,' Charlaine said to Perlmutter. She let the hand drop and stood. 'Not in front of my husband.'

22

Nursing home residents are always in and happy to have a visitor. Grace called the number and a perky woman answered.

'Starshine Assisted Living!'

'I'd like to know about visiting hours,' Grace said.

'We don't have them!' She spoke in exclamations.

'Excuse me?'

'No visiting hours. You can visit anytime, twenty-four-seven.'

'Oh. I'd like to visit Mr. Robert Dodd.'

'Bobby? Well, let me connect you to his room. Oh wait, it's eight. He'll be at exercise class. Bobby likes to keep in shape.'

'Is there a way I can make an appointment?'

'To visit?'

'Yes.'

'No need, just stop by.'

The drive would take her a little under two hours. It would be better than trying to explain over the phone, especially in light of the fact that she didn't have a clue what she wanted to ask him about. The elderly are better in person anyway.

'Do you think he'll be in this morning?'

'Oh sure. Bobby stopped driving two years ago. He'll be here.'

'Thank you.'

'My pleasure.'

At the breakfast table, Max dug his hand deep into the box of Cap'n Crunch. The sight – her child going for the toy – made her pause. It was all so normal. Children sense things. Grace knew that. But sometimes, well, sometimes children are wonderfully oblivious. Right now she was grateful for that.

'You already got the toy out,' she said.

Max stopped. 'I did?'

'So many boxes, so crummy a toy.'

'What?'

The truth was, she had done the same thing when she was a kid – digging to get the worthless prize. Come to think of it, with the same cereal. 'Never mind.'

She sliced up a banana and mixed it in with the cereal. Grace always tried to be sneaky here, gradually adding more banana and less of the Cap'n. For a while she added Cheerios – less sugar – but Max quickly caught on.

'Emma! Get up now!'

A groan. Her daughter was too young to start with the trouble-getting-out-of-bed bit. Grace hadn't pulled that until she was in high school. Okay, maybe middle school. But certainly, definitely, not when she was eight. She thought about her own parents, dead for so long now. Sometimes one of the kids did something that reminded Grace of her mother or father. Emma pursed her lips so much like Grace's mom that Grace sometimes froze in place. Max's smile was like her dad's. You could see the genetic echo, and Grace never knew if it was a comfort or a painful reminder.

'Emma, now!'

A sound. Might have been a child getting out of bed.

Grace started making one lunch. Max liked to buy it at school and Grace was all for the ease of that. Making lunches in the morning was a pain in the ass. For a while Emma would buy the school lunch too, but something recently grossed her out, some indiscernible smell in the cafeteria that caused an aversion so strong Emma would gag. She ate outside, even in the cold, but the smell, she soon realized, was also in the food. Now she stayed in the cafeteria and brought a Batman lunchbox with her.

'Emma!'

'I'm here.'

Emma wore her standard gym-rat garb: maroon athletic shorts, blue high-top Converse all-stars, and a New Jersey Nets jersey. Total clash, which may have been the point. Emma wouldn't wear anything the least bit feminine. Putting on a dress usually required a negotiation of Middle East sensitivity, with often an equally violent result.

'What would you like for lunch?' Grace asked.

'Peanut butter and jelly.'

Grace just stared at her.

Emma played innocent. 'What?'

'You've been attending this school for how long now?'

'Huh?'

'Four years, right? One year of kindergarten. And now you're in third grade. That's four years.'

'So?'

'In all that time how many times have you asked me for peanut butter in school?'

'I don't know.'

'Maybe a hundred?'

Shrug.

'And how many times have I told you that your school doesn't allow peanut butter because some children might have an allergic reaction?'

'Oh yeah.'

'Oh yeah.' Grace checked the clock. She had a few Oscar Mayer 'Lunchables,' a rather disgustingly processed premade lunch, that she kept around for emergencies – i.e., no time or desire to fix a lunch. The kids, of course, loved them. She asked Emma softly if she'd like one – softly because if Max heard, that would be the end of buying lunch. Emma graciously accepted it and jammed it into the Batman lunchbox.

They sat down to breakfast.

'Mom?'

It was Emma. 'Yep.'

'When you and Dad got married.' She stopped.

'What about it?'

Emma started again. 'When you and Dad got married – at the end, when the guy said now you may kiss the bride . . .'

'Right.'

'Well' – Emma cocked her head and closed one eye – 'did you have to?'

'Kiss him?'

'Yeah.'

'Have to? No, I guess not. I wanted to.'

'But do you have to?' Emma insisted. 'I mean, can't you just high-five instead?'

'High-five?'

'Instead of kiss. You know, turn to each other and high-five.' She demonstrated.

'I guess. If that's what you want.'

'That's what I want,' Emma said firmly.

Grace took them to the bus stop. This time she did not follow the bus to school. She stayed in place and bit down on her lower lip. The calm façade was slipping off again. Now that Emma and Max were gone, that would be okay.

When she got back to the house, Cora was awake and at the computer and groaning.

'Can I get you something?' Grace asked.

'An anesthesiologist,' Cora said. 'Straight preferred but not required.'

'I was thinking more like coffee.'

'Even better.' Cora's fingers danced across the keyboard. Her eyes narrowed. She frowned. 'Something's wrong here.'

'You mean with the e-mails off our spam, right?'

'We're not getting any replies.'

'I noticed that too.'

Cora sat back. Grace moved next to her and started biting a cuticle. After a few seconds, Cora leaned forward. 'Let me try something.' She brought up an e-mail, typed something in, sent it.

'What was that all about?'

'I just sent an e-mail to our spam address. I want to see if it arrives.'

They waited. No e-mail appeared.

'Hmm.' Cora leaned back. 'So either something is wrong with the mail system . . .'

'Or?'

'Or Gus is still ticked about that small wee-wee line.'

'How do we find out which?'

Cora kept staring at the computer. 'Who were you on the phone with before?'

'Bob Dodd Senior's nursing home. I'm going to pay him a visit this morning.'

'Good.' Cora's eyes stayed on the screen.

'What is it?'

'I want to check something out,' she said.

'What?'

'Nothing probably, just something with the phone bills.' Cora started typing again. 'I'll call you if I learn anything.'

Perlmutter left Charlaine Swain with the Bergen County sketch artist. He had forced the truth out of her, thereby unearthing a tawdry secret that would have been better left deep in the ground. Charlaine Swain had been right to keep it from him. It offered no help. The revelation was, at best, a sleazy and embarrassing distraction.

He sat with a doodle pad, wrote the word 'Windstar' and spent the next fifteen minutes circling it.

A Ford Windstar.

Kasselton was not a sleepy small town. They had thirty-eight cops on the payroll. They worked robberies. They checked on suspicious cars. They kept the school drug problems – suburban white-kid drugs – under control. They worked vandalism cases. They dealt with congestion in town, illegal parking, car accidents. They did their best to keep the urban decay of Paterson, a scant three miles from the border of Kasselton, at a safe distance. They answered too many false alarms emanating from the technological mating call of too many overpriced motion detectors.

Perlmutter had never fired his service revolver, except on a range. He had, in fact, never drawn his weapon in the line of duty. There had only been three deaths in the last three decades that fell under the possible heading of 'suspicious' and all three perpetrators were caught within hours. One was an ex-husband who got drunk and decided to profess his undying love by planning to kill the woman he purportedly adored before turning the shotgun on himself. Said ex-husband managed to get the first part right – two shotgun blasts to the ex's head – but like everything else in his pathetic life, he messed up the second part. He had only brought two shells. An hour later he was in custody. Suspicious Death Two was a teenage bully stabbed by a skinny, tormented elementary-school victim. The skinny kid served three years in juvie, where he learned the real meaning of being bullied and tormented. The final case was of a man dying of cancer who begged his wife of forty-eight years to end his suffering. She did. She got parole and Perlmutter suspected that it was worth it to her.

As for gunshots, well, there had been plenty in Kasselton but almost all were self-inflicted. Perlmutter wasn't much on politics. He wasn't sure of the relative merits of gun control, but he knew from personal experience that a gun bought for home protection was more likely – much, much, much more likely – to be used by the owner to commit suicide than to ward off a home invasion. In fact, in all his years in law enforcement, Perlmutter had never seen a case where the home gun had been used to shoot, stop, or scare away an intruder. Suicides by hand-guns, well, they were more plentiful than anyone wanted to let on.

Ford Windstar. He circled it again.

Now, after all these years, Perlmutter had a case in-volving attempted murder, bizarre abduction, unusually brutal assault – and, he suspected, much more. He started doodling again. He wrote the name *Jack Lawson* in the top left-hand corner. He wrote the name *Rocky Conwell* in the top right-hand corner. Both men, possibly missing, had crossed a toll plaza in a neighboring state at the same time. He drew a line from one name to the other.

Connection One.

Perlmutter wrote out Freddy Sykes's name, bottom left. The victim of a grievous assault. He wrote *Mike Swain* on the bottom right. Shot, attempted murder. The connection between these two men, Connection Two, was obvious. Swain's wife had seen the perpetrator of both acts, a stout Chinese guy she made sound like the Son of Odd Job from the old James Bond film.

But nothing really connected the four cases. Nothing connected the two disappearing men to the work of Odd Job's offspring. Except perhaps for one thing:

The Ford Windstar.

Jack Lawson had been driving a blue Ford Windstar when he disappeared. Mini Odd Job had been driving a blue Ford Windstar when he left the Sykes residence and shot Swain.

Granted this was a tenuous connection at best. Saying 'Ford Windstar' in this suburb was like saying 'implant' at a strip club. It wasn't much to go on, but when you add in the history of this town, the fact that stable fathers do not really just go missing, that this much activity never happens in a town like Kasselton . . . no, it wasn't a strong tie, but it wasn't far off for Perlmutter to draw a conclusion:

All of this was related.

Perlmutter had no idea how this was all related, and he really didn't want to think about it too much quite yet. Let the techies and lab guys do their jobs first. Let them scour the Sykes residence for fingerprints and hairs. Let the artist finish the sketch. Let Veronique Baltrus, their resident computer weenie and an honest-to-God knockout, sift through the Sykes computer. It was simply too early to make a guess.

'Captain?'

It was Daley.

'What's up?'

'We found Rocky Conwell's car.'

'Where?'

'You know the Park-n-Ride on Route 17?'

Perlmutter took off his reading glasses. 'The one down the street?'

Daley nodded. 'I know. It doesn't make sense. We know he left the state, right?'

'Who found it?'

'Pepe and Pashaian.'

'Tell them to secure the area,' he said, rising. 'We'll check the vehicle out ourselves.'

23

Grace threw on a Coldplay CD for the ride, hoping it'd distract her. It did and it didn't. On one level she understood exactly what was happening to her with no need for interpretation. But the truth, in a sense, was too stark. To face it straight on would paralyze. That was where the surrealism probably derived from – self-preservation, the need to protect and even filter what one saw. Surrealism gave her the strength to go on, to pursue the truth, to find her husband, as opposed to the eye of reality, stark and naked and alone, which made her want to crouch into a small ball or maybe scream until they took her away.

Her cell phone rang. She instinctively glanced at the display before hitting the hands-free. Again, no, not Jack. It was Cora. Grace picked up and said, 'Hey.'

'I won't classify the news as bad or good, so let me put it this way. Do you want the weird news first or the really weird news?'

'Weird.'

'I can't reach Gus of the small wee-wee. He won't answer his calls. I keep getting his voice mail.'

Coldplay started singing, appropriately enough, a haunting number entitled 'Shiver.' Grace kept both hands on the wheel, perfectly placed at ten and two o'clock. She stayed in the middle lane and drove exactly the speed limit. Cars flew by on both her right and left.

'And the really weird news?'

'Remember how we tried to see the calls from two nights ago? I mean, the ones Jack might have made?'

'Right.'

'Well, I called the cell phone company. I pretended I was you. I assumed you wouldn't mind.'

'Correct assumption.'

'Right. Anyway, it didn't matter. The only call Jack's made in the past three days was to your cell phone yesterday.'

'The call he made when I was at the police station.'

'Right.'

'So what's weird about that?'

'Nothing. The weird part was on your home phone.'

Silence. She stayed on the Merritt Parkway, her hands on the wheel at ten and two o'clock.

'What about it?'

'You know about the call to his sister's office?' Cora asked.

'Yeah. I found that one by hitting redial.'

'And his sister – what's her name again?'

'Sandra Koval.'

'Sandra Koval, right. She told you that she wasn't there. That they never talked.'

'Yes.'

'The phone call lasted nine minutes.'

A small shudder skipped through Grace. She forced her hands to stay at two and ten. 'Ergo she lied.'

'It would seem.'

'So what did Jack say to her?'

'And what did she say back?'

'And why did she lie about it?'

'Sorry to have to tell you,' Cora said.

'No, it's good.'

'How do you figure?'

'It's a lead. Before this, Sandra was a dead end. Now we know she's somehow involved.'

'What are you going to do about it?'

'I don't know,' Grace said. 'Confront her, I guess.'

They said good-bye and Grace hung up. She drove a

little farther, trying to run the scenarios through her head. 'Trouble' came on the CD player. She pulled into an Exxon station. New Jersey didn't have self-serve, so for a moment Grace just sat in her car, not realizing that she had to fill it up herself.

She bought a bottle of cold water at the station's mini-mart and dropped the change into a charity can. She wanted to think this through some more, this connection to Jack's sister, but there wasn't time for finesse here.

Grace remembered the number of the Burton and Crimstein law firm. She took out her phone and pressed in the digits. Two rings later she asked to be connected to Sandra Koval's line. She was surprised when Sandra herself said, 'Hello?'

'You lied to me.'

There was no reply. Grace walked back toward her car.

'The call lasted nine minutes. You talked to Jack.'

More silence.

'What's going on, Sandra?'

'I don't know.'

'Why did Jack call you?'

'I'm going to hang up now. Please don't try to contact me again.'

'Sandra?'

'You said he called you already.'

'Yes.'

'My advice is to wait until he calls again.'

'I don't want your advice, Sandra. I want to know what he said to you.'

'I think you should stop.'

'Stop what?'

'You're on a cell phone?'

'Yes.'

'Where are you?'

'I'm at gas station in Connecticut.'

'Why?'

'Sandra, I want you to listen to me.' There was a burst of static. Grace waited for it to pass. She finished filling the tank and grabbed her receipt. 'You're the last person to talk to my husband before he disappeared. You lied to me about it. You still won't tell me what he said to you. Why should I tell you anything?'

'Fair point, Grace. Now you listen to me. I'm going to leave you with one last thought before I hang up: Go home and take care of your children.'

The line went dead. Grace was back in the car now. She hit redial and asked to be connected to Sandra's office. Nobody answered. She tried again. Same thing. So now what? Try to show up in person again?

She pulled out of the gas station. Two miles later Grace saw a sign that said STARSHINE ASSISTED LIVING CENTER. Grace was not sure what she'd been expecting. The nursing home of her youth, she guessed, those one-level edifices of plain brick, the purest form of substance-over-style that, in a perverse way, reminded her of elementary schools. Life, alas, was cyclical. You start in one of those plain brick buildings, you end there. Turn, turn, turn.

But the Starshine Assisted Living Center was a three-story faux Victorian hotel. It had the turrets and the porches and the bright yellow of the painted ladies of old, all set against a ghastly aluminum siding. The grounds were manicured to the point where everything looked a tad too done, almost plastic. The place was aiming for cheery but it was trying too hard. The whole effect reminded Grace of Epcot Center at Disney World – a fun reproduction but you'd never mistake it for the real thing.

An old woman sat on a rocking chair on the front porch. She was reading the paper. She wished Grace a good morning and Grace did likewise. The lobby too tried to force up memories of a hotel from a bygone era. There were oil paintings in gaudy frames that looked like the kind of thing you'd buy at one of those Holiday Inn sales where everything was $19.99. It was obvious that they were reproductions of classics, even if you had never seen Renoir's *Luncheon of the Boating Party* or Hopper's *Nighthawks*.

The lobby was surprisingly busy. There were elderly people, of course, lots of them, in various states of degeneration. Some walked with no assistance, some shuffled, some had canes, some had walkers, some had wheelchairs. Many seemed spry; others slept.

The lobby was clean and bright but still had that – Grace hated herself for thinking like this – old-people smell, the odor of a sofa turning moldy. They tried to cover it up with something cherry, something that reminded Grace of those dangling tree fresheners in gypsy cabs, but there are some smells that you can never mask.

The singular young person in the room – a woman in her mid-twenties – sat behind a desk that was again aiming for the era but looked like something just bought at the Bombay Company. She smiled up at Grace.

'Good morning. I'm Lindsey Barclay.'

Grace recognized the voice from the phone. 'I'm here to see Mr. Dodd.'

'Bobby's in his room. Second floor, room 211. I'll take you.'

She rose. Lindsey was pretty in a way that only the young are, with that enthusiasm and smile that belong exclusively to the innocent or the cult recruiter.

'Do you mind taking the stairs?' she asked.

'Not at all.'

Many of the residents stopped and said hello. Lindsey had time for every one of them, cheerfully returning each greeting, though Grace the cynic couldn't help but wonder if this was a bit of a show for the visitor. Still Lindsey knew all the names. She always had something to say, something personal, and the residents seemed to appreciate that.

'Seems like mostly women,' Grace noted.

'When I was in school, they told us the national ratio in assisted living is five women for every one man.'

'Wow.'

'Yes. Bobby jokes that he's waited his whole life for that kind of odds.'

Grace smiled.

She waved a hand. 'Oh, but he's all talk. His wife – he calls her "his Maudie" – died almost thirty years ago. I don't think he's looked at a woman since.'

That silenced them. The corridor was done up in forest green and pink, the walls lined with the familiar – Rockwell prints, dogs playing poker, black-and-whites from old movies like *Casablanca* and *Strangers on a Train*. Grace limped along. Lindsey noticed it – Grace could tell the way she cut quick glances – but like most people, she said nothing.

'We have different neighborhoods at Starlight,' Lindsey explained. 'That's what we call the corridors like this. Neighborhoods. Each has a different theme. The one we're in now is called Nostalgia. We think the residents find it comforting.'

They stopped at a door. A nameplate on the right said 'B. Dodd.' She knocked on the door. 'Bobby?'

No reply. She opened the door anyway. They stepped into a small but comfortable room. There was a tiny kitchenette on the right. On the coffee table, ideally angled so that you could see it from both the door and the bed, was a large black-and-white photograph of a stunning woman who looked a bit like Lena Horne. The woman in the picture was maybe forty but you could tell that the picture was old.

'That's his Maudie.'

Grace nodded, lost for a moment in this image in the silver frame. She thought again about 'her Jack.' For the first time she allowed herself to consider the unthinkable: Jack might never come home. It was something she'd been avoiding from the moment she'd heard the minivan start up. She might never see Jack again. She might never hold him. She might never laugh at one of his corny jokes. She might never – and this was apropos to think here – grow old with him.

'Are you okay?'

'Fine.'

'Bobby must be up with Ira on Reminiscence. They play cards.'

They began to back out of the room. 'Is Reminiscence another, uh, neighborhood?'

'No. Reminiscence is what we call our third floor. It's for our residents with Alzheimer's.'

'Oh.'

'Ira doesn't recognize his own children, but he still plays a mean game of poker pinochle.'

They were back in the hall. Grace noticed a cluster of images next to Bobby Dodd's door. She took a closer look. It was one of those box frames people use to display trinkets. There were army medals. There was an old baseball, brown with age. There were photographs from every era of the man's life. One photograph was of his murdered son, Bob Dodd, the same one she'd seen on the computer last night.

Lindsey said, 'Memory box.'

'Nice,' Grace said, because she didn't know what else to say.

'Every patient has one by their door. It's a way to let everyone know about you.'

Grace nodded. Summing up a life in a twelve-by-eight box frame. Like everything else about this place, it managed to be both appropriate and creepy at the exact same time.

To get to the Reminiscence floor you had to use an elevator that worked by a coded numeric keypad. 'So the residents don't wander,' Lindsey explained, which again fit into the 'making sense yet giving the willies' style of this place.

The Reminiscence floor was comfortable, well appointed, well staffed, and terrifying. Some residents were functional, but most wilted in wheelchairs like dying flowers. Some stood and shuffled. Several muttered to themselves. All had that glazed, hundred-yard stare.

A woman deep into her eighties jangled her keys and started for the elevator.

Lindsey asked, 'Where are you going, Cecile?'

The old woman turned toward her. 'I have to pick up Danny from school. He'll be waiting for me.'

'It's okay,' Lindsey said. 'School won't be out for another two hours.'

'Are you sure?'

'Of course. Look, let's have some lunch and then you can pick up Danny, okay?'

'He has piano lessons today.'

'I know.'

A staff member came over and steered Cecile away. Lindsey watched her go. 'We use validation therapy,' she said, 'with our advanced Alzheimer's patients.'

'Validation therapy?'

'We don't argue with them or try to make them see the truth. I don't, for example, tell her that Danny is now a sixty-two-year-old banker with three grandchildren. We just try to redirect them.'

They walked down a corridor – no, 'neighborhood' – filled with life-size dolls of babies. There was a changing table and teddy bears.

'Nursery neighborhood,' she said.

'They play with dolls?'

'Those that are more high functioning. It helps them prepare for visits from great-grandchildren.'

'And the others?'

Lindsey kept walking. 'Some think they're young mothers. It helps soothe them.'

Subconsciously, or maybe not, they picked up the pace. A few seconds later, Lindsey said, 'Bobby?'

Bobby Dodd rose from the card table. The first word that came to mind: Dapper. He looked sprightly and fresh. He had dark black skin, thick wrinkles like something you might see on an alligator. He was a snappy dresser in a tweed jacket, two-tone loafers, red ascot with matching hanky. His gray hair was cropped close and slicked down.

His manner was upbeat, even after Grace explained that she wanted to talk to him about his murdered son. She looked for some signs of devastation – a wetness in the eye, a tremor in the voice – but Bobby Dodd showed nothing. Okay, yes, Grace was dealing in heavy generalities, but could it be that death and big-time tragedy did not hit the elderly as hard as the rest of us? Grace wondered. The elderly could be easily agitated by the little stuff – traffic delays, lines at airports, poor service. But it was as if the big things never quite reached them. Was there a strange selfishness that came with age? Was there something about being closer to the inevitable – having that perspective – that made one either internalize, block, or brush off the big calamities? Can frailty not handle the big blows, and thus a defense mechanism, a survival instinct, runs interference?

Bobby Dodd wanted to help, but he really didn't know much. Grace could see that almost right away. His son had visited twice a month. Yes, Bob's stuff had been packed up and sent to him, but he hadn't bothered opening it.

'It's in storage,' Lindsey told Grace.

'Do you mind if I look through it?'

Bobby Dodd patted her leg. 'Not at all, child.'

'We'll need to ship it to you,' Lindsey said. 'The storage facility is off site.'

'It's very important.'

'I can have it overnighted.'

'Thank you.'

Lindsey left them alone.

'Mr. Dodd –'

'Bobby, please.'

'Bobby,' Grace said. 'When was the last time your son visited you?'

'Three days before he was killed.'

The words came quickly and without thought. She finally saw a flicker behind the façade, and she wondered about her earlier observations, about old age making tragedy less hurtful – or does it merely make the mask more deft?

'Did he seem different at all?'

'Different?'

'More distracted, anything like that.'

'No.' Then: 'Or at least I didn't notice, if he did.'

'What did you talk about?'

'We never have much to say. Sometimes we talk about his momma. Most of the time we just watch TV. They got cable here, you know.'

'Did Jillian come with him?'

'No.'

He said that too quickly. Something in his face closed down.

'Did she ever come?'

'Sometimes.'

'But not the last time?'

'That's right.'

'Did that surprise you?'

'That? No, *that*' – big emphasis – 'didn't surprise me.'

'What did?'

He looked off and bit his lower lip. 'She wasn't at the funeral.'

Grace thought that she must have heard wrong. Bobby Dodd nodded as if he could read her thoughts.

'That's right. His own wife.'

'Were they having marital issues?'

'If they were, Bob never said anything to me.'

'Did they have any children?'

'No.' He adjusted the ascot and glanced away for a moment. 'Why are you bringing this all up, Mrs. Lawson?'

'Grace, please.'

He did not reply. He looked at her with eyes that spoke of wisdom and sadness. Maybe the answer to elderly coldness is far simpler: Those eyes had seen bad. They didn't want to see more.

'My own husband is missing,' Grace said. 'I think, I don't know, I think they're connected.'

'What's your husband's name?'

'Jack Lawson.'

He shook his head. The name meant nothing to him. She asked if he had a phone number or any idea how she could contact Jillian Dodd. He shook his head again. They headed to the elevator. Bobby didn't know the code, so an orderly escorted them down. They rode from floor three to one in silence.

When they reached the door, Grace thanked him for his time.

'Your husband,' he said. 'You love him, don't you?'

'Very much.'

'Hope you're stronger than me.' Bobby Dodd walked away then. Grace thought of that silver-framed picture in his room, of his Maudie, and then she showed herself out.

24

Perlmutter realized that they had no legal right to open Rocky Conwell's car. He pulled Daley over. 'Is DiBartola on duty?'

'No.'

'Call Rocky Conwell's wife. Ask her if she had a set of keys to the car. Tell her we found it and want her permission to go through it.'

'She's the ex-wife. Does she have any standing?'

'Enough for our purposes,' Perlmutter said.

'Okay.'

It took Daley no time. The wife cooperated. They stopped by the Maple Garden apartments on Maple Street. Daley ran up and retrieved the keys. Five minutes later they pulled into the Park-n-Ride.

There was no reason to be suspicious of foul play. If anything, finding the car here, at this depot, would lead one to the opposite conclusion. People parked here so that they could go elsewhere. One bus whisked the weary to the heart of midtown Manhattan. Another brought you to the northern tip of the famed isle, near the George Washington Bridge. Other buses took you to the three nearby major airports – JFK, LaGuardia, Newark Liberty – and ultimately anywhere in the world. So no, finding Rocky Conwell's car did not lead one to suspect foul play.

At least, not at first.

Pepe and Pashaian, the two cops who were watching the car, had not seen it. Perlmutter's eyes slid toward Daley. Nothing on his face either. They all looked complacent, expecting this would lead to a dead end.

Pepe and Pashaian hoisted their belts and sauntered toward Perlmutter. 'Hey, Captain.'

Perlmutter kept his eyes on the car.

'You want us to start questioning the ticket agents?' Pepe asked. 'Maybe one of them remembers selling Conwell a ticket.'

'I don't think so,' Perlmutter said.

The three younger men caught something in their superior's voice. They looked at each other and shrugged. Perlmutter did not explain.

Conwell's vehicle was a Toyota Celica. A small car, old model. But the size and age didn't really matter. Neither did the fact that there was rust along the wheel trims, that two hubcaps were gone, that the other two were so dirty you could not tell where metal ended and rubber began. No, none of that bothered Perlmutter.

He stared at the back of the car and thought about those small-town sheriffs in horror movies, you know the ones, where something is very wrong, where townspeople start acting strangely and the body count keeps rising and the sheriff, that good, smart, loyal, out-of-his-league law enforcement officer, is powerless to do anything about it. That was what Perlmutter felt now because the back of the car, the trunk area, was low.

Much too low.

There was only one explanation. Something heavy was in the trunk.

It could be anything, of course. Rocky Conwell had been a football player. He probably lifted weights. Maybe he was transferring a set of dumbbells. The answer could be as simple as that, good old Rocky moving his weights. Maybe he was bringing them back to the garden apartment on Maple Street, the one where his ex lived. She had worried about him. They were reconciling. Maybe Rocky loaded his car – okay, not his whole car, just his trunk, because Perlmutter could see that there was nothing in the backseat – anyway, maybe he loaded it up to move back in with her.

Perlmutter jangled the keys as he moved closer to the Toyota Celica. Daley, Pepe, and Pashaian hung back. Perlmutter glanced down at the set of keys. Rocky's wife – he thought that her name was Lorraine but he couldn't be sure – had a Penn State football helmet key chain. It looked old and scraped up. The Nittany Lion was barely visible. Perlmutter wondered what she thought about when she looked at the key chain, why she still used it.

He stopped at the trunk and sniffed the air. Not a hint. He put the key in the lock and turned. The trunk's lock popped open, the sound echoing. He began to lift the trunk. The air escaping was almost audible. And now, yes, the smell was unmistakable.

Something large had been squished into the trunk, like an oversize pillow. Without warning it sprang free like a giant jack-in-the-box. Perlmutter jumped back as the head fell out first, smacking the pavement hard.

Didn't matter, of course. Rocky Conwell was already dead.

25

Now what?

Grace was starved for one thing. She drove over the George Washington Bridge, took the Jones Road exit, and stopped to grab a bite at a Chinese restaurant called, interestingly enough, Baumgart's. She ate in silence, feeling as lonely as she had ever felt, and tried to hold herself together. What had happened? The day before yesterday – was it really only then? – she had picked up photographs at Photomat. That was all. Life was good. She had a husband she adored and two wonderful, inquisitive kids. She had time to paint. They all had their health, enough money in the bank. And then she had seen a photograph, an old one, and now . . .

Grace had almost forgotten about Josh the Fuzz Pellet.

He was the one who developed the roll of film. He was the one who mysteriously left the store not long after she picked up the pictures. He had to be the one, she was sure, who put that damn photograph in the middle of her pack.

She grabbed her cell phone, asked directory assistance for the number of the Photomat in Kasselton, and even paid the extra fee to be directly connected. On the third ring, the phone was picked up.

'Photomat.'

Grace said nothing. No question about it. She would recognize that bored yah-dude slur anywhere. It was Fuzz Pellet Josh. He was back at the store.

She considered just hanging up, but maybe, somehow, that would – she didn't know – tip him off somehow. Make him run. She changed her voice, added a little extra lilt, and asked what time they closed.

'Like, six,' Fuzz Pellet told her.

She thanked him, but he had hung up. The check was already on the table. She paid and tried not to sprint to her car. Route 4 was wide open. She sped past the plethora of malls and found a parking spot not far from the Photomat. Her cell phone rang.

'Hello?'

'It's Carl Vespa.'

'Oh, hi.'

'I'm sorry about yesterday. About springing Jimmy X on you like that.'

She debated telling him about Jimmy's late night visit, decided now was not the time. 'It's okay.'

'I know you don't care, but it looks like Wade Larue is going to get released.'

'Maybe it's the right thing,' she said.

'Maybe.' But Vespa sounded far from convinced. 'You sure you don't need any protection?'

'Positive.'

'If you change your mind . . .'

'I'll call.'

There was a funny pause. 'Any word from your husband?'

'No.'

'Does he have a sister?'

Grace changed hands. 'Yes. Why?'

'Her name Sandra Koval?'

'Yes. What does she have to do with this?'

'I'll talk to you later.'

He hung up. Grace stared at the phone. What the hell was that all about? She shook her head. It would be useless to call back. She tried to refocus.

Grace grabbed her purse and hurry-limped toward the Photomat. Her leg hurt. Walking was a chore. It felt as though someone were on the ground clinging to her ankle and she had to drag him along. Grace kept moving. She was three stores away when a man in a business suit stepped in her path.

'Ms. Lawson?'

A weird thought struck Grace as she looked at this stranger: His sandy hair was nearly the same color as his suit. It almost looked liked they were both made from the same material.

'May I help you?' she said.

The man reached into his coat pocket and pulled out a photograph. He held it up to her face so that she could see it. 'Did you post this on the Web?'

It was the cropped mystery photograph of the blonde and the redhead.

'Who are you?'

The sandy-haired man said, 'My name is Scott Duncan. I'm with the U.S. attorney's office.' He pointed to the blonde, the one who'd been looking up at Jack, the one with the X across her face.

'And this,' Scott Duncan said, 'is a picture of my sister.'

26

Perlmutter had broken the news to Lorraine Conwell as gently as he could.

He had delivered bad news plenty of times. Usually it involved car accidents on Route 4 or the Garden State Parkway. Lorraine Conwell had exploded into tears when he told her, but now the numb had seeped in and dried her eyes.

The stages of grief: Supposedly the first is denial. That was wrong. The first is just the opposite: Total acceptance. You hear the bad news and you understand exactly what is being said to you. You understand that your loved one – your spouse, your parent, your child – will never come home, that they are gone for good, that their life is over, and that you will never, ever, see them again. You understand that in a flash. Your legs buckle. Your heart gives out.

That was the first step – not just acceptance, not just understanding, but total truth. Human beings are not built to withstand that kind of hurt. That then is when the denial begins. Denial floods in quickly, salving the wounds or at least covering them. But there is still that moment, mercifully quick, the real Stage One, when you hear the news and stare into the abyss, and horrible as it is, you understand everything.

Lorraine Conwell sat ramrod. There was a quiver in her lips. Her eyes were dry. She looked small and alone and it took all Perlmutter had not to put his arms around her and pull her in close.

'Rocky and me,' she said. 'We were going to get back together.'

Perlmutter nodded, encouraging.

'It's my fault, you know. I made Rocky leave. I shouldn't have.' She looked up at him with those violet eyes. 'He was different when we met, you know? He had dreams then. He was so sure of himself. But when he couldn't play ball any more, it just ate away at him. I couldn't live with that.'

Perlmutter nodded again. He wanted to help her out, wanted to stay in her company, but he really did not have time for the unabridged life story. He needed to move this along and get out of here. 'Was there anyone who wanted to hurt Rocky? Did he have enemies or anything like that?'

She shook her head. 'No. No one.'

'He spent time in prison.'

'Yes. It was stupid. He got into a fight in a bar. It got out of hand.'

Perlmutter looked over at Daley. They knew about the fight. They were already on that, seeing if his victim had sought late revenge. It seemed doubtful.

'Was Rocky working?'

'Yes.'

'Where?'

'In Newark. He worked at the Budweiser plant. The one near the airport.'

'You called our office yesterday,' Perlmutter said.

She nodded, her eyes staring straight ahead.

'You spoke to an Officer DiBartola.'

'Yes. He was very nice.'

Right. 'You told him that Rocky hadn't come home from work.'

She nodded.

'You called in the early morning. You said he'd been working the night before.'

'That's right.'

'Did he work a night shift at the plant?'

'No. He'd taken a second job.' She squirmed a little. 'It was off the books.'

'Doing what?'

'He worked for this lady.'

'Doing what?'

She used one finger to wipe a tear. 'Rocky didn't talk about it much. He delivered subpoenas, I think, stuff like that.'

'Do you know the lady's name?'

'Something foreign. I can't pronounce it.'

Perlmutter did not need to think about it long. 'Indira Khariwalla?'

'That's it.' Lorraine Conwell looked up at him. 'You know her?'

He did. It had been a long time, but yes, Perlmutter knew her very well.

Grace had handed Scott Duncan the photograph, the one with all five people in it. He could not stop staring, especially at the image of his sister. He ran his finger over her face. Grace could barely look at him.

They were back at Grace's house now, sitting in the kitchen. They had been talking for the better part of half an hour.

'You got this two days ago?' Scott Duncan asked.

'Yes.'

'And then your husband . . . He's this one, right?' Scott Duncan pointed to Jack's image.

'Yes.'

'He ran off?'

'He vanished,' she said. 'He didn't run off.'

'Right. You think he was, what, kidnapped?'

'I don't know what happened to him. I only know he's in trouble.'

Scott Duncan's eyes stayed on the old photograph. 'Because he gave you some kind of warning? Something about needing space?'

'Mr. Duncan, I'd like to know how you came across this picture. And how you found me, for that matter.'

'You sent it out via some kind of spam. Someone recognized the picture and forwarded it to me. I traced back the spammer and put a little pressure on him.'

'Was that why we didn't receive any answers?'

Duncan nodded. 'I wanted to talk to you first.'

'I've told you everything I know. I was on my way to confront the guy in the Photomat when you showed up.'

'We'll question him, don't worry about that.'

He couldn't take his eyes off the picture. She had done all the talking. He had told her nothing, except that the woman in the photograph was his sister. Grace pointed at the crossed-out face. 'Tell me about her,' she said.

'Her name was Geri. Does her name mean anything to you?'

'I'm sorry, it doesn't.'

'Your husband never mentioned her? Geri Duncan.'

'Not that I remember.' Then: 'You said was.'

'What?'

'You said was. Her name *was* Geri.'

Scott Duncan nodded. 'She died in a fire when she was twenty-one years old. In her dorm room.'

Grace froze. 'She went to Tufts, right?'

'Yes. How did you know?'

Now it made sense – why the girl's face had seemed familiar. Grace hadn't known her, but there had been pictures in the newspapers at the time. Grace had been undergoing physical therapy and ripping through way too many periodicals. 'I remember reading about it. Wasn't it an accident? Electrical fire or something?'

'That was what I thought. Until three months ago.'

'What changed?'

'The U.S. attorney's office captured a man who goes by the name Monte Scanlon. He's a hired assassin. His job was to make it look like an accident.'

Grace tried to take it in. 'And you just learned this three months ago?'

'Yes.'

'Did you investigate?'

'I'm still investigating, but it's been a long time.' His voice was softer now. 'Not many clues after all these years.'

Grace turned away.

'I found out that Geri was dating a boy at the time, a local kid named Shane Alworth. The name mean anything to you?'

'No.'

'You're sure?'

'Pretty sure, yeah.'

'Shane Alworth had a rap sheet, nothing serious, but I checked him out.'

'And?'

'And he's gone.'

'Gone?'

'No sign of him. I can't find work records for him. I can't find any sign of a Shane Alworth on the tax payroll. I can't find any hit on his social security number.'

'For how long?'

'How long has he been gone?'

'Yes.'

'I've gone back ten years. Nothing.' Duncan reached into his coat pocket and pulled out another photograph. He handed it to Grace. 'Recognize him?'

She took a long look at the photograph. No question about it. It was the other guy in her photograph. She looked up at him for confirmation. Duncan nodded.

'Creepy, huh?'

'Where did you get this?' she asked.

'From Shane Alworth's mother. She claims her son lives in a small town in Mexico. That he's a missionary or something and that's why his name doesn't pop up. Shane also has a brother who lives in St. Louis. Works as a psychologist. He backs up what the mother said.'

'But you don't buy it.'

'Do you?'

Grace put the mystery photograph on the table. 'So we know about three people in this photograph,' she said, more to herself than Duncan. 'We have your sister, who was murdered. We have her boyfriend, Shane Alworth, the guy over here. He's missing. We have my husband, who disappeared right after seeing this photograph. That about right?'

'Pretty much.'

'What else did the mother say?'

'Shane was unreachable. He was in the Amazon jungle, she thought.'

'The Amazon jungle? In Mexico?'

'Her geography was fuzzy.'

Grace shook her head and pointed at the picture. 'So that leaves the other two women. Any clue who they are?'

'No, not yet. But we know more now. The redhead, we should get a bead on her pretty soon. The other one, the one with her back to the camera, I don't know if we'll ever know.'

'Did you learn anything else?'

'Not really. I've had Geri's body exhumed. That took some time to arrange. A full autopsy is being done, see if they can find any physical evidence, but it's a long shot. This' – he held up the picture from the Web – 'this is the first real lead I've had.'

She didn't like the pitch of hope in his voice. 'It might just be a picture,' she said.

'You don't believe that.'

Grace put her hands on the table. 'Do you think my husband had something to do with your sister's death?'

Duncan rubbed his chin. 'Good question,' he said.

She waited.

'Something to do with it, probably. But I don't think he killed her, if that's what you're asking. Something happened to them a long time ago. I don't know what. My sister was killed in a fire. Your husband ran overseas, I guess. France, you said?'

'Yes.'

'And Shane Alworth, too. I mean, it's all connected. It has to be.'

'My sister-in-law knows something.'

Scott Duncan nodded. 'You said she's a lawyer?'

'Yes. With Burton and Crimstein.'

'That's not good. I know Hester Crimstein. If she doesn't want to tell us anything, I won't be able to apply much pressure.'

'So what do we do?'

'We keep shaking the cage.'

'Shaking the cage?'

He nodded. 'Shaking cages is the only way you make progress.'

'So we should start with shaking Josh at the Photomat,' Grace said. 'He's the one who gave me that photograph.'

Duncan stood. 'Sounds like a plan.'

'You're going there now?'

'Yes.'

'I'd like to come along.'

'Let's go then.'

'As I live and breathe. Captain Perlmutter. To what do I owe the pleasure?'

Indira Khariwalla was small and wizened. Her dark skin – she was, as her name implied, from India, more specifically Bombay – had started to harden and thicken. She was still attractive but not the exotic temptress she had been in her heyday.

'Been a long time,' he said.

'Yes.' The smile, once a dazzler, took great effort now, almost cracking the skin. 'But I'd prefer not to rehash the past.'

'Me either.'

When Perlmutter started working in Kasselton, he had been partnered with a veteran a year from retirement named Steve Goedert, a great guy. They struck up a deep friendship. Goedert had three kids, all grown, and a wife named Susan. Perlmutter did not know how Goedert met Indira, but they started up. Susan found out.

Fast-forward past the ugly divorce.

Goedert had no money left once the lawyers were through with him. He ended up working as a private investigator but with a twist: He specialized in infidelity. Or at least that was what he claimed. To Perlmutter's thinking it was a scam – entrapment at its very worst. He would use Indira as bait. She would approach the husband, lure him in, and then Goedert would take pictures. Perlmutter told him to stop. Fidelity was not a game. It was not a prank, testing a man like that.

Goedert must have known it was wrong. He hit the bottle pretty good and never came out. He too had a gun in his house, and in the end he too did not use it to stop a home invasion. After his death, Indira struck out on her own. She took over the agency, keeping Goedert's name on the door.

'A long time ago,' she said softly.

'Did you love him?'

'None of your business.'

'You ruined his life.'

'Do you really think I can wield that kind of power over a man?' She shifted in her chair. 'What can I do for you, Captain Perlmutter?'

'You have an employee named Rocky Conwell.'

She did not respond.

'I know he's off the books. I don't care about that.'

Still nothing. He slapped down a crude Polaroid of Conwell's dead body.

Indira's eyes flicked to it, ready to dismiss, and then stared there. 'Dear Lord.'

Perlmutter waited, but Indira said nothing. She stared for a little while longer and then let her head drop back.

'His wife says he worked for you.'

She nodded.

'What did he do?'

'Night shifts.'

'What did he do on the night shifts?'

'Mostly repossession. He did a little subpoena work too.'

'What else?'

She said nothing.

'There was stuff in his car. We found a long-range camera and a pair of binoculars.'

'So?'

'So was he doing surveillance?'

She looked at him. There were tears in her eyes. 'You think he was killed on the job?'

'It's a logical assumption, but I won't know for certain until you tell me what he was doing.'

Indira looked away. She began to rock in the chair.

'Was he working a job the night before last?'

'Yes.'

More silence.

'What was he doing, Indira?'

'I can't say.'

'Why not?'

'I have clients. They have rights. You know the drill, Stu.'

'You're not a lawyer.'

'No, but I can work for one.'

'Are you saying this case was attorney work product?'

'I'm not saying anything.'

'You want to take another look at that photograph?'

She almost smiled. 'You think that will make me talk?' But Indira did take another look. 'I don't see any blood,' she said.

'There wasn't any.'

'He wasn't shot?'

'Nope. No gun, no knife.'

She looked confused. 'How was he killed?'

'I don't know yet. He's on the table. But I have a guess, if you want to hear it?'

She didn't. But she nodded slowly.

'He suffocated.'

'You mean like he was garroted?'

'Doubtful. There are no ligature marks on the neck.'

She frowned. 'Rocky was huge. He was strong as an ox. It had to be poison, something like that.'

'I don't think so. The M.E. said there was substantial damage to the larynx.'

She looked confused.

'In other words, his throat was crushed like an eggshell.'

'You mean he was strangled by hand?'

'We don't know.'

'He was too strong for that,' she said again.

'Who was he following?' Perlmutter asked.

'Let me make a call. You can wait in the hall.'

He did. The wait was not long.

When Indira came out, her voice was clipped. 'I can't speak to you,' she said. 'I'm sorry.'

'Attorney's orders?'

'I can't speak to you.'

'I'll be back. I'll get a warrant.'

'Good luck,' she said, turning away. And Perlmutter thought that maybe she meant it.

27

Grace and Scott Duncan headed back to the Photomat. Her heart sank when they entered and she saw no Fuzz Pellet.

Assistant Manager Bruce was there. He puffed out his chest. When Scott Duncan flashed his badge, the chest deflated. 'Josh is out on lunch break,' he said.

'Do you know where?'

'He usually goes to the Taco Bell. It's right down the block.'

Grace knew it. She hurried out first, afraid to lose his scent again. Scott Duncan followed. As soon as she entered the Taco Bell, the fragrance of lard rising up to assault her, she spotted Josh.

Equally important, Josh spotted her. His eyes widened. Scott Duncan stood at her side. 'That him?'

Grace nodded.

Fuzz Pellet Josh sat alone. His head was tilted down, his hair hanging in front of his face like a curtain. His expression – and Grace guessed that he only had this one – was sullen. He bit into the taco as if it insulted his favorite grunge group. The earphones were jammed into place. The cord fell into the sour cream. Grace hated to sound like an old biddy, but having this kind of music plugged directly into the brain all day could not be good for a person. Grace enjoyed music. When she was alone, she would turn the music up, sing along, dance, whatever. So it wasn't the music or even the volume. But what did it do to the mental health of a young mind to have music, probably angry and harsh, pounding in the ears all the time? An aural confinement, solitary walls of sound, to paraphrase Elton John, inescapable. No life noises let in. No talking. An artificial soundtrack to your life.

It could not be healthy.

Josh lowered his head, pretending he didn't see them. She watched him as they approached. He was so young. He looked pitiful, sitting there alone like that. She thought about his hopes and dreams and how he already looked set on the road of life-long disappointments. She thought about Josh's mother, about how she must have tried and how she must worry. She thought about her own son, her little Max, and about how she'd handle it if he started slipping in this direction.

She and Scott Duncan stopped in front of Josh's table. He took another bite and then slowly looked up. The music coming from his earphones was so loud that Grace could actually make out the lyrics. Something about bitches and ho's. Scott Duncan took the lead. She let him.

'Do you recognize this lady?' Scott asked.

Josh shrugged. He lowered the volume.

'Take those off,' Scott said. 'Now.'

He did as he was told, but he took his time.

'I asked you if you recognized this lady.'

Josh glanced in her direction. 'Yeah, I guess.'

'How do you know her?'

'From where I work.'

'You work at the Photomat, correct?'

'Yeah.'

'And Ms. Lawson here. She's a customer.'

'That's what I said.'

'Do you remember the last time she was in the store?'

'No.'

'Think.'

He shrugged.

'Does two days ago sound about right?'

Another shrug. 'Could be.'

Scott Duncan had the envelope from the Photomat. 'You developed this roll of film, correct?'

'You say so.'

'No, I'm asking you. Look at the envelope.'

He did. Grace stayed still. Josh had not asked Scott Duncan who he was. He had not asked them what they wanted. She wondered about that.

'Yeah, I developed that roll.'

Duncan took out the photograph with his sister in it. He put it on the table. 'Did you put this picture in Ms. Lawson's packet?'

'No,' Josh said.

'You sure?'

'Positive.'

Grace waited a beat. She knew that he was lying. She spoke for the first time. 'How do you know?' she asked.

They both looked at her. Josh said, 'Huh?'

'How do you develop rolls?'

He said, 'Huh?' again.

'You put the roll in that machine,' Grace said. 'They come out in a pile. Then you put the pile in an envelope. Isn't that right?'

'Yeah.'

'Do you look at every picture you develop?'

He said nothing. He looked around as if asking for help.

'I've seen you work,' Grace said. 'You read your magazines. You listen to your music. You do not check through all the pictures. So my question is, Josh, how do you know what pictures were in that pile?'

Josh glanced at Scott Duncan. No help there. He turned back to her. 'It's weird, that's all.'

Grace waited.

'That picture looks like it's a hundred years old or something. It's the right size, but that ain't Kodak paper. That's what I meant. I'd never seen it before.' Josh liked that. His eyes lit up, warming to his lie. 'Yeah, see, that's what I thought he meant. When he said did I put it in. Did I ever see it before?'

Grace just looked at him.

'Look, I don't know what goes through that machine. But I've never seen that print. That's all I know, okay?'

'Josh?'

It was Scott Duncan. Josh turned toward him.

'That picture ended up in Ms. Lawson's pack of pictures. Do you have any idea how that happened?'

'Maybe she took the picture.'

'No,' Duncan said.

Josh gave another elaborate shrug. He must have had very powerful shoulders from all the work they got.

'Tell me how it works,' Duncan said. 'How you develop the pictures.'

'It's like she said. I put the film into the machine. It does the rest. I just set the size and the count.'

'Count?'

'You know. One print from each negative, two prints, whatever.'

'And they come out in a pile?'

'Yeah.'

Josh was more relaxed now, on comfortable ground.

'And then you put them in an envelope?'

'Right. Same envelope the customer filled out. Then I file it in alphabetical order. That's it.'

Scott Duncan looked over at Grace. She said nothing. He took out his badge. 'Do you know what this badge means, Josh?'

'No.'

'It means I work for the U.S. attorney's office. It means I can make your life miserable if you cross me. Do you understand?'

Josh looked a little scared now. He managed a nod.

'So I'm going to ask you one more time: Do you know anything about this photograph?'

206

'No. I swear.' He looked around. 'I gotta get back to work now.'

He stood. Grace blocked his path. 'Why did you leave work early the other day?'

'Huh?'

'About an hour after I picked up my roll of film, I went back to the store. You were gone. And the next morning too. So what happened?'

'I got sick,' he said.

'Yeah?'

'Yeah.'

'Feeling better now?'

'Guess so.' He started pushing past her.

'Because,' Grace went on, 'your manager said you had a family emergency. Is that what you told him?'

'I gotta get back to work,' he said, and this time he pushed past her and nearly ran out the door.

Beatrice Smith was not home.

Eric Wu broke in without any trouble. He checked through the house. No one was there. With the gloves still on Wu flicked on the computer. Her software PIM – a fancy term for a date and phone book – was Time & Chaos. He opened it and checked her calendar.

Beatrice Smith was visiting her son, the doctor, in San Diego. She'd be home in two days – far enough away to save her life. Wu considered that, the fickle winds of fate. He couldn't help it. He glanced through Beatrice Smith's calendar two months in the past and two months in the future. There were no overnight trips. If he had come at any other time, Beatrice Smith would be dead. Wu liked to think about things like that, about how it was often the little things, the unconscious things, the things we can't know or control, that alter our lives. Call it fate, luck, odds, God. Wu found it fascinating.

Beatrice Smith had a two-car garage. Her tan Land

Rover took up the right side. The left side was empty. There was an oil stain on the ground. This, Wu figured, had been where Maury parked his car. She kept it empty now – Wu couldn't help but think of Freddy Sykes's mother – as if it was his side of the bed. Wu parked there. He opened the back. Jack Lawson looked shaky. Wu untied his legs so he could walk. The hands remained bound at the wrist. Wu led him inside. Jack Lawson fell twice. The blood had not fully circulated through the legs. Wu held him up by the scruff of his shirt.

'I'm taking the gag off,' Wu said.

Jack Lawson nodded. Wu could see it in his eyes. Lawson was broken. Wu had not hurt him much – not yet anyway – but when you spend enough time in the dark, alone with your thoughts, your mind turns inward and feasts. That was always a dangerous thing. The key to serenity, Wu knew, was to keep working, keep moving forward. When you're moving, you don't think about guilt or innocence. You don't think about your past or your dreams, your joys or disappointments. You just worry about survival. Hurt or be hurt. Kill or be killed.

Wu removed the gag. Lawson did not plead and beg or ask questions. That stage was over. Wu tied his legs to a chair. He searched the pantry and refrigerator. They both ate in silence. When they finished, Wu washed off the dishes and cleaned up. Jack Lawson stayed tied to the chair.

Wu's cell phone rang. 'Yes.'

'We have a problem.'

Wu waited.

'When you picked him up, he had a copy of that photograph, right?'

'Yes.'

'And he said there were no other copies?'

'Yes.'

'He was wrong.'

Wu said nothing.

'His wife has a copy of the picture. She's flashing it everywhere.'

'I see.'

'Will you take care of it?'

'No,' Wu said. 'I can't return to the area.'

'Why not?'

Wu did not respond.

'Forget I asked that. We'll use Martin. He has the information on her children.'

Wu said nothing. He did not like the idea, but he kept it to himself.

The voice on the phone said, 'We'll take care of it,' before hanging up.

28

Grace said, 'Josh is lying.'

They were back on Main Street. Clouds threatened, but for now humidity ruled the day. Scott Duncan gestured a few stores up with his chin. 'I could use a Starbucks,' he said.

'Wait. You don't think he's lying?'

'He's nervous. There's a difference.'

Scott Duncan pulled open the glass door. Grace entered. There was a line at Starbucks. There always seemed to be a line at Starbucks. The sound system played something old from a female warbly blues singer, a Billie Holiday or Dinah Washington or Nina Simone. The song ended and a girl-with-acoustic-guitar came on, Jewel or Aimee Mann or Lucinda Williams.

'What about his inconsistencies?' she asked.

Scott Duncan frowned.

'What?'

'Does our friend Josh look like the type who willingly cooperates with authority?'

'No.'

'So what would you expect him to say?'

'His boss said that he had a family emergency. He told us he was sick.'

'It is an inconsistency,' he agreed.

'But?'

Scott Duncan gave an exaggerated shrug, mimicking Josh. 'I've worked a lot of cases. You know what I've learned about inconsistencies?'

She shook her head. In the background the milk did

that froth thing, the machine making a noise like a car-wash vacuum.

'They exist. I'd be more suspicious if there weren't a few. The truth is always fuzzy. If his story had been clean, I'd be more concerned. I'd wonder if he rehearsed it. Keeping a lie consistent isn't that difficult, but in this guy's case, if you asked him what he ate for breakfast twice he'd mess it up.'

They moved forward in line. The *barista* asked for a drink order. Duncan looked at Grace. She ordered a venti iced Americano, no water. He nodded and said, 'Make that two.' He paid using one of those Starbucks debit cards. They waited for the drinks at the bar.

'So you think he was being truthful?' Grace asked.

'I don't know. But nothing he said raised much of a red flag.'

Grace wasn't so sure. 'It had to be him.'

'Why?'

'There was no one else.'

They picked up their drinks and found a table near the window. 'Run it through for me,' he said.

'Run what?'

'Go back. You picked up the pictures. Josh handed them to you. Did you look at them right away?'

Grace's eyes went up and to the right. She tried to remember the details. 'No.'

'Okay, so you took the packet. Did you stick it in your purse or something?'

'I held it.'

'And then what?'

'I got in my car.'

'The packet was still with you?'

'Yes.'

'Where?'

'On the console. Between the two front seats.'

'Where did you go?'

'To pick up Max from school.'

'Did you stop on the way?'

'No.'

'Were the pictures in your possession the whole time?'

Grace smiled in spite of herself. 'You sound like I'm checking in for a flight.'

'They don't ask that anymore.'

'It's been a while since I flew anywhere.' She smiled stupidly and realized why she had taken this inane detour in their conversation. He did too. She had spotted something – something she really didn't want to pursue.

'What?' he asked.

She shook her head.

'I might not have been able to tell if Josh was hiding something. You, however, make for an easier interrogation. What is it?'

'Nothing.'

'Come on, Grace.'

'The pictures were never out of my possession.'

'But?'

'Look, this is a waste of time. I know it was Josh. It had to be.'

'But?'

She took a deep breath. 'I'm just going to say this once, so we can dismiss it and get on with our lives.'

Duncan nodded.

'There was one person who *may* – I stress the word *may* – have had access.'

'Who?'

'I was sitting in the car waiting for Max. I opened the envelope and looked at the first few pictures. Then my friend Cora got in.'

'Got in your car?'

'Yes.'

'Where?'

'The passenger seat.'

'And the pictures were on the console next to it?'

'No, not anymore.' Her voice cracked now with annoyance. She was not enjoying this. 'I just told you. I was looking at them.'

'But you put them down?'

'Eventually, yeah, I guess.'

'On the console?'

'I guess. I don't remember.'

'So she had access.'

'No. I was there the whole time.'

'Who got out first?'

'We both got out at the same time, I think.'

'You limp.'

She looked at him. 'So?'

'So getting out must be something of an effort.'

'I do fine.'

'But come on, Grace, work with me here. It's possible – I'm not saying likely, I'm saying possible – that while you were stepping out, your friend could have slipped that picture into the envelope.'

'Possible, sure. But she didn't.'

'No way?'

'No way.'

'You trust her that much?'

'Yes. But even if I didn't, I mean, think about it. What was she doing – carrying around this picture in the hopes I'd have a packet of developed photos in my car?'

'Not necessarily. Maybe her plan was to plant it in your pocketbook. Or in the glove compartment. Or under the seat, I don't know. Then maybe she saw the roll of film and –'

'No.' Grace held up a hand. 'We're not going there. It's not Cora. It's a waste to even start down this road.'

'What's her last name?'

'It's not important.'

'Tell me that and I'll drop it.'

'Lindley. Cora Lindley.'

'Okay,' he said. 'I'll drop it.' But he was jotting on a small pad.

'Now what?' Grace asked.

Duncan checked his watch. 'I have to go back to work.'

'What should I do?'

'Search your house. If your husband was hiding something, maybe you'll get lucky.'

'Your suggestion is to spy on my husband?'

'Shake the cages, Grace.' He started for the car. 'Sit tight. I'll be back to you soon, promise.'

29

Life does not stop.

Grace had to do some food shopping. That might sound odd considering the circumstances. Her two children, she was sure, would gladly survive on a steady diet of delivered pizzas, but they still needed the basics: milk, orange juice (the kind with calcium and never, ever, pulp), a dozen eggs, sandwich meats, a couple of boxes of cereal, loaf of bread, box of pasta, a Prego sauce. Stuff like that. It might even feel good, food shopping. Doing the mundane, doing something so numbingly normal, would surely be, if not comforting, mildly therapeutic.

She hit the King's on Franklin Boulevard. Grace held no supermarket loyalties. Her friends had favorites and would never dream of shopping elsewhere. Cora liked the A&P in Midland Park. Her neighbor liked the Whole Foods in Ridgewood. Other acquaintances favored the Stop & Shop in Waldwick. Grace's selection was more haphazard because, to put it plainly, no matter where you shopped, Tropicana Orange Juice was Tropicana Orange Juice.

In this case the King's was the closest to Starbucks. Decision made.

She grabbed a cart and pretended that she was just an average citizen having an average day. That didn't last long. She thought about Scott Duncan, his sister, what that all meant.

Where, Grace wondered, do I go from here?

First off, the purported 'Cora Connection' – Grace dismissed it. There was simply no way. Duncan did not know Cora. His job was to be suspicious. Grace knew better.

Cora was out there, no question about it, but that was what had drawn Grace to her in the first place. They had met at a school concert when the Lawsons first moved to town. While their kids butchered the holiday standards, they'd both been forced to stand in the lobby because neither of them had arrived early enough to secure a seat. Cora had leaned over and whispered, 'I had an easier time getting front row for Springsteen.' Grace had laughed. And so, slowly, it began.

But forget that. Forget Grace's own biased viewpoint. What possible motive could Cora have? The smart money was still on Fuzz Pellet Josh. Yes, he would naturally be nervous. Yes, he was probably antiauthority. But there was more there, Grace was sure of it. So forget Cora. Concentrate on Josh. Figure an angle on that.

Max was on a bacon kick. There was some newfangled premade bacon he'd had at a friend's house during a playdate. He wanted her to buy it. Grace was checking the health claims. Like the rest of the country she was concentrating more on lowering the carb intake. This stuff had none. No carbs at all. Enough sodium to salt a large body of water. But no carbs.

She was checking the ingredients – an interesting potpourri of words she'd need to look up – when she felt, actually felt, someone's eyes on her. Still holding the box at eye level, she slowly shifted her gaze. Down the corridor, near the bologna and salami display, a man stood and openly stared at her. There was no one else in the aisle. He was average height, maybe five-ten or so. A razor hadn't glided across his face in at least two days. He wore blue jeans, a maroon T-shirt, and a shiny black Members Only windbreaker. His baseball cap had a Nike swoosh on it.

Grace had never seen the man before. He stared at her for another moment before he spoke. His voice was barely a whisper.

'Mrs. Lamb,' the man said to her. 'Room 17.'

For a moment the words did not register. Grace just stood there, unable to move. It wasn't that she hadn't heard him – she had – but his words were so out of context, so out of place coming from this stranger's lips, that her brain could not really comprehend the significance.

At first anyway. For a second or two. Then it all flooded in . . .

Mrs. Lamb. Room 17 . . .

Mrs. Lamb was Emma's teacher. Room 17 was Emma's classroom.

The man was already on the move, hurrying down the aisle.

'Wait!' Grace shouted. 'Hey!'

The man turned the corner. Grace went after him. She tried to pick up speed but the limp, that damn limp, kept her in check. She reached the end of the aisle, coming out on the back wall by the chicken parts. She looked left and right.

No sign of the man.

Now what?

Mrs. Lamb. Room 17 . . .

She moved to her right, checking down the aisles as she went. Her hand slid into her pocketbook, fumbled a bit, touched down on her cell phone.

Stay calm, she told herself. Call the school.

Grace tried to pick up the pace, but her leg dragged like a lead bar. The more she hurried, the more pronounced the limp became. When she really tried to run, she resembled Quasimodo heading up the belfry. Didn't matter, of course, what she looked like. The problem was function: She wasn't moving fast enough.

Mrs. Lamb. Room 17 . . .

If he's done anything to my baby, if he's so much as looked at her wrong . . .

Grace reached the last aisle, the refrigerated section that housed the milk and eggs, the aisle farthest from the entrance so as to encourage impulse buy. She started toward the front of the store, hoping that she'd find him when she doubled back. She fiddled with her phone as she moved, no easy task, scrolling through her saved phone numbers to see if she had the school's.

She didn't.

Damn. Grace bet those other mothers, the good mothers, the ones with the perky smiles and ideal after-school projects – she bet they had the school's phone number preprogrammed into their speed dial.

Mrs. Lamb. Room 17 . . .

Try directory assistance, stupid. Dial 411.

She hit the digits and the send button. When she reached the end of the aisle, she looked down the row of cashiers.

No sign of the man.

On the phone the thunder-deep voice of James Earl Jones announced: 'Verizon Wireless four-one-one.' Then a ding. A woman's voice now: 'For English please stay on the line. *Para español, por favor numero dos.*'

And it was then, listening to this Spanish option, that Grace spotted the man again.

He was outside the store now. She could see him through the plate glass window. He still wore the cap and the black windbreaker. He was strolling casually, too casually, whistling even, swinging his arms. She was about to start moving again when something – something in the man's hand – made her blood freeze.

It couldn't be.

Again it did not register immediately. The sight, the stimuli the eye was sending to the brain, would not compute, the information causing some sort of short circuit. Again not for long. Only for a second or two.

Grace's hand, the one with the phone in it, dropped to her side. The man kept walking. Terror – terror unlike anything she had ever experienced before, terror that made the Boston Massacre feel like an amusement park ride – hardened and banged against her chest. The man was almost out of sight now. There was a smile on his face. He was still whistling. His arms were still swinging.

And in his hand, his right hand, the hand closest to the window, he held a Batman lunchbox.

30

'Mrs. Lawson,' Sylvia Steiner, the principal of Willard School, said to Grace in that voice that principals use when dealing with hysterical parents, 'Emma is fine. So is Max.'

By the time Grace had made it to the door at King's, the man with the Batman lunchbox was gone. She started screaming, started asking for help, but her fellow shoppers looked at her as if she'd escaped from the county mental facility. There was no time to explain. She did her limp-run to her car, called the school while driving a speed that would have intimidated an Andretti, and burst straight into the main office.

'I spoke to both of their teachers. They're in class.'

'I want to see them.'

'Of course, that's your right, but may I make a suggestion?'

Sylvia Steiner spoke so damn slowly that Grace wanted to reach her hand down her throat and rip the words out.

'I'm sure you've had a terrible fright, but take a few deep breaths. Calm yourself first. You'll scare your children if they see you like this.'

Part of Grace wanted to grab her patronizing, smug, over-coiffed 'do and pull it off her head. But another part of her, a bigger part, realized that the woman was speaking the truth.

'I just need to see them,' Grace said.

'I understand. How about this? We can peek in on them from the window at the door. Would that work for you, Mrs. Lawson?'

Grace nodded.

'Come on then, I'll escort you.' Principal Steiner shot the woman working the desk a look. The woman at the desk, Mrs. Dinsmont, did everything she could not to roll her eyes. Every school has a seen-it-all woman like this at the front desk. State law or something.

The corridors were explosions of color. The artwork of children always broke Grace's heart. The pieces were like snapshots, a moment that is forever gone, a life-post, never to be repeated. Their artistic abilities will mature and change. The innocence will be gone, captured only in fingerpaint or coloring out of the lines, in uneven handwriting.

They reached Max's classroom first. Grace put her face to the glass. She spotted her son immediately. Max's back was to her, his face tilted up. He sat cross-legged in a circle on the floor. His teacher, Miss Lyons, was in a chair. She was reading a picture book, holding it up so the children could see it, while she read.

'Okay?' Principal Steiner asked.

Grace nodded.

They continued down the corridor. Grace saw number 17 . . .

Mrs. Lamb. Room 17 . . .

. . . on the door. She felt a fresh shiver and tried not to hurry. Principal Steiner, she knew, had noticed the limp. The leg ached in a way it hadn't in years. She peered through the glass. Her daughter was there, right where she should be. Grace had to fight back the tears. Emma had her head down. The eraser end of her pencil was in her mouth. She chewed on it, deep in thought. Why, Grace wondered, do we find such poignancy in watching our children when they don't know we're there? What exactly are we trying to see?

So now what?

Deep breaths. Calm. Her children were okay. That was

the key thing. Think it through. Be rational.

Call the police. That was the obvious move.

Principal Steiner faked a cough. Grace looked at her.

'I know this is going to sound nuts,' Grace said, 'but I need to see Emma's lunchbox.'

Grace expected a look of surprise or exasperation, but no, Sylvia Steiner just nodded. She did not ask why – had in fact not questioned her bizarre behavior in any way. Grace was grateful.

'All the lunchboxes are kept in the cafeteria,' she explained. 'Each class has their own bucket. Would you like me to show you?'

'Thank you.'

The buckets were all lined up in grade order. They found the big blue bucket marked 'Susan Lamb, Room 17' and started going through it.

'What does it look like?' Principal Steiner asked.

Just as she was about to reply Grace saw it. Batman. The word *POW!* in yellow caps. She slowly lifted it into view. Emma's name was written on the bottom.

'Is that it?'

Grace nodded.

'A popular one this year.'

It took all her effort not to clutch the lunchbox to her chest. She put it back as though it were Venetian glass. They headed back to the main office in silence. Grace was tempted to pull the kids out of school. It was two-thirty. They'd be let out in a half an hour anyway. But no, that wouldn't work. That would probably just freak them out. She needed time to think, to consider her response, and when she thought about it, weren't Emma and Max safest right here, surrounded by others?

Grace thanked the principal again. They shook hands.

'Is there anything else I can do?' the principal asked.

'No, I don't think so.'

Grace left then. She stood outside on the walk. She

closed her eyes for a moment. The fear was not so much dissolving as solidifying, turning into pure, primitive rage. She could feel the heat running up her neck. That bastard. That bastard had threatened her daughter.

Now what?

The police. She should call them. That was the obvious move. The phone was in her hand. She was about to dial when a simple thought stopped her: What exactly would she say?

Hi, I was in the supermarket today, see, and this man near the bologna section? Well, he whispered the name of my kid's teacher. Right, teacher. Oh, and her classroom number. Yes, at the bologna section, right there with the Oscar Mayer meats. And then the man ran off. But, I saw him later with my daughter's lunchbox. Outside the supermarket. What was he doing? Just walking, I guess. Well, no, it wasn't really Emma's lunchbox. It was the same kind. Batman. No, he didn't make any overt threats. Sorry? Yes, I'm the same woman who said her husband had been kidnapped yesterday. Right, then my husband called and said he needed space. Yep, that was me, the same hysterical broad . . .

Was there another option?

She ran it through again. The police already thought she was a whack job. Could she convince them otherwise? Perhaps. What would the cops do anyway? Would they assign a man full time to watch her children? Doubtful, even if she could somehow make them understand the urgency.

Then she remembered Scott Duncan.

He was with the U.S. attorney's office. That was like being a federal cop, right? He would have pull. He would have power. And most of all he would believe her.

Duncan had given her his cell number. She checked her pocket for it. Came up empty. Had she left it in the car? Probably. Didn't matter. He told her that he was heading back to work. The U.S. attorney's office was in Newark, she figured. Either that or Trenton. Trenton was too far a ride. Better to try Newark first. He should be there by now.

She stopped walking and turned to face the school. Her children were inside. Weird thought, but there it was. They spent their days here, away from her in this bastion of brick, and part of Grace found that oddly overwhelming. She dialed directory assistance and asked for the U.S. attorney's office in Newark. She spent the extra thirty-five cents to have the operator dial it for her.

'U.S. attorney for the state of New Jersey.'

'Scott Duncan, please.'

'Hold.'

Two rings and a woman answered. 'Goldberg,' she said.

'I'm looking for Scott Duncan.'

'What case?'

'Pardon?'

'What case is this in reference to?'

'No case. I just need to speak with Mr. Duncan.'

'May I ask what it's about?'

'It's a personal matter.'

'Sorry, I can't help you. Scott Duncan doesn't work here anymore. I'm covering most of his cases. If I can help you with that . . .'

Grace pulled the phone away from her ear. She looked at it as though from afar. She clicked the end button. She got into her car and again watched the brick building that currently housed her children. She watched it for a very long time, wondering if there was anyone she could truly trust, before deciding what to do.

She lifted the phone back into view. She pressed in the number.

'Yes?'

'This is Grace Lawson.'

Three seconds later, Carl Vespa said, 'Is everything okay?'

'I changed my mind,' Grace said. 'I do need your help.'

31

'His name is Eric Wu.'

Perlmutter was back at the hospital. He had been working on getting a warrant compelling Indira Khariwalla to tell him who her client was, but the county prosecutor was running into more interference than expected. In the meantime the lab boys were doing their thing. The fingerprints had been sent down to the NCIC, and now, if Daley was to be believed, they had an ID on the perp.

'Does he have a record?' Perlmutter asked.

'He was let out of Walden three months ago.'

'For?'

'Armed assault,' Daley said. 'Wu cut a deal on that Scope case. I called and asked around. This is one very bad man.'

'How bad?'

'Poop-in-your-pants bad. If ten percent of the rumors about this guy are true, I'm sleeping with my Barney the Dinosaur night-lite on.'

'I'm listening.'

'He grew up in North Korea. Orphaned at a young age. Spent time working for the state inside prisons for political dissidents. He has a talent with pressure points or something, I don't know. That's what he did with that Sykes guy, some kung-fu crap, practically severed his spine. One story I heard, he kidnapped some guy's wife, worked on her for like two hours. He calls the husband and tells him to listen up. The wife starts screaming. Then she tells him, the husband, that she hates his guts. Starts cursing him. That's the last thing the husband ever hears.'

'He killed the woman?'

Daley's face had never looked so solemn. 'That's just it. He didn't.'

The room's temperature dropped ten degrees. 'I don't understand.'

'Wu let her go. She hasn't spoken since. Just sits and rocks someplace. The husband comes near her, she freaks out and starts screaming.'

'Jesus.' Perlmutter felt the chill ease through him. 'You got an extra night-lite?'

'I got two, yeah, but I'm using both.'

'So what would this guy want with Freddy Sykes?'

'Not a clue.'

Charlaine Swain appeared down the corridor. She had not left the hospital since the shooting. They had finally gotten her to talk to Freddy Sykes. It had been a strange scene. Sykes kept crying. Charlaine had tried to get information. It'd worked to some extent. Freddy Sykes seemed to know nothing. He had no idea who his assailant was or why anyone would want to hurt him. Sykes was just a small-time accountant who lived alone – he seemed to be on no one's radar.

'It's all linked,' Perlmutter said.

'You have a theory?'

'I have some of it. Strands.'

'Let's hear.'

'Start with the E-ZPass records.'

'Okay.'

'We have Jack Lawson and Rocky Conwell crossing that exit at the same time,' Perlmutter said.

'Right.'

'I think now we know why. Conwell was working for a private investigator.'

'Your friend India Something.'

'Indira Khariwalla. And she's hardly a friend. But that's not important. What makes sense here, the only thing that makes sense really, is that Conwell was hired to follow Lawson.'

'Ipso facto, the E-ZPass timing explained.'

Perlmutter nodded, trying to put it together. 'So what happened next? Conwell ends up dead. The M.E. says he probably died that night before midnight. We know he crossed the tollbooth at 10:26 P.M. So sometime soon after that, Rocky Conwell met up with foul play.' Perlmutter rubbed his face. 'The logical suspect would be Jack Lawson. He realizes he's being followed. He confronts Conwell. He kills him.'

'Makes sense,' Daley said.

'But it doesn't. Think about it. Rocky Conwell was six-five, two-sixty, and in great shape. You think a guy like Lawson could have killed him like that? With his bare hands?'

'Sweet Jesus.' Daley saw it now. 'Eric Wu?'

Perlmutter nodded. 'It adds up. Somehow Conwell met up with Wu. Wu killed him, stuffed his body into a trunk, and left him at the Park-n-Ride. Charlaine Swain said that Wu was driving a Ford Windstar. Same model and color as Jack Lawson's.'

'So what's the connection between Lawson and Wu?'

'I don't know.'

'Maybe Wu works for him.'

'Could be. We just don't know. What we do know, however, is that Lawson's alive – or at least he was alive after Conwell was killed.'

'Right, because he called his wife. When she was at the station. So what happened next?'

'Damned if I know.'

Perlmutter watched Charlaine Swain. She just stood down the hall, staring through the window of her husband's room. Perlmutter considered going over, but really, what could he say?

Daley jostled him and they both turned to see Officer

Veronique Baltrus walk off the elevator. Baltrus had been with the department three years. She was thirty-eight, with tousled black hair and a constant tan. She was in a regulation police uniform that somehow hugged as much as anything with a belt and holster could, but in her off-hours she preferred Lycra workout clothes or anything that revealed the flat tan of her stomach. She was petite, with dark eyes, and every guy in the station, even Perlmutter, had a thing for her.

Veronique Baltrus was both exquisitely beautiful and a computer expert – an interesting albeit heart-racing combination. Six years ago she had been working for a bathing suit retailer in New York City when the stalking began. The stalker would call her. He would send e-mails. He would harass her at work. His main weapon was the computer, the best bastion for the anonymous and gutless. The police did not have the manpower to hunt him down. They also believed that this stalker, whoever he was, would probably not take it to the next level.

But he did.

On a calm fall evening Veronique Baltrus was savagely attacked. Her assailant got away. But Veronique recovered. Already good with computers, she now upped her ability and became an expert. She used her new knowledge to hunt down her assailant – he continued to send her e-mails discussing an encore – and bring him to justice. Then she quit her job and became a police officer.

Now, even though Baltrus wore a uniform and worked a regular shift, she was the county's unofficial computer expert. Nobody in the department but Perlmutter knew her back story. That was part of the deal when she applied for the job.

'You got something?' he asked her.

Veronique Baltrus smiled. She had a nice smile. Perlmutter's 'thing' for her was different than the rest of the guys'. It was not built simply on lust. Veronique Baltrus was the first woman to make him feel something since Marion's death. He wouldn't take it anywhere. It would be unprofessional. It would be unethical. And truth be told, Veronique was waaaaay out of his league.

She gestured down the corridor toward Charlaine Swain. 'We might have to thank her.'

'How so?'

'Al Singer.'

That, Sykes had told Charlaine, was the name Eric Wu used when he pretended to be making a delivery. When Charlaine asked who Al Singer was, Sykes jolted a little and denied knowing any Mr. Singer. He said he opened the door anyway out of curiosity. Perlmutter said, 'I thought Al Singer was a fake name.'

'Yes and no,' Baltrus said. 'I went through Mr. Sykes's computer pretty thoroughly. He'd signed up for an online dating service and had been corresponding fairly regularly with a man named Al Singer.'

Perlmutter made a face. 'A gay dating service?'

'Bisexual, actually. That a problem?'

'No. So Al Singer was, what, his online lover?'

'Al Singer doesn't exist. It was an alias.'

'Isn't that common online, especially at a gay dating service? Using an alias?'

'It is,' Baltrus agreed. 'But here's my point. Your Mr. Wu pretended to make a delivery. He used that name, Singer. How would Wu know about Al Singer unless . . . ?'

'You saying Eric Wu is Al Singer?'

Baltrus nodded, rested her hands on her hips. 'That would be my guess, sure. Here's what I think: Wu goes online. He uses the name Al Singer. He meets some people – potential victims – that way. In this case, he meets Freddy Sykes. He breaks into his home and assaults him. My guess is, he would have eventually killed Sykes.'

'You think he's done this before?'

'Yes.'

'So he's, what, some kind of serial bisexual basher?'

'That I don't know. But it fits the action I'm seeing on the computer.'

Perlmutter thought about it. 'Does this Al Singer have any other online partners?'

'Three more.'

'Have any of them been assaulted?'

'Not yet, no. They're all healthy.'

'So what makes you think it's serial?'

'It's too early to say for sure one way or the other. But Charlaine Swain did us a huge favor. Wu was using Sykes's computer. He probably planned on destroying it before he left, but Charlaine flushed him out before he had time. I'm piecing it together now, but there's definitely another on-line persona in there. I don't know the name yet, but he's working out of yenta-match.com. Jewish singles.'

'How do we know it's not Freddy Sykes?'

'Because whoever accessed this page did so in the past twenty-four hours.'

'So it had to be Wu.'

'Yes.'

'I still don't get it. Why would he go to another online dating service?'

'To find more victims,' she said. 'Here's how I think it works: This Wu has a bunch of different names and per-sonas at a bunch of different dating sites. Once he, shall we say, uses one, like Al Singer, he won't dip into that dat-ing pool again. He used Al Singer to get to Freddy Sykes. He'd have to know that an investigator could track that down.'

'So he stops using Al Singer.'

'Right. But he's been using other aliases at other sites. So he's ready for his next victim.'

'Do you have any of the other names yet?'

'Getting close,' Baltrus said. 'I just need a warrant for yenta-match.com.'

'You think a judge will grant it?'

'The only identity we know Wu accessed recently is the one at the yenta-match site. I think he was seeking out his next victim. If we can get a list of what name he used and who he contacted . . .'

'Keep digging.'

'Will do.'

Veronique Baltrus hurried out. Wrong as it felt – he was, after all, her superior – Perlmutter watched her go with a longing that made him remember Marion.

32

Ten minutes later Carl Vespa's driver – the infamous Cram
– met Grace two blocks away from the school.

Cram arrived on foot. Grace did not know how or
where his car was. She'd just been standing there, looking
at the school from afar, when she felt the tap on her shoulder. She leapt, her heart pounding. When she turned and
saw his face, well, the sight was hardly a comforting one.

Cram arched an eyebrow. 'You rang?'

'How did you get here?'

Cram shook his head. Up close, now that she was able
to get a really good look at him, the man was even more
hideous than she remembered. His skin was pockmarked.
His nose and mouth looked like an animal's snout, what
with the sea-predator smile locked on autopilot. Cram
was older than she'd thought, probably nearing sixty. He
was wiry though. He had the wild-eyed look she'd always
associated with serious psychosis, but there was a comfort
to that element of danger right now, the kind of guy you'd
want next to you in a foxhole and nowhere else.

'Tell me everything,' Cram said.

Grace started with Scott Duncan and moved on to arriving at the supermarket. She told him what the unshaven
man had said to her, about him darting down the aisle,
about him carrying the Batman lunchbox. Cram chewed on
a toothpick. He had thin fingers. His nails were too long.

'Describe him.'

She did as best she could. When she was done, Cram
spit out the toothpick and shook his head. 'For real?' he
said.

'What?'

'A Members Only jacket? What is this, 1986?'

Grace did not laugh.

'You're safe now,' he said. 'Your children are safe.'

She believed him.

'What time do they get out?'

'Three o'clock.'

'Fine.' He squinted at the school. 'Christ, I hated this place.'

'You went here?'

Cram nodded. 'A Willard graduate, 1957.' She tried to picture him as a little boy coming to this school. The image would not hold. He started walking away.

'Wait,' she said. 'What do you want me to do?'

'Pick up your kids. Bring them home.'

'Where will you be?'

Cram upped the grin. 'Around.' And then he was gone.

Grace waited by the fence. The mothers began to flock in, gather, chat. Grace folded her arms, trying to give off a 'keep away' vibe. There were days she could participate in the clatter. This was not one of them.

The cell phone rang. She put it to her ear and said hello.

'You get the message now?'

The voice was male and muffled. Grace felt her scalp tingle. 'Stop looking, stop asking questions, stop flashing the picture. Or we'll take Emma first.'

Click.

Grace did not scream. She would not scream. She put the phone away. Her hands shook. She looked down at them as if they belonged to someone else. She couldn't stop the shake. Her children would be coming out soon. She jammed her hands into her pockets and tried to force up a smile. It wouldn't come. She bit her lower lip and made herself not cry.

'Hey, you okay?'

Grace startled at the voice. It was Cora.

'What are you doing here?' Grace asked. The words came out with too sharp a snap.

'What do you think? I'm picking up Vickie.'

'I thought she was with her father.'

Cora looked puzzled. 'Just for last night. He dropped her off at school this morning. Jesus, what the hell happened?'

'I can't talk about it.'

Cora did not know how to react to that one. The bell sounded. Both women turned away. Grace did not know what to think. She knew that Scott Duncan was wrong about Cora – more than that, she now knew that Scott Duncan was a liar – and yet, once voiced, the suspicion about her friend would not leave. She couldn't flick it away.

'Look, I'm just scared, okay?'

Cora nodded. Vickie appeared first. 'If you need me . . .'

'Thank you.'

Cora moved away without another word. Grace waited alone, searching for the familiar faces in the stream of children pouring through the door. Emma stepped into the sunshine and shielded her eyes. When she spotted her mother, Emma's face broke into a smile. She waved.

Grace suppressed a cry of relief. Her fingers snaked through the chain-link, gripping hard, holding herself back so she wouldn't sprint over and scoop Emma into her arms.

When Grace, Emma, and Max reached home, Cram was already standing on their front stoop.

Emma looked a question at her mother, but before Grace could respond, Max sprinted up the walk. He stopped dead in front of Cram and craned his neck to look up at the sea-predator smile.

'Hey,' Max said to Cram.

'Hey.'

Max said, 'You were the guy driving that big car, right?'

'Right.'

'That cool? Driving that big car?'

'Very.'

'I'm Max.'

'I'm Cram.'

'Cool name.'

'Yeah. Yeah, it is.'

Max made a fist and held it up. Cram made one too and then they touched knuckles-against-knuckles in some newfangled high-five. Grace and Emma came up the walk.

'Cram is a family friend,' Grace said. 'He's going to help me a little.'

Emma did not like it. 'Help with what?' She aimed her 'eeuw gross' face in Cram's direction, which, under the circumstances, was both understandable and rude, but this was hardly the time for a correction. 'Where's Daddy?'

'He's on a business trip,' Grace said.

Emma did not say another word. She stepped into the house and ran upstairs.

Max squinted up at Cram. 'Can I ask you something?'

'Sure,' Cram said.

'Do all your friends call you Cram?'

'Yes.'

'Just Cram?'

'One word.' He wiggled his eyebrows. 'Like Cher or Fabio.'

'Who?'

Cram chuckled.

'Why do they call you that?' Max asked.

'Why do they call me Cram?'

'Yeah.'

'My teeth.' He opened his mouth wide. When Grace worked up the courage to look, she was greeted with a sight that resembled the mad experiment of a very deranged orthodontist. The teeth were all crammed together on the left, almost stacked. It looked like there were too many of them. Empty pockets of coarse pink where teeth should have been lined the right side of his mouth. 'Cram,' he said. 'You see?'

'Whoa,' Max said. 'That's so cool.'

'You want to know how my teeth got this way?'

Grace took that one. 'No, thank you.'

Cram glanced at her. 'Good answer.'

Cram. She took another look at the too-small teeth. Tic Tac might have been a more apt name.

'Max, you have homework?'

'Aw, Mom.'

'Now,' she said.

Max looked at Cram. 'Scram,' he said. 'We'll talk later.'

They shared another fist-knuckle salute before Max darted off with the abandon of a six-year-old. The phone rang. Grace checked the Caller ID. It was Scott Duncan. She decided to let the machine pick that one up – more important that she talk to Cram. They moved into the kitchen. There were two men sitting at the table. Grace pulled up short. Neither of the men looked up at her. They were whispering to each other. Grace was about to say something, but Cram signaled her to step outside.

'Who are they?'

'They work for me.'

'Doing?'

'Don't worry about it.'

She did, but right now there were more pressing matters. 'I got a call from the guy,' she said. 'On my cell phone.' She told him what the voice on the phone had said. Cram's expression did not change. When she finished, he pulled out a cigarette.

'You mind if I smoke?'

She told him to go ahead.

'I won't do it in the house.'

Grace looked around. 'Is that why we're out here?'

Cram did not reply. He lit the cigarette, drew a deep breath, let the smoke pour out of both nostrils. Grace looked toward the neighbor's yard. There was no one in sight. A dog barked. A lawn mower ripped through the air like a helicopter.

Grace looked at him. 'You've threatened people, right?'

'Yup.'

'So if I do what he says – if I stop – do you think they'll leave us alone?'

'Probably.' Cram took a puff so deep it looked like a doobie toke. 'But the real question is, why do they want you to stop?'

'Meaning?'

'Meaning you must have been getting close. You must have struck a nerve.'

'I can't imagine how.'

'Mr. Vespa called. He wants to see you tonight.'

'What about?'

Cram shrugged.

She looked off again.

'You ready for some more bad news?' Cram asked.

She turned to him.

'Your computer room. The one in the back.'

'What about it?'

'It's bugged. One listening device, one camera.'

'A camera?' She couldn't believe this. 'In my house?'

'Yeah. Hidden camera. It's in a book on the shelf. Fairly easy to spot if you're looking for it. You can get one at any spy shop. You've probably seen them online. You hide it in a clock or a smoke detector, that kind of thing.'

Grace tried to take this in. 'Someone is spying on us?'

'Yup.'

'Who?'

'No idea. I don't think it's the cops. It's a little too amateur for that. My boys have given the rest of the house a quick sweep. Nothing else so far.'

'How long . . .' She tried to comprehend what he was telling her. 'How long has the camera and – listening device, did you say? – how long have they been here?'.

'No way to know. That's why I dragged you out here. So we could talk freely. I know you've been hit with a lot, but you're ready to deal with this now?'

She nodded, though her head was swimming.

'Okay, first off. The equipment. It's not all that sophisticated. It only has a range of maybe a hundred feet. If it's a live feed, it goes to a van or something. Have you noticed any vans parked on the street for long periods of time?'

'No.'

'I didn't think so. It probably just goes to a video recorder.'

'Like a VCR?'

'Exactly like a VCR.'

'And it has to be within a hundred feet of the house?'

'Yep.'

She looked around as if it might be in the garden. 'How often would they need to change tape?'

'Every twenty-four hours tops.'

'Any idea where it is?'

'Not yet. Sometimes they keep the recorder in the basement or garage. They probably have access to the house, so they can fetch the tape and put in a new one.'

'Wait a second. What do you mean, they have access to the house?'

He shrugged. 'They got that camera and bug in somehow, right?'

The rage was back now, rising, smoldering behind her eyes. Grace started looking at her neighbors. Access to the house. Who had access to the house? she asked herself. And a small voice replied . . .

Cora.

Uh-uh, no way. Grace shook it off. 'So we need to find that recorder.'

'Yes.'

'And then we wait and watch,' she said. 'We see who picks up the tape.'

'That's one way of doing it,' Cram said.

'You have a better suggestion?'

'Not really.'

'Then, what, we follow the guy, see where it leads?'

'That's a possibility.'

'But . . . ?'

'It's risky. We could lose him.'

'What would you do?'

'If it were up to me, I'd grab him. I'd ask him some hard questions.'

'And if he refused to answer?'

Cram still wore the sea-predator smile. It was always a horrific sight, this man's face, but Grace was getting used to it. She also realized that he was not intentionally scaring her; whatever had been done to his mouth had made that become his permanent, natural expression. It spoke volumes, that face. It rendered her question rhetorical.

Grace wanted to protest, to tell him that she was civil and that they would handle this legally and ethically. But instead she said, 'They threatened my daughter.'

'So they did.'

She looked at him. 'I can't do what they asked. Even if I wanted to. I can't just walk away and leave it alone.'

He said nothing.

'I have no choice, do I? I have to fight them.'

'I don't see any other way.'

'You knew that all along.'

Cram cocked his head to the right. 'So did you.'

His cell phone went off. Cram flipped it open but did not speak, not even a hello. A few seconds later he snapped the phone shut and said, 'Someone is pulling up the drive.'

She looked out the screen door. A Ford Taurus came to a stop. Scott Duncan stepped out and approached the house.

'You know him?' Cram asked.

'That,' she said, 'is Scott Duncan.'

'The guy who lied about working for the U.S. attorney?'

Grace nodded.

'Maybe,' Cram said, 'I'll stick around.'

They remained outside. Scott Duncan stood next to Grace. Cram had stepped away. Duncan kept sneaking glances at Cram. 'Who is that?'

'You don't want to know.'

Grace gave Cram a look. He got the hint and headed back inside. She and Scott Duncan were alone now.

'What do you want?' she asked.

Duncan picked up on her tone. 'Something wrong, Grace?'

'I'm just surprised you got out of work already. I figured it'd be busier at the U.S. attorney's office.'

He said nothing.

'Cat got your tongue, Mr. Duncan?'

'You called my office.'

She touched her nose with her index finger, indicating a direct hit. Then: 'Oh wait, correction: I called the United States attorney's office. Apparently you don't work there.'

'It's not what you think.'

'How enlightening.'

'I should have told you up front.'

'Do tell.'

'Look, everything I said was true.'

'Except the part about working for the United States attorney. I mean, that wasn't true, was it? Or was Ms. Goldberg lying?'

'Do you want me to explain or not?'

Now his voice had a little steel. Grace gestured for him to continue.

'What I told you was true. I worked there. Three months ago this killer, this Monte Scanlon, he insisted on seeing me. No one could understand why. I was a low-level lawyer on political corruption. Why would a hit man insist on talking only to me? That was when he told me.'

'That he killed your sister.'

'Yes.'

She waited. They moved toward the porch furniture and sat down. Cram stood in a window watching them. He let his gaze wander toward Scott Duncan, hang there for a few heavy seconds, survey the grounds, go back to Duncan.

'He looks familiar,' Duncan said, gesturing toward Cram. 'Or maybe I'm flashing back to the Pirates of the Caribbean ride at Disney World. Shouldn't he have an eye patch?'

Grace shifted in her seat. 'You were telling me about why you lied?'

Duncan ran his hand through the sandy hair. 'When Scanlon said the fire was no accident . . . You can't understand what it did to me. I mean, one moment my life was one thing. The next . . .' He snapped his finger with a magician's flourish. 'It wasn't so much that everything was different now – it was more like the past fifteen years had all been different. Like someone had gone back in time and changed one event and it changed everything else. I wasn't the same guy. I wasn't a guy whose sister died in a tragic fire. I was a guy whose sister had been murdered and never avenged.'

'But now you have the killer,' Grace said. 'He confessed.'

Duncan smiled, but there was no joy there. 'Scanlon said it best. He was just a weapon. Like a gun. I wanted the person who pulled the trigger. It became an obsession.

I tried to do it part-time, you know, work my job while searching for the killer. But I started to neglect my cases. So my boss, she strongly suggested I take a leave.' He looked up at her.

'Why didn't you just tell me?'

'I didn't think it would be a great opening line, you know, telling you I was forced out like that. I still have connections in the office. I still have friends in law enforcement. But just so we're clear, everything I'm doing is off the books.'

Their eyes locked. Grace said, 'You're still holding something back.'

He hesitated.

'What is it?'

'We should get one thing straight.' Duncan stood, did the run through the sandy hair bit again, turned away from her. 'Right now we're both trying to find your husband. It's a temporary alliance. The truth is, we have separate agendas. I won't lie to you. What happens after we find Jack, well, do we both want the truth?'

'I just want my husband.'

He nodded. 'That's what I mean about separate agendas. About our alliance being temporary. You want your husband. I want my sister's killer.'

He looked at her now. She understood.

'So now what?' Grace asked.

He took out the mystery photograph and held it up. There was a hint of a smile on his face.

'What?'

Scott Duncan said, 'I know the name of the redhead in the photograph.' She waited.

'Her name is Sheila Lambert. Attended Vermont University the same time as your husband' – he pointed at Jack and then slid his finger to the right – 'and Shane Alworth.'

'Where is she now?'

'That's just the thing, Grace. No one knows.'

She closed her eyes. A shudder ran through her.

'I sent the photograph up to the school. A retired dean identified her. I ran a full check, but she's gone. There is no sign of Sheila Lambert's existence over the past decade – no payroll tax, no social security number hit, nothing.'

'Just like with Shane Alworth.'

'Exactly like Shane.'

Grace tried to put it together. 'Five people in the photograph. One, your sister, was murdered. Two others, Shane Alworth and Sheila Lambert, haven't been heard of in years. The fourth, my husband, ran overseas and is missing now. And the last one, well, we still don't know who she is.'

Duncan nodded.

'So where do we go from here?'

'You remember I said I talked to Shane Alworth's mother?'

'The one with the fuzzy Amazonian geography.'

'When I visited her the first time, I didn't know about this picture or your husband or any of that. I want to show her the picture now. I want to gauge her reaction. And I want you there.'

'Why?'

'I just have a feeling, that's all. Evelyn Alworth is an old woman. She's emotional and I think she's scared. I went in there the first time as an investigator. Maybe, I don't know, but maybe if you go in as a concerned mother, something will shake loose.'

Grace hesitated. 'Where does she live?'

'A condo in Bedminster. Shouldn't take us more than thirty minutes to get there.'

Cram came back into view. Scott Duncan nodded toward him.

'So what's with that scary guy?' Duncan asked.

'I can't go with you now.'

'Why not?'

'I have the kids. I can't just leave them here.'

'Bring them along. There's a playground right there. We won't take long.'

Cram came to the door now. He beckoned with his hand for Grace. She said, 'Excuse me' and headed toward Cram. Scott Duncan stayed where he was.

'What is it?' she asked Cram.

'Emma. She's upstairs crying.'

Grace found her daughter in classic cry position – face-down on her bed, pillow over her head. The sound was muted. It had been a while since Emma had cried like this. Grace sat on the edge of the bed. She knew what was coming. When Emma could speak, she asked where Daddy was. Grace told her that he was on a business trip. Emma said that she didn't believe her. That it was a lie. Emma demanded to know the truth. Grace repeated that Jack was just on a business trip. That everything was fine. Emma pushed. Where was he? Why hadn't Daddy called? When was he coming home? Grace made up rationales that sounded pretty believable in her ears – he was really busy, he was traveling in Europe, London right now, didn't know how long he'd be gone, he had called but Emma had been sleeping, remember that London is in a different time zone.

Did Emma buy it? Who knew?

Child-rearing experts – those namby-pamby, lobotomy-voiced Ph.D.s on cable TV – would probably tsk-tsk, but Grace was not one of those tell-kids-everything parents. Above all else a mother's job was to protect. Emma was not old enough to handle the truth. Plain and simple. Deception was a necessary part of parenting. Of course Grace could be wrong – she knew that – but the old adage is true: Kids don't come with instructions. We all mess up. Raising a child is pure impromptu.

A few minutes later she told Max and Emma to get

ready. They were going for a ride. Both children grabbed their Game Boys and piled into the back of the car. Scott Duncan moved toward the passenger seat. Cram cut him off.

'Problem?' Duncan said.

'I want to talk to Ms. Lawson before you go. Stay here.'

Duncan snapped a sarcastic salute. Cram gave him a look that could have held back a weather front. He and Grace stepped into the back room. Cram closed the door.

'You know you shouldn't go with him.'

'Maybe not. But I have to.'

Cram chewed on his lower lip. He didn't like it, but he understood. 'Do you carry a purse?'

'Yes.'

'Let me see it.'

She showed it to him. Cram pulled a gun out of his waist. It was small, almost toylike. 'This is a Glock nine-millimeter, model 26.'

Grace held up her hands. 'I don't want that.'

'Keep it in your purse. You can also wear it in an ankle holster but you'll need long pants.'

'I've never fired a gun in my life.'

'Experience is overrated. You aim for the middle of the chest, you squeeze the trigger. It's not complicated.'

'I don't like weapons.'

Cram shook his head.

'What?'

'Maybe I'm mistaken, but didn't somebody threaten your daughter today?'

That made her pause. Cram put the gun in her purse. She did not fight him.

'How long are you going to be gone?' Cram asked.

'Couple of hours, tops.'

'Mr. Vespa will be here at 7 P.M. He says it's important that he speaks to you.'

'I'll be here.'

245

'You sure you trust this Duncan guy?'

'I'm not sure. But I think we're safe with him.'

Cram nodded. 'Let me add a little insurance on that front.'

'How?'

Cram said nothing. He escorted her back. Scott Duncan was on his cell phone. Grace did not like what she saw on Duncan's face. He finished up his call when he spotted them.

'What?'

Scott Duncan shook his head. 'Can we go now?'

Cram walked toward him. Duncan did not back down, but there was definitely an understandable flinch. Cram stopped directly in front of him, stuck out his hand, wiggled his fingers. 'Let me see your wallet.'

'Pardon me?'

'Do I look like the kind of guy who enjoys repeating himself?'

Scott Duncan glanced at Grace. She nodded. Cram still had the fingers wiggling. Duncan handed Cram his wallet. Cram brought it over to a table and sat down. He quickly rifled through the contents, taking notes.

'What are you doing?' Duncan asked.

'While you're gone, Mr. Duncan, I'm going to learn everything about you.' He looked up. 'If Ms. Lawson is harmed in any way, my response will be' – Cram stopped, looked up as though searching for the word – 'disproportionate. I make myself clear?'

Duncan looked at Grace. 'Who the hell is this guy?'

Grace was already moving toward the car door. 'We'll be fine, Cram.'

Cram shrugged, tossed Duncan his wallet. 'Have a delightful drive.'

No one talked for the first five minutes of the ride. Max and Emma used their headphones with the Game Boys. Grace had bought the headphones recently because the beeps and buzzes and Luigi shouting 'Mamma Mia!' every two minutes gave her a headache. Scott Duncan sat next to her with his hands in his lap.

'So who was on the phone?' Grace asked.

'A coroner.'

Grace waited.

'Remember how I told you that I had my sister's body exhumed?' he said.

'Yes.'

'The police didn't really see a need for it. Too expensive. I understand, I guess. Anyway I paid for it myself. I know this person, used to work for a country M.E., who does private autopsies.'

'And he's the one who called you?'

'It's a she. Her name is Sally Li.'

'And?'

'And she says she needs to see me right away.' Duncan looked over at her. 'Her office is in Livingston. We can hit it on the way back.' He turned back away. 'I'd like you to come with me, if that's okay.'

'To a morgue?'

'No, nothing like that. Sally does the actual autopsy work at St. Barnabas Hospital. This is just an office where she does her paperwork. There's a waiting room we can stick the kids in.'

Grace did not reply.

The Bedminster condos were generic, which, when you're talking about condos, is something of a repetition in terms. They had the prefab light-brown aluminum siding, three levels, garages underneath, every building identical to the one to its right and to its left and behind it and in front of it. The complex was huge and sprawling, a khaki-coated ocean stretching as far as the eye could see.

For Grace, the route here had been familiar. Jack drove by this on his way to work. They had, for a very brief moment, debated moving into this condo development.

Neither Jack nor Grace was particularly good with their hands or enjoyed fix-the-old-home shows on cable. Condos held that appeal – you pay a monthly fee, you don't worry about the roof or an addition or the landscaping or any of that. There were tennis courts and a swimming pool and, yes, a playground for children. But in the end there was just so much conformity one could take. Suburbia is already a subworld of sameness. Why add insult to injury by making your physical abode conform too?

Max spotted the complicated, brightly hued playground before the car had come to a complete stop. He was raring to sprint for the swing set. Emma looked more bored with the prospect. She held onto her Game Boy. Normally Grace would have protested – Game Boy in the car only, especially when the alternative was fresh air – but again now did not seem the time.

Grace cupped her hand over her eyes as they started moving away. 'I can't leave them alone.'

'Mrs. Alworth lives right here,' Duncan said. 'We can stay in the doorway and watch them.'

They approached the door on the first level. The playground was quiet. The air was still. Grace inhaled deeply and smelled the freshly cut grass. They stood side-by-side, she and Duncan. He rang the bell. Grace waited by the door, feeling oddly like a Jehovah's Witness.

A cackling voice not unlike the witch in an old Disney film said, 'Who is it?'

'Mrs. Alworth?'

Again the cackle: 'Who is it?'

'Mrs. Alworth, it's Scott Duncan.'

'Who?'

'Scott Duncan. We spoke a few weeks ago. About your son, Shane.'

'Go away. I have nothing to say to you.'

Grace picked up an accent now. Boston area.

'We could really use your help.'

'I don't know nothing. Go away.'

'Please, Mrs. Alworth, I need to talk to you about your son.'

'I told you. Shane lives in Mexico. He's a good boy. He helps poor people.'

'We need to ask about some of his old friends.' Scott Duncan looked at Grace, nodded for her to say something.

'Mrs. Alworth,' Grace said.

The cackle was more wary now. 'Who's that?'

'My name is Grace Lawson. I think my husband knew your son.'

There was silence now. Grace turned away from the door and watched Max and Emma. Max was on a corkscrew slide. Emma sat cross-legged and played the Game Boy.

Through the door, the cackling voice asked, 'Who's your husband?'

'Jack Lawson.'

Nothing.

'Mrs. Alworth?'

'I don't know him.'

Scott Duncan said, 'We have a picture. We'd like to show it to you.'

The door opened. Mrs. Alworth wore a housedress that couldn't have been manufactured after the Bay of Pigs. She was in her mid-seventies, heavyset, the kind of big aunt who hugs you and you disappear in the folds. As a kid you hate the hug. As an adult you long for it. She had varicose veins that resembled sausage casing. Her reading glasses dangled against her enormous chest from a chain. She smelled faintly of cigarette smoke.

'I don't have all day,' she said. 'Show me this picture.'

Scott Duncan handed her the photograph.

For a long time the old woman said nothing.

'Mrs. Alworth?'

'Why did someone cross her out?' she asked.

'That was my sister,' Duncan said.

She flicked a glance his way. 'I thought you said you were an investigator.'

'I am. My sister was murdered. Her name was Geri Duncan.'

Mrs. Alworth's face went white. Her lip started to tremble. 'She's dead?'

'She was murdered. Fifteen years ago. Do you remember her?'

She seemed to have lost her bearings. She turned to Grace and snapped, 'What do you keep looking at?'

Grace was facing Max and Emma. 'My children.' She gestured toward the playground. Mrs. Alworth followed suit. She stiffened. She seemed lost now, confused.

'Did you know my sister?' Duncan asked.

'What does this have to do with me?'

His voice was stern now. 'Yes or no, did you know my sister?'

'I can't remember. It was a long time ago.'

'Your son dated her.'

'He dated a lot of girls. Shane was a handsome boy. So was his brother, Paul. He's a psychologist in Missouri. Why don't you leave me alone and talk to him?'

'Try to think.' Scott's voice rose a notch. 'My sister was murdered.' He pointed to the picture of Shane Alworth. 'That's your son, isn't it, Mrs. Alworth?'

She stared down at the strange photograph for a long time before nodding.

'Where is he?'

'I told you before. Shane lives in Mexico. He helps poor people.'

'When was the last time you spoke with him?'

'Last week.'

'He called you?'

'Yes.'

'Where?'

'What do you mean where?'

'Did Shane call you here?'

'Of course. Where else would he call?'

Scott Duncan took a step closer. 'I checked your phone records, Mrs. Alworth. You haven't gotten or made an international call in the past year.'

'Shane uses one of those phone cards,' she said too quickly. 'Maybe the phone companies don't pick those up, how I should know?'

Duncan took another step closer. 'Listen to me, Mrs. Alworth. And please listen closely. My sister is dead. There is no sign of your son anywhere. This man here' – he pointed to the picture of Jack – 'her husband, Jack Lawson, he's also missing. And this woman over here' – he pointed to the redheaded girl with the spaced-out eyes – 'her name is Sheila Lambert. There's been no sign of her for at least ten years.'

'This has got nothing to do with me,' Mrs. Alworth insisted.

'Five people in the photograph. We've been able to identify four of them. They're all gone. One we know is dead. For all we know, they all are.'

'I told you. Shane is –'

'You're lying, Mrs. Alworth. Your son graduated Vermont University. So did Jack Lawson and Sheila Lambert. They must have been friends. He dated my sister; we both know that. So what happened to them? Where is your son?'

Grace put a hand on Scott's arm. Mrs. Alworth was staring out now toward the playground, at the children. Her bottom lip was quivering. Her skin was ashen. Tears ran down both cheeks. She looked as if she'd fallen into a trance. Grace tried to step in her line of vision.

'Mrs. Alworth,' she said gently.

'I'm an old woman.'

Grace waited.

'I don't have nothing to say to you people.'

Grace said, 'I'm trying to find my husband.' Mrs. Alworth was still staring at the playground. 'I'm trying to find their father.'

'Shane is a good boy. He helps people.'

'What happened to him?' Grace asked.

'Leave me alone.'

Grace tried to meet the older woman's gaze, but the focus was gone from her eyes. 'His sister' – Grace gestured toward Duncan – 'my husband, your son. Whatever happened affected us all. We want to help.'

But the old woman shook her head and turned away. 'My son doesn't need your help. Now go away. Please.' She stepped back into her house and closed the door.

33

When they were back in the car, Grace said, 'When you told Mrs. Alworth you checked her phone records for international calls . . .'

Duncan nodded. 'It was a bluff.'

The children were plugged back into their Game Boys. Scott Duncan called the coroner. She was waiting for them.

Grace said, 'We're getting closer to the answer, aren't we?'

'I think so.'

'Mrs. Alworth might be telling the truth. I mean, as far as she knows.'

'How do you figure?' he asked.

'Something happened years ago. Jack ran away overseas. Maybe Shane Alworth and Sheila Lambert did too. Your sister, for whatever reason, hung around and ended up dead.'

He did not reply. His eyes were suddenly moist. There was a tremor in the corner of his mouth.

'Scott?'

'She called me. Geri. Two days before the fire.'

Grace waited.

'I was running out the door. You have to understand. Geri was a bit of a kook. She was always so melodramatic. She said she had to tell me something important, but I figured it could wait. I figured it was about whatever new thing she was into – aromatherapy, her new rock band, her etchings, whatever. I said I'd call her back.'

He stopped, shrugged. 'But I forgot.'

Grace wanted to say something, but nothing came to

her. Words of comfort would probably do more harm than good right now. She took hold of the wheel and glanced in the rearview mirror. Emma and Max both had their heads lowered, their thumbs working the buttons on the tiny console. She felt that overwhelmed thing coming on, that pure blast in the middle of normalcy, the bliss from the everyday.

'Do you mind if we stop at the coroner's now?' Duncan asked.

Grace hesitated.

'It's about a mile away. Just turn right at the next light.'

In for a penny, Grace thought. She drove. He gave directions. A minute later he pointed up ahead. 'It's that office building on the corner.'

The medical office seemed dominated by dentists and orthodontists. When they opened the door, there was that antiseptic smell Grace always associated with a voice telling her to rinse and spit. An ophthalmology group called Laser Today was listed for the second floor. Scott Duncan pointed to the name 'Sally Li, MD.' The directory said she was on the lower level.

There was no receptionist. The door chimed when they entered. The office was properly sparse. The furniture consisted of two distressed couches and one flickering lamp that wouldn't muster a price tag at a garage sale. The lone magazine was a catalogue of medical examiner tools.

An Asian woman, mid-forties and exhausted, stuck her head through the door of the inner office. 'Hey, Scott.'

'Hey, Sally.'

'Who's this?'

'Grace Lawson,' he said. 'She's helping me.'

'Charmed,' Sally said. 'Be with you in a sec.'

Grace told the kids that they could keep playing their Game Boys. The danger of video games was that they shut the world out. The beauty of video games was that they shut the world out.

Sally Li opened the door. 'Come on in.'

She wore clean surgical scrubs with high heels. A pack of Marlboros was jammed into the breast pocket. The office, if you could call it that, had that Early American Hurricane look going for it. There were papers everywhere. They seemed to be cascading off her desk and bookshelves, almost like a waterfall. Pathology textbooks were open. Her desk was old and metal, something bought at an old elementary school garage sale. There were no pictures on it, nothing personal, though a really big ashtray sat front and center. Magazines, lots of them, were stacked high all over the place. Some of the stacks had already collapsed. Sally Li had not bothered to clean them up. She dropped herself in the chair behind her desk.

'Just knock that stuff to the floor. Sit.'

Grace removed the papers from the chair and sat. Scott Duncan did the same. Sally Li folded her hands and put them on her lap.

'You know, Scott, that I'm not much with bedside manner.'

'I know.'

'The good thing is, my patients never complain.'

She laughed. No one else did.

'Okay, so now you see why I don't get dates.' Sally Li picked up a pair of reading glasses and started shuffling through files. 'You know how the really messy person is always so well organized? They always say something like, 'It might look like untidy but I know where everything is.' That's crap. I don't know where . . . Wait, here it is.'

Sally Li pulled out a manila file.

'Is that my sister's autopsy?' Duncan asked.

'Yep.'

She slid it toward him. He opened it. Grace leaned in next to him. On the top were the words DUNCAN, GERI. There were photographs too. Grace spotted one, a brown skeleton lying on a table. She turned away, as if she'd been caught invading someone's privacy.

Sally Li had her feet on the desk, her hands behind her head. 'Look, Scott, you want me to go through the rigmarole of how amazing the science of pathology has become, or do you want me to bottom-line it?'

'Skip the rigmarole.'

'At the time of her death, your sister was pregnant.'

Duncan's body convulsed as if she'd hit him with a cattle prod. Grace did not move.

'I can't tell you how long. No more than four, five months.'

'I don't understand,' Scott said. 'They must have done an autopsy the first time around.'

Sally Li nodded. 'I'm sure.'

'Why didn't they see it then?'

'My guess? They did.'

'But I never knew . . .'

'Why would you? You were, what, in law school? They may have told your mom or dad. But you were just a sibling. And her pregnancy has nothing to do with the cause of death. She died in a dorm fire. The fact that she was pregnant, if they knew, would be deemed irrelevant.'

Scott Duncan just sat there. He looked at Grace and then back at Sally Li. 'You can get DNA from the fetus?'

'Probably, yeah. Why?'

'How long will it take you to run a paternity test?'

Grace was not surprised by the question.

'Six weeks.'

'Any way to rush it?'

'I might be able to get some kind of rejection earlier. In other words, rule people out. But I can't say for sure.'

Scott turned to Grace. She knew what he was thinking. She said, 'Geri was dating Shane Alworth.'

'You saw the picture.'

She had. The way Geri looked up at Jack. She had not

256

known the camera was on her. They were all still getting ready to pose. But what was captured, the look on Geri Duncan's face, well, it was the way you look at someone who is much more than a friend.

'Let's run the test then,' Grace said.

34

Charlaine was holding Mike's hand when his eyes finally fluttered open.

She screamed for a doctor, who declared, in a moment of true obviousness, that this was a 'good sign.' Mike was in tremendous pain. The doctor put a morphine pump on him. Mike did not want to go back to sleep. He grimaced and tried to ride it out. Charlaine stayed bedside and held his hand. When the pain got bad, he squeezed hard.

'Go home,' Mike said. 'The kids need you.'

She shushed him. 'Try to rest.'

'Nothing you can do for me here. Go home.'

'Shh.'

Mike began to drift off. She looked down at him. She remembered the days at Vanderbilt. The range of emotions overwhelmed her. There was love and affection, sure, but what troubled Charlaine right now – even as she held his hand, even as she felt a strong bond with this man who shared her life, even as she prayed and made deals with a God she'd ignored for far too long – was that she knew that these feelings would not last. That was the terrible part. In the middle of this intensity Charlaine knew that her feelings would ebb away, that the emotions were fleeting, and she hated herself for knowing that.

Three years ago Charlaine attended a huge self-help rally at Continental Arena in East Rutherford. The speaker had been dynamic. Charlaine loved it. She bought all the tapes. She started doing exactly what he said – making goals, sticking to them, figuring out what she wanted from life, trying to put things in perspective, organizing and restructuring her priorities so that she could achieve – but even as she went through the motions, even as her life began to change for the better, she knew that it would not last. That this would all be a temporary change. A new regimen, an exercise program, a diet – that was how this felt too.

It would not be happily ever after.

The door behind her opened. 'I hear your husband woke up.'

It was Captain Perlmutter. 'Yes.'

'I was hoping to talk to him.'

'You'll have to wait.'

Perlmutter took another step into the room. 'Are the children still with their uncle?'

'He took them to school. We want things to feel normal for them.' Perlmutter moved next to her. She kept her eyes on Mike. 'Have you learned anything?' she asked.

'The man who shot your husband. His name is Eric Wu. Does that mean anything to you?'

She shook her head. 'How did you figure that out?'

'His fingerprints in Sykes's house.'

'Has he been arrested before?'

'Yes. In fact he's on parole.'

'What did he do?'

'He was convicted of assault and battery, but it's believed that he's committed a number of crimes.'

She was not surprised. 'Violent crimes?'

Perlmutter nodded. 'Can I ask you something?'

She shrugged.

'Does the name Jack Lawson mean anything to you?'

Charlaine frowned. 'Does he have two kids at Willard?'

'Yes.'

'I don't know him personally, but Clay, my youngest, is still at Willard. I see his wife sometimes when we do pick-ups.'

'That would be Grace Lawson?'

'I think that's her name. Pretty woman. She has a daughter named Emma, I think. She's a year or two behind my Clay.'

'Do you know her at all?'

'Not really, no. I see her at the school holiday concert, stuff like that. Why?'

'It's probably nothing.'

Charlaine frowned. 'You just picked that name out of a hat?'

'Early conjecture,' he said, trying to dismiss it. 'I also wanted to thank you.'

'For?'

'For talking to Mr. Sykes.'

'He didn't tell me much.'

'He told you that Wu used the name Al Singer.'

'So?'

'Our computer expert found that name on Sykes's computer. Al Singer. We think Wu used that alias for an online dating service. That's how he met Freddy Sykes.'

'He used the name Al Singer?'

'Yes.'

'It was a gay dating service then?'

'Bisexual.'

Charlaine shook her head and came close to chuckling. *Ain't that something?* She looked at Perlmutter, daring him to laugh. He was stone-faced. They both looked down at Mike again. Mike started. He opened his eyes and smiled at her. Charlaine smiled back and smoothed his hair. He closed his eyes and drifted back to sleep.

'Captain Perlmutter?'

'Yes.'

'Please leave,' she said.

35

While waiting for Carl Vespa to arrive, Grace started picking up the bedroom. Jack, she knew, was a great husband and father. He was smart, funny, loving, caring, and devoted. To counter that, God had blessed him with the organization skills of a citrus beverage. He was, in sum, a slob. Nagging him about it – and Grace had tried – did no good. So she stopped. If living happily was about compromise, this seemed to her like a pretty good one to make.

Grace had long ago given up on Jack clearing out the pile of magazines next to his bed. His post-shower wet towel never ended up back on the rack. Not every article of clothing made it to its ultimate destination. Right now, there was a T-shirt draped half-in, half-out of the hamper as if it'd been shot trying to escape.

For a moment Grace just stared down at the T-shirt. It was green with the word FUBU plastered across the front, and it might have one day been in vogue. Jack bought it for $6.99 at T.J. Maxx, a discount clothing store where hip goes to die. He'd put it on with a pair of too-baggy shorts. He stood in front of the mirror and started wrapping his arms around his body in a bizarre variety of ways.

'What are you doing?' Grace had asked him.

'Gangsta poses. Yo, whatchya think?'

'That I should get you seizure medication.'

'Phat,' he said. 'Bling-bling.'

'Right. Emma needs a ride to Christina's.'

'Word. Dawg. Hit dat.'

'Please go. Immediately.'

Grace picked up the shirt now. She had always been

cynical about the male species. She was guarded with her feelings. She did not open up easily. She had never believed in love at first sight – she still didn't – but when she met Jack, the attraction had been immediate, flutters in her stomach, and deny it now as much as she wanted, a small voice had told her right then and there, first meeting, that this was the man she was going to marry.

Cram was in the kitchen with Emma and Max. Emma had recovered from her earlier histrionics. She had recovered the way only kids can – fast and with very little residue. They were all eating fish sticks, Cram included, and ignoring the side dish of peas. Emma was reading a poem to Cram. Cram was a great audience. His laugh was the kind that not only filled a room but pushed against the panes of glass. You heard it, you had to either smile or cringe.

There was still time before Carl Vespa arrived. She didn't want to think about Geri Duncan, her death, her pregnancy, the way she looked at Jack in that damned photograph. Scott Duncan had asked her what she ultimately wanted. She'd said her husband back. That was still very much the case. But maybe, with all that was happening, she needed the truth too.

With that in mind Grace headed downstairs and flipped on the computer. She brought up Google and typed in 'Jack Lawson.' Twelve hundred hits. Too many to do any good. She tried 'Shane Alworth.' Hmm, no hits. Interesting. Grace tried 'Sheila Lambert.' Hits about a woman basketball player with the same name. Nothing relevant. Then she began trying combinations.

Jack Lawson, Shane Alworth, Sheila Lambert, and Geri Duncan: These four people were together in this picture. They had to be linked in some other way. She tried various combinations. She tried one first name, one last name. Nothing of interest popped. She was still typing, going through the useless 227 hits on the words 'Lawson' and

'Alworth' when the phone rang.

Grace looked at the Caller ID and saw it was Cora. She picked up. 'Hey.'

'Hey.'

'I'm sorry,' Grace said.

'Don't worry about it. Bitch.'

Grace smiled and kept hitting the down arrow. The hits were useless.

'So do you still want my help?' Cora asked.

'Yeah, I guess.'

'Enthusiasm. I love that. Okay, fill me in.'

Grace kept it vague. She trusted Cora, but she didn't want to have to trust her. Yeah, that made little sense. It was like this: If Grace's life were in jeopardy, she'd call Cora immediately. But if the kids were in danger . . . well, she'd hesitate. The scary thing was, she probably trusted Cora more than anybody, which was to say that she had never felt more isolated in her life.

'So you're putting the names through search engines?' Cora asked.

'Yes.'

'Any relevant hits so far?'

'Not a one.' Then: 'Wait, hold on.'

'What?'

But now again, trust or no trust, Grace wondered what would be the point in telling Cora more than she needed to know. 'I gotta run. I'll call you back.'

'Okay. Bitch.'

Grace hung up and stared at the screen. Her pulse started giddying up, just a little faster now. She had pretty much used up all the name combinations when she'd remembered an artist friend name Marlon Coburn. He was constantly complaining because his name was misspelled. Marlon would be spelled Marlin or Marlan or Marlen and Coburn would be Cohen or Corburn. Anyway Grace figured she'd give it a go.

The fourth 'typo' combo she tried was 'Lawson' and 'Allworth' – two Ls instead of one.

There were three hundred hits – neither name was that uncommon – but it was the fourth one that jumped out at her. She looked at the top line first:

Crazy Davey's Blog

Grace knew vaguely that a blog was a sort of public diary. People wrote down their random thoughts. Other people, for some odd reason, enjoyed reading them. A diary used to be about being private. Now it was about trying to be shrill enough to reach the masses.

The little sample bit under the link line read:

'... John Lawson on keyboards and Sean Allworth who was wicked on guitar ...'

John was Jack's real name. Sean was pretty close to Shane. Grace clicked the link. The page was forever long. She went back, clicked 'cache.' When she returned to the page, the words Lawson and Allworth would be highlighted. She scrolled down and found an entry from two years ago:

April 26
    Hey, gang. Terese and I took a weekend up in Vermont. We stayed at the Westerly's bed and breakfasts. It was great. They had a fireplace and at night we played checkers ...

Crazy Davey went on and on. Grace shook her head. Who the hell read this nonsense? She skipped three more paragraphs.

That night I went with Rick, an old college bud, to Wino's. It's an old college bar. Total dump. We used to go when we went to Vermont University. Get this, we played Condom Roulette like the old days. Ever play? Every guy guesses a color – there's Hot Red, Stallion

Black, Lemon Yellow, Orange Orange. Okay, the last two are jokes, but you get the point. There's this condom dispenser in the bathroom. It's still there! So each guy puts a buck on the table. One guy gets a quarter and buys a condom. He brings it to the table. You open it and whammo, if it's your color, you win! Rick guessed the first one right. He bought us a pitcher. The band that night sucked. I remembered hearing a group when I was a freshman named Allaw. There were two chicks in that band and two guys. I remember one chick played drums. The guys were John Lawson on keyboards and Sean Allworth who was wicked on guitar. That was how they got the name, I think. Allworth and Lawson. Combine it into Allaw. Rick never heard of them. Anyway we finished up the pitcher. A couple of hot chicks came in but they ignored us. We started feeling old . . .

That was it. Nothing more.

Grace did a search for 'Allaw.' Nothing.

She tried more combinations. Nothing else. Only this one mention in a blog. Crazy Davey had gotten both Shane's first and last name wrong. Jack had gone by Jack, well, for as long as Grace had known him, but maybe he was John back then. Or maybe the guy remembered it wrong or saw it written down.

But Crazy Davey had mentioned four people – two women, two men. There were five people in the picture, but the one woman, the one who was pretty much a blur near the edge of the photograph – maybe she wasn't part of the group. And what had Scott said about his sister's last phone call?

I figured it was about whatever new thing she was into – aromatherapy, her new rock band . . .

Rock band. Could that be it? Was it a picture of a rock group?

She searched Crazy Davey's site for a phone number or a full name. There was only an e-mail. Grace hit the link and typed quickly:

'I need your help. I have a very important question about Allaw, the band you saw in college. Please call me collect.'

She listed her phone number and then hit the send button.

So what does this mean?

She tried to put it together in a dozen different ways. Nothing fit. A few minutes later the limousine pulled up the driveway. Grace glanced out the window. Carl Vespa was here.

He had a new driver now, a mammoth muscleman with a crewcut and matching scowl who did not look half as dangerous as Cram. She bookmarked Crazy Davey's blog before heading down the corridor to open the door.

Vespa stepped in without saying hello. He still looked natty, still wearing a blazer that seemed to have been tailored by the gods, but the rest of him looked strangely unruly. His hair was always unkempt – that was his look – but there is a fine line between unkempt and not touched at all. It had crossed that line. His eyes were red. The lines around his mouth were deeper, more pronounced.

'What's wrong?'

'Somewhere we can talk?' Vespa asked.

'The kids are with Cram in the kitchen. We can use the living room.'

He nodded. From a distance they heard Max's full-bodied laugh. The sound made Vespa pull up. 'Your son is six, right?'

'Yes.'

Vespa smiled now. Grace did not know what he was thinking, but the smile broke her heart. 'When Ryan was six, he was into baseball cards.'

'Max is into Yu-Gi-Oh!'

'Yu-Gi-what?'

She shook her head to indicate that it wasn't worth explaining.

He went on: 'Ryan used to play this game with his cards. He'd break them up into teams. Then he'd lay them out on the carpet like it was a ball field. You know, the third baseman – Graig Nettles back then – actually playing third, three guys in the outfield – he even kept the extra pitchers in a bullpen out in right field.'

His face glowed in the memory. He looked at Grace. She smiled at him, as gently as she could, but the mood still burst. Vespa's face fell.

'He's getting released on probation.'

Grace said nothing.

'Wade Larue. They're rushing his release. He'll be out tomorrow.'

'Oh.'

'How do you feel about it?'

'He's been in jail for almost fifteen years,' she said.

'Eighteen people died.'

She did not want to have this conversation with him. That number – eighteen – was not relevant. Just one mattered. Ryan. From the kitchen Max laughed again. The sound shredded the room. Vespa kept his face steady but Grace could see something going on inside of him. A roiling. He did not speak. He did not have to, the thoughts obvious: Suppose it had been Max or Emma. Would she rationalize it as a stoned loser getting high and panicking? Would she be so quick to forgive?

'Do you remember that security guard, Gordon MacKenzie?' Vespa asked.

Grace nodded. He had been the hero of the night, finding a way to open up two locked emergency exits.

'He died a few weeks ago. He had a brain tumor.'

'I know.' They had given Gordon MacKenzie the biggest spread in the anniversary pieces.

'Do you believe in life after death, Grace?'

'I don't know.'

'How about your parents? Will you see them one day?'

'I don't know.'

'Come on, Grace. I want to know what you think.'

Vespa's eyes bored into hers. She shifted in her seat. 'On the phone. You asked if Jack had a sister.'

'Sandra Koval.'

'Why did you ask me that?'

'In a minute,' Vespa said. 'I want to know what you think. Where do we go when we die, Grace?'

She could see that it would be useless to argue with him. There was a wrong vibe here, something out of sorts. He was not asking as a friend, a father figure, out of curiosity. There was challenge in his voice. Anger even. She wondered if he'd been drinking.

'There's a Shakespeare quote,' she said. 'From Hamlet. He says that death is – and I think I have the quote right – "an undiscovered country from whose borne no traveler returns."'

He made a face. 'In other words, we don't have a clue.'

'Pretty much.'

'You know that's crap.'

She didn't say anything.

'You know that there's nothing. That I will never see Ryan again. It's just too hard for people to accept. The weak-minded invent invisible gods and gardens and reunions in paradise. Or some, like you, won't buy into that nonsense, but it's still too painful to admit the truth. So you come up with this "how can we know?" rationale. But you do know, Grace, don't you?'

'I'm sorry, Carl.'

'For what?'

'I'm sorry that you're in pain. But please don't tell me what I believe.'

Something happened to Vespa's eyes. They expanded

268

for a moment and it was almost as if something behind them exploded. 'How did you meet your husband?'

'What?'

'How did you meet Jack?'

'What does that have to do with anything?'

He took a quick step closer. A threatening step. He looked down at her, and for the first time Grace knew that all the stories, all the rumors about what he was, what he did, they were true. 'How did you two meet?'

Grace tried not to cringe. 'You already know.'

'In France?'

'Right.'

He stared at her hard.

'What's going on, Carl?'

'Wade Larue is getting out.'

'So you said.'

'Tomorrow his lawyer is holding a press conference in New York. The families will be there. I want you there.'

She waited. She knew there was more.

'His lawyer was terrific. She really dazzled the parole board. I bet she'll dazzle the press too.'

He stopped and waited. Grace was puzzled for a few moments, but then something cold started in the center of her chest and spread through her limbs. Carl Vespa saw it. He nodded and stepped back.

'Tell me about Sandra Koval,' he said. 'Because, see, I can't understand how your sister-in-law, of all people, ended up representing someone like Wade Larue.'

36

Indira Khariwalla waited for the visitor.

Her office was dark. All the private detection was done for the day. Indira liked sitting with the lights out. The problem with the West, she was convinced, was overstimulation. She fell prey to it too, of course. That was the thing. No one was above it. The West seduced you with stimulation, a constant barrage of color and light and sound. It never stopped. So whenever possible, especially at the end of the day, Indira liked to sit with the lights off. Not to meditate, as one might assume because of her heritage. Not sitting in lotus position with her thumbs and forefingers making two circles.

No, just darkness.

At 10 P.M., there was a light rap on the door. 'Come on in.'

Scott Duncan entered the room. He did not bother turning on the light. Indira was glad. It would make this easier.

'What's so important?' he asked.

'Rocky Conwell was murdered,' Indira said.

'I heard about that on the radio. Who is he?'

'The man I hired to follow Jack Lawson.'

Scott Duncan said nothing.

'Do you know who Stu Perlmutter is?' she continued.

'The cop?'

'Yes. He visited me yesterday. He asked about Conwell.'

'Did you claim attorney-client?'

'I did. He wants to get a judge to compel me to answer.'

Scott Duncan turned away.

'Scott?'

'Don't worry about it,' he said. 'You don't know anything.'

Indira was not so sure. 'What are you going to do?'

Duncan stepped out of the office. He reached behind him, grabbed the knob, and started closing the door behind him. 'Nip this in the bud,' he said.

37

The press conference was at 10 A.M. Grace took the children to school first. Cram drove. He wore an oversized flannel shirt left untucked. He had a gun under it, she knew. The children hopped out. They said good-bye to Cram and hurried away. Cram shifted the car into gear.

'Don't go yet,' Grace said.

She watched until they were safely inside. Then she nodded that it was okay for the car to start moving again.

'Don't worry,' Cram said. 'I have a man watching.'

She turned to him. 'Can I ask you something?'

'Shoot.'

'How long have you been with Mr. Vespa?'

'You were there when Ryan died, right?'

The question threw her. 'Yes.'

'He was my godson.'

The streets were quiet. She looked at him. She had no idea what to do. She could not trust them – not with her children, not after she'd seen Vespa's face last night. But what choice did she have? Maybe she should try the police again, but would they really be willing or able to protect them? And Scott Duncan, well, even he had admitted that their alliance only went so far.

As if reading her thoughts, Cram said, 'Mr. Vespa still trusts you.'

'And what if he decides he doesn't anymore?'

'He'd never hurt you.'

'You're that sure?'

'Mr. Vespa will meet us in the city. At the press conference. You want to listen to the radio?'

The traffic was not bad, considering the hour. The George Washington Bridge was still crawling with cops, a hangover from September 11 that Grace could not get over. The press conference was being held at the Crowne Plaza Hotel near Times Square. Vespa told her that there'd been talk about conducting it in Boston – that would seem more appropriate – but someone in the Larue camp realized that it might be too emotionally jarring to return so close to the scene. They also hoped that fewer family members would show up if it were held in New York.

Cram dropped her off on the sidewalk and headed into the lot next door. Grace stood on the street for a moment and tried to gather herself. Her cell phone sounded. She checked the Caller ID. The number was unfamiliar. Six-one-seven area code. That was the Boston area, if she remembered correctly.

'Hello?'

'Hi. This is David Roff.'

She was near Times Square in New York. People were, of course, everywhere. No one seemed to be talking. No horns were honking. But the roar in her ear was still deafening. 'Who?'

'Uh, well, I guess you might know me better as Crazy Davey. From my blog. I got your e-mail. Is this a bad time?'

'No, not at all.' Grace realized that she was shouting to be heard. She stuck a finger in her free ear. 'Thanks for calling me back.'

'I know you said to call collect, but I got some new phone service where all long distance is included, so I figured what the hell, you know.'

'I appreciate it.'

'You made it sound kind of important.'

'It is. On your blog you mentioned a band named Allaw.'

'Right.'

'I'm trying to find out anything I can about them.'

'I figured that, yeah, but I don't think I can really help you. I mean, I just saw them that one night. Me and some buddies got totally wasted, spent the whole night there. We met some girls, did a lot of dancing, did a lot more drinking. We talked to the band afterward. That's why I remember it so well.'

'My name is Grace Lawson. My husband was Jack.'

'Lawson? That was the lead guy, right? I remember him.'

'Were they any good?'

'The band? Truth is, I don't remember, but I think so. I remember having a blast and getting wasted. Had a hangover that still makes me cringe to this day. You trying to put a surprise together for him?'

'A surprise?'

'Yeah, like a surprise party or a scrapbook about his old days.'

'I'm just trying to find out anything I can about the people in the group.'

'I wish I could help. I don't think they lasted that long. Never heard them again, though I know they had another gig at the Lost Tavern. That was in Manchester. That's all I know, I'm sorry.'

'I appreciate your calling me back.'

'Sure, no problem. Oh wait. This might be fun trivia for a scrapbook.'

'What's that?'

'The gig Allaw played in Manchester? They opened for Still Night.'

Waves of pedestrians rushed past her. Grace huddled near a wall, trying to avoid the masses. 'I'm not familiar with Still Night.'

'Well, only real music buffs would be, I guess. Still Night didn't last too long either. At least not in that incarnation.' There was a static crackle, but Grace still heard Crazy Davey's next words too clearly: 'But their lead singer was Jimmy X.'

Grace felt her grip on the phone go slack.

'Hello?'

'I'm still here,' Grace said.

'You know who Jimmy X is, right? "Pale Ink"? The Boston Massacre?'

'Yes.' Her voice sounded very far away. 'I remember.'

Cram came out of the parking lot. He spotted her face and picked up his pace again. Grace thanked Crazy Davey and hung up. She had his number on her cell phone now. She could always call him back.

'Everything okay?'

She tried to shake it off, this feeling of cold. It wouldn't happen. She managed to utter, 'Fine.'

'Who was that?'

'You my social secretary now?'

'Easy.' He held up both hands. 'Just asking.'

They headed inside the Crowne Plaza. Grace tried to process what she had just heard. A coincidence. That was all. A bizarre coincidence. Her husband had played in a bar band in college. So had a zillion other people. He happened to play on the same bill once as Jimmy X. Again so what? They were both in the same area at around the same time. This would have been at least a year, probably two, before the Boston Massacre. And Jack might not have mentioned it to her because he figured that it was irrelevant and might, in any case, upset his wife. A Jimmy X concert had traumatized her. It had left her partially crippled. So he maybe didn't see a need to mention that slight connection.

No big deal, right?

Except that Jack had never even mentioned playing in a band. Except that the members of Allaw were all now either dead or missing.

She tried to gather some of the pieces. When exactly

had Geri Duncan been murdered anyway? Grace had been undergoing physical therapy when she read about the fire. That meant it probably happened a few months after the massacre. Grace would need to check the exact date. She would need to check the entire time line because, let's face it, there was no way the Allaw–Jimmy X connection was a coincidence.

But how did it work? Nothing about it made sense.

She ran it through one more time. Her husband plays in a band. One time the band plays at the same time as a band featuring Jimmy X. A year or two later – depending on if Jack had been a senior or a year postgrad – the now famous Jimmy X plays a concert that she, young Grace Sharpe, attends. She gets injured in a melee that night. Another three years pass. She meets Jack Lawson on an entirely different continent and they fall in love.

It didn't mesh.

The elevator dinged on the ground level. Cram said, 'You sure you're okay?'

'Groovy,' she said.

'Still twenty minutes until the press conference begins. I figured it would be better if you went alone, try to grab your sister-in-law beforehand.'

'You're a fount of ideas, Cram.'

The doors opened. 'Third floor,' he said. Grace stepped inside and let the elevator swallow her whole. She was alone. There would not be much time. She took out her cell phone and the card Jimmy X had given her. She pressed in the number and hit send. It went immediately into his voice mail. Grace waited for the beep:

'I know about Still Night playing with Allaw. Call me.'

She left her number and hung up. The elevator came to a stop. When she stepped off, there was one of those black signs with the changeable white letters, the kind that tell you in what room the Ratzenberg bar mitzvah or Smith-Jones wedding is being held. This one read:

'Burton-Crimstein Press Conference.' Advertising the firm. She followed the arrow to a door, took a deep breath, and pushed it open.

The whole thing was like one of those courthouse movie scenes – that pinnacle cinematic moment when the surprise witness bursts through the double doors. When Grace walked in, there was that sort of collective gasp. The room hushed. Grace felt lost. She glanced around and what she saw made her head spin. She took a step back. The faces of grief, older but no more at peace, swirled about her. There they were again – the Garrisons, the Reeds, the Weiders. She flashed back to the early days at the hospital. She had seen everything through the haze of Halcion, as if through a shower curtain. It felt the same today. They approached in silence. They hugged her. None of them said a word. They didn't have to. Grace accepted the embraces. She could still feel the sadness emanating from them.

She saw the widow of Lieutenant Gordon MacKenzie. Some said that he had been responsible for pulling Grace to safety. Like most true heroes, Gordon MacKenzie rarely talked about it. He claimed not to remember what he did exactly, that yes, he opened doors and pulled people out, but that it was more out of reaction than anything approaching bravery.

Grace gave Mrs. MacKenzie an extra long hug.

'I'm sorry for your loss,' Grace said.

'He found God.' Mrs. MacKenzie held on. 'He's with Him now.'

There was really nothing to say to that, so Grace just nodded. She let her go and looked over the woman's shoulder. Sandra Koval had entered the room from the other side. She spotted Grace at almost the same moment and a strange thing happened. Her sister-in-law smiled, almost as if she'd expected this. Grace stepped away from Mrs. MacKenzie. Sandra tilted her head, signaling her to step forward. There was a velvet rope. A security guard stepped in her way.

'It's okay, Frank,' Sandra said. He let Grace pass.

Sandra led the way. She hurried down a corridor. Grace limped behind, unable to catch up. No matter. Sandra stopped and opened a door. They stepped into a huge ballroom. Waiters busily laid out the silverware. Sandra led her to a corner. She grabbed two chairs and turned them so that they faced each other.

'You don't seem surprised to see me,' Grace said.

Sandra shrugged. 'I figured you were following the case in the news.'

'I wasn't.'

'Doesn't matter, I guess. Until two days ago you didn't know who I was.'

'What's going on, Sandra?'

She did not answer right away. The tinkling of the silverware provided background music. Sandra let her gaze wander toward the waiters in the center room.

'Why are you representing Wade Larue?'

'He was charged with a crime. I'm a criminal defense lawyer. It's what I do.'

'Don't patronize me.'

'You want to know how I stumbled upon this particular client, is that it?'

Grace said nothing.

'Isn't it obvious?'

'Not to me.'

'You, Grace.' She smiled. 'You're the reason I represent Mr. Larue.'

Grace opened her mouth, closed it, started again. 'What are you talking about?'

'You never really knew about me. You just knew that Jack had a sister. But I knew all about you.'

'I'm still not following.'

'It's simple, Grace. You married my brother.'

'So?'

'When I learned you were going to be my sister-in-law, I was curious. I wanted to learn about you. Makes sense, right? So I had one of my investigators do a background check. Your paintings are wonderful, by the way. I bought two. Anonymously. They're in my home out in Los Angeles. Spectacular stuff, really. My older daughter, Karen – she's seventeen – loves them. She wants to be an artist.'

'I don't see what this has to do with Wade Larue.'

'Really?' Her voice was strangely cheerful. 'I've worked criminal defense since I graduated law school. I started by working with Burton and Crimstein in Boston. I lived there, Grace. I knew all about the Boston Massacre. And now my brother had fallen in love with one of the Massacre's major players. It piqued my curiosity even more. I started reading up on the case – and guess what I realized?'

'What?'

'That Wade Larue had been railroaded by an incompetent lawyer.'

'Wade Larue was responsible for the death of eighteen people.'

'He fired a gun, Grace. He didn't even hit anyone. The lights went out. People were screaming. He was under the influence of drugs and alcohol. He panicked. He believed – or at least, honestly imagined – that he was in imminent danger. There was no way, no way at all, that he could have known what the outcome would be. His first lawyer should have cut a deal. Probation, eighteen months away tops. But no one really wanted to work this case. Larue was sent to jail to rot. So yes, Grace, I read about him because of you. Wade Larue had been shafted. His old attorney screwed him and ran.'

'So you took the case?'

Sandra Koval nodded. 'Pro bono. I came to him two years ago. We started preparing for the parole hearing.'

Something clicked. 'Jack knew, didn't he?'

'That I don't know. We don't talk, Grace.'

'Are you still going to tell me you didn't talk to him that night? Nine minutes, Sandra. The phone company says the call lasted nine minutes.'

'Jack's call had nothing to do with Wade Larue.'

'What did it have to do with?'

'That photograph.'

'What about it?'

Sandra leaned forward. 'First you answer a question for me. And I need the truth here. Where did you get that picture?'

'I told you. It was in my packet of film.'

Sandra shook her head, not believing her. 'And you think the guy from Photomat stuck it in there?'

'I don't know anymore. But you still haven't explained – what about the picture made him call you?'

Sandra hesitated.

'I know about Geri Duncan,' Grace said.

'You know what about Geri Duncan?'

'That she's the girl in the picture. And that she was murdered.'

That made Sandra sit up. 'She died in a fire. It was an accident.'

Grace shook her head. 'It was set intentionally.'

'Who told you that?'

'Her brother.'

'Wait, how do you know her brother?'

'She was pregnant, you know. Geri Duncan. When she died in that fire, she was carrying a baby.'

Sandra stopped and looked up in horror. 'Grace, what are you doing?'

'I'm trying to find my husband.'

'And you think this is helping?'

'You told me yesterday you didn't know anyone in the picture. But you just admitted you knew Geri Duncan, that she died in a fire.'

Sandra closed her eyes.

'Did you know Shane Alworth or Sheila Lambert?'

Her voice was soft. 'Not really, no.'

'Not really. So their names are not totally unfamiliar to you?'

'Shane Alworth was a classmate of Jack's. Sheila Lambert, I think, was a friend from a sister college or something. So what?'

'Did you know that the four of them played together in a band?'

'For a mònth maybe. Again so what?'

'The fifth person in the picture. The one with her head turned. Do you know who she is?'

'No.'

'Is it you, Sandra?'

She looked up at Grace. 'Me?'

'Yes. Is it you?'

There was a funny look on Sandra's face now. 'No, Grace, it's not me.'

'Did Jack kill Geri Duncan?'

The words just came out. Sandra's eyes opened as if she'd been slapped. 'Are you out of your mind?'

'I want the truth.'

'Jack had nothing to do with her death. He was overseas already.'

'So why did the picture freak him out?'

She hesitated.

'Why, dammit?'

'Because he didn't know Geri was dead until then.'

Grace looked confused. 'Were they lovers?'

'Lovers,' she repeated, as if she'd never heard the word before. 'That's a pretty mature term for what they were.'

'Wasn't she dating Shane Alworth?'

'I guess. But they were all just kids.'

'Jack was fooling around with his friend's girlfriend?'

'I don't know how friendly Jack and Shane were. But yes, Jack slept with her.'

Grace's head began to whirl. 'And Geri Duncan got pregnant.'

'I don't know anything about that.'

'But you know she's dead.'

'Yes.'

'And you know Jack ran away.'

'Before she died.'

'Before she was pregnant?'

'I just told you. I never knew she was pregnant.'

'And Shane Alworth and Sheila Lambert, they're both missing too. You want to tell me it's all a coincidence, Sandra?'

'I don't know.'

'So what did Jack say when he called you?'

She let loose a deep sigh. Her head dropped. She was silent for a while.

'Sandra?'

'Look, that picture has to be, what, fifteen, sixteen years old? When you just gave it to him like that, out of the blue . . . how did you think he'd react? With Geri's face crossed out. So Jack went to the computer. He did a Web search – I think he used the *Boston Globe*'s archives. He found out she's been dead this whole time. That was why he called me. He wanted to know what happened to her. I told him.'

'Told him what?'

'What I knew. That she died in a fire.'

'Why would that make Jack run out?'

'That I don't know.'

'What made him run overseas in the first place?'

'You have to let this go.'

'What happened to them, Sandra?'

She shook her head. 'Forget the fact that I'm his attorney and that it's protected. It is simply not my place. He's my brother.'

Grace reached out and took Sandra's hands in hers. 'I think he's in trouble.'

'Then what I know can't help him.'

'They threatened my children today.'

Sandra closed her eyes.

'Did you hear what I said?'

A man in a business suit leaned into the room. He said, 'It's time, Sandra.' She nodded and thanked him. Sandra pulled her hands away, stood, smoothed out the lines of her suit.

'You have to stop this, Grace. You have to go home now. You have to protect your family. It's what Jack would want you to do.'

38

The threat at the supermarket had not taken.

Wu was not surprised. He had been raised in an environment that stressed the power of men and the subordination of women, but Wu had always found it to be more hope than truth. Women were harder. They were more unpredictable. They handled physical pain better – he knew this from personal experience. When it came to protecting their loved ones, they were far more ruthless. Men would sacrifice themselves out of machismo or stupidity or the blind belief that they would be victorious. Women would sacrifice themselves without self-deception.

He had not been in favor of making the threat in the first place. Threats left enemies and uncertainty. Eliminating Grace Lawson earlier would have been routine. Eliminating her now would be riskier.

Wu would have to return and handle the job himself.

He was in Beatrice Smith's shower, dyeing his hair back to its original color. Wu usually wore it bleached blond. He did this for two reasons. The first reason was basic: He liked the way it looked. Vanity, perhaps, but when Wu looked in the mirror he thought the surfer-blond, gel-spiked style worked on him. Reason two, the color – a garish yellow – was useful because it was what most people remembered. When he brought his hair back to its natural state of everyday Asian-black, flattened it down, when he changed his clothes from the modern hip style to something more conservative, donned a pair of wire-rimmed spectacles, well, the transformation was very effective.

He grabbed Jack Lawson and dragged him down into

the basement. Lawson did not resist. He was barely conscious. He was not doing well. His mind, already stretched, had perhaps snapped. He would not survive much longer.

The basement was unfinished and damp. Wu remembered the last time he'd been in a similar setting, out in San Mateo, California. The instructions had been specific. He had been hired to torture a man for exactly eight hours – why eight Wu had never learned – and then break bones in both the man's legs and arms. Wu had manipulated the broken bones so that the jagged edges sat next to nerve bundles or near the surface of the skin. Any movement, even the slightest, would cause excruciating pain. Wu locked the basement and left the man by himself. He checked up on him once a day. The man would plead, but Wu would just stare silently. It took eleven days for the man to die of starvation.

Wu found a strong pipe and chained Lawson to it. He also cuffed his arms behind his back around a support wall. He put the gag back into his mouth.

Then he decided to test the binds.

'You should have gotten every copy of that photograph,' Wu whispered.

Jack Lawson's eyes rolled up.

'Now I'll have to pay your wife a visit.'

Their gazes locked. A second passed, no more, and then Lawson sprang to life. He began to flail. Wu watched him. Yes, this would be a good test. Lawson struggled for several minutes, a fish dying on the line. Nothing gave way.

Wu left him alone then, still fighting his chains, to find Grace Lawson.

39

Grace did not want to stay for the press conference.

Being in the same room with all these mourners . . . She didn't like to use the term 'aura,' but it seemed to fit. The room had a bad aura. Shattered eyes stared at her with a yearning that was palpable. Grace understood, of course. She was no longer the conduit to their lost children – too much time had passed for that. Now she was the survivor. She was there, alive and breathing, while their children rotted in the grave. On the surface there was still affection, but beneath that Grace could feel rage at the unfairness of it all. She had lived – their children had not. The years had offered no reprieve. Now that Grace had children of her own, she understood in a way that would have been impossible fifteen years ago.

She was about to slide out the back door when a hand took firm hold of her wrist. She turned and saw it was Carl Vespa.

'Where are you going?' he asked.

'Home.'

'I'll give you a ride.'

'That's okay. I can hire a car.'

His hand, still on her wrist, tightened for a brief moment and again Grace thought she saw something detonate behind his eyes. 'Stay,' he said.

It was not a request. She searched his face, but it was oddly calm. Too calm. His demeanor – so off with the surroundings, so different from the flash of fury she'd seen last night – frightened her anew. Was this really the man she was trusting with her children's lives?

She sat next to him and watched Sandra Koval and Wade Larue take to the podium. Sandra pulled the microphone closer and started up with the standard clichés about forgiveness and starting over and rehabilitation. Grace watched the faces around her shut down. Some cried. Some pursed their lips. Some visibly shook.

Carl Vespa did none of that.

He crossed his legs and leaned back. He surveyed the proceedings with a casualness that scared her more than the worst scowl. Five minutes into Sandra Koval's statement, Vespa's eyes shifted toward Grace. He saw that she'd been watching him. Then he did something that made her shiver.

He winked at her.

'Come on,' he whispered. 'Let's get out of here.'

With Sandra still talking, Carl Vespa rose and headed for the door. Heads turned and there was a brief hush. Grace followed. They took the elevator down in silence. The limousine was right out front. The big burly guy was in the driver's seat.

'Where's Cram?' Grace asked.

'On an errand,' Vespa said, and Grace thought she saw the trace of a smile. 'Tell me about your meeting with Ms. Koval.'

Grace recounted her conversation with her sister-in-law. Vespa stayed silent, gazing out the window, his index finger gently tapping his chin. When she finished, he asked, 'Is that everything?'

'Yes.'

'Are you sure?'

She did not like the lilt in his tone.

'What about your recent' – Vespa looked up, scanning for the word – 'visitor?'

'You mean Scott Duncan?'

Vespa had the oddest grin. 'You are aware, of course, that Scott Duncan works for the U.S. attorney's office.'

'Used to,' she corrected.

'Yes, used to.' His voice was too relaxed. 'What did he want with you?'

'I told you.'

'Did you?' He shifted in his chair, but he still did not face her. 'Did you tell me everything?'

'What's that supposed to mean?'

'Just a question. Was this Mr. Duncan your only recent visitor?'

Grace did not like how this was going. She hesitated.

'Nobody else you'd like to tell me about?' he continued.

She tried to search his face for a clue, but he kept it turned away from her. What was he talking about? She mulled it over, replayed the past few days . . .

Jimmy X?

Could Vespa somehow know about Jimmy stopping by after his concert? It was possible, of course. He had found Jimmy in the first place – it would stand to reason that he'd have someone following him. So what should Grace do here? Would saying something now just compound the issue? Maybe he didn't know about Jimmy. Maybe opening her mouth now would just get her in deeper trouble.

Play it vague, she thought. See where it goes. 'I know I asked for your help,' she said, her tone deliberate. 'But I think I'd like to handle this on my own now.'

Vespa finally turned toward her and faced her full. 'Really?'

She waited.

'Why is that, Grace?'

'Truth?'

'Preferably.'

'You're scaring me.'

'You think I'd harm you?'

'No.'

'Then?'

'I just think it might be best –'

'What did you tell him about me?'

The interruption caught her off guard. 'Scott Duncan?'

'Is there anyone else you talked to about me?'

'What? No.'

'So what did you say to Scott Duncan about me?'

'Nothing.' Grace tried to think. 'What could I tell him anyway?'

'Good point.' He nodded, more to himself than at Grace. 'But you were never very specific on why Mr. Duncan paid you this visit.' Vespa folded his hands and put them on his lap. 'I'd very much like to know the details.'

She didn't want to tell him – didn't want him involved anymore – but there was no way to avoid it. 'It's about his sister.'

'What about her?'

'Do you remember the girl crossed out in that picture?'

'Yes.'

'Her name was Geri Duncan. She was his sister.'

Vespa frowned. 'And that's why he came to you?'

'Yes.'

'Because his sister was in the photograph?'

'Yes.'

He sat back. 'So what happened to her, this sister?'

'She died in a fire fifteen years ago.'

Vespa surprised Grace then. He didn't ask a follow-up question. He didn't ask for clarification. He simply turned away and stared out the window. He did not speak again until the car pulled into the driveway. Grace opened the door to get out, but there was some kind of locking system on it, like the safety lock she'd used when the kids were small, and she could not open it from the inside. The burly driver came around and took hold of the door handle. She wanted to ask Carl Vespa what he planned on doing now, if he'd indeed leave them alone, but his body language was wrong.

Calling him in the first place had been a mistake. Telling

him she wanted him out of this may have compounded it.

'I'll keep my men on until you pick up the children from school,' he said, still not facing her. 'Then you'll be on your own.'

'Thank you.'

'Grace?'

She looked back at him.

'You should never lie to me,' he said.

His voice was ice. Grace swallowed hard. She wanted to argue, to tell him that she hadn't, but she worried that it would sound too defensive – protesting too much. So she simply nodded.

There were no good-byes. Grace headed up the walk alone. Her step teetered from something more than the limp.

What had she done?

She wondered about her next step. Her sister-in-law had said it best: Protect the children. If Grace were in Jack's shoes, if she had gone missing for whatever reason, that would be what she'd want. *Forget me,* she'd tell him. *Keep the children safe.*

So now, like it or not, Grace was out of the rescue business. Jack was on his own.

She'd pack now. She'd wait until three o'clock, until school was let out, and then she'd pick up the children and drive to Pennsylvania. She'd find a hotel where you didn't need a credit card. Or a B&B. Or a rooming house. Whatever. She'd call the police, maybe that Perlmutter even. She'd tell him what was going on. But first she needed her children. Once they were safe, once she had them in her car and was on the road, she'd be okay.

She reached her front door. There was a package on the step. She bent down and picked it up. The box had a *New Hampshire Post* logo on it. The return address read: Bobby Dodd, Sunrise Assisted Living.

It was Bob Dodd's files.

40

Wade Larue sat next to his lawyer, Sandra Koval.

He wore brand-new clothes. The room did not smell of prison, that horrid combination of decay and disinfectant, of fat guards and urine, of stains that never come out, and that in and of itself was a strange adjustment. Prison becomes your world, getting out an impossible daydream, like imagining life on other planets. Wade Larue had gone inside at the age of twenty-two. He was now thirty-seven. That meant he had spent pretty much all his adult years inside that place. That smell, that horrid smell, was all he knew. Yes, he was still young. He had, as Sandra Koval repeated mantralike, his whole life in front of him.

It didn't feel like that right now.

Wade Larue's life had been ruined by a school play. Growing up in a small town in Maine everyone agreed that Wade had the acting chops. He was a crummy student. He was not much of an athlete. But he could sing and dance and, most important, he had what one local reviewer called – this after seeing Wade star as Nathan Detroit in *Guys and Dolls* sophomore year – 'supernatural charisma.' Wade had that something special, that intangible that separated talented wannabes from the real deals.

Before his senior year of high school, Mr. Pearson, the high-school play director, called Wade into his office to tell him about his 'impossible dream.' Mr. Pearson had always wanted to put on *Man of La Mancha*, but he never had a student, not until now, who could handle the role of Don Quixote. Now, for the first time, he wanted to give it a go with Wade.

But come September Mr. Pearson moved away and Mr. Arnett took over as director. He held tryouts – usually a formality for Wade Larue – but Mr. Arnett was hostile. To the shock of everyone in town he ended up picking Kenny Thomas, a total no-talent, to play Don Quixote. Kenny's father was a bookie and Mr. Arnett, rumor had it, was into him for over twenty grand. You do the math. Wade was offered the role of the barber – one song! – and ended up quitting.

Here was how naïve Wade was: He thought that his quitting would cause a town-wide uproar. High schools are made up of types. The handsome quarterback. The basketball captain. The school president. The lead in every school play. He thought the townsfolk would rally against the injustice that had befallen him. But no one said a thing. At first, Wade figured that they were scared of Kenny's father and his possible mob connections, but the truth was far simpler: They didn't care. Why should they?

It is so easy to inch your way into foul territory. The line is so thin, so flimsy. You just step over it, just for a second, and sometimes, well, sometimes you can't make your way back. Three weeks later Wade Larue got drunk, broke into the school, and vandalized the sets for the play. He was caught by the police and suspended from school.

And so the slide began.

Wade ended up taking too many drugs, moving to Boston to help sell and distribute, grew paranoid, carried a gun. And now here he was, sitting at this podium, a famous felon blamed for the death of eighteen people.

The faces glaring up at him were familiar from his trial fifteen years ago. Wade knew most of the names. At the trial they would stare with a combination of grief and bewilderment, still woozy from the sudden blow. Wade had understood back then, sympathized even. Now, fifteen years later, the glares were more hostile. Their grief and bewilderment had crystallized into a purer cut of anger and hate. At the trial, Wade Larue had avoided the glares. But no more. He kept his head up. He met their eyes. His sympathy, his understanding, had been decimated by their lack of forgiveness. He had never meant to hurt anyone. They knew that. He had apologized. He had paid a huge price. They, these families, still chose hate.

To hell with them.

Sandra Koval waxed eloquent from the seat next to him. She spoke of apologies and forgiveness, of turning corners and transformations, of understanding and the human desire for a second chance. Larue tuned her out. He spotted Grace Lawson sitting next to Carl Vespa. He should have felt tremendous fear seeing Vespa in the flesh, but no, he was beyond that now. When Wade was first put in prison, he had been badly beaten – first by people working for Vespa and then by those hoping to curry favor. Guards included. There had been no escape from the constant fear. Fear, like the smell, had become a natural part of him, his world. Maybe that explained why he was immune to it now.

Larue eventually made friends at Walden, but prison is no character-builder, despite what Sandra Koval was now telling this audience. Prison strips you down to your barest state, the state of nature, and what you do to survive is never pretty. No matter. He was out now. That was in the past. You move on.

But not quite yet.

The room was beyond silent, a vacuuming feel, as if the very air had been sucked out of it. The families all sat there, unmoved both physically and emotionally. But there was no energy there. They were hollow entities, devastated and powerless. They could not hurt him. Not any more.

Without warning Carl Vespa rose. For a second – no longer than that – Sandra Koval was thrown. Grace Lawson stood too. Wade Larue could not understand why they were together. It made no sense. He wondered if it changed anything, if he would soon meet Grace Lawson.

Did it matter?

When Sandra Koval finished, she leaned over to him and whispered, 'Come on, Wade. You can take the back way out.'

Ten minutes later, out on the streets of Manhattan, Wade Larue was free for the first time in fifteen years.

He stared up at the skyscrapers. Times Square was his first destination. It would be noisy and crowded with people – real, live nonconvicts. Larue did not want solitude. He did not crave green grass or trees – you could see those from his prison cell in the sticks of Walden. He wanted lights and sounds and people, real people, not prisoners, and yes, perhaps, the company of a good (or better, bad) woman.

But that would have to wait. Wade Larue checked his watch. It was almost time.

He started west on Forty-third Street. There was still a chance to back out of this. He was achingly close to the Port Authority bus terminal. He could hop on a bus, any bus, and start anew someplace. He could change his name, maybe his face a little, and try out for local theater. He was still young. He still had the chops. He still had that supernatural charisma.

Soon, he thought.

He needed to clear this up. Put it behind him. When he was being released, one of the prison counselors had given him the standard lecture about this being either a new start or a bad end, it was all up to him. The counselor was right. Today he would either put this all behind him or he would die. Wade doubted that there would be an in-between.

Up ahead he saw a black sedan. He recognized the man leaning against the side, his arms crossed. It was the mouth you couldn't forget, the way the teeth were all twisted together. He had been the first to beat Larue all those years ago. He wanted to know what had happened the night of the Boston Massacre. Larue had told him the truth: He didn't know.

Now he did.

'Hey, Wade.'

'Cram.'

Cram opened the door. Wade Larue slid into the back. Five minutes later they were on the West Side Highway heading toward the endgame.

41

Eric Wu watched the limousine pull up to the Lawson residence.

A large man who looked like anything but a chauffeur stepped out of the car, pulled his jacket together hard so he could work the button, and opened the back door. Grace Lawson stepped out. She headed for her front door without saying good-bye or looking behind her. The large man watched her pick up a package and go inside. Then he got back in the car and pulled out.

Wu wondered about him, the large man. Grace Lawson, he'd been told, might have protection now. She had been threatened. Her children had been threatened. The large chauffeur was not with the police. Wu was certain of that. But he was no simple driver either.

Best to be cautious.

Keeping a good distance away, Wu began to circle the perimeter. The day was clear, the foliage bursting with green. There were many places to hide. Wu did not have binoculars – it would have made the task easier – but that was not important. He spotted one man within minutes. The man was stationed behind the detached garage. Wu crept closer. The man was communicating with a cellphone walkie-talkie. Wu listened. He only picked up snippets, but it was enough. There was someone in the house too. Probably another man on the perimeter, on the other side of the street.

This was not good.

Wu could still handle it. He knew that. But he would have to strike fast. He would first have to know the exact location of the other perimeter man. He would take one out with his hands and one with the gun. He would need to rush the house. It could be done. There would be lots of bodies. The man inside could be tipped off. But it could be done.

Wu checked his watch. Twenty minutes until three.

He started circling back toward the street when the back door of the Lawson home opened. Grace stepped out. She had a suitcase. Wu stopped and watched. She put the suitcase in the trunk. She went back inside. She came out with another suitcase and a package – the same one, he thought, that he'd seen her pick up at the front door.

Wu hurried back to the car he was using – ironically enough, her Ford Windstar, though he'd switched license plates at the Palisades Mall and slapped on some bumper stickers to draw attention away from that fact. People remembered bumper stickers more than license plates or even makes. There was one about him being a proud parent of an honor roll student. A second, for the New York Knicks, read ONE TEAM, ONE NEW YORK.

Grace Lawson got behind the wheel of her car and started it up. Good, Wu thought. It would be much easier to grab her wherever she stopped. His instructions were clear. Find out what she knows. Get rid of the body. He put the Windstar in gear but kept his foot on the brake. He wanted to see if anyone else followed. No one pulled out after her. Wu kept his distance.

There were no other tails.

The men had been ordered to protect the house, he guessed, not her. Wu wondered about the suitcases, about where she might be headed, about how long this journey might take. He was surprised when she started taking small side streets. He was even more surprised when she pulled to a stop near a schoolyard.

Of course. It was nearing three o'clock. She was picking up her children from school.

He thought again about the suitcases and what they might mean. Was her intention to pick up her children and take a trip? If that was the case, it might be someplace far away. It might be hours before she stopped.

Wu did not want to wait hours.

On the other hand she might head straight back home, back into the protection of the two men on the perimeter and the one in the house. That was not good either. He would have the old set of problems, plus, in either case, children would now be involved. Wu was neither blood-thirsty nor sentimental. He was pragmatic. Grabbing a woman whose husband had already run off may raise suspicions and even police involvement, but if you add dead bodies, possibly two dead children, the attention becomes nearly intolerable.

No, Wu realized. It would be best to grab Grace Lawson here and now. Before the children came out of the schoolyard.

That did not give him much time.

Mothers began to congregate and mingle, but Grace Lawson stayed in her car. She seemed to be reading something. The time was 2:50 P.M. That gave Wu ten minutes. Then he remembered the earlier threat. They had told her that they would take her children. If that was the case, it was entirely possible that there were men watching the school too.

He had to check fast.

It didn't take long. The van was parked a block away, at the end of a cul-de-sac. So obvious. Wu considered the possibility that there was more than one. He did a quick scan and saw nothing. No time anyway. He had to strike. The school would be letting out in five minutes. Once the kids were present, it would complicate everything exponentially.

Wu had dark hair now. He put on gold-framed glasses. He had the loose-fitting casual clothes. He tried to make himself look timid as he was walked toward the van. He looked around as if lost. He moved straight to the back door and was about to open it when a bald man with a sweaty brow popped his head out.

'What do you want, pal?'

The man was dressed in a blue velour sweat suit. There was no shirt under the jacket, just mounds of chest hair. He was big and gruff. Wu reached out with his right hand and cupped the back of the man's head. He snapped his arm forward and planted his left elbow deep in the man's adam's apple. The throat simply collapsed. The entire windpipe gave way like a brittle branch. The man went down, his body thrashing like a fish on the dock. Wu pushed him deeper into the van and slid inside.

There was the same cell-phone walkie-talkie, a pair of binoculars, a gun. Wu jammed the weapon into his waist. The man still thrashed. He would not live much longer.

Three minutes until the bell rang.

Wu locked the van's door behind him and hurried out. He made it back to the street where Grace Lawson was parked. Mothers lined the fence in anticipation of school being let out. Grace Lawson was out of her car now, standing by herself. That was good.

Wu walked toward her.

On the other side of the schoolyard, Charlaine Swain was thinking about chain reactions and falling dominoes.

If she and Mike hadn't had problems.

If she had not started up that perverted dance with Freddy Sykes.

If she had not looked out that window when Eric Wu was there.

If she had not opened the hide-a-key and called the police.

But right now, as she passed the playground, the dominoes were falling more in the present: If Mike had not woken up, if he had not insisted she take care of the children, if Perlmutter had not asked her about Jack Lawson, well, without all of that, Charlaine would not have been looking in Grace Lawson's direction.

But Mike had insisted. He had reminded her that the children needed her. So here she was. Picking up Clay from school. And Perlmutter had indeed asked Charlaine if she knew Jack Lawson. So when Charlaine arrived at the schoolyard, it was natural, if not inevitable, that she would start scanning the grounds for the man's wife.

That was how Charlaine came to be looking at Grace Lawson.

She had even been tempted to approach – hadn't that been part of the reason she had agreed to pick up Clay in the first place? – but then she saw Grace pick up her cell phone and start talking into it. Charlaine decided to keep her distance.

'Hi, Charlaine.'

A woman, a popular yappy mom who had never deigned to give Charlaine the time before, now stood before her with a look of feigned concern. The newspaper had not mentioned Mike's name, just that there was a shooting, but small towns and gossip and all that.

'I heard about Mike. Is he okay?'

'Fine.'

'What happened?'

Another woman sidled up to her right. Two others began to mosey over. Then two more. They came from every direction now, these approaching mothers, getting in her way, almost blocking Charlaine's view.

Almost.

For a moment Charlaine could not move. She stood frozen, watching as he approached Grace Lawson.

He had changed his appearance. He wore glasses now. His hair wasn't blond anymore. But there was no doubt. It was the same man.

It was Eric Wu.

From more than a hundred feet away Charlaine felt the shiver when Wu put his hand on Grace Lawson's shoulder. She saw him bend down and whisper something into her ear.

And then she saw Grace Lawson's whole body go rigid.

Grace wondered about the Asian man walking toward her.

She figured that he would just walk by her. He was too young to be a parent. Grace knew most of the teachers. He wasn't one of them. He was probably a new student teacher. That was probably it. She really did not give him much thought. Her mind was concerned with other things.

She had packed enough clothes for a few days anyway. Grace had a cousin who lived near Penn State, smack in the middle of Pennsylvania. Maybe she would drive out there. Grace had not called ahead to see. She did not want to leave any trail.

After throwing clothes in the suitcases, she had closed the door to her bedroom. She took out the small gun Cram had given her and set it on the bed. For a long time she just stared at it. She had always been fervently anti-gun. Like most rational people she was scared of what a weapon like this could do lying around the house. But Cram had put it succinctly yesterday: Hadn't her children been threatened?

The trump card.

Grace wrapped the nylon ankle holster around her good leg. It felt itchy and uncomfortable. She changed into jeans with a small flare at the bottom. The gun was covered now, but there was some room down there. There was still a small bulge in the area, but no more so than if she were wearing a boot.

She grabbed the box of Bob Dodd files from his office at the *New Hampshire Post* and drove to the school. She had a few minutes now, so she stayed in the car and started

going through it. Grace had no idea what she expected to find. There were plenty of desk knickknacks – a small American flag, a Ziggy coffee mug, a return address stamper,
a small Lucite paperweight. There were pens, pencils, erasers, paperclips, whiteout, thumbtacks, Post-it notes, staples.

Grace wanted to skip past that stuff and dive into the files, but the pickings were slim. Dodd must have done all his work on a computer. She found a few diskettes, all unmarked. Maybe there would be a clue on one of those. She'd check when she got access to a computer.

As for paperwork, all she found was press clippings. Articles written by Bob Dodd. Grace skimmed through them. Cora had been right. His stories were mostly small-time exposés. People would write in with a complaint. Bob Dodd would investigate. Hardly the sort of stuff that gets you killed, but who knows? The little things have a way of rippling.

She was just about to give up – had given up really – when she located the desk photo in the bottom. The frame was facedown. More out of curiosity than anything else she flipped the frame over and took a look. The photograph was a classic vacation shot. Bob Dodd and his wife Jillian stood on a beach, both smiling with dazzling white teeth, both wearing Hawaiian shirts. Jillian had red hair. Her eyes were widely spaced apart. Grace suddenly understood Bob Dodd's involvement. It had nothing to do with the fact that he was a reporter.

His wife, Jillian Dodd, was Sheila Lambert.

Grace closed her eyes and rubbed the bridge of her nose. Then she carefully put everything back in the package. She stuck it in the backseat and slipped out of the car. She needed time to think and put it together.

The four members of Allaw – it all came back to them. Sheila Lambert, Grace now knew, had stayed in the country. She had changed her identity and gotten married. Jack had taken off for a small village in France. Shane Alworth was either dead or in parts unknown – maybe, as his mother suggested, helping the poor in Mexico. Geri Duncan had been murdered.

Grace checked her watch. The bell would ring in a few minutes. She felt the buzz of her cell phone on her belt. 'Hello?'

'Ms. Lawson, this is Captain Perlmutter.'

'Yes, Captain, what can I do for you?'

'I need to ask you some questions.'

'I'm picking up my children at school right now.'

'Would you like me to come by your house? We can meet there.'

'They'll be out in two more minutes. I'll swing by the station.' A sense of relief rushed over her. This half-baked idea of running off to Pennsylvania – that might be too much. Maybe Perlmutter knew something. Maybe, with all she now knew about that picture, he would finally believe her. 'Will that be okay?'

'That'll be fine. I'll be here waiting.'

The very moment Grace snapped the receiver closed, she felt a hand touch down on her shoulder. She turned. The hand belonged to the young Asian man. He bent his head toward her ear.

'I have your husband,' he whispered.

42

'Charlaine? Are you okay?'

It was the popular yappy mother. Charlaine ignored her.

Okay, Charlaine, think.

What, she wondered, would the dumb heroine do? That was how she'd try to play it in the past – imagine what the waif would do and do the opposite.

C'mon, c'mon . . .

Charlaine tried to battle through the near-paralyzing fear. She had not expected to see this man ever again. Eric Wu was wanted. He had shot Mike. He had assaulted Freddy and held him captive. The police had his fingerprints. They knew who he was. They would send him back to prison. So what was he doing here?

Who cares, Charlaine? Do something.

The answer was a no-brainer: Call the police.

She reached into her pocketbook and pulled out her Motorola. The mothers were still barking like small dogs. Charlaine flipped the phone open.

It was dead.

Typical, and yet it made sense. She had used it during the chase. She had left it on all this time. The phone was two years old. The damn thing was always going dead. She glanced back across the schoolyard. Eric Wu was talking to Grace Lawson. They both began to walk away.

The same woman asked again: 'Is something wrong, Charlaine?'

'I need to use your cell phone,' she said. 'Now.'

*

Grace just stared at the man.

'If you come with me quietly, I will take you to your husband. You will see him. You will be back in an hour. But the school bell rings in one minute. If you do not come with me, I will take out a gun. I will shoot your children. I will shoot random children. Do you understand?'

Grace could not speak.

'You don't have much time.'

She found her voice. 'I'll go with you.'

'You drive. Just walk calmly with me. Please do not make the mistake of trying to signal someone. I will kill them. Do you understand?'

'Yes.'

'You may be wondering about the man assigned to protect you,' he went on. 'Let me assure you that he will not interfere.'

'Who are you?' Grace asked.

'The bell is about to ring.' He looked off, a tiny smile on his lips. 'Do you want me to be here when your children come out?'

Scream, Grace thought. Scream like a lunatic and start running. But she could see the bulge of the gun. She could see the man's eyes. This was no bluff. He meant it. He would kill people.

And he had her husband.

They began to walk to her car, side by side, like two friends. Grace's eyes darted about the playground. She spotted Cora. Cora gave her a puzzled look. Grace did not want to risk it. She looked away.

Grace kept walking. They reached her car. She had just unlocked the doors when the school bell rang.

The yappy woman rummaged through her purse. 'We have a terrible calling plan. Hal is so cheap sometimes. We run out of minutes in the first week and then we need to watch ourselves the rest of the month.'

Charlaine looked at the other faces. She did not want to cause a panic, so she kept her voice even. 'Please, does anyone have a phone I can borrow?'

She kept her eyes on Wu and Lawson. They were across the street, by Grace's car now. She saw Grace use one of those remote controls to unlock the doors. Grace stood by the driver's door. Wu was by the passenger's. Grace Lawson made no move to run away. It was hard to see her face, but she didn't look as if she was being coerced.

The bell sounded.

The mothers all turned toward the doors, a Pavlovian response, and waited for their children to emerge.

'Here, Charlaine.'

One of the mothers, eyes on the school door, handed Charlaine her cell phone. Charlaine tried not to grab it too quickly. She was raising it to her ear when she glanced over at Grace and Wu one more time. She stopped cold.

Wu was staring directly at her.

When Wu saw that woman again, he started for his gun.

He was going to shoot her. Right here. Right now. Right in front of everyone.

Wu was not a superstitious man. He realized that the odds of her being here were reasonable. She had children. She lived in the area. There must have been two or three hundred mothers here. It would make sense that she would be one of them.

But he still wanted to kill her.

On the superstitious side, he would kill this demon.

On the practical side, he would prevent her from calling the police. He would also cause a panic that would allow him to escape. If he shot her, everyone would run toward the fallen woman. It would be the ideal diversion.

But there were problems too.

First, the woman stood at least a hundred feet away. Eric Wu knew his strengths and weaknesses. In hand-to-hand he had no equal. With a gun, he was merely decent. He might only wound or, worse, miss altogether. Yes, there would be a panic, but without a body falling, it might not be the sort of diversion he wanted.

His real target – the reason he was here – was Grace Lawson. He had her now. She was listening to him. She was pliable because she still held out hope that her family could survive this. If she were to see him fire a shot, standing as she was out of his reach, there was a chance that Grace Lawson would panic and bolt.

'Get in,' he said.

Grace Lawson opened her car door. Eric Wu stared at the woman across the schoolyard. When their eyes met, he slowly shook his head and gestured toward his waist. He wanted her to understand. She had crossed him before and he had fired. He would do so again.

He waited until the woman lowered the phone. Still keeping his eyes on her, Wu slid into the car. They pulled out and disappeared down Morningside Drive.

43

Perlmutter sat across from Scott Duncan. They were in the captain's office at the station. The air-conditioning was on the fritz. Dozens of cops in full uniform all day and no air-conditioning – the place was starting to reek.

'So you're on leave from the U.S. attorney's office,' Perlmutter said.

'That's correct,' Duncan replied. 'I'm working in private practice right now.'

'I see. And your client hired Indira Khariwalla – check that, you hired Ms. Khariwalla on behalf of a client.'

'I will neither confirm nor deny that.'

'And you won't tell me if your client wanted Jack Lawson followed. Or why.'

'That's correct.'

Perlmutter spread his hands. 'So what exactly do you want, Mr. Duncan?'

'I want to know what you've learned about Jack Lawson's disappearance.'

Perlmutter smiled. 'Okay, let me make sure I have this straight. I'm supposed to tell you everything I know about a murder and missing person investigation, even though your client may very well be involved. You, in turn, are supposed to tell me squat. That about cover it?'

'No, that's not correct.'

'Well, help me here.'

'This has nothing to do with a client.' Duncan crossed his ankle over his knee. 'I have a personal involvement in the Lawson case.'

'Come again?'

'Ms. Lawson showed you the photograph.'

'Right, I remember.'

'The girl with her face crossed out,' he said, 'was my sister.'

Perlmutter leaned back and whistled low. 'Maybe you should start at the beginning.'

'It's a long story.'

'I'd say I have all day, but that would be a lie.'

As if proving the point, the door flew open. Daley jammed his head in.

'Line two.'

'What is it?'

'Charlaine Swain. She says she just saw Eric Wu at the schoolyard.'

Carl Vespa stared at the painting.

Grace was the artist. He owned eight of her paintings, though this was the one that moved him most. It was, he suspected, a portrait of Ryan's last moments. Grace's memory of that night was hazy. She hated to sound pompous about it, but this vision – this seemingly ordinary painting of a young man somehow on the verge of a nightmare – had come to her in something of an artistic trance. Grace Lawson claimed that she dreamed about that night. That, she said, was the only place that the memories existed.

Vespa wondered.

His home was in Englewood, New Jersey. The block had at one time been old money. Now Eddie Murphy lived at the end of the street. A power forward for the New Jersey Nets was two houses down. Vespa's property, once owned by a Vanderbilt, was sprawling and secluded. In 1988 Sharon, his then-wife, had torn down the turn-of-the-century stone edifice and built what was then considered modern. It had not aged well. The house looked like a bunch of glass cubes, stacked haphazardly. There were too many windows. The house got ridiculously hot in the summer. It looked and felt like a damn greenhouse.

Sharon was gone now too. She had not wanted the house in the divorce. She really did not want very much at all. Vespa did not try to stop her. Ryan had been their main connection, in his death more than life. That was never a healthy thing.

Vespa checked the security monitor for the driveway. The sedan was pulling up.

He and Sharon had wanted more children, but it was not to be. Vespa's sperm count was too low. He told no one, of course, subtly implying that the fault lay with Sharon. Awful to say now, but Vespa believed that if they had more children, if Ryan had at least one sibling, it would have made the tragedy, if not easier, at least bearable. The problem with tragedy is that you have to go on. There is no choice. You cannot just pull off the road and wait it out – much as you might want to. If you have other children you understand that right away. Your life may be over, but you get out of bed for others.

Put simply, there was no reason for him to get out of bed anymore.

Vespa headed outside and watched the sedan come to a stop. Cram got out first, a cell phone glued to his ear. Wade Larue followed. Larue did not look frightened. He looked oddly at peace, gazing at the lush surroundings. Cram mumbled something to Larue – Vespa couldn't hear what he said – and then started up the stairs. Wade Larue wandered away as if he was on retreat.

Cram said, 'We got a problem.'

Vespa waited, following Wade Larue with his eyes.

'Richie is not answering his radio.'

'Where was he stationed?'

'In a van near the kids' school.'

'Where is Grace?'

'We don't know.'

Vespa looked at Cram.

'It was three o'clock. We knew she'd gone to pick up Emma and Max. Richie was supposed to tail her from there. She got to the school, we know that. Richie radioed that in. Since then, nothing.'

'Did you send someone over?'

'Simon went to check on the van.'

'And?'

'It's still there. Parked in the same spot. But there are cops in the area now.'

'What about the kids?'

'We don't know yet. Simon thinks he sees them in the schoolyard. But he doesn't want to get too close with the cops around.'

Vespa closes his fists. 'We have to find Grace.'

Cram said nothing.

'What?'

Cram shrugged. 'I think you have it wrong, that's all.'

Neither one of them said anything after that. They stood and watched Wade Larue. He strolled the grounds, cigarette in tow. From the top of the property there was a magnificent view of the George Washington Bridge and, behind it, the distant skyline of Manhattan. It had been there that Vespa and Cram had watched the smoke billow as if from Hades when the towers fell. Vespa had known Cram for thirty-eight years. Cram was the best with a gun or a knife Vespa had ever seen. He scared people with little more than a glance. The vilest men, the most violent psychotics, begged for mercy before Cram even touched them. But on that day, standing silently in the yard, watching the smoke not dissipate, Vespa had seen even Cram break down and cry.

They looked over at Wade Larue.

'Did you talk to him at all?' Vespa asked.

Cram shook his head. 'Not a word.'

'He looks pretty calm.'

Cram said nothing. Vespa started toward Larue. Cram stayed where he was. Larue did not turn around. Vespa stopped about ten feet away and said, 'You wanted to see me?'

Larue kept staring out at the bridge. 'Beautiful view,' he said.

'You're not here to admire it.'

He shrugged. 'Doesn't mean I can't.'

Vespa waited. Wade Larue did not turn around. 'You confessed.'

'Yes.'

'Did you mean it?' Vespa asked.

'At the time? No.'

'What does that mean, at the time?'

'You want to know if I fired those two shots that night.' Wade Larue finally turned and faced Vespa full. 'Why?'

'I want to know if you killed my boy.'

'Either way I didn't shoot him.'

'You know what I mean.'

'Can I ask you something?'

Vespa waited.

'Are you doing this for you? Or your son?'

Vespa thought about that. 'It's not for me.'

'Then your son?'

'He's dead. It won't do him any good.'

'Who then?'

'It doesn't matter.'

'It does to me. If it's not about you or your son, why do you still need revenge?'

'It needs to be done.'

Larue nodded.

'The world needs balance,' Vespa went on.

'Yin and yang?'

'Something like that. Eighteen people died. Someone has to pay.'

'Or the world is out of balance?'

'Yes.'

Larue took out a pack of cigarettes. He offered one to

Vespa. Vespa shook his head.

'Did you fire those shots that night?' Vespa asked.

'Yes.'

That was when Vespa exploded. His temper was like that. He went from zero to uncontrolled rage in a snap. There was an adrenaline rush, like a thermometer spiking up in a cartoon. He cocked his fist and smashed it into Larue's face. Larue went down hard on his back. He sat up, put his hand to his nose. There was blood. Larue smiled at Vespa. 'That give you balance?'

Vespa was breathing hard. 'It's a start.'

'Yin and yang,' Larue said. 'I like that theory.' He wiped his face with his forearm. 'Thing is, this universal balancing act – does it stretch across generations?'

'What the hell is that supposed to mean?'

Larue smiled. There was blood on his teeth. 'I think you know.'

'I'm going to kill you. You know that.'

'Because I did something bad? So I should pay a price?'

'Yes.'

Larue got to his feet. 'But what about you, Mr. Vespa?'

Vespa tightened his fists, but the adrenaline rush was quieting.

'You've done bad. Did you pay the price?' Larue cocked his head. 'Or did your son pay it for you?'

Vespa hit Larue deep in the gut. Larue folded. Vespa punched him in the head. Larue fell again. Vespa kicked him in the face. Larue was flat on his back now. Vespa took a step closer. Blood dripped out of Larue's mouth, but the man still laughed. The only tears were on Vespa's face, not Larue's.

'What are you laughing at?'

'I was like you. I craved revenge.'

'For what?'

'For being in that cell.'

'That was your fault.'

Larue sat up. 'Yes and no.'

Vespa took a step back. He looked behind him. Cram stood perfectly still and watched. 'You said you wanted to talk.'

'I'll wait till you're done beating me.'

'Tell me why you called.'

Wade Larue sat up, checked his mouth for blood. He seemed almost happy to see it. 'I wanted vengeance. I can't tell you how badly. But now, today, when I got out, when I was suddenly free . . . I don't want that anymore. I spent fifteen years in prison. But my sentence is over. Your sentence, well, the truth is yours will never end, will it, Mr. Vespa?'

'What do you want?'

Larue stood. He walked over to Vespa. 'You're in such pain.' His voice was soft now, as intimate as a caress. 'I want you to know everything, Mr. Vespa. I want you to learn the truth. This has to end. Today. One way or another. I want to live my life. I don't want to look over my shoulder. So I'm going to tell you what I know. I'm going to tell you everything. And then you can decide what you need to do.'

'I thought you said you fired those shots.'

Larue ignored that. 'Do you remember Lieutenant Gordon MacKenzie?'

The question surprised Vespa. 'The security guard. Of course.'

'He visited me in prison.'

'When?'

'Three months ago.'

'Why?'

Larue smiled. 'That balance thing again. Making things right. You call it yin and yang. MacKenzie called it God.'

'I don't understand.'

'Gordon MacKenzie was dying.' Larue put his hand on Vespa's shoulder. 'So before he went, he needed to confess his sins.'

44

The gun was in Grace's ankle holster.

She started up the car. The Asian man sat next to her. 'Head up the road and turn left.'

Grace was scared, of course, but there was an odd calmness too. Something about being in the eye of the storm, she guessed. Something was happening. There was a potential to find answers here. She tried to prioritize.

First: Get him far away from the children.

That was the number one thing here. Emma and Max would be fine. The teachers stayed outside until all the children were picked up. When she didn't show, they would give an impatient sigh and bring them to the office. That old battleaxe of a receptionist, Mrs. Dinsmont, would gleefully cluck her tongue about the neglectful mother and make the children wait. There had been an incident about six months ago when Grace got caught up by construction and arrived late. She'd been wracked with guilt, picturing Max waiting like a scene from *Oliver Twist*, but when she got there he was in the office coloring a picture of a dinosaur. He wanted to stay.

The school was out of sight now. 'Turn right.'

Grace obeyed.

Her captor, if that's what you wanted to call him, had said that he was taking her to Jack. She did not know if that was true or not, but she somehow suspected that it was. She was sure, of course, that he was not doing this out of the goodness of his heart. She had been warned. She had gotten too close. He was dangerous – she didn't need to see the gun in his waistband to know that. There was a crackle around him, an electricity, and you knew, just knew, that this man always left devastation in his path.

But Grace desperately needed to see where this led. She had her gun in the ankle holster. If she stayed smart, if she was careful, she would have the element of surprise. That was something. So for now she would go along. There was really no alternative anyway.

She was worried about working the gun and the holster. Would the gun come out smoothly? Would the gun really just fire when she pulled the trigger? Did you really just aim and pull? And even if she could get the gun from the holster in time – something doubtful with the way this guy was watching her – what would she do? Point it at him and demand he take her to Jack?

She couldn't imagine that working.

She couldn't just shoot him either. Forget the ethical dilemma or the question of if she'd be brave enough to pull the trigger. He, this man, might be her only connection to Jack. If she killed him, where would that leave her? She'd have silenced her only solid clue, maybe her only chance, to find Jack.

Better to wait and play it out. As if she had a choice.

'Who are you?' Grace asked.

Total stone face. He took hold of her purse and emptied the contents into his lap. He went through it, sifting and tossing items into the backseat. He found her cell phone, removed the battery, threw it in the back.

She kept peppering him with questions – where is my husband, what do you want with us – but he continued to ignore her. When they reached a stoplight, the man did something that she did not expect.

He rested his hand on her bad knee.

'Your leg was damaged,' he said.

Grace was not sure how to respond to this. His touch was light, almost feathery. And then without warning his fingers dug down with steel talons. They actually burrowed beneath the kneecap. Grace buckled. The tips of the man's fingers disappeared into the hollow where the knee meets the shinbone. The pain was so sudden, so enormous, that Grace could not even scream. She reached out and grabbed his fingers, tried to pry them out of her knee, but there was absolutely no give. His hand felt like a concrete block.

His voice was barely a whisper. 'If I dig in a little more and then pull . . .'

Her head was swimming. She was close to losing consciousness.

'. . . I could tear your kneecap right off.'

When the light turned green, he let go. Grace nearly collapsed in relief. The whole incident had probably taken less than five seconds. The man looked at her. There was the smallest hint of a smile on his face.

'I'd like you to stop talking now, okay?'

Grace nodded.

He faced forward. 'Keep driving.'

Perlmutter called in the APB. Charlaine Swain had had the good sense to get both the make and license plate. The car was registered to Grace Lawson. No surprise there. Perlmutter was in an unmarked car now, heading toward the school. Scott Duncan was with him.

'So who is this Eric Wu?' Duncan asked.

Perlmutter debated what to tell him but saw no reason to hold this back. 'To date we know he broke into a house, assaulted the owner in such a way as to leave him temporarily paralyzed, shot another man, and my guess is, he killed Rocky Conwell, the guy who was following Lawson.'

Duncan had no response.

Two other police cars were already on the scene. Perlmutter did not like that – marked cars at a school. They'd had the good sense, at least, to not use their sirens. That was something. The parents picking up offspring reacted in two ways. Some hurried their kids to their cars, hands on their shoulders, shielding them as though from gunfire. Others let curiosity rule the day. They walked over, oblivious or in a state of denial that there could be any danger in so innocent a setting.

Charlaine Swain was there. Perlmutter and Duncan hurried toward her. A young uniformed cop named Dempsey was asking her questions and taking notes. Perlmutter shooed him away and asked, 'What happened?'

Charlaine told him about coming to school, keeping an eye out for Grace Lawson because of what he, Perlmutter, had said. She told him about seeing Eric Wu with Grace.

'There was no overt threat?' he asked.

Charlaine said, 'No.'

'So she might have gone him with him voluntarily.'

Charlaine Swain flicked a glance at Scott Duncan, then back to Perlmutter. 'No. She didn't go voluntarily.'

'How do you know?'

'Because Grace came alone to pick up her kids,' Charlaine said.

'So?'

'So she wouldn't just voluntarily leave them like that. Look, I couldn't call you guys right away when I saw him. He was able to make me freeze from across a schoolyard.'

Perlmutter said, 'I'm not sure I understand.'

'If Wu could do that to me from that far away,' Charlaine said, 'imagine what he'd be able to do to Grace Lawson when he was right next to her, whispering in her ear.'

Another uniformed officer named Jackson came sprinting over to Perlmutter. His eyes were wide and Perlmutter could see he was trying everything he could not to panic. The parents picked up on it too. They took a step away.

'We found something,' Jackson said.

'What?'

He leaned in closer so no one would overhear. 'A van parked two blocks away. I think you should come see this.'

*

She should use the gun now.

Grace's knee throbbed. It felt as if someone had set off a bomb inside the joint. Her eyes were wet from holding back tears. She wondered if she'd be able to walk when they stopped.

She sneaked glances at the man who had hurt her so. Whenever she did, he was watching her, that bemused look still on his face. She tried to think, tried to organize her thoughts, but she kept flashing back to his hand on her knee.

He had been so casual about causing her such pain. It would have been one thing if he'd been emotional about it, one way or the other, if he'd been moved to either ecstasy or revulsion, but there had been nothing there. Like hurting someone was paperwork. No strain, no sweat. His boast, if you want to call it that, had not been idle: If he'd so desired, he could have twisted off her kneecap like a bottle top.

They had crossed the state line and were in New York now. She was on Interstate 287 heading toward the Tappan Zee Bridge. Grace did not dare speak. Her mind, naturally enough, kept going back to the children. Emma and Max would have come out of the school by now. They would have looked for her. Would they have been brought to the office? Cora had seen Grace in the schoolyard. So had several other mothers, Grace was sure. Would they say or do something?

This was all irrelevant and, more than that, a waste of mental energy. Nothing she could do about it. Time to concentrate on the task at hand.

Think about the gun.

Grace tried to rehearse in her mind how it would go. She would reach down with both hands. She would pull her cuff up with her left and grab the weapon with her right. How was it strapped in? Grace tried to remember.

There was a strip covering the top, wasn't there? She had snapped it into place. It kept the gun secure, so it wouldn't jerk around. She'd have to unsnap that. If she just tried to pull the gun free, it would get caught.

Okay, good. Remember that: Unsnap first. Then pull.

She thought about timing. The man was incredibly strong. She had seen that. He probably had a fair amount of experience with violence. She would have to wait for an opportunity. First – and this was obvious – she couldn't be driving when she made her move. They would either need to be at a stoplight or parked or . . . or better, wait until they were getting out of the car. That might work.

Second, the man would have to be distracted. He watched her a lot. He was also armed. He had a weapon in his waistband. He would be able to draw it out far faster than she could. So she had to make sure that he was not looking at her – that his attention was, in some way, diverted.

'Take this exit.'

The sign read ARMONK. They had only been on 287 for maybe three or four miles. They were not going to be crossing the Tappan Zee Bridge. She had thought that perhaps the bridge would have provided another opportunity. There were tollbooths there. She could have tried to escape or somehow signal the toll worker, though she couldn't imagine that working. Her captor would be watching her if they'd pulled up to the tollbooth. He would, she bet, have put his hand on her knee.

She veered to the right and up the ramp. She began to work it out in her head again. When you really thought about it, Grace's best bet would be to wait until they reached their destination. For one thing, if indeed he really was taking her to Jack, well, Jack would be there, right? That made some sense.

But more than that, when they stopped the car, they would both have to get out. Obvious, yes, but it would provide an opportunity. He would get out on his side. She would get out on hers.

This could be her diversion.

Again she started rehearsing it in her head. She would open the car door. As she swung her legs out, she'd pull up the cuff. Her legs would be on the ground and blocked by the car. He wouldn't see. If she timed it right, he would be getting out on his side of the car at the same time. He'd turn his back. She'd be able to pull out the weapon.

'Take the next right,' he said. 'And then the second left.'

They were moving through a town Grace didn't know. There were more trees here than in Kasselton. The houses looked older, more lived-in, more private.

'Pull into the driveway over there. Third on the left.'

Grace's hands stayed tight on the wheel. She pulled into the driveway. He told her to stop in front of the house.

She took a breath and waited for him to open the door and get out.

Perlmutter had never seen anything like it.

The guy in the van, an overweight man with a standard issue mafiosa sweat suit, was dead. His last few moments had not been pleasant. The big man's neck was, well, flat, totally flat, as if a steamroller had somehow managed to roll over only the man's throat, leaving his head and torso intact.

Daley, never one at a loss for words, said, 'Serious grossness.' Then he added, 'He looks familiar.'

'Richie Jovan,' Perlmutter said. 'Works low level for Carl Vespa.'

'Vespa?' Daley repeated. 'He's involved in this?'

Perlmutter shrugged. 'This has to be Wu's handiwork.'

Scott Duncan was turning white. 'What the hell is going on?'

'It's simple, Mr. Duncan.' Perlmutter turned to face him. 'Rocky Conwell worked for Indira Khariwalla, a private investigator you hired. The same man – Eric Wu – murdered Conwell, killed this poor schmuck, and was last seen driving away from that school with Grace Lawson.' Perlmutter moved toward him. 'You want to tell us what's going on now?'

Another police car screeched to a stop. Veronique Baltrus came flying out. 'Got it.'

'What?'

'Eric Wu at yenta-match.com. He was using the name Stephen Fleisher.' She sprinted over to them, the raven hair tied back in a tight bun. 'Yenta-match sets up Jewish widows and widowers. Wu had three online flirtations going on at the same time. One woman is from Washington, DC. Another lives in Wheeling, West Virginia. And the last one, a Beatrice Smith, resides in Armonk, New York.'

Perlmutter broke into a run. No doubt, he thought. That was where Wu had gone. Scott Duncan followed. The ride to Armonk would take no more than twenty minutes.

'Call the Armonk Police Department,' he shouted to Baltrus. 'Tell them to send every available unit right away.'

45

Grace waited for the man to get out.

The lot was wooded so that the house was hard to see from the road. There were cathedral points and lots of deck space. Grace could see an aging barbecue. There were a string of lights, the old lantern kind, but the lanterns were weathered and torn. There was a rusted swing set in the back, like ruins from another era. There had been parties here once. A family. People who liked to entertain friends. The house had the feel of a ghost town: you expected tumbleweeds to roll past.

'Turn off the ignition.'

Grace ran it over again. Open the door. Swing the legs out. Pull out the gun. Take aim . . .

And then what? Tell him to put his hands up? Just shoot him in the chest? What?

She flicked off the ignition and waited for him to get out first. He reached for the door handle. She readied herself. His eyes were on the front door of the house. She slid her hand down a little.

Should she go for it now?

No. Wait until he starts getting out. Don't hesitate. Any hesitation and she would lose the edge.

The man stopped with his hand on the handle. Then he turned around, made a fist, and hit Grace so hard in the lower ribs she thought the whole cage would cave in like a bird's nest. There was a thud and a crack.

Pain exploded across Grace's side.

She thought that her whole body would simply give out. The man grabbed her head with one hand. With the other he traced his hand down the side of her rib cage. His index finger came to rest on the spot he'd just hit, at the bottom of the rib cage.

His voice was gentle. 'Please tell me how you got that picture.'

She opened her mouth but nothing came out. He nodded as if he'd expected that. His hand dropped off her. He opened the car door and got out. Grace was dizzy from the pain.

The gun, she thought. Get the goddamn gun!

But he was already on the other side of the car. He opened her door. His hand took hold of her neck, his thumb on one side, his index finger on the other. He squeezed the pressure points and started to lift. Grace tried to stay with him. The movement jarred her ribs. It felt like someone had jammed a screwdriver between two bones and was jerking it up and down.

He dragged her out by the neck. Every step was a new adventure in pain. She tried not to breathe. When she did, even that slight expansion of the ribs made the tendons feel like they were being freshly ripped. He yanked her toward the house. The front door was unlocked. He turned the knob, pushed it open, and tossed her inside. She fell hard, nearly passing out.

'Please tell me how you got that picture.'

He slowly moved toward her. Fear cleared her head. She talked fast.

'I picked up a packet of film at the Photomat,' she began.

He nodded in the way someone does when they are not listening. He kept coming closer. Grace kept talking and tried to scoot back. There was nothing on his face, a man going about a mundane task, planting seeds, hammering a nail, putting in a buy order, whittling wood.

He was on her now. She tried to struggle but he was ridiculously strong. He lifted her enough to flip her onto her stomach. The ribs banged against the floor. A different pain, a new pain, seared through her. Her vision started going hazy. They were still in the front foyer. He straddled her back. She tried to kick, but there was nothing behind it. He pinned her down.

Grace couldn't move.

'Please tell me how you got that picture.'

She felt the tears coming, but she would not let herself cry. Stupid. Macho. But she would not cry. She said it again, about going to the Photomat, and getting that packet. Still straddling her back, his knees on the other side of her hips, he put his index finger on the damaged bottom of the rib cage. Grace tried to buck. He found the spot where it hurt the most and rested the tip of his finger right there. For a moment he did not do anything. She bucked more. She flung her head back and forth. She flailed. He just waited a second. Then another.

And then he jammed the finger between two broken ribs.

Grace screamed.

The voice unchanged: 'Please tell me how you got that picture.'

Now she did cry. He let her. She started explaining again, changing her words, hoping it would sound more believable, more convincing. He did not say a word.

He rested the index finger on the damaged rib again.

That was when a cell phone rang.

The man sighed. He put his hands on her back and lifted himself off. The ribs screamed again. Grace heard a whimpering sound and realized that it was coming from her. She made herself stop. She managed to glance over her shoulder. He kept his eyes on her, took the phone from his pocket, snapped it open.

'Yes.'

One thought in her head: Go for the gun.

He stared down at her. She almost didn't care. Going

for the gun right now would be suicide, but her thoughts were base – escape the pain. Whatever the cost. Whatever the risk. Escape the pain.

The man kept the phone by his ear.

Emma and Max. Their faces floated toward her in something of a haze. Grace encouraged the vision. And something odd happened then.

Lying there, still on her stomach, her cheek pressed to the floor, Grace smiled. Actually smiled. Not from feelings of maternal warmth, though that might be part of it, but with specific memory.

When she was pregnant with Emma, she told Jack that she wanted to do natural childbirth and that she did not want to take any drugs. She and Jack dutifully attended Lamaze class every Monday night for three months. They practiced breathing techniques. Jack would sit behind her and rub her belly. He would go 'hee hee hoo hoo.' She would copy him. Jack even bought a shirt that read 'Coach' on the front and 'Team Healthy Baby' on the back. He wore a whistle around his neck.

When the contractions began, they rushed to the hospital all prepared, all ready for their hard work to pay off dividends. Once there, Grace felt a stronger contraction. They started doing their breathing. Jack would go 'hee hee hoo hoo.' Grace would follow suit. It worked wonderfully well right up until the very moment Grace started to, well, started to feel pain.

Then the insanity of their plan – when did 'breathing' become a euphemism for 'painkiller'? – became apparent. It washed away the macho idiocy of 'taking the hurt,' a concept idiotically male in the first place, and reason, calm reason, finally came to her.

She reached out then, grabbed a part of Jack's anatomy, pulled him close so he could hear her. She told him to find an anesthesiologist. Now. Jack said he would, the moment she released said anatomy. She obliged. He ran and found an anesthesiologist. But by then it was too late. The contractions were too far along.

And the reason Grace was smiling now, some eight years after the fact, was that the pain that day was at least this bad, probably worse. She had taken it. For her daughter. And then, miraculously, she had been willing to risk it again for Max.

So bring it on, she thought.

Maybe she was delirious. Nothing maybe about it. She was. But she didn't care. The smile stayed in place. Grace could see Emma's beautiful face. She saw Max's face too. She blinked and they were gone. But that didn't matter anymore. She looked at the cruel man on the phone.

Bring it on, you sick son of a bitch. Bring it on.

He finished with his phone call. He moved back toward her. She was still on her stomach. He straddled her again. Grace closed her eyes. Tears squeezed out of them. She waited.

The man took hold of both of her hands and pulled them behind her back. He wrapped duct tape around them and stood. He pulled her so that she was on her knees, her hands bound behind her back. The ribs ached but the pain was manageable for now.

She looked up at him.

He said, 'Don't move.'

He turned away and left her alone then. She listened. She heard a door open and then the sound of footsteps.

He was heading down into the basement.

She was alone.

Grace struggled to free her arms, but they were wrapped tightly. No way to reach the gun. She debated trying to stand and run, but that would be futile at best. The position of her arms, the searing pain in her ribs, and of course, the fact that she was a major gimp under the best of circumstances – add it up and it didn't look like a sound alternative.

But could she slip her hands under herself?

If she could do that, if she could get her hands, even bound, to the front of her body, she could go for the gun.

It was a plan.

Grace had no idea how long he'd be gone – not long, she figured – but she had to chance it.

Her shoulders rolled back in their sockets. Her arms straightened. Every movement – every breath – set the ribs afire. She fought through it. She stood and bent at the waist. She forced her hands down.

Progress.

Still standing, she bent the knees and squirmed. She was getting close. Footsteps again.

Damn, he was heading back up the stairs.

She was caught in the middle, her bound hands under her buttocks.

Hurry, dammit. One way or the other. Put the hands back behind her or keep going.

She chose to keep going. Keep going forward.

This was going to end here and now.

The footsteps were slow. Heavier. It sounded like he was dragging something with him.

Grace pushed harder. Her hands were stuck. She bent more at the waist and knees. The pain made her head swim. She closed her eyes and swayed. She pulled up, willing to dislocate her shoulders if it would help her get through.

The footsteps stopped. A door closed. He was here.

She forced her arms through. It worked. They came out in front of her.

But it was too late. The man was back. He stood in the room, not five feet from her. He saw what she had done. But Grace did not notice that. She was, in fact, not looking at the man's face at all. She stared openmouthed at the man's right hand.

The man let go. And there, falling to the floor by his side, was Jack.

46

Grace dove toward him.

'Jack? Jack?'

His eyes were closed. His hair was matted to his forehead. Her hands were still bound, but she was able to hold his face. Jack's skin was clammy. His lips were dry and caked over. There was duct tape around his legs. A handcuff hung around his right wrist. She could see scabs on his left wrist. It had been cuffed too, for a long time judging by the marks.

She called his name again. Nothing. She lowered her ear to his mouth. He was breathing. She could see that. Shallow, but he was breathing. She shifted around and put his head in her lap. Her rib pain screamed but that was irrelevant now. He lay flat on his back, her lap his pillow. Her mind fell back to the grape groves in that vineyard in Saint-Emilion. They'd been together about three months by then, totally infatuated, jammed neatly in that sprint-across-the-park, thumping-of-the-heart-when-ever-you-see-the-person stage. She packed some pâté, some cheese, wine of course. The day had been sun-kissed, the sky the kind of blue that made you believe in the angels. They'd lain down on a red tartan blanket, his head in her lap like this, she stroking his hair. She'd spent more time staring at him than the natural wonders that surrounded them. She'd traced his face with her fingers.

Grace made her voice soft, tried to ease up on the panic.

'Jack?'

His eyes fluttered open. His pupils were too large. It took him a moment to focus, and then he saw her. For a moment his caked lips cracked into a smile. Grace wondered if he too was flashing back to that same picnic. Her heart burst, but she managed to smile back. There was a serene moment, no more, and then reality flooded in. Jack's eyes widened in panic. The smile vanished. His face crumbled into anguish.

'Oh God.'

'It's okay,' she said, even though that was about as dumb a statement as one could make under the circumstances.

He was trying not to cry. 'I'm so sorry, Grace.'

'Shhh, it's okay.'

Jack's eyes searched like beacons, finding their captor. 'She doesn't know anything,' he said to the man. 'Let her go.'

The man took a step closer. He bent down on his haunches. 'If you speak again,' he said to Jack, 'I will hurt her. Not you. Her. I will hurt her very badly. Do you understand?'

Jack closed his eyes and nodded.

He stood back up. He kicked Jack off her lap, grabbed Grace by the hair, and pulled her to a standing position. With his other hand he clutched Jack by the neck.

'We need to take a ride,' he said.

47

Perlmutter and Duncan had just gotten off the Garden State Parkway at Interstate 287, no more than five miles from the house in Armonk, when the call was radioed in:

'They were here – Lawson's Saab is still in the driveway – but they're gone now.'

'How about Beatrice Smith?'

'Nowhere in sight. We just got here. We're still checking the residence.'

Perlmutter thought about it. 'Wu would figure that Charlaine Swain would report seeing him. He'd know he had to get rid of the Saab. Do you know if Beatrice Smith had a car?'

'Not yet, no.'

'Is there any other car in the driveway or garage?'

'Hold on.' Perlmutter waited. Duncan looked at him. Ten seconds later: 'No other car.'

'Then they took hers. Find out the make and license plate. Get an APB out right away.'

'Okay, got it. Wait, hold on a second, Captain.' He was gone again.

Scott Duncan said, 'Your computer expert. She thought that Wu was maybe a serial killer.'

'She thought it was a possibility.'

'You don't believe it though.'

Perlmutter shook his head. 'He's a pro. He doesn't pick victims for jollies. Sykes lived alone. Beatrice Smith is a widow. Wu needs a place to stay and operate. This is how he finds those places.'

'So he's a gun for hire.'

'Something like that.'

'Any thoughts on who he's working for?'

Perlmutter held the wheel. He took the Armonk exit. They were only about a mile away now. 'I was hoping you or your client might have an idea.'

The radio crackled. 'Captain? You still there?'

'I am.'

'One car registered to Mrs. Beatrice Smith. A tan Land Rover. License plate 472-JXY.'

'Get an APB out on it. They can't be far.'

48

The tan Land Rover stayed on side roads. Grace had no idea where they were headed. Jack was lying on the floor of the backseat. He had passed out. His legs were duct-taped together. His hands were cuffed behind him. Grace's hands were still bound in front of her. Her captor, she figured, had seen no reason to make her put them back.

In the backseat Jack groaned like a wounded animal. Grace looked at their captor, his placid face, one hand on the wheel like a father taking the family out for a Sunday drive. She ached. Every breath was a reminder of what he'd done to her ribs. Her knee felt as if it'd been ripped apart by shrapnel.

'What did you do to him?' she asked.

She tensed, awaiting the blow. She almost didn't care. She was beyond that. But the man did not lash out. He did not stay silent either. He pointed with his thumb toward Jack.

'Not as much,' he said, 'as he did to you.'

She stiffened. 'What the hell is that supposed to mean?'

Now, for the first time, she saw a genuine smile. 'I think you know.'

'I don't have the slightest idea,' she said.

He still smiled, and maybe, somewhere deep inside of her, the gnawing started to grow. She tried to cast it off, tried to concentrate on getting out of this, on saving Jack. She asked, 'Where are you taking us?'

He did not reply.

'I said —'

'You're brave,' he interrupted.

She said nothing.

'Your husband loves you. You love him. It makes this easier.'

'Makes what easier?'

He glanced toward her. 'You both may be willing to risk pain. But are you willing to let me hurt your husband?'

She did not reply.

'The same thing I said to him: If you talk again, I won't hurt you. I'll hurt him.'

The man was right. It worked. She kept silent. She gazed out the window and let the trees blur. They veered onto a two-lane highway. Grace had no idea where. The area was rural. She could see that. They took two more roads and now Grace knew where they were – the Palisades Parkway heading south, back down toward New Jersey.

The Glock was still in the ankle holster.

The feel of it was constant now. The weapon seemed to be calling to her, mocking her, so close and yet out of reach.

Grace would have to figure a way to get to it. There was no other choice. This man was going to kill them. She was sure of that. He wanted some information first – the origin of that photograph, for one thing – but once he had it, once he realized that she was telling the truth on that score, he would kill them both.

She had to go for the gun.

The man kept sneaking glances at her. There was no opening. She thought about it. Wait until he stopped the car? She had tried that before – it hadn't worked. Just go for it? Just pull it out and take her chances? A possibility but she really did not think she'd be fast enough. Pulling up the leg cuff, unsnapping that safety strap, getting her hand around the gun, withdrawing it . . . all before he reacted?

No way.

She debated the slow approach. Lower her hands a little to the side. Try to work her cuff up a bit at a time. Pretend like she had an itch.

Grace shifted in her seat and looked down at her leg. And that was when she felt her heart slam into her throat . . .

Her cuff had ridden up.

The ankle holster. It was visible now.

Panic spread through her. She cut a glance at her captor, hoping that he hadn't seen it. But he had. His eyes suddenly widened. He was looking right at her leg.

Now or never.

But even as she reached, Grace could see that she had no chance. There was simply no way to get there in time. Her captor put his hand on her knee again and squeezed. Pain blasted violently through her, nearly knocking her unconscious. She screamed. Her body went rigid. Her hands dropped, useless now.

He had her.

She turned toward him, looked into his eyes, saw nothing. Then, without warning, there was movement coming from behind him. Grace gasped.

It was Jack.

Somehow he had risen up from the backseat like an apparition. The man turned, more curious than concerned. After all, Jack's hands and legs were bound. He was totally spent. What harm could he do?

Wild-eyed and looking something like an animal, Jack reared back his head and whipped it forward. The surprise caught the man off guard. Jack's forehead connected with the man's right cheek. The sound was a deep, hollow clunk. The car shrieked to a stop. The man let go of Grace's knee.

'Run, Grace!'

It was Jack's voice. Grace fumbled for the gun. She unsnapped the safety strap. But the man was back up again. He used one hand to grab Jack's neck. With the other he went after her knee again. She pulled away. He tried again.

Grace knew that there was no time to get the gun. Jack could no longer help. He had used up everything, sacrificed himself, for that one blow.

It would all be for nothing.

The man punched Grace in the ribs again. Hot knives blasted through her. Nausea swam through her stomach and head. She felt consciousness start ebbing away.

She couldn't hang on . . .

Jack tried to thrash away, but he was little more than a nuisance. The man squeezed Jack's neck. Jack made a sound and went still.

The man reached for her again. Grace grabbed the door handle.

His hand clasped her arm.

She could not move.

Jack's lifeless head slid down the man's shoulder. It stopped on the forearm. And there, with his eyes closed, Jack opened his mouth and bit down hard.

The man howled and released his grip. He started shaking his arm, trying to get Jack off. Jack clenched his jaw and hung on like a bulldog. The man slammed his free palm into Jack's head. Jack slumped off.

Grace pulled the door handle, leaned her body against it.

She fell out of the car and landed on the pavement. She rolled away, anything to get farther away from her captor. She actually rolled into the other lane of the highway. A car swerved past her.

Get the gun!

She reached down again. The safety strap was off. She turned toward the car. The man was getting out. He pulled up his shirt. Grace saw his gun. She saw him reaching for it. Grace's own gun came loose.

There was no question now. There was no ethical dilemma. There was no thought about maybe yelling out a warning, telling him to freeze, asking him to put his hands on his head. There was no moral outrage. There was no culture, no humanity, no years of civilization or breeding.

Grace pulled the trigger. The gun went off. She pulled it again. And again. The man staggered. She pulled it again. The sound of sirens grew. And Grace fired again.

49

Two ambulances arrived. One whisked Jack away before Grace could even see him. Two paramedics worked on her. They were in constant motion, asking questions as they worked, but their words did not register. She was strapped to a stretcher and wheeled toward the ambulance. Perlmutter was there now.

'Where are Emma and Max?' she asked.

'At the station. They're safe.'

An hour later Jack was in surgery. That was all they would tell her. He was in surgery.

The young doctor ran a battery of tests on Grace. The ribs were indeed cracked, but there was nothing you could really do for cracked ribs. The doctor wrapped them with an Ace bandage and gave her a shot. The pain began to subside. An orthopedic surgeon checked out her knee and just shook his head.

Perlmutter came into her room and asked a lot of questions. For the most part Grace answered. On some subjects she was intentionally vague. It wasn't that she wanted to keep anything from the police. Or maybe, well, maybe she did.

Perlmutter was pretty vague too. Her dead captor's name was Eric Wu. He had been in prison. In Walden. That did not surprise Grace. Wade Larue had been in Walden too. It was all linked. That old photograph. Jack's group, Allaw. The Jimmy X Band. Wade Larue. And yes, even Eric Wu.

Perlmutter deflected most of her questions. She did not push it. Scott Duncan was in the room too. He stayed in the corner and did not speak.

Grace asked, 'How did you know I was with this Eric Wu?'

Perlmutter clearly did not mind answering this one. 'Do you know Charlaine Swain?'

'No.'

'Her son Clay goes to Willard.'

'Okay, right. I've met her.'

Perlmutter filled her in on Charlaine Swain's own ordeal at the hands of Eric Wu. He was expansive on the subject, purposefully, Grace thought, so that he could keep mum about the rest of it. Perlmutter's cell phone rang. He excused himself and headed into the corridor. Grace was alone with Scott Duncan.

'What are they thinking?' she asked.

Scott came closer. 'The popular theory is that Eric Wu was working for Wade Larue.'

'How do they figure?'

'They know you went to Larue's press conference today, so that's link one. Wu and Larue were not only in Walden at the same time, but they were cellmates for three months.'

'Link two,' she said. 'So what do they think Larue was after?'

'Revenge.'

'On?'

'On you, for starters. You testified against him.'

'I testified at his trial, but not really against him. I don't even remember the stampede.'

'Still. There is a solid link between Eric Wu and Wade Larue – we checked the prison phone records, they've been in touch – and there is a solid link between Larue and you.'

'But even if Wade Larue was out for vengeance, why not take me? Why take Jack?'

'They think maybe Larue was trying to hurt you by hurting your family. Make you suffer.'

She shook her head. 'And that weird photograph arriving? How do they figure that into the mix? Or your sister's murder? Or Shane Alworth or Sheila Lambert? Or Bob Dodd getting killed in New Hampshire?'

'It is a theory,' Duncan said, 'with lots of holes. But remember – and this plugs most of them – they don't see all these connections the way we do. My sister may have been murdered fifteen years ago, but that doesn't have anything to do with now. Neither does Bob Dodd, a reporter who was shot gangland style. For now they're keeping it simple: Wu gets out of jail. He grabs your husband. Maybe he would have grabbed others, who knows?'

'And the reason he didn't just kill Jack?'

'Wu was holding him until Wade Larue is released.'

'Which was today.'

'Right, today. Then Wu grabs you both. He was taking you to Larue when you escaped.'

'So Larue could, what, kill us himself?'

Duncan shrugged.

'That doesn't make sense, Scott. Eric Wu broke my ribs because he wanted to know how I got that photograph. He stopped because he got an unexpected call. Then he suddenly packed us in that car. None of that was planned.'

'Perlmutter just learned all that. They may now alter their theory.'

'And where is Wade Larue anyway?'

'No one seems to know. They're searching for him.'

Grace dropped back on her pillow. Her bones felt so damned heavy. The tears started flooding her eyes. 'How bad is Jack?'

'Bad.'

'Is he going to live?'

'They don't know.'

'Don't let them lie to me.'

'I won't, Grace. But try to get some sleep, okay?'

*

In the corridor Perlmutter spoke to the captain of the Armonk Police Department, Anthony Dellapelle. They were still combing through the home of Beatrice Smith.

'We just checked the basement,' Dellapelle said. 'Someone was kept locked up down there.'

'Jack Lawson. We know that.'

Dellapelle paused and said, 'Maybe.'

'What's that supposed to mean?'

'There's still a set of handcuffs against a pipe.'

'Wu unlocked him. He probably left them there.'

'That could be. There's also blood down there – not much of it, but it's fairly fresh.'

'Lawson had some cuts on him.'

There was a pause.

'What's going on?' Perlmutter asked.

'Where are you right now, Stu?'

'Valley Hospital.'

'How long would it take you to get here?'

'Fifteen minutes with the sirens,' Perlmutter said. 'Why?'

'There's something else down here,' Dellapelle said. 'Something you might want to see for yourself.'

At midnight Grace pulled herself out of bed and started down the corridor. Her children had visited briefly. Grace insisted that they let her get out of bed for that. Scott Duncan bought her some regular clothes – an Adidas sweat suit – because she did not want to greet her children in a hospital gown. She took a major pain injection so as to quiet the screaming in her ribs. Grace wanted the children to see that she was all right, that she was safe, that they were safe. She put on a brave face that lasted right up until the moment she saw that Emma had brought her poetry journal. Then she started crying.

You can only be strong for so long.

The children were spending the night in their own beds.

Cora would stay in the master bedroom. Cora's daughter, Vickie, would sleep in the bed next to Emma. Perlmutter had assigned a female cop to stay the night too. Grace was grateful.

The hospital was dark now. Grace managed to stand upright. It took her forever. The hot scream was back in her ribs. Her knee felt more like shards of shattered glass than a joint.

The corridor was quiet. Grace had a specific destination in mind. Someone would try to stop her, she was sure, but that didn't really concern her. She was determined.

'Grace?'

She turned toward the female voice, readying to do battle. But that wouldn't be the case here. Grace recognized the woman from the playground. 'You're Charlaine Swain.'

The woman nodded. They moved toward each other, eyes locked, sharing something neither one of them could really articulate.

'I guess I owe you a thanks,' Grace said.

'Vice versa,' Charlaine said. 'You killed him. The nightmare is over for us.'

'How is your husband?' Grace asked.

'He's going to be fine.'

Grace nodded.

Charlaine said, 'I hear yours isn't doing well.' They were both beyond phony platitudes. Grace appreciated the honesty.

'He's in a coma.'

'Have you seen him?'

'I'm going there now.'

'Sneaking in?'

'Yes.'

Charlaine nodded. 'Let me help you.'

Grace leaned on Charlaine Swain. The woman was strong. The corridor was empty. In the distance they heard

342

the sharp clack of heels on tile. The lights were low. They passed an empty nurse station and got into the elevator. Jack was on the third floor, in intensive care. Having Charlaine Swain with her felt oddly right to Grace. She could not say why.

This particular section of the intensive care unit had four rooms with glass walls. A nurse sat in the middle, thus able to monitor them all at once, but right now, only one room had a patient in it.

They both pulled up. Jack was in the bed. The first thing Grace noticed was that her powerful husband, the gruff six-two hunk who'd always made her feel safe, looked so small and fragile in that bed. She knew that it was her imagination. It had only been two days. He had lost some weight. He had been totally dehydrated. But that wasn't what this was.

Jack's eyes were closed. He had a tube coming out of his throat. There was another tube in his mouth. Both were taped with white adhesive. Yet another tube was in his nose. Still another in his right arm. There was an IV. There were machines surrounding him, straight out of some futuristic nightmare.

Grace felt herself starting to fall. Charlaine held her up. Grace steadied herself and moved toward the door.

The nurse said, 'You can't go in there.'

'She just wants to sit with him,' Charlaine said. 'Please.'

The nurse glanced around then back at Grace. 'Two minutes.'

Grace let go of Charlaine. Charlaine pushed opened the door for her. Grace went in alone. There were beeps and dings and a hellish sound like drops of water being sucked up a straw. Grace sat down next to the bed. She did not reach for Jack's hand. She did not kiss Jack's cheek.

'You're going to love the last verse,' Grace said.

She opened Emma's journal and started reading:

'Baseball, baseball,
Who's your best friend?
Is it the bat,
Who hits your rear end?'

Grace laughed and turned the page, but the next page – in fact, the rest of the journal – was blank.

50

A few minutes before Wade Larue died, he thought he had finally found true peace.

He had let vengeance go. He no longer needed to know the full truth. He knew enough. He knew where he was to blame and where he was not. It was time to put it behind him.

Carl Vespa had no choice. He would never be able to recover. The same was true for that awful swirl of faces – that blur of grief – he had been forced to see in the courtroom and again today at the press conference. Wade had lost time. But time is relative. Death is not.

He had told Vespa all he knew. Vespa was a bad man, no doubt about it. The man was capable of unspeakable cruelty. Over the past fifteen years Wade Larue had met a lot of people like that, but few were that simple. With the exception of full-blown psychopaths, most people, even the most evil, have the ability to love someone, to care about them, to make connections. That was not inconsistent. That was simply human.

Larue spoke. Vespa listened. Sometime in the middle of his explanation, Cram appeared with a towel and ice. He handed it to Larue. Larue thanked him. He took the towel – the ice would be too bulky – and dabbed the blood off his face. Vespa's blows no longer hurt. Larue had dealt with much worse over the years. When you've had enough of beatings, you go one way or the other – you fear them so much that you will do anything to avoid them, or you just ride them out and realize that this too shall pass. Somewhere during his incarceration Larue had joined that second camp.

Carl Vespa did not say a word. He did not interrupt or ask for clarification. When Larue finished Vespa stood there, his face unchanged, waiting for more. There was nothing. Without a word Vespa turned and left. He nodded at Cram. Cram started toward him. Larue lifted his head. He would not run. He was through with running.

'Come on, let's go,' Cram said.

Cram dropped him off in the center of Manhattan. Larue debated calling Eric Wu, but he knew that would be pointless at this stage. He started toward the Port Authority bus terminal. He was ready now for the rest of his life to begin. He was going to head to Portland, Oregon. He wasn't sure why. He had read about Portland in prison and it seemed to fit the bill. He wanted a big city with a liberal feel. From what he'd read, Portland sounded like a hippy commune that had turned into a major metropolis. He might get a fair shake out there.

He would have to change his name. Grow a beard. Dye his hair. He didn't think it would take that much to change him, to help him escape the past fifteen years. Naïve to think it, yes, but Wade Larue still thought that an acting career was a possibility. He still had the chops. He still had the supernatural charisma. So why not give it a go? If not, he'd get a regular job. He wasn't afraid of a little hard work. He'd be in a big city again. He'd be free.

But Wade Larue didn't go to the Port Authority bus station.

The past still had too strong a pull. He couldn't go quite yet. He stopped a block away. He saw the buses churning out to the viaduct. He watched for a moment and then turned to the row of pay phones.

He had to make one last phone call. He had to know one last truth.

Now, an hour later, the barrel of a gun was pressed against that soft hollow under his ear. It was funny what you thought of a moment before death. The soft hollow –

that was one of Eric Wu's favorite pressure-point spots. Wu had explained to him that knowing the location was fairly meaningless. You could not just stick your finger in there and push. That might hurt, but it would never incapacitate an opponent.

That was it. That pitiful thought, beyond pitiful, was Wade Larue's last before the bullet entered his brain and ended his life.

51

Dellapelle led Perlmutter into the basement. There was enough light, but Dellapelle still used the flashlight. He pointed it at the floor.

'There.'

Perlmutter stared down at the concrete and felt a fresh chill.

'You thinking what I'm thinking?' Dellapelle asked him.

'That maybe' – Perlmutter stopped, trying to figure this into the equation – 'that maybe Jack Lawson wasn't the only one being held down here.'

Dellapelle nodded. 'So where is the other guy?'

Perlmutter did not say anything. He just stared at the floor. Someone had indeed been held down. Someone who found a pebble and scratched two words into the floor, all in caps. A name actually, another person from that strange photograph, a name he'd just heard from Grace Lawson:

'SHANE ALWORTH.'

Charlaine Swain stayed to help Grace back to her room. Their silence was comfortable. Grace wondered about that. She wondered about a lot of things. She wondered why Jack had run away all those years ago. She wondered why he'd never touched that trust fund, why he let his sister and father control his percentage. She wondered why he'd run away not long after the Boston Massacre. She wondered about Geri Duncan and why she ended up dead two months later. And she wondered, perhaps most of all, if meeting Jack in France that day, if falling in love with him, had been more than just a coincidence.

She no longer wondered if it was all connected. She knew that it was. When they reached Grace's room, Charlaine helped her get back into bed. She turned to go.

'Do you want to stay a few minutes?' Grace asked.

Charlaine nodded. 'I'd like that.'

They talked. They started with what they had in common – children – but it was clear neither one of them wanted to stay on the subject long. An hour passed in a moment. Grace was not sure what they'd even discussed exactly. Just that she was grateful.

At nearly two in the morning the hospital phone next to Grace rang. For a moment they both just stared at it. Then Grace reached over and picked it up.

'Hello?'

'I got your message. About Allaw and Still Night.'

She recognized the voice. It was Jimmy X.

'Where are you?'

'In the hospital. I'm downstairs. They won't let me up.'

'I'll be down in a minute.'

The hospital lobby was quiet.

Grace was not sure how to handle this. Jimmy X sat with his forearms resting against his thighs. He didn't look up as she hobbled toward him. The receptionist read a magazine. The security guard whistled softly. Grace wondered if the guard would be able to protect her. She suddenly missed that gun.

She stopped in front of Jimmy X, stood over him, and waited. He looked up. Their eyes met and Grace knew. She didn't know the details. She barely knew the outline. But she knew.

His voice was almost a plea. 'How did you learn about Allaw?'

'My husband.'

Jimmy looked confused.

349

'My husband is Jack Lawson.'

His jaw dropped. 'John?'

'That's what he went by back then, I guess. He's upstairs right now. He may very well die.'

'Oh God.' Jimmy buried his face in his hands.

Grace said, 'You know what always bothered me?'

He did not reply.

'Your running away. It doesn't happen very much – a rock star just giving up like that. There are rumors about Elvis or Jim Morrison, but that's because they're dead. There was that movie, *Eddie and the Cruisers,* but that was a movie. In reality, well, like I said before, the Who didn't run away after Cincinnati. The Stones didn't after Altamont Speedway. So why, Jimmy? Why did you run?'

He kept his head low.

'I know about the Allaw connection. It's just a matter of time before someone puts it together.'

She waited. He dropped his hands away from his face and rubbed them together. He looked toward the security guard. Grace almost took a step back, but she held her ground.

'Do you know why rock concerts used to always start so late?' Jimmy asked.

The question threw her. 'What?'

'I said . . .'

'I heard what you said. No, I don't know why.'

'It's because we're so wasted – drunk, stoned, whatever – that our handlers need time to get us sobered up enough to perform.'

'Your point being?'

'That night I nearly passed out from cocaine and alcohol.' His gaze drifted off then, his eyes red. 'That's why there was such a long delay. That was why the crowd got so impatient. If I had been sober, if I had taken the stage on time . . .' He let his voice drift off with a 'who knows' shrug.

She didn't want excuses anymore. 'Tell me about Allaw.'

'I can't believe it.' He shook his head. 'John Lawson is your husband? How the hell did that happen?'

She didn't have an answer. She wondered if she ever would. The heart, she knew, was strange terrain. Could that have been part of the initial attraction, something subconscious, a knowing that they had both survived that terrible night? She flashed back to meeting Jack on that beach. Had it been fate, preordained – or planned? Did Jack want to meet the woman who had come to embody the Boston Massacre?

'Was my husband at the concert that night?' she asked.

'What, you don't know?'

'We can play this two ways, Jimmy. One, I can pretend I know everything and just want confirmation. But I don't. I may never know the truth, if you don't tell me. You may be able to keep your secret. But I'll keep looking. So will Carl Vespa and the Garrisons and the Reeds and the Weiders.'

He looked up, his face so like a child's.

'But two – and I think this is more important – you can't live with yourself anymore. You came to my house needing absolution. You know it's time.'

He lowered his head. Grace heard the sobs. They wracked his body. Grace did not say a word. She did not put a hand on his shoulder. The security guard glanced over. The receptionist looked up from her magazine. But that was all. This was a hospital. Adults weeping were hardly foreign in this environment. They both looked away. A minute later Jimmy's sobs started to quiet. His shoulders no longer shook.

'We met at a gig in Manchester,' Jimmy said, wiping his nose with his sleeve. 'I was with a group called Still Night. There were four bands on the roster. One of them was Allaw. That's how I met your husband. We hung out backstage, getting stoned. He was charming and all, but you have to understand. For me the music was everything. I wanted to make *Born to Run*, you know. I wanted to change the landscape of music. I ate, slept, dreamed, shat music. Lawson didn't take it too seriously. The band was fun, that's all. They had some decent songs, but the vocals and arrangement were totally amateur. Lawson didn't have any grand illusions about making it big or anything.'

The security guard was whistling again. The receptionist had her nose back in the magazine. A car drove up to the entrance. The guard headed outside and pointed toward the ER.

'Allaw broke up a few months later, I think. So did Still Night. But Lawson and I stayed in touch. When I started up the Jimmy X Band, I almost thought of asking him to join.'

'Why didn't you?'

'I didn't think he was that good a musician.'

Jimmy stood so suddenly that he startled Grace. She took a step back. She kept her eyes on him, still searching to make eye contact, as if that alone could keep him in place.

'Yeah, your husband was at the concert that night. I got him five tickets in the front pit. He brought some of his old band members with him. He even brought a couple backstage.'

He stopped then. They stood there. He looked off and for a moment Grace feared that she was losing him.

'Do you remember who they were?' she asked.

'The old band members?'

'Yes.'

'Two girls. One had this bright red hair.'

Sheila Lambert. 'Was the other girl Geri Duncan?'

'I never knew her name.'

'How about Shane Alworth? Was he there?'

'Was that the guy on keyboard?'

'Yes.'

'Not backstage. I only saw Lawson and the two girls.'

He shut his eyes.

'What happened, Jimmy?'

His face sagged and he suddenly looked older. 'I was pretty wasted. I could hear the crowd. Twenty thousand strong. They would chant my name. They would clap. Anything to get the concert started. But I could barely move. My manager came in. I told him I'd need more time. He left. I was alone. And then Lawson and those two chicks came into the room.'

Jimmy blinked and looked at Grace. 'Is there a cafeteria in this place?'

'It's closed.'

'I could use a cup of coffee.'

'Tough.'

Jimmy started pacing.

Grace asked, 'What happened after they came in the room?'

'I don't know how they got backstage. I never gave them passes. But all of a sudden Lawson comes up to me and is all "hey how's it going?" I was happy to see him, I guess. But then, I don't know, something went really wrong.'

'What?'

'Lawson. He went crazy. I don't know, he must have been higher than I was. He started pushing me, making threats. He shouted that I was a thief.'

'A thief?'

Jimmy nodded. 'It was all nonsense. He said . . .' He finally stayed still and met her eyes. 'He said I stole his song.'

'What song?'

'"Pale Ink."'

Grace could not move. The tremor started moving down her left side. There was a flutter in her chest.

'Lawson and that other guy, Alworth, wrote this song

for Allaw called "Invisible Ink." That was pretty much the only similarity between the songs. That part of the title. You know the lyrics to 'Pale Ink,' right?'

She nodded. She didn't even try to speak.

'"Invisible Ink" had a similar theme, I guess. Both about how fragile memory can be. But that was it. I told John that. But he was just out of his mind. Whatever I said just pissed him off more. He kept pushing me. One of the girls, she had this really dark hair, was egging him on too. She started saying they'd break my legs or something. I called for help. Lawson punched me. You remember the reports that I was injured in the melee?'

She nodded again.

'I wasn't. It was your husband. He hit my jaw, and then he jumped me. I tried to push him off. He started shouting how he was going to kill me. It was, I don't know, the whole thing was surreal. He said he was going to cut me up.'

The flutter expanded and grew cold. Grace was holding her breath. This couldn't be. Please, this just couldn't be.

'By now it was just so out of hand, one of the girls, the redhead, told him to calm down. It's not worth it, she said. She pleaded with him to forget it. But he wasn't listening. He just smiled at me and then . . . then he took out a knife.'

Grace shook her head.

'He said he was going to stab me in the heart. You remember how I said I was stoned out of my mind? Well, that sobered me up. You want to sober someone up? Threaten to stick a knife in their chest.' He went quiet again.

'What did you do?'

Had she spoken? Grace wasn't sure. The voice sounded like hers, but it seemed as though it'd come from someplace else, someplace tinny and distant.

Jimmy's face, lost in the memory, went slack. 'I wasn't going to just let him stab me. So I jumped him. He dropped the knife. We started wrestling. The girls were screaming now. They came over and tried to pull us apart. And then, when we were on the floor like that, I heard a gunshot.'

Grace was still shaking her head. Not Jack. Jack wasn't there that night, no way, no chance at all . . .

'It was so loud, you know. Like the gun was behind my ear or something. All hell broke loose then. There were screams. And then there were two, maybe three more shots. Not in the room. They were from far away. I heard more screams. Lawson stopped moving. There was blood on the floor. He'd been hit in the back. I pushed him off and then I saw that security guard, Gordon MacKenzie, still pointing his gun.'

Grace closed her eyes. 'Wait a second. Are you telling me Gordon MacKenzie fired the first shot?'

Jimmy nodded. 'He heard the commotion, heard me calling for help and . . .' Again his voice trailed off. 'We just stared at each other for a second. The girls were screaming, but by now they were being drowned out by the crowd. That sound, I don't know, people talk about the most terrible sound, like maybe it's a wounded animal, but I've never heard anything that comes close to the sound of fear and panic. But you know that.'

She didn't. The head trauma had wiped out the memory. But she nodded so that he'd keep talking.

'Anyway, MacKenzie stood there for a second, stunned. And then he just ran. The two girls grabbed Lawson and started dragging him out.' He shrugged. 'You know the rest, Grace.'

She tried to take it all in. She tried to understand the implications, tried to fit it into her own reality. She had been standing yards away from all this, the other side of the stage. Jack. Her husband. He'd been right there. How could that be?

'No,' she said.

'No what?'

'No, I don't know the rest, Jimmy.'

He said nothing.

'The story didn't end there. Allaw had four members. I've been checking out the time line. Two months after the stampede someone hired a hit man to kill one of the members, Geri Duncan. My husband, the one who you say attacked you, ran overseas, shaved his beard, and started going by Jack. According to Shane Alworth's mother, he's overseas too, but I think she's lying about that. Sheila Lambert, the redhead, changed her name. Her husband was recently murdered and she disappeared again.'

Jimmy shook his head. 'I don't know anything about any of that.'

'You think it's all just a big coincidence?'

'No, I guess not,' Jimmy said. 'Maybe they were scared of what would happen if the truth came out. You remember what it was like those first few months – everyone wanting blood. They could have gone to jail, maybe worse.'

Grace shook her head. 'And what about you, Jimmy?'

'What about me?'

'Why did you keep this secret all these years?'

He said nothing.

'If what you just told me is true, you didn't do anything wrong. You were the one attacked. Why didn't you just tell the police what happened?'

He opened his mouth, closed it, tried again. 'This was bigger than me. Gordon MacKenzie was part of it, too. He came out the hero, remember? If the world ever learned that he fired that first shot, what do you think would have happened to him?'

'Are you saying you lied all these years to protect Gordon MacKenzie?'

He didn't reply.

'Why, Jimmy? Why didn't you say anything? Why did you run away?'

His eyes started shifting. 'Look, I told you everything I know. I'm going home now.'

Grace moved closer. 'You did steal that song, didn't you?'

'What? No.'

But she saw it now. 'That was why you felt responsible. You stole that song. If you hadn't, none of this would have happened.'

He just kept shaking his head. 'That's not it.'

'That's why you ran away. It wasn't just that you were stoned. You stole the song that made you. That was where it all started. You heard Allaw play in Manchester. You liked their song. You stole it.'

He shook his head, but there was nothing behind it. 'There were similarities . . .'

And another thought struck her with a deep, hard pang: 'How far would you go to keep your secret, Jimmy?'

He looked at her.

'"Pale Ink" became even bigger after the stampede. That album ended up selling millions. Who has that money?'

He shook his head. 'You're wrong, Grace.'

'Did you already know I was married to Jack Lawson?'

'What? Of course not.'

'Is that why you came by my house that night? Were you trying to figure out what I knew?'

He kept shaking his head, tears on his cheeks. 'That's not true. I never meant to hurt anyone.'

'Who killed Geri Duncan?'

'I don't know anything about that.'

'Was she going to talk? Is that what happened? And then, fifteen years later, someone goes after Sheila Lambert aka Jillian Dodd, but her husband gets in the way. Was she going to talk, Jimmy? Did she know you were back?'

'I have to go.'

She stepped in his path. 'You can't run away again. There's been too much of that.'

'I know,' he said, his voice a plea. 'I know that better than anyone.'

He pushed past her and ran outside. Grace was tempted to yell, 'Stop! Grab him!' but she doubted the whistling guard would be able to do much. Jimmy was already outside, almost out of sight. She limped after him.

Gunshots – three of them – shattered the night. There was the squeal of tires. The receptionist dropped her magazine and picked up the phone. The security guard stopped whistling and sprinted toward the door. Grace hurried behind him.

When Grace got outside, she saw a car shoot down the exit ramp and disappear into the night. Grace had not seen who was in the car. But she thought she knew. The security guard bent down over the body. Two doctors ran out, nearly knocking Grace down. But it was too late.

Fifteen years after the stampede began, the Boston Massacre claimed its most elusive victim.

52

Maybe, Grace thought, we are not supposed to know the entire truth. And maybe the truth does not matter.

There were plenty of questions in the end. Grace thought that she would never know all the answers. Too many of the players were dead now.

Jimmy X, real name James Xavier Farmington, died from three gunshot wounds to the chest.

Wade Larue's body was found near the Port Authority Bus Terminal in New York City less than twenty-four hours after his release. He'd been shot in the head at point-blank range. There was only one significant clue: A reporter for the New York *Daily News* managed to follow Wade Larue after he left the press conference at the Crowne Plaza. According to the reporter, Larue got into a black sedan with a man fitting Cram's description. That was the last time anyone saw Larue alive.

No arrests have been made, but the answer seemed clear.

Grace tried to understand what Carl Vespa had done. Fifteen years had passed, and his son was still dead. Weird to put it that way, but maybe it was apropos. For Vespa, nothing had changed. Time had not been enough.

Captain Perlmutter would try to make a case against him. But Vespa was pretty good about covering his tracks.

Both Perlmutter and Duncan came to the hospital after Jimmy was killed. Grace told them everything. There was nothing to hide anymore. Perlmutter mentioned almost in passing that the words *Shane Alworth* had been scratched into the concrete floor.

'So what does that mean?' Grace asked.

'We're checking the physical evidence, but maybe your husband wasn't alone in that basement.'

It made sense, Grace guessed. Fifteen years later they were all coming back. Everyone in that photograph.

At four in the morning Grace was back in her hospital bed. Her room was dark when the door opened. A silhouette slid in quietly. He thought that she was asleep. For a moment Grace didn't say anything. She waited until he was in the chair again, just like fifteen years ago, before she said, 'Hello, Carl.'

'How are you feeling?' Vespa asked.

'Did you kill Jimmy X?'

There was a long pause. The shadow did not move. 'What happened that night,' he said at last. 'It was his fault.'

'It's hard to know.'

Vespa's face was no more than a shadow. 'You see too many shades of gray.'

Grace tried to sit up, but her rib cage would not cooperate. 'How did you find out about Jimmy?'

'From Wade Larue,' he said.

'You killed him too.'

'Do you want to make accusations, Grace, or do you want to know the truth?'

She wanted to ask if that was all he wanted, the truth, but she knew the answer. The truth would never be enough. Vengeance and justice would never be enough.

'Wade Larue reached out to me the day before he was released,' Vespa said. 'He asked if we could talk.'

'Talk about what?'

'He wouldn't say. I had Cram pick him up in the city. He came out to my house. He started in with some touchy-feely crap about understanding my pain. He said he was suddenly all at peace with himself, that he didn't want vengeance anymore. I didn't want to hear any of that. I

360

wanted him to get to the point.'

'Did he?'

'Yes.' The shadow was still again. Grace debated reaching for the light switch and decided against it. 'He told me that Gordon MacKenzie had visited him in prison three months ago. Do you know why?'

Grace nodded, seeing it now. 'MacKenzie had terminal cancer.'

'Right. He was still hoping to buy a last-minute ticket to the Promised Land. All of a sudden he can't live with what he's done.' Vespa cocked his head and smiled. 'Amazing how that happens right before you're going to die anyway, isn't it? Ironic timing when you think about it. He confesses when there is no personal cost, and hey, if you buy into that confess-and-forgive nonsense, there could be a big upside.'

Grace knew not to comment. She stayed still.

'Anyway, Gordon MacKenzie took the blame. He was working the backstage entrance. He let some pretty young thing distract him. He said that Lawson and two girls sneaked past him. You know all this, don't you?'

'Some of it.'

'You know that MacKenzie shot your husband?'

'Yes.'

'And that's what started the riot. MacKenzie met up with Jimmy X after the whole thing went down. They both agreed to keep it quiet. They worried a little about Jack's injury or if those girls were going to come forward, but hey, those three had plenty to lose too.'

'So everyone just kept quiet.'

'Pretty much. MacKenzie became a hero. He got a job with the Boston police from that. He rose to captain. All off his heroics from that night.'

'So what did Larue do after MacKenzie confessed all this?'

'What do you think? He wanted the truth to come out.

He wanted vengeance and exoneration.'

'So why didn't Larue tell anyone?'

'Oh, he did.' Vespa smiled. 'Three guesses who.'

Grace saw it. 'He told his lawyer.'

Vespa spread his hands. 'Give the lady a kewpie doll.'

'But how did Sandra Koval convince him to keep quiet?'

'Oh, this part is brilliant. Somehow – and let's give the lady credit – she did what was best for her client *and* her brother.'

'How?'

'She told Larue that he'd have a better chance of getting out on parole if he didn't tell the truth.'

'I don't understand.'

'You don't know much about parole, do you?'

She shrugged.

'You see, the parole board doesn't want to hear that you're innocent. They want to hear your mea culpas. If you want to get out, you have to hang your head in shame. You did wrong, you tell them. You've accepted blame – that's the first step toward rehabilitation. If you keep insisting you're innocent, you're not going to get better.'

'Couldn't MacKenzie testify?'

'He was too ill by then. You see, Larue's innocence wasn't the parole board's concern. If Larue wanted to take that route, he'd have to request a new trial. It would take months, maybe years. According to Sandra Koval – and she was telling the truth here – Larue's best chance of getting out was to admit his guilt.'

'And she was right,' Grace said.

'Yes.'

'And Larue never knew that Sandra and Jack were brother and sister?'

Again Vespa spread his hands. 'How would he?'

Grace shook her head.

'But, you see, it's not over for Wade Larue. He still wants vengeance and exoneration. He just knows he'll have to wait until he's out of jail. The question is, how? He knows the truth, but how will he prove it? Who will, pardon the expression, feel his wrath? Who is really to blame for what happened that night?'

Grace nodded as something else fell into place. 'So he went after Jack.'

'The one who pulled the knife, yep. So Larue got his old prison buddy Eric Wu to grab your husband. Larue's plan was to hook up with Wu the moment he got released. He'd make Jack tell the truth, film it, and then, he wasn't sure, but probably kill him.'

'Find exoneration and then commit murder?'

Vespa shrugged. 'He was angry, Grace. He might have ended up just beating him up or breaking his legs. Who knows?'

'So what happened?'

'Wade Larue had a change of heart.'

Grace frowned.

'You should have heard him talk about it. His eyes were so clear. I'd just punched him in the face. I'd kicked him and threatened his life. But the peace on his face . . . it just stayed there. The moment Larue was free, he realized that he would be able to get past it.'

'What do you mean, past it?'

'Exactly that. His punishment was in the past. He could never really be exonerated because he wasn't blameless. He fired shots in the middle of the crowd. That raised the hysteria level. But more than that, it was like he told me: He was truly free. Nothing was left to tie him to the past. He was no longer in prison, but my son would always be dead. You see?'

'I think so.'

'Larue just wanted to live his life. He was also afraid of what I'd do to him. So he wanted to trade. He told me the truth. He gave me Wu's number. And in exchange, I'd leave him alone.'

'So it was you who called Wu?'

'Actually Larue made the call. But yes, I spoke to him.'

'And you told Wu to bring us to you?'

'I didn't realize you were there. I thought it was just Jack.'

'What was your plan, Carl?'

He said nothing.

'Would you have killed Jack too?'

'Does it matter anymore?'

'And what would you have done with me?'

He took his time. 'There were things that made me wonder,' he said.

'About?'

'About you.'

Seconds passed. There were footsteps in the corridor. A stretcher with a squeaky wheel rolled past the door. Grace listened to the sound recede. She tried to slow her breath.

'Here you were nearly killed in the Boston Massacre – yet you end up marrying the man responsible for it all. I also know that Jimmy X came to visit your house after we saw him at that rehearsal. You never told me about that. And then there's the fact that you remember so little of what happened. Not just that night, but for almost a week before.'

She tried to keep her breaths even. 'You thought –'

'I didn't know what to think. But now maybe I do. I think your husband is a good man who made a terrible mistake. I think he ran away after the stampede. I think he felt guilty. That was why he wanted to meet you. He saw the press reports and wanted to know you were okay. Maybe he even planned on apologizing. So he found you on the beach in France. And then he fell in love with you.'

She closed her eyes and leaned back.

'It's over now, Grace.'

They sat in silence. There was nothing else to say. A few minutes later Vespa stole out, silent as the night.

53

But it wasn't over.

Four days passed. Grace got better. She went home that first afternoon. Cora and Vickie stayed with them. Cram came by that first day too, but Grace asked him to leave. He nodded and complied.

The media went crazy, of course. They only knew bits and pieces, but the fact that the notorious Jimmy X had resurfaced only to be murdered had been enough to send them into a total state of derangement. Perlmutter set up a patrol car in front of Grace's house. Emma and Max still went to school. Grace spent most of her days in the hospital with Jack. Charlaine Swain kept her company a lot.

Grace thought about the photograph that started it all. She now figured that one of the four members of Allaw had found a way to get it in her packet. Why? That was harder to answer. Perhaps one of them realized that the eighteen ghosts would never sleep.

But then there was the question of timing: Why now? Why after fifteen years?

There was no shortage of possibilities. It could have been the release of Wade Larue. It could have been the death of Gordon MacKenzie. It could have been all the anniversary coverage. But most likely, what made the most sense, was that the return of Jimmy X set everything in motion.

Who really was to blame for what happened that tragic night? Was it Jimmy for stealing the song? Jack for attacking him? Gordon MacKenzie for firing a weapon under those circumstances? Wade Larue for illegally carrying a gun, panicking, and firing more shots into an already frenzied crowd? Grace did not know. Small ripples. All of this carnage had not started with some big conspiracy. It had started with two small-time bands playing some dive in Manchester.

There were still holes, of course. Lots of them. But they would have to wait.

There are some things more important than the truth.

Now, right now, Grace stared at Jack. He lay still in his hospital bed. His doctor, a man named Stan Walker, sat next to her. Dr. Walker folded his hands and used his gravest voice. Grace listened. Emma and Max waited in the corridor. They wanted to be there. Grace didn't know what to do. What was the call on this one?

She wished that she could ask Jack.

She did not want to ask him why he had lied to her for so long. She did not want an explanation for what he had done that terrible night. She did not want to ask him how he'd happened by her on the beach that day, if he had been intentionally seeking her out, if that was why they fell in love. She didn't want to ask Jack any of that.

She only wanted to ask him one last question: Did he want his children by his bedside when he died?

In the end Grace let them stay. The four of them gathered as a family for the last time. Emma cried. Max sat there, his eyes trained on the tile floor. And then, with a gentle tug at her heart, Grace felt Jack leave for good.

54

The funeral was a major blur. Grace usually wore contact lenses. She took them off that day and did not wear her glasses. Everything seemed a little easier to handle in the blur. She sat in the front pew and thought about Jack. She did not picture him in the vineyards or on the beach anymore. The sight she remembered best, the sight she would always carry with her, was Jack holding Emma after she was born, the way his big hands held the little wonder, carrying her as if afraid she'd break, scared he might hurt her, the way he turned to Grace and looked at her in pure awe. That was what she saw.

The rest, all she now knew about his past, was white noise.

Sandra Koval came to the funeral. She stayed in the back. She apologized that their father could not come. He was elderly and ill. Grace said that she understood. The two women did not embrace. Scott Duncan was there. So were Stu Perlmutter and Cora. Grace had no idea how many people showed up. She didn't much care either. She held her two children and fought her way through it.

Two weeks later the children went back to school. There were issues, of course. Both Emma and Max were suffering separation anxieties. That was normal, she knew. Grace walked them into school. She was there before the bell rang to pick them up. They were hurting. That, Grace knew, was the price you paid for having a kind and loving father. The hurt never goes away.

But now it was time to end this.

Jack's autopsy.

Some would say that the autopsy, when she read and understood it, was what sent Grace's world off kilter again. But that really wasn't it. The autopsy was merely independent confirmation of what she already knew. Jack had been her husband. She had loved him. They had been together for thirteen years. They had two children together. And while he had clearly kept secrets, there were some things a man cannot hide.

Some things must truly remain on the surface.

So Grace knew.

She knew his body. She knew his skin. She knew every muscle on his back. So she really did not need the autopsy. She did not need to see the results of the full-exterior examination to tell her what she already knew.

Jack had no major scars.

And that meant that – despite what Jimmy had said, despite what Gordon MacKenzie had told Wade Larue – Jack had never been shot.

First Grace visited the Photomat and found Fuzz Pellet Josh. Then she drove back down to Bedminster, to the condominium development where Shane Alworth's mother resided. After that, she plowed through the legal work on Jack's family trust. Grace knew a lawyer from Livingston who now worked as a sports agent in Manhattan. He set up plenty of trusts for his wealthy athletes. He went through the paperwork and explained enough for her to understand.

And then, when she had all the facts pretty much down, she visited Sandra Koval, her dear sister-in-law, at the offices of Burton and Crimstein in New York City.

Sandra Koval did not meet her in the reception area this time. Grace was inspecting the photo gallery, stopping again at the shot of the wrestler, Little Pocahontas, when a peasant-bloused woman told her to come this way. She led Grace down the corridor and into the exact same conference room where she and Sandra had first talked a lifetime ago.

'Ms. Koval will be with you shortly.'

'Great.'

She left her alone. The room was set up exactly the same as last time, except now there was a yellow legal pad and a Bic pen in front of each seat. Grace did not want to sit. She did her own version of a pace, more a limp-pace, and ran it over in her head again. Her cell phone buzzed. She spoke briefly and then snapped it off. She kept it close. Just in case.

'Hi, Grace.'

Sandra Koval swept into the room like a turbulent weather front. She headed straight for the little refrigerator, opened it and peered inside.

'Can I get you something to drink?'

'No.'

With her head still in the mini-fridge, she asked, 'How are the children?'

Grace did not reply. Sandra Koval dug out a Perrier. She twisted the top off and sat.

'So what's up?'

Should she test the temperature with her toe or just jump in? Grace chose the latter. 'You didn't take on Wade Larue as a client because of me,' she began without preamble. 'You took him on because you wanted to stay close to him.'

Sandra Koval poured the Perrier into a glass. 'That might – hypothetically – be true.'

'Hypothetically?'

'Yes. I may, in a hypothetical world, have represented Wade Larue to protect a certain family member. But if I had, I would have still made sure that I represented my client to the best of my ability.'

369

'Two birds with one stone?'

'Perhaps.'

'And the certain family member. That would be your brother?'

'It would be possible.'

'Possible,' Grace said. 'But that wasn't what happened here. You weren't out to protect your brother.'

Their eyes met.

'I know,' Grace said.

'Oh?' Sandra took a sip. 'Then why don't you clue me in.'

'You were, what, twenty-seven years old? Fresh out of law school and working as a criminal lawyer?'

'Yes.'

'You were married. Your daughter was two years old. You were on your way to a promising career. And then your brother messed it all up for you. You were there that night, Sandra. At the Boston Garden. You were the other woman backstage, not Geri Duncan.'

'I see,' she said without a trace of worry. 'And you know this how?'

'Jimmy X said one woman was a redhead – that's Sheila Lambert – and the other, the one who was egging Jack on, had dark hair. Geri Duncan was a blonde. You, Sandra, had dark hair.'

She laughed. 'And that's supposed to be proof of something?'

'No, not in and of itself. I'm not even sure it's relevant. Geri Duncan was probably there too. She might have been the one who distracted Gordon MacKenzie so you three could sneak backstage.'

Sandra Koval gave her a vague wave of the hand. 'Go on, this is interesting.'

'Shall I just get to the heart of the matter?'

'Please do.'

'According to both Jimmy X and Gordon MacKenzie, your brother was shot that night.'

'He was,' Sandra said. 'He was in the hospital for three weeks.'

'Which hospital?'

There was no hesitation, no eye twitch, no give at all. 'Mass General.'

Grace shook her head.

Sandra made a face. 'Are you telling me you checked every hospital in the Boston area?'

'No need,' Grace said. 'There was no scar.'

Silence.

'You see, the bullet wound would have left a scar, Sandra. It's simple logic. Your brother was shot. My husband had no scar. There's only one way that can be so.' Grace put her hands on the table. They were quaking.

'I was never married to your brother.'

Sandra Koval said nothing.

'Your brother, John Lawson, was shot that day. You and Sheila Lambert helped drag him out during the melee. But his wounds were lethal. At least I hope they were, because the alternative is that you killed him.'

'And why would I do that?'

'Because if you took him to a hospital, they would have to report the shooting. If you showed up with a dead body – or even if you just dumped him on the street – someone would investigate and realize where and how he was shot. You, the promising lawyer, were terrified. I bet Sheila Lambert was too. The world went crazy when this happened. The Boston DA – hell, Carl Vespa – was on television demanding blood. So were all the families. If you got caught up in that, you'd be arrested or worse.'

Sandra Koval stayed quiet.

'Did you call your father? Did you ask him what to do? Did you contact one of your old criminal clients to help you? Or did you just get rid of the body on your own?'

She chuckled. 'You have some imagination, Grace. Can I ask you something now?'

371

'Sure.'

'If John Lawson died fifteen years ago, who did you marry?'

'I married *Jack* Lawson,' Grace said. 'Who used to be known as Shane Alworth.'

Eric Wu hadn't held two men in the basement, Grace now realized. Just one. One who had sacrificed himself to save her. One who probably knew that he was going to die and wanted to scratch out some last truth in the only way left to him.

Sandra Koval almost smiled. 'That's a hell of a theory.'

'One that will be easy to prove.'

She leaned back and folded her arms. 'I don't understand something about your scenario. Why didn't I just hide my brother's body and pretend he ran away?'

'Too many people would ask questions,' Grace said.

'But that's what happened to Shane Alworth and Sheila Lambert. They just disappeared.'

'True enough,' Grace admitted. 'And maybe the answer has to do with your family trust.'

That made Sandra's face freeze. 'The trust?'

'I found the papers on the trust in Jack's desk. I took them to a friend who's a lawyer. It seems your grandfather set up six trusts. He had two children and four grandchildren. Forget the money for a second. Let's talk about voting power. All of you got equal voting shares, divided six ways, with your father getting the extra four percent. That way your side of the family kept control of the business, fifty-two percent to forty-eight. But – and I'm not good with this stuff so bear with me – Grandpa wanted to keep it all in the family. If any of you died before the age of twenty-five, the voting power would be divided equally among the five survivors. If your brother died the night of the concert, for example, that would mean that your side of the family, you and your father, would no longer hold a majority position.'

'You're out of your mind.'

'Could be,' Grace said. 'But tell me, Sandra. What drove you? Was it fear of being caught – or were you worried about losing control of the family business? Probably a combination of both. Either way, I know you got Shane Alworth to take your brother's place. It'll be easy to prove. We'll dig up old pictures. We can run a DNA test. I mean, it's over.'

Sandra started drumming the table with her fingertips. 'If that's true,' she said, 'the man you loved lied to you all these years.'

'That's true no matter what,' Grace said. 'How did you get him to cooperate anyway?'

'That question is supposed to be rhetorical, right?'

Grace shrugged. 'Mrs. Alworth tells me that they were dirt poor. His brother Paul couldn't afford college. She was living in a dump. But my guess is, you made a threat. If one member of Allaw went down for this, they all would. He probably thought he had no choice.'

'Come on, Grace. Do you really think a poor kid like Shane Alworth could pull off being my brother?'

'How hard would it be? You and your father helped, I'm sure. Getting an ID would be no problem. You had your brother's birth certificate and the pertinent paperwork. You just say he had his wallet stolen. Screening was easier back then. He'd have gotten a new driver's license, new passport, whatever. You found a new trust lawyer in Boston – my friend noticed the change from the one in Los Angeles – someone who wouldn't know what John Lawson looked like. You, your dad, and Shane go in to his office together, all with proper ID – who would question that? Your brother had already graduated from Vermont University, so it wasn't like he'd have to show up there with a new face. Shane could go overseas now. If someone bumped into him, well, he'd go by Jack and just say he was another John Lawson. It's not an uncommon name.'

Grace waited.

Sandra folded her arms. 'Is this the part where I'm supposed to crack and confess everything?'

'You? No, I don't think so. But come on, you know it's over. It won't be any problem to prove that my husband wasn't your brother.'

Sandra Koval took her time. 'That may well be,' she said, her words coming out more measured now. 'But I'm not sure I see any crime here.'

'How's that?'

'Let's say – again hypothetically – that you're right. Let's say I did get your husband to pretend to be my brother. That was fifteen years ago. There's a statute of limitations. My cousins might try to fight me on the trust issue, but they wouldn't want the scandal. We'd work it out. And even if what you said is true, my crime was hardly a big one. If I was at the concert that night, well, in the early days of that rabid frenzy, who could blame me for being scared?'

Grace's voice was soft. 'I wouldn't blame you for that.'

'Right, so there you go.'

'And at first you didn't really do anything that terrible. You went to that concert seeking justice for your brother. You confronted a man who stole a song your brother and his friend wrote. That's not a crime. Things went wrong. Your brother died. There was nothing you could do to bring him back. So you did what you thought best. You played the terrible hand you were dealt.'

Sandra Koval opened her arms. 'Then what do you want here, Grace?'

'Answers, I guess.'

'It seems as if you already got some of those.' Then she raised her index finger and added, 'Hypothetically speaking.'

'And maybe I want justice.'

'What justice? You just said yourself that what happened was understandable.'

'That part,' Grace said, her voice still soft. 'If it ended there, yeah, I'd probably just walk away. But it didn't.'

Sandra Koval sat back and waited.

'Sheila Lambert was scared too. She knew that her best move would be to change her name and disappear. You all agreed to disperse and stay silent. Geri Duncan, she stayed where she was. That was okay, at first. But then Geri found out she was pregnant.'

Sandra just shut her eyes.

'When he agreed to be John Lawson, Shane, my Jack, had to cut all ties and go overseas. Geri Duncan couldn't find him. A month later she learns that she's pregnant. She's desperate to find the father. So she came to see you. She probably wanted to start new. She wanted to tell the truth and have her baby with a clean slate. You knew my husband. He would never turn his back on her if she insisted on having a child. Maybe he'd want to wipe the slate clean too. And then what would happen to you, Sandra?'

Grace looked down at her hands. They were still shaking.

'So you had to silence Geri. You're a criminal defense attorney. You repped criminals. And one of them helped you find a hit man named Monte Scanlon.'

Sandra said, 'You can't prove any of this.'

'The years pass,' Grace went on. 'My husband is now Jack Lawson.' Grace stopped and remembered what Carl Vespa had said about Jack Lawson seeking her out. Something there still didn't mesh. 'We have children now. I tell Jack I want to go back stateside. He doesn't want to. I push him on it. We have kids. I want to be back in the United States. That's my fault, I guess. I wish he had just told me the truth –'

'And how would you have reacted, Grace?'

She thought about it. 'I don't know.'

Sandra Koval smiled. 'Neither, I guess, did he.'

It was, Grace knew, a fair point, but this was not the

time for that sort of contemplation. She pressed on. 'We ended up moving to New York. But I don't know what happened next, Sandra, so you're going to have to help me with this part. I think what with the anniversary and with Wade Larue coming free, Sheila Lambert – or maybe even Jack – decided it was time to tell the truth. Jack never slept well. Maybe they both needed to ease their guilt, I don't know. You couldn't go along with that, of course. They might be granted forgiveness but not you. You had Geri Duncan killed.'

'And again I ask: The proof of that is . . . ?'

'We'll get to that,' Grace said. 'You've lied to me from the start, but you did tell the truth about one thing.'

'Oh goodie.' The sarcasm was thick now. 'What was that?'

'When Jack saw that old picture in the kitchen, he did look up Geri Duncan on the computer. He found out she'd died in a fire, but he suspected it was no accident. So he called you. That was the nine-minute phone call. You were afraid he was about to crack, so you knew that you had to strike fast. You told Jack that you'd explain everything but not over the phone. You set up a meet off the New York Thruway. Then you called Larue and told him that this would be a perfect time to get his revenge. You figured Larue would have Wu kill Jack, not hold him like that.'

'I don't have to listen to this.'

But Grace did not stop. 'My big mistake was showing you the photograph that first day. Jack didn't know I'd made a copy. There it was, a photograph of your dead brother and his new identity for all the world to see. You needed to keep me quiet too. So you sent that guy, the one with my daughter's lunchbox, to scare me off. But I didn't listen. So you used Wu. He was supposed to find out what I knew and then kill me.'

'Okay, I've had enough.' Sandra Koval stood. 'Get out of my office.'

'Nothing to add?'

'I'm still waiting for proof.'

'I don't really have any,' Grace said. 'But maybe you'll confess.'

She laughed at that one. 'What, you don't think I know you're wired? I haven't said or done one thing that'll incriminate me.'

'Look out the window, Sandra.'

'What?'

'The window. Look down at the sidewalk. Come on, I'll show you.'

Grace limped toward the huge picture window and pointed down. Sandra Koval moved warily, as if she expected that Grace would push her through it. But that wasn't it. That wasn't it at all.

When Sandra Koval looked down, a small gasp escaped her lips. On the sidewalk below them, pacing like two lions, were Carl Vespa and Cram. Grace turned away and started for the door.

'Where are you going?' Sandra asked.

'Oh,' Grace said. She wrote something down on a piece of paper. 'This is Captain Perlmutter's phone number. You have your choice. You can call and leave with him. Or you can take your chances with the sidewalk.'

She put the piece of paper on the conference table. And then, without looking back, Grace left the room.

Epilogue

Sandra Koval chose to call Captain Stuart Perlmutter. She then lawyered up. Hester Crimstein, the legend herself, was going to represent her. It would be a tough case to make, but the DA thought, because of certain developments, that he could do it.

One of those developments was the return of Allaw's redheaded member, Sheila Lambert. When Sheila read about the arrest – and the media appeal for her help – she came forward. The man who shot her husband fit the description of the man who threatened Grace at the supermarket. His name was Martin Brayboy. He'd been caught and had agreed to testify for the prosecution.

Sheila Lambert also told prosecutors that Shane Alworth had been at the concert that night but that he had decided at the last minute not to go backstage and confront Jimmy X. Sheila Lambert wasn't sure why he'd changed his mind, but she speculated that Shane realized John Lawson was too high, too wired, too willing to snap.

Grace was supposed to find comfort in that, but she's not sure she did.

Captain Stuart Perlmutter had hooked up with Scott Duncan's old boss, Linda Morgan, the U.S. attorney. They managed to turn one of the men from Carl Vespa's inner circle. Rumor has it they'll be arresting him soon, though it will be hard to nail him on Jimmy X's murder. Cram called Grace one afternoon. He told her Vespa wasn't fighting back. He stayed in bed a lot. 'It's like watching a slow death,' he told her. She didn't really want to hear it.

Charlaine Swain brought Mike home from the hospital. They returned to their regularly scheduled lives. Mike is back at work. They watch TV together now instead of in separate rooms. Mike still falls asleep early. They've upped their lovemaking somewhat, but it's all too self-conscious. Charlaine and Grace have become close friends. Charlaine never complains but Grace can see the desperation. Something, Grace knows, will soon give.

Freddy Sykes is still recuperating. He put his house up for sale and is buying a condo in Fair Lawn, New Jersey.

Cora remained Cora. Enough said on that subject.

Evelyn and Paul Alworth, Jack's – or in this case, she should say, Shane's – mother and brother, have also come forward. Over the years Jack had used the trust money to pay for Paul's schooling. When he started working with Pentocol Pharmaceuticals, Jack moved his mother into that condominium development so they could be closer. They had lunch together at the condo at least once a week. Both Evelyn and Paul wanted very much to be a part of the children's lives – they were, after all, Emma and Max's grandmother and uncle – but they understood that it would be best to take it slow.

As for Emma and Max, they handled the tragedy in very different ways.

Max likes to talk about his father. He wants to know where Daddy is, what heaven is like, if Daddy really sees them. He wants to be assured that his father can still observe the key events of his young life. Grace tries to answer him the best she can – tries to sell it, as it were – but her words have the stilted hollow of the dubious. Max wants Grace to make up 'Jenny Jenkins' rhymes with him in the tub, like Jack used to do, and when she does, Max laughs and he sounds so much like his father that Grace thinks her heart might explode right then and there.

Emma, her father's princess, never talks about Jack. She does not ask questions. She does not look at photographs or reminisce. Grace tries to facilitate her daughter's needs, but she is never sure what approach to take. Psychiatrists talk about opening up. Grace, who has suffered her share of tragedies, is not so sure. There is, she's learned, something to be said for denial, for severing and compartmentalizing.

Strangely enough, Emma seems happy. She's doing well in school. She has lots of friends. But Grace knows better. Emma never writes poetry anymore. She won't even look at her journal. She insists now on sleeping with her door shut. Grace stands outside her daughter's bedroom at night, often very late, and sometimes she thinks she hears soft sobs. In the morning, after Emma goes to school, Grace checks her daughter's room.

Her pillow is always wet.

People naturally assume that if Jack were still alive, Grace would have a lot of questions for him. That's true, but she no longer cares about the details of what a stoned, scared kid of twenty did in the face of that devastation and aftermath. In hindsight he should have told her. But then again suppose he had? Suppose Jack had told her right in the beginning? Or a month into their relationship? A year? How would she have reacted? Would she have stayed? She thinks about Emma and Max, about the simple fact that they are here, and the road untraveled brings a shiver.

So late at night, when Grace lies alone in their too-large bed and talks to Jack, feeling very strange because, really, she doesn't believe he's listening, her questions are more basic: Max wants to sign up for the Kasselton traveling soccer team, but isn't he too young for that kind of commitment? The school wants to put Emma in an accelerated English program, but will that put too much pressure on her? Should we still go to Disney World in February, without you, or will that be too painful a reminder? And what, Jack, should I do about those damn tears on Emma's pillow?

Questions like that.

Scott Duncan came by a week after Sandra's arrest. When she opened the door, he said, 'I found something.'

'What?'

'This was in Geri's stuff,' Duncan said.

He handed her a beat-up cassette. There was no label on it but faintly, in black ink, someone had written: ALLAW.

They moved silently into the den. Grace stuck the cassette in her player and pressed the play button.

'Invisible Ink' was the third song.

There were similarities to 'Pale Ink.' Would a court of law have found Jimmy guilty of plagiarism? It would be a close call, but Grace figured that the answer, after all these years, was probably no. There were plenty of songs that sounded alike. There was also a fine line between influence and plagiarism. 'Pale Ink,' it seemed to her, probably straddled that blurry line.

So much that went wrong did – straddled a blurry line, that is.

'Scott?'

He did not turn toward her.

'Don't you think it's time we cleared the air?'

He nodded slowly.

She was not sure how to put this. 'When you found out your sister was murdered, you investigated with a passion. You left your job. You went all out.'

'Yes.'

'It wouldn't have been hard to find out she had an old boyfriend.'

'Not hard at all,' Duncan agreed.

'And you would have found out that his name was Shane Alworth.'

'I knew about Shane before all this. They dated for six months. But I thought Geri had died in a fire. There was no reason to follow up with him.'

'Right. But now, after you talked to Monte Scanlon, you did.'

'Yes,' he said. 'It was the first thing I did.'

'You learned that he'd disappeared right around the time of your sister's murder.'

'Right.'

'And that made you suspicious.'

'To put it mildly.'

'You probably, I don't know, checked his old college records, his old high school records even. You talked to his mom. It wouldn't have taken much. Not when you're looking for it.'

Scott Duncan nodded.

'So you knew, before we even met, that Jack was Shane Alworth.'

'Yes,' he said. 'I knew.'

'You suspected him of killing your sister?'

Duncan smiled, but there was no joy in it. 'A man is dating your sister. He breaks up with her. She's murdered. He changes identity and disappears for fifteen years.' He shrugged. 'What would you think?'

Grace nodded. 'You told me you like to shake the cages. That was the way to make progress in a case.'

'Right.'

'And you knew that you couldn't just ask Jack about your sister. You had nothing on him.'

'Right again.'

'So,' she said, 'you shook the cage.'

Silence.

'I checked with Josh at the Photomat,' Grace said.

'Ah. How much did you pay him?'

'A thousand dollars.'

Duncan snorted. 'I only paid him five hundred.'

'To put that picture in my envelope.'

'Yes.'

The song changed. Allaw was now singing a song about

voices and wind. Their sound was raw, but there was potential there too.

'You cast suspicion on Cora to distract me from pressuring Josh.'

'Yes.'

'You insisted I go with you to see Mrs. Alworth. You wanted to see her reaction when she saw her grandchildren.'

'More cage shaking,' he agreed. 'Did you see the look in her eyes when she saw Emma and Max?'

She had. She just hadn't known what it meant or why Mrs. Alworth ended up living in a condo right on Jack's route to work. Now, of course, she did. 'And because you were forced to take a leave, you couldn't use the FBI for surveillance. So you hired a private detective, the one who used Rocky Conwell. And you put that camera in our house. If you were going to shake the cage, you'd need to see how your suspect would react.'

'All true.'

She thought of the end result. 'A lot of people died because of what you did.'

'I was investigating my sister's murder. You can't expect me to apologize for that.'

Blame, she thought again. So much of it to go around. 'You could have told me.'

'No. No, Grace, I could never trust you.'

'You said our alliance was temporary.'

He looked at her. There was something dark there now. 'That,' he said, 'was a lie. We never had an alliance.'

She sat up and turned the music down.

'You don't remember the massacre, do you, Grace?'

'That's not uncommon,' she said. 'It's not amnesia or anything like that. I was hit so hard in the head I was in a coma.'

'Head trauma,' he said with a nod. 'I know all about it. I've seen in it lots of cases. The Central Park jogger, for one. Most cases, like yours, you don't even remember the days before it.'

'So?'

'So how did you get into the front pit that night?'

The question, coming out of nowhere like that, made her sit up. She searched his face for a give. There was none. 'What?'

'Ryan Vespa, well, his father scalped the ticket for four hundred bucks. The members of Allaw got them from Jimmy himself. The only way to get up there was to shell out a ton of dough or know someone.' He leaned forward. 'How did you get into that front pit, Grace?'

'My boyfriend got tickets.'

'That would be Todd Woodcroft? The one who never visited you at the hospital?'

'Yes.'

'You sure about that? Because before you said you don't remember.'

She opened her mouth and then closed it. He leaned closer.

'Grace, I talked to Todd Woodcroft. He didn't go to the concert.'

Something inside her chest lurched to the side. Her body went cold.

'Todd didn't visit you because you'd broken up with him two days before the show. He thought it'd be weird. And you know what, Grace? Shane Alworth broke up with my sister on that same day. Geri never went to the concert. So who do you think Shane took instead?'

Grace shivered and felt the tremor spread. 'I don't understand.'

He pulled out the photograph. 'This is the original Polaroid I had blown up and put into your envelope. My sister wrote the date on the back. The picture was taken the day before the concert.'

She shook her head.

'That mystery woman on the far right, the one we can barely see? You thought it was Sandra Koval. Well, maybe, Grace – just maybe – that's you.'

'No . . .'

'And maybe, while we're looking for more people to blame, maybe we should wonder about the pretty girl who distracted Gordon MacKenzie so the others could get to Jimmy X. We know it wasn't my sister or Sheila Lambert or Sandra Koval.'

Grace kept shaking her head, but then she flashed back to that day at the beach, the first time she laid eyes on Jack, that feeling, that instant grab of the gut. Where had that come from? It was the kind of thing you feel . . .

. . . when you've met someone before.

The strangest sort of déjà-vu. The kind where you've already connected with someone, gotten that first head rush of infatuation. You hold hands, and when the turmoil begins, there's that stomach-dropping feel of his hand slipping from yours . . .

'No,' Grace said, more firmly now. 'You got it wrong. It can't be. I'd have remembered that.'

Scott Duncan nodded. 'You're probably right.'

He stood and popped the cassette out of the machine. He handed it to her. 'This is all just crazy conjecture. I mean, for all we know, maybe that mystery woman was the reason Shane didn't go backstage. Maybe she talked him out of it. Or maybe he realized that there was something more important right there, in that front pit, than anything he could find in a song. Maybe, even three years later, he made sure he found it again.'

Scott Duncan left then. Grace stood and headed into her studio. She had not painted since Jack's death. She put the cassette into her portable player and pressed the play button.

She picked up a brush and tried to paint. She wanted to paint him. She wanted to paint Jack – not John, not Shane.

Jack. She thought it would come out muddled and confused, but that wasn't what happened at all. The brush soared and danced across the canvas. She started thinking again about how we can never know everything about our loved ones. And maybe, if you think about it hard, we don't even know everything about ourselves.

The cassette ended. She rewound it and started it again. She worked in a delirious and delightful frenzy. Tears ran down her cheeks. She did not brush them away. At some point she glanced at a clock. Soon it would be time to stop. School would be letting out. She had to get the kids. Emma had piano today. Max had traveling-team soccer practice.

Grace grabbed her purse and locked the door behind her.